Harry Bowling was born in Bermondsey, London, and left school at fourteen to supplement the family income as an office boy in a Wholesale provisions' merchant. He was called up for National Service in the 1950s. Before becoming a writer, he was variously employed as a lorry driver, milkman, meat cutter, carpenter and decorator, and community worker. He lived with his wife and family, dividing his time between Lancashire and Deptford before his death in 1999.

HARRY BOWLING

The Farrans of
Fellmonger Street

headline

First published in 1994 by
HEADLINE BOOK PUBLISHING PLC

This edition published in paperback in 2016 by
HEADLINE PUBLISHING GROUP

1

Cataloguing in Publication Data is available from the British Library

ISBN 978 0 7553 4042 2

Typeset in Times by Palimpsest Book Production Limited,
Falkirk, Stirlingshire

Printed and bound in Great Britain by Clays Ltd, St Ives plc

HEADLINE PUBLISHING GROUP
An Hachette UK Company
Carmelite House
50 Victoria Embankment
London EC4Y 0DZ

www.headline.co.uk
www.hachette.co.uk

To Shannon, Nina
with love.

Prologue

1949 had been a bad year for the Farrans. On a cold and damp November morning towards its end, Rose Farran took a tighter grip of her young brother's hand and hurried him across the busy junction as a weak red sun climbed above the Bermondsey rooftops. Up ahead of them the brewery drays were parked at the kerb outside the transport cafe as usual, and a tram was waiting for the points to be switched at the busy Tooley Street intersection. To their left the imposing stone structure of Tower Bridge loomed up through the morning fog, and away to the right Rose caught sight of the familiar iron railway bridge that spanned the Tower Bridge Road.

Billy sniffed and pulled on his sister's arm as the two of them reached the safety of the pavement. 'Mind me finger, Rose, it's sore,' he grumbled.

The slim young girl released her grip on Billy's hand and moved round to his other side. 'Now don't make a fuss, I'll bathe it when we get back 'ome,' she told him hastily. 'We've gotta get this business over wiv first.'

The twelve-year-old lad suddenly stopped in his tracks and turned to face his sister. 'If they try ter lock me up I'll run away,' he said quickly, his pale blue eyes narrowing. 'I'll go down Kent an' stay wiv the gypsies. They'll never find me down Kent.'

Rose Farran slipped a reassuring arm around Billy's shoulders and steered him the few remaining yards to the magistrates' court. 'There's no need ter worry if yer remember what I told yer,' she said. 'Just be polite an' don't ferget yer manners. "Yes sir, no sir," an' stop that awful sniffin'. Where's that 'ankey I gave yer?'

'I fergot ter bring it.'

'Well, use mine, 'ere you are, an' be quick or we'll be late,' she sighed.

The juvenile court had been set up at the rear of the building, and as they entered through the fastened back doors Billy cast an anxious glance at his sister. Rose tried to hide her nervousness as she led him to the trestle table where a policeman was seated, busily sifting through a pile of papers, and she coughed to attract the officer's attention. Billy's wide eyes fixed immediately on the police helmet which was sitting on the table at the man's elbow and the sick feeling grew in his stomach as Rose coughed again and shuffled her feet.

'Name?'

'Rose Farran.'

The duty officer glanced through the papers again. 'There's no Rose Farran listed 'ere,' he replied. 'There's a William Farran.'

'That's right,' Rose said quickly. 'I thought yer wanted my name. I'm Billy's sister an' I've gotta be wiv 'im.'

The policeman's face relaxed and he gave Rose a disarming smile. 'That's all right, luv. They usually come wiv their mums an' dads,' he told her.

'Our dad's dead. 'E was killed in the war,' the young girl replied in a matter-of-fact voice.

'What about yer muvver?' the officer asked, his eyes softening.

2

'She's gone away an' I'm in charge o' the family,' Rose told him.

'There's more at 'ome then?'

'Yeah,' she answered tersely.

The officer studied the girl's proud, open face and was struck by the look of determination in her widely spaced blue eyes. Her small nose, full lips and her slightly pointed chin reminded him of his own young daughter, and he gazed for a moment at her hair. It was very fair and long, reaching almost down to her waist.

'If yer'll take a seat over there yer'll be called soon,' he told her in a pleasant tone.

Rose nodded, rubbing the palm of her hand down the lapel of her shabby grey winter coat as she steered Billy over to the polished wooden bench in the far corner of the large, lofty room.

Billy's steel-tipped shoes sounded loudly on the wooden floorboards and he sat down with a nervous puff of breath and reached down to pull up his knee-length socks, sniffing loudly.

'What did I tell yer about that sniffin',' Rose admonished him.

'I can't 'elp it,' Billy replied, wincing as he pressed the swollen area around his fingernail.

Rose took the lad's hand in hers. 'It looks like a whitlow,' she said. 'I'll fix it later.'

Billy pulled a face and scratched at his unruly fair hair. 'What's a whitlow?' he asked her.

'It's a poisoned finger.'

'Can yer die from whitlows?' he asked fearfully.

'I shouldn't fink so,' his sister replied smiling.

Billy slumped on the bench, his back resting against the cream-painted wall, and he slipped the offending finger inside the lapel of his navy-blue coat with an exaggerated expression of suffering on his pale face.

Rose studied her brother's appearance and reached over to adjust his grey woollen tie. 'Yer can't stay tidy fer two minutes, can yer?' she sighed, noticing that he had managed to smudge the collar of his white shirt.

All around them people were milling about. Uniformed policemen came in and out of the large room and officious-looking individuals talked with worried parents who had accompanied their children, some of whom looked overawed, while others seemed indifferent to all the goings-on around them. Rose glanced at Billy's vacant expression and was suddenly filled with a sense of guilt. It was all her fault that this had happened, she thought with a sad sigh. If only she had kept control of herself that evening a couple of weeks ago, instead of sounding off the way she had. It wasn't the kids' fault that their mother had finally left them all to fend for themselves. It wasn't their fault either that their father had been killed on the D-Day landing. They now looked to her, the eldest of the Farrans, to take care of them all and provide for them. How could they be expected to understand the feeling of despair that had suddenly overwhelmed her and reduced her to tears.

Looking back on it now it all seemed so trivial, but every-thing had conspired to happen at once. Seven-year-old Susan had refused to eat her meal and then Joey, who was almost ten years old, calmly announced that he had walked through the sole of his only pair of shoes, and to crown it all Billy had confessed that he had skipped school that day to go over to watch the fish porters at work in Billingsgate market, and he wanted a sick note for school. Rose remembered clearly how she had led off at Billy and tearful young Susan, and then been subjected to an outburst from her sixteen-year-old brother Don, who felt that she was being heavy-handed with them all. She had tried to tell him that it wasn't easy taking her mother's place and still trying to hold her job down at the tin-bashers, not to mention the worry of being the sole breadwinner for them all.

Billy had put his arm around her that teatime and tried to comfort her, saying that everything would be all right and she shouldn't worry any more. A few days later on Saturday afternoon he came in the flat with a big grin on his face and tipped a bagful of tinned fruit and vegetables out on to the table. His explanation was that he had been given the tins by one of the market men for helping out in the shop, but Rose had her doubts. On Sunday morning her suspicions were confirmed when a policeman knocked at the door and said that he wanted to talk to Billy about a break-in at the East Lane barrow sheds.

''Ow much longer we gotta wait, Rose? My finger's really sore,' Billy moaned.

At that moment a tall, bespectacled man approached them. 'I'm Mr Brown, the welfare officer,' he said in a tired voice. 'Before we go in I need to ask a few more questions. There's nothing to worry about. I'm sure that the magistrate will look kindly at the circumstances of this misdemeanour. Now, William is twelve years old and this is the first time he's been in any sort of trouble, correct?'

The sun had risen above the cloud and the last of the fog had disappeared by the time Rose and Billy walked out of Tower Bridge juvenile court. Billy's face was still flushed from the dressing-down he had been given by the woman magistrate but he was elated at having escaped the punishment of being sent to Borstal. Rose felt humbled after the ordeal of having to approach the bench with her prepared statement on her young brother's behalf, and she remained silent as she walked home with Billy along the busy Tower Bridge Road. The young girl recalled how nervous she had felt as she faced the stern magistrate and how she had been embarrassed by the official's response. The woman had been very free with her praise for the way in which Rose was caring for the family and had taken into consideration her feeling that Billy's criminal act was undertaken solely out of need, and the desire to help his sister. 'It is only the fact that you are coping well with your situation in providing a happy home and ample care for your younger brothers and sisters that stays the hand of this court from seeking a care order,' she had declared. 'The alternative would have been that your family were fostered out. You are to be admired for the way you are coping, and for the way you have conducted yourself since your mother's departure.'

The magistrate's words reverberated in Rose's mind and she fought back anxious tears. What would the woman's response have been had she known the full truth of the matter. Rose Farran, just eighteen, single, and solely responsible for her family's welfare, had managed to get herself pregnant.

'We'll be all right now, won't we, Rose?' Billy asked anxiously.

The young girl squeezed his hand in hers and gulped hard before replying. ''Course we will, Billy.'

Chapter One

Abbey Street had always existed in one way or another, following the same track since the days when Bermondsey was pasture land, open fields and clear water streams. The Cluniac monks had found the area a pleasant place in which to settle and an abbey was built just about one mile from the wide river that flowed inland westwards from the dangerous coastline. The place was peaceful and fertile, and crops grew in abundance. For the purpose of trade and communication the monks often journeyed to the river along the straight country path, and they named it Abbey Path.

By the time King Henry VIII dissolved the monasteries the abbey path had become a wide, well-trodden byway, travelled now by merchants and adventurers who refreshed themselves in the streams and drank from the cool flowing water. Artisans and tradesmen skilled in leathercraft who had fled from persecution on the Continent saw Bermondsey as an ideal spot to settle and a tanning industry prospered. In the process of time Abbey Path became Abbey Street, a long cobbled road that led through the heart of old Bermondsey, past the ruins of the Cluniac Abbey and on to rural areas further inland.

By the middle of the nineteenth century Bermondsey had become a sprawling mass of factories surrounded by filthy, insanitary hovels for the growing army of workers. Around Abbey Street tenement blocks sprang up to house the tannery workers, and in 1879 a three-storeyed building was erected in Fellmonger Street, a narrow turning that led off from the cobbled thoroughfare and where the fellmongers had once gathered to trade in skins and hides.

Imperial Buildings had four blocks, designated simply A, B, C and D. Each block contained six two-bedroomed flats, and a twisting wooden staircase led up to the landings. The buildings were illuminated by gas lamps, lit every evening by the porter Fred Albury, an elderly man who lived with his wife Muriel in Number 1, A block. Each morning Fred Albury was required to extinguish the gas lamps, and he did so, when he was good and ready. On cold dark mornings it made little sense getting out of a warm bed at the crack of dawn to put out the lamps, Fred reasoned. His working day was long enough anyway, what with keeping the blocks swept clean and answering calls to change tap washers or let tenants in when they had locked themselves out of their flats.

From Joe Diamond's shop on the corner with Abbey Street, Imperial Buildings stretched down to a flattened and boarded-up bombsite which took up the rest of Fellmonger Street on the right-hand side. On the opposite side of the small turning there was a horse transport firm situated in the middle of a line of two-up, two-down houses. The firm and the house next to it on the far side were owned by Tommy Caulfield, a large jovial character who contracted to cart skins and hides. Apart from his house, which was boarded up and currently used as a store, all the housefronts had whitened doorsteps and lace curtains in the windows. The far end of the turning led into the middle of Basin Street, which boasted two rows of small houses and a corner pub, The Anchor.

At number four, C block, the first block past the corner shop, Don Farran looked into the cracked mirror over the stone sink in the scullery and ran his fingers through his thick dark hair. He studied the few hairs on his chin and winced at the large spot on his left cheek, then he tightened the knot of his grey and blue striped tie and leaned his head round the doorway. 'There's a few creases in this collar, Rose,' he said irritably.

'I can't 'elp that,' his sister replied sharply. 'Yer didn't give me much warnin' yer needed a clean shirt.'

Don bit back on an angry retort. He remembered the last time he had shouted at his sister and he regretted the way it had affected her. She was the best, was Rose, and it wasn't easy for her trying to look after them all. Maybe he should learn how to iron, he thought. It didn't seem too hard, and then he would always have a shirt ready for important times such as tonight.

'Don't be late in,' Rose called out from the living room. 'The fog seems ter be comin' back.'

'Don't worry, Sis, I don't s'pose I'll meet up wiv Jack the Ripper,' Don told her cheerfully as he walked back into the room. 'Anyway if I did bump into 'im I'd just give the geezer a bunch o' fives an' knock 'im spark out. They don't mess wiv Don Farran.'

Rose managed a smile as she watched her brother shadow-boxing in the doorway. 'Remember what I said an' keep away from those Morgan boys,' she urged him. 'They're a bad lot an' I don't want you up the magistrates' court.'

Don buttoned up his blue serge suit and stood with his feet apart, his hands held away from his body. 'Well, 'ow do I look?' he asked.

'You'll do,' Rose replied, looking back down at the dress she was ironing.

Don let himself out of the first-floor flat in Fellmonger Street and Rose glanced up and listened to the hurried footsteps on the stairs as her sixteen-year-old brother went off to meet the Morgan boys. He was her main worry, she thought, apart from her condition. Don was certainly a handsome young man and so like their dead father. He had similar colouring and manner, and the same confident air about him. Don had started an apprenticeship with an electrical firm in Rotherhithe in the spring of that year, about the time their mother had run off, and he was unable to contribute any money to the family. To be fair to him, he had wanted to give it all up so that he could bring in a much-needed wage but Rose had been adamant that he should stay where he was, with the chance of learning a worthwhile trade. She had finally prevailed by reminding him that he had promised his father he would complete an apprenticeship. Don was a nice lad, but quick to anger and volatile at times, she told herself, and that was the trouble. He was getting in with the Morgan family, who everyone local knew to be a bad lot. The Morgans' father had spent quite a few years behind bars for one offence or another and every time he came home he managed to father another son and then get himself into more trouble. The eldest two boys had married and settled down in other parts of London, but the younger four were always getting into one scrape after another. John Morgan at twenty-two was the worst of the lot and he had already been given a dishonourable discharge from the army for battering his drill sergeant during the early days of his National Service.

Rose put the hot iron down in the hearth to cool and folded the ironing blanket. Susan was getting tired and fretful, and Billy was slowly getting agitated by Joey's refusal to accept defeat in their game of draughts.

'Yer can't go over two spaces,' Billy stormed, pointing at the draughtboard with his bandaged finger.

'Yes I can, it's a new rule. Frankie Lester told me,' Joey replied with a smug grin.

'Well, Frankie Lester can't play anyfing prop'ly. 'E's stupid,' Billy replied scowling.

'I'll tell 'im what yer said,' Joey countered quickly.

'I ain't scared o' Frankie Lester,' Billy shouted at his younger brother. 'I can fight 'im any day.'

Rose sighed deeply and banged her hand down on the table. 'Right, you two, that's enough. It's school in the mornin' an' I want yer both ready fer bed early ternight,' she said with authority.

Susan picked up her one-eyed doll and tucked the loose cottonwool back into the hole under the toy's arm. 'I'm tired, Rose,' she said yawning widely.

Rose swept the child up into her arms and kissed her on the cheek. 'Come on, darlin', let's get yer washed before the boys collar the scullery,' she said smiling.

At seven thirty the pretty young child was tucked into her small bed and as Rose brushed a strand of loose hair from her eyes Susan looked up at her. 'Will Mummy come back one day?' she asked.

'One day, now off ter sleep, baby,' Rose replied softly, leaning down to plant a kiss on the child's cool forehead.

Don Farran sat with John and Albert Morgan in the public bar of the Anchor, his eyes fixed on the elder brother who was speaking in a low voice.

'The ole git won't be no trouble at all,' he was saying. 'All we do is stick a sack over 'is 'ead an' bundle 'im in the office. We just warn 'im that if 'e tries anyfing we'll bash 'is 'ead in. Those cases are full o' fags an' cigars. Gotta be a fortune in it.'

'What about if 'e recognises us, John?' Albert queried.

'Don't worry about that, the ole goat's blind as a bat,' John replied. 'I dunno why they take on ole geezers ter watch places like Jackson's. If they get done it's their look-out.'

The other two young men nodded and Don fished into his trouser pocket. 'I'll get the next one,' he said, hoping that Albert would insist on buying a round instead.

'Cheers, Don,' Albert said, leaving him to count his coppers.

'I'm a bit dodgy about 'im,' John said quietly, nodding in Don's direction as the young man walked to the counter. ''E acts big but 'e ain't done nuffink. 'E might start flappin'.'

'Don's all right,' Albert assured his older brother. 'Me an' Don are good mates. 'E won't let us down.'

''E's only a kid yet,' John persisted.

''E's goin' on seventeen an' 'e's knocked a bit o' gear out fer me more than once,' Albert went on. 'Besides, Don don't earn much bein' an apprentice.'

'Why did yer let 'im buy the round then?' John asked. 'You're flush after that load o' shoes yer got rid of.'

''E likes ter buy a round,' Albert replied with a lop-sided grin.

As Don Farran walked back to the corner table carrying three pints of bitter on a tin tray, Sammy McGarry the pub landlord cast his wife a look of resignation. For some time Beryl had wanted her husband to ban the Morgans from the pub, knowing that the small-time villains were giving the place a bad name, but Sammy had declined. He had spent a few years as a professional boxer and had worked in the docks before going into the Anchor; he had kept company with men every bit as hard as the Morgans and they held no fear for him, but he was all for a quiet life now he was in his late fifties. Besides, there were the few perks he got from the villains now and then.

'Yer know that one's only sixteen,' Beryl reminded him in a low voice.

Sammy sighed and scratched at his balding head. 'Look, gel, I can't go askin' fer all the young bucks' birth certificates,' he replied. 'Anyway, 'e looks eighteen at least.'

'I bet young Rose Farran don't know 'e's in 'ere,' Beryl told him.

'Don't you go tellin' 'er,' Sammy said sharply. 'That poor cow's got enough on 'er plate. I was talkin' ter Fred Albury this mornin'. 'E said that Rose was up the court wiv 'er Billy. Somefing ter do wiv 'im breakin' inter some barrer sheds.'

Beryl finished pumping out a pint of ale and handed the brimming glass to the elderly Ted Baxter. 'There we are, Ted. 'Ow's yer missus?' she asked him.

Ted shook his head slowly. 'She can't get aroun' much since that fall,' he replied. 'The orspital said it was lucky she didn't break 'er 'ip. She's got rheumatics, yer see. It plays on that bad 'ip.'

Beryl nodded briefly in the direction of the young conspirators. 'Young Don Farran's gettin' in bad company, I see,' she remarked.

Ted Baxter nodded sadly. 'Bloody shame what 'appened ter that family,' he replied. ''E was a smashin' bloke, young Gerry. I remember the night before 'e went back off leave. 'E was tellin' me that 'is mob expected ter be on the invasion at any time an' I swear 'e knew 'e was gonna cop it. It was jus' somefing 'e said. Mind yer, it might 'ave bin the beer talkin', but yer know what 'e said?'

Beryl remained silent, knowing that Ted was going to tell her anyway.

'Gerry said ter me, "I wish fings could 'ave bin different wiv me an' Ida," that's what 'e said. So I ses to 'im, "You two are gonna get fings sorted out when this lot's over, Gerry," an' 'e turns round an' gives me a funny grin. "It's too late fer me, ole mate." 'E knew, Beryl. Gerry knew right enough that 'e wasn't comin' back.'

'Leave orf, Ted, yer makin' me go all cold an' miserable,' the landlady said with a pronounced shudder.

'She was a bad one, that ole woman of 'is,' Ted went on regardless. 'A real bitch in my book. D'yer know what? My ole dutch told me that as soon as young Gerry got called up she was orf out wiv a fancy bloke. She used ter go up West wiv the Yanks. Brought one 'ome 'ere once. Nice bloke 'e was. 'E bought me an' my missus a drink or two right in this very bar. Gawd knows 'ow those kids of 'ers got on in those days. She left 'em wiv anybody who was silly enough ter take it on. Gawd knows what would 'ave 'appened ter those poor mites if it wasn't fer the neighbours in those buildin's. They gave those kids more than she ever did. Young Rose Farran was only about twelve or firteen at the time an' she 'ad ter look after young Susie. The kid was only about two year old then. Bloody shame if yer ask me.'

Beryl gave her husband a sideways glance and leaned on the counter, facing the elderly ex-docker. 'What's the latest on Ida Farran? I 'eard she upped an' left fer good.'

Ted showed his distaste by shaking his head slowly. 'She run orf wiv a bloody bus inspector, would yer believe? Left all those kids fer a bloody bus inspector she did,' he growled. 'I tell yer, Beryl, if it'd bin my wife I'd 'ave sorted the pair of 'em out. I'd 'ave give 'im bus inspector. I'd put the bleeder's 'ead under a bus, then I'd give 'er a right pastin' an' drag 'er back by the scruff of 'er neck.'

'Trouble is, there's no man ter do it, as far as the Farrans are concerned,' Beryl pointed out. 'Who Ida Farran goes out wiv is 'er concern, but she shouldn't neglect those kids. Ter be honest, I thought they'd 'ave taken 'em away. The welfare, I mean.'

'They did go roun' ter see the kids, accordin' ter my Amy,' Ted informed her. 'Young Rose was doin' a good job an' they seemed ter fink the kids was better orf wiv 'er. That boy is gonna 'ave ter watch 'imself though,' he said nodding in Don Farran's direction. ''E's only sixteen yer know. 'E shouldn't be in 'ere, not drinkin'.'

'I know, I've told 'im,' Beryl replied with a flick of her eyes at Sammy who was pulling a pint at the other end of the bar. ''E don't take a blind bit o' notice what I say. Might as well talk ter the brick wall.'

Albert Morgan sauntered over to the counter, having finally been persuaded to buy a round. 'Might 'ave a bit o' stuff for yer pretty soon, Sammy,' he said under his breath.

The landlord winced as he spotted Beryl giving him an old-fashioned look. 'Don't mention anyfing while the missus is 'ere,' he hissed. 'She gets all worried.'

Albert winked and stood with his hands in his trouser pockets while the pints were drawn, then he pulled out a roll of one-pound notes and peeled one off. 'Get yerself a drink too, an' one fer the missus,' he said, grinning slyly out of the corner of his mouth.

Sammy rang the till and handed Albert the change. 'I'd keep that young Farran boy out o' yer duckin'-an'-divin',' he advised. 'Yer know the welfare are on the family's back. If that lad got into any sort o' trouble they could well split the family up.'

'Don't worry, I'll look after 'im,' Albert Morgan said dismissively.

The young man under discussion was feeling excited at the prospect of being accepted into the inner circle at last. John Morgan was right, he reasoned. People shouldn't put an old man to watch over a warehouse full of valuable stock. If the firm got robbed it was their own fault.

'Right then, we'll go over the plan once more, then we'll meet up at Teacake Ted's at five sharp next Tuesday evenin','

John told them. 'The cafe stays open till six o'clock, so we'll 'ave time fer a bite to eat while we watch points. The firm's dead opposite Ted's cafe so we can see it all from the winder. Soon as the last worker leaves the ole boy shuts the place up. I've checked it out wiv our contact. The stuff's goin' in on Tuesday mornin' so there should be some nice pickin's. One fing I need ter say,' he stressed, looking at both the young men in turn. 'No gabbin'. If any o' this gets out, there may be somebody who'll take the opportunity o' puttin' us away. We've got a few enemies round 'ere an' it's all down ter jealousy. Us Morgans walk around in good gear, an' we 'ave a few bob ter spend. 'Alf of 'em want the same but they ain't got the bottle ter do anyfing about it. So remember what I say. Keep schtoom.'

The first-floor flat in Imperial Buildings was quiet on that cold November night. Susan slept peacefully in the bedroom, but in the second bedroom where they shared a double bed, Joey and Billy were talking quietly.

'Don's late,' Billy said, glancing at the empty single bed.

'I bet Rose is really mad,' Joey replied.

'She'd be madder if she knew where Don's gone,' Billy whispered.

'Where's 'e gone to?' the younger brother asked.

'I can't tell yer. Don would give me a clout if 'e knew I told yer,' Billy said seriously.

'I wouldn't say anyfing, cross me 'eart an' 'ope ter die,' Joey urged.

Billy turned over to face him. 'Don's gone ter meet the Morgans. I 'eard 'im makin' the arrangements yesterday outside the block. 'E didn't know I was sittin' on the bottom o' the stairs wiv me mates. They've gone ter that pub in Basin Street. There's something goin' on, Joey, but yer mustn't breave a word or Rose'll go mad at Don an' then 'e'll scream an' shout back like 'e did last time. We don't wanna be split up an' 'ave ter go an' live wiv strange people.'

'What d'yer mean, Billy?' Joey asked him.

'Well yer see, Rose told me that we've gotta stick tergever an' not cause any trouble,' Billy explained. 'She said that if people 'ear us all shoutin' an' arguin' amongst ourselves they might report us ter the welfare people an' they'll fink Rose can't look after us all prop'ly. We'll be put in different 'omes an' not see each ovver fer years.'

'I wish muvver never left us,' Joey said, suddenly wanting to cry.

'Well she did, an' if she really cared what 'appened to us she wouldn't 'ave left us, so it's no good wishin' fer 'er ter come back,' Billy said firmly. 'We gotta 'elp Rose best we can.'

'If I say me prayers will Jesus 'elp Rose?' Joey asked.

'Yeah, I fink so,' Billy told him, then after a few minutes deep in thought he said, 'G'night, Joey.'

'I was sayin' me prayers,' the younger boy puffed loudly. 'G'night, Billy.'

Chapter Two

Rose Farran left the flat and hurried down the damp, creaking staircase and out into the street. It was five minutes to eight, barely enough time for her to reach her workplace, the Bromilow sheet-metal works at Dockhead. Susan had been slow in rousing that morning and Billy's sore finger had had to be re-dressed. It seemed to be festering and needed to be looked at, Rose thought as she walked quickly down Abbey Street. Tomorrow was Saturday and the medical mission would be open until twelve. She would have to take him there to get it lanced in case of blood poisoning.

The works manager was standing just inside the entrance to the factory and he gave her a cold stare. 'You almost lost a quarter,' he growled as Rose grabbed her card from the rack and pushed it into the time-clock.

'Better luck next time,' she said in anger at the fat little man as he stood arms folded and feet apart.

'None of yer cheek, my gel, or yer'll soon find yerself queuin' up down the labour exchange,' he warned her.

Rose bit back on a sharp reply and struggled into her heavy apron and cap as she hurried to her place at the stamping machine. One day that little squirt was going to get his comeuppance, she told herself. He had been nasty to her since she had spurned his advances on the stairway a few weeks previously. He had put his arm around her waist and tried to fix up a date, and when she shook her head vigorously he had stormed off in a huff with a look that spelt trouble ahead for her.

The belts were turning and the noise of the heavy machinery was deafening as Rose set to work, trying to shut her mind off from her troubles and trying desperately to ignore the large clock high up on the stone wall to her left. Her job entailed feeding large sheets of tin into a stamping machine which cut the metal into strips. Further along the workshop the strips were rolled ready for soldering into tin cans. All morning the noise was incessant as the women took their tea break in groups, so as to keep the belts turning. As Rose fed the constant supply of sheets into the hungry press, she worried. She worried about Susan, about Billy's septic finger, and about the baby growing inside her. It was stupid and unforgivable that she had allowed him to seduce her. It would have been different if it was just she alone who would suffer the consequences, but there was the family to consider. She had let them all down badly.

The huge press lifted and fell with an unending thump, never varying a second nor changing its tune, and in her desperation Rose dwelt on the Mag Dolan tragedy. Mag had worked a press at Bromilow's and one day she had suddenly stopped talking to her workmates. None of them paid much attention to the girl's strange behaviour. For a whole week she never uttered a single word to anyone, and on the Friday evening, just before the factory whistle signalled that the working week was over, Mag put her head under the press. The newspapers carried the story and everyone then knew the reason for the tragic girl's behaviour. Mag Dolan, a staunch Catholic girl from Dublin, had got herself pregnant.

Rose felt that she understood the awful dilemma Mag must have been faced with and she shuddered as the machinery thundered relentlessly on. Suicide had been the answer for Mag Dolan, but it wasn't going to be her way out. She still had some time yet before her condition became apparent to anyone else. One answer would be to get an abortion. Rose knew at least two factory girls who had decided to get rid of their unborn babies. One, Kath Wilson, had gone to a chemist in Whitechapel and he had given her some 'black and whites'. Kath had been quite open about it all one day in the canteen.

'We ain't got a barf in our 'ouse,' she had said, 'so I 'ad ter go roun' the Spa Road municipal barf. I tell yer, gels, that barf was the 'ottest one I ever 'ad in me life. Sweatin' like a pig, I was. Anyway, I takes these two white pills while I'm in the barf an' I shouts out to ole Maggie Moses fer more 'ot water in number two. She can't believe it. "More 'ot water?" she shouts out. "Yeah, more 'ot, Maggie," I tells 'er. Now I'm expectin' miracles, gels, but all I got was the feelin' I was gonna faint because o' the steam. Anyway, I finally gets out o' that barf lookin' like a bleedin' stewed plum an' I dries meself down an' takes the black pills like the chemist bloke told me, an' d'you know what, I nearly never made it 'ome. The pains! They were like nuffink I've ever 'ad in me life. Gripin' me up they were. When I got 'ome my ole lady was goin' orf about one fing an' anuvver an' I pushes past 'er fer the closet an' she shouts out somefing or the ovver. "Shut up, yer silly ole cow," I tells 'er, "I'm dyin'!" I really did fink I was a gonna, Gawd strike me dead if I'm tellin' a lie. Well, ter cut a long story short it was all over there an' then.'

'What was in the pills?' one of the girls asked.

'I fink the white ones were made out o' crab apples an' the black ones were liquorice,' Kath told her.

Rose thought about Kath Wilson's confession, and about the

other Bromilow girl who had become pregnant. Ellie Braden was married and already had five children, and she had decided that enough was enough. Ellie went to an abortionist and was back at work two days later. Rose felt a revulsion as she dwelt on the two factory girls' experiences and suddenly her head started to pound. A reddish mist swam in front of her eyes and then blackness.

Joey Farran took his younger sister's hand as they left Caxton primary school and walked the few streets home to Imperial Buildings. Circumstances had forced young Joey to be responsible and reliable beyond his years in looking after Susan and as the rain started to fall he opened his coat and let his sister nestle her head against him, sheltering her from the heavy rainspots. 'Come on, Sue, 'fore we get soaked,' he urged her.

The two children reached the buildings and climbed the flight of stairs, Joey fishing for the front-door key which was tied to a piece of ribbon round his neck. Joey usually made a pot of tea for them, as Billy normally got home from his school a few minutes later, but on this occasion the children were surprised to see that Rose was already home.

''Ave yer got the sack?' Joey asked quickly.

Rose smiled and shook her head. 'I got sent 'ome early 'cos I was feelin' a bit sick,' she said. 'I'm all right now though. 'Ow was school?'

Susan pulled a face and Joey puffed as he sat down on the tatty armchair beside the gas fire. 'I've got 'omework ter do,' he said.

Rose filled two cups with tea from a blue china teapot and added a spoonful of goat's milk to each cup. Just then Billy came in and sat down without saying a word. He looked pale and he held his bandaged finger up, supporting his wrist with the other hand.

Rose could see that the boy was in some pain and she immediately reached up for her coat. 'C'mon, Billy, we're goin' straight roun' the mission,' she told him. 'If we're lucky they might still be open.'

'Can't I 'ave a cup o' tea first, Rose?' he asked.

'Later. Let's get that finger looked at first.'

Billy started to protest but his sister knelt down and put her hand on his knee. 'Look, luv, if we leave it any longer blood poisonin' might set in an' yer'll 'ave ter go in 'ospital,' she said firmly. 'Now c'mon, no arguments.'

The rain was now falling heavily and Rose opened up her umbrella as she stepped out into the street. Billy walked close to her as they hurried along Abbey Street and took a narrow turning that led out into the main Grange Road. They passed by the fur factory, the row of tall terraced houses that had steps leading up to the front doors and then turned left into Crimscott Street.

The small medical mission was just a few yards along the street, dwarfed by the huge Crosse and Blackwell food factory. The clinic had originally been opened by women missionaries who had returned from India after long service in the subcontinent, and it catered for women and children of the borough. When Rose stepped into the passageway with her arm around a nervous Billy she breathed a tired sigh of relief to find it open; she could hear a child crying and the reassuring voice of the elderly sister who was in charge.

The door in front of her was wedged open and as she walked through into a narrow corridor she saw two children sitting on the wooden bench waiting patiently for treatment. Billy looked frightened and Rose gave him a smile and kept her arm round his shoulders as they sat down. Billy struggled free and tried to look grown-up, aware that the two children sitting next to him had become curious.

'I gotta 'ave drops in me ears,' the little boy told him matter-of-factly.

'I gotta 'ave me stitches out,' the boy's companion announced proudly. 'I cut me 'ead open on the ruins. Fifteen stitches I 'ad.'

'Don't tell lies. It was only two stitches,' the first boy corrected him.

Billy held out his finger. 'It's poisoned,' he replied. 'I might 'ave ter get it chopped off.'

'Don't be wicked, Billy, it's only a bit festered,' Rose said quickly, smiling at the two shocked children.

A young woman carrying a baby emerged from the surgery at the end of the corridor, followed by a tall, lean woman with a very lined face. She was dressed in a light blue uniform and she wore a white linen hat with a large diamond-shaped piece of cloth hanging down from the back as far as her shoulders. The sister stood with hands on hips and looked along the bench. 'Next one,' she said in a singsong voice.

The boy who needed his stitches removed got up and followed her into the surgery.

'It's only two stitches,' the other boy whispered to Billy. 'I bet 'e cries. 'E's a cowardy-custard.'

A sudden wail broke the silence and then came the sister's loud voice. 'Now keep still. There's only one more to come out and I'm sure it doesn't hurt that much.'

'Drops 'urt more than stitches but I ain't scared,' the boy told Billy.

Billy's finger was throbbing and he gave the boy a sickly grin. 'I ain't scared neivver,' he said without much conviction.

The first boy came out of the surgery looking rather sheepish and hurried off home. Soon it was Billy's turn, and as he went in with Rose and sat down his eyes fixed on the steaming steriliser in the corner of the room. The sister gently undid the bandage and stared down at the swelling. Humming to herself she removed some instruments from the steriliser and sat herself down facing Billy. She pulled a cloth across her lap and took his hand in hers. 'Now I want you to look up at the ceiling and tell me what you see,' she said, indicating to Rose to hold the boy's head up.

As he lifted his head Billy felt a sharp pain and he tried to look down at his finger. Rose had her hand under his chin, her eyes fixed on what the sister was doing. She had quickly and expertly made a small incision to release the pus, and Rose had to take a deep breath. She had already passed out once that day and she felt queasy as she saw the result of the nursing sister's efforts. Billy seemed to relax against her and she patted his face. 'There, that didn't take long, did it?'

Soon the young lad's finger was cleaned and bandaged, and he looked cheerful as he walked home beside his sister. The throbbing had ceased and for the first time that week he did not feel any pain.

On Saturdays it was pie and mash for lunch at the Farrans', and when the table had been cleared Rose brought in a surprise sweet of plain pudding and syrup.

'Cor! My favourite,' Joey said, licking his lips.

Susan managed to drop a large piece of sticky pudding on her lap and Don gave Rose a grin as he scooped it up with his spoon and put it back on to her plate. 'C'mon, eat it all up, babes, or yer won't get a big gel,' he joked.

Rose sat back and watched her brothers and sister as they devoured the pudding. She had told them that she did not like plain and syrup, but in fact there was only just enough for four small portions. It was nice to see them all enjoying the sweet and she wanted to savour the moment. The future was uncertain and there was a strong possibility that the family would have to be split up, she realised, once the welfare knew of her condition.

'I got an extra job o' work next Tuesday, Rose,' Don said suddenly. 'It's a bit of overtime an' I'll be paid a full rate. The guv'nor said it's money in the 'and, so I'll be able ter put a few bob in the 'ouse-keepin' tin.'

'I could get a paper round,' Joey butted in. 'I could put some money in then.'

'Never mind about paper rounds, you've gotta look after Susan while I'm at work,' Rose reminded him.

'I'll be firteen next March an' then one year later I'll be able ter start work,' Billy said. 'I'm gonna try an' get a job in the tannery. My mate's dad works in a tannery an' 'e gets good wages. 'E's a dipper.'

'That's a right dirty job, skin-dippin',' Don told him. 'Yer don't want none o' that. Yer gotta try an' get a job wiv a future, like me. When I'm twenty-one I'll be a fully-fledged electrician.'

'Can I go an' play out, Rose?' Joey asked.

'Yeah but stay round 'ere,' Rose told him, 'I don't wanna come lookin' for yer when it's time ter come in.'

Billy slipped out of his chair and sidled up to Rose. 'I'm gonna call fer Danny, all right?'

Rose brushed her hand over her brother's tousled fair hair and nodded with a smile. The two younger boys were so alike, she thought. Both Joey and Billy were like her in colouring and they all favoured their mother. They had pale blue eyes, fair hair and fresh complexions. Only Don and young Susan were dark like their late father. Both had large expressive brown eyes and dark complexions. Don was growing into a living image of him.

Susan was now sitting comfortably in the armchair by the fire, busy talking to her favourite doll, and as she watched, Rose promised herself that she would sew up the arm of the toy and try to replace the missing eye as soon as possible.

'Young Billy seems ter be very close ter you lately,' Don remarked suddenly.

'It's understandable,' Rose replied, turning to face him. 'I've 'ad ter do a bit o' muvverin' wiv Billy lately. There was the court business an' then that finger of 'is. They lanced it at the mission an' 'e never murmured. I fink 'e wanted ter show me 'ow grown-up 'e was.'

'Are you all right, Rose?' Don asked, giving her an enquiring look.

'Yeah, I'm fine. Why d'yer ask?'

'I dunno. It's just that yer look all worried lately,' he told her. 'I don't mean about us lot. It's like yer got somefing else on yer mind.'

'No, there's nuffink worryin' me outside the family,' Rose lied. 'I've bin a bit fed up wiv me job this last few weeks an' I've bin a bit off colour terday.'

Don reached into his shirt pocket and pulled out a packet of Woodbines and a box of matches. 'A smoke might do yer good,' he said, taking a cigarette from the packet.

Rose shook her head. 'You shouldn't smoke, it'll stunt yer growth,' she told him.

Don smiled briefly and lit the cigarette, inhaling deeply and then puffing a cloud of smoke towards the ceiling. 'Did yer manage ter find out any more about who's payin' our rent?' he asked.

'I got the same answer from the manager at the Crown Estate office as I did when I asked the rent collector,' Rose replied. 'A woman pays our rent when she pays 'er own, directly ter the office. The manager said the woman wouldn't say who gave 'er our rent money. She's bin told not to.'

Don studied the glowing end of his cigarette. 'It's very strange. I mean ter say, who would wanna pay our rent week after week, if it ain't Muvver?'

Rose laughed bitterly. 'Muvver? Gawd, Don, I 'ad ter get a loan off o' Mrs Greenfield ter pay the arrears before Muvver left. She only paid the rent when it suited 'er. I've only just finished repaying that loan.'

'Yer don't fink Farvver left any instructions wiv anyone before 'e went back off leave, do yer?' Don asked.

'Yer've asked me before an' I still say the same fing. Our farvver didn't 'ave a penny ter bless 'imself wiv. Muvver saw ter that. She bled 'im dry,' Rose replied with bitterness in her voice.

'It's certainly puzzlin',' Don said, puffing on his cigarette.

Rose shrugged her shoulders. 'I've stopped finkin' about it ter tell yer the trufe,' she said. 'This family's 'ad a fair share o' knocks an' we've got ourselves a good fairy. I'm content ter leave it at that. One day we may find out an' then I'll try ter repay the debt. Fer the time bein' just do what I do an' say a prayer fer 'im or 'er, whoever it is.'

Chapter Three

On Monday morning Rose walked to work through the swirling, chilling fog. The previous Friday morning she had heard one of the girls say that the firm was starting Saturday working until Christmas and Rose hoped that it was not just a rumour. The extra money would certainly come in handy for the family's Christmas presents, she thought.

'You're bright an' early this mornin', Farran,' the manager remarked as he stood in his usual position by the time clock.

Rose gave him a brief smile, not wanting to antagonise the man in case he took it out on her by not offering her the chance of Saturday overtime.

'Before yer start work I'd like a word in my office,' he told her, forcing a smile before he turned his back on her and strutted off.

Rose followed him along the corridor and into the office that looked on to the main workshop.

'Sit yerself down, I won't be five minutes. Somefing I've gotta take care of,' he said.

Rose sat on a hard chair beside the cluttered desk, wondering why the works manager should want to speak with her. It was probably about her fainting on Friday morning, she thought.

Bernard Collis walked out of the office humming nervously to himself. He had worked with Bromilow's since leaving school and his aptitude for mechanical engineering had been spotted by the company, which sent him on a course at the local polytechnic. Bernard had eventually risen to be assistant works manager, and when the manager himself neared retirement he became increasingly impatient to take over the job. Bob Myers had been a good manager who had the interests of his workers at heart, but the years had taken their toll and he had become rather forgetful. Occasionally important maintenance jobs on the large machines tended to get overlooked, and although Bernard Collis did not fail to notice, he found it suited his plan not to remind his boss, whose job it was to supervise the maintenance. One day the main cutter broke down and it was found to have a dry bearing. The firm lost two days' production and the emergency meeting held by the directors recommended that Bob Myers be given early retirement and his assistant Bernard Collis be approached about replacing him.

At the outbreak of war Bromilow's went on to essential war work and works manager Bernard Collis was granted an exemption from call-up. All through the war he strutted about the factory making himself more and more unpopular. The factory girls knew him to be a lecherous creep who took advantage of the fact that the workforce could not readily leave of their own accord, and they were forced to suffer the man's nasty ways.

After the war, when the women workers came and went, Bernard Collis was forced to act a little more respectfully towards the girls, but it did not stop him getting to know which of his workers were desperate for the job, and when it suited him he made their lives a misery.

Rose Farran was soon to learn the ulterior motives for being summoned to the office when Collis came back after a few minutes and sat himself down, puffing loudly.

'You know we're startin' Saturday workin' from this Saturday,' he said, leaning back in his seat and clasping his hands together. 'Unfortunately you'd gone 'ome sick when the list came round. I'm sorry you're not on it, an' I'm afraid it's full now. We only wanted 'alf the workers in this week.'

Rose tried not to show her disappointment but Collis had caught the look in her eyes. 'I might be able ter swing somefing, it all depends on a few fings,' he said, a hint of a smile showing on his podgy red face.

'A few fings?' Rose repeated.

'I'm a friendly sort o' bloke an' yer don't wanna listen ter rumours ter the contrary,' Collis said, the smile now evident. 'I know yer need the extra money, what wiv Christmas comin' on. What say yer leave it ter me? I'll do me best an' see what I can do. In the meantime you go back ter work an' we can 'ave a little talk later. By the way I usually go in the Pagoda on Tuesday nights. Why don't yer pop in there an' let me buy yer a drink. Yer know where the Pagoda is, don't yer?'

Rose nodded and stood up, feeling sick inside. The leering face of her manager left her in no doubt what he had in mind. 'I'm sorry, I don't get the chance ter get out much,' she answered.

'Just fink about it,' Collis said, lowering his head to the mess of papers on his desk by way of dismissal.

The afternoon sun had made a few brief appearances through the heavy cloud but it disappeared for the day as the November fog started to roll in from the river. Outside C block, Imperial Buildings, two elderly women stood chatting after walking back from Joe Diamond's corner shop together. Mrs Campbell and her good friend Mrs Stratton both lived on the ground floor of C block and they were concerned about the Farrans.

'She's gorn fer good, that's fer sure,' Ivy Campbell remarked.

'I knew that right from the start. Never 'ad any time fer those kids of 'ers,' Rene Stratton replied, pulling up the collar of her heavy coat against the damp late afternoon. 'I often saw that fancy man of 'ers 'angin' round on the corner. Sickenin' it was ter see the two of 'em tergevver. I wouldn't mind if 'e was some sort o' catch. Bloody bloke looked like a good dinner wouldn't do 'im any 'arm.'

Ivy Campbell nodded. ''E's married, yer know.'

'Go on.'

'Yeah. Four kids 'e's got.'

'Good Gawd.'

'I know the woman's bin widowed, an' nobody begrudges 'er a bit o' life, but ter leave those little mites the way she did was disgraceful,' Ivy went on. 'I tell yer, Rene, if it wasn't fer that eldest gel Rose they'd all be took away by the welfare people. Stan's ter reason. After all, young Susie can't be no more than six or seven.'

'The welfare people called round a few times makin' enquiries. They're keepin' their eye on 'em, I expect,' Rene said.

'I feel sorry fer that Rose,' Ivy continued. 'She's only eighteen. She's got a burden.'

'She works at the tin bashers in Dock'ead, so she told me,' Rene added. 'What a bloody place ter work. I worked there once. Two days I lasted. The bloody noise o' those machines nearly drove me ter drink. My ole man told me ter pack the job up or e'd go round there an' drag me out.'

Ivy quickly looked right and left to make sure no one was in earshot. ''E's gonna 'ave ter watch 'imself,' she said in a low voice.

'Who's that?'

'That Don Farran.'

'Why's that, then?'

''E's bin gettin' in wiv those Morgans.'

Rene shook her head slowly. 'They're prison bait, that lot. Charlie Morgan's doin' a five stretch an' then there's the ole man. 'E's bin in an' out the nick more times than enough, I can tell yer. 'E's waitin' ter come up fer assault now, by all accounts.'

'I was finkin' o' mentionin' it ter young Rose. I bet she don't know,' Ivy said. 'Trouble is yer don't know if yer doin' right from wrong. I'd only get the name o' bein' a busybody.'

'Mind yer, if yer did mention it the gel would only 'ave somefing else ter worry about, an' besides, I don't s'pose Don would take any notice of 'er,' Rene remarked.

'All bloody trouble ain't it, one way an' anuvver,' Ivy said finally as she took a key from her purse.

Rene Stratton tucked the evening paper under her arm and followed her friend into the block. 'See yer tomorrer, luv. 'E'll be waitin' fer 'is read.'

At five o'clock that evening Tommy Caulfield stepped out of his transport yard through the wicket-gate and clicked it shut. He was a big man, standing well over six feet tall, with a build like a heavyweight wrestler. His heavy round face was ruddy and his deep blue eyes were friendly, though on this particular evening they had a worried look.

Tommy pulled his trilby hat down over one eye and turned up the collar of his tweed overcoat as he walked quickly out of the street, turning his steps towards the transport cafe in Jamaica Road where he had arranged to meet an old friend, Chief Inspector Bill Grogan, the policeman in charge at Dockhead. Grogan had phoned Tommy that morning, suggesting that they met somewhere they could have a quiet chat. Sid Baines' place had seemed a suitable venue. Sid was the soul of discretion and his cafe was a regular stopping-place for

Tommy when he was out on business in the area, as well as for his car men.

''Ello, Tom, a couple o' yer boys were in 'ere terday. 'Ow's business?'

Tommy gave the cafe owner a friendly smile and was pleased to find that there were no other customers in the shop. 'Can't complain, Sid,' he replied. 'Give us a large one, an' a bacon sandwich, will yer.'

Sidney Baines filled a large mug full of strong tea from a huge metal teapot and scooped in two spoonfuls of sugar. He knew just how Tommy liked his tea, and as he stirred it Sid noticed that Tommy wasn't his usual self.

'Yer look tired, old mate. Ain't bin overdoin' fings lately, 'ave yer?' he remarked.

The contractor forced a smile as he made himself comfortable in one of the bench seats. 'I'm OK, Sid, just a bit tired,' he told him.

Sid put two thin rashers of bacon into a large frying-pan of hot fat and reached for two thick slices of new bread. ''Ow's the missus, Tom?' he asked.

'She's fine. I'll tell 'er you asked after 'er,' Tommy replied, running his large gnarled hand over his forehead. 'By the way, is your clock right?'

'Spot on, mate, accordin' ter Big Ben.'

'What time yer shuttin'?'

'Six sharp, as usual.'

'I'm meetin' someone 'ere, Sid. Shouldn't be too long,' Tommy told him.

Sid took the strips of streaky bacon out of the pan with the end of his carving knife and laid them on a thickly buttered slice of bread and with a deft movement he flipped the other slice over and slid the knife under his arched hand to halve the sandwich. Normally Sid's customers collected their

33

sandwiches and tea from the counter, but on this occasion Tommy made no move. The cafe owner looked at him as he sat deep in thought, then slipped round the counter and put the mug of tea and the sandwich down in front of him. 'Service wiv a smile,' he said. ''Ere, you sure you're all right?' he asked.

Tommy nodded quickly and as he took his first bite from the bacon sandwich a tall lean man walked in, unbuttoning his heavy overcoat as he slid on to the bench seat facing him. 'Sorry I'm late. There's a lot on at the station at the moment,' he said.

'You sounded a bit mysterious over the phone, Bill,' the contractor said. 'What's up?'

The inspector adjusted the collar of his shirt and leaned forward over the table. 'Give us a large tea,' he called over to Sid.

Tommy watched closely as his friend settled himself. 'This place is as good as anywhere fer a private chat, an' Sid's an ole pal,' he told him.

Bill Grogan nodded. 'I'll come straight to the point, Tommy,' he said. 'I got the word this morning from a reliable source that somebody's been putting the frighteners in. That's why I gave you a ring.'

'Fright'ners? Nah, they got it wrong, Bill,' the contractor replied quickly. 'Why should anybody wanna do that?'

'Stan Archer sounds as good a reason as any I can think of,' the inspector said quietly, watching his old friend's reaction.

'Stan Archer don't work for me anymore,' Tommy replied, trying to remain calm.

Chief Inspector Bill Grogan afforded himself a smile. 'Now, why don't you enlighten me, Tommy?' he said familiarly. 'We go back a long way. I'll give you my word that anything you tell me will be in confidence.'

The contractor took a sip from his mug of tea and then

clasped his hands together on the table. 'All right, Bill, but yer gotta promise me yer won't let me down,' he said anxiously.

'My word's always meant something, hasn't it?' Grogan reminded him.

The contractor sighed deeply and studied his thumbs for a moment or two. 'About six weeks ago I got paid a visit by Frankie Morgan,' he began. 'I've known Frankie since we ran the streets tergevver as kids, an' we've always bin on friendly terms. Anyway, Frankie was upset. 'E told me that I 'ad a grass workin' fer me an' I'd do well ter give the bloke the boot.'

'You're talking about Stanley Archer?' the inspector cut in.

Tommy nodded. 'Stan was a good worker an' I couldn't find any reason fer sackin' the man,' he went on. 'Besides, I don't take kindly ter bein' told 'ow ter run my business, Bill, who I should or shouldn't employ. What it was, though, Frankie told me 'e'd got word it was Stan Archer who put 'is boy Charlie away fer that affray in the Crown. 'E said that Archer contacted the police and named names. Don't ask me 'ow Frankie got the info on Stan. 'E didn't tell me, anyway. I warned Stan Archer, told 'im ter be careful, an' then two weeks later 'e asked fer 'is cards. That was that, until I read in the paper about 'im gettin' done over, an' Frankie bein' up on an assault charge.'

Sid brought over a mug of tea and as soon as he had left Tommy reached into his coat pocket and took out an envelope which he put down in front of the inspector. 'After Frankie Morgan was charged I got this letter pushed under the gate,' he said.

Grogan took out the folded sheet of paper and read the short message:

'Remember Pat Reagan. Don't you make the same mistake.'

'Reagan was the cartage contractor who got put out of business over the union troubles back in the thirties, wasn't he?' he asked.

Tommy nodded. 'I've got no trouble wiv the Transport Union. All my lads carry union cards an' I pay over the union rates,' he said. 'I do a fair bit o' dock work an' it suits me that my lads are union men. That message is clear ter me, Bill. What it really ses is, I shouldn't go upsettin' the wrong people or I'll be put out o' business.'

The inspector nodded. 'I can see that, but what makes you think Morgan wrote this note? Someone else might be holding a grudge against you.'

Tommy leaned forward over the table. 'Listen, Bill, I'm gonna be honest wiv yer,' he said in a low voice. 'When Stan Archer was lyin' in Guy's 'Ospital after Frankie Morgan beat 'im up an' your lads were makin' enquiries they called on me as yer know, and you also know what I told 'em. I just said that Archer was a good worker wiv no known enemies as far as I was aware. Well, yer know now that I wasn't tellin' the trufe, but yer gotta realise I 'ave ter live wiv these people an' I get me livin' in the borough. I got me wife ter fink about an' she ain't bin too well lately. I can't afford ter go upsettin' the likes o' Frankie Morgan an' 'is boys. You know what they're like. They're animals, Bill.'

'And you're going to be plagued with that sort until you and people like you decide that enough is enough,' the inspector told him firmly.

The contractor studied his clasped hands for a moment or two, then he looked up at the policeman. 'We've known each ovver fer quite a few years, Bill,' he began, 'an' I know yer can understand my position. Well, yesterday mornin' when I got ter the yard one o' the lads showed me a bundle o' charred rags lyin' near the cart shed. Somebody 'ad obviously lobbed 'em over the wall the previous night. Luckily fer me they'd burned out on the cobbles. If they'd landed on one o' my carts or on the shed the 'ole yard could 'ave gone up in smoke. So now yer know. Yes, I've 'ad the fright'ners put in, an' I reckon it's 'cos someone spotted your blokes when they paid me a visit last week. They're makin' sure that I don't go in the stand an' tell about the visit I got from Frankie Morgan.'

Bill Grogan folded up the note and put it back into the envelope before handing it back. 'Look, Tommy, you're not down to give evidence so you can sleep easy on that score,' he said reassuringly.

Tommy sighed deeply. 'As far as Frankie Morgan's concerned I don't 'ave ter give evidence on the witness stand, I could 'ave already told you what I know in confidence, ter put yer on the right road. That's what the Morgans suspect, I'm sure of it.'

The inspector drained his mug of tea and put it down in front of him with a wry smile. 'We got Frankie Morgan fair and square,' he said, 'though not the way we would've wanted. The police were called to an affray in the Crown, the same pub where Frankie's boy Charlie caused trouble. It was the pub manager who called us, knowing that if he tried to cover it up, especially after the first affray, then he was down to lose his licence. As it happens there are witnesses to say that Stan Archer started the fight and Morgan was defending himself. Archer sustained the fractured skull when he fell and hit his head on the bar rail. There were no other injuries, apart from a small bruising from a punch on the jaw. This is in confidence, of course. Anyway, with a few independent witnesses coming forward Frankie Morgan looks like he's going to get off this one, so why should he make things worse for himself by terrorising you?'

'Frankie Morgan might fink I'm gonna volunteer ter be a witness fer the prosecution because 'e might 'ave found out that Stan Archer is family,' Tommy explained.

'Family?'

'Yeah. Yer see, Stan Archer's livin' wiv my sister Lil,' the contractor went on. 'If I went in the box an' testified that Morgan knew Archer 'ad put 'is boy away then it could shed a new light on the 'ole affair.'

The inspector gazed down at the table thoughtfully. 'It's all a bit iffy. Besides, Morgan's got strong witnesses,' he said with a frown. 'He could deny that the conversation ever took place between the two of you, and remember that your statement to the police might be read out, if the defence request it. That's where you didn't do yourself any favours, old son. Or us, come to that.'

The two men finally left the cafe in Jamaica Road and shook hands as they parted company at Tower Bridge Road. 'As I said, Bill, I've gotta live an' trade in the area,' Tommy sighed, shrugging his broad shoulders. 'I can't mess wiv the Morgans, but at least I've put the record straight. If my place does go up in smoke at least yer'll 'ave somefing ter go on. Those Morgans are a plague, an' like most respectable people on this manor I wanna see the lot of 'em banged away fer a long time. Until then, we've all got problems. Take care, ole friend.'

Chapter Four

After Don Farran left for work on Tuesday morning Rose roused Susan and the two younger boys with cups of sweet tea, only to find that her young sister had a heavy cold coming on. As she helped Susan get dressed Rose realised that she would have to call on Mrs Arrowsmith once more.

Freda Arrowsmith lived at number 3 across the landing and Rose felt grateful to her for being such a good friend to the family. She was in her late forties with two grown-up sons who worked in the docks, and her husband who was ten years older than her was a tally clerk at the Surrey Docks. She left the flats at six o'clock sharp every morning to go to her part-time job cleaning offices in Tooley Street and she was always home before eight o'clock. She had looked after Susan on more than one occasion when the child was off colour and had also helped the family out with the occasional bottle of milk or packet of tea. Freda was a large, cheerful and obliging woman with a warm smile, and not prone to gossiping.

''Course yer can. Bring 'er in, gel, she'll be all right wiv me,' Freda replied, grinning at Rose's anxious expression. 'I'll stoke up the fire, it's a bleedin' perisher this mornin'.'

Rose set off for work feeling the cold wind on her face and

she noticed how leaden the sky looked. Snow was on the way, she thought, making a mental note to call in to Joe Diamond's shop for a supply of candles on her way home. The flats in Imperial Buildings had had electric lighting installed two years ago, though gas lighting was still used on the stairways and landings, and since the conversion there had been a few power cuts during the winter months.

Rose hurried into the factory ten minutes late through having to arrange things with Freda. At least Susan would be quite comfortable with her and the boys could be relied on to make sure the flat was warmed through before they collected her after school, Rose told herself.

'Late night, last night, then?' Bernard Collis asked, giving her a probing look that made the young woman want to shout an angry reply. Instead, she shook her head and said quietly, 'I overslept.'

'I've put a gel on your machine, you're on the bin terday,' the manager told her before turning on his heel and striding off along the corridor.

Rose breathed a sigh of relief. Getting into work late usually meant being allocated one of the worst jobs, but doing the binning wasn't too bad, she thought. It entailed collecting the metal waste from the machines in large containers and then dragging them out to the rear of the factory on four-wheeled trolleys. Although the task was hard physically it gave the girls a chance to get away from the neverending din for a short period, making the day seem a little less tedious than when standing in front of a machine for eight hours.

As Rose pulled a heavy trolley along the gangway Collis approached her. 'I might 'ave a vacancy on the Saturday list,' he said out of the corner of his mouth.

The young woman gave him a cold stare, knowing only too well the implication. Unless she gave in to his overtures there was no way she would get the extra overtime. The family would have to make do this Christmas. All that mattered was that they stayed together, were warm enough and had enough food to eat. There would be a few small presents for the boys and Susan but Don would have to go without. He was old enough to understand anyway.

'Don't ferget what I said,' the manager mumbled as he walked off.

'That's right, piss orf, you four-eyed, fat little bastard.'

Rose turned round to see one of the factory girls walking along behind the trolley.

'As soon as I get meself fixed up wiv anuvver job I'm gonna go in that office an' smack 'im right in the chops,' the girl went on.

Rose smiled at her. 'I know 'ow yer feel,' she said. 'I got told yesterday that I wasn't on the Saturday list. Now 'e's just said that there might be a vacancy, if I played me cards right.'

'Dirty little git,' the girl growled. 'One o' these days that goat's gonna get what's comin' to 'im. By the way, my name's Alice Copeland an' I normally work on the solderin'. Where d'you work?'

'Rose Farran. I'm on the big press,' she said, pointing over to the far side of the workshop. 'I got in late this mornin', that's why I got put on this job.'

'I'm tryin' ter place yer face. I know yer from somewhere,' Alice said.

Rose studied the girl for a moment or two. She was tall and dark-eyed; strands of dark hair showed from beneath her factory cap, and her face was round with rosy cheeks and a dimpled chin.

Alice suddenly smiled widely. 'I know where! The young women's club near the Tunnel. That's where I've seen yer.'

Rose felt her stomach tighten. 'I used ter go there wiv a

couple o' the gels who worked 'ere, but I stopped goin' in the spring,' she replied, mindful that it was at a club dance that she had met the man who made her pregnant.

'What made yer stop?' Alice asked.

'I just got bored wiv it,' Rose lied.

'Bored? There's plenty ter do there, an' there ain't much else ter do in the evenin's, unless yer courtin',' Alice went on.

Rose looked into the young woman's large enquiring eyes and felt that she could safely tell her the truth in confidence. 'As a matter o' fact I 'ad ter leave. Me muvver ran off an' I got younger bruvvers an' a sister ter look after,' she explained. 'I don't get much time ter go out at nights.'

'You poor cow,' Alice said, her open face full of sympathy. 'Can't yer get out fer the Saturday night dances? They still 'ave 'em now an' again, yer know.'

Rose shook her head. 'I don't fink so. It's very difficult.'

Alice nodded, her face becoming serious. 'I understand,' she said quietly. 'It was like that fer me once, but that's anuvver story.' She glanced up and muttered quickly, 'Look out! There's that ugly-lookin' ole goat comin' this way.'

'The machines won't get sorted out by themselves, yer know,' Collis growled as he reached the two young women.

'Just goin' ter the bog, Mr Collis,' Alice said sweetly, pulling a face at the back of his head as he walked on. Then she turned to Rose, looking suddenly sad. 'I remember now. Yer dad got killed on the invasion. I remember somebody tellin' me. So yer gotta look after the kids as well as workin' in this bloody place. Gawd 'elp us, 'ow d'yer manage?'

'I manage,' Rose said staidly. 'The kids look after each ovver till I get in.'

Alice put her hand on Rose's arm. 'I fink yer a brick, really I do,' she said as she walked off quickly with a friendly grin.

*

Don Farran had told Rose that he was doing overtime that evening and when he finished for the day he walked the short distance to Teacake Ted's cafe in Creek Road. John and Albert Morgan were already there when he arrived and he noticed that they both looked tense as he sat down on the wooden bench facing them.

'Yer better get somefing,' John said sharply. 'We've just ordered a roll each.'

Don went to the counter and ordered a large tea and a cheese roll. The shop was warm but he shivered with excitement as he went back to his seat. The food soon arrived and as the three sat munching their rolls they looked just like any other customers.

'Bruvver Ernie's just gone by,' John hissed. ''E flashed 'is lights.'

The other two peered through the steamy window and saw the two-ton Bedford van turn down the narrow street that ran along the side of Jackson's warehouse. Don swallowed hard and Albert began drumming his fingers on the table top. John Morgan sat rigid, his face set in a hard line.

Two customers in paint-splashed overalls left and Ted's wife came out from behind the counter to collect the empty cups and plates. At five forty-five the last of the workers left Jackson's factory and the elderly night watchman could be seen locking the iron gates from the inside. Albert Morgan looked anxious to get started but his older brother was in no hurry. 'There's time yet. Let's get anuvver cuppa,' he said.

It was dark as the three conspirators left Teacake Ted's at a couple of minutes to six and crossed the main road. They walked purposefully into the side turning and immediately saw the van parked without lights beside the high factory wall. John waved his hand and the van started up and jumped the kerb, pulling up inches away from the wall. Without a word the three clambered on to the bonnet and up on to the top of the van. John led the way and as the three of them clambered over the wall and dropped into the yard Ernie Morgan pulled off the pavement and cut the engine.

Jack Dobson hung the front-gate keys on the hook above the filing cabinet and set about making himself a cup of tea. Later he would do his rounds of the yard and then settle down for a good night's sleep in the comfortable office chair. He felt secure in his locked office, and in the fifteen years that he had been a night watchman Jack had never had any cause for alarm, other than from the air raids during the war when there had been fire watchers on the premises anyway.

The scratching on the office door made Jack start and he looked through the barred window into the yard. Bloody cats are a nuisance, he thought as he spooned sugar into his cracked mug. The scratching persisted and he cursed as he walked over to the door and gave it a kick with his boot. For a few minutes it was quiet and then the noise started again. Jack Dobson picked up the key and slipped it into the lock, swearing to himself that he would boot the cat over the wall. As he opened the door he was pounced on. He had no time to see his attackers or shout for help as he was spun round and pinioned by a pair of strong arms. A piece of sticking plaster was slapped on to his mouth and a large sack was slipped over his head.

'One sound outta you an' we'll shut yer up fer good. Understand?' a voice growled at him.

The watchman wondered how he was supposed to utter a sound with the plaster over his face and the sack over his head but he nodded vigorously. He was bundled into the office chair and ropes were tightly bound round his chest. He found it hard to breathe and he decided to relax as best he could for fear of having a heart attack. Three pounds seventeen and sixpence per week did not warrant him becoming a hero, and as long as the robbers did not do him any harm they could take what they wanted.

John Morgan took down all the keys from the rack and the three men hurried out into the yard. It took them barely a minute to find the right key for the main warehouse door and then Don Farran was told to sort out the front-door key and let the van in. In less than fifteen minutes the raid was over and as the laden van drove out Don pulled the gates shut and leapt into the cab as they pulled away and accelerated along Creek Road.

'Turn right 'ere, Em,' John ordered.

As the vehicle swung left and right through a maze of backstreets Don started to breathe more easily. It had worked as planned and the watchman had been unharmed.

The van finally pulled up outside a small yard and John Morgan jumped out and opened the gates. Ernie backed the van in beside a row of barrows and stalls and they quickly set about unloading it. There were six large cartons bound with thick string and it took only seconds to bundle them off, stashing them at the rear of the yard and covering them with a large tarpaulin sheet.

'Right, that's that fer now. Let's get back ter the Anchor fer a drink, lads, we've earned it,' John said cheerfully.

At six o'clock on Tuesday evening Herbert James Rideout opened his eyes and tried to focus on the alarm-clock by his bedside. It seemed to be wavering around on the chair and Herbert closed his eyes and brought a shaking hand up to his forehead. 'Sod it,' he growled, deciding to wait a few moments more before trying to pin down the clock. Just then the alarm went off and with a curse Herbert reached out from under the tattered blanket and grabbed the clock. He slipped it under the bare pillow and tried to ignore the ringing. Finally he turned over on to his back and opened his eyes. The electric light hanging over his head eventually stopped swinging and the alarm-clock bell stopped ringing. For a few minutes Herbert lay perfectly still in his bed, not wanting to move in case something else happened and jarred his frayed nerves. It remained quiet, and with a heroic effort the middle-aged drunkard dragged himself from his bed and staggered to the door. The passage was in darkness and as he searched for the light switch he suddenly remembered that the bulb needed replacing. 'Bloody nuisance,' he grumbled, still trying desperately to pull himself together.

At six fifteen Herbert had roused himself sufficiently to boil an egg, and as he sat munching the sandwich he had stuck together, the soft egg yoke dripped down on to his creased trousers. The suffering inebriate finished the last crusts and washed them down with black coffee, then he staggered slowly to his feet, picked up the saucepan containing the still-warm egg water and took it over to the stone sink. Dipping his shaving-brush into the saucepan he began to make a lather from a well-worn shaving stick and shakily applied the foam to his face. The two-day growth of beard was finally scraped away and Herbert looked into the broken mirror resting on the window-sill and surveyed the cuts and scratches on his face and chin. 'Bloody blade must be blunt,' he told himself aloud, not wishing to blame the damage on his shaking hand and unsteady legs.

Herbert James Rideout was forty-five years of age and stood five-eleven in his stockinged feet, when he was standing upright, which wasn't too often. He detested the name Herbert and ever since he was a very young man he had always been known to everyone as Jimmy. Herbert, or rather Jimmy, had once been a successful market trader with stalls in the markets on both sides of the river. At the outbreak of war he had volunteered for the navy and spent some time on a mine sweeper and on destroyers guarding the Arctic convoys to Russia. In 1944 he was invalided out of the navy with a back injury and he had tried to pick up the pieces of his life. At first he was in constant pain from the shrapnel wound to his back and he found that the regular painkillers he was required to take were slowly killing him. Alcohol seemed to be more effective and Jimmy started to drink heavily.

By the end of the war Jimmy's back pain was less of a problem than his intake of drink had become. His wife Doreen had had enough of his drunkenness and decided to leave him for a Canadian soldier, finally divorcing him and going to settle in Alberta. Jimmy's business suffered too and finally he was left with one stall in the East Lane market and a barrow outside London Bridge Station. All was not lost, however, and he found a couple of trusted friends to run the stalls for him when he was not too capable. The arrangement suited him and now his friends managed the stalls on a permanent basis, with Jimmy picking up a weekly income which paid for his drink, and his idleness.

At six forty-five Jimmy Rideout left his ground-floor flat in Imperial Buildings and walked into the Anchor public house where he ordered his usual pint of bitter. He cast a bleary eye at the three young men sitting talking in low voices in one corner and glanced back to the big, buxom Beryl McGarry, whom he had long lusted after. 'You're lookin' very nice this evenin' darlin',' he smiled, resting his aching back by leaning against the counter. ''Ow's that miserable ole sod of an 'usband doin' these days? I don't see much of 'im lately.'

'Yer don't 'ave ter look far. 'E's 'ere,' Beryl replied, smiling broadly.

'P'raps it's 'cos I don't wanna see 'im,' Jimmy joked. 'It's you who's stole me 'eart, gel. Come away wiv me an' let that silly ole sod fend fer 'imself.'

Beryl put the pint of beer down in front of Jimmy and tapped his wrist playfully. 'Mind yerself or my ole man might take it into 'is 'ead ter bar yer,' she replied, her slightly raised voice and warning tone lost on the drunkard.

Jimmy fished into his waistcoat pocket and took out a crumpled ten-shilling note. ''Ere, get yerself a drink, an' one fer that ole fella of yours,' he said loudly.

Sammy McGarry glanced at him and came over. 'I wanna word in yer ear, Jimmy,' he said, looking serious.

Jimmy blinked once or twice and gave the landlord a dutiful stare. 'I'm listenin',' he slurred.

'Last night,' the publican said.

'Yeah, what about last night?'

'You was pissed.'

'Gawd, that makes a change.'

'Yer got a bit stroppy wiv a couple o' customers.'

'Did I?'

'Yes, yer did. I want no more of it, Jimmy,' Sammy told him. 'If yer can't 'old yer booze then yer'll 'ave ter take yer custom elsewhere. I run a respectable pub an' I can't afford to 'ave my regulars upset by the likes o' you. So be warned.'

'Pity yer don't bar the right ones,' Beryl hissed at her husband as she went to serve a customer.

'I put my 'and on me 'eart, Sammy. I'll be the soul o' discretion,' Jimmy said earnestly. 'Yer won't need ter worry any more. 'Ere, d'yer fink yer missus might care ter run orf wiv me?'

'Yer couldn't 'andle 'er, Jimmy. Now go over there an' sit down, an' be'ave yerself,' Sammy told him, hiding a smile.

Jimmy stayed where he was, leaning against the counter, his red-rimmed eyes moving round the bar. Suddenly he spotted Don Farran and he picked up his pint and walked slowly over to where he was sitting. ''Ello, me son,' he said pleasantly. ''Ow's the tribe doin' these days?'

John and his brother Albert gave the drunkard wicked looks but Don smiled. 'They're OK, Jimmy,' he replied.

'That's good. Luvverly kids. Does me old 'eart good ter see 'em,' Jimmy said. 'Is young Rose all right?'

'She's fine.'

'I saw the boys the ovver day. Growin' up a treat. Credit ter yer farvver, those boys,' Jimmy slurred, 'an' so are you, me son.'

'If yer don't mind, we got fings ter talk about,' Albert cut in sharply.

'Go on then, talk. I wasn't talkin' ter you anyway, yer saucy little sod,' Jimmy replied, his eyes widening as he tried to focus clearly.

Albert stiffened and pushed his glass away, but John laid a hand on his arm. 'Take no notice, 'e's pissed,' he said quickly.

'Who's pissed?'

'You're pissed.'

Don could see trouble erupting and he looked up to catch Jimmy's unsteady eye. 'I'll talk ter yer later, Jimmy,' he said, winking.

'I'm gonna sod off, 'cos I know where I'm not wanted,' Jimmy said with a flourish. 'I'll talk to yer later, son.'

Once Jimmy had left John Morgan pulled out a roll of pound notes. 'Look, it's gonna take a few days ter get the business sorted out,' he said, 'so 'ere's a fiver each ter be gettin' on wiv.'

Albert gave his brother a sly grin and Don Farran's eyes lit up as he quickly pocketed the note. 'This'll come in 'andy fer Christmas,' he said.

Chapter Five

Rose had become resigned to the fact that it was going to be tight for money this Christmas. It would be the first Christmas without their mother and young Susan was bound to miss her. The younger boys would be a little upset too, but Don would not be troubled much. He had never been all that close to his mother, not in the way he had been to his father, and he was in no doubts about his mother's conduct towards them all. As for herself, Rose had mixed feelings. There had been times, a few times, when her mother was friendly and loving towards her, but there had usually been an ulterior motive. When the shouting and banging stopped and her attitude changed it was because there was someone new in her life and it meant that she would be expecting Rose to take over and manage the home and family during her absence.

As she sat beside the fire on Saturday evening Rose looked around her at the dark, stained ceiling and the old, faded wallpaper, peeling and torn, and she sighed in resignation. There was little chance of doing much about it, but she would be able to wash the paintwork down and add a few paper chains and balloons to hide the dirty ceiling and walls. The armchairs were tatty but she might be able to unpick the cushions and give them a wash. As for the mats, well a good beating and brushing would have to suffice. The presents were going to be a problem. Mrs Arrowsmith was knitting a jumper for Susan and she had already made two pullovers, one for each of the boys. She had them parcelled up in Christmas paper and was holding on to them until Christmas Eve.

Freda was a good woman and so were the people in the two flats above. Sadie Jones lived at number 5 with her three daughters Joan, Jennie and Josie. Like Rose's father, Sadie's husband had been killed in the war, while serving in the Auxiliary Fire Service during the height of the blitz. In the flat facing Sadie were the Prices, George and Ethel. Their two sons were serving in the army and their daughter Molly had just got married and moved away. Both the Prices and Sadie Jones had promised to help out as best they could and Rose felt confident that the family would enjoy their Christmas somehow.

Susan was playing with her faithful rag doll and the boys were quietly reading comics as they shared the armchair. Don was out, but that morning he had put three pounds into the cracked teapot and it was going to be a big help. Rose got up from her chair, reached up to the top shelf of the dresser and took down the teapot. She tipped out the coins, and the notes that Don had added, and started to count it once more. It came to five pounds seven and fourpence, and Rose hoped to make it a round six pounds by Christmas. It was now the first of December and it was going to be a squeeze, she knew.

As she put the money back into the teapot Rose suddenly remembered she was out of sugar and she glanced up at the clock on the mantelshelf. It was five minutes to five and she knew that Joe Diamond's shop closed around five. 'Keep yer eyes on Sue, I've gotta run down the road a minute,' she told the boys.

Joe was putting up his shutters as Rose reached his shop and he gave her a grin. 'Cuttin' it fine, ain't yer?' he said.

'Gis a pound o' sugar, Joe, and 'alf a pound o' broken biscuits, will yer,' she said breathlessly. It was a little extravagant but she knew how the boys and Susan liked broken biscuits.

As Rose was going out of the door she was stopped by Mrs Campbell, who had the usual tide of information to tell the young woman. While they were talking an old man wearing a tattered overcoat that reached down to his feet walked into the street muttering to himself as he passed by.

'Not 'im again,' Ivy Campbell groaned. ''E's makin' it a bloody 'abit.'

The old man carried on to the centre of the street and stood in the middle of the road facing the buildings. He took off his cap and placed it down at his feet, then he proceeded to sing in a loud deep voice. The words were a jumble of 'oohs' and 'ahs', with the occasional long-drawnout note that seemed to come from his boots. A window lifted and two pennies clattered to the pavement in front of him. The old man ignored the money and continued to sing out his baritone melody.

At number 4, C block the window remained closed but three faces were pressed against it as the Farran children stared down.

'Poor ole man,' Susan said sadly.

'I bet 'e's starvin' 'ungry. That's why 'e's singin' fer money,' Joey added.

Billy laughed. 'Look at 'is coat. I bet 'e 'as ter wear a long coat 'cos 'e ain't got no trousers on.'

Joey laughed loudly but Susan continued to look down with a sad face at the vagabond. 'Poor man. Yer shouldn't laugh at 'im, it's wicked,' she admonished her brothers.

Joey stopped laughing and stared down at the man for a few moments, then he turned to Billy. 'I wish we 'ad some money fer 'im,' he said.

Billy nodded, and as he turned away from the window he

caught sight of the teapot lying on the table. 'We could give 'im a few coppers out o' the teapot,' he suggested.

'That's what Rose's savin' up fer Christmas,' Joey reminded him.

'Rose wouldn't mind us givin' the man some money,' Susan urged them. 'I bet she'd give 'im some if she was 'ere.'

Billy fished his fingers into the teapot and drew out a shilling piece. 'Let's give 'im this,' he said, looking at the others.

'Yeah, let's!' Susan squealed.

Joey was not too sure but he nodded anyway.

Billy slid the window up a fraction and threw the silver coin out. He lost sight of it falling but heard the tinkle as it hit the ground before he shut the window down quickly, remembering his big sister's strict instructions that none of them must ever open the windows while she was out.

Down below the old man heard the tinkle of the coin as it hit the pavement and his sharp eye saw the glint of silver. As he moved forward to retrieve it he saw it roll from the kerb straight down into the drain.

Cursing his luck, and the aim of the donor, he picked up the two pennies lying on the pavement and swore at the first-floor window as he put on his cap and walked quickly out of the turning.

On Sunday morning Don Farran woke up and saw the winter sun streaming through the bedroom window. It looked to be a cold bright day and he realised that he had slept late. He could hear laughter coming from the living room and he sat up and slipped his feet down on to the cold oilcloth. He smelt bacon cooking. Rose always did bacon sandwiches on Sunday mornings. He dressed quickly, but before he left the bedroom he searched through his trouser pockets and counted the money he was left with. After giving Rose three pounds he had changed a pound note at work and paid back a ten-shilling loan from one of the electricians. He had changed the other ten-shilling note in the pub on Saturday evening and spent seven shillings. There was one pound three shillings left. It was enough for what he had in mind. It was about time they all had a day out, he told himself later as he munched on a crispy bacon sandwich.

Rose walked along clasping Susan's hand. She wore her only coat, but although it was rather shabby at least it was warm. Susan had on her coat and leggings and she wore a scarf wrapped around her throat and ears to keep out the winter chill. Billy and Joey walked side by side behind her and on their outside Don strolled along whistling quietly. The boys were warm in their heavy coats but Don felt the chill going through his light serge suit. He put his hands in his pockets and pretended not to notice as the family walked out into Tower Bridge Road on the cold, bright December sabbath.

'Where we goin'?' Susan asked her big sister.

'Yer'll soon find out,' Rose replied, hugging the child to her as they boarded a number thirty-six tram at the Bricklayer's Arms.

They found seats on the lower deck, and as the boys chattered happily together in the seat in front Rose turned to Don who was sitting beside her. 'I know I shouldn't be ungrateful, Don, but yer shouldn't 'ave gambled. We can do wiv every penny fer Christmas,' she said in a low voice.

Don smiled and shrugged his shoulders. 'I just felt lucky,' he told her. 'Besides it was only sixpence each way. One shillin' wouldn't 'ave made much difference an' look what I won. At least we can 'ave a day out, so don't worry.'

Rose settled down and glanced out of the window at the shuttered shops, nagging fear for the family worrying at her mind. At least they could enjoy the day together, she told herself. There would be enough time in the future for the heartaches.

'Elephant an' Castle next stop,' the conductor called out in a sing-song voice, winking at Susan.

The family stepped down from the tram and Don led the way into the tube station and bought tickets. A warm gust of air hit the Farrans as they stepped out of the large lift and walked along a sloping corridor to the platform. They had little time to wait and a gush of wind heralded the arrival of the train which would take them to Piccadilly. Susan had never been on a tube train before and the noise of the wheels made her cling tightly to Rose, but the boys sat wide-eyed, watching the lights dip and then glow brightly as the train thundered along the dark tunnel.

The sun was still shining as they all walked out from the station into the milling Christmas crowds. They strolled along into Regent Street, gazing into the shop windows that were gaily decorated with tinsel and holly, then they turned into a side street where a man was shuffling hot chestnuts over a coke brazier. Don stopped and bought them each a bagful of the hot nuts, giving them all a chance to warm their hands from the heat of the fire, and then they retraced their steps to Shaftesbury Avenue and walked along through Soho to Charing Cross Road. Susan had become tired and Don picked her up and carried her in his arms until they reached Trafalgar Square.

Rose stood beside Don on the edge of the Square, leaning against the balustrade overlooking the large paved area. The boys had taken their young sister off to feed the pigeons with peanuts that Don had bought from an old man with a tray strapped round his neck who looked blue with cold.

'They're enjoyin' this,' Rose said, giving Don a warm smile.

'I love it up West,' he replied. 'It's so big an' lively.'

Rose looked down at her clasped hands for a few moments,

thinking that her brother would soon have to be told that she was pregnant. It was only right, bearing in mind that he would have to take on more of the responsibility for the others. How would he react? She wondered. He would want to know who the father was and most likely rant and rave. It was only natural.

'Don, d'yer fink I'm doin' all right fer us all?' she said suddenly.

The young man turned to her and grinned. 'You're a bit of an ole moaner at times, but we understand,' he said, his large dark eyes bright and mischievous.

'I want us all ter stay tergevver, Don. I can't bear the thought of us bein' split up,' she said, her voice faltering.

'Look, Rose, nobody's gonna split us up,' he told her. ''Ow can they?'

'The welfare could, if they thought I wasn't carin' fer the boys an' Susan prop'ly,' Rose replied. 'They could put 'em in foster 'omes. It 'appened ter the Corrigans when their parents were killed in the bombin'.'

'That was different,' Don said quickly. 'There were all steps an' bloody stairs. The oldest was only ten or eleven. In our case there's you an' me. We're both classed as adults now.'

'Well, I am, but what about if anyfing 'appened ter me?' Rose reminded him.

'Like what? Like you runnin' off, or gettin' pregnant or somefing?' Don said grinning.

His reply was intended to raise a smile but it was as though an arrow had pierced her heart and Rose suddenly found that she could not look at him. She turned away from his laughing eyes and stared out over the Square, sighing deeply with anguish.

Her response to his remark surprised Don and he laid a gentle hand on her arm. 'Yer've not done anyfing silly, 'ave yer, Rose?' he asked her.

She bit on her lip, tears flooding into her eyes. 'I wish it was all a nightmare an' I could wake up an' see Mum an' Dad back 'ome tergevver again, just like they used to be,' she said, brushing a tear away from her cheek.

'Gawd Almighty, Rose. Yer not, are yer?' Don gasped.

'I'm two months gone,' she replied, still gazing down on to the Square, afraid of her brother's reaction.

Don turned away from her and leaned his arm on the balustrade, gazing down at the laughing children. For a minute or two his eyes wandered to the tall column, the lofty buildings surrounding the square, and the cold afternoon sun that was beginning to dip down in the winter sky. Then he turned to face his sister and his voice was soft and calm as he spoke. 'Look at me, Rose. Who's the farvver?'

'I can't tell yer. It doesn't matter anyway,' she replied, staring ahead as she fought to control her emotions.

'What d'yer mean, it doesn't matter?' Don asked her quietly. ''E's got a responsibility towards yer, or the baby at least.'

'I don't want a man ter come ter me out of a sense o' responsibility, Don,' she said, turning to face him.

'Is 'e married?' Don asked.

Rose shook her head. 'It was my fault. 'E never took advantage of me. It's too 'ard to explain. You wouldn't understand.'

'Try me,' he said.

Rose sighed and turned her eyes to the tall column in front of them. 'I was feelin' very low at the time,' she began. 'I 'adn't 'ad a night out fer months an' one evenin' as I was comin' 'ome from work I bumped inter one o' the girls who used ter work at Bromilow's. She told me about the dance that was comin' up at the Tunnel club I used ter belong to. She persuaded me ter go wiv 'er. It was on a Friday night. You remember. It was the night when Freda next door came in ter look after Susan an' the boys. Well, that was the night I got pregnant.'

Don did not say anything in reply. Rose saw that he was shocked, but she was a little relieved to find that he did not seem angry.

'The band was playin' all the best tunes an' everyone was 'avin' a lovely time,' she went on. 'They didn't serve beer or spirits at the dance, only lemonade and orange juice, but some o' the fellers brought their own drinks. There was a couple o' the girls I knew talkin' ter these three fellers. They called me over to even the numbers, an' one o' the blokes started passin' this bottle o' whisky around. I only took a few tiny sips but it made me feel good. I was glowin' inside, an' yer know what, Don? Fer the frist time since our muvver run off I didn't care. I lost the feelin' that 'ad nagged at me insides and I wanted the night ter go on forever. Anyway we split up inter couples an' I danced wiv my feller fer the rest o' the evenin'. I remember it got very stuffy an' we went outside fer a breath o' fresh air. We snogged fer a bit, an' then fings started ter get serious. I should 'ave seen the danger, but like I said, it was all too good. I could 'ave made 'im stop, but I didn't, an' because I didn't I've got the rest o' me life to regret it.'

Don rested his hand on Rose's arm again and tried to find words that might comfort her. 'Look, gel, I understand more than you fink,' he said quietly. 'I'm not exactly a kid, yer know. I can imagine what it's like ter be a muvver an' farvver ter the rest of us. Most gels o' your age are out an' about wiv boyfriends an' they can ferget fings fer a while. Wiv you it's all work. Yer got that poxy job at the tin bashers an' then yer got shoppin' an' 'ousework ter do every night. There's meals ter get, an' the worry o' the money. Well, I tell yer straight. Fings are gonna be different from now on. I'm gonna do more in the 'ouse. An' I tell yer somefing else too. Yer gotta 'ave one night out a week. I'll stop in an' look after the kids, an' don't worry about the money neivver. I got fings goin' fer me. I can look after the money side.'

Rose suddenly turned to face him again. 'I don't want yer ter pack up that apprenticeship, Don,' she said sharply. 'It's what Dad wanted. Anuvver fing. No more gamblin'. It's a mug's game. All right you 'ad a win, but yer lose more than yer win. We can manage the way we're goin' fer the time bein'. I'll sort fings out fer us all.'

Don squeezed her arm. 'Promise me somefing, Rose,' he said. 'Promise me yer won't try an' get rid o' the baby. It could kill yer. Look what 'appened ter that gel in the Buildin's. What was 'er name?'

'Pat Brody.'

'Pat Brody, that's right,' Don went on. 'She went ter one o' those women ter get rid of 'er baby an' she got blood poisonin'. Gawd almighty, Rose, yer don't want me ter spell it out ter yer, do yer? The woman stuck 'er wiv a steel knittin' needle. It was in the papers. The ole witch got eighteen months fer what she done.'

Rose smiled at him and patted his hand. 'You've grown up quickly,' she replied. 'Don't worry. I won't try anyfing silly. I promise.' She sighed. 'I'm sorry, Don, but I 'ad ter tell yer. You've got a right ter know. I'm just terrified what's gonna 'appen when the welfare people find out.'

'Sod the welfare,' Don said dismissively. 'I'll tell 'em ter mind their own business. If they come sniffin' I'll tell 'em ter piss off.'

'It is their business, that's the trouble,' Rose replied. 'We're on their list an' they 'ave ter keep an eye on us. It's not us two they'll be worried about, we're old enough ter look after ourselves. It's them three.'

Don looked down into the Square and saw the children coming towards them, Susan being half carried along as she clasped the boys' hands. Her face was flushed and she was laughing happily.

'They're not takin' those kids away, that's fer sure,' he growled.

Rose stood up straight and pulled the collar of her coat round her neck as the wind got up. 'Yer made me promise not ter do anyfing silly, an' now I'm askin' you ter promise me somefing, Don,' she said in a measured voice. 'Promise me yer'll not do anyfing that'll get yer inter trouble. Yer know what I mean. Stay at yer job, an' stay away from those Morgan boys. They're a real bad lot.'

Don's face relaxed and he gave his sister a broad smile. 'All right, I promise,' he replied.

'If you get put in prison it'd kill me, I know it would,' she said with passion.

'It's all right, yer got nuffink ter worry about. I promised, didn't I?' he said as the children came up the steps and hurried over to them.

'We're 'ungry,' Billy shouted.

Don picked up Susan and hugged her to him. 'Come on, kids. Let's go down the Strand. I know a place where we can get a luvverly 'ot meat pie an' chips.'

As the night closed in and the tram rattled towards Abbey Street Susan slept, nestled against Rose. The two boys were quiet, worn out but happy. Don sat deep in thought. There was money due to him from the robbery and he would have to be careful now that he had promised to keep away from the Morgans. He yawned widely and turned to his sister. 'I fink they're goin' on to a bonus scheme at work an' us apprentices are gonna be included. Should be a few bob extra each week,' he said as casually as he could.

Chapter Six

It was the Thursday evening of Christmas week and the Anchor was filling up. John Morgan stood at the bar talking to his brothers Ernie and Albert and the conversation came round to Ernie's impending army medical.

'I'm lookin' forward ter goin' in,' Ernie was saying, much to the disgust of the other two. 'There's a chance ter go abroad an' see places.'

'Yeah, or get posted ter some dead-an'-alive 'ole in this country,' John replied.

'Do yerself a favour an' play up on yer ears,' Albert advised him. 'Yer don't wanna go frew what John went frew. Bloody stupid ponces tellin' yer what ter do, like that sergeant 'e belted.'

'Yeah, too bloody true,' the older brother growled. 'I stood it as long as I could an' all the time I was finkin', who the bloody 'ell does 'e fink 'e is, an' when the stupid git 'ad the cheek ter tell me I looked like a pregnant kipper I upped an' put one on 'is chops. Trouble was the bloke didn't know when 'e was beat. 'E come back at me, didn't 'e, so I 'ad ter put the boot in or I'd 'ave got a smack meself.'

'Cost yer though, didn't it?' Ernie remarked. 'Yer done

twelve months in the glass'ouse over it. Yer might 'ave bin better off soldierin' on.'

Albert took a large gulp of his beer. 'Jus' do as I did an' play up on yer ears,' he repeated.

'Yeah, but you've got perforated eardrums. They don't take people in wiv dodgy eardrums,' Ernie replied. 'There's nuffink wrong wiv my ears.'

'Well, there's ovver fings yer can play up on,' John said. 'Yer could play the fairy. When yer go fer yer medical grab 'old o' the doctor an' give 'im a kiss. They don't take poofs in the services.'

The bar was filling up and when Jimmy Rideout walked in and stood at the counter John Morgan nodded to his brothers. 'C'mon, let's grab a seat, I don't want 'im chattin' to us.'

When they had sat down in a corner Albert took out a cigarette and lit it with a silver Ronson lighter. ''Ere, John, what we gonna do about Don Farran?' he said. 'We'll 'ave ter pay 'im a few bob.'

The older brother smirked. 'I'll give 'im a tenner an' tell 'im there'll be anuvver few bob ter come later,' he replied. 'After all, it was us what set it up an' all 'e did was 'elp wiv the unloadin'. I didn't see 'im give us much of an 'and wiv the ole geezer. Frightened of 'urtin' 'im, I s'pose.'

Albert shrugged his shoulders. He was nineteen, darkhaired and thickset like his brothers. He liked Don Farran and had managed to convince his brother that the young man could use a few bob and was to be trusted. However, he knew that it wasn't sensible to argue with John's decisions and he kept silent.

'That's all right wiv you, ain't it, Ern?' John asked.

'Suits me fine,' Ernie replied. 'As yer say, 'e didn't do much. Be different if 'e was in the team. 'E's only a sprog.'

'I gotta pay the contact off, then there's the geezer at the barrer sheds. We gotta pay 'im fer storage,' John went on. 'On top o' that we've got the loan o' the lorry ter sort out. We gotta keep Fat Arfur 'appy or 'e won't lend it to us again.'

'Anyway, it's sorted us out fer Christmas,' Albert remarked. 'Come nice an' 'andy, that.'

John Morgan sipped his beer. 'I got somefing else comin' up that's gonna be in readies,' he said in a low voice as he put his glass down on the table. 'I ain't sayin' anyfing about it yet, not till I make a few more enquiries, but yer in on it, ain't yer?'

'Bet yer life,' Albert said.

They both looked at Ernie, who had not answered. 'Well, Ern. What about you?' John asked.

'Sorry. What was yer sayin'?' Ernie said, dragging his eyes away from the counter.

'Never mind,' John replied.

''E reckoned there was nuffink wrong wiv 'is ears,' Albert joked. 'Play it like that an' yer 'ome an' dry, bruv.'

'Sorry, I was clockin' that geezer standin' at the counter,' Ernie said thoughtfully, his eyes glancing back briefly at a tall thin man in a grey suit and trilby hat.

John Morgan followed his brother's glance. 'Who yer talkin' about?' he queried.

'The one talkin' ter Sammy,' Ernie told him.

John looked back at his brothers. 'Bloody 'ell. That's a 'tec,' he said under his breath.

'I 'ope it ain't got nuffink ter do wiv us,' Albert said anxiously.

''E might be after gettin' some info fer the old man's case,' John said. ''E's comin' up the first week in the new year.'

'Yeah, yer could be right,' Albert replied. 'Sammy's pretty fick wiv Tommy Caulfield an' that 'tec might be pumpin' 'im ter see if Caulfield's said anyfing to 'im about what 'appened the ovver night.'

'Pity yer didn't aim a bit better an' burn the poxy yard down,' Ernie growled.

'That wasn't the idea,' John told him, playfully tapping his brother on the cheek. 'It was meant ter put the frighteners in. The old man was adamant there mustn't be no cock-up. Caulfield's got the message right enough an' I don't fink fer one minute 'e'll be blabbin' ter the coppers.'

Chief Inspector Bill Grogan drained his glass of ale and licked his lips. He knew that his presence in the pub had been duly noted by the Morgan boys, and that had been his main aim. He had wanted to have a few words with Sammy McGarry as well. The landlord allowed the Morgan family to use his pub, even though it meant that some of the locals had stopped going in. Either the man was frightened to ban the family or he was involved in their shady dealings. In any case, Sammy would be pondering over why the Chief Inspector of Dockhead had decided to stop in at the backstreet pub, and that pleased Bill Grogan.

Rose had managed to put another few shillings into the teapot to make it up to a round six pounds, and after the younger children had gone to bed on Thursday evening she sat at the table thinking about the presents she had to buy. Saturday was Christmas Eve and she wanted to have it all sorted out by then. It would mean going out after work tomorrow to buy all the bits and pieces but at least most of the shops would be staying open late.

Rose looked at the list she had made. A new doll for Susan was the first item she had thought of. A toy teaset and maybe one of those model sweet shops with the tiny jars of sweets and a pair of scales. Susan would play for hours with something like that, she thought. The boys would have to make do this year. A cap gun each for Billy and Joey and a couple of table games such as snakes and ladders and ludo. They had been asking about football boots and socks but that was out, they were far too expensive. Don would get a tie, a pair of socks and cufflinks, and if there was any money left over she might be able to manage a few extra decorations to make the flat look really festive.

As she got up to take down the teapot for a last check Rose heard Susan calling out, and when she went into the bedroom she saw the child sitting upright in bed clutching her tattered doll to her and rubbing her eyes.

'It's all right, luv, yer've bin dreamin',' she said in a comforting voice. 'C'mon let's get yer tucked down 'cos it'll soon be Christmas an' Farvver Christmas's fairies are makin' sure that all the children are bein' good an' goin' asleep early.'

Susan laid her head back on the pillow with a sigh and as Rose bent over her she looked up at her. 'Will Mummy come 'ome fer Christmas, Rose?' she asked.

'I don't know, darlin', but I'll be 'ere, and Billy an' Joey, an' Don,' Rose replied. 'Now you just shut yer eyes an' go ter sleep. I'll sit 'ere fer a while, all right?'

The child seemed reassured and she closed her eyes, the tattered doll clasped tightly to her. Rose sighed sadly. She looked around the bedroom which was illuminated by a night-light flickering in a saucer of water. On top of the wardrobe she saw her old teddy bear, the one her father had bought her when she was a young child. She had never been able to part with it, although her mother had often been on to her to get rid of it. She saw the framed picture of a guardian angel with hands held out over two young children, and the few picture books lying on a shelf above the iron trunk in the corner. This bedroom was in dire need of paint and wallpaper, she realised. The whole flat needed so much done to it, but it would all have to wait.

Susan was sleeping soundly now and Rose got up quietly and left the room with a heavy heart. She remembered her friends at work saying how they were wishing the old year out and looking forward to a more prosperous and happy new year. Things were not going to get any better next year for the Farrans, Rose thought, barring some miracle.

Jimmy Rideout walked unsteadily back to his flat in the Buildings. The pain in his back had eased but his head felt heavy and he shivered as a cold wind caught him head on when he turned the corner. He pulled up the collar of his overcoat and thought about the promise he had made to himself only a few days ago. After Christmas he was going to give up the drink and make a few changes to his life, he had vowed. Drink had cost him heavily. His wife had run off, his business had all but gone, and he was looking like a tramp. His last pair of shoes were stuffed with cardboard and his one remaining suit was so bad that the cleaners had nearly refused to accept it for cleaning.

'Just wait, you'll see,' Jimmy muttered aloud as he reached the entrance to A Block. 'There's gonna be a few changes made, mark my words.'

As he fished in his coat pocket for his front-door key Fred Albury walked into the block carrying a tool bag. ''Ello, Jim, 'ow's tricks?' he asked.

'Not so bad, apart from a bloody 'eadache, a pain in me back an' a touch o' the miseries,' Jimmy replied with a lopsided grin.

Fred had a soft spot for the street's drunkard despite the man's reputation, and he chuckled as he put down his heavy bag and scratched at his bald head. 'We've all got our problems, mate,' he said. 'I've just bin up ter that scatty mare Iris Ford in D Block. She 'ad a leaky tap an' I was stuck up there nearly

66

an hour. I couldn't get away from the silly ole cow. My ole dutch is gonna go orf alarmin'. I'm sure she finks I'm up ter no good.'

Jimmy was having trouble finding his key. 'I'm sure I brought that poxy key out wiv me,' he said, pulling on his chin as he tried to remember. 'Can yer let us in, Fred?'

The porter nodded with an indulgent grin. ''Ang on while I dump this bag indoors,' he told him.

Jimmy heard a few heated words exchanged and when the porter came back out of his flat clutching a bunch of keys he looked agitated. 'Told yer, didn't I? Bloody silly mare,' he growled. 'I can't be gone five minutes wivout she wants a bleedin' autopsy. Gawd 'elp us, a bloke would 'ave ter be really 'ard up ter fancy Iris Ford. Right, 'ere we are.'

Jimmy stood back while Fred turned the key in the lock and then he saw the look of concern on the porter's face.

''Ere, you ain't left a pot on, 'ave yer?' he asked.

Jimmy put his head into the passage. 'Bloody blimey, it's me clean socks,' he shouted as he staggered into the flat.

Fred followed Jimmy in and saw the charred remains of the socks lying over the gas stove. The gas jet was on a low flame and the place felt like an oven. 'You was lucky there, Jim boy,' he said with emphasis. 'The 'ole buildin's could 'ave caught light if they'd gone on the floor.'

Jimmy scooped the pile of newspapers from the chair beside the table and sat down heavily. 'Funny fing, I was only just finkin' about the promise I made ter meself a few days ago,' he said, leaning his arm on the table and cupping his chin in the palm of his hand. 'I'm gonna pack up drinkin' after Christmas. I can't go on like this fer much longer. It's gettin' worse. Last week I ruined me grey flannels wiv the iron, an' then I let the kettle boil away. Bloody great 'ole in it, there is. Fing is, I stop in one night ter try an' do wivout a drink, then the next night I can't get enough of it.'

Fred was anxious to get back to his irate wife and he nodded sympathetically. 'Well, Jimmy, I've gotta go, yer know the score wiv Muriel,' he said with a shrug. 'I gotta keep 'er sweet or I'll be on bread an' water.'

As he got to the door Fred turned. ''Ere, Jim, I don't know if yer interested but that Iris was tellin' me she does a bit o' dressmakin'. She might come in 'andy fer you now an' again.'

'What do I want a dress for, yer silly git?' Jimmy growled.

'Nah, I mean fer alterations or repairs ter yer strides,' Fred told him.

'Yeah OK, Fred. An' fanks fer lettin' me in,' Jimmy replied.

After he had made himself a cup of tea Jimmy sat back in his chair and cocked his feet up on the table. For a while he sat sipping the hot sweet tea, then suddenly his eyes caught sight of the old photograph album on the dresser. He remembered finding it at the back of a cupboard when he was searching for some socks and he had left it handy, telling himself that he would browse through it later. With a grunt he got up and picked up the heavy, leather-bound album. His ex-wife Doreen had filled it with photographs but for some reason she had chosen to leave it behind. How it had come to be buried at the back of the cupboard was a mystery to Jimmy, and he put it down to just another of his unaccountable actions when he was the worse for drink.

As he turned the pages the memories came flooding back and Jimmy sighed sadly. There was a photo of him and Doreen standing together outside the block. There was another of him together with some of his old naval friends and he could hardly recognise himself. On the last page he saw the photo of a vivacious young blonde woman, and after staring at it for some time Jimmy closed the album and let it rest on his lap while he stared up at the ceiling, deep in thought. 'Dolly Farran,' he said aloud. How long ago it all seemed now. Dolly was

Gerry Farran's young sister and she would have been about twenty then, with all the young men in the street eager to win her hand. He had succeeded in taking her out on one or two occasions, but as Dolly had told him, she was not ready for a life at the kitchen sink with a tribe of children tugging at her apron. She was something, he had to admit. Dolly was the prettiest girl he had ever laid eyes on. She was a flirt, a bubbling, beautiful creature who remained free as the air, untamed and unsullied.

It had all changed as the war clouds gathered in 1938, Jimmy remembered. Dolly suddenly left the area and her disappearance remained a mystery for a while. He had asked after her when he and Gerry Farran had a farewell drink together before they both joined up, a few days after the outbreak of war. Gerry told him then that Dolly had got married and was living somewhere in Kent. He had seemed reluctant to enlarge on the matter, and at that time there were other things to occupy their minds.

Now, as he sat thinking about Dolly Farran, the years seemed to weigh down heavily on the lonely, inebriate man. Was this to be his destiny? Was he to drink himself into an early grave, with no one to mourn his passing? No. He could pull himself together and rid himself of the demon. The new year would be one he would look back on with pride.

The clock struck eleven and Jimmy stood up. Next year, certainly, but now it was Christmastime, the season of good cheer, and if he had to drink alone then so be it. With the good intentions still uppermost in his bleary head, Jimmy Rideout reached into the dresser cupboard for a bottle of whisky and poured himself a large measure.

Chapter Seven

On Friday evening the Bromilow factory closed at five o'clock as usual and some of the girls planned to have a drink together at the Horseshoe public house in Tower Bridge Road. Alice Copeland had managed to find Rose that lunchtime and she lost no time in trying to persuade her new-found friend to join the rest of them at the pub.

'C'mon, luv, it's only once a year, an' yer never know, yer might find yerself a bit o' spare,' she said laughing.

'I'd love to, but I gotta do all the shoppin' an' there's the presents ter get,' Rose replied.

Alice pulled a face. 'I wish you could come wiv us. It'd make a nice break. I got money so yer needn't worry,' she said, her rosy cheeks flushed with excitement.

Rose shook her head, feeling sad at having to refuse the girl. Alice was nice, she thought, but there was too much to do and this Christmas had to be special.

'I 'ope yer won't be offended, but I got yer somefing,' Alice said hesitantly.

Rose looked down at the small parcel in her friend's hands and up into the girl's open face and she suddenly felt a surge of emotion. It was the look in Alice's wide dark eyes that did it, a mixture of sadness and happiness that overwhelmed her. 'Yer shouldn't 'ave. I – I couldn't buy you anyfing,' she blurted out.

Alice tried to hide her own embarrassment, waving her hand. 'I'm very pleased yer didn't,' she said quickly. 'Yer got enough ter do. Just 'ave a lovely Christmas an' don't worry, fings ain't always as bad as they seem.'

Rose felt the tears starting and she suddenly hugged her blushing friend. 'Fanks, luv,' she said gratefully. 'You 'ave a good Christmas, too, an' be careful.'

As she hurried towards the market Rose clutched her handbag tightly. Inside was the small package Alice had given her and an envelope with the contents of the teapot, six pounds exactly. If all went well she would be able to get everything she needed in Tower Bridge Road and be home before the children got too tired to eat their tea. First there was Susan's and the boys' presents to get at the toyshop, then she could call in to the men's shop opposite for Don's tie and cufflinks.

The market stalls were piled high with fruit and vegetables and lit with large Tilley lamps. People were milling around between them and going in and out of the market shops, and young children wrapped in warm clothes and woollen scarves held on tightly to their mother's hands, their faces glowing with the excitement of the season. Old women, bowed down with shopping-bags and parcels, trudged through the market on tired legs and aching feet, wishing for the fireside and cups of strong hot tea. Traders shouted loudly, encouraging the shoppers to buy, and as the darkness closed in so the first few snowflakes started to fall.

Rose crossed the main thoroughfare, holding on to the children's presents, and stood for a few moments looking at the display of ties in the shop window. There was one tie which caught her eye. It had thin stripes of black and royal blue, and under the display there were boxes of cufflinks and tie-pins. She hurried in, aware that she had taken longer than she wanted choosing the children's toys. The shop manager wrapped up the tie and cufflinks and then waited expressionless as Rose counted out nineteen shillings and elevenpence from the envelope.

'Will that be all, madam?' he said haughtily as Rose picked up the parcel.

'For now,' she replied, matching his stare before hurrying out of the shop.

As she waited to cross back into the market Rose made a quick calculation. So far the presents had come to five pounds fifteen and elevenpence, which left four shillings and a penny. She saw a gap in the traffic and dashed across the road, stopping at a fruit stall where she bought apples, oranges and a bag of Brazil nuts, which came to half a crown. There should have been one shilling and sevenpence left in the envelope but there was only sevenpence. Rose was puzzled as she walked back through the market. She had counted the money over and over again and felt certain that she had added the right amount to make it up to the even six pounds. As she was trying to work it out she stopped distractedly to look at a stall selling packets of decorations and balloons.

''Ere you are, luv. Two bob each. Best value in the market,' the trader told her. 'Make yer place look like fairyland. C'mon, give the kids a treat.'

Rose opened her handbag and tore open her pay packet to search for a two-shilling piece. 'I'll take one,' she said quickly.

'What about a couple o' paper lanterns, luv?' the stall owner pressed her. 'Now wiv these fings it really will be fairyland.'

Rose shook her head but the man persisted. 'I tell yer what. They're goin' for one an' fivepence each,' he said. 'I'll give yer two fer 'alf a crown. Go on, be darin', after all, Christmas only comes once a year.'

The young woman delved back into her pay packet. The man was right, she thought with a smile.

When she arrived home Rose was pleasantly surprised. Don had already given the children their tea, and as she sat down to remove her shoes from her tired feet he brought her a cup of tea. 'Yer look all in,' he said with concern on his face.

Later that evening Rose sat facing Don beside the glowing gas fire. She had been thinking about the teapot money and decided to tackle him about it.

'Yer don't ever take money out o' the teapot, do yer, Don?' she asked him. 'Just ter borrer, I mean.'

He shook his head emphatically. 'I've never touched it, Rose, except that time when yer said I could borrer ten bob. That went back the next week. I gave it ter you, remember?'

'It's all right, I'm not doubtin' yer,' Rose replied. 'It's just that I counted that money out time an' time again. I know I 'ad five pounds seven an' fourpence in that pot ter start wiv. I added the rest since then ter make it up ter six quid exactly an' before I went ter work this mornin' I put the money in an envelope. I done all me shoppin' an' right at the end I was one shillin' short. I can't understand it.'

'P'raps one o' the shops short-changed yer,' Don offered.

Rose shook her head. 'The money was mostly coppers an' silver. At each shop and stall I counted out the right amount. So I know I didn't get short-changed.'

Don grinned at his sister's serious face. 'Don't let it worry yer, Rose,' he said. 'Yer could 'ave made a mistake, even you ain't perfect.'

'It just gets me, I'd sooner give it away than lose it,' she replied.

'Well, we know the kids ain't touched it,' Don remarked. 'They never go near the teapot. They can't reach it where you keep it anyway.'

Rose suddenly remembered when she had run out to Joe Diamond's shop and left the teapot on the table. The children would not have touched the money, surely, she told herself.

Susan came over and leaned her head on Rose's lap. 'I'm tired an' I wanna go ter sleep,' she said yawning.

Rose picked the child up in her arms and kissed her on the forehead. 'C'mon then, sweet, let's get yer tucked up in bed all nice an' warm,' she said.

Susan sighed contentedly as Rose pulled the bedclothes up around her ears. 'Rose, the man was 'ere again while you was out,' she said as she clasped her ragged doll to her.

'What man?' Rose asked, intrigued.

'The singin' man,' Susan replied.

'What singin' man?'

'The one who sings in the street, but we 'ad no money ter give 'im this time,' Susan went on. 'I wanted Billy ter chuck 'im a slice o' bread but 'e wouldn't. The poor man must be very 'ungry.'

Rose kissed the child's head and smiled at her sad expression. 'So yer give 'im money last time, then?' she said, realising now what had happened to the missing shilling.

'I didn't, but I told Billy an' 'e chucked the money out to 'im,' Susan replied, looking suddenly frightened. ''E only pushed the winder up a tiny bit, Rose, 'cos 'e knew 'e mustn't open it. It was only fer the singin' man.'

'I see, an' Billy got the money fer the man from the teapot,' Rose said, trying to keep a straight face. 'So Billy gave the man a shillin'.'

'I dunno 'ow much Billy gave the man but it wasn't much, 'cos 'e said so,' Susan told her with a wide yawn.

'Well, that's all right,' Rose said quietly. 'Now you go ter sleep, an' when yer wake up it'll be Christmas Eve, an' on

Christmas-Eve night Farvver Christmas brings the children their presents.'

'Will I get some this year?' Susan asked.

'Of course yer will.'

'Will Billy an' Joey get some too?'

'Yes, they will.'

'I wish Don would get a present.'

''E will too.'

'Even you?'

'Even me.'

Rose left the bedroom a few minutes later when she saw that Susan was sleeping soundly. She could hear Don singing to himself in the scullery and she settled down beside the fire. Later she would wrap the presents, but there was time for a short nap first, she thought, suddenly feeling exhausted.

'I'm meetin' a mate o' mine, Rose. Shan't be late,' Don announced.

Rose mumbled a reply as Don left the flat, little realising that he was on his way to meet the Morgan boys and collect his share of the proceeds from the robbery.

In the boys' bedroom Billy Farran settled down beneath the bedclothes tired and eager for the next day to dawn, but Joey was wide awake.

''Ere Billy. Where do Christmas trees come from?' he asked.

'I dunno. Christmas land, I s'pose,' came a muffled reply.

'I've never 'eard o' Christmas land.'

'Well, p'raps they come from somewhere else.'

'Like where?'

'Like where the Eskimos an' the reindeer come from.'

'Rose said we can't 'ave a tree this year,' Joey went on. 'I s'pose it's 'cos we're poor.'

Billy turned over to face his brother. 'Look, if yer go ter

sleep right away I'll take yer down the market termorrer an' find out 'ow much Christmas trees cost,' he told him.

Joey closed his eyes and was quiet for a few minutes, then he opened them and said, 'I don't believe in Farvver Christmas, do you?'

Billy was already fast asleep and Joey turned on his back and stared up at the ceiling which glowed with the light from the street lamp outside. Sounds from the street carried up to the first-floor flat in Imperial Buildings, as revellers came along, singing, and a market trader pushed his empty barrow through the cobbled turning. Tiredness finally overtook the disbeliever, and as he sank into a dreamless sleep the snow began to settle.

Both bars of the Anchor were packed when Don pushed open the door of the public bar and walked in. He found John and Albert Morgan sitting at their usual table and he went over and nodded to Albert. There was no vacant seat and for a few moments the young Farran boy stood looking uneasy. 'I'm sorry but I can't get yer a drink. I'm boracie lint,' he said.

John Morgan flipped a ten-shilling note down on the table in front of Albert. 'Get 'im a drink,' he said coldly.

When Albert left the table John motioned Don to sit. 'Look, I've 'ad a bit o' trouble gettin' the money. There's certain people ter be paid off an' I've 'ad ter shell out from me own pocket. It's gonna be after Christmas before I can collect the dosh,' he told the young man.

Don sagged in his seat as Morgan reached into his waistcoat pocket. 'Look, here's a fiver ter carry yer over. Some o' the fags were marked fer the NAAFI an' I'll 'ave a job gettin' rid of 'em. I expect I'll only get a fraction o' the true price if I can place 'em, so I don't 'old out much 'ope of any more dosh,' he said gruffly.

Don pocketed the note. 'I fink it was a big risk ter take fer a few quid,' he said. 'What about the cigars? There was a couple o' cases, wasn't there?'

John Morgan's eyes narrowed disdainfully. 'Look, I only took you along on the job 'cos bruvver Albert told us you was 'is mate,' he said in a low voice full of menace. 'We could 'ave done the job wivout your 'elp. Just fink yerself lucky. Yer've earned a tenner in all. As fer the cigars, they ain't much cop. A lot o' people don't smoke cigars like they do fags. They'll take a bit o' gettin' rid of. If there's any more dosh ter come yer'll be rode in. Now as far as I'm concerned, that's my final say on the matter, all right?'

Don's face had flushed with anger and he clenched his hands into fists under the table. 'OK. If that's yer attitude then yer can leave me out of any ovver clever plans yer might 'ave,' he retorted scornfully. 'I ain't gonna take those sort o' chances fer peanuts.'

'Don't get flash wiv me, son, or I might ferget yer Albert's mate,' John Morgan hissed, leering forward across the table top.

Don got up quickly. 'Don't let that stop yer,' he growled.

Albert was coming back to the table and could see the confrontation taking place. ''Old up, Don, I got yer a pint 'ere,' he said quickly.

'Give it to 'im, 'e's the big man,' Don sneered as he turned on his heel and walked quickly out of the pub.

The saloon bar of the Anchor was small and comfortably furnished. It was usually frequented by local traders and a few elderly couples who were prepared to pay the extra penny for the privilege of a little luxury. Frankie Morgan used the saloon as a rule, and on that Friday evening he sat chatting to a couple of well-dressed men of about his own age.

Frankie was a big man with dark, greying hair that was swept back, partially covering his ears and lying on his collar, and he was dressed in an expensive suit. His heavy face bore the marks of violence. There was a long white scar running along one cheek to his ear and another over his left eye, the results of a bar-room brawl back in the thirties when he was a minder for a local bookmaker. His eyes were closely spaced under thick dark eyebrows and his complexion was pasty, with two patches of red over his cheekbones. When Frankie was angry or under the influence of drink the patches of colour flared, and tonight they were prominent.

Frankie was feeling very relaxed and a little drunk. Early in January his case was due to be heard at the Old Bailey and he was confident of the outcome. There had been no comeback from the warning message he had got his son to deliver over the wall of Tommy Caulfield's yard, and as his solicitor had said only last week, the case was almost a non-starter. The defence witnesses were solid and it looked as though Stan Archer was a certainty to be broken down under cross-examination.

One of the men sitting with Frankie Morgan looked cautiously around the bar and then leaned forward over the table. He was a tall, thin man in a smart grey suit with an immaculate white shirt and silver tie. He wore gold-rimmed spectacles and his eyes were deep-set beneath a sloping forehead. 'This is a big one, Frankie,' he began. 'I can tell you now that it's a West End jeweller's shop and there's a guaranteed grand in it for you up front, with another grand after the proceeds have been sold, which I would expect to be in about three months at the very outside. Basically, your three boys will be hired as the muscle. Our man is good, very good, and you'll be meeting him soon. I've no doubts about this operation whatsoever. It'll go off like a dream, providing your lads do as they're told without question. We've spent a lot of time setting this one up and I have to stress that the timing is crucial. Our man goes in the shop fifteen minutes before closing time and he'll look like the everyday customer. On his signal your boys go in and take care of the staff and they follow our man's instructions to the letter. The getaway method is all sorted out, but we'll talk more about that later.'

'Where are my boys gonna be waitin'?' Frankie cut in.

The thin man smiled indulgently. 'As I just said, we'll go through all the finer points when we finalise the plans,' he replied. 'For the time being all you need to know is that the shop is an old-established concern; it's well belled-up as you would imagine, but the owner and the two assistants working there are all knocking on a bit, so we don't anticipate heroics of any sort. I have to tell you that the more valuable pieces in the haul will be too hot to market anywhere in London. That's where we come in. Our organisation has the contacts to market the stuff on the Continent.'

Frankie nodded slowly, stroking his chin with his thumb and forefinger thoughtfully.

The other man, who had been sitting quietly, took his cue and coughed to clear his throat. He was thick-set and older-looking than his colleague. His face was pallid and he gave the impression of a life spent behind a desk. When he spoke his voice was clear and measured, however, and he commanded attention. 'The actual date of the operation has not been set yet. We're waiting on more information, but it'll be before the end of January,' he began. 'You see, the shop is due to take delivery of their spring collection some time in January. As soon as we get the go-ahead I'll contact you, Mr Morgan, and we'll finalise everything. Of course we'll need your answer within the next few days. You've been recommended, but if you feel that this is too big for you to handle, then feel free to say so. There'll be no hard feelings.'

'What do you say, Frankie?' his companion cut in. 'We need muscle for this one and I know your boys fit the bill admirably.'

Frankie Morgan stood up and pulled out a roll of pound notes from his trouser pockets. 'I'll get us all anuvver round, an' we'll drink ter success, if that answers your question,' he said, grinning evilly.

An hour later the two distinguished-looking visitors left the saloon bar of the Anchor feeling pleased with the outcome. Frankie remained at the table sipping his Scotch. He knew that his boys would jump at the chance of earning some real money, and when he put the proposition to them he knew that there would be no doubt about their response.

Chapter Eight

Billy and his younger brother Joey walked through the Tower Bridge Road market, their faces glowing and their hands tucked down deep in their trouser pockets. On Saturday mornings the market was always busy but today, Christmas Eve, it was heaving. Billy and Joey squeezed between some shoppers and stood beside a fruit and vegetable stall that was also selling small Christmas trees.

''Ow much fer the trees, mister?' Billy asked the roubust-looking trader.

'All of 'em or just one?' the man answered with a grin.

'That one there,' Billy asked, pointing to the largest tree that was about a foot taller than he was.

'That'll cost yer a dollar,' the trader told him. 'Or there's that one next to it. Yer can 'ave that one fer four an' a tanner.'

'We'll come back later,' Billy replied, grabbing Joey's coat sleeve and propelling him away from the stall.

'I wish we 'ad five bob, that was a big tree fer five bob,' Billy said knowledgeably. 'Yer could get a load o' stuff on a tree like that.'

'I bet we could do it better than that one at my school,' Joey remarked.

The two boys stopped at the doughnut shop and Billy fished into his coat pocket for the sixpence Rose had given him. 'C'mon, let's get two jam doughnuts,' he said.

They came out and turned into Weston Street to eat their doughnuts without being jostled. The snow had been cleared from the market area and had turned to a greyish-brown slush on the main road, but in the backstreets it still lay firm and white. Billy brushed the top of a low brick wall clear before they sat themselves down.

'It really looks like Christmas wiv all the snow,' Joey said eagerly, jam spurting out of his doughnut as he took a huge bite.

'I reckon we could sell a dollar's werf o' firewood if we could get any,' Billy said as he screwed up his paper bag and threw it into the gutter.

'Yeah, but by the time we got enough dosh those trees'd be all sold,' Joey replied, licking the sugar and jam from round his mouth.

'C'mon, let's go an' 'ave anuvver look,' Billy said, sliding down from the wall.

As they turned back into the market Joey caught sight of Jimmy Rideout, who was remonstrating with a stallholder.

'I ain't 'avin' them,' Jimmy protested. 'Yer took 'em all from the front. I like nice firm ones, not those soddin' fings.'

The trader took one of the tomatoes from the scale pan and waved it under Jimmy's nose. 'Wassa matter wiv that one?' he said loudly. 'That ain't soft, yer silly ole sod.'

Jimmy looked peeved, swaying back on his heels as he focused his bleary eyes on it. 'Those ovvers are,' he said.

The trader sighed in resignation. 'All right I'll weigh yer up a pound from the back o' the pile. 'Ow's that suit yer?' he growled.

'I should bloody well fink so,' Jimmy mumbled.

'What d'you say?' the trader said quickly.

'I just said bloody good show,' the inebriate replied with a lopsided smile.

Billy and Joey watched as the tomatoes were carefully selected and placed on the scales. 'That man's always drunk,' Billy said. ''E was singin' really loud the ovver night when we was in bed. I looked out the winder an' I saw 'im sittin' on the kerb. 'E was drunk as anyfing.'

The boys walked on and stopped at the fruit stall further along to take another look at the Christmas trees. 'If we lived in Iceland we could just go out an' get one fer nuffink,' Joey said.

'Well, we don't so it's no good wishin',' Billy replied.

''Ello, you two. What yer doin' 'ere?'

The boys turned to see Jimmy Rideout standing behind them. He was eating a tomato, a brown paper bag clutched to his chest.

'We're lookin' at the trees,' Joey replied.

''Ave yer got a Christmas tree?' Jimmy asked. 'I ain't bovvered ter get one.'

'We ain't bovvered neivver,' Billy said, shrugging his shoulders.

'We would 'ave 'ad one, but they cost five bob. Well, that one does,' Joey told him, nodding towards the largest tree.

'C'mon, Joey, we've gotta get back 'ome,' Billy said.

'I'm goin' back 'ome too. 'Ere, 'ave a tomater,' Jimmy said, holding out the bag.

'No fanks,' Billy replied.

'I'll 'ave one,' his brother said quickly while the bag was still in reach.

'They're good for yer. Keep yer fightin' fit. Look at me,' Jimmy said, sticking his chest out.

The boys set off home with the drunk stepping along beside them.

'I knew yer farvver. Me an' yer farvver was ole mates,' Jimmy announced, puffing with the effort of keeping up with them.

'Was you in the army?' Billy asked.

'Navy. Leadin' seaman James Rideout reportin', sir.'

The two boys smiled as Jimmy saluted.

'Our dad was killed on D-day,' Billy said. 'We got 'is medals in a drawer.'

'Yer farvver was a brave man, an' I know, 'cos me an' 'im was good pals,' Jimmy told them.

Suddenly a passing shopper caught the drunk's arm and knocked the paper bag out of his hand. The few remaining tomatoes spilled on to the pavement. A woman stepped on one and Joey ran to retrieve another which had rolled into the gutter.

'Never fear,' Jimmy said smiling as the young boy handed him the bruised tomato. 'That clumsy ole mare did me a favour. They didn't taste very nice anyway. Now as I was sayin'. Me an' yer farvver was ole pals, since we was both no older than you two. An' yer know what? I've bin keepin' me eye on you lot. Oh yes, I know yer very well. I know yer sister Rose, yer bruvver Don, an' that little Susie. Yer may not fink it, but I bin keepin' me eye out fer the lot o' yer. If anybody upsets yer you come an' see ole Jimmy. 'E'll soon sort 'em out for yer.'

The unlikely trio had left the market and were walking along beside the Trocette cinema. Snow carpeted the pavement and a few flakes whirled in the wind. ''Ere, you two, slow down a bit or I'll be finkin' yer don't wanna be seen wiv me,' Jimmy gasped.

'Sorry, Jimmy, but we can't stop out too long or our sister'll get worried. She looks after us, yer see,' Joey told him.

'I know very well she does,' Jimmy replied. 'Yer shouldn't go too far away or yer could get lost.'

'We know as far as the market,' Joey went on. 'Billy brings me all the time an' we come terday ter see 'ow much the Christmas trees cost.'

'They wasn't all that good,' Billy piped in.

'I bet yer'd like one though, wouldn't yer?' the drunk said. 'It's very nice ter sit round the tree at Christmas, 'specially when it's bin all decorated wiv paper chains an' tinsel. I 'ad one once, many years ago. I put a lot o' stuff on it an' I even 'ung silver bells on it. Lovely it was.'

'If we wasn't very poor we'd 'ave a big tree wiv lots o' stuff on it,' Joey said. 'We'd put all kinds o' fings on it. Then we'd all sit under it an' eat sweets an' oranges, an' we'd stay up really late.'

Jimmy suddenly stopped. ''Ere, you two. I've just remembered,' he told them. 'I gotta go an' get me shoes soled an' 'eeled. I better do it before I ferget. We'll 'ave to 'ave anuvver chat later.'

Rose had finished hanging the paper chains round the walls and across the room. She had hung the two large paper lanterns from the ceiling and was busy blowing up balloons when Don walked in.

'That looks very nice,' he said, standing with hands on hips as he admired his sister's efforts. 'At least it 'ides the dirty ceilin'.'

Rose smiled. 'We'll 'ave ter get it whitewashed after Christmas,' she told him.

'Where's the kids?' he asked as he took off his coat.

'Susan's over wiv Freda an' the boys 'ave gone down the market,' she replied.

Don sat down in the armchair. 'Give us those balloons, I'll blow 'em up fer yer,' he said, seeing that Rose's face was becoming red from straining.

'While yer doin' them I'll make a cuppa,' she said. 'I'll 'ave ter collect Susan soon, I don't wanna take liberties wiv the woman.'

Don blew up a balloon, knotted the neck of it and gave it a tap, idly watching as it rose to the ceiling and floated back down to the floor. ''Ere, I was finkin',' he called out to the scullery. ''Ave yer bin ter the doctor's about the baby yet, Rose? Will yer 'ave it 'ere, or will yer 'ave ter go in the 'ospital?' he asked.

'I ain't bin nowhere yet,' Rose called out. 'I'll 'ave ter wait an' see.'

Don took another balloon from the packet. 'Yer should get support from the farvver, yer know,' he told her. ''E should be made ter pay yer somefing each week.'

Rose came into the room and stood facing her brother. 'Look, I already told yer I want nuffink ter do wiv 'im,' she said quickly. 'I was as much ter blame as 'e was, so let's leave it at that. We'll manage some'ow.'

Just then they heard footsteps on the stairs. 'That sounds like the boys,' she said as she hurried back into the scullery.

Jimmy Rideout had walked back into the market feeling uncomfortable. His feet were cold and wet and he cursed to himself, realising that the cobbler would not be too happy about having to repair wet shoes. He carried on past the shoemender's and hurried across the main road through the slush to the shoe shop, which was packed with people. 'I wanna see a pair o' brown brogues in size ten,' he told the shop assistant as he sat down on the last vacant seat beside a very large woman.

The young man looked down at Jimmy's soaking wet suede shoes and then hurried out to the storeroom. Jimmy gazed benignly at the woman next to him who was puffing loudly as she struggled into a pair of high heels.

'Looks like yer could do wiv the next size,' he remarked to her casually.

'I know what size I take,' she replied indignantly.

'Those sort o' shoes are dangerous in this weavver, missus,' he told her.

'Look, mate, I'll 'ave ter make these shoes do till next Christmas an' I don't s'pose fer one minute the snow's gonna last that long, do you?'

'I'm only just sayin',' that's all, but you please yerself,' Jimmy replied.

The woman gave him a cold stare and looked down at his shoes, a smile forming on her fat face. 'You got a lot o' room ter talk,' she countered. 'Those fings you got on ain't exactly ideal fer the snow.'

'That's why I'm gettin' a pair o' brogues. Last fer ever, they do,' Jimmy said smugly.

More people were coming into the shop and when the assistant came back carrying a box he looked harassed. 'I could only find this one pair,' he said.

'I only want one pair,' Jimmy answered grinning. 'All right, let's try the left one on.'

The assistant hurried away to serve another customer and Jimmy slipped off his left shoe, to reveal a large hole in the toe of his sopping wet sock. The woman next to him raised her eyes to the ceiling as she caught the look of disgust on another customer's face, then she stood up in her new high heels to test them.

Jimmy pulled the sock forward and folded the holed toepiece back under his foot, struggling into the brown brogue with the help of a large shoehorn that the assistant had left with him. It fitted well and he stood up next to the fat woman. ''Ow's it look?' he asked her.

She ignored him and he sat down again to try on the other shoe.

People were waiting to be served and Jimmy saw that the shop assistant was run off his feet. The large woman was trying to attract the man's attention and was getting angry at having to wait. Finally the assistant noticed the woman's gesturings and hurried over. Just then Jimmy stood up and handed him the shoe box. 'Sorry, mate, they're too tight,' he said. 'I'll come back when it's quieter.'

As he crossed back into the market Jimmy smiled to himself, wondering what the assistant would say when the next customer asked for size ten brown brogues and he discovered the sodden old suedes in the box. I must remember not to visit that shop again for a while, he told himself as he walked up to the fruit stall.

The snow was falling heavily outside as Rose sat alone sipping her tea in the gaily decorated living room. Don had gone out earlier and the children were all sleeping soundly. As she sat comfortably in the armchair beside the fire Rose stared over at the wrapped presents that she had laid out in the corner of the room and wondered about the present Alice Copeland had given her. She had wanted to open it but resisted the temptation. The children would feel happy that she had an extra present to open on Christmas morning. Amongst the pile of gifts were five parcels from Freda, one for each of them. Both her ground-floor neighbours had called that evening too. Rene Stratton had brought a large tin of pineapple and a pot of strawberry jam, and soon after Ivy Campbell had knocked at the door with a large bag of mixed nuts and five chocolate bars. The little gifts had lifted the young woman's spirits. It was nice to feel the neighbours' genuine concern for them, and Rose knew that she and the rest of the family were going to need all the help they could get in the coming year.

The noise on the stairs startled her and she got up quickly

and put her ear against the front door. She heard what sounded like the porter's voice, and another louder voice protesting.

'Don't bend it like that or yer'll snap the bloody top off it.'

'Don't talk daft, I gotta bend it ovverwise it won't go.'

'All right but be careful. No, not like that.'

'Gawd almighty, I ain't a contortionist. I gotta stay at the back.'

There was a loud clatter and then a pregnant pause. 'Bloody 'ell, I could've broke me back,' someone said.

Rose's curiosity got the better of her and she opened the front door gingerly, only to find a red-faced Fred Albury standing on the landing with the biggest Christmas tree she had ever seen at his feet. Jimmy Rideout was coming up the stairs towards him holding his head. 'I just done a bleedin' somersault,' he groaned. 'Arse over tip from top ter bottom I went.'

'Well, it was yer own bloody fault. I told yer ter let me 'ave it but yer wouldn't listen,' Fred rebuked him.

Jimmy saw Rose standing at her door and his face broke into a huge grin. ''Ere, love, this is fer you, no fanks to 'im.'

'Well, sod yer then if that's me fanks,' Fred grumbled. 'Anuvver bloke would've let yer cart it up on yer own.'

'Yer right, Fred ole son. I'm sorry fer not bein' more grateful but yer do go on a bit, don't 'e,' he laughed, looking at Rose.

The young woman had her hand up to her mouth. 'Fer me?' she said incredulously.

'It's all yours, lovey. Best bleedin' Christmas tree in Bermondsey, I should fink,' Jimmy announced.

'I don't understand,' Rose said, staring at the drunk.

'I shouldn't try, luv,' Fred told her. 'Nuffink this bloke does surprises me an' I've known 'im fer a few years. I don't understand 'im eivver.'

Jimmy leaned against the wall for a few moments then he straightened up again. 'When the boys wake up termorrer mornin' just tell 'em that I didn't get me shoes mended after all,' he said with a wink.

Fred shook his head. ''E's mad, stark ravin' mad, I'm sure 'e is.'

Jimmy grinned widely. 'C'mon, Fred, let's give 'er an 'and ter get it in place or we'll be 'ere all night. Now take the end of it. No, not like that, yer silly git.'

With a lot of cursing, puffing and blowing the huge Christmas tree was installed in the corner of the room. Fred had to snap a foot off the top of the tree to get it upright and Jimmy supervised the operation. The smell of pine filled the room, and when at last the two tired men and the delighted young woman sat drinking tea Jimmy explained.

'What got ter me, gel, was what your young Joey said when I bumped into 'im an' Billy terday,' he began. ''E told me yer 'adn't got a tree this year. I'd seen those kids down the market starin' at the trees on a stall. They even priced 'em, would yer believe. Anyway, we was chattin' away as I walked 'ome wiv 'em, then I got this idea. It's too long ter go inter details but I managed ter save a few bob on a pair o' shoes an' I decided ter get yer a tree. Them ones the kids were lookin' at wasn't much good fer the price. They wanted a dollar for 'em. Bloody scandalous. Well, I know this bloke on London Bridge Station who 'ad some beauties. Saw 'em yesterday when I was up there. Now I got 'im ter save me the best one of 'em an' when 'e was finished fer the day 'e put the tree on 'is barrer an' carted it down ter the barrer sheds in Long Lane. I carried it 'ome from there meself an' by the time I got ter the Buildin's I was absolutely cattled. Anyway, my old mate Fred saw me strugglin', an' like the nice feller 'e is 'e 'elped me the rest o' the way.'

Fred remained impassive, secretly enjoying the praise, but his face dropped when Jimmy continued.

'Trouble is, Fred can be a bit obstinate at times. If I'd 'ave left it to 'im the bloody tree would've bin ruined. So there you are. Well, I'd better get goin'. It looks a picture in that corner, even if I say so meself.'

As the two men left, Rose put her arms around Jimmy and planted a kiss on his cheek, while Fred stood in the doorway, smiling at the drunk's embarrassment.

'Put 'im down, gel, yer don't know where 'e's bin,' he joked.

Rose watched as they walked down the stairs and she heard Jimmy say, 'C'mon, ole sport, let's buy you an' yer miserable ole missus a pint.'

Chapter Nine

As the last minute of 1949 ticked away, Don Farran took the top off a bottle of brown ale and shared it between two glasses. The gas fire was turned up and the flat was warm and quiet. Outside the settled snow had turned to ice as the temperature dropped below freezing and the wind rattled the windows and howled along the landings and stairways of Imperial Buildings.

Rose picked up her glass and took a long draught. 'I'll be glad ter see the end o' this year,' she said with a deep sigh.

Don nodded. 'I just 'ope next year's gonna be a good one,' he said as he put down his drink and went over to turn up the volume on the wireless.

The BBC was broadcasting a programme from Scotland, and as the skirl of the bagpipes died the first booming gong of midnight rang out. Suddenly the sound of Scottish voices singing 'Auld Lang Syne' filled the room and Don clinked glasses with Rose as the two drank a toast to 1950.

The young man sat back in the armchair and looked at the Christmas tree which had already started to shed its needles. 'Well, it was a better Christmas than we expected, Rose,' he said quietly. 'An' the people round 'ere come up trumps, that's fer sure.'

Rose smiled, recalling the episode on the stairs with Jimmy and the porter. 'Those presents from Freda were lovely,' she said. 'The cardigans she made fer the boys were just the right fit, an' Susan's jumper looks smashin' on 'er. An' I got these earrin's from you,' she added, turning her head left and right and puckering up her nose at Don. 'Then there was that pair o' nylons from Alice at work.'

'Well, we 'ad plenty to eat an' the chicken was really tasty,' Don replied.

Rose spread her feet out before the fire. 'D'yer know what really made it fer me this Christmas, Don? It was the kids' faces when they got up on Christmas mornin' an' saw the tree standin' there. Susan's eyes nearly popped out, an' the boys looked really surprised.'

Don got up and turned off the wireless. 'Well, I'll be seventeen in a few weeks' time,' he sighed. 'This time next year I'll be gettin' ready fer me call up.'

Rose's face dropped. 'P'raps it'll all be stopped by then,' she said hopefully.

Don laughed. 'Yer gotta be kiddin'. There's talk of extendin' it from eighteen months ter two years, what wiv the way the Russians are playin' up.'

'Yer don't fink there'll be anuvver war, do yer, Don?' Rose asked fearfully.

'Nah, the Russians wouldn't start anyfing,' he replied. 'They know that if they dropped an atom bomb on us they'd get two back. They're just spoutin' off.'

'If yer 'ave ter do National Service what would yer put down for?' Rose asked.

'I'd go in Dad's old regiment. I s'pect the Royal Marines'd take someone whose farvver got killed servin' wiv 'em, that's if I measure up OK.'

'Measure up?'

'Yeah, they don't take any ole mug, yer know.'

'They'll take you, Don,' Rose said, smiling affectionately at him.

The two lapsed into silence, sipping their drinks thoughtfully, then Rose suddenly remembered the letter which had dropped on the mat just after Christmas. It was from the welfare, saying that a call would be made on the evening of 4 January. The young woman had put it to the back of her mind, but now that there was time to think, she began to worry.

'I don't show yet, do I?' she asked her brother.

'No. Why d'yer ask?'

'I'm worried about the letter from the welfare.'

'I wouldn't get worried if I were you.'

'But I am worried.'

Don put down his drink and straightened up in the chair. 'Look, they're just doin' the usual call. Everyfing's all right 'ere an' the kids are all lookin' fit an' well,' he said reassuringly. 'I'm the only one who knows yer carryin', so stop worryin', will yer.'

'I s'pose yer right,' Rose sighed.

They finished their drinks and after a few minutes Don got up and stretched. 'Well, I'm off ter bed,' he said. 'G'night, Rose.'

'Night, Don, an' fanks.'

'Fer what?'

'Oh, you know. Fer the present, fer the money yer put in, an' fer bein' understandin' about everyfing,' she said.

Don looked at her and grinned. 'Look, Rose, I know what's what,' he said quietly. 'I know 'ow yer always fink of us before yerself, an' 'ow 'ard it must be, workin' at that poxy job o' yours. Then there's the worry o' the baby. It won't always be like it is now. One day yer'll meet the right bloke an' yer'll be very 'appy. One day we'll all look back, the kids as well, an' we'll all be very grateful fer what yer done fer the lot of us.'

Rose pouted at him. 'Stop it, yer makin' me feel old,' she told him.

'C'mon, Rose, yer should get some sleep,' he reminded her.

'I won't be long,' she replied. 'I just gotta finish patchin' Joey's trousers.'

In Basin Street, the Morgan family were gathered around the table in their house at the end of the turning. It was just seconds into the new year and Frankie Morgan poured out a large measure of whisky and passed the bottle across the table to his son John. 'It's gonna be a good year, lads,' he said. 'I can feel it in me water.'

John poured himself a drink and studied the glass for a few moments in silence, then he looked across the table at his father. 'I'm a little bit puzzled about those pals o' yours,' he said. 'Ter be honest they worry me. 'Ow come they sorted us out fer the job?'

Frankie smiled indulgently. 'Now listen ter me fer a few minutes,' he began. 'When I was moved ter Pentonville ter see out me stretch I shared a cell wiv this geezer by the name o' Tom Reilly. 'E was a big, dangerous-lookin' character who seemed ter get very well treated by the screws. I soon sussed that a couple of 'em were bein' paid ter smuggle in fags an' a few extra comforts. Anyway, me an' Reilly got pally, an' I got ter know quite a lot about 'is background. I found out that 'e was a minder an' bag man fer Big Joe Andretti.'

'Who's Big Joe Andretti?' Ernie butted in.

''E's the wop who runs the Cable Street mob,' John told him.

Frankie snorted. 'Big Joe Andretti 'appens ter be Maltese, an' fer your information 'e's about the biggest villain in the East End. 'E runs the gamblin' set up an' all the prossers from Wappin' ter Cannin' Town. Anyway, when I was gettin' out Reilly asked me ter go an' see Andretti.'

'What for?' Ernie asked.

'Reilly 'ad some information ter pass on ter the big man,' Frankie continued, 'somefing important 'e'd managed ter get frew the grapevine. Reilly couldn't read or write so 'e couldn't send a letter, an' in any case letters are vetted by the screws. When yer banged away in a cell fer months on end wiv someone yer get ter know each ovver very well, as yer can imagine. I'd told Reilly what I was in for an' about the villainry I got up to, an' I s'pose 'e saw me as somebody 'e could trust. So as soon as I got out I went ter see Andretti. I told 'im I was Reilly's cell mate an' when I gave 'im the message 'e looked pleased an' 'e bought me a drink. We 'ad a long talk, as it 'appened, an' 'e seemed interested in what I was up to. Anyway, yer remember that load o' salmon we nicked from Chamber's Wharf last October? Well, most of it went Big Joe Andretti's way. The Malt must 'ave earned a nice few quid on that lot, 'cos 'e got in touch a few weeks ago. 'E told me that 'e might 'ave somefing for me. Next fing I know, those two blokes come ter see me an' they mention Big Joe. This is big business, not like that tuppenny-'a'penny stunt you boys pulled before Christmas.'

'Why don't the Malt do this one 'imself if it's that good?' Albert asked.

'It's not the sort o' fing 'e gets involved wiv, an' besides, it's all about territory,' Frankie said, spreading his hands out over the table. 'When yer get as big as Joe Andretti yer've got enough ter do lookin' after yer own manor wivout venturin' out all over the place. Now we've bin goin' on long enough so let's cut the cackle an' 'ave anuvver drink. We'll drink a toast ter success. If we do this one right we'll all be in the money.'

Albert leaned towards his brother John. ''Ere, what's a bag man?' he asked.

''E's a bloke who carries wages an' dodgy money to an' from. Someone who's not likely ter get waylaid,' John told him.

Frankie held up his filled glass. ''Ere's ter success,' he said, downing the whisky in one gulp. 'An' before we all piss orf I wanna impress on yer the need ter keep yer traps shut. Remember that the cozzers are sniffin' about on the manor.'

At lunchtime on Sunday the first day of 1950 Albert Morgan sought out his friend Don Farran, whom he had not seen since the disagreement in the Anchor on Christmas week. Albert felt that Don was a genuine bloke and had been hard done by over the proceeds of the Creek Road robbery. He had felt guilty at not being more firm with his brothers, John in particular, over the share-out and he wanted Don to know.

As he picked his way carefully through the frozen snow Albert was feeling a little apprehensive. The coming robbery would be the biggest job the Morgans had done. The proceeds would make any previous money he had earned look like peanuts, but he was aware that the penalty for a jewller's shop hold-up would be as much as ten years for his father, what with his record. They were not used to working with anyone else either, and if there was a slip up and someone got killed the lot of them would swing. Brother John did not appear to be worried at all, and Ernie looked like he was in a trance half the time. As far as the old man went, he did not seem to have a nerve in his body.

Albert was still fretting over the coming raid when he put his head into the Swan at Dockhead. He and Don occasionally had a drink at the place and he assumed that if his friend was out he might well be there. He was not disappointed. Don was talking to a couple of young men whom Albert knew by sight. Don caught his eye and turned away as though he had not seen him, but Albert was not to be put off. He came over and nodded to the group. 'Don, can yer spare a minute, I'd like a word,' he said.

Don excused himself to his mates and followed Albert to the counter.

'What yer drinkin'?' Albert asked.

Don held up his half pint of ale. 'I'm all right,' he said stiffly.

Albert ordered a pint of bitter and waited, feeling increasingly awkward.

'I reckoned I'd find yer in 'ere,' he said.

'So?' Don replied, looking directly at him.

The pint arrived and Albert picked it up quickly and took a large gulp as though seeking the courage to say his piece. 'I come down ter say I'm sorry about the ovver night, Don,' he began. 'I was out of order not speakin' up, but if it makes any difference I'm gonna 'ave words wiv our John.'

'I shouldn't bovver,' Don told him coldly. 'As far as your bruvver John's concerned I'm some flash young git who don't know what day it is. Well, I tell yer somefing, Albert. Don't ever ask me ter go wiv yer again. Yer took advantage of our friendship an' I ain't fergettin' it.'

Albert's face coloured up slightly and he lowered his head. 'I ain't blamin' yer, Don, but yer gotta see it my way,' he replied. 'I ain't really got much sway where John's concerned. 'E makes the rules an' does the organisin'. As far as Ernie goes, it's like 'e's in anuvver world most o' the time. It's a case o' John shouts an' we all jump. Well, I'm gonna 'ave a talk wiv 'im anyway. I ain't lettin' 'im mess everyfing up. We've bin pals since school. You did yer share that night an' took the same risks. If there's any more dosh comin' it's gonna be shared equally.'

Don lost a little of his anger. Albert had been his best friend and he was obviously upset at what had happened. 'Look, Albert, I'm not blamin' you,' he said quickly, 'but I'm really narked at that flash bruvver o' yours.'

Albert nodded and gazed down at his feet for a few moments, then he took another large gulp from his beer and put the glass down on the counter. 'I'll be off then. I just 'ad ter tell yer 'ow I felt,' he said quickly.

Suddenly Don's face relaxed and his mouth parted in a wide grin. 'I've never known you leave beer in yer glass,' he said.

Albert smiled sheepishly. 'Fer a minute I lost the taste fer it,' he replied.

'Let's sit down over there,' Don said, pointing to a corner table.

The Swan was a favourite haunt of the dock workers and on that particular Sunday it was filling up rapidly. Albert glanced around him to see if there were any familiar faces, and then he looked back at Don with a quizzical smile. 'Maybe yer better off givin' us the old elbow,' he said suddenly.

Don laughed. 'Funny you should say that. Our sister Rose told me I should keep well clear o' you lot. Mind yer, she's bein' the muvver at the moment so I can understand 'er feelin's. It's nuffink against you personally, but yer know 'ow it is.'

Albert's face was serious. 'I meant what I just said, Don. There's somefing comin' up an' it's big,' he said in a low, urgent voice.

'Oh, an' what's that then?' Don asked casually.

'I can't say no more, but the thought of it scares the life out o' me,' Albert told him. 'I got a bad feelin' about this job. If fings 'adn't turned out the way they did you might 'ave bin in on this one as well. Just feel 'appy that you're well out of it.'

'If yer that worried about doin' the job why don't yer tell that bruvver o' yours that yer don't wanna know?' Don said.

'It's family stuff. We always stick tergevver, an' the ole man's settin' this one up,' Albert replied. 'Don't say a word to a soul about all this, fer Gawd sake, or I'm in dead trouble.'

'Don't worry, I ain't 'eard anyfing,' Don said with a reassuring smile. 'Now let's buy yer a pint, Alb. Yer look like yer could do wiv anuvver one.'

Chapter Ten

Rose walked into work on Wednesday morning feeling apprehensive about that evening's visit from the welfare people, and as usual the manager was hovering near the time-clock.

Alice Copeland rushed in puffing loudly and gave Rose a big grin. 'I nearly missed the bus this mornin',' she gasped. 'I thought I was gonna lose a quarter.'

Rose punched her card and slipped it back into the rack, aware of the manager looking over at her. 'I'll see yer at lunch-time,' she said quickly to Alice.

'Look at that miserable git starin' at us,' Alice growled. 'I'd like ter put 'is 'ead under a press.'

As Rose walked into the factory Bernard Collis came up to her, pushing his glasses off the tip of his nose. 'I got a different job fer you, Farran,' he said with a hint of a smile. 'Yer'll be on the rollers terday.'

Rose's heart sank. The job entailed sliding wired bundles of thin tin sheets into position on the rollers so they could be fed into the cutter. The bundles were heavy and had to be manoeuvred into position and then the wire bindings had to be snipped off before the sheets were individually picked up by the cutter. Bundles were brought in on trolleys by two young men who lifted them on to the bench next to the wide metal rollers, and as Rose took up her position beside the machine one of the loaders came up and gave her a sympathetic smile. 'What did yer do to upset ole cod's eyes?' he said.

Rose shrugged her shoulders. 'I must 'ave fergot ter say good mornin',' she replied, returning the smile.

The other loader strolled up to the machine. 'I see Big Mary's done 'erself a bit o' good then,' he remarked, grinning knowingly at his mate.

Rose slid the first of the bundles into position, pushing hard to get it level. It slid too far over and she had to pull back on it to set it right. As she picked up the large snippers the first loader pushed the bundle slightly further over. 'Yer need ter get it level wiv that guide or it won't slide straight,' he advised her.

Rose nodded as she opened the snippers and clamped them over the thick wire binding. It took some pressure to snap the wire, and when she had finally succeeded in removing the two binders the loader gave her a friendly wink. 'Yer look a bit too little fer this job, if yer don't mind me sayin',' he remarked. 'I dunno why 'e took Big Mary off this job. She's built like a tank.'

'I know why,' the other loader piped in. 'Cod's eyes an' Mary are 'avin' it orf. 'E's put 'er on the lids. It's a doddle, that job.'

Rose spotted the manager walking along the gangway and she warned the two young men who hurried off smartly.

Bernard Collis came up to her, a look of satisfaction on his fat face. 'Make sure you keep the machine goin',' he said sharply, 'an' don't leave them binders layin' all over the floor. Bend 'em up an' put 'em in the bin.'

Rose gave him a perfunctory nod as she pushed hard on the next bundle and with some difficulty managed to get it into the correct position. The manager stood for a few moments watching her exertions, then he turned on his heel without another word, smiling smugly to himself as he walked off.

The morning seemed to pass quickly and by lunchtime Rose found that she was feeling more tired than usual. The bottom of her stomach was starting to ache and the palms of her hands felt sore and bruised from using the heavy snippers. As she walked into the canteen carrying her sandwiches and joined the queue at the tea counter Alice joined her.

'I just seen Big Mary outside talkin' ter that ugly bastard Collis,' she said angrily. 'She was all over 'im. I bet any money yer like that's why she got took orf the rollers.'

'Yeah, I got 'er job,' Rose said, smiling stoically.

'I know. One o' the loaders told me,' Alice replied.

Rose picked up her mug of tea and stood waiting while Alice collected hers. The two walked over to a vacant table and sat down.

'You look a bit pale. You all right?' Alice asked.

Rose leaned forward in her chair. 'Yeah, I'm OK. I got a bit of a stomach ache, that's all,' she answered.

'It's that bloody job yer on. They should put the fellers on the rollers, it's too 'eavy fer us gels. Big Mary excepted, of course,' Alice said pointedly.

Rose opened her parcel of sandwiches and offered Alice one. 'It's breakfast sausage,' she said.

'Yer can 'ave one o' mine, it's Spam,' Alice replied.

For a while they sat eating their lunch and sipping the strong tea, then Alice screwed up her empty paper bag and licked her lips.

''Ave yer thought any more about the club dances?' she asked. 'There's one comin' up in two weeks' time.'

'I'd like ter come, but it's awkward, really,' Rose replied. 'I can't leave the kids, an' I don't really wanna ask the woman on our landin' ter sit in. I don't like takin' liberties. She's always good in an emergency.'

'I understand,' Alice said with a resigned smile, patting down her dark hair. 'Fancy a stroll?'

Rose had been feeling sharp twinges at the pit of her stomach and she shook her head. 'I'd sooner sit 'ere till we go back ter work. Don't let me stop you though,' she told her.

'Nah, I'll stay 'ere wiv you. You sure you're all right?' Alice queried.

Rose suddenly began to feel quite emotional. The worry of the welfare people's visit that evening and her anger at being put on the heavy job had left her edgy, and Alice's concern for her made her feel suddenly vulnerable. Tears came into her eyes and she wiped them away quickly, feeling a little silly. 'It's nuffink,' she said, forcing a brief smile.

Alice looked down at her clasped hands for a moment or two while Rose recovered her composure, then she looked up at her. 'If there's anyfing wrong yer can tell me,' she said quietly. 'I'm not one ter go round shoutin' me mouth off ter this lot.'

Rose had to force back her tears as she saw the genuine look of concern in Alice's large dark eyes. She was a decent friend and it might be good to confide in someone like her, she told herself. Everyone in the factory would know sooner or later anyway.

Rose sighed deeply. 'Keep this ter yerself, Alice. I'm pregnant.'

'Oh my good Gawd!' Alice gasped. 'You poor cow. I knew there was somefing wrong, I just knew. I could see by yer face. Yer look all in.'

'I'm gonna 'ang on as long as I can, but I can't 'ide it much longer,' Rose told her.

''Ow far gone are yer?' Alice asked, still looking shocked.

'Almost three months,' Rose replied.

'Well, you ain't showin' yet,' Alice remarked.

'I know the date when it 'appened an' I've bin feeling sick in the mornin's,' Rose told her. 'My clothes 'ave started ter feel tighter so I won't be able to 'ide it fer more than a couple o' weeks, three at the most I should fink.'

Alice's face suddenly took on a worried look. 'Those pains in yer stomach,' she said quickly. 'That's a warnin' ter take it easy. 'Ow the bloody 'ell yer gonna take it easy on that poxy roller?'

'I'll be all right,' Rose said dismissively.

'All right, me arse. Yer'll 'ave ter come off that job, that's fer sure, unless yer wanna lose the baby,' Alice told her firmly. 'D'yer wanna lose the baby, Rose?'

The young woman shook her head slowly. 'At first I was finkin' o' gettin' rid of it, but I couldn't bring meself ter go anywhere,' she said quietly. 'It just didn't seem right. I know I've got the family ter consider, but I just couldn't do it, Alice.'

'What about the farrver?' Alice asked. 'Does 'e know yer condition?'

Once again Rose shook her head. 'I don't want 'im ter know. It was somefing that just 'appened. I was as much ter blame as 'e was.'

'Yeah, but us gels 'ave ter pick up the bill, don't we?' Alice replied. ''E should be made to pay 'is due. Yer entitled ter maintenance. Anyway that's in the future. What we gotta do is get yer off that poxy job yer on.'

'I can't tell the manager that I'm carryin',' Rose said quickly.

Alice gave her a wicked grin. 'My ole gran'muvver used ter say there's more than one way ter skin a cat, an' believe you me, that ole lady knew what she was talkin' about. Don't worry, just you leave it ter me.'

'Don't go gettin' yerself inter trouble on my account,' Rose said anxiously.

The factory whistle sounded and as the two got up to go back to work Alice squeezed Rose's arm. 'I'll see yer later,' she said, giving her a scheming wink and hurrying off.

Bernard Collis shuffled the pile of papers on his desk and slipped them into a large folder. Everything seemed to be going according to plan, he thought smugly. Big Mary had promised to meet him that evening for a drink and if he played his cards right the weekend in Brighton would be very enjoyable. Mary had been going on for some time about how he should put her on an easier job and now she was going to repay him. Pity about young Farran. She would have been a good catch. She was pretty and had a good figure, but she had made it plain that she wasn't interested in him. Well, she might still change her mind, after a week or two on the rollers. In the meantime there was Big Mary. She had a reputation with the men and certainly knew what it was all about. There would be no comeback either. Mary was a widow and could do as she liked. He could too, up to a point. When Tessie had found out about his previous fling with Rita from the packing department she had slept in the spare room and the two of them had started to lead separate lives, agreeing to stay under the same roof for the sake of the children, until they were older.

Bernard leaned back in his chair and sipped his afternoon tea. That Johnson woman on the stamper would have to go, he decided. She had too much chat for her own good. Copeland was another one for the chop as soon as possible. She was too impertinent. Her time-keeping left a lot to be desired too. Maybe another warning would put the frighteners in there, he gloated.

The tap on the door made him sit up straight in his seat. 'Enter,' he called out imperiously.

106

Alice Copeland walked in almost apologetically and gave him a big smile. 'Can I 'ave a quick word, Mr Collis, if you're not too busy?' she said sweetly.

'What is it, Copeland?' he asked irritably.

'Well, it's a bit difficult, you see . . .'

'C'mon, I've got work ter do and so 'ave you,' he reminded her.

'Well, I thought I should come an' see yer, Mr Collis,' she began hesitantly, ''cos yer've always bin fair wiv me. As I said ter the gels on my bench, that Mr Collis is strict but fair, an' we can't ask fer much more than that, can we.'

The manager sighed impatiently, 'Get ter the point, please,' he pleaded.

Alice drew in a deep breath. 'It's like this, yer see. There's a rumour flyin' around an' it concerns you.'

'Oh, an' what are they sayin'?' he asked with raised eyebrows.

'I really didn't wanna say anyfing, Mr Collis, but like I say, yer've always treated me right an' I wouldn't like ter see yer get inter trouble wiv the management,' Alice told him.

The manager sucked in his breath sharply. 'Go on,' he prompted.

'Well, there's a petition goin' round an' a lot o' the gels 'ave signed it,' she explained. 'It's about Big Mary Alcroft. The women feel that she's bin given special treatment an' one o' the gels is takin' the petition ter Mr Penrose. They're complainin' about the way you ogle the gels as well, an' one o' 'em put down on the petition that yer keep touchin' 'er bum.'

Bernard Collis gulped hard and ran his finger round the inside of his tight collar as he stared up at the young woman in front of him. 'I've never touched anyone's bum, er, bottom,' he said quickly.

'Yer did touch my bum once, but I didn't mind,' Alice said, smiling shyly.

'I never did,' Bernard spluttered. 'Who's the woman who's organisin' this petition?'

'I tried ter find out, but they wouldn't tell me which one it was. It was because I refused to sign it,' Alice told him. 'Like I said, yer've always bin fair wiv me.'

Bernard realised that he could land himself in serious trouble with the bosses over something like this. George Penrose did not like him and might well demand his resignation. He drummed his fingers nervously on the desktop as he desperately sought an answer to the sudden crisis he was faced with.

'Can I say somefing?' Alice said in a low voice.

'You've told me enough already,' Bernard growled. 'What more?'

'Well, I 'eard the women say they were 'opin' yer wouldn't put Big Mary back on the rollers until they got some more names after the whistle went, or they wouldn't 'ave a case,' she said slyly. 'I thought I'd better tell yer, so yer could do somefing about it.'

Bernard sighed deeply, suddenly feeling a little better. 'Thank you fer comin' to see me, Copeland. I appreciate it,' he said grudgingly.

'Well, like I say . . .'

'Yes all right, now go back ter work,' he cut her short.

Alice smiled sweetly once more and slipped out of the office, feeling very pleased with her performance. On the way back to her machine she passed the rollers and called out above the din of the machinery, 'Rose, take it easy, there's relief on the way, if I'm not mistaken.'

Alice was right. Ten minutes later Big Mary was reinstated on the rollers, and she had something to say about it.

'If you fink I'd go out fer a drink wiv you yer must be out o' yer simple bloody mind,' she hissed at the chastened manager. 'Piss orf an' leave me alone.'

Chapter Eleven

Rose Farran hurried home on Wednesday evening still marvelling at how quickly she had been given back her original job on the press. Alice was obviously responsible but Rose could think of no way her friend would have been able to persuade the manager to make the change without telling him that she was pregnant. She felt sure that Alice would not have given her secret away and realised that she had found a very good friend in the bright, amiable young woman. She had not been able to speak with her before she quickly left work that evening and there had been no time to stop and seek her out. The welfare were calling at seven and there was so much to do.

Rose hurried into Fellmonger Street still feeling the heaviness in the pit of her stomach. She trudged quickly up the wooden stairs of the buildings and let herself into the flat. Billy and Joey were sitting quietly at the table playing draughts and they looked up as she walked in. Susan ran to her and held out her arms for her usual hug.

'Billy said the welfare's comin' ternight. Can I stay up ter see 'em?' Susan asked.

'If you're a good gel an' eat all yer tea I'll let yer stay up,' Rose said, planting a big kiss on the child's cheek.

'We ain't gonna tell 'em anyfing,' Billy announced quickly.

'Nah, we don't like nosy parkers,' Joey added.

Rose slipped off her coat and sat at the table. 'Now look, you two, there's nuffink ter worry about,' she said firmly. 'They're nice people at the welfare an' they're only comin' ter see if we're all right. But yer all gotta 'elp me. I'm gonna get the tea ready an' you boys can lay the table. Get a clean table-cloth out o' the dresser drawer.'

'Can I 'elp too?' Susan cried.

'Yes, I've got a special job fer you, darlin',' Rose told her. 'I want you ter sit in that armchair an' do a nice drawin' fer me. Use those colourin' pencils Don bought yer. I want it ter be a really lovely picture so I can show the welfare lady 'ow clever you are, all right?'

Susan was pleased with her special task and she delved into the corner for her pencil box and drawing pad. Rose went out to the scullery and hurriedly peeled the potatoes and sliced the large green cabbage on the draining board, still feeling apprehensive about the imminent visit. Soon the pots of vegetables were coming to the boil and she opened a large tin of corned beef and cut the block thinly, laying four slices on Don's plate and three slices each for the rest of them. The boys were doing a good job laying the table and she hurried into the living room to glance at the clock.

By the time Don came in at twenty minutes to six the tea was being served up.

'C'mon, Don, wash yer 'ands quickly,' Rose told him, 'we gotta get tea over. Yer know who's comin' ternight, don't yer?'

Don nodded, pulling a face as he took the evening paper from his coat pocket and threw it down in the armchair. 'They're a bloody nuisance,' he growled.

'Mind what yer say in front o' the kids,' Rose reminded him sharply.

'They're bloody nosy parkers,' Joey added.

'That's enough o' that, young man,' Rose said sternly. 'Now, let's sit down an' eat.'

The clock on the mantelshelf showed ten minutes to seven and the flat looked clean and tidy. The tea things had been cleared away and Don had washed up while Rose got Susan ready for bed. The cushions had been straightened and the toys put away for the night; the kettle was simmering on the gas stove and the bits and pieces of bric-a-brac on the shelves and mantelshelf had been dusted and rearranged. Rose surveyed the room and looked down at herself as she straightened her clean dress. It was the one she had worn that evening at the dance, a green organza with puffed sleeves which was loose fitting and less likely to reveal any tell-tale changes in her figure. She could not see any difference just yet, apart from her breasts which seemed to feel heavier.

Footsteps sounded on the stairs and along the landing and there was a loud double knock. Rose took a deep breath and quickly brushed her hands down the front of her dress before going into the passage and pulling open the front door. She was confronted by a rather plumpish woman in a brown tweed suit and a mustard-coloured hat which was tilted to one side of her head. She was wearing gold-rimmed glasses and carried a large handbag over her shoulder. 'I'm Miss Grant, Welfare Services,' she said. 'You received my letter?'

'Yes, come in,' Rose replied, stepping to one side.

The woman walked in and stood in the centre of the living room, staring at the children for a moment or two before casting her trained eye around the room.

'Billy, get up and let Miss, er . . .'

'Miss Grant,' she said again as she sat down and pulled her

tweed skirt down over her knees. 'So this is Billy, and who might you be?' she asked Joey.

'I'm Joey,' the lad told her. 'Me name's really Joseph, but I reckon Joseph stinks. Everybody calls me Joey.'

'And this is Susan, I believe,' the welfare officer said, smiling at the dark-haired child. 'You are a pretty one, and I see that you have a dolly. Has she got a name?'

'Yes. I call 'er Sarah, but Billy calls 'er rude names some-times,' Susan replied.

Rose glanced quickly at Don and flicked her eyes up at the ceiling. 'Susan's just off ter bed. Say goodnight ter the nice lady, Susan,' she said, picking up her baby sister.

'G'night, nice lady,' Susan said shyly.

Don sat watching as the woman unzipped her large handbag and took out a writing pad and fountain pen. She seems friendly enough, he thought, but just a bit too self-important. It always was like that with those sort. The woman he saw at the Labour Exchange was similar. She had that same smug expression on her face. Perhaps they were trained to look like that, just to make people feel uneasy.

Rose came back into the room. 'She's tucked up fer the night,' she announced. 'I always get Susan ter bed by seven.'

'That's very good. Children of her age do need their sleep,' Miss Grant replied as she unscrewed the top of her fountain pen. 'Now, let me see. Your father was a serving soldier and was killed during the war. 1944, I believe?'

''E was killed on D-Day,' Billy cut in. 'Our dad was in the Royal Marines. D'yer wanna see 'is medals? They're in the drawer.'

'Not just now, Billy. I'd like to talk to your sister,' the welfare officer said quickly.

'Billy, you an' Joey go an' get washed ready fer bed, it's nearly your bedtime now,' Rose told him.

Billy walked out into the tiny scullery without more ado but Joey stood his ground. 'We can't both get washed at once, Rose,' he protested. 'Yer said yerself there ain't enough room out there ter swing a cat round.'

Rose's eyes widened menacingly. 'Joey. Do as yer told.'

The lad walked out to join Billy who was pulling faces behind the welfare officer's back, while Don slouched down in his chair, his eyes half closed as he studied the woman.

'Your mother left the family home last June, was it?' she queried, looking at her notepad.

'Last May,' Rose corrected her. 'It was the end o' May.'

'She run off wiv a bus inspector, would yer believe?' Don said mockingly.

'Well, we don't need to know the sordid details,' Miss Grant said sharply as she glared over at him.

'Well, it might be important ter know the details,' Don replied, equally sharply.

'Oh and why is that?' the woman asked him.

Don sat up straight, his handsome face flushed slightly. 'Well, the fact that she run off wiv a bus inspector ain't the same as 'er runnin' orf wiv a bookmaker or a grocer, is it?' he explained. 'After all, bus inspectors don't earn that much, an' 'e's got a wife an' kids ter support by all accounts. Our ole lady could get fed up wiv it all an' decide ter come back. Now if she'd run orf wiv somebody who 'ad a few bob, like a grocer or a bookmaker . . .'

'Yes, I take your point,' the officer interrupted him. 'Does your mother make any provision for you all?'

'Not a brass farthin',' Don said quickly.

The woman scribbled into the notebook for a few seconds, then looked up at Rose. 'Can you tell me where you work?'

'Bromilow's at Dock'ead.'

'The sheet metal works?'

'Yeah, that's right.'

'I understand it's a heavy job, for a woman, I mean.'

'It's not easy, but the money's good, compared wiv the rest o' the factories round 'ere,' Rose told her.

'It must be very tiring, what with the added responsibility of caring for the family,' the woman went on.

'I manage. I'm fit an' strong,' Rose said quickly.

'I have to be honest with you,' the officer said, looking first at Don and then back at Rose. 'Our concern of course is for the welfare of the three younger children, you must understand. We have to be satisfied that their needs are fully catered for. We have to know that they get enough to eat and are clothed properly, that they attend school regularly, and that they are not at risk in any way. A home without a mother can be a sad and sometimes frightening place for young children.'

Don had heard enough and he got up quickly, his face dark with anger, and he brushed away Rose's arm as she tried to restrain him. 'Now, look 'ere, Miss whatever-yer-name is. Me an' Rose go ter work an' bring in enough ter feed an' clothe those kids,' he told her in a loud voice. 'They're very 'appy wiv the way fings are, an' I don't fink yer necessarily right when yer talk about an 'ome wivout a muvver. In our case our muvver drank the rent away in booze. She got us inter debt an' we 'ad ter go ter the local moneylender ter borrer a month's rent. Since she left us someone's bin payin' our rent every week wivout fail, an' don't bovver to ask who it is 'cos we don't know. I can tell yer one fing fer sure though, it ain't our muvver what's payin' it. I tell yer somefing else too. Christmas gone the neighbours rallied round wiv presents, an' that Christmas tree, an' they give us food, not that we were starvin', mind yer. They were smashin'. They wouldn't see us go short. An' last of all, I tell yer this. As good as the neighbours are, they'd soon shop us ter you an' the police if we was neglectin' the kids in any way.'

Miss Grant had sat impassive as Don went on, but when he stopped speaking she slipped the pen and notepad back into her large bag and stood up. She smiled at the young man and Rose in turn. 'I think I've learned enough here this evening,' she said indulgently. 'I have to admit I was a little dubious when I first walked in here, but you and your brother have let me see that you are passionately devoted to the children and you are both doing a very good job with their upbringing. I don't think we have anything to worry about in the circumstances. There is just one thing I'd like to ask though, before I leave you. The bit of trouble that Billy got into . . .'

''E was just worried about us 'avin' enough food an' 'e broke inter some barrer sheds,' Rose explained. 'It wasn't more than two bob's werf what 'e took.'

'I understand from the court report that the magistrate praised you highly. Well done, Rose. Well done, the pair of you,' the officer said smiling. 'Well, I'd better be off. I'd like to wish you both a happy new year.'

As soon as the front door closed behind her Rose and Don gave a huge sigh of relief. 'I thought yer was gonna put yer foot right in it when yer went off the way yer did,' Rose said, shaking her head in disbelief.

Don smiled nonchalantly. 'It pays ter speak yer mind at times,' he answered. 'Now stop worryin', 'cos there's no need fer the time bein' at least. Termorrer can take care of itself. Now what about you puttin' yer feet up fer five minutes an' I'll make us both a nice cup o' Rosie Lee.'

The cold weather had continued into the new year and the first week of January was bitterly cold. The icy streets were all but deserted after the local factories shut for the day and folk spent their evenings huddled around their fires for warmth. Not many people ventured out to the pubs and the hardy few who did were well wrapped up in overcoats, hats and scarves.

One middle-aged woman braved the elements as she stepped out of a taxi in Bermondsey Square and trudged up to number 6 carrying a small suitcase. She looked up at the high windows for a few moments before climbing the few stone steps to the front door. Her knock was answered by an elderly man wearing thick-lensed spectacles.

'I phoned earlier. I'm Mrs Morgan,' she said.

'Oh yes, do come in,' the man answered. 'I'll show you to your rooms. I took the liberty of putting the gas fire on and there's some tea, sugar and milk in the kitchen.'

The woman followed him up the long, thickly carpeted flight of stairs. On the landing he paused for breath. 'There's the convenience and bathroom, and these are your rooms,' he told her.

She stood back while he selected a key from a large bunch and opened the door. 'I'm sure you'll be comfortable,' he said, moving out of the way to let her enter. 'If there's anything more you need you just give me or my wife a call. We're on the ground floor.'

She thanked him and put her suitcase down beside the armchair as he closed the door behind him. For a moment she stood in the centre of the room and looked around. It was a large room, with heavy, mustard-coloured curtains already drawn across the window. A thick carpet covered the floor and it looked expensive, though well worn in places. There was a small gate-legged table folded down in front of the curtains and two armchairs placed near the gas fire. A large oak sideboard stood against the wall facing the fire and the walls themselves were decorated with flower-patterned paper. There were one or two pictures of country scenes hanging from a wooden picture rail and the ceiling looked freshly painted. The room felt cosy and she sighed as she sat herself down in one of the armchairs and kicked off her tight shoes to warm her feet.

For a while Dolly Morgan sat still, giving herself time to grow accustomed to the newness of her surroundings as memories of her old life drifted into her mind. Despite all the trouble and heartache the passing years had been kind to her, and though she was forty-seven years old her round full face was still unlined. Wide, deep blue eyes, full red lips and a compact nose framed by honey-blonde hair created a quite striking appearance. Her chin was dimpled, and when she smile the dimples in her cheeks were prominent and her eyes lit up mischievously. Her ample figure and wide shoulders gave the impression that she was taller than average, and when she moved about a room she had a commanding presence; it had been that way since she was a very young woman, and it was a quality that had attracted Bob to her.

Thinking of her late husband made Dolly feel suddenly sad and lonely and she got up to see what was in the sideboard. It contained cutlery, plates, and cups and saucers as well as a cruet set and breadboard, and when she walked out into the tiny kitchen she discovered a gas stove and a white porcelain sink with an attached draining board. Cupboards around the walls revealed the usual range of kitchen utensils and Dolly smiled to herself as she walked back into the lounge. So far so good. The flat was certainly as nice as she had been led to believe. There was just the bedroom to inspect. She opened the door to the left of the fireplace and stepped inside. It was a small room but it looked clean and well maintained. The bed was covered with a large white eiderdown and there was a dressing-table just in front of the window. A single wardrobe stood in a recess between the bed and the window and on the other side there was a small low table with a bedside lamp perched on it. The pale blue curtains were drawn tight and Dolly noticed that the room smelled of lavender. She tried the lamp and it cast a soft light across the counterpane. She decided that the flat would be ideal, for the time being at least.

Outside, the wind was rising again and when Dolly peeped through the curtains she could see a stretch of the Tower Bridge Road, its covering of ice and snow white and glistening in the light of a full moon. For a few moments she stood looking down on the deserted thoroughfare, then she turned away and went back into the tiny kitchen to make herself a strong cup of tea. Tomorrow she would go and see a few old friends, and take a look around a war-scarred Bermondsey. It was a home-coming, to the place where she was born and grew up. It had been a happy place once, and there were lots of happy memories, but Dolly's face tightened with anger as she recalled the circumstances which had caused her and Bob to leave the area so suddenly, all of twelve years ago.

It was Bob who had persuaded her that they should move away, and her deep love for him which had prevented her from arguing too strongly against it, even though she wanted desperately for the two of them to stay and fight the injustice done to her husband by his own family. She had known from the start that Bob was a one-off. The youngest son of Samuel and Martha Morgan, his father had been a cooper who started up in his own business and built up a very successful firm. Bob and his brothers, Conrad, Jack and Frankie, all spent some time working in the family business, but the others had preferred to go their own way, leaving Bob to run the company when their father died in his late fifties from a burst ulcer, brought on by excessive drinking.

Con, Jack and Frankie were all cursed with the same bad blood, Dolly recalled. They were wild, irresponsible and, like their father, prone to drink. Con was killed in the First World War and Jack finally drank himself to death in the early thirties after his marriage had broken up. Frankie had slipped into a life of crime and had spent many of his adult years behind bars.

The shock that she felt that day in August 1938 when the business failed had turned to anger and disgust when she learned the full story. She and Bob had just married and their aspirations of a bright and prosperous future together were suddenly dashed. On that day in August the future had looked decidedly grim.

With the move to Kent things had turned out better than they could have hoped for. Dolly and her husband had run the Pheasant in Westover for more than ten years, and they had been happy years, despite the war. When Bob suffered his heart attack they had become even closer, with Dolly taking on the burden of organising the running of the pub and Bob doing as much as he could. He seemed to have made a full recovery and then in 1944, at the time of the invasion of Europe, he suffered a stroke and was paralysed completely.

Now, after his death, Dolly was back in Bermondsey, and she vowed to herself that Frankie Morgan would live to rue the day.

Chapter Twelve

Rose had been pleased at the outcome of the welfare woman's visit, but now she was getting increasingly worried about her condition. She could see the change in her figure and would not be able to hide it for very much longer. She would have to go and see the doctor soon to make arrangements and it would not be long before the welfare found out. She would not be able to disguise things any more when the patronising Miss Grant made her next visit, and it was quite possible that one of the neighbours would let the cat out of the bag, even if they didn't mean to. Some of them visited the clinic in Grange Road and people were inclined to talk.

Rose was worried about her job too. She might be able to remain at work for another few weeks but Bernard Collis was on the warpath and he was unpredictable. He had apparently made enquiries and was convinced that Alice had been lying to him about the petition. Alice told her about being summoned into the office and confronted by the very angry manager. He had accused her of making the story up and warned her in no uncertain terms that she was on borrowed time at Bromilow's.

''E told me straight that the first opportunity 'e gets I'm out on me ear,' Alice told her, 'so I'm lookin' fer anuvver job. I'm

120

gonna try the wine stores down Tooley Street. Pity yer can't come wiv me, 'cos the first chance cod's eyes gets 'e's gonna put yer back on the rollers.'

Rose knew that her friend was not exaggerating. Collis would hang around that time-clock like a vulture and the next time Alice came in late he would pounce. The poor girl was often late, and the fact that she lived Downtown and relied on the bridges not being swung open at the wrong time cut no ice as far as Collis was concerned. Alice pointed out that the manager had seen the two of them chatting together and he would assume that they had been in collusion. She was worried about what he might do now.

'I'm sorry if I've dropped yer in it, luv, but I thought it might work,' she said, pulling a despondent face. 'I didn't know that greasy cow Milly Ashley was gonna go blabbin' about me makin' it all up. A couple o' the women told me it was 'er.'

'Yer got me off that job so it worked, fer a while anyway,' Rose told her, smiling affectionately. 'I'll be leavin' soon anyway.'

'Yeah, but yer don't want anuvver spell on the rollers in your condition,' Alice said anxiously.

As Rose worked the press she thought about what Alice had said. She was right. Another spell on the heavy work might well induce a miscarriage. True, it would solve her problem, but it was a baby growing inside her, a human being, and it had the right to life, regardless of the fact that it had been conceived accidentally. Perhaps she could refuse to go on the rollers if she was told to. She could complain that she was being victimised, but she knew only too well that it would make no difference. This workforce had no union to fight for them and the other girls could not be expected to rally to the cause. Most of them worked in fear of being victimised themselves or losing their jobs.

The morning seemed to pass very slowly and just before the lunchtime whistle sounded Bernard Collis came marching along the gangway and stopped at the press Rose was operating. 'I may 'ave ter take yer off this an' put yer on the roller fer a week,' he said coldly. 'The woman doin' the job went off sick this mornin'. I've found a replacement fer the rest o' the day but we'll 'ave ter see if she's in termorrer.'

'What about one o' the ovver girls?' Rose said angrily. 'Surely yer got someone else ter take a turn.'

'I make the decisions,' Collis replied, 'an' if yer don't like it there's always the door.'

Rose watched him storm off, her jaws clamped tight with temper. How right Alice was. It was only a matter of time before she found herself back on the rollers. Maybe she should follow Alice's lead and seek work at the wine cellars. At least she would be sitting down and able to stay at work until the last few weeks of her pregnancy. The problem was, when young women started in new factory work they were always asked if they were pregnant. No, it was no use. She would have to grin and bear it, and hope that the heavy work did not harm her baby.

The factory whistle sounded and as Rose hurried off to the canteen Alice caught up with her, a wide grin on her flushed face. 'Yer never guess,' she said.

'Guess what?'

'Guess who's bin put on the rollers.'

'Not you?'

Alice shrugged her shoulders. 'I can do the job wiv one 'and tied be'ind me back,' she said dismissively. 'That boss-eyed no-good git of a manager ain't gonna beat me. I'll show 'im. 'E finks Big Mary's the only one who can do the job wivout flaggin'. You jus' watch me.'

They reached the canteen and as they lined up at the tea

counter Rose took her friend by the arm. 'Listen, Alice, yer shouldn't overdo it just to impress 'im,' she said solicitously. 'At best yer'll get stuck on the job fer good, an' at the worst yer could strain yer insides.'

Alice grinned. 'Don't worry, I'm as tough as ole boots. 'Ere, I bin finkin' about goin' down ter that union office in Tooley Street ter find out about gettin' us gels in the trade union when I finish work ternight. Ovver firms 'ave done it an' the workers get a better deal. The union blokes would really clamp down on the likes of ole four-eyes.'

'It's a good idea,' Rose replied as they found themselves a table. 'I wish I was gonna be around 'ere long enough ter get involved.'

'Don't matter what 'appens, Rose, you an' me 'ave gotta keep in touch,' Alice said. 'I could call round one night maybe an' get yer up ter date wiv what's goin' on.'

'I'd like that,' Rose replied.

'Good, so that's settled then.'

The two ate their sandwiches in silence and then Alice pulled out some knitting from her large handbag. 'I'm makin' a pair o' bootees,' she said shyly. 'I'm doin' 'em in white 'cos I don't know what sex the baby's gonna be. I started 'em the ovver night.'

Rose gave her an intimate smile. 'They'll be smashin',' she replied. 'I'm surprised you 'ave the time. Don't yer go out nights? I mean wiv mates. Or a boyfriend . . .?'

'I've got a boyfriend, but we don't go out in the week,' Alice told her. 'John's muvver ain't too well at the moment an' 'e 'as ter do everyfing for 'er. I offered to 'elp 'im nights, but 'e won't let me. 'E's too proud. 'Is muvver suffers from chronic arthritis an' every ovver fing yer can fink of. I fink she plays on my John's good nature an' I told 'im so the ovver night. Nearly caused a barney it did, 'cos 'e's devoted to 'er an' won't 'ave a word said against 'er. So the long an' the short of it is, 'e looks after the ole gel an' I sit in knittin'. Life's a bitch at times, don't yer fink?'

Rose laughed aloud. 'Yer wouldn't fink so, lookin' at you. Yer never get miserable. Don't yer ever get screwed up, really screwed up, I mean? Don't yer ever feel like yer wanna walk out o' this dump an' say, sod it. Sod everyfing?'

'Every day, Rose, but I knuckle down like we all do,' Alice said smiling. 'I s'pose I jus' got one o' those faces that don't show me true feelin's. I'll tell yer though. Sometimes, when the day's goin' slow an' that bloody clock on the wall seems ter be goin' backwards, I fink o' bein' whisked out of 'ere by some 'andsome feller wiv lots o' dosh. 'E'll take me on 'is yacht an' 'ave 'is wicked way wiv me, then when I tell 'im I'm leavin' 'e'll go down on 'is 'ands an' knees an' tell me 'e can't live wivout me. Mind you, I wouldn't be silly enough ter leave. I'd marry 'im an' live the rest o' me life in luxury. I'd make 'im pander ter my every wish. Gawd, Rose, if pigs could fly.'

The short time they had spent together and Alice's light-hearted persiflage seemed to lift Rose's spirits and she returned to work feeling less miserable. Her respite did not last long; at four o'clock Bernard Collis came up to her again and told her that she was to go back on the roller first thing next morning.

The day had been a bit hazy for Jimmy Rideout and as he was searching the bottom of his wardrobe for a clean pair of socks he realised that he had not eaten since yesterday suppertime, when he brought home cod and chips. Jimmy remembered the promise he had made to himself before Christmas and sighed. If he was to kick the habit he would have to do it in stages. First thing would be to make sure that he ate regularly. It would mean going out and buying a new set of saucepans. The only one he possessed was used for everything from boiling potatoes to shaving out of. He sometimes used the disgusting frying pan but that had now become so bad that the eggs and bacon he cooked in it tasted absolutely vile. That stale fat must have been in it for months, he realised. Well, anyway, there was no time like the present. He would put the frying pan in the dustbin right away and go out and buy a new one. He would get a couple of saucepans while he was at it and maybe a new kettle. The old one was leaking at the seams after many years' good service.

Jimmy's big problem was that he had lost the measure of the nights and days. His world was a lingering blur of twilight, where time stood still and no one else ever slept. His inability to rejoin the normal routine of daily living caused him endless difficulties. He went shopping at mid-night and got up to have breakfast at three in the afternoon. He had knocked the long-suffering Fred Albury up at four o' clock one morning to ask for a box of matches, and he had been seen camping on the front doorstep of the Anchor at nine o'clock one Sunday morning, expecting the pub to open at any minute. Jimmy was a friendly sort who wanted to do right by everyone, but his lack of tact coupled with a tendency to talk to all and sundry caused him no end of troubles. Mrs James in the next street had stopped speaking to him after he told her that she reminded him of his mother. It was meant to be a compliment, but Mrs James knew that Jimmy's mother was approaching her eightieth birthday, and she was only forty-two. Mr Brown who lived in the Buildings had almost hit Jimmy when he told him with his best interests at heart to get a move on as they were crossing the Tower Bridge Road together. Mr Brown was seventy-two and in poor health. He was finding it difficult to stand, let alone walk, and he did not take very kindly to Jimmy's concern that he might be hit by a tram, especially since there was no traffic in sight. One experience that Jimmy shivered to think of was the time when he saw a woman approaching him one dark night and mistook her for Fred Albury's wife Muriel. As a joke he asked her if she would like to go for a romantic drink with him and she floored him with her handbag in sheer terror before running off screaming at the top of her voice.

As he sorted through a tangled heap of clothing Jimmy found the socks. They did not exactly make a pair, but wearing one black and one grey sock was better than freezing his ankles off. At least his shoes were nice and new. Shame he couldn't find the laces, but never mind, a piece of string would serve the purpose, and it wouldn't show if he turned his turnups down. Must remember to get a couple of pairs of laces at Cheap Jack's stall, he told himself. Goodrich's would sell pots and pans and he could get the kettle there as well.

At seven o'clock Jimmy put on his overcoat and tied it together with the dog lead he had found in the street, and before leaving he suddenly remembered to turn down the bottoms of his threadbare trousers. Outside it felt cold and seemed strangely dark to the inebriate, and slowly it dawned on him that the market would be closed. Must have been a long time getting ready, he told himself as he walked instinctively in the opposite direction to the market, towards the Anchor public house.

The cold weather and icy wind made Jimmy gasp and he blinked his watery eyes constantly as he made his way along Fellmonger Street and turned left into Basin Street. He could see the lights of the corner pub up ahead and he licked his lips. The food could come later, he decided; first a stiff drink to whet his appetite. Suddenly Jimmy saw the woman coming towards him, and remembering his last encounter in a darkened street with a person of the fairer sex he decided to hold his tongue. The woman was getting nearer, walking slowly through the slippery street. She was well built and her head was wrapped in a silk scarf She had a long light-coloured coat on and carried a handbag over her shoulder. He could see her face now and it was full and round.

'No! It couldn't be!' he gasped aloud.

The woman had almost reached him and she suddenly looked aprehensive. She took a tighter grip of her handbag and clenched her fists ready to protect herself from the gawking stranger who had stopped to stare at her.

Jimmy's face was wreathed in a broad smile, displaying his yellow teeth as he stood directly in her path. 'Bloody blimey, it's you. Dolly. Dolly Farran. Gawd 'elp us, gel it *is* you!'

Dolly looked hard at the drunk, frowning at his daft expression, then she suddenly dropped her tensed shoulders and smiled back. 'If it ain't Jimmy Rideout,' she said with relief. 'I ain't seen you since before the war. I didn't recognise yer at first. Yer look different.'

'Yeah, I imagine,' Jimmy replied, still grinning. 'What yer doin' round 'ere, gel? Last time I 'eard about yer I was wiv yer bruvver Gerry. We was in the pub an' 'e told me yer upped an' got married. 'E said yer moved down ter Kent somewhere. Gawd almighty, Dolly, yer don't look a day older than when me an' you tripped the light fantastic on that river boat.'

Dolly pulled the collar of her coat up around her ears. 'Where you off to?' she asked.

'I was goin' down the market but I left it too late. I'm now gonna refresh meself wiv a drop o' tiddly before I eat,' he replied with as much dignity as he could muster. 'Would yer care ter join an old suitor?'

Dolly had just left one of her old friends who used to go hop-picking every year and had always made a point of visiting her pub with the latest news of Bermondsey. Although she was rather tired she was still feeling quite nostalgic, and the surprise of seeing Jimmy Rideout was like an electric shock. He was one of the old crowd, many of whom had sadly not survived the war. She looked him up and down for a moment and shook her head in disbelief. 'Why not?' she smiled.

Jimmy stood up straight and threw his shoulders back as he took Dolly by the arm and led her the few remaining yards to the public bar of the Anchor. Dolly looked at him closely, and his unshaven face and the scruffy overcoat he was wearing over his string-tied boots made her pause. She preferred to drink in saloon bars and the state of her companion might prove to be a problem, but then again on a night like this the publican would welcome customers and couldn't afford to be too fussy about whom he admitted and whom he did not. 'No, the saloon bar, Jimmy. I want a comfortable sit-down,' she told him.

Jimmy stroked his bristles thoughtfully for a moment or two. Even he knew that he wasn't exactly dressed for drinking in saloon bars and Sammy McGarry would no doubt have something to say to him as soon as he crossed the threshold.

'C'mon then, yer gonna stand there all night?' Dolly said sharply.

'Still the same old Dolly,' Jimmy replied, grinning as he opened the door and stepped into the carpeted saloon.

'Yer in the wrong bar,' Sammy called out to Jimmy and the drunk turned to leave.

'No 'e's not. 'E's wiv me,' Dolly said as she stepped into Sammy's view.

The publican's eyes nearly popped and he stood as though transfixed. Here was the scruffiest man he had ever allowed into his public bar, and now he was in company with a very smart and good-looking woman who was obviously a friend of his. Or was she? he wondered.

'I'll 'ave a large gin an' tonic wiv a slice o' lemon, an' whatever my friend wants,' Dolly said to the shocked Sammy.

'I'll 'ave a nice pint o' bitter,' Jimmy said, looking very pleased with himself as he smiled at the publican. 'I want yer ter meet a very old an' dear friend o' mine,' he announced. 'This is Dolly Farran, as far as I was concerned the best-lookin' sort in Bermondsey. She's still a doll, ain't yer, Doll?'

'It's Dolly Morgan. Pleased ter meet yer,' she said.

Sammy's face grew even more surprised. 'Dolly Morgan? Any relation ter the Morgan family?' he asked.

'I married one of 'em,' she replied curtly.

Sammy put the gin and tonic down in front of Dolly and set about pulling the pint of bitter. 'One o' Frankie Morgan's bruvvers?' he probed.

'Bob Morgan, the best o' the lot,' Dolly replied before sipping her drink.

'I've not met Bob,' Sammy said, as he put the frothing pint down on the polished counter.

'No, yer not likely to. Bob's dead,' Dolly said without emotion.

Jimmy was looking around the bar and gazing at the only two other customers sitting there. They were young and totally wrapped up in each other. 'Quiet ternight,' he remarked.

'Yeah, but yer can't expect many people ter come out in this weavver,' Sammy said pleasantly, feeling he should refrain from a sarcastic reply while the drunk was in such refined company.

Dolly and Jimmy sat down at a table near the coal fire and the drunk took a long draught of his beer. 'Gawd, gel, yer could 'ave knocked me over wiv a feavver when I saw yer comin' terwards me,' he exclaimed. 'Yer look like a film star.'

Dolly smiled. 'Yer look down at 'eel, Jimmy, if yer don't mind me sayin',' she replied. 'Ain't yer workin'?'

'I still got a couple o' stalls. Well, I share 'em as a matter o' fact wiv a couple o' pals,' Jimmy told her. 'I do all right though. Me missues left me, yer know.'

'No, I didn't,' Dolly answered, looking at him with compassion and noticing the shake of his hand as he picked up his drink. 'Yer still livin' in Basin Street?'

'Nah. I got a flat in Imperial Buildin's. It suits me needs,' he said. 'By the way, I'm sorry to 'ear about yer ole man. I didn't know yer married one o' the Morgan boys.'

'You was a good pal o' Gerry's if I remember right,' Dolly said, changing the subject.

'Yeah, we were good ole mates,' Jimmy replied. 'As a matter o' fact me an' Gerry 'ad a drink tergevver just before we both left ter join up. That was the last time I clapped eyes on 'im 'cos when 'e was on leave I was at sea. Lovely feller 'e was. I still bloody well miss 'im.'

''Ow's Ida coped wiv the kids an' 'ow are they all?' Dolly asked. 'This is the first time I bin back 'ere since I left the year before the war broke out.'

Jimmy shook his head. 'She pissed orf last year. Left the lot of 'em fer a bleedin' bus inspector, would yer believe,' he growled.

Dolly was visibly shocked. 'Who's lookin' after 'em?' she asked.

'Why young Rose, Gawd love 'er, an' young Don. Smashin' kids they are. Billy and Joey are right little lads, an' that young Susan's a beauty,' Jimmy went on. 'They all manage, wiv a bit of 'elp from us neighbours from time ter time.'

Dolly finished her drink. ''Ere, let's refill yer glass,' she said convivially. 'It seems a lot's 'appened since I left.'

'Well, it's bin twelve years or more,' Jimmy reminded her. 'An' bearin' in mind there was the war too.'

'There's one or two people who's gonna fink the third world war's broken out very soon, mark my words,' Dolly said malevolently.

Jimmy ignored the remark and sat sipping his drink thoughtfully. ''Ere, where yer stayin'?' he asked finally.

'I got rooms in Bermondsey Square. It's a temporary arrangement till I can get me clothes an' fings from the pub,' Dolly told him.

The two people sat chatting in front of the flaring fire with another drink, and when it was time to leave Dolly walked back over to the counter. 'I understand Frankie Morgan drinks 'ere,' she said in a measured voice. 'Well, would yer do me a favour? Next time yer see that mongrel, tell 'im Dolly's back in town.'

Chapter Thirteen

The Friday evening whistle sounded and the Bromilow work-force hurried from the large, grim factory, sighing with relief at the prospect of another brief weekend away from the clatter of tins and the loud, constant thump of the heavy machinery. The bitterly cold weather of the last week had relented somewhat and the ice had started to thaw. It was slippery underfoot as Rose walked out into the cold air alongside her friend Alice, and as they crossed the busy Dockhead thoroughfare the two girls linked arms. Things had not worked out as they had expected. Bernard Collis had not carried out his threat to put Rose back on the rollers and Alice was sure she had worked out his motives.

'I know what the dirty git's up to,' she growled. ''E finks 'e'll get me ter go cryin' to 'im fer a bit o' pity. Well, Mr bleedin' Collis is gonna wait fer ever if that's 'is game. I ain't givin' 'im the pleasure of 'avin' me crawl to 'im.'

Rose felt bad about the way her friend was being treated and blamed herself. Alice had alienated the manager through sticking up for her and now she was paying the price. Rose knew too that she had been in touch with the union people after lobbying a few of the girls and it would not be long before

Collis found out. He seemed to have his spies on the factory floor and he would soon find a reason to get rid of her.

The two friends reached the tram stop and Alice joined the queue for a tram to Rotherhithe. 'Well, luv, 'ave a nice weekend, an' take it easy. I'll see yer Monday,' she said cheerfully.

Rose waved goodbye and turned into Abbey Street feeling tired and jaded. She had felt physically sick every morning for the past week and the drudgery at the factory made her depressed and irritable. The only bright note was having escaped another week on the rollers, thanks to Alice. Next week could be a different story, she realised. Her friend was on borrowed time at the factory and Collis would know where to look for a replacement on the rollers once he got rid of her.

The young woman reached Fellmonger Street and went into Joe Diamond's corner shop. Joe was a big jovial man in his fifties, a confirmed bachelor, and he seemed to know all that was going on in the area. He sold groceries, papers and tobacco, as well as numerous other bits and pieces, and he had an assistant by the name of Lizzie Carroll, a diminutive woman of about Joe's age. She picked up as many snippets of gossip as her employer, and between the two of them nothing of the goings-on in the immediate vicinity was ever missed.

''Ello, young Rose,' Joe said, looking over his metal-rimmed glasses. ''Ow's the kids?'

'They was all right this mornin',' she replied. 'Give us a quarter o' tea an' a jar o' strawberry jam, will yer, Joe.'

The shopkeeper placed the items down on the counter and picked up the ten-shilling note, giving Rose a wink and a sly grin as he ignored the ration book she held out to him. Joe had always managed to keep a good stock of foodstuffs and during the war he had produced from under the counter luxury items such as tinned salmon and ham for a few coppers extra, unlike a lot of the other shopkeepers, who tended to charge a lot more.

Rose was quite happy to pay the extra penny on the tea, knowing that her ration book would be left unstamped for the week.

''Ave you 'eard about ole Jimmy Rideout?' Joe said as he placed the change down in front of the young woman.

'No, what's 'appened?' she asked.

''E's 'ad a fall, comin' out the block by all accounts,' Joe informed her. 'Cut 'is 'ead on the kerb. Nasty one it was. Fred Albury picked 'im up an' took 'im in. Muriel bandaged 'is crust. The silly sod refused ter go ter the 'ospital even though she told 'im it needed a few stiches.'

'When did it 'appen?' Rose asked him.

'This mornin'. All right, I know Jimmy's a boozer, but I don't fink 'e eats enough,' Joe remarked. 'Bloody shame really.'

Rose left the shop and hurried into the Buildings, and as she climbed the flight of stairs she felt the nagging pain start up again in the pit of her stomach. As she opened the door and stepped into the passage she heard the children's laughter and the warmth of the flat felt good. Don greeted her with a grin. 'I got away early this evenin',' he said. 'Yer look all in.'

'Fanks fer the compliment,' Rose replied, casting a sideways glance at him as she gave Susan her usual kiss.

Billy looked unusually quiet but Joey wore a big smile as he gazed up at his sister. 'Billy's got a letter from 'is teacher,' he said quickly.

'All right, big mouth,' Billy growled. 'I was gonna tell 'er.'

Rose frowned as she tore open the envelope that was lying on the table. 'She wants ter see me as soon as possible,' she told Don, and turning to Billy. 'What yer bin up to?'

'It wasn't me, it was Charlie Fletcher. 'E brought fags inter school an' when we was in the playground at playtime Charlie said 'e was gonna go in the lavs to 'ave a puff,' Billy explained. 'Me an' some o' the boys went in ter watch. Honest, Rose. We wasn't gonna 'ave a smoke ourselves. Anyway Charlie got sick an' 'e give me the fag to 'old while 'e was bein' sick an' that's when Mr Norris caught us. 'E was on playground duty.'

Rose puffed loudly as she sat down and kicked off her shoes. 'Are you tellin' me the trufe, Billy?' she asked him.

'Cross me 'eart an' 'ope ter die,' Billy replied quickly.

Don hid a grin as he handed Rose a cup of tea. 'Yer better not let me catch yer smokin',' he said firmly to his sad-faced young brother.

'You smoke,' Joey butted in.

'It's different wiv me. I'm grown up. Anyway, smokin' stunts yer growth,' Don told him. 'D'yer wanna be a shrimp all yer life?'

'I don't smoke,' Joey replied with a cheeky grin.

'Nor do I,' Billy cut in loudly. 'I told yer, I was only mindin' the fag fer Charlie.'

'All right, all right,' Rose shouted. 'Now let's 'ear no more about it. I'll go an' see yer teacher an' sort it out on Monday mornin'. Now be quiet or I'll send the two of yer ter bed early.'

Don sat down in the armchair facing his sister and folded his arms as he leaned back. 'I fink I'll go out fer a drink ternight,' he said casually. 'Albert Morgan's asked me out.'

'I told yer ter keep away from that crowd,' Rose said quickly, her face growing stern.

'I'm a bit too old ter be told what ter do,' Don replied quietly.

'No, yer not,' Rose retorted.

'Look, Rose, Albert's OK. 'E's not like the rest of 'em,' Don said placatingly. 'In fact 'e told me somefing the ovver night. 'E's dead worried.'

'What about?' Rose asked.

'Between you an' me, the Morgans are plannin' somefing,' Don began in a quiet voice, glancing over to make sure the boys were not paying any attention. 'I fink it's a big robbery an' Albert's got the jitters. 'E don't wanna get involved but' e's frightened ter back out.'

''E told yer that?' Rose queried.

'Yeah. 'E looked really worried,' Don went on. 'Trouble wiv Albert is, 'e's frightened o' John. 'E's the big I-am an' 'e expects the bruvvers ter fall in wiv everyfing 'e ses. As far as Ernie goes, 'e's as fick as two short planks, but Albert's got more sense. 'E can see the danger. The ole man's in on this one an' that's what's worryin' 'im.'

'Don't you get involved in the Morgans' business, Don,' Rose implored him. 'That family spell trouble an' I don't wanna see you get locked up. I got enough ter worry about, wivout 'avin' ter come an' visit you in the nick.'

'Don't worry yerself, I'm only gonna 'ave a chat wiv Albert. That can't do no 'arm,' Don said with a shrug of his broad shoulders.

Rose busied herself with preparing the evening meal, trying not to dwell on what Don had just told her, but the nagging fear that everything was soon going to fall apart would not leave her.

Tommy Caulfield sat in the yard office, a glass of brandy in front of him, and he looked very pensive as he gazed out of the window at the darkening clouds. The last of his car men had left fifteen minutes ago and usually he wasted no time in locking up and getting home to Doris. She had become more immobile of late with her arthritis and quickly grew anxious if he was late home. On this particular Friday evening, however, Tommy needed time to think. His old friend Bill Grogan had seemed sure that Frankie Morgan would be cleared in court the following Monday, but there was always the possibility that something would go wrong. The warning he had received by way of the burning rags worried the transport contractor. If Frankie did go down he would be in the firing line. The Morgans would be convinced that he had had something to do with it, whatever came out in court.

Tommy took a swig of brandy as he sat slumped in his comfortable desk chair and wondered whether he should accept Brandon's offer to buy him out. It was a reasonable bid and it would set him up for the rest of his life. He would also be able to spend more time with Doris, though that prospect was not something he relished. His wife was one of the best and he loved her dearly, but she could be trying at times. She would get irritable with him under her feet all day, and he would no doubt get bored himself after a lifetime in business.

The yard bell sounded loudly and Tommy got up to go to the gate, a puzzled look on his florid face. It was unusual for anyone to call at this time, he thought.

As the contractor bent down and opened the wicket-gate his eyes widened in surprise. 'Well, this is a turn-up fer the book,' he said smiling. 'C'mon in.'

Dolly Morgan stepped into the yard. 'I'm back 'ere ter live, Tommy, an' I thought I'd look yer up. I'm doin' the rounds, yer see,' she said smiling broadly.

Tommy led the way to his office and pulled up a chair to his desk. 'Sit yerself down, Doll. Bloody 'ell, I still can't believe it's you. Yer do look well,' he told her, shaking his head slowly.

Dolly crossed her legs and adjusted her skirt, all the while appraising the man in front of her. 'Yer put on a lot o' weight, Tommy, but yer still look bright an' breezy,' she remarked.

Tommy laughed. 'I 'eard yer was back from Sammy McGarry in the Anchor,' he said, reaching into his desk drawer for another glass. 'Care fer a snort? I've only got brandy.'

Dolly smiled. 'I'll take a drink wiv yer, Tommy, fer ole times' sake,' she said. 'Brandy'll do nicely. I saw there was a light on in the yard so I took a chance.'

'I'm glad yer did,' he replied. 'Sammy told me about Bob.

Sorry to 'ear it. 'E was a good man, was Bob. Pity I can't say the same fer the rest o' the family.'

'You ain't gettin' no grief from 'em, are yer?' Dolly said, her eyes narrowing.

'No, not really, but there's a court case comin' up next Monday an' Frankie Morgan's in the dock,' Tommy told her. ''E knocked seven bells out o' one o' my car men. Nuffink ter do wiv me, but I'm a bit appre'ensive o' the outcome. Anyway, enough o' my troubles. What's your plans now yer back?'

'Well, first of all I've gotta find a place ter live,' Dolly replied. 'I'm in rooms at the moment. It's nice an' comfortable, but it's not like yer own place wiv yer own front door. Then soon as I get meself prop'ly settled I've got a long overdue bit o' business ter sort out wiv Frankie Morgan. That's gonna be interestin', ter say the least.'

'I bet it will,' Tommy said quickly, feeling suddenly uneasy as he passed her the filled glass.

Dolly took a sip and grimaced. 'That's bloody strong,' she gasped.

'It's good stuff. Sammy gets it for me,' Tommy told her, studying her furtively.

'This Sammy. Is 'e a mate o' Frankie Morgan's?' Dolly asked, her eyes narrowing.

'Not really. Sammy's wife Beryl can't stand the sight of Frankie but Sammy's just out fer a quiet life. I fink 'e just tolerates the bloke,' Tommy replied. 'Why d'yer ask?'

'Oh nuffink. Just curious, that's all,' Dolly said casually.

The contractor took another swig and refilled his glass. 'Anuvver?'

Dolly shook her head. 'Not this early, Tom. I need a clear 'ead ternight. I got anuvver visit ter make.'

'Not to Morgan?'

'Nah, 'e can await my pleasure,' she replied with a cruel smile.

Tommy leaned back in his chair and shook his head slowly as he looked at the big blonde woman. 'Bloody 'ell, Dolly, it's really nice seein' yer back after all this time. Remember the ole days? Gerry, Jimmy Rideout, Bert Adams, an' the Westleys. Remember Jack Lyons an' the kid wiv the club foot? I could never remember 'is name.'

'Les Nunn,' Dolly replied, smiling as the memory of them all came flooding back. 'They was good times. I bumped inter Jimmy Rideout the ovver day but I ain't seen many ole faces I recognise.'

Tommy sighed sadly. 'Bert Adams was killed on the invasion, a few days after your Gerry, an' Stan Westley went down wiv the *Repulse* out in the Far East. Stan's younger bruvver survived the war. 'E married inter money an' moved over the water somewhere. Doin' quite well fer 'imself, last I 'eard.'

'Jack Lyons?' Dolly prompted.

Tommy shook his head. 'Jack got invalided out o' the army after Dunkirk. Poor git was sufferin' from shell shock. Never really recovered. One day terwards the end o' the war 'e chucked 'imself in the Thames. The lightermen pulled 'im out. Poor ole Jack couldn't do anyfing right. 'E was the one who always got caught, d'yer remember?'

Dolly nodded sadly as she ran her forefinger round the edge of her glass. 'Jack got a few slaps, didn't 'e. Is 'e still alive?'

'Yeah, 'e's a night watchman on the Council,' Tommy told her. 'I saw 'im only the ovver week as I was goin' 'ome. Sittin' in 'is 'ut cookin' a bit o' toast in front of a coke fire. Mumblin' to 'imself 'e was. Sad, very sad.'

'An' Les Nunn?'

'Gawd knows. Never seen 'ide nor 'air of 'im since the blitz. Could 'ave bin killed in the bombin', I s'pose,' Tommy said with a heavy sigh.

Dolly drained her glass. 'Well, it's bin nice talkin' ter yer,

Tommy. I gotta go. We should 'ave a drink tergevver soon,' she said as she got up.

The contractor walked across the yard with her and opened the wicket-gate. 'By the way,' he said suddenly. 'Yer mentioned bumpin' inter Jimmy Rideout. Sammy was tellin' me that Jimmy took a bad fall this mornin'. Cracked 'is 'ead open apparently. Comin' out o' the Buildin's. The porter's wife bandaged 'im up but 'e wouldn't go ter the 'ospital. You know 'ow funny Jimmy is.'

Dolly nodded. 'Yeah, I know. Anyway, nice seein' yer, Tommy. Take care,' she said, kissing him on the cheek before stepping out into Fellmonger Street.

'Don't ferget about that drink,' Tommy called out to her as she walked away.

Chapter Fourteen

Albert Morgan felt more than a little conspicuous as he stood alone in the public bar of the Swan, wearing his dark-brown pinstripe suit and white shirt with a narrow, grey silk tie which he had borrowed from his brother Ernie. Albert always liked to look smart when he went out for the evening, but as he looked around at the rivermen and transport workers who filled the public bar he wished he had worn his working overcoat and scarf instead. Most of the men there had come straight from work and they stood around in groups, talking loudly and arguing over the respective merits of their favourite football teams. In the far corner of the bar two transport union officials sat collecting subscriptions from drivers and car men, and in the opposite corner a game of darts was in progress. Albert remembered seeing the two young players talking with Don and he felt a little uneasy at the curious glances they occasionally gave him.

The game over, the two players walked over to the counter and one of them ordered fresh drinks.

'You're a mate o' Don Farran's, ain't yer?' the young man said to Albert.

''S'right,' Albert replied curtly.

'Waitin' fer 'im, are yer?'

'Are you Albert Morgan?' the other young man said before Albert could answer.

'Yeah. What's it ter you?' Albert said quickly.

The young man shrugged his shoulders. 'Nuffink, just askin',' he replied, looking a little abashed as his friend handed him his pint of ale.

Albert picked up his pint and took a large swig. 'I'm waitin' fer Don,' he said, putting down and the glass and tugging at his shirt cuffs which were secured with small brass cufflinks and showed below the sleeve of his suit.

The young men took their drinks back to the dartboard and were joined by another young man who looked briefly in Albert's direction and scowled.

'Right flash git, ain't 'e,' the shorter of the two said to the newcomer.

'It don't do ter get on the wrong side o' that family,' the young man replied. 'I've seen Frankie Morgan walk into a pub carryin' a chopper, lookin' fer someone who'd upset 'im.'

'What's Don Farran doin' mixin' wiv 'im?' the tall one asked.

'They've bin pals fer some time. They was at the same school,' the young man informed him. 'That geezer must be a couple o' years older than Don though, 'cos 'e's bin fer 'is army medical. Failed wiv 'is ears apparently. The older bruvver John done a year in the glass'ouse an' got a DD.'

'What's a DD?'

'Dishonourable discharge. 'E got it fer whackin' a sergeant. A real 'ard git John is.'

Albert stood with his back to the dart players, aware that they were most probably discussing him, and he hoped that Don would show up soon. Being identified as one of the Morgans worried him. He knew full well that the family had made a few enemies in Bermondsey over the years and one day someone was going to come looking. Brother John would no doubt relish such a confrontation and Ernie could be expected to react violently and do whatever John said, but the prospect of a vendetta scared Albert.

As he drained his glass Albert saw Don enter the pub and he ordered two pints of bitter. 'I was gettin' ready ter leave,' he said gruffly. 'I feel like a bloody poppy show in 'ere.'

Don grinned. 'Yer look pretty nifty, if you ask me,' he replied, acknowledging the dart players with a wave of his hand.

'Who are they?' Albert asked.

'Just local lads,' Don told him as he picked up his pint. 'Cheers, Alb.'

'The ole man comes up on Monday,' Albert said suddenly.

Don leaned on the counter, looking at him closely. 'Yer not worried about 'im goin' down, are yer?' he asked.

Albert shook his head emphatically. 'No chance. The ole man's brief's got it sewed up,' he replied.

'Are yer still worried about what yer told me?' Don enquired. 'Yer look a bit troubled.'

Albert took a sip of his beer and then leaned his elbow on the bar as he moved closer to Don. 'Once the trial's out o' the way fings are gonna start movin',' he said in a low voice.

Don looked around quickly to make sure they were not being overheard. 'What fings?' he asked.

Albert looked at his friend for a few minutes then he dropped his eyes. 'What I told yer about,' he said quietly.

'Yer didn't tell me much, only that yer 'ad somefing planned an' yer ole man was organisin' it,' Don replied.

'We're doin' a job up West. It's a jeweller's,' Albert whispered.

Don blew through his pinched lips. 'Bloody 'ell, Alb, no wonder yer worried. That's a bit out o' your league, ain't it? Yer can get ten years fer that sort o' robbery.'

Albert nodded nervously. 'I've bin 'avin' nightmares about it,' he sighed.

Don leaned closer to him. 'Listen, pal. If I were you I'd pull out while yer still can. Tell the ole man straight out yer not gonna go on this one.'

'Yeah, but you're not me, are yer?' Albert said quickly. 'Yer don't understand what the ole man's like. Yer don't argue wiv 'im. Not even John argues. I'll tell yer somefing. We 'ad a family get-tergevver an' our ole man put it to us plain as day. Was we in or out. 'E knew the answer before 'e put the question. As far as 'e was concerned it's playin' games. I never 'ad the guts ter front 'im, Don. I'm in, like it or not.'

Don shook his head slowly. 'Yer right, Albert. I don't understand,' he replied. 'But I tell yer what. One day yer gonna stand up to 'im, like it or not, an' the longer yer put it off the 'arder it's gonna be. Surely yer can find a way ter talk ter yer own farvver. Tell 'im the trufe. Tell 'im yer concerned. There's no disgrace in that.'

Albert smiled sardonically. 'When ovver kids' farvvers were takin' 'em up the park or ter football matches my old man was in nick,' he explained with a snort. 'None of us grew up wiv 'im around. Even our muvver can't talk sense to 'im without gettin' 'er 'ead bit off. It's not like 'avin' a farvver.'

'Why don't yer leave 'ome then?' Don suggested. 'At least yer got a job.'

Albert shrugged his shoulders. Don was right, he had to admit. He should leave home and get away from the family influence. Unlike John and Ernie he had always been in work. The window-cleaning job paid well, if he put the time and effort into it. Maybe he could get a flat and start up in business on his own. Perhaps he could get a stall in the market. If Jimmy Rideout could do it so could he. 'I might just find a flat,' he said unconvincingly.

'I'd ask yer ter come as a lodger, but trouble is, yer'd 'ave ter sleep in the coal cupboard,' Don joked. 'We're a bit short o' space in our flat.'

Albert smiled. 'I bin goin' on about me own troubles. 'Ow about yours? Is Rose an' the kids keepin' well?'

Don nodded. 'Yeah, we get by,' he said. 'It's a struggle though. I wish I could put a bit more inter the 'ome. That's why I got so uptight about gettin' took on by that bruvver o' yours. That few bob would 'ave come in 'andy fer Christmas. Still, we managed. Trouble is, it's all down ter Rose mainly. She's got a right poxy job but the pay's good.'

'Yeah, she's a great gal,' Albert said, a faraway look coming into his eyes.

Don gazed at him and grinned, noting the tone in his friend's voice. 'I thought at one time that you an' Rose might get tergevver,' he remarked.

'Yeah, but yer muvver scotched that, didn't she?' Albert replied. 'Yer remember that time I called fer yer an' she told me ter piss off? That was when she found out me name was Morgan. I'm sure she thought I was after datin' Rose.'

'Well yer was, wasn't yer?' Don said laughing.

Albert ignored the question as he pushed his empty glass across the counter. 'I'll get these. I'm a bit more flush than you,' he said.

At number 2 Imperial Buildings Jimmy Rideout sat back in his armchair feeling sorry for himself. His head throbbed and his hip felt stiff and sore. The coal fire was burning low and the temperature in the room was falling. He had made himself a brawn sandwich earlier and he had just used up the last of the coffee. Now as he stared up at the stained ceiling he realised that he badly needed a drink. Maybe he could manage to get to the Anchor for just one. He wouldn't be out long and perhaps the cold air would shift his headache.

Jimmy eased himself out of the chair slowly, feeling the tightness in his hip, and then as he straightened up the room seemed to swim before his eyes and he flopped back into the armchair. It was no good. Better if he got into bed and slept, he decided. At least it would be preferable to sitting here feeling sorry for himself. It didn't do to sit brooding about how things were, and how things could have been, given different circumstances. It was the war that had caused him to be the way he was. It had changed him the same as it had changed many people, and there was no use arguing the fact, he told himself.

The knock on the door startled him and he gingerly eased himself out of his comfortable chair, holding his head this time as he clutched at the sideboard to steady himself and reached for the doorhandle. He shuffled slowly and painfully into the cold dark passage and opened the front door.

'I'm sorry if I disturbed yer, Jimmy, but I 'ad ter call when I 'eard yer'd 'ad a fall,' Dolly said, full of concern.

Jimmy leaned his suffering body against the door jamb, a huge stupid smile spreading across his face. 'I'd ask yer in but I ain't done me cleanin' up terday,' he replied.

Dolly stepped into the passage past him and closed the door behind her, taking him by the arm like an invalid. 'C'mon, no arguin'. Let's get yer sat down,' she said firmly.

The drunk allowed himself to be guided into the armchair and he looked up at Dolly, wincing.

'Does it 'urt much?' she said quickly.

'Nah, I'm just ashamed o' you seein' the place the way it is,' Jimmy replied. 'I usually give it a good goin'-over once a week, on Fridays as it 'appens. That's why it's so scruffy.'

Dolly looked around the flat, taking in every detail. She could see that Jimmy had not put a duster or broom to the place for weeks. She noticed the dirty plate and mug standing on the table and the newspapers that were scattered about the room, the ashes in the grate and the dying fire, the filthy curtains and the pile of clothes resting in a corner of the room. There was a stale smell about the flat and she could see the brown stained ceiling showing up above the shadeless electric lightbulb.

'Jimmy, yer a dirty ole git,' she said, standing in front of him with her hands on her hips. 'This gaff looks like it ain't bin cleaned fer bloody years, never mind weeks. Yer can't live in a place like this or yer'll get ill. It's like a bleedin' igloo in 'ere. Ain't yer got any coal?'

'I was gonna get a bit off 'im next door till the coalman come,' Jimmy explained, 'but I come over giddy when I got up out o' the chair.'

'Where d'yer store it, in the yard?' Dolly asked.

'No, in the coal cupboard, in the passage, but I told yer I'm right out of it,' Jimmy said as Dolly walked out of the room.

After a few seconds she was back. 'Right, there's enough dust ter make some coal bricks,' she told him. 'Now, where's yer tea fings kept?'

'In the scullery on the shelf. But I'm out o' tea an' coffee,' Jimmy moaned.

'You're a bloody useless git, Jim Rideout, an' you ought ter be ashamed o' yerself lettin' the place go the way you' ave,' Dolly said scathingly. 'What 'appened ter the proud Jimmy I used ter know?'

The drunk slumped down in his chair, looking very sheepish. 'I ain't bin feelin' too well lately,' he said in a subdued voice.

'No, course yer wouldn't,' Dolly went on aggressively. 'It's the booze, I can tell. When was the last time you 'ad a good meat an' two veg inside yer?'

'I usually cook meself a fry-up, but the pan needs a good clean out an' I ain't got round ter doin it,' Jimmy told her.

Dolly shook her head slowly. 'Give us yer key,' she demanded.

'What for?'

'So I can let meself in again.'

'Why, where yer goin'?'

'Never you mind. The key I said.'

Jimmy pointed to the mantelshelf. 'I was just goin' ter bed when yer knocked,' he said in a sorry voice.

'Just sit there an' wait till I get back,' she told him firmly.

Dolly hurried out of the flat and picked her way through the snow that was hardening in the cold evening air. She knocked on the side door of Joe Diamond's shop and produced a suitably worried look as he opened the door. 'I'm very sorry ter trouble yer, but we've just found an old feller sufferin' from the cold,' she said appealingly. 'We gotta warm 'im up some'ow. Can yer let me 'ave a packet o' tea an' some milk an' sugar?'

Joe Diamond mumbled something under his breath and disappeared into the back of his shop, emerging in a few moments with a brown carrier bag.

'You are a love,' Dolly said sweetly as she handed him two half-crowns. 'Yer'll get yer reward in 'eaven. 'Ere, yer don't sell bags o' coal, do yer?'

Joe went in again and came back carrying a heavy bag. 'This is the last o' the best nuts,' he said puffing.

Dolly dipped into her purse and took out another half-crown 'That's seven an' six I've give yer. Keep the change fer yer trouble,' she told him.

'Fanks, missus,' he said smiling. 'Can yer manage this?'

'Put it in me arm,' Dolly told him. 'Yer a dear.'

'Who was it yer said yer found?' Joe asked.

'This man. Sorry I can't stop to explain, it's a matter o' life an' death,' she said, hugging the bag of coal to her bosom.

The sharp wind felt icy on Dolly's face as she walked back along Fellmonger Street carrying a bag of best coal nuts in her arm and clutching the carrier bag in her other hand. She let herself into Jimmy's flat with some difficulty and puffed loudly as she dropped the big bag into the hearth. 'Right. First fings first,' she said as she picked pieces of coal from the split bag and laid them on the dying fire.

'Where d'yer get that?' Jimmy asked, looking very surprised.

'The corner shop. I knocked 'im up,' Dolly said as she raked out the ash from under the fire.

Jimmy looked even more surprised. 'I've never known Joe Diamond ter be knocked up fer anyone,' he remarked.

'Well, there's always a first time fer everyfing,' she told him.

Jimmy sat back and watched as Dolly bustled herself about the room. It took her mere minutes to get the place in some sort of order, and then when she was reasonably satisfied she took the carrier bag out into the scullery. Ten minutes later she sat down facing Jimmy and watched him sip his tea gratefully.

'That's the best cup o' tea I've 'ad in years,' he said, smiling happily as the warmth of the flaring fire reached his aching bones.

'Right, now I'm gonna wash up a couple o' those dirty rotten plates and then I'm gonna go an' get us some fish an' chips,' she said. 'I s'pose yer out o' salt an' vinegar, ain't yer?'

'There's plenty in the cupboard, as it goes,' he said with a mischievous twinkle in his eyes.

At nine thirty that evening Dolly got up and stretched her arms above her head. 'Well, I'd better make tracks,' she told him. 'Can I 'elp yer inter bed?'

'Nah, I fink I'll kip 'ere in the warm,' Jimmy replied.

Dolly went into the bedroom and came back carrying a

blanket. ''Ere, wrap yourself up in this,' she said. 'It'll be cold when the fire dies down.'

The drunk looked up at her with gratitude showing on his face. 'Yer a bloody diamond, d'yer know?' he said.

'So I've bin told. Now get some sleep. I'll try an' look in termorrer some time,' she replied, picking up her handbag.

Jimmy looked contented as he snuggled down beneath the blanket. ''Ere, Dolly, yer wouldn't like ter do me one more favour, would yer?'

'What's that?'

'Marry me,' he grinned.

Chapter Fifteen

On Saturday morning the temperature rose and a sudden thaw turned the backstreets into rivers of running water. The drains and pipes gurgled; streams flowed along the kerbsides and by early evening the last of the snow had disappeared.

At number 4 Imperial Buildings Rose Farran finished the washing up and then hurried into the living room to quieten the two boys who were involved in a heated argument over a torn comic paper.

'Now look, you two. I've warned yer once an' I'm not gonna tell yer again. If yer can't be quiet an' play prop'ly yer'll go ter bed at six, an' I mean it,' she shouted.

'It wasn't me, Rose,' Joey said, glaring at Billy. ''E sat on me comic. Look at it, it's all screwed up.'

'I didn't do it on purpose, Rose, honest,' Billy told her. ''E shouldn't leave it on the armchair where people could sit on it.'

'I'll sit on you two if yer don't shut up,' Rose retorted. 'Now get yer games out an' play tergevver like two sensible kids. Look at yer sister. She's playin' nice an' quiet.'

Susan was sitting on the mat in front of the gas fire carefully poking the stuffing back into her tattered doll, and she looked up wide-eyed. 'Them two are always arguin',' she said, giving the boys a scornful look.

Rose sat down and brushed a strand of her fair hair away from her forehead. 'Why don't yer play wiv yer new dolly?' she asked the child. 'Don't yer like it?'

'I do like it, Rose, but I like this one as well. I wish it could 'ave two eyes, though,' she said, cuddling the toy to her.

'Don't worry, luv, I'll see if I can mend it soon. Promise,' Rose told her, realising that she had promised to get the doll fixed before on more than one occasion. It was strange the love Susan had for the ragged thing. Even though she had a new doll with strands of hair, a pretty dress and eyes that opened and closed, she still insisted on taking the tattered one to bed with her.

The boys had heeded the threat of early bed and they were now playing draughts. Don sat facing Rose, idly watching her unpicking the seam of a dress with a pair of small scissors. His few shillings pocket money had all but gone on Friday night and he knew that his sister was going to rant and rave at him when he told her of the decision he had made. Now was not the time though. Better to wait until the children were in bed, he thought. Susan was easily upset when they rowed, and row they would if Rose tried to dissuade him.

Footsteps sounded on the wooden stairs and Rose pricked up her ears. She had got to recognise the treads of all her neighbours and she knew instinctively when it was a strange step. The loud knock was repeated before Don reached the front door and Rose barely had time to put down the split dress and get up before Don came back into the room followed by a large blonde woman.

''Ello, Rose,' she said smiling. 'Yer don't remember me, do yer? I'm yer aunt Dolly, yer dad's sister.'

Rose held out her hand. 'I'm pleased ter meet yer,' she

said quickly, trying to hide her sudden embarrassment as she moved her sewing box from the side of the armchair. 'Won't yer sit down?'

Don looked equally embarrassed and he motioned towards the scullery. 'I'll go an' put the kettle on,' he said.

Dolly made herself comfortable in the armchair and then smiled widely at the curious children. 'Let me see. Now, you'll be Joey an' you're Billy,' she said.

'No, I'm Billy. 'E's Joey.'

'An' you must be Susan.'

The child nodded slowly as she got up and went to Rose's side, burying her head in the fold of her elder sister's cotton skirt. Rose sat down in the chair vacated by Don and pulled Susan on to her lap. 'I remember me dad talkin' about yer, but I can't remember yer,' she told Dolly.

'I don't s'pose yer would, luv. The last time I called 'ere was before the war,' Dolly replied. 'You was only a child then. About Susan's age. Don was toddlin' around, an' of course these little luvvies were still a twinkle in yer farvver's eye.'

Don stood by the scullery doorway studying the big blonde who seemed to fill the armchair. She was a very attractive woman and he noticed how her features resembled those of his dead father although her colouring was so different. Her eyes were big and expressive like his, and she seemed to hold herself upright, even while sitting.

'Was that the last time yer saw me dad?' Rose asked.

Dolly shook her head. ''E used ter come ter Kent where I was livin'. Last time I saw 'im was while 'e was on embarkation leave,' she replied. 'Yer dad used ter tell me all about yer an' 'ow yer was all gettin' on. As a matter o' fact 'e 'ad some photos of you all in 'is wallet. You was all standin' outside the Buildin's. Did yer ever get the photos back?'

Rose shook her head. 'I never saw 'em after we got the

telegram about Dad,' she said ruefully. 'P'raps me muvver 'ad 'em. There's none 'ere, though.'

Dolly looked up at Don. 'You're the spittin' image of yer dad,' she told him. 'The same build an' looks. Yer a nice-lookin' lad, Don. Sorry if I'm embarrasin' yer.'

Don smiled, colouring up slightly. 'So people tell me – I mean about lookin' like 'im,' he said quickly, his face growing more flushed.

Dolly switched her attentions to the child on Rose's lap. 'I meant ter tell yer. I got somefing in me bag for you,' she said in an encouraging voice. 'Wanna 'elp me find it?'

Susan shook her head.

'Never mind, I'll see if I've still got it,' Dolly went on.

Billy and Joel moved away from the table and hovered near Dolly's chair, both looking curious as the big woman made an exaggerated search of her handbag. 'There we are,' she said triumphantly, pulling out three bars of white chocolate. 'One fer you, an' you, an' one fer little Susan.'

The boys thanked Dolly but Susan took the bar hesitantly and nestled back against Rose.

'Say fanks to Aunt Dolly,' Rose prompted her.

The child mumbled her thanks and Dolly reached out and playfully tickled her. 'I was gonna call last night but I 'ad ter make anuvver call first an' it was gettin' late before I could get away,' she said, placing her handbag down by her side. 'Still, better late than never.'

'Are yer not still livin' down Kent?' Rose said.

Dolly shook her head. 'My 'usband died last year an' I decided ter move back,' she explained. 'We 'ad a pub yer see, an' after my Bob went I 'ad ter get away. Besides, there's fings I've gotta take care of – fings I couldn't do before, but that's anuvver story. Anyway, I 'ad ter come an' see you all, 'specially after I was told yer muvver left.'

Rose had been looking closely at the big blonde woman while she was listening and she found herself feeling at ease with her. Her presence seemed to fill the room and her eyes were soft and kind. She was certainly attractive and smartly dressed, and her mouth seemed to have a humorous curl when she spoke.

'We do OK,' Rose told her. 'It took the boys an' Susan some time ter get used to it, but they're better now. Susan still gets a bit tearful, but it's only natural, I s'pose.'

'I can't understand 'ow she could go off like that,' Dolly said, shaking her head sadly.

''Ave you got children?' Rose asked, hoping to get her away from the subject.

'No, I couldn't 'ave any,' Dolly told her. 'I 'ad two miscarriages an' the doctor told me I shouldn't try anymore. I got pretty ill each time, yer see.'

Don had quietly slipped back into the scullery while they were talking and he re-emerged carrying a tray containing tea things, which he set down on the table. 'We've already 'ad our tea but I can easily get yer somefing,' Rose said, smiling at Dolly.

'No, just a cuppa, luv. I could just go a nice cup o' tea,' she replied.

Rose got up and poured the tea and was pleased to see that Don had put a plate of cream biscuits on the tray. 'Would yer like a biscuit?' she asked.

Dolly shook her head. 'No fanks, I'm tryin' not ter get too fat. I put weight on so quick.'

Rose suddenly looked vaguely embarrassed and instinctively brushed her hand down the front of her loose skirt as she passed over the tea, and Dolly's quick eye spotted the movement. 'I s'pose yer don't get much chance ter get out much, what wiv all you 'ave ter do round the 'ouse,' she remarked.

'I work at the tin factory at Dock'ead,' Rose told her as she sat down again. 'Don's doin' an apprenticeship. 'E's gonna be an electrician.'

'That's nice,' Dolly replied, glancing in the young man's direction. 'D'yer like it, Don?'

'I'm finkin' o' chuckin' it in,' he said, giving Rose a quick glance. 'It's the money, yer see. I could get much more workin' at the sawmills or in a ware'ouse.'

'Yeah, but yer gotta fink o' the future,' Rose cut in quickly. 'Besides, it was what Dad wanted for yer.'

Dolly gave Don a sympathetic smile. 'Never mind. One day yer'll earn good money. Once yer get yer trade qualification you could start up on yer own p'raps.'

Don shrugged his shoulders. He had already made his decision and had vowed that there was to be no going back, whatever Rose said.

Dolly finished her tea and reached for her handbag. 'Well, I'd better be off,' she said. 'Yer wouldn't mind if I called again soon, would yer?'

'Yer welcome any time,' Rose replied smiling. 'We'd like ter see yer, wouldn't we, Don.'

Don nodded. 'It'd be nice fer Rose too,' he said. 'I can get out now an' then but she don't get no break.'

'Do yer use the pubs round 'ere?' Dolly asked as she stood up.

'Yeah, I meet me mates there,' Don told her.

'D'yer know the Morgan family who live in Basin Street?' she asked.

'Yeah, Albert Morgan's a mate o' mine.'

'My 'usband Bob was Frankie Morgan's bruvver,' Dolly informed him. 'Mind yer, Bob was the odd one out in that family, an' I 'ave ter tell yer that I'm not their favourite in-law.'

'I keep on at Don ter stay away from the Morgans,' Rose

said pointedly. 'They're a bad lot. I don't want Don gettin' inter trouble.'

'I couldn't agree more,' Dolly rejoined. 'Take notice of what yer sister ses, Don. They are trouble. They've caused me enough.'

Rose followed Dolly to the door, and as she stepped out on to the landing the big woman turned to face her. 'I'm in rooms at the moment, but I'm lookin' fer a flat round 'ere, so I 'ope we'll see a lot of each ovver in the future, Rose,' she said.

'Yeah, me too,' the young woman replied.

Dolly started off down the stairs. 'Take it easy, luv,' she said with emphasis, her gaze dropping momentarily to Rose's stomach.

Don was clearing away the teacups when Rose walked back into the room. 'That was a turn-up fer the books,' he said lightly.

Rose followed her brother out into the scullery looking thoughtful. 'She knows. I could tell,' she said.

'Knows yer carryin'?' Don queried. ''Ow could she? You 'ardly show, 'specially wiv that skirt on.'

'Women can tell,' Rose told him. 'Dolly knows, I'm positive.'

'Well, it won't be a secret fer much longer, that's fer sure,' Don said, leaning against the draining board, 'an' that's why I'm gonna tell yer what I intend ter do.'

'Don't start again about packin' yer job in,' Rose said sharply. 'We've bin over this time an' time again.'

Don took a deep breath. 'Now look,' he began in a deliberate tone. 'I know yer only want the best fer me, fer all of us come ter that, but yer not a magician. Yer can't magic money out of a top 'at. So I want yer ter listen wivout jumpin' down me froat. All right?'

Rose remained silent and he went on. 'I've decided ter go in on Monday an' put me notice in. There's vacancies at the sawmills in Dock'ead an' there's plenty o' jobs goin' in the ware'ouses in Tooley Street. I can earn more money than you're gettin' at the tin bashers. That way we'll be OK when you 'ave ter pack up workin'. It's no good you tryin' ter talk me out of it by goin' on about what Dad wanted. Our dad wouldn't expect me ter carry on only earnin' a bloody pittance while you slog away till the last minute. Besides I'm finkin' about the kids. We gotta stay tergevver, an' 'ow we gonna do that wiv no money comin' in? No, Rose. Me mind's made up, so let's leave it at that.'

The young woman folded her arms and stared down at her feet for a few moments. It was all starting to fall to pieces, she thought sadly. Don was going to give up his chance to learn a trade, and even if he managed to provide the money to keep the home going the welfare would most probably argue that the flat was overcrowded and put the kids into foster homes when the baby arrived. Perhaps she should do something about getting rid of the baby. It was a new life growing inside her, true, but there were three other lives to consider, apart from Don. Why had she been so stupid? Why hadn't she thought of the consequences before allowing herself to get pregnant?

'You all right? I thought yer was gonna give me an ear'ole-bashin',' Don said smiling.

'I dunno, Don, where's it all gonna end?' she asked, looking into her brother's troubled eyes.

'It was Christmas day in the work'ouse an' the snow . . .'

'Don't joke about it, Don, it's not funny,' Rose cut in sharply.

The young man raised his hands in front of him. 'Sorry, I was only tryin' ter raise a smile,' he said quietly. 'By the way, when yer gonna go an' see the doctor? Yer can't put it off much longer, yer know.'

'I'm gonna take Monday mornin' off an' go up the school ter see about Billy, then I'll call in the doctor's,' Rose told him.

'Want me ter come wiv yer?' Don offered. 'I can go lookin' fer a job straight after,'

'No, I don't want yer to 'old me 'and,' Rose said, smiling wryly at him. 'I've only gotta get a letter fer the antenatal clinic in Grange Road.'

Susan walked into the scullery carrying her tattered doll. 'I'm tired, Rose,' she said.

Rose picked the child up and cuddled her. 'All right, darlin', we'll get yer washed an' then I'll read yer a story.'

'I want Don ter read me a story,' Susan said.

'Yeah, course I will,' Don told her, reaching out and taking the child from Rose as he noticed his sister wince suddenly. 'C'mon, I'll tell yer a story right now. Once upon a time . . .'

Rose leaned against the cupboard and bit on her bottom lip as Don walked into the living room with Susan snuggled up in his arms. The painful twinges had been coming and going all day but they felt stronger. She would have to tell the doctor about it when she saw him on Monday. Perhaps it was a normal occurrence, she thought, taking a deep breath as the pain left her. Anyway this was not the time to ponder. There were the children to see to, and the ironing was beginning to pile up . . .

Jimmy Rideout stood up and pulled a face as he hobbled over to the fire. There were still some pieces of coal left in the bag and he worked out that it would last him over the weekend if he went sparingly. His thigh felt stiff but the headache had left him, and he hummed to himself as he carefully banked up the fire. Dolly coming back into the area was like a sign from heaven, he felt sure. Things were going to be different now, he vowed. No more boozing. Well, no more drunken antics at least. No more slouching around living like a slob either. He couldn't have Dolly calling on him any more and finding the place like this. 'It's like a bloody pigsty,' he said aloud.

Jimmy straightened himself up and stood there thinking. If things were to work out the way he planned, then drastic changes would have to be made. From now on there was to be no shaving in the egg water, no sitting around with his overcoat over his long johns, and no letting the heaps of dirty clothes pile up. Muriel next door would do the washing and ironing if he paid her a few bob, and maybe that lazy husband of hers would give him a hand to spruce the place up a bit. It wouldn't take much. Just a few rolls of wallpaper, and a large tin of whitewash for the ceiling. The doors and skirting boards would need a coat of paint though. Maybe a nice purple brown. There wasn't much that could be done about the furniture. The stuffing was coming out of the armchairs and one of the table legs was loose. Perhaps he should have a word with the Salvation Army lady who was always calling into the Anchor to sell the *War Cry*. Sometimes they had furniture and bits and pieces for deserving cases. Would she consider him to be a deserving case though, Jimmy wondered. Perhaps not, considering the last turnout at the pub when he put his arms round the huge woman and tried to steal a kiss. Anyway, there were a lot of things he could do to tidy up the flat, and himself, and it would be a start.

Jimmy sat down again, suddenly feeling tired with all the planning. Must get a decent suit, and a couple of white shirts, he told himself. Could do with another pair of shoes for Sundays too, and a tie. His overcoat had seen better days but he would have to make do for the time being. It would look more present-able, however, if he sewed a couple of buttons on it instead of holding it together with that dog lead. One thing was for sure. Dolly walked out of his life once and he was not going to let it happen again. As soon as he straightened himself out he would ask Dolly to step out with him.

The fire burned bright and the room felt cosy, and for the first time in a long while Jimmy Rideout felt good inside.

Chapter Sixteen

Ivy Campbell and her next-door neighbour Rene Stratton walked back from the market together, both carrying shopping bags. They were old friends and both worked as office cleaners in the Strand. Rene's husband Ken was a gas fitter and they had two sons who had served in the army during the latter part of the war. Both the boys had married and Rene now had time on her hands during the day. She was a slim, sharp-featured woman in her fifties and she constantly wore a worried frown.

Ivy Campbell was the opposite. She was short, fat and jovial, her hair seemingly never out of curlers and always covered with a cotton headscarf. Ivy's husband Bill worked for the Borough Council as a ganger who looked after a team of road-sweepers. Like their next-door neighbours', the Campbell's children, two daughters and one son, had all married.

When they reached the grimy-looking buildings in Fellmonger Street the two friends put down their shopping bags for their usual few words outside the block, even though they had chatted all the way to the market and back. They were constantly popping into each other's flats for cups of tea and chats during the day too, but both women felt that to go straight in without a few words would seem a bit abrupt, not to say rude.

'I wonder 'ow ole Jimmy Rideout is,' Ivy said, stretching backwards and massaging the side of her back.

'Gawd knows,' Rene replied, rubbing her numb fingers. 'That was a nasty fall apparently. Muriel said that cut should 'ave bin stitched but the silly sod wouldn't go anywhere.'

'Tough as ole boots, 'e is,' Ivy remarked. 'Bloody shame 'ow 'e's let 'imself go. 'E was a very smart man once upon a time. Looked a treat in 'is uniform. Bit of a lad wiv the gels too.'

'The war done it fer 'im,' Rene replied. ''E was badly wounded. My Ken told me it was shrapnel in 'is back. Lucky ter be alive, Ken reckons.'

'Seen anyfing o' Mrs Price lately?' Ivy asked.

'She's bin laid up wiv 'er back,' Rene told her. 'I bumped inter George Price yesterday mornin' down the stairs ter get the papers. 'E was tellin' me their eldest boy's gettin' demobbed soon.'

'Who, Bert?'

'Nah, Joe. Bert's the youngest. Bert's not bin in long.'

'I always get them two mixed up. Nice boys they are.'

'Yeah. They're a nice family. Very sociable.'

'I ain't seen much of 'er at number five.'

'Who, Sadie Jones?'

'Yeah, Sadie.'

'She's up an' down. Bloody 'andful she's got wiv those gels of 'ers,' Rene went on. ''Er eldest daughter Joan's gettin' married next month an' Jennie an' Josie are courtin' strong. It'll cost 'er a packet, what wiv three weddin's in the family.'

'Mind yer, Sadie works full time an' she gets a pension from the Fire Service,' Ivy remarked.

'It's a wonder she ain't married again,' Rene said. 'Tom's bin dead nearly ten years now.'

'It'll be ten years this October. 'E was a lovely feller,' Ivy said, shaking her head sadly.

The grey morning and the dampness in the air did not seem to deter the two old friends and they were still talking together when they spotted Rose coming towards them.

''Ello, luv. Not at work then?' Ivy said smiling.

'No, I 'ad ter go up Billy's school,' Rose told her.

'Not in trouble is 'e?'

'Sort of. 'E was caught smokin'. Well 'e wasn't really, but the ovver boys 'e was wiv were, so our Billy got roped in,' Rose explained with a grin.

'Back ter work this afternoon then?' Rene asked.

'No, I'll go in termorrer. It'll give me a chance ter straighten up a bit,' Rose replied.

Ivy picked up her shopping bag. 'Well, this won't get me work done,' she said smiling.

Rose excused herself and climbed the stairs to the flat. Don was sitting in the living room reading the morning paper and when she walked in he gave her a big smile. 'I start next Monday at Gilbey's in Dock'ead,' he announced.

'Is that the sawmills?' she asked him.

'Yeah. I'm on four quid a week an' there's some overtime now an' then. Better than that pittance I've bin gettin',' he replied.

Rose sat down in the armchair, still in her coat, and stretched out her hands to the fire. Don got up and went into the scullery and he was soon back with a cup of tea. 'I've only just made it,' he said, passing it over. ''Ow did fings go?'

'Well, the teacher was very nice,' Rose replied. 'She said she didn't fink Billy was actually smokin', but anyway she gave me a nice report. She said Billy's very good at 'is work an' 'e's well be'aved.'

'What about the doctor?' Don asked. 'Did yer go?'

'Yeah, 'e gave me a letter fer the clinic. I gotta go there this Thursday evenin' at seven,' Rose told him.

'I bin waitin' fer yer ter get back. I'm goin' in ter work this afternoon an' puttin' me notice in,' Don said, looking pleased with himself.

'I'm gonna 'ave a tidy-up, then I fink I'll make us a nice stew fer tea,' Rose said, sipping her tea gratefully.

True to his word, Jimmy Rideout had spent the whole of Monday tidying up his flat. Old papers had been bundled up and he had managed to get his dirty washing sorted out ready for Muriel Albury. The curtains had been opened and the fire cleared of ashes and laid ready to be lit. All the used crockery that had accumulated in the scullery was now washed and stowed away in the cupboard, and Jimmy felt exhausted. He had changed the bed and swept the flat through too, as well as shaking the mats outside the block, to the disgust of one of his neighbours who had been passing at the time.

Jimmy looked at the clock on the mantelshelf and it showed ten minutes past seven. He had wound the clock up that morning for the first time in months and had set the correct time from the wireless. Progress had been made and all the hard work called for some reward, he felt, bearing in mind however that whenever he went out for a livener it turned into two or more, usually more, and all his good intentions and promises went out the window. This time he would smarten himself up with a wash and shave and put on his new shoes. There was time too for a repair job with a needle and cotton. The slit in the arm of his overcoat had spread and he had to find some buttons.

At eight thirty that evening a very uncharacteristically tidy Jimmy Rideout stepped from his flat and pulled up the collar of his renovated overcoat as he made his way to the Anchor. He was clean-shaven and he had replaced the bandage for a large plaster which fully covered the nasty gash on the left-hand side of his forehead. His new shoes squeaked as he walked and he felt constricted by the buttoned-up overcoat, but he was satisfied with his appearance.

As he stepped into the public bar Jimmy noticed that it was unusually busy. There were some strange faces and it seemed very noisy. He reached the counter and caught Beryl's eye. 'Give us a pint o' bitter, darlin',' he said cheerfully.

It was some time before the landlady got round to serving him and when she finally placed his drink in front of him she pulled a face. 'The ovver mob's in the saloon,' she said out of the corner of her mouth.

'Who's that then?' Jimmy asked.

'The Morgans,' she hissed. 'They're all celebratin'. I didn't know they 'ad that many friends.'

'Never mind, it's good fer business,' Jimmy told her.

'I can do wivout their patronage, fank you very much,' Beryl said sharply. 'It's a bloody menagerie in 'ere ternight. The saloon bar's packed out an' some o' Frankie's cronies 'ave come round this side ter get served.'

Jimmy noticed that Beryl had two young women helping her behind the counter and guessed that Sammy was looking after the saloon along with his usual barman. The reforming drunk picked up his pint and took a long swig. If he was to keep to his promise then this pint would have to last him for a while. There could be no whisky for him either, he vowed.

A group of young men standing in a corner were laughing loudly while others pushed their way to the counter impatiently shouting their orders, and Jimmy moved along the bar to the far wall where he could rest his arm on the counter and survey the scene in comparative comfort. After a while he noticed John and Ernie Morgan come into the bar and push their way to the counter. Both men looked drunk and they acknowledged greetings from various people with raised hands and nods.

Jimmy watched the revelry for some time, occasionally

sipping his drink, and then suddenly he caught sight of both the Morgan boys who seemed to be leering at him. He turned and rested his other arm on the counter, feeling strangely uncomfortable as he watched Beryl and her helpers pulling pints and filling glasses of spirit from the optics. They appeared to be working flat out and Beryl looked decidedly irritable and stressed.

'Well, well. What we got 'ere? If it ain't Jimmy the piss artist.'

Jimmy looked round and saw John Morgan leaning on the counter next to him. Ernie was standing beside his brother and he wore an evil grin on his broad, swarthy face.

'We're celebratin' ternight, Jimmy boy,' John said, slurring slightly.

'Oh yeah?' Jimmy replied.

'Yeah. Our ole man got the verdict terday,' Ernie told him.

Jimmy took another sip from his glass. 'That's nice,' he said.

'It's more than nice, it's bloody marvellous,' Ernie replied.

'Don't yer fink it's marvellous?' John asked, leaning towards him.

'Yeah, it's marvellous,' Jimmy replied.

'Well, yer don't sound too sure,' Ernie sneered.

'Look, I've come in 'ere fer a quiet drink,' Jimmy said, looking directly at Ernie. 'I've got a bit of an 'eadache, so if yer don't mind.'

'I didn't fink piss artists got 'eadaches,' Ernie said to his brother.

'Nah, it's that lump 'e got fallin' down the ovver day,' John told him. 'We 'eard all about that, didn't we bruv? Pissed was yer?'

Jimmy took another swig, ignoring the jibes.

'We're buyin' ternight,' John said. ''Ave one wiv us.'

Jimmy shook his head. 'I'm takin' it easy,' he replied. 'This'll do me nice.'

'Yer nearly empty,' Ernie said. ''Ave anuvver. What about a whisky? Yer drink whisky, I know yer do, 'cos I've seen yer knockin' it back in 'ere plenty o' times.'

'I've give it up,' Jimmy said quickly.

'Nah, not ternight,' Ernie said, a hint of menace in his voice. 'Ternight we're drinkin' ter celebrate an' we expect our friends ter celebrate wiv us. Don't we, John?'

John Morgan called one of the barmaids over. 'Give our pal a double Scotch, sweetie,' he told her, 'an' me an' my bruv will 'ave a large gin an' tonic. Take one fer yerself as well.'

Jimmy stood up straight. 'Look, I told yer I'm off the spirits,' he said quietly. 'I'm pleased yer ole man got off but I don't wanna drink. Now leave us alone, fer Gawd sake.'

'Oh dear. Did you 'ear that, Ern? Our pal doesn't wanna drink wiv us,' John said, feigning surprise. 'Everyone's 'avin' a drink wiv us ternight an' that includes you, Jimmy the piss artist.'

The barmaid brought the drinks and John picked up the Scotch and set it down in front of the older man. 'Right now, let's see yer drink it. C'mon now, get it down in one gulp. It won't 'urt yer,' he sneered.

One or two of John's mates had sidled up to see the fun, and Jimmy could see that he had been well and truly set up. He racked his brains desperately trying to work out what he could do. If he drank the whisky the Morgans would give him more until he was reduced to a sorry state and then the fun would really start. Better if he fronted them now, while he was still capable of thinking straight.

'Drink it yerself,' he said sharply. 'You bought it, you drink it.'

'Oh dear. I fink our pal's got a bee in 'is bonnet,' Ernie remarked. 'If yer don't drink it we'll fink it's a downright bloody insult, an' not only to us but to our ole man. 'E wants everyone to 'ave a drink on 'im.'

Jimmy ignored him and turned to lean on the counter, only to be spun round by the lapels of his coat. 'Drink it,' John ordered.

Ted Baxter the ex-docker had been watching events and he pushed his way through the onlookers to face the Morgan brothers. 'Why don't yer leave 'im alone,' he growled. ''E ain't 'urtin' you.'

Ernie pushed him aside and glared at Jimmy. 'You 'eard me bruvver. Drink it,' he snarled.

Ted Baxter was trying to push his way forward again but was forcibly restrained by two heavily built young men. Beryl had seen the confrontation getting very dangerous and she hurried into the saloon bar to fetch Sammy.

Jimmy looked down at the glass of whisky and very slowly he reached out his hand and picked it up. For a few moments he stared at the drink, then slowly and deliberately he tipped the glass up, spilling the spirit over the polished counter. 'Now piss off,' he said quietly.

John Morgan's face turned purple and veins bulged in his forehead. Jimmy got ready for the punch but his tormentor turned to one of the young men. 'Give us yer flask,' he ordered.

'All right then, what's goin' on?' Sammy called out from behind the counter.

'Just a bit o' fun, no one's gettin' 'urt,' Ernie replied.

'Right, grab 'im!' John shouted.

Jimmy found his arms pinioned behind him and someone yanked his head back by the hair. His nose was squeezed and he had to open his mouth to breathe.

'Keep 'im still,' John yelled, moving forward with a silver whisky flask.

'Right, that's enough,' Sammy shouted.

'Go round an' stop it, yer big slob,' Beryl told him angrily.

Sammy leapt over the counter just as the Morgan boy tipped

the flask up to Jimmy's open mouth. Suddenly the young man standing next to John was bundled out of the way and John himself was knocked sideways by a backhander in the face. Jimmy struggled to free himself, managing to spit out the whisky that had been poured into his mouth, and when he looked up he saw Dolly standing with her feet apart, eyes blazing. The young men had moved away from her and John Morgan was left leaning on the counter blinking to clear his vision. Ernie tried to remonstrate with the irate woman, unaware of who she was, but she pushed him away as she faced his startled brother. 'Wanna try yer 'and at makin' me drink that, son?' she sneered.

John blinked again, hardly believing his eyes. 'You!' he gasped.

'Yeah, me,' Dolly said calmly. 'You ain't changed a bit. You always was a bully, even as a kid.'

'Who is she?' Ernie hissed.

'That's our Aunt Dolly, would yer believe,' John replied as he stroked his sore face, his eyes fixed on the big blonde woman. 'Yer remember the ole man tellin' us about 'er? 'E was right ter call 'er an interferin' bitch. It seems she ain't changed much eivver. What business is it of 'ers.'

'I'm makin' it my business,' she growled.

Sammy had been as shocked as the rest of the customers and he stood waiting for the next move, only to be prodded sharply in the ribs by Beryl. 'I want the lot of 'em out now!' she screamed at him.

'Right, the fun's over,' Sammy said loudly, quickly reasserting himself as he faced the Morgans and their friends. 'I mean all of yer. If yer not out in two minutes I'm phonin' the police.'

Slowly the young men dispersed. John and Ernie Morgan stood back, their hostile eyes fixed on Dolly as she took a shaken Jimmy by the arm.

'Don't fink yer gonna get away wiv this,' John snarled at her.

Sammy turned to front the brothers. 'C'mon, you as well. Out!' he shouted.

Dolly walked to the door, still holding on to Jimmy's arm. 'I called round ter see yer an' Muriel next door said I'd just missed yer. I knew where ter find yer but I didn't expect yer ter be playin' games,' she said, smiling wickedly.

Jimmy gave her a sheepish grin. 'I wasn't gonna drink wiv 'em, if they clobbered me,' he said firmly. 'Mind yer, luv, I could do wiv a stiff whisky right now. I'm all of a tremble.'

Dolly laughed as she propelled Jimmy out of the pub.

'Where we goin'?' he asked confusedly.

'I gotta call in the saloon first,' Dolly told him calmly.

Jimmy looked horrified. 'No. Not after what's just 'appened, surely,' he said incredulously.

'C'mon, it won't take five minutes,' she told him, gripping his arm tightly.

The news of the fracas in the public bar had been relayed swiftly to the saloon and when Dolly walked in with Jimmy the customers all stared in silence.

Sammy had resumed his place behind the counter and he was visibly put out at seeing the big blonde back in the pub. 'I'd prefer it if yer took 'im 'ome,' he said to her.

'I fink the man's entitled ter one drink on the 'ouse after what 'e's bin frew,' she replied trenchantly. 'Give 'im a Scotch, will yer.'

The revellers filling the saloon bar stood watching curiously but Frankie Morgan's face went white as he recognised his dead brother's wife. Dolly had marked him and she waited until the disconcerted landlord had passed over the Scotch before she turned towards him.

'I 'ope yer got the message, Frankie,' she said, her eyes narrowing as she stared at him.

'I got it,' he replied curtly.

'I'll tell yer somefing else too,' she growled. 'Yer wanna keep those mongrels o' yours in order before somebody sorts 'em out good an' proper. C'mon, Jimmy, let's get out o' this place. I don't like the smell.'

Jimmy swallowed his drink and followed Dolly out into the cold night air. 'D'yer know somefing. You're a bloody maniac,' he said, shaking his head in disbelief.

'It's a good job I come round tonight,' Dolly muttered, a satisfied look on her face.

'What did yer come round for?' Jimmy asked her curiously.

'Ter pick up yer dirty washin', yer scruffy git,' she said, hiding a smile. 'Muriel ain't too pleased about you givin' it to 'er.'

'She could 'ave said,' Jimmy replied humbly.

The two turned into Fellmonger Street and Dolly sighed. 'The woman feels sorry for yer,' she told him. 'I can't fink why.'

Chapter Seventeen

The din of machinery was suddenly muted as Bernard Collis closed his office door and took his seat. He ignored the anxious-looking young woman who had followed him into his den, leaving her standing waiting while he fiddled with some papers and made a meal of straightening his desk. When he finally decided that he had finished he looked up over his glasses and grunted irritably. 'You were absent yesterday,' he said. 'Sickness, was it?'

'Yes,' Rose replied.

The manager studied the pencil that he was rolling between his fingers for a few moments then he looked up again. 'I've noticed that you an' Alice Copeland are very chummy,' he said.

'I know 'er,' Rose replied, looking puzzled.

'Well, as it 'appens she was absent yesterday as well,' Collis said, his eyes narrowing.

'What's that got ter do wiv me?' Rose asked him.

'Alice Copeland's bin spreadin' that union filth around,' he replied sharply. 'It's got back ter me that she's bin stirrin' the gels up, tryin' ter get 'em interested in the union. What's more, I was called upstairs yesterday afternoon ter be told by Mr Penrose that 'e'd received a phone call from the Transport an'

172

General Worker's Union. They wanna open talks wiv our company about union recognition.'

'I still don't see what that's got ter do wiv me,' Rose said quickly.

'Oh, you don't. Well I 'appen ter know that Alice Copeland took yesterday off ter meet with the union,' Collis said sardonically. 'It seems more than a coincidence that you just 'appened ter take the day off as well. Did you go wiv 'er ter meet those Bolshie troublemakers?'

'I don't see as it's any of your business,' Rose answered with a brave show of defiance, 'but the reason I didn't come in yesterday was 'cos I was feelin' ill.'

The manager pushed his glasses up on to the bridge of his nose with a podgy forefinger and looked down at his desk. 'Well. I've got ter see Copeland this mornin', an' in the meantime I want you ter take 'er place on the rollers,' he informed her with a sneering look on his fat face. 'I'll 'ave anuvver job sorted out fer Copeland. You can go now. Take 'er place an' tell 'er ter come an' see me straight away.'

Rose left the manager's office feeling very angry and frustrated, and as she walked along the gangway to the end of the factory she saw Alice arguing with the two young loaders.

'I don't care what yer fink. This job should be done by men, not us women,' she was saying.

'Alice. I've gotta take over yer job,' Rose cut in. 'Shit-face wants yer in 'is office right away.'

The agitated Alice smiled briefly at seeing her friend and then turned back to the flushed young man. ''Ave you got any idea what this job could do to a woman?' she growled. 'We ain't made the same as you.'

'I could 'ave told yer that,' the other young man said, smirking.

'I ain't talkin' ter you, Spiv,' Alice said quickly. 'I'm talkin' to 'im.' Then, rounding on the more timid of the two, she said, 'Listen ter me, Dennis. This firm's gonna get union recognition very shortly, an' when it does this job is out, as far as us women are concerned.'

'All I was sayin' is, Big Mary's bin doin' this job fer ages wivout any trouble,' the young man explained. 'I agree it shouldn't be done by women but I don't make the rules, I only take orders like everybody else 'ere.'

Alice looked a little less angry, knowing that the young man was right. 'Anyway, when the union do come in make sure you an' Spiv join,' she told him. 'We want 'undred per cent support, or we'll get picked off.'

'Suits me,' Dennis replied. 'My ole man works in the docks an' 'e reckons the union does a lot o' good.'

'I dunno if I'll join,' Spiv Richards said, winking at his friend. 'I fink they're more trouble than they're werf.'

'Listen, stupid,' Alice growled. 'This stinkin' firm pays a few bob over the odds ter keep us 'ere. Ovver firms round 'ere look after their workers much better. We're treated more like animals in this poxy place. Still, I s'pose you're too dopey ter see it. Bromilow's loves the likes o' you.'

Spiv shrugged his shoulders and tried to hide his grin. 'I might join, I'll 'ave ter fink about it first,' he said, walking away.

Bernard Collis had become impatient and he suddenly appeared in the gangway. 'Copeland! Get in my office!' he exclaimed loudly.

Alice gave Rose a lopsided grin as she walked away from the rollers, and when she stepped into the manager's office she faced a tirade.

'Copeland. Yer've got about the worst record 'ere fer time lost. What was it this time, anuvver 'eadache?' he ranted. 'There's barely a single week goes by wivout you bein' absent

174

one day at least. I can't run the business like this. I've gotta keep switchin' the gels about ter cover fer you an' it causes friction. What's more, I've bin told that you're tryin' ter get the gels ter join the union. Well, you just listen ter me. We don't want no union in this firm, comin' in tellin' us 'ow ter run the factory. So in future, will yer get on wiv yer job an' stop pesterin' the rest o' the workforce or I'll be forced ter sack yer on the spot. Is that clearly understood?'

Alice took a deep breath and glared at the red-faced manager. She had been waiting for this moment to speak her mind and after the meeting she had had the previous day with union officials she felt confident. 'No, it's not,' she began. 'First yer tell me that I got the worst record 'ere fer sickness, which ain't true, an' you know it. Then yer tell me yer gonna sack me on the spot fer incitin' the gels ter join the union. Well, let me tell you that I did take the day off ter go an' see the union an' I'm quite prepared ter be docked a day's pay. But if you wanna sack me fer goin' ter the union then I'm refusin' the sack until I get it from Mr Penrose.'

Bernard Collis was unused to his workforce answering him back and his face clouded. He opened his mouth to speak but Alice carried on talking in a loud voice. 'The top union official at Tooley Street told me that they'd bin tryin' fer some time ter get the firm ter recognise the union an' they were makin' progress. This bloke told me point blank that if you sacked me fer goin' ter see 'im then they'd mark your card. Those were 'is exact words. Who knows, yer might even find yerself out of a job, when it all comes out.'

'When what comes out?' Collis spluttered, hardly believing his own ears.

'You know,' Alice said coldly.

Collis slumped down in his chair and glared at the young woman for a few seconds, trying desperately to compose himself. 'Maybe I exaggerated a bit about yer work record, Copeland,' he began, 'but it leaves a lot ter be desired. As fer the ovver fing, I'm perfectly entitled ter sack you on the spot fer leavin' yer place o' work an' incitin' the workforce ter walk out on strike.'

'I've not bin leavin' my machine, nor askin' the gels ter strike,' Alice said sharply.

'Well, I've bin under a misappre'ension then,' Collis replied, fidgeting uncomfortably in his seat. ''An' I've always treated you gels fair an' square. I've no worry on that score. The union don't frighten me.'

'So I can go back ter work then?' Alice said.

'I'm keepin' Farran on the rollers fer the rest o' the week. You can go on the baler until furvver notice,' Collis told her. 'That'll be all, Copeland.'

Alice left the office feeling gratified at having faced the manager down. Next week the union talks would begin and at least she would be around to see the outcome, as long as she stayed clear of any more trouble. Working on the baler would ensure that. From his office window Collis could see clearly the bench where the cartons of tin cans were wired ready for dispatch. She would have no chance to leave her position and Collis knew it.

Albert Morgan leaned his extension ladder against the office wall and squeezed out his sopping leather over the bucket. Tooley Street was a hive of industry on that damp and dreary Tuesday morning, and as he climbed to the first floor and set about removing the grime and grit from the large window Albert was worried. Inside he could see the clerks and typists sitting at their desks and he wished that he could find a job that kept him out of the cold and rain. It was nice in the summer being a window cleaner, though. He was finished by three o'clock at the latest, and Frank Spires didn't trouble him, as long as he completed his daily quota of work. Frank was elderly and would be retiring soon, and he had promised that Albert could buy the business from him at a reasonable price.

Albert thought over his predicament as he took the piece of cheesecloth from his back pocket and quickly polished the pane of glass. The young typist sitting near the window had given him a nice smile and it would make a pleasant break to swap a few words with her when he went into the office to clean the inside of the glass. Normally he would have been flashing his smile at her but today he had other things on his mind. His father's trial had ended in his acquittal, as expected, and now it was nearing decision time. His brothers John and Ernie were straining at the traces to get on with the robbery and their father was preparing to meet with the two men who had organised it to finalise the plan.

Albert came down the ladder and moved it to the next window, thinking about the previous evening. He had purposely distanced himself from the celebrations in the Anchor after making an early appearance, and considering what had happened he was glad that he had. The goings-on there last night had been way out of order. His brothers were always the same when they had had too much to drink. There was no cause to pick on Jimmy Rideout anyway. He was a nuisance, but he was harmless and inoffensive. Sammy had been within his rights to evict them from his pub, but to hear John and Ernie talk anyone would have thought that they were the aggrieved party. They never seemed to listen. The Anchor was the family's local and it wasn't the place to start trouble. The old man had been strangely quiet after Aunt Dolly confronted them all, according to Ernie, and that too worried Albert. What did it all mean?

All through the early afternoon the young man worked doggedly to complete his quota, but it was nearly four o'clock by the time he finally finished for the day. He had not been able to keep his mind on the job, and as he strapped his ladders into the side cart and pedalled his bicycle towards the store in Bermondsey Street Albert's fears grew stronger. John and Ernie had come to suspect that he was unhappy about the impending raid and they had started to make snide remarks. It was supposedly in fun but the innuendo was there, and before long he would have to make a decision.

Dolly Morgan stood looking out on the busy scene below her. The evening traffic was heavy and the buses and trams crawled along full of homeward-bound workers. Things had certainly been hectic since her return, and it was not going to change much until her main business was settled. Frankie Morgan had been shocked to see her and his bullying sons had felt her anger, at least one of them had. Her future dealings with the Morgans, and with Frankie in particular, would have to be very carefully planned. He was a dangerous man, vicious, and without compunction or sense of fair play when it came to meting out his own brand of justice.

Dolly crossed the room and sat down in the comfortable armchair, idly flipping through the leather-bound photograph album which she had brought back with her when she first arrived. She had finally managed to get most of her personal possessions sent on from the pub, and apart from her clothes and jewellery, the photos and a briefcase of papers which she kept at her lodgings, all the other items, including books, ornaments and a few small pieces of furniture, had been crated up and were being stored at Tommy Caulfield's transport yard for the time being. Tommy had been happy to oblige when she went back to see him and they had chatted together lightheartedly for some time, but behind the jovial facade Dolly suspected that her old friend was troubled in some way. It was just a feeling she had, nothing tangible that she could put her finger on, but the lingering suspicion stayed with her as she thumbed through the old photographs.

Rain was falling as Tommy Caulfield left his yard and made for Tower Bridge Road on his way home, his overcoat collar turned up and his trilby hat pulled down over his forehead against the weather. Tommy lived in a quiet turning off the New Kent Road, just a mile from his place of business. His house was one of a row of Victorian-built properties, spacious and comfortably furnished, but he had long cherished a dream of selling the place and buying a property down in Kent, maybe a cottage with a nice garden. He had talked it over with Doris some time ago but she was against the idea. He could understand her point of view. There were no children from their marriage and Doris would be on her own all day. Her condition meant that she could not get out much and would not be able to do much in the garden, while in London she was close to her old friends, who often called on her during the day.

As a rule Tommy would walk home, but tonight the rain was becoming heavy and he intended to catch a tram. His mind was full of troubled thoughts and before he realised it he had reached the Bricklayer's Arms. He crossed the busy main thoroughfare into New Kent Road and decided to go into the King's Arms public house to shelter from the sheeting downpour. The pub was quiet at that time of the evening and he ordered a pint of ale.

It had been a big relief to hear that Frankie Morgan had been acquitted of the assault charge, but now there was much more to worry about. When Sammy McGarry had told him about Dolly Morgan it felt as though he had been hit with a bolt of lightning, and when Dolly called on him she had confirmed his worst fears: that she was out for revenge. He had found it difficult to act as though he was pleased to see her after all those years, for he knew that before long it was all going to come out; the buried past was going to be exhumed, and his part in it all would be laid bare.

The contractor thought about his options as he sipped his drink. He could try to persuade Dolly to let bygones be bygones, using the excuse that she was putting herself in jeopardy by tangling with Frankie Morgan, but he dismissed the thought instantly. Dolly was not that easily frightened, and Sammy's account of her stepping in when Jimmy Rideout was being tormented bore testimony to that. The publican had told him all about it only that morning when he had gone into the Anchor for his usual lunchtime drink. Maybe he should accept the offer from Brandon's to buy him out. It was a good one but he would have to persuade Doris to agree first. She might well, if he told her everything. The problem was, his wife was a born worrier, and for that reason he had made sure that she knew nothing of what went on all those years ago. To tell her now would be cruel, and could prove disastrous.

What other course of action was there, Tommy asked himself anxiously. He could do nothing and bluff it out, hoping that Dolly would not make enough progress to uncover properly what really happened that August of '38. That was assuming that she did not get her hands on any evidence to speak of, but it seemed unlikely that she would have come back to seek revenge without at least having a good start on Morgan.

The rain was beginning to ease and as Tommy Caulfield drained his glass he knew that the only other solution was for Frankie Morgan to be got rid of, and the thought of it made him shudder.

Chapter Eighteen

All through the week it rained on and off and the dreary weather seemed to take effect on the Bromilow workforce. Big Mary had a confrontation with one of the girls in the canteen on Wednesday and the girl left in tears. Bernard Collis seemed more grumpy and nasty than ever, and even the effervescent Alice Copeland was looking decidedly miserable when she sat down with Rose Farran on Friday lunchtime.

'I can't understand it,' she said despondently. 'The union bloke told me that 'e was definitely gonna make contact wiv the firm this week an' 'e'd make a point of seein' me before 'e left. The bloke said I'd make a good shop steward an' 'e was gonna talk ter me about it.'

'P'raps 'e's comin' terday,' Rose suggested.

'Yeah, or maybe 'e saw Collis an' that slimy git told 'im I was off sick or somefing. I wouldn't put it past 'im,' Alice growled.

The two friends finished their sandwiches and Alice took out her knitting. Rose smiled as she watched Alice struggle to unravel the strands of wool and then begin picking up the stitches. The young woman handled the steel knitting needles expertly and Rose sat intrigued at the quick clicking sound and the way Alice draped the thin white strand of wool round her crooked forefinger and fed it into the needles. She had never managed to master the skill herself, and after watching for a few minutes she leaned back in her chair and folded her arms. 'Who taught yer ter knit?' she asked.

'My mum,' Alice told her. 'My muvver was a good knitter once. She don't do much now though. Can't you knit?'

Rose shook her head. 'I tried a few times but I never seemed ter get the knack,' she replied.

Alice put the needles down to search in her carrier bag for another ball of wool. ''Ere, I gotta tell yer, Rose,' she said with an eager grin; 'One o' the gels saw me knittin' an' she asked me who it was for. I told 'er it was fer me. Course then she give me an ole-fashioned look an' I said it's all right I ain't in the pudden club just yet, but I'm livin' in 'ope!'

'They'll all be watchin' you closely now,' Rose laughed.

'Well, that'll keep 'em away from noticin' you,' Alice replied with a large wink.

'I don't show yet, do I?' Rose asked anxiously.

'Nah, yer still look like a deal-board,' Alice grinned. 'I fink I'll start comin' ter work wiv a cushion tucked down me dress, that'll give 'em somefing ter talk about, 'specially now they've noticed I'm knittin'.'

The factory whistle sounded and the women hurried out of the canteen. Rose was feeling tired and the lower part of her back ached as she set to work again. The young loaders had left a fresh batch of sheet tin beside the rollers and one bundle had been placed up on the stand. Rose pulled it towards her and grunted as she slipped it into position ready for the machine. She snipped the steel bands and pushed it sideways towards the mouth of the cutter, only to see that one of the bands had snagged the rollers and was being drawn along under the weighty pile of tin sheets. She stooped and put the heel of her hand under the corner of the bundle, and as she pulled on the band with her other hand she pushed up hard. Suddenly she felt a sharp, severe pain in the bottom of her stomach, and as the band jerked free she staggered back, doubling in agony, and lost her footing. She felt herself falling backwards and there was an explosion in her head.

Spiv Richards came running as he saw Rose lying stretched out on the factory floor, closely followed by his friend Dennis, and as the two young men knelt down to help her she groaned and moved her head to one side.

'She must 'ave fainted,' Spiv said. 'We better sit 'er up.'

'Look, there's blood! She's cut the back of 'er 'ead open,' Dennis said, looking horrified. 'We better leave 'er. I'll stay 'ere, Spiv, an' you run an' get Collis.'

Don Farren walked home through the rain whistling happily. He had said goodbye to his workmates at the electrical contractors and was looking forward to earning some decent money at last. As he hurried up the stairs Ivy Campbell came out of her flat and watched him. The poor lad was in for a shock, she thought as she went back inside and closed her front door.

Don let himself in and immediately saw a strange young woman comforting a tearful Susan, who was cuddling her tattered doll. Billy and Joey stood nearby looking very worried. 'What's 'appened? Where's Rose?' he asked quickly.

'I'm afraid she's 'ad a bit of an accident at work,' Alice replied as she got up from the chair. 'It's not serious, but they've decided ter keep 'er in 'ospital fer the night, just as a precaution. She fell an' cut 'er 'ead, yer see.'

'What 'ospital's she in?' Don asked her, his face ashen.

'St Olave's,' Alice told him. 'I said I'd come round ter tell yer. Me an' Rose are good mates, yer see.'

'Are you Alice?' Don asked.

'Yeah. The woman on the ground floor told me which flat yer lived in, an' she said you'd be in soon,' Alice replied. 'Billy let me in. I 'ope yer don't mind.'

'Course not,' he told her. 'I'm grateful.'

'Would any o' the neighbours look after the children while you go ter the 'ospital?' Alice asked.

'Yeah, I'll go an' see Freda. She's good as gold,' Don said. 'I won't be a minute.'

He was back within seconds. 'C'mon, kids, Freda's gonna give yer some tea. I won't be very long. Now be'ave yerselves, d'you 'ear?'

The boys nodded and Susan wiped a tear away as they were shepherded across the landing and Don turned to Alice. 'Fanks fer lookin' after 'em,' he said quickly.

'Would yer mind if I came wiv yer ter the 'ospital?' Alice asked.

'Course not,' he replied.

The two hurried from the flat and walked through the rain to the end of Abbey Street just as a tram lumbered round the bend. Don took Alice by the arm as they ran across the road to the tram stop and when they were safely seated he turned to her and said, 'Did yer see what 'appened?'

Alice shook her head. 'Rose was on a really 'eavy job an' I fink she must 'ave blacked out, accordin' ter the young lads who found 'er lyin' on the floor,' she explained. 'She caught 'er 'ead on the leg of a machine. I asked the ambulance man if it was a bad cut an' 'e said it wasn't serious. Our stupid manager was gonna send the police round ter tell yer but I volunteered ter come instead.'

Don looked at Alice closely. Rose had told him quite a lot about her and how she had stood up to the manager on her behalf. 'Rose said you an' 'er were good friends,' he told her. 'I understand yer got a right evil git of a manager.'

'Evil's right,' Alice said. ''Is name's Collis, Bernard Collis, an' no one can stand 'im. Rose should never 'ave bin put on that job, it's not a job fer women. I've 'ad a spell on it as well. Collis puts all the gels on it 'e don't like.'

''E sounds a right bastard,' Don muttered. 'What did you two do ter get in 'is bad books?'

'Well, between you an' me, I fink 'e 'ad designs on your Rose, but she let 'im see 'e was wastin' 'is time,' Alice told him. 'As fer me, I've bin tryin' ter get the gels ter join the union an' 'e found out.'

'Rose did mention somefing about the union,' Don replied.

The tram rattled along Jamaica Road towards the Rotherhithe Tunnel and Alice took the opportunity of studying the young man. Rose had told her that her brother was nice-looking but inclined to be a bit short-tempered, and as she furtively glanced at him Alice was impressed. His thick dark hair was slightly wavy and his small ears sat close to his head. He had large brown eyes, and his square chin was attractively masculine.

''Ave yer got a gelfriend?' she asked suddenly, giving him a casual smile.

He laughed briefly and Alice saw his even white teeth. 'Nah, not a regular gelfriend,' he told her. 'I bin doin' an apprentice-ship, yer see, an' the money don't go ter takin' gels out. I just about manage a couple o' pints a week an' that's about it.'

'You go in pubs?' Alice queried.

'Yeah, well, the publicans don't seem ter worry. I s'pose they fink I'm over eighteen,' Don said, looking through the window to see if they had reached the tunnel.

''Ow old are you exactly?' Alice asked, becoming curious.

'I'm seventeen next week,' he replied.

The tram swung round by Rotherhithe Tunnel and ground to a halt. The two young people jumped down and hurried through the old hospital gates and along a path between two flowerbeds to the main entrance. The receptionist ran her finger down the page of a large flat admissions book.

'Miss Farran is in McMillan Ward,' she smiled. 'Go to the end of the corridor and take the stairs. The ward's on the first floor.'

Rose Farran sat propped up with pillows and she looked pale and tired. Her head was swathed in bandages and she gave the two a meek smile. Don bent over the bed and kissed his sister gently on the forehead and Alice held her hand as she sat down on the chair next to the bed.

'What you bin doin' then? Don asked breezily.

'Dodgin' the column I should fink,' Alice joked. ''Ow d'yer feel, luv?'

'Well, I've got a bit of an 'eadache but the doctor said it's nuffink ter worry about,' Rose replied. 'They was more concerned about my ovver problem.' Don looked at her and glanced briefly at Alice. 'It's all right, Don, Alice knows about the baby,' she told him.

'I should fink they were concerned, what wiv the luggin' yer bin doin' all the week,' Alice said quickly.

'The doctor said 'e finks the baby'll be OK but I gotta stop in bed fer a couple o' days,' Rose told them. 'I'm worried about the kids.'

Before Don could reply Alice jumped in. 'Don't worry about a fing. Me an' yer bruv'll sort it out, won't we, Don?'

Rose looked from one to the other and smiled weakly. ''Ow are the kids? Is young Susan all right?'

'They're fine,' Don told her. 'Everyfing'll be all right. You jus' rest like the doctor said.'

Alice leaned forward and gave her workmate a bit of gossip while Don cast his eyes about the ward, feeling a little uncomfortable. Alice's anecdotes brought a few smiles to Rose's pale face, and for a while the girls sat chatting together. It was Don who made the first move to leave. 'We'd better be goin' now, Rose,' he said apologetically. 'I wanna make sure the kids don't get ter bed too late.'

As they left the hospital Don turned to Alice and gave her a smile. 'I'm really grateful fer what yer did,' he told her.

'It wasn't much,' Alice said, returning his smile. 'Like I say, your Rose is a friend o' mine. We get on well tergevver.'

Don studied his shoes for a few moments. 'Look, I'd like ter see yer again, if yer want to – I mean if yer 'aven't already got a boyfriend . . .' he faltered.

'As a matter o' fact I did 'ave a boyfriend till very recently, but it's sort of over now,' Alice replied. 'We don't really see anyfing of each over anymore.'

Don gazed at her bright eyes. 'I'm gonna be tied up wiv the kids till Rose gets on 'er feet again,' he said a little nervously, 'but I'd like – I mean ter say, it'd be nice ter take yer ter the pictures soon as I can, if yer can make it . . .'

'I'd like that,' Alice replied.

The two parted company outside the hospital gates, Don walking the few yards to the tram stop and Alice crossing the road to catch the Downtown bus. As one pulled up she turned and gave him a wave and Don waved back, suddenly feeling elated.

Following his ordeal at the hands of John and Ernie Morgan, Jimmy Rideout had decided to keep out of the Anchor, but then on reflection he thought why the bloody hell should he, he wasn't to blame for the upset. It was his local after all, and to keep out of the place would show that he was running scared. Jimmy knew his limitations and was well aware that he tended to get people's backs up, but he did not for a minute deem himself a coward. He would face the Morgans any time, and in that spirit he went into the public bar on Tuesday night and ordered his usual pint. Ted Baxter bought him a pint and Sammy gave him a pint on the house, and then Jimmy realised suddenly that his good intentions were beginning to evaporate. With a rare show of willpower he refused the next pint offered him, and walked off home feeling a little taller and much happier than he had felt for a long time.

On Wednesday evening Jimmy had two pints in the Anchor and then left for home. On Thursday evening he did the same, and as he was getting ready to go to the pub on Friday evening Dolly called.

'I was beginnin' ter fink yer'd deserted me,' he joked as he waved her into a chair.

'I'm sorry, Jimmy, I've bin really busy,' she told him. 'I've 'ad people ter see an' fings ter do.'

Jimmy nodded as he stood in front of the mantelshelf struggling to fix his tie. 'Bloody fings are a nuisance,' he growled.

Dolly got up and spun him round by the shoulders. ''Ere, let me fix it,' she said grinning. 'I dunno why yer poncin' yerself up. 'Ave yer got someone ter meet?'

Jimmy held up his chin to let her knot the tie properly. 'I'm jus' tryin' ter smarten meself up, that's all,' he told her, and then he noticed that she was twitching her nostrils. 'What's up?' he said quickly.

'What yer wearin'?' Dolly asked, looking at him curiously.

'It's a drop o' rosewater I found in the bedroom. I fink it belonged ter Doreen,' he told her. 'I used it on me face after I shaved.'

'Well, I'm sorry ter tell yer that it's sour, Jimmy. Yer smell like a vinegar factory,' she replied, puckering her nose.

The reforming drunk looked downcast and Dolly immediately felt guilty for her lack of tact. Jimmy was doing well trying to get himself in shape and she had to admit that he looked ten times better than the first time she had seen him in Basin Street. His face was shining from the close shave, although he had nicked himself in a few places, and the prospects for future improvement looked good. Once he got his system working properly and started eating regular meals he would be a new man, and quite attractive into the bargain, she felt.

Jimmy studied his neatly knotted tie in the mirror for a few moments then turned to Dolly. 'D'yer feel all right after that bloody turn out the ovver night?' he asked her with concern.

'Yeah, course I do,' she replied quickly. ''Ow about you?'

'I'm fine,' he told her. 'I've bin in the Anchor since, but I ain't seem nuffink o' the Morgan boys, nor the ole man. Mind yer, 'e don't drink in the public bar anyway.'

Dolly sat down again. 'You ain't goin' out yet, are yer?' she asked him.

'Well, not just yet. D'yer fancy a cuppa, Dolly?'

'That'll be nice.'

Jimmy strolled out into the scullery. ''Ow many sugars?' he shouted back.

'Only one, I gotta watch me weight,' Dolly called out.

'Looks quite nice ter me.'

'Why fank you very much, kind sir.'

Jimmy poked his head round the door. 'Yer know I always 'ad a fing fer you, even when yer gave me the elbow I still reckoned yer, Dolly,' he said grinning.

'What d'yer mean, give yer the elbow? I told yer straight I wasn't gonna play second fiddle ter no one, but you wouldn't listen,' Dolly told him firmly. 'You was out ter date every gel yer laid eyes on at the time. Mind yer, we was only sixteen.'

When Jimmy brought the two cups of tea into the living room he saw that Dolly had kicked off her shoes and stretched her feet out towards the hearth. Suddenly the urge to go out to the pub left him. The prospect of a quiet chat with Dolly in front of the fire seemed a much better proposition.

For a while they sipped their tea in silence and then Jimmy looked up at his childhood sweetheart.

'This business wiv Frankie Morgan. What's it all about, gel?' he asked her quietly.

Dolly's face became serious. 'Tell me, Jimmy. What d'yer know about it all?' she enquired.

He shrugged his shoulders. 'Only what everyone else who was around at the time knows,' he replied. 'Yer remember you disappeared off the manor before the war. Nineteen thirty-eight wasn't it? Well, even though I was married I still used ter fancy yer. I'd seen yer about occasionally up until then. Like I said before, it was your Gerry who told me that yer'd got married an' moved away. I felt sad when 'e told me. I thought of what could 'ave bin wiv me an' you. Anyway there was the war an' everyfing, but after it was all over I used to 'ear bits an' pieces o' gossip. The Morgans were beginnin' ter make a nuisance o' themselves an' any talk concernin' them an' their activities was news. I 'eard that the Morgans' cooperage 'ad gone bust before the war an' one o' the bruvvers 'ad run off wiv what was left o' the money. Word was, 'is name was Bob. Your 'usband, Dolly.'

The big blonde eased herself in the armchair and smiled cynically. 'It was Frankie Morgan who put that story about,' she said darkly. 'My Bob worked 'is fingers ter the bone tryin' ter keep that cooperage business goin' after ole Samuel Morgan died. The rest o' the bruvvers 'ad worked there fer a time but it was Bob who stuck it out. Frankie stayed fer a while but what Bob didn't realise was that 'is bruvver was milkin' the profits. It was a limited company, yer see. Anyway, in '37 Bob decided it was time ter modernise the place – get in new machinery an' build an extension on spare land at the back. There was a lot o' business ter be 'ad, what wiv the new wine merchants that were takin' over the arches in Bermondsey. The idea was sound an' the bank agreed. They put up some o' the capital needed an' the rest was gonna come from the family. Frankie agreed ter put in 'is bit and their ole mum was ter supply the rest. Samuel 'ad left 'er comfortably off an' she 'ad plenty ter last 'er out. Well, ter cut a long story short, everyfing got under way an' when all the bills 'ad ter be settled Frankie Morgan couldn't pay 'is share. 'E'd bin fritterin' 'is money away, but worst of all 'e'd bin systematically fleecin' 'is ole mum. Gawd knows 'ow much 'e took off of 'er but there wasn't much left in 'er account when it all came out.'

Jimmy sat listening intently to Dolly's revelations, his eyes never leaving hers, and he saw the hard look on her face as she went on.

'Well, as yer can gavver, my Bob 'ad signed all the agreements in good faith on be'alf o' the family an' 'e was the one the creditors came after. There was no choice but ter sell the business ter raise the money fer payin' off the bank, an' what little money the old lady 'ad left in 'er account paid off the contractors. She died later that year, which was a blessin', I s'pose. Anyway, all the new machinery was sent back an' at the end o' the day Bob an' me were left wiv the clothes we stood up in. That was after years of sweat an' toil ter keep the business goin'.'

'Good Gawd,' Jimmy gasped. 'I'd 'ave killed the bastard if that was me.'

'So would most men, but Bob was a one-off. 'E was soft. Not weak, but soft, like an innocent child,' Dolly said in a quiet voice. 'Frankie was still family an' it wasn't in my man's nature to 'arm 'im physically. Mind yer, there was a terrible row an' the outcome was Bob turned 'is back on Frankie an' said 'e never wanted ter lay eyes on 'im again. That was why we moved away that year. We moved into a pub in Kent as managers an' in time the brewers let us buy it. Bob never really got over what 'ad 'appened an' I'm certain the constant broodin' over it all brought on 'is stroke. Bob was still quite a young man really, Jimmy.'

'So yer back on the manor an' after Frankie's blood,' Jimmy said nodding slowly. 'What d'yer expect ter get, Dolly? Frankie blew 'is money. After all, yer can't get blood out of a stone.'

'Frankie Morgan wasn't as stupid as people thought,' Dolly replied, her pale blue eyes narrowing. ''E'd salted money away, a lot o' money.'

''Ow d'yer know that?' Jimmy asked, intrigued.

'About a month before Bob 'ad 'is stroke we 'ad a visitor come ter stay at the pub,' Dolly went on. 'We did bed an' breakfast at the time. This bloke was an accountant fer a broker's, an' it so 'appened that 'e recognised Bob. 'E stayed fer a week while 'e did business in the area, an' 'im an' Bob got ter talkin'. It turned out that in 1939, just before the war broke out, Frankie Morgan 'ad put a lot o' money into a local company. The accountant couldn't, or wouldn't, tell my feller exactly which company it was. 'E said that 'e wasn't involved directly in the transaction, but it was a colleague who'd done the work. So yer see Frankie didn't just fritter the money away. 'E robbed Bob an' me, an' 'e robbed 'is own muvver.'

'What did your feller 'ave ter say when 'e found out about the money?' Jimmy asked her.

'Bob just shrugged it off an' said it was all in the past,' Dolly replied. 'But I know it really upset 'im, even though 'e made light of it. Anyway, this last week I've bin makin' a lot of enquiries an' very soon I'll 'ave enough on Frankie Morgan ter finish 'im.'

Jimmy Rideout felt a sudden pang of concern for his old friend's safety. She was big and strong, and she had no fear, but she was up against a very callous and brutal villain, a man who would give no quarter.

Chapter Nineteen

Annie Morgan sat beside the fire in her tidy parlour and looked across at her husband. He was nodding off to sleep, his hands clasped in his lap, and Annie sighed in resignation as she folded up the letter she had just received from her eldest son, Joe. She took off her glasses and put them back into the metal case. He was a good boy, Joe, she reflected, and he had done well for himself. He had married Carol soon after getting demobbed and had moved away to Brentwood in Essex, going into the plumbing business. He owned his own house now and the two kids were doing well at school. Joe had asked her in the letter to come and stay with him and Carol for a few days and Annie thought that it would be a good idea to take up his offer. Joe knew that she loved to spend some time with her grandchildren and Carol always made her feel welcome.

Michael, the second eldest, was a good boy too, and like Joe he was married and doing well for himself since he had opened a greengrocery shop over in Barking. His wife Peggy came from Stepney, but unlike Joe's wife she was a bit stuck-up, Annie felt, and did not make her feel so welcome on the odd occasion when she paid them a visit. Michael and Peggy had no children and always seemed to be gallivanting about.

At least Joe and Michael were both earning an honest living though, not like the rest of them, Annie sighed sadly. Charlie was doing a five-year stretch in prison, and it looked as if the rest had another job coming up soon, if the conversation around the dinner table that day was anything to go by. No one had bothered to put her in the picture, but that was nothing unusual. Frankie and the boys seemed to be talking in riddles half the time and Annie had become used to it over the years. She cooked and cleaned for them and put up with Frankie's moods, and occasionally, when things between them got too bad, she went to stay with Joe and Carol for a spell.

Annie folded Joe's letter and put it into her apron pocket. She was a slim woman in her late fifties with mousy hair and deep-set eyes. She constantly wore a troubled look and tended to be shunned by her neighbours, which did not bother her too much. She preferred not to stand chatting with them, and in any case Frankie suspected that they were only out to learn what they could and were envious of the fact that he was a good provider, unlike most of their husbands who kept them short.

Annie could not deny that Frankie was a good provider. He saw to it that she always had enough money for food and clothes, although she hardly ever bought herself a new coat or a smart dress. There was little need, she reasoned. He hardly ever took her out anywhere, and when he did it was only to the Anchor for a drink, on the very rare occasion when he was in one of his more generous moods.

Annie puffed irritably as Frankie stirred in his chair and started to snore. He had told her to wake him in good time as he was going out that evening to see someone. That was it. No discussion, no confiding in her, nothing, and it had always been like that, right from the early days. Annie sometimes wondered what she had ever seen in him. She had been a caring wife and had given him six sons, only to see four of them turn out just like him. Of those four, only Albert was in a regular job and showed her any respect, but it seemed that he was slowly becoming as wild as the others. Well, if this latest job they were planning went wrong and they got put away she would do as Joe had urged her many times. Leave them all and move in with him and Carol.

Don Farran felt pleased with himself as he hurried out of the Buildings on the cold Saturday evening to visit Rose in hospital. He had done the shopping, got the tea ready and managed to get Susan ready for bed before he left. Freda next door was minding her and had promised to tuck her up in bed at the usual time. The two boys could be trusted to look after themselves until he got back and he had left them with a bag of sweets and a bar of chocolate to share between them. He had bought Rose a small box of chocolates too and remembered to gather up a few toiletry items that she had asked him to take in to her.

As he reached the end of the turning he spotted Albert coming towards him. He was wearing his black Crombie overcoat with the collar turned up against the wind, his hands thrust into the pockets. He looked worried but he smiled quickly as he spotted his friend. 'I jus' bin fer a walk,' he said simply.

'On a night like this?' Don replied, giving him a critical look.

'Yeah well, I needed time ter fink,' Albert told him with a miserable expression on his handsome face. 'We've got a meetin' arranged fer termorrer night.'

Don felt that he had enough troubles of his own without spending time listening to Albert's problems and he made to move off. 'I'll see yer later, Alb, I gotta dash,' he said quickly.

'Where you off to in such an 'urry?' Albert asked.

'I'm goin' in the 'ospital ter see Rose,' Don told him.

'Rose? What's wrong wiv 'er?' Albert asked frowning.

'She 'ad a fall at work. She cut 'er 'ead open an' they took 'er in,' Don explained. 'She's OK. It's just a precaution. I can't stop now or I'll be late. I'll see yer later.'

Albert stood staring after Don as the young man hurried away and then he made a snap decision, turning on his heel and retracing his steps back into Abbey Street.

Rose sat up in bed feeling rested, happy with the doctor's visit that afternoon. He told her that everything was fine and she could look forward to having her baby in the first week of July. Don had been pleased to see her looking so well when he came in that evening and he had told her how worried he had been that she would harm herself trying to get rid of the baby. They had talked together during the visiting hour and Rose felt that she had succeeded in assuring Don of her intentions. What had happened was meant to be or she would have lost the baby, she pointed out. It would be difficult at first, but they would manage somehow, the way they always had since their mother first walked out on them. The only worry nagging at Rose was how the welfare people would react when they discovered that she was having a baby. She had made light of it that evening when Don mentioned the welfare, and when he left he had given her a kiss and his usual carefree smile.

It was eight thirty and the evening cocoa was being brought round by the nurse when Albert Morgan walked into the ward carrying a bunch of flowers and looking very nervous. He came up to Rose's bed and gave her a brief smile.

'I 'ope yer didn't mind me comin' in, Rose,' he said, his face flushed. 'Don told me about what 'appened an' I wanted ter come an' see yer.'

Rose had been taken aback to see him coming along the

ward towards her and her face grew suddenly hot. 'No, it's OK,' she said quickly.

Albert put the flowers down on the bottom of the bed and stood looking very uncomfortable. 'The sister said visitin' was finished but I told 'er I was in the army an' was goin' back off leave ternight,' he said, grinning boyishly. 'I told 'er you was my cousin.'

Rose smiled at his discomfort and pointed to the chair by the bed. 'Yer'd better sit down,' she told him.

'I won't stop if yer'd sooner not see me,' Albert said quickly.

'No, it's all right. Sit down,' she told him.

The young man did as he was bid and sat rigid in the chair, still looking uncomfortable as he glanced around him. 'Don said you 'ad a fall,' he told her.

'Yeah I cut the back o' me 'ead. They put a few stitches in but I'm all right,' she replied.

''Ow long yer in for?' Albert asked.

'I'll be out in a few days,' Rose said as she reached for the box of chocolates. 'You can 'ave one,' she told him, opening the box.

Albert shook his head. 'I've missed seein' yer about,' he said shyly.

'Well, I don't get much time these days,' Rose replied. 'I s'pose Don told yer about our muvver runnin' off.'

'Yeah, 'e did.'

'That's why I ain't bin ter the dances.'

'Yeah, I guessed.'

'D'you still go?'

Albert nodded and lowered his head while he mustered up the courage to go on. 'Look, Rose, I'm sorry about what 'appened that night,' he said quietly, raising his eyes and looking directly at the young woman. 'I felt terrible afterwards. I don't s'pose yer fink I did, but I'm tellin' yer the trufe.'

Rose gave him a smile. 'Why should yer feel bad about it? I didn't.'

'Didn't yer?'

'Course not. I knew what I was doin', or at least I thought I did,' she said.

Albert looked at her closely. 'Yer don't fink any less o' me then?' he asked.

Rose reached out and touched him on the arm momentarily. 'Look, Albert. It was just one o' those fings,' she said quietly. 'We wanted each ovver an' we did it. There's no sense in regrettin' it.'

Albert leaned forward in his seat. 'Tell me somefing, Rose,' he said in a hushed voice. 'Is there any chance fer me an' you ter see each ovver after yer get out of 'ere? I mean, I could call round p'raps an' . . .'

'No, Albert,' she cut in. 'I can't make any commitment, the way fings are. We can still be friends though.'

The young man dropped his gaze for a few moments. 'I've always liked you a lot, Rose,' he said, looking up slowly. 'I used ter make excuses ter call on Don, just ter see yer. I told yer all this that night at the dance, but it's true, honest. Yer muvver put the block on it though. She told me straight she didn't want a daughter of 'ers goin' around wiv a Morgan. All right, I know us Morgans 'ave got a bad name round 'ere an' I'm not disputin' it, but I wouldn't do anyfink to 'urt you, Rose. I got a regular job winder cleanin' an' I've got a chance ter buy the business soon. If me an' you walked out tergevver I'd never do anyfing dodgy again, an' that's a promise.'

The ward sister came marching along the aisle between the beds. 'Right, young man, we've got a ward to run. Say goodbye now,' she ordered.

Albert looked at Rose, his dark eyes open wide. 'What d'yer say, Rose?' he asked.

She shook her head slowly, fighting back tears of anguish. 'Let's leave it the way it is, Albert,' she said softly.

Albert leaned down and gently squeezed her arm. 'I'll see yer about,' he said quietly. 'Good luck.'

Rose watched him walk off along the ward, tears blurring her sight.

Albert reached the sister's office and turned to wave but Rose had her head buried and he cursed under his breath as he passed the office door.

'Excuse me, young man.'

Albert put his head into the office. 'Yeah?'

'You asked me about Miss Farran when you came in,' the sister said. 'Well, I've just had a word with the doctor. Your cousin should be able to go home on Wednesday, after the consultant sees her. The baby's fine, it's just routine.'

Albert went suddenly white and he leaned against the door jamb. 'She's 'avin a baby?' he gasped.

'Yes, I thought you knew,' the sister said quickly, looking confused. 'Oh dear, I . . .'

Albert had not stopped to hear the sister's last few words. He was almost running back down the ward, to the amusement of the patients. 'Rose! Why didn't yer tell me?' he gasped. 'You're 'avin' my baby! Why didn't yer tell me?'

The elderly woman in the next bed chuckled as she watched the confrontation. 'Yeah, why didn't yer tell 'im, luv?' she said. 'These fellers get orf too bloody lightly if yer ask me.'

Rose rubbed the tears away with the back of her hand. 'I wasn't gonna put yer under any pressure ter do the right fing by me,' she hissed, glancing quickly at the woman in the next bed who was straining to listen. 'In any case I wouldn't want yer under those terms.'

Albert's face was flushed with excitement. 'I asked yer ter step out wiv me before I knew yer was carryin' my child, remember,' he said quickly. 'Well, the offer still stands. Will yer walk out wiv me?'

'I–I dunno,' Rose mumbled.

'What she say?' the elderly woman asked Albert.

'She dunno yet,' Albert told her.

'Look, I'm sorry about the confusion,' the sister said, hurrying up to the bed, 'but I can't have my ward turned into a marriage bureau. It's lights out in ten minutes so will you please kiss the girl and leave now,' she said firmly.

'Go on, give 'er a kiss,' the nosy patient said, chuckling loudly.

Albert bent down and pressed his lips against Rose's. 'Look, I've gotta go out on business wiv my ole man termorrer night, but I'm comin' in on Monday night fer yer answer,' he said, and as he turned away he waved to the patient in the next bed and strode out of the ward feeling ten feet tall.

In the saloon bar of the Anchor the Morgans were gathered for a meeting. Frankie had just bought a round and as he carried the drinks over to a table near the fire he fixed Ernie with a hard look. 'I thought I told yer ter make sure Albert got 'ere sharp on eight,' he growled.

'I told 'im what yer said, I can't do no more,' Ernie replied, shrugging his shoulders.

'I gotta go over Whitechapel ter see those two geezers ternight, an' they expect me ter be there at nine,' Frankie told them gruffly. 'I gotta know now if we're all in this or not.'

'Course we are,' John said sipping his beer.

'We don't know, do we?' Frankie snapped. 'That bloody Albert's bin 'edgin' lately an' I gotta get it from 'im. This job's too big fer anyone who ain't got 'is 'eart in it.'

'P'raps we should row Albert out on this one an' bring in Fat Danny,' Ernie suggested.

'Oh no,' Frankie said quickly. 'I want this one ter stay in the family. Fat Danny's kosher, but 'e ain't family. Now where's that bloody boy o' mine got to?'

At nine thirty Albert Morgan walked into the Anchor to be met by his anxious brothers. 'Where the 'ell 'ave you bin?' John said acusingly. 'The ole man's ravin'.'

''E's 'ad ter shoot over Whitechapel,' Ernie butted in. ''E's rowed you in on this one, but 'e wanted yer ter tell 'im straight if yer still 'ad the bottle for it.'

Albert looked at Ernie and then John. 'The ole man's gonna 'ave ter find someone ter take me place,' he said calmly.

John grabbed his brother by the lapels, his face a dark mask. 'You bottly bastard,' he snarled.

Ernie shouldered in between them. 'C'mon, John, we don't want no more trouble 'ere. Remember we promised the ole man.'

Albert stepped back as his brother released him. 'Yer a bloody lunatic,' he growled.

'Why ain't yer wiv us on this one, Albert?' Ernie appealed to him.

'It's no big mystery,' Albert replied. 'It's just that I'm gonna be a farvver.'

Chapter Twenty

Ivy Campbell and Rene Stratton walked into Joe Diamond's shop together on Monday morning complaining about the cold weather, the prices at the market and any other subject they could think of to moan about. Lizzie Carroll was eager for any titbits of gossip as usual and she guided the two women on to the subject of Frankie Morgan's trial.

''E got off scot-free then,' she prompted.

'Who, Frankie Morgan?'

'Yeah, I reckon the bloody judge was paid off, don't you?'

Ivy pulled a face. 'My ole man 'eard that the bloke Frankie 'ad walloped 'ad started it. It was in the *South London* an' the *Mercury*, by all accounts,' she told Lizzie.

'I ain't read the papers,' Lizzie lied. 'Was that right?'

Rene shrugged her shoulders. 'They get away wiv bleedin' murder that lot,' she puffed. 'I tell yer, Liz, if my ole man 'ad done what Frankie Morgan done 'e would 'ave gone down fer sure.'

Joe Diamond was used to his regulars spending a few minutes chatting in his shop with Lizzie and he smiled to himself as he restocked his shelves. Lizzie was at it again and before the day was out she would have gathered more evidence than the Bermondsey CID.

''Cos yer know that the bloke who Frankie walloped was one o' Tommy Caulfield's car men,' Rene remarked.

Lizzie nodded and slipped her hands into the armholes of her white apron. 'Yeah, Stan Archer, 'im wiv the cocky walk. Always bowled along wiv 'is thumbs tucked in 'is waistcoat,' she told the two women. ''E used ter come in 'ere fer 'is fags, didn't 'e, Joe?'

Joe Diamond nodded vaguely, not wishing to become embroiled in the conversation.

Ivy leaned forward over the counter. 'I 'eard that Stan Archer was livin' wiv Tommy's sister, Lil. Set up 'ome tergevver by all accounts.'

'No,' Lizzie said, looking wide-eyed at Ivy.

''S'right,' Rene joined in. 'I 'eard it too. Fred Albury's wife Muriel told me 'er an' Fred saw 'em tergevver in the Crown one night. All over each ovver they was. Stan Archer's married, yer know, an' Lil's ole man pissed orf years ago. What a carryon.'

Lizzie shook her head in mock disgust. 'The fings you 'ear,' she sighed.

Rene picked up her few groceries and put them in her shopping bag, smiling gratefully as Lizzie pushed the ration book away. Ivy gathered up the laden canvas shopping bag that was resting at her feet and made to leave. 'By the way, I fergot ter tell yer, Liz,' she said suddenly. 'Yer know that Farran gel? She's in 'ospital.'

'Good Gawd. What's the matter wiv 'er?' Lizzie asked.

'She 'ad an accident at work. Cut 'er 'ead open,' Ivy informed her.

'She works at Bromilow's, don't she?' Lizzie replied. 'What a bloody dump that is. Dangerous too. I 'eard that the gels are always 'avin accidents there.'

'One o' the gels from Bromilow's called ter tell young Don

Farran the news,' Ivy went on. 'The poor sod looked really worried when I saw 'im. Bloody shame, she's such a nice kid, is Rose. They all are. Those two young boys are not a bit o' trouble an' that Susan, she's like a little doll, so sweet.'

'Must 'ave bin a bad cut. They don't keep people in 'ospital fer a cut 'ead usually, unless they fink it might be serious,' Lizzie remarked.

'Yeah, but it might 'ave bin somefing else caused the accident,' Rene butted in. 'When I saw Don goin' out fer the papers yesterday I asked 'im 'ow Rose was an' 'e told me she's bin under observation, in case she 'ad a fractured skull. She's all right though. She's due out on Wednesday, so 'e told me. Apparently she fainted an' caught 'er 'ead as she fell.'

'She ain't pregnant, is she?' Lizzie said, giving Rene a quick glance.

'I shouldn't fink so,' Ivy told her. 'The kid never seems ter go out. She's got enough on 'er plate lookin' after that lot.'

'Still, yer never know,' Lizzie replied. 'Gels get pregnant at work, an' that place she works ain't exactly a nunnery. There's fellers workin' there.'

Rene nodded. 'Funny fing now yer come ter mention it, but I've noticed a few fings this last week or so,' she said, stroking the side of her face with the palm of her hand.

''Ave yer?' Lizzie prompted.

'Well, yer tend ter notice certain fings,' Rene went on. 'The ovver mornin' I saw 'er comin' down the stairs an' she looked white as a sheet. Could be mornin' sickness. She looks like she's puttin' on weight too. Not the usual fat but 'ow yer bust an' 'ips look when yer carryin'. Mind yer, I ain't sayin' she is, but it makes yer fink.'

'Well, I 'ope she ain't in the puddin' club fer 'er sake. That would be the last straw, wouldn't it?' Ivy said. 'As if she ain't got enough ter worry about.'

'Oh well, c'mon, Ivy, we can't stand chattin' all day,' Rene said, feeling a little guilty for casting aspersions.

Joe Diamond breathed a sigh of relief when the two women walked out of his shop. The poor kid was in hospital with a cut head and those two were already spreading gossip. 'I shouldn't fink the kid's pregnant,' he remarked to his assistant. 'She looked all right when she came in 'ere the ovver day.'

'You blokes don't notice such fings until it's starin' yer in the face,' Lizzie replied. 'Us women can tell very early on.'

Joe shrugged his shoulders and went out into the store room for another carton of canned peas. He was not feeling up to a lesson on pregnancy and he had other things on his mind. The weekly delivery from his wholesaler was due soon and he was hoping for a few extra cases of tinned fruit. The last lot he had got went in two days and the driver had promised him some tinned ham this time.

That Monday at lunchtime the delivery arrived and while Joe was busy in the back of the shop Freda Arrowsmith came in with Ethel Price.

Lizzie was her usual enquiring self and she quickly started them off in the right direction. 'I 'eard this mornin' that young Rose Farran's in 'ospital,' she remarked blithely.

Ethel Price had come in to see if Joe could let her have some extra rations for the party she had planned in a few weeks' time, and she felt that it was a good idea to start off on the right foot.

'Yeah, Ivy Campbell told me, Liz,' she replied. 'Bloody shame. She's such a nice kid.'

Freda nodded. 'I've bin lookin' after the little one while Don goes in ter see 'er,' she told Lizzie. 'She's doin' all right though an' she's due out on Wednesday.'

'She fainted at work, so I 'eard,' Lizzie went on. 'Mind yer, I ain't surprised. That Bromilow's factory is a terrible place ter work. There's all that noise an' din, an' ter tell yer the trufe I don't fink that gel gets enough to eat. Yer know what it's like when yer got a family ter feed. The muvver usually 'as ter put up wiv what's left, an' after all, young Rose is a muvver ter those kids. I mean ter say, if she was out an' about yer might fink she was carryin', what wiv 'er faintin' the way she did. I shouldn't fink it was the cause in that gel's case though. If it was, I'd be very surprised.'

'So would I,' Freda said quickly, hardly disguising her distaste at Lizzie's sly implication.

Ethel merely smiled. She was hoping Joe would come into the shop so that she could have a discreet word in his ear.

Freda motioned to the top shelf. 'I'll 'ave a tin o' those pears, a quarter o' Brooke Bond divi, a pound o' sugar an' two ounces o' those dolly mixtures please, Liz, oh an' a packet of Lux flakes,' she said in one breath, hoping not to be kept chatting for too long.

Just then Joe walked through looking pleased with himself and he nodded to the two women.

''Ere, Joe, any chance of some tinned 'am?' Ethel asked him quietly. 'My boy Joe's gettin' demobbed next month an' we're 'avin a party fer 'im.'

Joe winked as he leaned over the counter. 'I just got a nice tin o' shoulder 'am if yer want it,' he whispered. 'I ain't unpacked it yet so see me termorrer.'

As Ethel and Freda left the shop together Lizzie Carroll turned to her employer. 'That Freda Arrowsmith looks after the Farran kids quite a lot an' what she just said 'as got me finkin',' she told him.

'What was that then?' Joe asked.

'Well, it wasn't exactly what she said, more the way she said it,' Lizzie replied deeply.

Joe was getting a little tired of his assistant harping on the day's news. 'Yeah,' he said in a weary voice.

Lizzie quickly cast a glance sideways, though no one else was in the shop. 'Well, I 'appened ter say that if Rose Farran was always out an' about yer could understand people finkin' she might be carryin', 'er faintin' the way she did, but I said I didn't fink fer one minute that the gel was carryin' an' if she was I'd be very surprised. Well, Freda jumped down me froat. "So would I," she said in a right off 'and way.'

'Why should that make yer fink?' Joe asked her with a deep sigh.

'Well, she's a friend o' the Farran family an' she'd be protective, wouldn't she, if the gel was pregnant,' Lizzie explained. 'I dunno, it was just the way she said it. It makes yer fink.'

'Well, don't fink too 'ard, Lizzie, I wanna get them shelves sorted out,' Joe told her, and then as Dora Kennedy walked into the shop his face dropped.

Lizzie's eyes lit up as the big woman waddled up to the counter. Dora knew a bit about everybody in the neighbourhood and she would have something to say about the latest gossip.

Rose Farran had been allowed out of bed on Monday morning and she had made a special effort to look nice for the evening visiting. Don would be in as usual and it looked likely that she would have another visitor too. She had managed to borrow curling tongs from one of the nurses, and one of the patients who worked in a hairdresser's had volunteered to wave her hair for her. Don had brought in her pink quilted dressing gown and Freda had sent her in a pretty pink nightdress to match.

The elderly woman in the next bed had been quick to put two and two together and she called Rose over during the afternoon. 'I expect 'e will come ter see yer, luv. They usually come round ter pick up the pieces, once they've smashed the bloody mould,' she said, nodding her wise old head. 'Still, yer gotta take fings as they come. I always 'ave an' it didn't do me any 'arm. 'Ere, reach in my locker, will yer. See the bottle? It's in there somewhere.'

Rose pulled out a small bottle of Evening in Paris perfume. 'Is this it?' she asked.

'That's it. You take it,' the old lady told her. 'I ain't got no use fer the likes o' that. Be fair, luv, what the bloody 'ell is that stuff gonna do fer me, apart from makin' me smell like a Lisle Street whore. Stuff like that's fer the likes o' you young people. Stick a drop o' that be'ind yer ears an' on yer cleavage an' that feller'll be jumpin' inter bed wiv yer, afore yer can say Jack Robinson.'

Rose laughed aloud and bent down to give the old lady a kiss on her lined forehead. 'I'll let yer know 'ow 'e responds,' she said with a wink.

The rest of the afternoon seemed to drag, and when the tea things were being cleared away from the ward Rose took another walk to the toilet and surveyed herself in the mirror over the hand basin. She could see that most of her colour had returned and her short, thick hair had been styled to hide the square of sticking-plaster. She turned sideways and noticed the very slight roundness of her belly and the fullness of her breasts. She faced the mirror again and bared her teeth, then she stretched her lips tight while she carefully applied a pale shade of lipstick. A touch of Evening in Paris on the places designated by the old lady and a final look in the mirror was enough to make her feel that she had done her best to look nice.

The hands of the clock moved slowly and at ten minutes to seven Rose was feeling nervous. Perhaps Albert wouldn't come to see her tonight. Perhaps he had met up with Don and there had been trouble between the two, she fretted. It was silly of her not to have told Don the whole truth about Albert when he called in on Sunday afternoon to see her, but it had been too soon after Albert called the previous evening and she had not really had time to think it all through. It was different now. She had lain awake half the night and finally made her mind up to have it all out with Albert before telling her brother. One thing was certain. Albert would have to come to her in love, not out of pity, or to fulfil his obligations as a father. She could never allow that. She had her pride, and an overwhelming desire to bring her child up in a house full of love and happiness.

Albert Morgan worked all day Monday in a state of shock. The knowledge that he was going to become a father saw him lurching from elation to despair. He imagined himself taking his son for walks in the park. He would teach him to kick a ball properly and to swim, and the boy would grow tall and strong. Supposing it was a girl? Well, she would be pretty, as pretty as her mother and she would adore him. He would be protective and when she grew into a beautiful young woman he would buy her her first party dress. He would vet her boyfriends and they would protect her with their lives for fear of his terrible wrath.

Albert came down to earth heavily as he thought about the meeting that would take place that evening. His father and brothers were going over to Whitechapel to finalise the plans for the raid, which had suddenly been set for Wednesday. His father had raved and ranted at him on his return from the initial meeting in the East End on Saturday evening, and as he sat in the cafe in Tooley Street the young man relived the angry confrontation.

'Yer knew I wanted you at the pub before I left,' his father had barked at him. 'The boys said you was bottlin' out, but I didn't listen. I don't want a son o' mine ter be a snivv'lin' coward. 'Ow could I go over an' tell the geezers I wasn't sure about yer intentions? I'd 'ave bin a laughin'-stock. I 'ad ter row you in an' you'll go on that job, like it or not.'

'You can't make me go, Farvver,' he told him adamantly. 'I

got new responsibilities now. I'm gonna go straight, an' that's final.'

The ensuing events were like a blur. His father had cuffed him roughly across the face with the back of his hand and it was only the timely intervention of his mother, who had somehow got between them, that had prevented a more serious attack. He had staggered across the room and been bundled out into the street by Ernie, who had the sense to see the danger. He had stood outside the house for a while, listening to his father raging and his mother answering him back with every vile name she could lay her tongue to. Albert recalled walking the streets until the early hours and then, when tiredness finally overtook him, he had let himself into the sheds where he kept his ladders and slept until late on Sunday morning. John and Ernie had been out early looking for him at their mother's instigation and when they found him wandering in Abbey Street, Ernie had told him that it would be best if he found somewhere else to live, at least until after the raid. Ernie had been sympathetic, but John had been very cold towards him and had little to say.

Albert was sure in his mind that the family bond had been severed, and there was no way he could ever again live in his father's house. Tonight he was being allowed home at seven o'clock to pack his things. His father had made it clear that he was to be gone by the time he got back at eight o'clock. Ernie had passed on the message and had told him that their father wanted nothing more to do with him.

Albert finished his rounds and as he prepared to collect his things he knew that, as bad as it had all turned out, he had made the right decision. His criminal days were over once and for all. He had always loved Rose and he would make her love him. His future now was with her and the baby, if she would have him.

Chapter Twenty-One

Dora Kennedy had two grown-up daughters who, like their mother, were both prone to gossiping whenever they found time; and like their mother, Jessica and Monica usually found the time. Both were very fertile, and despite Dora's warning that too many children weighed a woman down, the girls continued to produce. It was no hardship, they argued. They both lived in Basin Street, both their husbands worked in the docks, and they were both pregnant again. Jessica, the elder by two years, was having her fourth and she glowed with good health as she sat chatting to Monica, who was into her third pregnancy.

The children were playing happily together in a very untidy parlour and Jessica sighed in resignation as she cast her eye around the room. 'It's no good gettin' all worked up about it,' she said to her younger sister. 'Yer can't expect ter keep a place tidy where kids are concerned. Let 'em play is what I say. There's plenty o' time to 'ave a straighten-up once they're tucked up in bed.'

'Yeah, yer right,' Monica replied as she sipped her tea. 'I gave up tryin' ter be tidy in the 'ouse when I 'ad Judy. Arfur don't seem ter mind comin' in to a shit-tip. 'E knows I don't get much time fer that sort o' fing durin' the day, an' 'e's good about the place.'

'Same wiv my Billy,' Jessica remarked. ''E never complains. Mind yer I did tell 'im right from the start. If yer want kids yer gotta make the sacrifices, I told 'im. Anyway we both wanted a big family, but I 'ave ter say I'm finkin' of 'avin' a word when we go ter the clinic this afternoon. Enough's enough, an' like Muvver ses, they do pull yer down.'

Dora Kennedy walked into the house at that moment with her usual bag of sweets for the children and both the girls got their coats on. 'Yer wanna show the nurse your leg, Jess,' she said. 'It could be the start o' varicose veins. They'll prob'ly give yer a crepe bandage fer support.'

Jessica pulled a face. 'I don't think I'll bovver,' she replied. 'I don't wanna look like a bloody race 'orse.'

'Fat chance o' that wiv your shape,' Monica laughed. 'C'mon or we'll be too late fer the tea an' biscuits.'

''Ere, before yer go, I just bin in Joe Diamond's an' I was talkin' ter that Lizzie Carroll who works there,' Dora told them. 'Well, she was sayin' that the Farran gel's in 'ospital.'

'Who, Rose? That's a shame. What's up wiv 'er?' Jessica asked.

'Well, accordin' ter Lizzie the kid's pregnant,' Dora went on. 'She fainted at work an' cracked 'er 'ead an' they took 'er in the ambulance. I s'pose they found out at the 'ospital.'

'Well, they would, wouldn't they?' Monica chimed in.

'Gawd 'elp 'er,' Dora said. 'The poor cow's got enough on 'er plate wivout this.'

''Ow did Lizzie get ter find out?' Jessica asked.

'She gets to know everyfing does Lizzie,' Dora told her. 'She's a nosy cow really. She wants ter know the ins an' outs of a nag's arse.'

'Well, we better get goin', Mum,' Monica said. 'Now be good

fer Gran'ma, you lot, an' no arguin' over those toys. Judy, don't poke that doll in Terry's face.'

'No, Stanley, don't squeeze Judy like that, yer'll 'urt 'er,' Jessica told him.

'Will yer two get goin' an' leave the kids ter me,' Dora groaned. 'They'll be all right, I'll share the sweets out once yer've gone.'

The two women made their way to the antenatal clinic which was situated in a large building in Grange Road, a ten-minute walk from Fellmonger Street. For Dora's daughters, however, the journey took thirty minutes. Jessica told her younger sister that she had developed this strange craving for jam-filled doughnuts smothered in sugar, and a short detour to the doughnut shop provided the opportunity to indulge in a little bit of window-shopping at several stops along the way. When they finally arrived they were disappointed to learn that the refreshments had already been served. Jessica used her persuasive powers to scrounge two cups of tea, and when they were at last seen by the nurse the young women were both told that all was going well, though Jessica's leg did indeed appear to need some support if she were to avoid varicose veins.

'Bloody 'ell, that's all I want,' she moaned to Monica. 'I'll look charmin'.'

'That's part of the joys o' muvver'ood,' Monica laughed. ''Ere, did yer tell 'er about not wantin' any more kids?'

'Nah, there's plenty o' time,' Jessica said as they strolled leisurely out of the welfare centre. 'Mind yer though, she was nice ter talk to, not like that miserable cow we saw last time. She does 'ome visits down our way an' she said she knows quite a lot o' people in Fellmonger Street. I was askin' 'er if she knew the Farran family.'

'What'd she say?' Monica asked.

'She said she didn't but one o' the ovvers calls on the family occasionally.'

'What's that for then?'

'Well, the Farran's muvver run off wiv a married man last year, didn't she, an' the welfare are keepin' their eye on 'em 'cos o' the kids. The littlest is only seven.'

'I didn't know she run off. Bloody woman wants shootin',' Monica growled.

'Shootin's too good fer the likes of 'er,' Jessica replied. 'Fancy runnin' off an' leavin' yer kids. Imagine us two runnin' off.'

'Who'd 'ave us?' Monica said as they crossed the main road.

'I dunno, we ain't so bad. I s'pose if it was Robert Taylor or Stewart Granger I'd 'ave ter fink about it,' Jessica joked.

'Well, I don't care who it was, I wouldn't leave my kids,' Monica said firmly.

'Nah, me neivver,' her sister replied.

By the time Dora Kennedy's two daughters had reached home on that Monday afternoon things were moving at a rapid pace back at the welfare centre. Miss Grant, welfare visitor for the Abbey Street area, had been summoned into the district manager's office.

'Sit down, Peggy. I want to go over your visiting schedule for the next two weeks,' the district officer said. 'I've had some information from Nurse Thompson concerning the Farran family and I'd like you to make a call as soon as you can.'

'Oh, I see, and what was the information?' Peggy asked, taking out a notepad from her handbag and putting on her gold-rimmed glasses.

'Well, it appears that Rose Farran has had a mishap at work and been admitted into hospital, but most importantly, the girl's apparently got herself pregnant,' the officer told her.

'Oh dear. Oh dear, oh dear,' Peggy sighed. 'Such a nice family too. I was very pleased with the situation on my last visit. You have my report.'

'Yes, I've just been going through it, but this throws a

different light on the subject entirely,' the officer said quickly. 'There are a number of reasons why we'll have to seek fostering for the under-age three. The two boys share a bedroom with their sixteen, nearly seventeen-year-old brother, and Rose shares the small back bedroom with seven-year-old Susan. It's a small flat and the facilities are very limited. We have a classic over-crowding situation here, and although we know that the new baby only counts as half a person in the council reckoning for rehousing we have to look at it in a more practical light, as I'm sure you understand.'

'Exactly,' Peggy replied. 'There's no room for a cot in the back bedroom.'

'Yes, and we have the confinement to consider,' the district officer went on. 'I see that you assessed Don Farran as being a very sensible young man who is considerate towards the children, but he has a job to hold down and the neighbours can't be expected to help out more than they do at the moment.'

'So we go for fostering,' Peggy said compliantly.

'Yes, I'll make the necessary arrangements with Ben Griffiths,' the officer said, opening a folder, 'and I'd like you to see the family as soon as possible. Perhaps you might be able to visit the Farran girl in hospital. Let's see now. She would have been admitted either to Guy's or St Olave's as a casualty. I'll ring both and find out which one she's at. She may have been discharged, but I'll try anyway.'

The ward clock showed ten minutes to eight and Don frowned as he noticed Rose glancing over his shoulder again. 'Look, sis, if yer bored wiv me company I don't 'ave ter wait until the bell goes. I could leave now,' he said with a smile. 'Ever since I got 'ere you've bin givin' that clock the eye.'

Rose smiled and shifted uncomfortably in the large cush-ioned chair. She had thought about this evening with a lot of trepidation and now it looked very much like Albert was not coming in. She had wondered how she was going to handle the situation, and whether Albert would say anything about the baby while Don was there. Her brother would have to know sooner or later that Albert was the baby's father, though it was her fear that Don might harm him in some way that had prevented her telling him in the first place. He had been very good, she had to admit. Another brother might have tried to prise the identity of the father from her.

'Don, I'm sorry if I seem edgy, but there's somefing on me mind, somefing I should 'ave told yer before now,' she began.

Don leaned forward in his seat and put a cupped hand to his ear. His attempt at humour was lost on Rose and she adjusted her dressing gown as she got up out of the chair. 'C'mon, let's take a walk down the corridor,' she said. 'There's a waitin' room fer visitors an' we can talk better there than in 'ere.'

Granny Thorpe in the next bed cursed under her breath as she feigned sleep. Never mind, she told herself. The young woman would no doubt put her in the picture as soon as visiting was over. Shame about the other young man though, she thought with a frown. Rose had really been looking forward to him coming in that evening. Well, if he came in tomorrow she would have quite a bit to say to him herself. It was scandalous the way some men treated their women. It would not have happened in her day. Not to her anyway.

Albert Morgan had killed time by going to the fish shop in the Old Kent Road for his tea, and when he knocked at his front door at seven sharp his mother had greeted him with open arms. She had been very tearful and had plied him with lots of questions, desperate to convince him that she didn't want him to leave the family home and had tried to get his father to relent without success. Albert did not have to be told. His father had always been a hard man, whose orders were absolute and final. His mother had shown a lot of courage in standing up to him and it might have meant her feeling the back of his hand too, though Albert had to admit he had never known his father to lay a finger on her.

The young Morgan had managed to find a room in Abbey Street with a friendly couple whose lodger had left to get married. He had been given the address by his employer who cleaned the windows along that turning, and Albert was satisfied with his digs. The room was clean and tidy and there was a small gas fire in the hearth. The single bed fitted neatly into one corner and there was a table and two chairs as well as a comfortable easy chair placed beside the fire. The wardrobe was big enough to hold his clothes and there was also a small sideboard which took up the wall facing the window. The arrangement was that Albert should pay the woman of the house for his food and he would eat with her and her husband, which suited him fine. He had never had to boil more than a kettle at home and along with his father and brothers he had always sat down to good, wholesome meals.

Albert had completed the move using his window-cleaning bicycle, finding that the two large suitcases sat comfortably in the side cart. He had been out of the house by ten minutes to eight after a tearful farewell with his mother, who promised to call in at his new address occasionally to make sure he was well. The young man stowed his cases in his new room and hung up his two suits, then he decided to go down to the Swan for a quiet drink to think things over.

Albert walked along towards Dockhead deep in thought, and with his eyes on the ground he almost bumped straight into Don Farran. He saw the hard look on his friend's face and smiled a greeting.

'Well, I reckon yer a no-good bastard after what you done,' Don said sharply, his face white with temper.

'Look, Don, I . . . I've always cared for Rose, you know that. What 'appened was one o' those fings. I never forced 'er ter do anyfink, honest I never. I . . .'

Don's anger spilled over and suddenly he lashed out, whacking his fist into the side of Albert's mouth. The young man staggered back, his hand going up to his face as he steadied himself.

'Yer don't understand . . .' he started.

'Don't understand?' Don shouted, his throat dry. 'I understand right enough. I'm not on about yer makin' 'er pregnant. I'm on about yer not goin' in ter see 'er after what yer told 'er. She was really lookin' forward ter seein' yer tonight. She got 'erself all smartened up an' she looked a picture. Yer don't deserve 'er.'

Albert stood with his feet spread, waiting for another blow to land. He was two years older than Don and heavier by a stone, but Don was powerfully built with a big pair of shoulders and muscular arms. He was shaking with temper too and Albert knew that he was going to have a fight on his hands. 'Listen fer one moment, then we can fight if yer like,' he said quickly, spitting blood from his split lip. 'I love Rose an' I was gonna go in ternight ter tell 'er I wanted ter marry 'er, if she'd 'ave me, but I couldn't.'

'Couldn't? Why couldn't yer?' Don asked, his fists still clenched.

'I got chucked out o' me 'ouse an' I 'ad ter go an' get me fings ternight, that's why,' Albert told him. 'The old man said I was ter go while 'e was out an' I 'ad ter be out o' the 'ouse by eight o'clock when 'e got back. I was finkin' of goin' in ter see Rose after hours but they wouldn't let me in, not after the turn-out on Saturday night. The sister almost chucked me out o' the ward.'

Don's shoulders sagged and he wiped his sweating hands down the sides of his trousers. 'I didn't know,' he said quietly.

'There's a lot yer don't know,' Albert went on, feeling more confident now that Don had relaxed a little. 'I told my old man straight that I was finished wiv all the villainry. 'E'd already rowed me in on that job they're pullin' off an' 'e gave me a back'ander when I refused ter be a part of it. I told 'im I was gonna be a farvver an' from now on I was goin' straight.'

Don held out his hands, palms up. 'I'm sorry I clouted yer, Albert. I should 'ave given yer time to explain.'

'It ain't no big fing,' Albert said, spitting some more blood and wincing as he raised a smile. 'I ain't lost any teef. If it was my sister I'd do the same as you did. I was a mug really. I should 'ave gone in fer Rose's answer last night, but I told 'er I 'ad ter go out on business wiv me farvver. I needed time ter get fings sorted out wiv 'im, yer see. I knew there'd be trouble, but I didn't expect 'im ter chuck me out.'

Don nodded slowly as Albert finished, then he moved forward and held out his hand. 'Pals?'

'Sure. Pals,' Albert said. 'Got time fer a quick'un at the Swan?'

'Why not, yer gonna be me bruvver-in-law soon,' Don answered grinning. 'If she'll 'ave yer.'

Chapter Twenty-Two

On Tuesday morning Peggy Grant, the welfare visitor, called in to the hospital to see Rose. She knew that it was not going to be a pleasant task, spelling everything out at such a time, but decisions had already been made and the district officer was setting the wheels in motion.

''Ow did yer find out I was in 'ere?' Rose asked as soon as the welfare officer sat down beside her bed.

'You know how it is,' Peggy replied. 'Word gets around and we do get to know these things, eventually.'

'I'm goin' 'ome termorrer an' the children are all bein' well looked after,' Rose said quickly.

'Yes, I'm sure they are,' Peggy replied, 'but you see it's different now, you must see that.'

'I don't know what yer mean,' Rose said.

'Well, I'm thinking about your condition. You can't be expected to look after the children as well as your own baby. They take a lot of your time and . . .'

Rose looked horrified as she stared hard at the officer. 'Yer mean yer know I'm pregnant?' she gasped. 'It was the 'ospital. They told yer.'

'No, it was just something we picked up at the welfare

220

session yesterday,' Peggy corrected her. 'Like I just said, word does get around, and you have to remember that a lot of mums from your part of Bermondsey attend our clinic.'

'I never told anyone, no one outside the family that is,' Rose replied with a troubled frown. 'I wasn't gonna say anyfing just yet, not until I could make some arrangements about the boys an' Susan.'

The welfare officer laid her hand on Rose's arm. 'Look, my dear. What we're intending to do is for the best. The two boys can be fostered by one family, hopefully, and Susan will soon settle in with her foster parents. They will most probably have other children about Susan's age.'

Rose snatched her arm away as anxious tears filled her eyes. 'I won't let yer take those kids away from me. They'd fret, I know they would. No, yer can't 'ave 'em,' she said quickly, her voice faltering.

'Unfortunately, it's something that has to be done. Once the court agrees that the children need to be taken into care there's nothing you, or anyone else, can do. The process will begin.'

'Process?' Rose almost shouted. 'This is my family you're talkin' about. They're not sheets o' paper ter be shuffled about. I won't let 'em go. I can manage, an' I'll 'ave the baby at 'ome. Don can manage the kids fer a few days until I get back on me feet.'

'But your brother has got a job to think about,' Peggy tried to explain. 'He has to bring in some money. Surely you can appreciate the situation. Anyway it won't be for ever. Once things settle down the children can come home.'

'Yeah, an' 'ow long would they be away?' Rose asked, tears beginning to fall.

'That depends,' the officer said quietly. 'It could be one year, or two, perhaps a little less than that. We have to make sure that you will be able to care for the children when there's an infant to think about as well.'

'You're not takin' 'em. I won't let you split my family up just because there's anuvver little mouth ter feed,' Rose said passionately.

'It's not only a matter of care. The flat you live in barely caters for your family as it is,' the officer went on. 'Be sensible, Rose. Where would you put the cot?'

'I'm gonna apply ter the council fer a flat. Ovver people 'ave got flats when their families grew,' the young woman said, biting her lip in anguish.

'I want you to think carefully about what I've just said, Rose,' the officer told her. 'I'm sure you'll very soon come to realise that we're acting in the best interests of the children. Now I must go. I'll call in to your flat on Friday and we'll talk further.'

'Never. I'll never let 'em go, even if yer lock me up,' Rose said gravely, her face set hard.

'They may even do that, if you resist the court order,' Peggy said quietly as she stood up. 'Until Friday then.'

Rose watched her leave the ward and then slumped down against the pillow crying.

'Oi, sister. What's that bloody woman doin' upsettin' our Rose?' the old lady in the next bed called out as the ward sister came up to the young woman's bed. 'If I could 'ave, I'd 'ave give 'er what for.'

'It's none of your business, Maggie,' the sister told her sternly. 'Now just stay quiet. You know what the doctor said. No excitement.'

'Sod the doctor. What's 'e know, 'e's only a bit of a boy,' Maggie growled. 'She was all right till that ponced-up cow come ter see 'er. Where's she from, I'd like ter know?'

'Maggie, I won't tell you again,' the sister scolded her. 'Now if you don't lie quiet I'll get the nurse to give you an enema right away instead of waiting for nature to take its course. Do you understand?'

'Yeah, all right,' the old lady said grudgingly. 'Can yer do me one favour though?'

The ward sister sighed in resignation. 'What is it now?'

'Stick yer paw in my locker, will yer. There's a bag o' bull's eyes in there. Give 'em to our Rose, they might cheer 'er up a bit.'

On Tuesday lunchtime Don Farran left the sawmills and walked quickly along Abbey Street, taking a narrow turning that led out into Spa Road. He was still wearing his dusty overalls and as he hurried up the steps into the Town Hall he was stopped by a uniformed doorman. 'Can I 'elp you, young man?' he asked.

'I want the 'ousin' office,' Don told him.

'Out 'ere, turn left, second door on yer left,' the doorman said in a tired voice, feeling a little irritated by the number of people he had directed to that particular place during the past few weeks.

'I wanna see about gettin' me name down on the council list fer a three or four-bedroom flat,' Don said to a young man wearing tin-rimmed spectacles at a desk nearest the counter.

'Ar yes, now let me see,' he said frowning. 'Brenda, have we those green forms? You know the ones. 20674s.'

The young woman at the next desk still looked a little blank and she shook her head.

'Look, those by your arm. Yes, those,' the young man said, giving Don a look of despair. 'She's only been here a couple of weeks. Can't get any sense out of her at all. I don't know what the Council's coming to,' he groaned as he came to the counter carrying the stack of forms. 'Right now. If you fill in all the details in this space. Then get your doctor to sign there, then you can post it off.'

'Can't I bring it in?' Don asked.

The clerk shook his head slowly. 'If you come in and give it to Brenda it's most likely to find its way into the Mayor's chambers or the fumigation department,' he said, smiling at his own joke. 'Brenda's got a way with forms. She just puts them in the nearest tray available. No, you must post it. It's the rule.'

'Tell me. 'Ow long's the waitin' list?' Don asked him.

'How long's a piece of string?' the clerk replied with a shrug of his shoulders. 'Seriously, it could be anything up to five years, the way things are moving here.'

Don walked back to work feeling that he had wasted a lunchtime. Rose had said it was time they tried to get a bigger flat and he wanted to go into the hospital and cheer her up, but the Council looked hopeless. Suddenly he remembered the Dunton Estates. Maybe they would be more likely to help. The office was just round the corner and it was only twelve thirty.

'I'm sorry, but there's nothing going at the moment,' the Dunton Estates clerk told him.

Don nodded. 'Can I get on the waitin' list?' he asked.

'I'm afraid it's full, and we don't like to add names to an overfull list. It raises false hopes, you see,' the clerk said apologetically. 'Mind you, we are likely to have one or two large houses available for rent in the near future. Out of this area, though.'

'Whereabouts?'

'The Isle of Dogs.'

'No fanks.'

'I don't blame you. The properties are next to the glueworks,' the clerk informed him. 'Terrible smells, and not a good place to bring children up, I would think.'

Feeling thoroughly depressed, Don walked back to work and was met in the yard by the foreman. 'Sorry, lad, but the over-time's off tonight,' he said. 'The bloody delivery's bin delayed. The lorry's broke down over the Isle o' Dogs by all accounts.'

Don remembered the glue-works and wanted to say some-thing sarcastic about sticking the lorry, but he thought better of it.

Jimmy Rideout went to London Bridge Station to see his stallholder friend and the news was good. Trade was up by ten per cent on last week, with the prospect of another increase now that the bad weather was lifting slightly. Jimmy did not know exactly what it all meant, except that his mate was an honest trader and there would be a few more shillings coming in that week.

His friend gave him an old-fashioned look up and down and stroked his chin thoughtfully. 'You're lookin' a bit spruce, Jimmy,' he said with a saucy smile. 'I like the suit. And the tie's a beaut. It's all right, yer can take it orf now I've got the joke.'

Jimmy brushed a hand down his front. 'Two an' a tanner in Burton's.'

'What, the suit?' his friend queried.

'No, the bloody tie, yer dope,' Jimmy said indignantly.

'Well, I 'ave ter say yer do look well, Jim. Bin on the wagon?' the stallholder enquired.

'Nah, just pullin' meself tergevver a bit,' Jimmy told him. 'I got good reason to, yer see.'

'Oh yeah? Got yerself a bit o' fluff then?'

'Yer could say.'

'Nice to 'ear it. Anyone I know?'

'I wouldn't be seen wiv anyone you know,' Jimmy said.

'Sharp too. Never mind, Jim boy. Keep takin' the tablets an' mind yer don't go strainin' that ole clacker valve.'

'Piss orf.'

The stallholder watched Jimmy Rideout walk off with a smile on his face. It was nice to see the change in the man, he thought. It was about time Jimmy sorted himself out.

Tommy Caulfield often went into the saloon bar of the Anchor at lunchtime and it was not unusual to see Frankie Morgan there. Tommy would stand at the counter and chat with Sammy McGarry while he sipped his pint, and apart from the normal nod of acknowledgement in Frankie's direction the contractor avoided the man's company. The villain always stood in the far corner of the bar with a few of his associates, and because of one or two nasty experiences he never stood with his back to the door.

On Tuesday morning Frankie saw Tommy Caulfield come in and he immediately walked over with a grin on his swarthy face. "Ow's it goin' then?' he asked.

Tommy shrugged his shoulders. 'Not bad, Frank. Trade's slow but it's the usual fing until the weavver brightens up,' he told him.

Frankie looked over the bar at Sammy. 'Give us the same again, an' put one in there fer Tommy,' he ordered.

Tommy felt it was useless to refuse the drink. Frankie would go on pressing him anyway. 'What about you?' he enquired.

The villain leaned his elbow on the counter, his eyes casting around the bar. 'Can't complain,' he said smiling. 'There's some business comin' up soon. I gotta take it while I can.'

Tommy knew the sort of business Frankie was referring to and he felt it good policy not to pursue the matter. 'I got a surprise visit the ovver evenin',' he said quietly.

'Don't tell me, let me guess,' Frankie replied, his face darkening.

Tommy raised his thick eyebrows. 'The same. She was the

last person I expected ter call on me. I thought she'd said goodbye ter Bermondsey fer ever.'

'Yer know she's back ter make trouble,' Franke said as he picked up his fresh drink.

'She didn't give me that impression,' Tommy lied. 'She just talked about Bob an' the old days. 'As she spoke ter you yet?'

'Yeah, she came in 'ere wiv that piss artist Rideout the ovver night an' made it clear she wanted ter talk,' Frankie growled. 'I don't like it. It could get all unnecessary.'

'I don't fink there's any cause ter worry,' Tommy went on, still putting on a front. 'We're talkin' about a lot o' years ago. I wouldn't fink there's anyfing she could pick up on.'

'Dolly's a very determined bitch,' Frankie reminded him. 'She's bin that way ever since I've known 'er, an' when she got 'er claws into our Bob she really come into 'er own. No, Tommy, I ain't underestimatin' the cow. I reckon she's gonna try an' make it as uncomfortable as possible, so just you be on yer guard.'

Tommy finished his drink and looked at the villain. 'Let me get yer one,' he offered.

Frankie shook his head. 'Nah, I'm in company,' he replied quickly. 'I just come over ter put yer in the picture.'

Tommy ordered another drink. It was unusual for him to have more than two pints at lunchtime but he needed to quell the nagging feeling in his insides. His options were diminishing, for only that morning Brandon's had withdrawn their offer to buy him out.

Dolly sat in the carriage deep in thought as the train rumbled towards the outskirts of London. She had been back to Westover to sort out a few things and now she felt that her links with the place that had been her home for over twelve years were finally severed. Her future was in Bermondsey now, and there were old scores to settle. The initial meeting with Grantham's, the investment brokers, had been a start and she had been pointed in the right direction.

The train pulled into Sidcup Station and the last of the other passengers in her compartment got out. Dolly glanced idly at the elderly man on sticks as he walked along the platform and was reminded of her own mortality. She was nearing fifty, widowed and facing an uncertain future. Coming back to Bermondsey was painful in many respects, though it had been nice to meet up again with Jimmy Rideout. He had rekindled a few happy memories when he jokingly told her that he had a thing about her. She had had a crush on him once. Jimmy had been a handsome young man in his youth, and he had certainly made her heart flutter. It had been a shock seeing him in such down-and-out circumstances, although he had assured her he was surviving. The war had scarred him, like so many of the young men she had known.

Dolly was still absorbed in her thoughts when the train pulled into London Bridge Station. The January evening was cold and damp, and there was a chill in the air as she walked out into the forecourt, pulling the collar of her heavy fawn coat up around her ears. She had been in Kent for three days, purposely staying at a small village pub a few miles away from Westover. Dennis Friar, the landlord of her old pub, and his wife had both wanted her to stay with them while she was in Kent, but Dolly had seen the danger signs. Dennis still looked at her in that secretive way he had, and it would have been terrible if his wife found out now about the fleeting moments of comfort they had once shared together.

A long flight of stone steps took Dolly down to St Thomas's Street and from there it was only a ten-minute walk to her rooms in Bermondsey Street. She had spent her time in Kent tying up a lot of loose ends and it had mostly been a very painful business. She was still left with a dull ache deep inside her that would not ease, and the thought of going back to her lonely lodgings and making tea was a prospect she did not relish. She felt a desperate need for company, for someone who could share a few light-hearted moments with her and bring a smile to her face. At the present time there was only one person who fitted the bill, and Dolly turned into Abbey Street and took a left into Fellmonger Street.

Chapter Twenty-Three

On Tuesday evening Albert Morgan put on his best suit, shirt and tie and then slipped into his dark blue Crombie overcoat, studying himself for a few moments in the wardrobe mirror before hurrying out into the damp night air. He caught a tram to Rotherhithe and before going into the hospital he bought a bunch of flowers from a stall outside the main gates.

''Ere we are, luvvy. The choice is limited this time o' year but they look nice an' presentable,' the big jovial woman told him with a broad smile. 'Fer someone special, is it?'

Albert nodded awkwardly and walked into the hospital carrying the flowers down at his side, as though they might spring up and bite him. The large wall clock said seven fifteen as he hurried down the long corridor and ran up the stone stairs to the first floor. The ward sister gave him a cautious smile as she blocked his path. 'Only two people are allowed round the beds, I'm afraid,' she said.

Albert stood wondering what to do. He looked along the ward and saw Don with Rose and another young woman with them. The three seemed to be chatting and suddenly Rose happened to glance in his direction. She said something to Don and then he stood up along with the young woman and the two of them came down the ward.

Don held out his hand. 'Glad yer made it, Alb,' he said as they shook hands. 'This is Alice, she's one of Rose's workmates.'

Alice gave him a smile and held out her hand. 'Pleased ter meet yer,' she said. 'Rose 'as bin expectin' yer. Try an' cheer 'er up.'

Albert gave Alice a puzzled look and turned to Don. 'Is she all right?' he asked quickly.

Don nodded. 'Yeah, but the welfare woman's bin in an' she's all worried.'

Albert felt embarrassed as he walked along the ward carrying the flowers at his side, and when he reached the bed he bent over and kissed Rose on the cheek. He caught a whiff of perfume and felt the smooth warmth of her skin. She looked up at him, flushed with excitement. 'I didn't fink yer was comin' in ter see me,' she said.

'I knew 'e would,' Maggie said with a wicked glint in her rheumy eyes. 'I can see jus' looking' at 'im that 'e's a nice boy. You are a good boy, ain't yer?'

Rose and Albert looked at each other and suddenly they both laughed aloud, and the young man shook his head slowly as he sat down beside the bed and took Rose's hand in his. 'This is just stupid,' he said.

'What is?' Rose asked him, suddenly frowning.

'Well, me 'avin' ter come in 'ere ter tell yer that I want yer, want ter marry yer.'

'If yer don't want to, yer don't 'ave to,' she replied quickly.

'No, yer don't understand,' Albert told her, sighing with frustration. 'Look, Rose. I've always wanted you, but I allowed fings ter get in the way. There was yer muvver. She sent me off wiv a flea in me ear. She said 'er daughter was too good fer a Morgan boy. I should 'ave took no notice an' tried ter see yer, but I didn't. I s'pose I thought maybe she was right. Us Morgans ain't exactly pillars o' society, are we? Then there was that night at the dance. It was the most wonderful night I can remember. Not just . . .'

Rose put her hand on his arm and turned to look at Maggie who was leaning almost out of her bed in an effort to follow the conversation. 'Maggie, why don't you turn over an' 'ave forty winks,' she said kindly.

The old lady pulled a face and slumped down in the pillows, closing her eyes compliantly, and Rose turned back to Albert. 'You was sayin'?' she prompted with a saucy smile playing on her lips.

Albert sighed as he reached out and squeezed her hand in his. 'That night at the dance was just great,' he continued. 'Not only us makin' love, but just bein' tergevver. It was the music, the dancin', an' me an' you jus' talkin' tergevver the way we did. It was the best night I've ever 'ad. I thought about it fer ages, but yer stopped comin' ter the club. I didn't know the real reason. I thought it was 'cos yer didn't wanna see me any more. I thought yer was angry an' upset that I took advantage of yer. P'raps I did, but . . .'

'No yer didn't, Albert. Like I said before, I wanted you just as much as you wanted me. Yer know the reason I 'ad ter stay away. Don's told yer all that. The problem fer me now is, I'm carryin' yer child inside me an' I can't see any way forward for us. I've got the family ter fink about. They need me, Albert.'

'I need yer, Rose,' he answered, his eyes burning into hers.

'But I'm the muvver ter those kids. I'm all they've got,' she said, squeezing the sheet in her hand.

'The baby yer carryin' is gonna need a farvver, Rose,' he appealed to her. 'Yer can't deny that, unless yer don't feel anyfing for me.'

'I do, Albert. I've thought about that night at the dance,

many times. You are special ter me an' I want yer, but what can I do?' she sighed.

'Look, I'm not askin' yer ter run away wiv me,' Albert said in a low voice. 'I wanna see yer, be wiv yer. I wanna be a part of yer. All right, I understand the way it is, but fings 'ave got a way o' workin' out. Don't ask me 'ow. Just let me inter yer life. Gimme the chance ter show yer 'ow much I love yer.'

Rose looked into his dark eyes for a moment and saw how sincere he was, and she leaned her head forward slowly until their lips met in a tender kiss, soft and thrilling. He could feel the passion in her warm lips and his heart leapt.

'I love you,' she whispered as they moved together.

'I love you too,' he told her.

Alice was coming along the ward and when she reached the bed she laid a hand on Albert's shoulder and smiled at Rose. 'Don's just told me about this feller. I feel like cryin',' she said, biting her lip. 'I'm so 'appy for yer.'

Rose leaned forward as Alice kissed her and they clasped hands.

'I'll see yer soon. I'll call round,' Alice said as she moved away from the bed.

Albert stood up. 'I'd better leave now. I'll send Don in,' he said, leaning towards her. This time Rose put her arms around him and their kiss was strong and vibrant. 'Love you,' he whispered as he backed away.

The incorrigible old lady turned over in her bed and smiled at Rose. 'Yer'll 'ave ter tell me all about it when the visitin's over,' she said, grinning slyly.

In a small room behind a delicatessen in the East End's Whitechapel Road five men sat around a clean-scrubbed wooden table that held a bottle of Scotch and five glasses. The thick-set man speaking was one of the two who had originally met with

Frankie in the Anchor public house before Christmas. John and Ernie Morgan sat listening intently, their eyes fixed on him. Frankie toyed with his half-empty glass, his eyes lowered as the man held forth.

'Now as I said before, and I can't impress it on you strongly enough, the success or failure of this operation depends on timing,' he told them. 'I mean timing to the second, in fact. There'll be no margin for error, however slight. Now then, gentlemen, let's go through it once more, shall we?'

The stranger in the group leaned forward over the table and clasped his hands together. He was of medium height and average build. His fair hair was receding and his high fore-head bore two small scars just below the hairline. His jaw was square and his small flat nose seemed out of place on his wide pale face, but the one feature which stood out was his eyes. They were very pale blue, almost colourless, and they were cold and menacing. The man spoke softly and confidently, looking at each of them in turn as he went over the plan.

'I'll be in Berkeley Street at four forty-five. At four fifty exactly I'll walk into the shop. I'll present this ring and ask if it can be made larger. When I think it's appropriate I'll take off my hat as the signal. While you boys keep the staff happy I'll take the proprietor into the back room and clear the safe. As soon as I give the word we fill the bags with the display items and leave the shop.'

The thick-set man nodded. 'Right. Mr Morgan?'

Frankie looked up. 'We'll be ready outside the wine merchants opposite. I watch fer the signal, then we go. We cover up our faces an' put on the gloves as we reach the shop an' me two boys take the assistants inter the back room, tie 'em up an' gag 'em. I turn the sign ter closed, drop the door shutter an' slide the bolts. I watch through the blinds until I spot the cab pull up, then I give the word ter leave on the signal from the cab passenger.'

The thick-set man nodded again. 'Good. Now you must be out of the shop by five o'clock exactly,' he said firmly. 'Whatever happens you must leave on time, regardless of how many trays you've managed to empty into the bags, or there could be a problem with the taxi. We don't want a fare to pinch our cab and leave us stranded, do we?'

The men around the table smiled and Frankie reached for the bottle of Scotch. 'Just one fing,' he said. 'S'posin' there's some concealed alarms, apart from the ones under the counter. One might get set off.'

The organiser smiled indulgently. 'Great care has gone into this operation, Mr Morgan,' he replied. 'We have the complete alarm system diagram. I can assure you that there are no secret alarms to trip us up. There's nothing to worry about on that score.'

'I've got one question,' John cut in. 'What if the taxi gets 'eld up in traffic? It could be jammed up at that time o' night.'

The organiser nodded. 'It's a consideration, but our driver is an expert. He'll judge the traffic and be in Berkeley Square in plenty of time. In the very unlikely event that he isn't, you must wait in the shop until he arrives. All right then. Any more questions?'

The Morgans finished their drinks and shook hands with the other two men, and when they left the delicatessen they went straight to a nearby pub for a drink.

John looked thoughtful as he sipped his beer. 'I didn't like the look o' that geezer,' he said to his father.

Frankie nodded. 'Yeah, there was somefink about the eyes,' he remarked. 'I just 'ope the jeweller don't try an' argue wiv 'im.'

Ernie was looking blank as usual, although he was actually

deep in thought, and it provoked a gibe from his brother. 'You wiv us, Ern?' he asked grinning.

'I was jus' finkin',' Ernie replied. 'We might be able ter slip a tray or two in our own pockets, as a sort o' bonus.'

'That's a thought,' John said, glancing at his father.

'Don't even fink about it,' Frankie told him quickly. 'We're not involved wiv mugs on this one. I bet that geezer's got eyes up 'is arse. We're gettin' a good payment so let's be satisfied.'

John nodded acquiescently. He thought it was unusual for his father to preach caution, but he had to admit that he was probably right. It wouldn't do to upset those sort of people.

Frankie sipped his beer in silence, his thoughts turning to the altercation with Albert. He had had to tell the organiser that he would be taking his son's place on the job and the man hadn't looked too happy at first. It had been settled though and Frankie felt that the meeting had gone off quite well. In the morning he was to call in at the delicatessen to collect one thousand pounds up front, and tomorrow evening was the off. Everything had to be perfect.

Alice Copeland waved goodbye to Don and stepped on to the number 82 bus that would take her over the bridges into Downtown. She sat thinking about the handsome young man she had got to know through her friendship with Rose and she smiled to herself, recalling his embarrassment when she slipped her arm through his as they were walking out of the hospital. He was obviously inexperienced where girls were concerned but he had tried to make her think otherwise. He had talked about going to the pictures together once Rose was out of hospital, and Alice wondered if he would steer her to the back seats and slip his arm around her during the performance. Boys usually did. He might steal a kiss or two, and then with a little encouragement he might get really passionate. It was nice to think about it, but she suddenly became afraid that Don might be put off asking her out once his sister warned him that she had a regular boyfriend. She had told Don herself that they were not seeing each other anymore, but she worried that he might not believe her. She wished now that she had been honest and told Rose the truth, that there was no man in her life, and never had been.

Alice was nearing nineteen, the second of two daughters born to Benjamin and Sarah Copeland, stalwarts of the Pentecostal church. Benjamin had ruled the household with a rod of iron, spurred on by his fervent belief in the certainty of salvation for him and his God-fearing family when the world came to an end in the very near future. There could be no normal childhood for Alice and Beatrice, her elder sister. They had to attend church regularly and study the scriptures at home, under their father's watchful eye. There could be no dirty boys visiting, no music, other than hymns and songs of praise, nor newspapers to spread and encourage wickedness and licentious behaviour. The world was on a downward spiral, said Benjamin, and the end was nigh.

Beatrice was two years older than Alice and just eighteen when she met Alan Moody, a young man who came to work in the City shipping office where Beatrice was employed as a typist. It was love at first sight, and when Beatrice tentatively broke the news to her parents about her romantic involvement Benjamin raised the roof. She had no right to form an attachment with anyone who was not a true believer.

The bond of love between the two young people was strong enough to prevail, and finally Beatrice made her decision. She left the family home and ran away with Alan, travelling with him to Gretna Green where they were married over a blacksmith's anvil. She had escaped from a harsh, miserable existence to lead a normal happy life, but for Alice the misery continued. There was badness in the blood. A wicked seed had been passed down and it must be purged, raved Benjamin.

One night he had gone unannounced into Alice's bedroom and caught her reading a copy of Emily Brontë's *Wuthering Heights,* and his anger knew no bounds. He took off his thick leather belt and beat Alice mercilessly, until even his docile and obedient wife felt compelled to intervene. The enraged patriarch then made them all kneel in the parlour while he asked forgiveness for his daughter's sins, praying for her to be raised from the depths of iniquity so that she might join them on the high place when the waters came to cover the earth and the fires of hell consumed the screaming damned.

Alice could stand it no more and she ran from the house, bleeding and terrified, making for the only sanctuary she could think of: Downtown and the home of her maternal grandmother, who had long sorrowed at her own daughter being brainwashed by that 'bible-punchin' maniac', as she described him. Now, almost a year later, Alice still lived with her ageing grandmother and loved her dearly, but she was very much aware of the void in her life. She had gone to work at Bromilow's factory and very soon learned the language and the ways of the factory girls. There was much time to be made up, and her freed spirit burned to spread its crumpled wings. She learned quickly and faced the harsh realities of life head on, but like Don Farran, Alice was inexperienced in the ways of love, and she was eager to bite on the forbidden fruit.

Chapter Twenty-Four

On Wednesday lunchtime Rose arrived home escorted by her neighbour Freda, who had taken her clothes into the hospital. Freda had tidied up her flat earlier and lit the gas fire to warm the room. She had also bought a few groceries and refused to take money for them. Rose felt a debt of gratitude to her kind and caring neighbour and realised how much more difficult things would have been without her help. Freda was always there to mind Susan or watch out for the two boys, and nothing seemed too much trouble.

The knock on the door startled Rose out of her reverie, and when she went to answer it she was surprised to see Dolly standing on the landing, breathing heavily from climbing the stairs.

'I must be gettin' old,' she joked.

'Come in, Dolly. I've just got in meself,' Rose replied, leading the way into the cosy living room.

Dolly unfastened her coat and sat herself down facing Rose. 'I 'ad ter come an' see yer,' she said. 'I 'eard from Jimmy Rideout that yer'd bin in 'ospital. 'E told me you was comin' out this mornin'. Are yer feelin' all right?'

'Yeah, I'm fine,' Rose assured her.

'Yer look pale. Mind yer it's ter be expected,' Dolly went on. 'Jimmy 'eard from the porter that yer'd cracked yer 'ead open. 'E told me when I popped in ter see 'im last night. I'd bin down ter my old pub ter sort a few fings out. Anyway, 'ow's the kids, an' Don?'

'They're all fine,' Rose replied.

Dolly loosened her scarf, feeling suddenly hot, and Rose stood up. 'Let me take yer coat,' she said. 'I'll put the kettle on.'

''Ere you sit yerself down. I'll make the tea,' Dolly said quickly. 'You need ter rest up a bit.'

Rose tried to object but Dolly was insistent. She quickly filled the iron kettle and set it over the gas jet, then she came back into the room and sat down again with a sigh. ''Ow yer goin' on fer money?' she asked. 'The firm'll 'ave ter pay yer while yer off sick, won't they?'

'We get 'alf pay fer sickness,' Rose replied.

'Yeah, but an accident's different,' Dolly told her. 'They're obliged ter pay full wages. Anyway look, there's a couple o' bob ter tide yer over,' she said, taking a couple of one-pound notes out of her handbag.

'No, I couldn't,' Rose protested. 'You can't afford that.'

'I can afford it, so put it in yer pocket,' Dolly pressed her.

'It's very good of yer,' Rose said gratefully.

'Fink nuffink of it. You're family after all. Sick or not, the rent's still got ter be paid,' Dolly reminded her.

Rose eased back in the chair. 'That's one fing we don't 'ave ter worry about,' she replied. 'Someone pays our rent every week. This old lady takes it ter the estate offices regular as clockwork. Whoever's payin' it don't want us ter know. The estate office 'ave been told not ter divulge who it is.'

'It's not yer muvver who pays the rent, is it?' Dolly asked.

'No. Our muvver couldn't pay the rent when she was 'ere,'

Rose told her. 'In fact she got us inter debt. When she left there was over a month's rent due.'

'That's strange,' Dolly said, looking thoughtful.

They lapsed into silence for a minute or two. 'Are yer still in rooms,' Rose asked eventually.

Dolly nodded. 'I ain't 'ad much time ter look around yet,' she replied, 'but it's all right where I am, fer the time bein'.'

'Don's bin ter the Council ter try an' get us a bigger place, but it don't look too 'opeful,' Rose told her. 'They gave 'im forms ter fill in an' they said it could be a couple o' years.'

'What about your landlord?' Dolly asked.

'Don went there as well. They said there was nuffink available yet an' the waitin' list is closed,' Rose replied.

'It must be difficult for yer,' Dolly said sympathetically. 'This flat's very small. What is it, two bedrooms?'

'Yeah. Don should 'ave 'is own room really. 'E sleeps in the front bedroom wiv the boys an' me an' Susan's got the small back bedroom,' Rose told her. 'C'mon, I'll show yer.'

The wind had dropped and rain had started to fall while the two women sat chatting in the cosy living room. Dolly had eased off her tight-fitting shoes and was feeling relaxed in Rose's company. She could not help thinking how like her father she was, though her colouring was fair while his had been dark. She could see that there was something on the young woman's mind.

Rose had now come to accept that it was useless trying to hide her condition any longer. The neighbours were talking and Dolly was going to find out before long, if she hadn't already heard.

'The welfare woman came ter see me while I was in the 'ospital,' she began, taking a deep breath. 'She said that Susan an' the boys would 'ave ter go inter care.'

'Why, 'cos you was in 'ospital?' Dolly queried, her eyes wide with surprise.

'No, it's more serious than that,' Rose said flatly. 'Yer see, Dolly, I'm pregnant.'

'I guessed it,' Dolly replied quickly. 'I 'ad that feelin' last time I called. I just sensed it.'

'Well, it's 'appened an' I'm not proud about it,' Rose continued. 'Trouble is it's the kids who's gonna suffer. The welfare woman told me they were gonna get a court order or somefing ter get the boys an' Susan fostered out. They said I couldn't manage ter look after 'em prop'ly, what wiv me own baby ter care for. Then there was the flat ter fink of. She told me that we were overcrowded.'

'What did you say?' Dolly asked her.

'What could I say, ovver than they was gonna 'ave ter fight me over those kids,' Rose replied, her voice quavering. 'I ain't lettin' 'em go, Dolly. Susan's still missin' our muvver an' I've just got 'er settled down. I can manage. I know it's gonna be 'ard, but I can manage.'

Dolly could see the tears welling up in her niece's eyes and she was so saddened that she could have burst into tears herself. 'What about the neighbours?' she asked. 'Would any of 'em 'elp out, even if it's just fer the time bein'?'

'Freda across the landin's bin really good an' she'd 'elp, but the welfare said it's not enough,' Rose explained. 'I dunno 'ow I'm gonna sort it all out. Gawd knows 'ow I'm gonna tell those kids.'

'It'll all work out, some'ow,' Dolly said, not knowing what she could say to comfort her.

Rose shook her head slowly. 'It's all my fault. Why did I 'ave ter get pregnant?' she sighed.

'Ter make the world go round, I s'pose,' Dolly replied.

'These fings 'appen. You're not the first one ter slip up, an' yer won't be the last, that's fer sure.'

'At first I thought about gettin' rid o' the baby, but I just couldn't,' Rose told her. 'Oh, I could 'ave 'ad an abortion or took some pills, but I couldn't bring meself ter do it. I know it would 'ave bin a way out, but it wasn't the answer as far as I was concerned.'

'What about the farvver?' Dolly asked her.

''E wants us ter get married but 'e knows the problems I've got,' Rose replied.

'D'yer love 'im?'

'Yes, I do.'

'Will 'e wait?'

'Yeah, I fink so.'

'Well, it's not all bad, luv,' Dolly said smiling. 'I got this feelin' that it's all gonna work out. You just mark my words.'

The Morgan family had been up and about early that Wednesday morning, and Annie knew instinctively that whatever they had planned to do, today was the day. Frankie was not his usual grumpy self at breakfast and John was brighter than usual. Ernie on the other hand was edgy, which was unlike him, and when they left together early in the afternoon they all looked very serious.

Annie busied herself about the house to take her mind off things. She had bought a few presents for her eldest son's children and a new hat and stockings for herself ready for her visit, stowing everything away out of Frankie's sight. She did not like telling him in advance when she planned an extended visit to her son, and why should she. Frankie and the boys never seemed to confide in her.

The day had been wet and dreary, and now that the winter's night was drawing in it became colder. People were hurrying about and the traffic was heavy in Piccadilly as John and Ernie Morgan crossed the main thoroughfare and turned into Berkeley Street. They did not go too quickly, and with their loose black mackintoshes and collars and ties they could have passed for everyday office or shop workers. Frankie walked behind them, keeping a good distance. He too wore a loose mackintosh, his hands stuffed in the pockets.

Up ahead the street looked comparatively clear of traffic and lights glimmered on the wet pavements. John and Ernie slowed down and ambled up to the wine merchant's shop on the right-hand side of the road, both seeming to take an interest in the bottles of French wines lying in the window. Out of the corners of their eyes they saw the jeweller's shop opposite, with the ornate sign over the window saying, 'Jameson's, Court Jewellers'. It was exactly four forty-four.

Frankie Morgan glanced at his watch and stopped to look at a smart red Bentley that was parked in the kerb, and then after a few moments he strolled on. He had seen their man coming along, wearing the disguise he had described at the briefing. He was stooped, leaning on a cane walking stick, and he had on a beige gaberdine topcoat and a tan fedora. His face was unrecognisable behind the full beard, bushy moustache and dark, thick-rimmed glasses.

The man reached the jeweller's shop, paused to glance at his wristwatch, then stepped inside. Frankie had to admire the man's coolness. He was obviously a professional.

The two Morgan boys had seen the man enter the shop and they turned their attention to the wines, waiting for the signal from their father as arranged. It was good planning, John thought. If anyone saw three men standing opposite a jeweller's shop with their eyes fixed on the window it would look suspicious. One man ambling along on his own and turning back to keep the window in view would not be so obvious.

'Do you young men like French wine? I think it's much more fruity than the Portuguese, don't you?'

The Morgans turned to eye the thin young man who had spoken to them in a cultured voice, and as John started to give him a sharp reply Ernie gripped his forearm. 'It's a matter o' taste, I s'pose,' he said, winking at his brother.

'It's all a matter of taste, dear,' the effeminate young man persisted, giving Ernie a sweet smile. 'Now me, I like a bit of rough, know what I mean?'

Ernie could hardly stop himself from laughing but his brother glared at the young man. 'You'll get some rough if yer don't piss off, Percy, right on yer poncy 'ooter.'

'Suit yourself, love,' the man said, looking peeved as he hurried away.

'Right, let's go!' Frankie hissed, leading his sons across the street.

They reached the shop, managed to slip on their black cotton masks and gloves without being noticed and went inside. They saw their man standing at the counter facing the two middle aged assistants and the jeweller himself, all three backed against the glass case looking terrified as they stared at the revolver in the thief's hand. John and Ernie hurried round the counter and seized the two assistants roughly by their coat collars, pulling them towards the back room.

'Door!' the leader spat out, galvanising Frankie into action.

The Morgan boys were busy trussing up their victims with the thin ropes they had brought with them when the gunman forced the elderly jeweller into the back room.

'Open the safe!'

'I–I can't,' the elderly man stuttered in terror.

'Pity. Now I'll count up to three so you've time to think again,' the gunman said in a calm, cold voice. 'Then I pull the trigger, all right? One, two . . .'

'All right, all right,' the jeweller gasped, bending down and spinning the tumblers with a shaking hand.

'You two fill the bags,' the man told the Morgan boys. 'Quickly now.'

John and Ernie hurried into the front of the shop, unbuttoning their mackintoshes to remove the canvas bags strapped to their bodies. Frankie took his eye away from the window just long enough to see the trays of rings and jewellery being quickly emptied, then he turned back and saw the taxi pull up a few yards past the shop. A tall, well-dressed man in an overcoat and trilby got out. It was all going like clockwork, he thought. Just as they planned.

When the elderly jeweller straightened up to pull open the safe door the gunman pushed him against the wall and pressed the gun in his spine. With his free hand he pulled open the heavy door and reached into the safe, took out a purple-coloured velvet bundle and slipped it inside his coat.

As he pulled the jeweller away from the wall by his coat collar the old man staggered forward and reached out to save himself by clasping a stool near the workbench. The gunman knew about the secret alarm button underneath the bench and smashed the butt of the revolver into the jeweller's head.

'Bloody old fool!' he growled, glancing quickly at his watch. 'Right, it's five o'clock exactly. That's it!'

Frankie suddenly saw the taxi fare raise his hat to the driver and turn to leave. 'Let's go!' he shouted, slipping the bolts.

The Bermondsey villain led the way, walking quickly to the waiting taxi. His two sons followed, the filled bags partly hidden under their unbuttoned topcoats. The gunman turned, closed the door and calmly tried the lock as a couple of office workers went by, then he walked to the taxi, still holding on to his cane walking stick.

The taxi pulled away and swung round Berkeley Square,

joining the throng of traffic that was making its way towards Oxford Street. After a few minutes it turned into a mews and parked outside a garage. The four robbers leapt out and hurried into the house next door, leaving the driver to manoeuvre the cab out of sight. Ten minutes later the vehicle was back in service, now with its correct registration and number plates. Fifteen minutes after arriving, Frankie and his two sons left the house at two-minute intervals and met up in the ticket hall of Oxford Circle underground station. The three men boarded a train to the Elephant and Castle, and when they arrived they ambled up into the street and went inside the Trocadera cinema. They had timed it just right. The newsreel was showing when they took their seats and they were able to watch the main feature from the beginning, having made sure that their ticket stubs were safely pocketed.

At five sharp the House went into recess and the Right Honourable Hamish MacKenzie MP, Under Secretary at the War Office, put on his overcoat, took down his bowler hat from the peg and set it on his head with a double tap of his fingers, something he had always done, then he removed his rolled umbrella from the rack and strolled into the Commons Yard. His official car was waiting, and having briefed his chauffeur he sat back comfortably against the luxurious upholstery as the limousine moved out into Parliament Square. The detour took fifteen minutes and at six o'clock that Wednesday evening the right honourable gentleman took his first-class seat on the express train to Inverness, smiling to himself as he put a hand to the left-hand side of his jacket and tapped the purple-coloured velvet bundle.

Chapter Twenty-Five

Albert Morgan first heard of the West End jewel robbery on the nine o'clock news while he was sitting chatting with his landlady Mrs Gorman in her comfortable parlour, and her immediate comment sent an icy shiver down his spine.

'Gawd, it makes yer fink, Albert,' she said as she turned off the wireless. 'The chances some people take. If that jeweller's man dies they'll get the rope when they're caught, an' they'll catch 'em all, yer can bet a pound to a pinch o' shit.'

Albert excused himself as soon as he could and went to his room. For some time he sat motionless on the edge of the bed, and as he stared out through the partly drawn curtains at the clear night sky he felt sick with fear. According to the report the elderly jeweller had been taken to hospital and was still in a critical condition after being brutally clubbed by one of the armed robbers. The haul had included the Cape Diamonds, and was estimated to be in excess of one hundred thousand pounds. The newsreader had gone on to say that the diamonds were a special collection that were to be set into a tiara for the Marchioness of Roxburgh, an old and esteemed customer of Jameson's.

The fact that it had been an armed robbery shocked Albert.

248

His father and brothers had never handled guns and it was very unlikely that they would have been persuaded to take them on a job. They had been recruited as heavies and if the estimated value of the haul was correct, treated like idiots, considering their share. If the jeweller died, his father and brothers would face the rope for just two thousand pounds.

He had been right about the raid. Right from the start he had had that strange feeling that something would go wrong. Perhaps he was being too pessimistic though. The report had said that the robbers had made a clean getaway and there were no witnesses. Hopefully the jeweller would recover and then in a few weeks' time all the fuss would die down and the raid would hardly be remembered.

Albert climbed into bed and lay for a while staring up at the ceiling. All he could do was be thankful that he was well out of it, he told himself. He had more important matters to think about now. He would see if his employer was ready to let him buy the business for a start. He had to get some money together quickly if he was to provide a home for Rose and the baby.

Albert turned on to his side but sleep would not come. He could see his father and brothers in his mind, and they were all looking at him with hate in their eyes. He saw his mother, and she was crying as they led her from the court. He heard a distant clock strike the hour and the mournful sound of a tug whistle, and he felt suddenly ice cold.

On Thursday morning all the newspapers carried the story of the West End jeweller's raid, and when Don Farran sat reading the story in the *Daily Mirror* during his morning break at the sawmills he immediately thought of what his friend Albert had told him. He had said that it was going to be something big, but this job had been carried out by real professionals, according to the account in the paper. This was surely too big for the Morgans to have been involved.

Try as he would, Don could not get the raid out of his mind, and he knew he would have to see Albert at his lodgings that evening to lay his doubts to rest. Albert would be worried sick if it was his father and brothers who had carried out the raid, considering the condition of the elderly jeweller.

When Don got home from work at ten minutes past five Rose was busy getting the evening meal prepared and she looked pale and drawn. He knew that the worry of the children being taken from her in the near future was obviously playing on her mind, and he could see that all three youngsters seemed to have sensed that something was wrong. Susan was standing beside Rose while she peeled the potatoes and the boys sat talking together quietly. Don picked Susan up and gave her a big cuddle but she seemed eager to go to Rose. The two boys would normally have come up to him with plenty to say for themselves but today they were unusually quiet.

It was later that evening when Rose told Don that she had let the children know about the baby. 'I 'ad ter tell 'em, Don,' she said with a sad sigh. 'Susan just looked at me an' I could see that it was all too much for 'er to understand, especially when I tried to explain that she'd be the baby's auntie. 'Ow do yer tell a kid that age?'

'What about the boys?' Don asked.

'Well, Joey said 'e wanted it ter be a boy, an' of course 'e asked a few awkward questions, like, "'Ow comes you're 'avin' a baby wivout bein' married?"' Rose said smiling briefly. 'I told 'im it 'appens ter some gels. What else could I say? Billy was the difficult one. 'E came right out wiv it. "Who's the baby's farvver?" he asked. I told 'im it was Albert Morgan an' the reason we weren't married was 'cos I 'ad ter look after the family till they were all grown up. Billy said ter me, "Why don't yer marry Albert an' let 'im come an' live 'ere?" I said there was no room, an' then I broke it to all of 'em as best I could about when the baby's born.' Rose paused and frowned, chewing her lip. 'I said that I'd 'ave ter get someone who was very nice ter look after 'em when I was gettin' ready to 'ave the baby an' then they could all come back 'ome after a few weeks.'

Don's face darkened at the painful thought of the children going away and he shook his head sadly. 'They must all be wonderin' just what's gonna 'appen to 'em,' he muttered. 'First their muvver runs off, an' now they're told that they're gonna go an' live wiv someone else.'

'I 'ad ter start preparin' 'em, Don. I couldn't leave it till it was all fixed up,' Rose replied, her eyes misting.

'Yeah, I know,' Don said softly. 'Yer doin' the right fing, but it seems so cruel ter take kids away from their own an' put 'em wiv strangers.'

'I just wish there was anuvver way out of all this, but there's not,' Rose sighed sadly. 'I can't stop 'em goin' if the welfare gets that court order.'

'If we could only get a bigger place it'd 'elp,' Don remarked. 'At least they couldn't get us fer overcrowdin'.'

'It's no use wishin',' Rose told him sharply. 'Yer've tried already. What was it the Council said, two years?'

Don slumped down in his armchair looking dejected and didn't answer. Rose glanced at him and felt suddenly sorry for her angry reply. None of this was his fault. Another brother might well have told her that the blame rested on her shoulders. It was her getting pregnant which had brought all this on the family. Don had never uttered an angry word against her and he had had to make sacrifices too.

'Don.'

'Yeah?'

'I'm sorry.'

'Sorry? What for?'

'Fer everyfing.'

'Don't be stupid.'

'But . . .'

'Now look,' he interrupted. 'When our muvver ran off an' the welfare came ter see us they could 'ave took Susan an' the boys away then, but they saw that you was capable o' lookin' after 'em. It was you what kept this family tergevver. What's 'appened since is jus' one o' those fings. It could 'ave 'appened to anybody. Even if the kids do get fostered it might only be fer a few weeks, like yer told 'em. Anyway it's not 'appened yet, Rose. P'raps somefing'll come up.'

'We're gonna need a miracle, Don,' she told him.

Don stood up and looked down at her. 'Miracles 'ave bin known to 'appen,' he said, going to the door and taking down his coat.

'Where you off to?' she asked.

'I'm gonna pop round an' see Albert, an' while I'm there I'm gonna tell 'im 'e's welcome ter call on yer,' Don chuckled. 'All right?'

Jimmy Rideout had spent some time attempting to smarten his flat up but Dolly's unexpected call on Tuesday evening had caught him in the middle of things. He had wanted to have the ceiling finished and the doors painted before she came round, but she had seemed impressed with his progress, which was encouraging. She had said she would call again on Thursday evening, and while Jimmy waited for her to arrive he decided to make good use of his time. He searched through the bundle of ironing that Muriel had left and found a white tablecloth, which he spread carefully over the paint-stained table. Next job was the lightshade, he told himself. Dolly had remarked on the bare electric light bulb hanging down from the ceiling, saying that a home looked poverty-stricken without a lightshade.

Jimmy unwrapped the pink-coloured glass shade he had bought that morning in the market, placing it carefully on the table before switching off the light and climbing up on to a chair. He reached into his pocket and took out a hand-kerchief to remove the hot bulb and at the same time grasped the bulb-holder with his other hand. Suddenly the chair moved and he arched backwards, pulling the wire flex and the rose from the ceiling in a shower of plaster. He managed to regain his balance on the rickety chair but when he saw the damage he had done he swore out loud. Dolly would be here soon and there was a gaping hole where the light-rose had been.

Jimmy got down carefully and scratched his head as he stared at the damage in the meagre light from the fire. He could see two wires hanging down from the hole in the ceiling and he realised that he had to think quickly. There was only one answer, he decided, and he got back on to the chair again and tied the two loose wires to the end of the light flex. At least the light was nearer the ceiling now. Taking care not to pull on the suspect knotted wire Jimmy fitted the glass shade to the bulb-holder and stood down to admire his work. It was fine, providing he did not switch the light on and short out the wires.

Fifteen minutes later when Dolly knocked on Jimmy's front door he was ready to greet her. He had cleared up the plaster on the floor, tidied the cushions, and added another few touches that he hoped would impress his visitor.

Dolly walked in and saw that the room was lit by candles. There was one standing in a saucer on the mantelshelf, another on the dresser, and a third in an enamel candle-holder at the centre of the table, which was covered with a spotless white linen tablecloth and adorned with a vase that held a spray of heather. Dolly looked up at the pink lightshade above the table and smiled with satisfaction. 'Jimmy, it looks very nice,' she purred. 'Tell me though. Why the candles?'

'Well, I thought it'd look more romantic,' he grinned.

'Now don't go gettin' any ideas,' she said, giving him a sideways glance. 'Flowers too, I see.'

'Yeah, I got 'em at the market. There was this ole gipsy woman an' she said a sprig of 'eavver would bring me luck, so I bought two,' Jimmy told her smiling.

'Why don't yer put the light on an' save the candles,' Dolly said, making for the light switch.

'No!' Jimmy shouted, quickly lowering his voice. 'It's better like this.'

Dolly sat down and kicked off her shoes, watching her host as he went to the sideboard and picked up a bottle of gin. He seemed a little nervous, she thought. And he had obviously taken pains to look clean and tidy. He had shaved and put on a crisp blue shirt, and his trousers looked freshly pressed. Muriel must have been very busy.

Jimmy came over to her with a glass of gin and lemon. 'There you are,' he said smiling. 'It's all right, I ain't swamped it.'

'Where's yours?' Dolly asked him.

'I'll 'ave one later,' he said quickly, sitting down facing her. 'What's new? Did yer manage ter see the accountant?'

'Yeah, I saw 'im, but I dunno, Jimmy,' she replied. 'I spent all that time down in Kent goin' frew Bob's ole papers an' it seems there still ain't enough ter go on.'

'But I thought yer said you almost 'ad enough on Morgan ter nail 'im good an' proper, an' there was only a few more bits an' pieces ter sort out,' Jimmy queried.

'Yeah I did, an' I honestly believed that once I got Bob's papers tergevver I'd 'ave all I needed ter go ter court,' Dolly said sighing. 'It's what my solicitor led me ter believe after 'e spoke wiv the accountant. Yer see, Bob took all the firm's account books and ledgers wiv 'im when we moved ter Kent. They were all stored in a garage be'ind the pub an' I spent hours sortin' 'em all out. I parcelled 'em all up in a tea-chest an' I 'ad it sent ter the accountant by van while I was still down there. When I saw the accountant this mornin' 'e told me 'e's bin all frew the papers an' stuff an' it still ain't enough ter go on. The trouble is, we need positive proof that Frankie was actually saltin' money away an' then puttin' it into anuvver company.'

'Yeah, but are yer sure Frankie Morgan did put money into anuvver company?' Jimmy asked. 'After all, yer've only got that feller's word fer it, the one who stayed at the pub that time.'

'I'm sure,' Dolly said emphatically. 'As I told yer before, Frankie's ole muvver was well taken care of by 'er 'usband before 'e died. She 'ad a tidy sum in 'er account, Bob vouched fer that. 'E saw the bank balance. Frankie 'ad access to it 'cos the ole lady was too infirm ter get ter the bank 'erself. She was also goin' a bit vacant in 'er old age an' it was quite easy fer Frankie ter take large amounts out over a period an' bank it in anuvver account. She wasn't any the wiser an' in 'er condition she wouldn't 'ave bin able to understand the bank statements anyway. No, Jimmy, I can't believe Frankie Morgan frittered all that amount away, an' why should the accountant lie ter Bob?'

'Well, where d'yer go from 'ere?' Jimmy asked.

For a few moments Dolly stared down at her clasped hands, then she looked up at him, her pale blue eyes wide and frank. 'As a matter o' fact I've decided ter put it all on the back burner,' she told him with a brief smile.

'After all the work yer put into it?' he queried.

'I didn't say I was gonna turn the gas out, Jimmy, it's just that I've come ter realise there's more important fings ter consider,' she said, a distant look appearing on her face.

'Like me an' you?' Jimmy asked, his face brightening.

'I'm talkin' about a young woman tryin' ter keep a family tergevver,' Dolly said quietly. 'I went ter see young Rose yesterday. She's pregnant.'

'Bloody 'ell!' Jimmy exclaimed.

'It seems the welfare found out an' they're gonna take the kids away from 'er,' Dolly told him.

'Poor little cow must be worried out of 'er mind,' Jimmy said, shaking his head sadly.

'I can't let 'em take those kids from 'er, Jimmy. They're my bruvver's kids, after all's said an' done,' Dolly reminded him.

'But what can you do?' Jimmy asked.

'I bin finkin' about that,' she replied. 'As a matter o' fact I've thought of little else since yesterday.'

Jimmy leaned forward in his chair and rested his hands on his knees. 'Don't tell me, Dolly, let me guess. You're gonna move in there.'

'I can't, they're overcrowded as it is,' she replied. 'But I am gonna make meself responsible fer that family. No one's gonna split 'em up, Jimmy. I won't let 'em.'

'What about the Council, or the estate office? Wouldn't they be able to 'elp?' Jimmy asked.

'Rose said they've already tried. There's nuffink at all,' Dolly told him.

Jimmy got up and took the empty glass from her. 'Let me get yer a top-up. Yer look like you could do wiv it,' he said smiling.

The candles burned low and Dolly began to feel more relaxed as the gin and lemon slowly took effect. Jimmy had poured himself only one drink and there was still some left in the bottom of his glass as he chatted away. She had to admire his self-control. He was making a bold effort in fighting his addiction, and he had worked hard to turn his shabby hovel into something resembling a home. She had found him easy to talk to and someone to whom she could unburden herself. He had made no secret of the fact that he still had a crush on her, but he had never once made her feel threatened in any way. Jimmy was a good man and she could do a lot worse, she thought.

'Will yer 'ave anuvver?' he asked her.

Dolly shook her head. 'Jimmy?'

'Yeah?'

'Yer won't mind if I ask yer a personal question, will yer?'

'O' course not.'

'Did yer change yer sheets like I told yer?'

'As a matter o' fact I got Muriel ter do a wash for me,' he replied grinning. 'I got clean sheets on the bed, clean pillowcases, an' what's more I got meself a nice new pair o' blankets from that shop in Long Lane you was tellin' me about. Why d'yer ask?'

'Well, ter be honest, Jimmy, I don't fancy goin' back ter that lonely flat o' mine ternight,' she said quietly.

Jimmy stood up quickly. 'Bloody 'ell!' he exclaimed. 'D'yer mind if I 'ave one?'

'It's your booze,' she said, giving him a warm smile, and as Jimmy walked over to the sideboard and reached for the bottle of gin she said, 'While yer there put a light on the subject, will yer?'

Without thinking he flipped the light switch and suddenly there was a bright flash and an explosion and the pink lightshade crashed down on to the table.

Dolly jumped out of her chair in fright. 'You can't do nuffink right, can yer?' she groaned.

Jimmy's face suddenly creased into a wide grin. 'Tell me in the mornin', darlin',' he said, holding out his arms to her.

*

As flashes of lightning split the night sky and the first heavy spots of rain hit the pavement, Gus Lazaar hurried up the few steps to the front door of number 5 Grafton Place, Paddington, glancing warily left and right along the deserted street as he let himself in. Gus prided himself on his training and experience of many tight situations and he did not need to be told that he was in jeopardy. His life was in danger, of that he was certain, and his every move from now on would need to be carefully thought out.

Gus climbed the carpeted stairs to his first-floor flat, and before he inserted his key in the Yale lock he unbuttoned his overcoat to allow himself quick access to his service revolver. The stocky man's ice-cold eyes widened with anticipation as he went inside, his hand hovering over the butt of his weapon that rested snugly in a shoulder holster. Everything looked as he had left it and he took the evening paper from his coat pocket and threw it on to the table before making a quick inspection of the bathroom and bedroom.

The organisation had contacted him on two previous occasions and each time he had been paid handsomely for his services. Two unsolved murders had been added to Scotland Yard's files and the organisation had been happy with his work. On this occasion he had been recruited for a special job and he had been required to work with others, something which had not pleased him. He was a loner and carried out his business in his own way and in his own time. The bonus agreed in excess of his usual high fee had been inducement enough, however, and Gus Lazaar had gone along with the arrangement. Now, however, he wished he had not compromised himself. The new story on the front page of the evening papers changed everything. Now things would move fast, and he had no intention of being offered up on a sacrificial altar to placate those in high places.

Gus poured himself a stiff brandy and sat down to check through his travel documents. The boarding particulars for passage to the Canary Islands on the Geest line banana boat, his passport and the visa all looked in order. He had received his payment in full, and only just in time to make his plans. The morning papers had fully covered the jewellery shop raid, but they had been too late to report fully on the story that was all over the evening editions. That morning it had just about made the stop press, but Gus had spotted it. It read, 'Express to Inverness derailed at Glenboig. Hamish MacKenzie MP reported to be amongst the badly injured.'

Chapter Twenty-Six

Rose Farran left the Buildings on Monday morning and hurried along Abbey Street, still dwelling on the past weekend. Albert had called round on Friday evening and he had looked very uncomfortable at first, but the children with their innocent curiosity had helped him settle down. Susan had been unusually talkative and even allowed herself to sit on his lap for a short while. The boys were a little reticent at first but Joey soon started chatting away and Billy joined in, bringing an embarrassed smile to Albert's face when he suddenly asked him if he was still going to marry Rose, and when. It had been a start, Rosie felt, smiling to herself as she recalled the hurried, self-conscious kiss Albert had given her at the front door when he left.

On Saturday evening Alice Copeland had called to see her and she had looked very smart in her fawn coat and high-heeled shoes. Her hair looked nice too, and she had obviously taken pains with her make-up, Rose thought. Don had been impressed, judging by the look in his eyes, and he had coloured quite a bit when he falteringly asked her if she fancied going to the pictures with him. Albert had called later that same evening and he had looked worried. They had discussed getting married as soon as possible, even though it meant that they would have to live apart until he could find a bigger place for them all. He had been very understanding about the way things were, and he had reproached himself for causing all the trouble in the first place. His considerate manner and the sad look on his handsome face had stirred something in Rose, and she felt a warm glow as she recalled how they had stood together in the quiet room and held each other close. Albert had kissed her tenderly and been nervous about holding her too tightly, until she reassured him that it wouldn't harm the baby inside her.

The morning sky was leaden and mist drifting in from the river hung in the damp air as Rose neared Dockhead, her mind still full of the weekend's events. Albert had seemed to have something troubling him, though his kisses had given her all the reassurance she needed. He had been very delicate with her and had restrained himself from caressing her in the way she wanted him to. She needed him to love her fully, and soon. She wanted him to take her, and help her to forget her cares and worries for just a few brief, wonderful moments in time. She wanted to show him just how much love she had in her heart for him and let him see that they could, and would, be happy together.

As Rose turned the corner she saw that something was wrong. There were people standing outside the factory entrance and a heated discussion seemed to be going on between some of the girls and two men who both wore dufflecoats. Other girls stood apart talking in small groups, and as Rose got nearer she could see that her friend Alice was leading the discussion.

'I don't care what yer say, we ain't goin' in till yer sort fings out once and fer all,' she said angrily to the two men.

'That's right, Alice, you tell 'em,' another girl shouted.

'What's 'appenin?' Rose asked the nearest girl as she reached the gates.

'They've sacked Alice,' she replied sharply. 'That bastard Collis told 'er soon as he walked frew the door this mornin'.'

'Who are they?' Rose asked, nodding towards the two men.

'They were 'ere first fing. They're from the union,' the girl told her. 'They're givin' out union papers fer us ter sign.'

As more workers arrived and heard the news the situation became more tense. Angry shouts grew louder. 'String the bastard up!' someone called out.

'One out, all out!' another shouted as two of the women moved to go into the factory. Workers blocked their way and there was a scuffle as one girl tried to attack the two women. Another girl came up to Rose. 'Collis saw the union men standin' outside when 'e came in this mornin' an' 'e took it out on Alice,' she said angrily. 'The ole git told 'er she was on the rollers fer good an' Alice told 'im ter get knotted. She said it was victimisation an' 'e sacked 'er there an' then.'

One of the men raised his arms in the air as he sought to restore order. 'Now listen, all of yer,' he shouted. 'The Transport an' General Workers Union ain't got no clout 'ere. The firm's non-union an' all we can do is seek ter get a dialogue goin' wiv yer employers. Now I'm askin' yer ter go ter work while we see what we can do.'

'What about Alice?' someone shouted out.

'We'll 'ave ter wait an' see if we can get a meetin' off the ground,' he told her. 'If we're successful we'll appeal ter the firm ter reinstate your colleague. That'll be our first priority, an' that's a promise.'

'Well, it ain't good enough,' a big woman shouted at the official as she barged her way to the front. 'I was 'ere at 'alf seven this mornin' an' you two was already givin' out those forms. If yer so anxious ter get us all enrolled in the union why don't yer go in there an' tell that slimy git Collis ter fink again. 'E's gorn too far this time an' we ain't budgin' from 'ere till yer tell 'im straight.'

Voices of approval greeted the woman's remarks but there was one dissenter. 'I can't afford ter stand out 'ere. I got no ole man ter fend fer me an' my kids,' a middle-aged woman said sharply.

The big woman turned to face her. 'Listen, luv. We all know 'ow that four-eyed git Collis takes it out on us fer every little fing. One day it might be your turn an' what's gonna 'appen then? I say we make a stand, 'cos if we don't we're all gonna suffer one way or the ovver.'

A chorus of approval went up and the official raised his hands again, a brief smile appearing on his face. 'All right, if that's yer answer I suggest yer sort out an organised picket an' the rest of yer move away from the factory,' he advised. 'Let's show 'em we're gonna do it right an' proper. We'll go in right now an' ask ter see the management. We'll meet 'ere at nine o'clock fer a report back. 'Ow's that sound?'

Once again voices were raised in support and spontaneous clapping broke out as the two men walked into the factory entrance.

Rose walked over to where Alice was talking to the big woman who had pressured the union men and saw that her friend's face was flushed with emotion. Alice gave her a welcome smile and raised her eyes to the sky comically. 'It seems I've caused a bit o' trouble this mornin',' she said sheepishly.

Rose laughed and took her arm. 'We've got an hour ter kill, let's go an' get a cuppa,' she suggested.

The two walked along the turning and turned into River Lane. Horse carts and lorries were parked beside the wharves and warehouses and dockworkers and car men exchanged curses and ribald comments as potentially dangerous man-oeuvres took place beneath cranes and pulley ropes. The mist was still drifting in from the river and there was a chill in the late January air as the two young women walked arm in arm to the street-corner cafe.

Corned beef Sam was busy buttering rounds of toast and he gave them a broad smile. 'No work this mornin', luvs?' he enquired in his camp voice.

'We're on strike,' Alice told him.

'You gels from the tin basher's?' Sam asked. 'I 'eard there was some trouble there.'

'Give us two large teas, Sam, an' no conversation please,' Alice said jokingly.

'Get 'er,' Sam said out loud, picking up the huge metal teapot and looking at the seated car men for effect. 'I dunno as I should serve troublemakers. Gawd knows what this country's comin' to what wiv one fing an' anuvver.'

Alice and Rose exchanged smiles as they took their mugs of tea and found a vacant table. The cafe felt warm after having stood outside the factory in the chill air and Rose found her face beginning to glow.

''Ow yer feelin'?' Alice asked as she sipped her steaming hot tea.

'I'm much better now,' Rose told her.

'What a day ter come back ter work,' Alice said. 'I was really surprised the gels acted the way they did. One of 'em 'eard ole cod's eyes tellin' me I was sacked as she come in an' it spread like anyfing. Before I knew it there was a group o' the early starters stoppin' all the gels as they arrived. Not one of 'em clocked in.'

'One o' the gels told me yer got sacked fer tellin' Collis ter get knotted,' Rose said.

'Well, it was words ter that effect,' Alice replied grinning. 'When Collis told me I was goin' on the rollers permanently I just saw red.'

'Did yer know the union men were gonna be at the factory this mornin'?' Rose asked.

Alice nodded. 'Yeah, an' it was a good job they were there. I've bin tryin' ter tell 'em what was 'appenin' at Bromilow's an' I'm sure they didn't believe me; well not everyfing I told 'em,' she said grinning.

Rose sipped her tea. 'Did you enjoy the pictures?' she asked after a while.

'Yeah, it was smashin',' Alice said enthusiastically. 'We went in the back seats an' Don put 'is arm round me. It was just like I expected it ter be. Don's really nice an' 'e finks the world o' you, Rose.'

'Yeah, I know, an' I love 'im too,' Rose replied, putting her mug down on the table. 'I wouldn't like 'im ter get 'urt, Alice,' she said gently.

Alice frowned and nodded. 'I wouldn't 'urt 'im,' she said quietly. 'I like 'im a lot.'

''E likes you too, 'e told me so,' Rose went on quietly. 'That's why I said about 'im gettin' 'urt.'

'We've arranged ter go out again on Friday,' Alice told her.

'What about yer regular boyfriend?' Rose asked.

Alice moved the empty mug over a wet patch on the table, her eyes averted from her friend's. 'I got a confession ter make, Rose,' she said in a low voice. 'I ain't got a regular boyfriend. I made 'im up. I just got niggled at all the gels talkin' about the fellers in their lives an' I didn't want any of 'em pokin' fun at me 'cos I didn't 'ave a feller. Yer know 'ow 'orrible they can get.'

Rose reached out and patted the back of her friend's hand. 'Yeah, I know,' she replied.

Alice smiled sadly. 'The trouble was my dad's a religious fanatic an' 'e made our lives a misery. When most gels were off out in the evenin's an' datin' fellers I 'ad ter stop in an' do the chores. Then I 'ad ter read the Bible every day. My farvver was ferever goin' on about the end o' the world comin' soon an' 'e scared the life out o' me an' my sister. She was older than me an' she'd met a nice feller where she worked. Anyway, one day, she just packed 'er bags an' ran away ter get married. I was left to answer fer 'er as well as meself. One day I'll tell yer the full story, but it ain't very nice, Rose.'

Rose looked into Alice's wide dark eyes and saw her struggling with her hidden pain. 'Don's a smashin' bruvver, an' 'e'll make a good 'usband fer some gel one day,' she said, trying to comfort her.

'I 'ope that gel's me,' Alice replied quickly, and seeing her friend's look of surprise she added, 'I know it's silly ter talk o' fings like marriage after only the first date, but I do like Don very much an' I want 'im ter be my steady feller, if 'e'll 'ave me. There's nuffink wrong wiv that, is there?'

Rose smiled warmly. 'No, there's nuffink wrong wiv that, Alice,' she answered. 'I 'ope it works out right for yer. Fing is though, our Don's gonna be called up soon as 'e's eighteen.'

'Yeah, I know,' Alice replied, looking downcast.

'Anyway, that's a year off an' maybe it'll all be squashed by then,' Rose said encouragingly.

Alice nodded and stared down at her tea for a few moments. 'What about you, Rose?' she asked. 'Does it worry you 'avin' ter get married so soon? Don told me you were intendin' to.'

'I'm nineteen in March,' Rose replied quickly. 'Anyway, it doesn't worry me in the slightest. Albert Morgan's a real nice feller, despite what all the neighbours fink. 'E's nineteen an' 'e's got a steady job.'

The cafe was beginning to fill up and the two young women left, Alice slipping her arm through Rose's as they walked quickly back to the Bromilow factory. The two union men were waiting outside and there was a buzz of expectation when one of the men beckoned the workers to gather round him.

'Firstly, we've made good progress an' the management 'ave agreed ter recognise the union,' he began. 'Secondly, the disputed job on the rollers is now gonna be done by men.'

'What about Alice Copeland?' the big woman butted in.

The union man looked around at the women before replying. 'Alice Copeland was sacked fer insubordination,' he said. 'I'm afraid we've got a problem there.'

'Insubordination, my arse,' the woman shouted. 'She told that no-good whoreson what ter do wiv the roller job. Any one of us would 'ave done the same. If the union let the firm get away wiv this we might as well not bovver ter join.'

'Listen,' the union official said in a loud voice. 'Fer the moment, Alice Copeland is suspended pendin' an enquiry. We'll be sittin' in on it, an' I can assure yer that we'll be puttin' pressure on the firm regardin' what we consider ter be a clear case o' victimisation. Now my advice is fer you all ter return ter work an' let us do our bit ter get Alice reinstated.'

At nine fifteen the Bromilow workforce marched into the factory feeling that they had won the first round. Bernard Collis looked unusually subdued as he allotted the daily tasks to the women, and Nora Collins, the big woman who had spoken up for Alice, was unusually confident as she faced the works manager. 'I 'ope yer not gonna make trouble over Alice,' she said pointedly. 'We've got union backin' now, let me tell yer.'

Collis ignored the remark but his face darkened in anger. He was due to see the directors later that morning to explain fully his decision to sack Alice and he did not relish the prospect. The factory women were a lazy, ignorant lot, in his opinion, and half of them deserved to be sacked.

*

The weekend had been very nice, as far as Jimmy Rideout was concerned. Dolly had called round on Saturday evening and the two of them had gone to the Anchor for a couple of drinks, and then, after a fish-and-chip supper in 'Old Joe's', at the Bricklayer's Arms Jimmy had invited Dolly back to his place for a nightcap. She had spent the night with him and he had been at pains to convince her that he was the right man for her, holding her in his arms and listening patiently as she unburdened herself. He knew full well that she still grieved for her dead husband and worried about how best to help the Farrans, but Jimmy was happy to think that by listening he was sharing her pain, anxieties and fears. He also knew that behind the hard shell and tough image there was a soft, warm and loving person who had much to offer.

'I don't remember seein' you in 'ere before.'

Jimmy looked up from the table and saw Tommy Caulfield standing over him. 'No, I always used ter use the public bar, but I don't like the company in there these days,' he replied quickly.

'Mind if I sit down?' Tommy asked.

'Take a seat, Tommy. 'Ow yer doin'?'

'No so bad. 'Ow are you? Yer looked deep in thought.'

Jimmy smiled. 'I was enjoyin' it, mate.'

'I 'eard you an' Dolly are keepin' company,' Tommy said.

'You 'eard right, ole son.'

'Good fer you. She's the best.'

'Don't I know it,' Jimmy said with a wink and a sideways nod of his head.

Tommy sipped his beer thoughtfully then he put the glass down on the polished table and folded his arms. 'I can understand yer not fancyin' the public bar after the turnout you 'ad wiv the Morgan boys,' he begun, 'but yer can't get away from the family so easy, can yer. Frankie uses this bar.'

'Yeah, I know,' Jimmy replied, 'but 'e keeps 'is own company. 'E don't trouble me. I might 'ave changed bars, but I certainly ain't changin' pubs just fer that pile o' shite.'

Tommy nodded and took another sip from his glass. 'Frankie ain't one o' Dolly's favourites eivver,' he went on. 'The word is she's out fer blood. I'd tell 'er ter play it very careful if I was you, Jimmy.'

'Yer've no need ter worry on that score,' Jimmy replied. 'Dolly's got ovver fings on 'er mind at the moment. She's concerned about the Farrans. Young Rose got 'erself pregnant an' it looks like the kids are gonna be took away from 'er.'

'I'm sorry to 'ear it,' Tommy said. 'Still there's not a lot Dolly can do, is there?'

'The Farrans are 'er bruvver's kids an' she's made 'erself responsible,' Jimmy told him. 'Dolly's lookin' fer a bigger place an' then she'll move in an' take over. That way she can keep the family tergevver. That's our Dolly.'

'What's the chances?' Tommy asked.

'Not a lot, if you ask me,' Jimmy replied. 'The Council's got a waitin' list as long as yer arm an' there's no private places available.'

'There's no room where the family's livin' now then?'

'Bloody 'ell, Tommy, they've only got two bedrooms as it is,' Jimmy said indignantly. 'That's part o' the trouble. The welfare told young Rose that what wiv a new baby an' all they'd 'ave ter take the kids away. It's a real mess.'

Tommy Caulfield shook his head and quickly finished his drink. 'Well, I'd better get back ter the yard,' he said. 'Can I get yer one before I go?'

Jimmy waved his hand. 'No fanks, mate, I'm takin' it easy these days.'

The cartage contractor left the pub and strolled back to the yard office, his mind working overtime. The chance meeting with Jimmy Rideout had started him thinking. A short time ago, when Dolly first made her appearance, he had realised that once she started her delving it would only be a matter of time before his complicity with Frankie Morgan was discovered. He had had to consider his options and one of them was to sell his business and move away from the area. When the prospective buyer pulled out of the deal he had been left with little room for manoeuvre, but now there was another possibility he could consider. It was not an ideal solution for him, but as he walked into the yard and sat down heavily in his office chair Tommy reminded himself sagely that a drowning man clutches at any straws. He raised a cynical smile too, as he recalled another old adage. You don't bite the hand that feeds you.

Chapter Twenty-Seven

On Monday afternoon after school Billy and Joey Farran sat down in their front room to discuss the current situation. It did not take them long to decide that with the way things were going they should run away before they were taken away.

'What about Susan?' Joey asked. 'We can't leave 'er 'ere on 'er own. S'posin' she burns 'erself in the fire or sets the place alight.'

'We'll take 'er wiv us, stupid,' Billy replied quickly.

'Yeah, but she can't walk very far wivout gettin' tired, an' she don't like ter be out in the dark,' Joey reminded him.

'Look, I got it all planned,' Billy said, his eyes wide with excitement. 'Termorrer afternoon I'll cut some bread an' marge as soon as we get in an' you fill that empty medicine bottle wiv water. I've got a tanner in me money box so we'll take 'alf a crown out o' the teapot an' that'll do fer fares, an' then we'll go ter London Bridge an' get the train ter Kent.'

'That's stealin',' Joey told him. 'Rose said we mustn't never touch that money 'cos it's fer food.'

'I know that,' Billy said quickly, 'but this is different. Rose wouldn't like us ter run away wiv nuffink, would she?'

'I shouldn't fink so,' Joey answered.

'We'll get two one-an'-sixes an' I'll carry Susan. We won't 'ave ter pay for 'er that way.'

'We could 'ide 'er under the seat,' Joey suggested.

'Yeah, we could,' Billy said brightly.

''Ere, what we goin' ter Kent for?' Joey asked suddenly.

'Well, there's fousands o' Gypsies in Kent,' Billy told him. 'Charlie Barker said so. 'E goes down 'oppin' every year. The Gypsies live in smashin' caravans an' they take yer in if yer run away from 'ome.'

'I still fink Susan's gonna cry when we tell 'er we're runnin' away,' Joey said, shaking his head.

'We ain't gonna tell 'er we're runnin' away, stupid,' Billy went on. 'We're just gonna tell 'er we're goin' on 'oliday fer a week.'

'What about food? We can't live on two slices o' bread an' marge fer a week,' Joey reminded him.

'The Gypsies feed yer. They got stewpots an' they cook their dinner over a fire, just like the cowboys an' indians,' Billy told him.

'But we ain't got no money, so 'ow we gonna pay 'em?' Joey asked.

'Yer don't 'ave ter pay 'em. Yer just 'ave ter make pegs an' pick flowers so the Gypsy ladies can go roun' door-knockin',' Billy explained.

''Ow d'yer know all this?'

'Charlie told me.'

'Charlie Barker tells fibs.'

'Yeah, but not about fings like Gypsies. Charlie went ter live wiv 'em once.'

'Cor!'

'Yeah, an' 'e can make pegs quick as anyfing. I see 'im do it.'

'What, make pegs?'

'Yeah, wiv a Tarzan knife that 'e brought ter school.'

'Wish I 'ad a Tarzan knife,' Joey sighed.

Susan walked in from her bedroom cuddling her favourite doll. 'Dolly's sick,' she said sadly.

'Never mind, we're going on 'oliday termorrer after school,' Billy told her, winking at Joey.

'All of us?' Susan asked excitedly.

'No, just us,' Billy told her. 'We're only goin' fer a week. We're gonna live wiv the Gypsies.'

Susan looked wide-eyed at the boys. 'Those ladies who come round knockin' at doors wiv flowers are Gypsies. Rose told me,' she said.

'Yer mustn't say anyfing about us goin' ter Rose or Don,' Billy warned her.

'Did Rose say we couldn't go?' Susan asked.

'Yeah, but she won't mind. Yer mustn't say anyfing though. Promise,' Billy said.

'I promise.'

'If yer breaks yer promise yer tongue'll go black,' Joey reminded her.

Susan looked tearful and Joey puffed loudly. 'Yer shouldn't 'ave told 'er till termorrer,' he moaned at his brother.

'It's your fault fer talkin' rubbish,' Billy countered.

'We won't starve even if the Gypsies don't give us any food,' Joey said cheerfully. 'We can go scrumpin' an' light a fire ter keep warm.'

'Yeah, we'll 'ave ter take matches,' Billy told them.

Susan looked up at him. 'Can I take dolly?' she asked.

'Yeah, if she's feelin' better.'

'I'm gonna make a catapult an' shoot rabbits. We can cook 'em over the fire,' Joey said, sighting an imaginary rabbit and pulling back on his invisible sling.

Susan disappeared into her bedroom to tuck her doll up for

the night and the two boys sat talking about the coming adventure. Billy was beginning to have doubts about taking Susan with them, and Joey was having second thoughts about going himself. He had heard strange tales about the Gypsies and the curses they were supposed to cast on people, and children never being seen again . . .

'If we decide it's too cold termorrer we could always go the next day,' Billy said after a long silence.

'Yeah, it might be too cold termorrer,' Joey replied.

'I don't like spiders,' Billy said. 'Trouble is there's fousands o' spiders in the country.'

'I bet there's 'undreds o' fousands in Kent,' Joey remarked.

'Charlie said there's snakes too,' Billy told him.

'I don't fink it'll be warm enough ter go termorrer.'

'No, nor do I.'

'We could go next week.'

'Or in the summer.'

'Yeah, it's best in the summer.'

Late on Monday evening Gus Lazaar buttoned up his trench coat and picked up his canvas grip-bag and suitcase, looking around the flat for the last time as he patted the comforting bulge in his breast pocket. The ship was sailing on the midnight tide and it was essential that he boarded as late as possible to avoid waiting too long in the customs shed at the quayside. Lazaar left the flat and hurried down the few stairs into the dark street. It was deserted, with a welcome mist beginning to thicken, and the fugitive smiled to himself as he thought about the prospect of a leisurely few weeks in the sunny Canary Islands. The organisation's men would already be scouring his various London haunts in their search for him, and if Lady Luck continued to smile on him a little longer he would soon be enjoying a stiff drink as the Geest banana boat sailed out of London and down the estuary into the English Channel.

Gus Lazaar walked the length of the quiet street and turned into Praed Street, feeling exposed beneath the bright street-lights, but he was soon sitting comfortably in a taxicab as it journeyed across London to New Fresh Wharf at the foot of London Bridge. So far so good, he thought. He had been very careful about his travel plans. All the arrangements had been made from a call-box and he had only visited the travel agents once to pay for his passage and collect the ticket.

The traffic was heavy around Marble Arch and the fugitive looked out of the window at the gathering fog and felt reassured. He leaned back against the leather seat as the taxi drove into Park Lane and took a Gold Flake from a silver cigarette case. It would be extremely difficult for anyone to follow him in this traffic and with the fog closing in, he thought. It would be unlikely anyway. He had been very careful to stay off the streets as much as possible during his short stay in Paddington, though he had slept with his revolver under the pillow. The men who had hired him were professionals, and it did not do to underestimate them.

The taxi rounded Hyde Park Corner and turned into the park, a short cut to Westminster Bridge and the Embankment. The road behind was clear and Gus Lazaar puffed on his Gold Flake as he thought about the freak accident involving the night train to Inverness and its perilous consequences. The evening papers had first reported that the derailment had claimed seven lives, including those of the train driver and fireman, and that the accident had been caused by a sudden landslip as the train passed through a cutting near Glenboig. The latest news in the *Evening Standard* was that another person had died as a result of injuries but Hamish MacKenzie MP had regained consciousness, though he was still in a critical condition. Gus knew that the organisation would go to any lengths to ensure that they were not implicated in the robbery and would stop at nothing to get him. He had passed over the Cape Diamonds to the Minister of State and knew too much to be allowed to live. It was different with the Bermondsey gang. They were just stupid thugs who would no doubt be turned in to the police to keep people happy, especially now that the police had recovered the diamonds. If, as seemed likely, the eminent Minister of State at the War Office pulled through, then big wheels would inevitably start to turn, and in due course Hamish MacKenzie would retire from politics to concentrate on farming at his country estate.

The taxicab moved steadily along the Embankment and into the deserted City streets. Gus looked at his wristwatch. It was ten forty-five. At the end of Cannon Street the driver turned right and took a sharp left into Billingsgate fish market. Up ahead was the main entrance to New Fresh Wharf and the fugitive ordered the driver to stop at the gates. As the car passed the corner Lazaar noticed the scruffily dressed men standing round a flaring brazier a few yards along Lower Thames Street and he felt a strange twinge of pity for them, grateful that he did not share their fate: penny-up-the-hill men, down-and-outs who earned a few shillings a week by helping to push the laden barrows of the Billingsgate fish porters, sleeping rough at night in the alleyways that wormed all through the area.

Charles Emberson pulled the collar of his tattered overcoat up against the cold night air and warmed his hands over the brazier. He had worked for the organisation for more than ten years as bag-man, negotiator and go-between, and it was he who had first met with Frankie Morgan and his sons. Emberson was used to arranging meetings and recruiting particular individuals on behalf of his employers and he had long ceased to be amazed at their power and influence. The organisation had a dossier on all those who were involved with them and it had come as no surprise to him during his morning briefing to be told that Gus Lazaar was planning to flee the country that same evening. His name was on the passenger list of the Geest line ship now lying berthed at New Fresh Wharf and Emberson had guessed rightly that the information had come from a dockside source, most probably the captain himself.

Emberson shuddered in his old clothes and scratched beneath his tattered and greasy trilby hat. To all intents and purposes he was just another lost soul who worked for pennies by pushing the laden fish barrows up the steep cobbled hills of the market, another piece of flotsam who had come along to the communal brazier to warm himself. The bag-man did not expect to be challenged by the down-and-outs. They were only too glad to share their fire, as long as any newcomer preserved the protocol of silence.

Emberson stood staring down at the flaring wood and watched out of the corner of his eye as the heavily built man approached the brazier. He was humming tunelessly to himself and as he reached the fire he looked directly at the tram ticket which was protruding from the bag-man's scruffy trilby. The newcomer's cold eyes flickered a recognition, and a faint smile creased his lips as he took a tram ticket from his pocket and threw it into the fire. In answer Emberson casually removed the ticket from his hat and threw it among the flames, briefly returning the smile.

Twenty minutes later a taxicab pulled up outside the wharf gates and Emberson's sharp eye spotted the fugitive alight and slide out his luggage from beside the driver. As the cab drew away the bag-man mumbled a few words into the ear of the man standing next to him and then immediately walked away in the direction of London Bridge. Emberson was quite happy to be going home after the evening vigil. He was shivering with more than the cold and he was eager to put a few miles between him and the damp, evil-smelling fish market.

The man Emberson had identified paused for a few seconds at the gate while he buttoned up his fawn overcoat, then he picked up the suitcase and walked into the yard. Directly ahead was the customs shed and he could see passengers standing in line at the far end where two customs officers were busy examining passports. As he started to walk towards the shed Gus Lazaar suddenly noticed a scruffy-looking individual walk out of the shadows a few yards to his left.

'Got a few coppers fer a cup o' tea, guv?' the man asked him.

The fugitive put down his suitcase and made to slip his hand inside his trench coat pocket. It was then that the bullet hit him squarely between the eyes and he sank down in a heap.

Tommy Caulfield was lost in his thoughts as he walked steadily towards his house off the New Kent Road on that cold, damp Monday evening. What had happened in the past could not be undone and it was no good dwelling on it, he told himself. Times had been hard then and he had seen a way to get out of the miserable existence that was grinding him down. Doris had been dragging her heels over his proposal of marriage and had told him in no uncertain terms that she wanted more out of life than being stuck in poverty as wife to a skin dresser. The chance of going into the cartage business came out of the blue and he had approached the banks for the necessary capital, only to be refused. It was then that Frankie Morgan had come up with his proposal.

Tommy sighed to himself as he recalled that evening in the Anchor. Frankie and some of his cronies were drinking in the public bar and the villain had chanced to remark on his downtrodden look. Tommy confided in him and Frankie was quick to capitalise. He made an offer which was too good to refuse and with his financial backing the transport business was founded. Frankie went in as a silent partner with money which belonged to his own family. He had explained quite openly at the time that the cooperage concern was being managed by his brother Bob who was keen to plough in all the available money to build up the business. A profitable return for the investment would take a few years and Frankie was not prepared to wait. Through Tommy he had seen a more lucrative way of using his mother's inheritance.

Tommy recalled the struggle he had had providing Frankie Morgan with his expected cut every week, though he had managed somehow. The war years had seen his business grow and during that time the villain had been convicted of black market dealings and sentenced to three years' imprisonment. On his release Frankie had sought to raise money for a new venture and agreed to sell his share of the business. The contractor remembered how good it had felt to be his own man once more, and only last summer he had paid the final loan instalment to the bank. The guilt persisted, however, for Tommy knew full well that while he had been getting his firm off the ground another firm had floundered because of him.

As he reached his front door and took out his key the contractor smiled to himself. He would not say anything to Doris about what he was planning. She was not aware of his past shady dealings, and if his new idea was successful, and there was no reason why it shouldn't be, then she need never know.

Chapter Twenty-Eight

On Tuesday morning the union met with the directors of Bromilow's and agreement was reached which allowed the firm's workforce to become members of the Transport and General Workers' Union. There had been no serious differences to hold up the decision, and the directorate had been quick to state that Bromilow's paid tuppence an hour more than their local business rivals. They also pointed out that there was a canteen available for the workers and all the machines had safety-guards and emergency stopping-devices in place.

The local branch secretary and convenor felt obliged to praise the efforts of the company in providing good conditions for their workers, and then they set about the outstanding item of business.

'It appears, from the information we've gavvered, that your shopfloor manager provoked the suspended worker inter makin' a rude remark,' the convenor began.

George Penrose, the technical services director, hid a smile as he nodded. 'Alice Copeland, the young woman in question, told him to get knotted, as I understand,' he said.

''Ardly a sackin' offence, surely,' the convenor replied quickly. 'I've 'eard worse language in offices.'

'Copeland also made a further remark,' Philip Bromilow, the managing director, cut in.

'Oh?'

'Apparently Copeland called Collis a four-eyed old git,' Penrose said for him, unable to resist it.

'Her remarks were seen as a refusal to carry out a daily task,' the managing director added.

'A task which 'as since been agreed as unsuitable fer women, and which is now bein' carried out by men,' the other union man replied.

'That's beside the point,' Bromilow told him. 'The woman in question also has a bad attendance record. She's been repeatedly warned about her lateness.'

'I understand that Alice Copeland lives Downtown,' the convenor went on. 'I'd appreciate it if you'd supply us wiv lateness records for all yer ovver workers who live Downtown. We all know about the delays due ter the bridges goin' up at all times.'

George Penrose raised his hand. 'I think we can dispense with that,' he said quickly. 'Alice Copeland was suspended by our manager for insubordination.'

The convenor leaned forward, his eyes suddenly narrowing. 'I beg ter differ,' he said firmly. 'Our union feels that Alice Copeland was suspended 'cos she was active in seekin' union recognition. Collis used 'er remark as an excuse ter suspend her. I fink we need ter look at the attitude of your manager.'

'Bernard Collis has been here ever since he was a lad and he has worked his way up from the shopfloor,' Bromilow countered. 'As far as we are concerned he is efficient and fair-minded, and he knows his job backwards.'

George Penrose hid his displeasure at the managing director's defence of Bernard Collis but he refrained from joining the rest of the directors who were nodding their approval. He disliked the shopfloor manager intensely and wanted to see the back of him.

'I feel that I may be in some way to blame for what has happened,' he said quietly. 'Mr Collis has been under a lot of pressure lately and I feel that I should have made it my duty to be more involved in the day-to-day running of the company at shopfloor level. I think it'll be a good idea if I liaise with Mr Collis on practical shopfloor matters in future. It'll certainly lighten his workload.'

Heads nodded and the managing director stared along the table at his technical director. It was a smart move, he thought. Like Collis, George Penrose had risen through the ranks and he was never happier than when he was involved on the shopfloor. 'I think we can discuss that matter at our monthly meeting,' he said, looking around the table.

'Which brings us ter the suspension,' the convenor cut in. 'Can we suggest that we 'ave a clean start by you agreein' ter reinstate Miss Copeland?'

Philip Bromilow looked around at his associates and seeing no obvious objections he nodded his head. 'I think we can afford to be magnanimous on this occasion,' he said tartly.

The convenor knew from long experience of sitting round negotiation tables that for his union to be taken seriously they could not afford to adopt the cap-in-hand approach. 'I fink sensible would be a better word,' he replied. 'None of us want ter see pickets outside yer gates.'

George Penrose clasped his hands on the table. 'I hope we can have a sensible working relationship,' he said quietly, wishing to defuse any bad feelings around the table.

The convenor leaned down to retrieve his briefcase before getting up. Then he looked around at the directors. 'I'm sure we can,' he replied, glancing quickly at his colleague. 'Good day, gentlemen.'

On Tuesday morning Tommy Caulfield saw Fred Albury going into the end block to switch off the landing gas lamps and he hurried across the street. 'If yer see Jimmy Rideout tell 'im ter pop in an' see me, will yer, Fred?' he asked.

The porter of Imperial Buildings was never very talkative early in the morning and he merely nodded. He had a busy day in front of him and he did not relish the jobs in hand. There were two tap-washers to change and there was that leak in Ethel Price's back bedroom. On top of that Ivy Campbell had nagged him again about her stiff front-room window although he was at a loss to understand why the woman should be bothering about it, the weather being the way it was. Fred persevered with this task nevertheless, and it was early afternoon before he had a chance to knock at Jimmy's flat with Tommy Caulfield's message.

The contractor had been hard at work all morning and into the afternoon and when Jimmy walked into the yard he had just about sorted things out. 'Jimmy, I want yer ter take a look at my store rooms,' he said.

'What for?' Jimmy asked, looking puzzled.

'Just come wiv me,' he said mysteriously.

Ten minutes later the two men sat down together in the yard office to talk further, and when Jimmy left the yard he was whistling happily.

In the Farran household that evening everything seemed to be going wrong. Billy and Joey, having decided that the weather was still much too cold for rabbit-hunting and scrumping in Kent, started to sort out their books, toy soldiers and various other bits and pieces. Rose had decided to sew a button on Susan's freshly laundered dress while the tea was cooking, and she was scolding the boys for making a mess when Don walked in from work carrying a bundle of wood offcuts. The boys suddenly became involved in a heated argument over who owned what and Susan, tiring of playing nurse to her sick doll, went over to the table and started fishing into Rose's needlework box for pretty buttons.

'Don, don't leave that wood there, it's in the way,' Rose groaned.

'I'll give yer a bunch o' fives if yer don't gimme that book back,' Joey shouted at Billy.

'Where can I put this wood then, Rose?' Don asked, scratching his head.

'I don't know, do I. Billy, give that book back. Susan, stop pullin' my box ter pieces. Joey, stop tuggin' on that book or yer'll tear it,' Rose went on, her voice rising at each reprimand.

Don picked up the bundle of wood and the string broke, which set the two boys into fits of laughter. Seeing that her big sister had been distracted, Susan delved deeper into the needlework box for more coloured buttons and promptly pricked her finger on a loose needle. She burst into tears and at that moment the potato pot boiled over.

'Fer goodness' sake, stop that cryin'!' Rose shouted as she dashed into the tiny scullery to turn off the gas.

The loud rat-tat startled them, and when Don opened the door he saw Peggy Grant, the welfare visitor, standing there looking very concerned.

Don stepped back to let her enter, a hostile look on his face, and Rose came out of the scullery looking very agitated with her cheeks flushed. 'I'm sorry, but yer've come at an awkward time,' she said flatly.

'I seem to have done,' the officer said quickly, stepping over the pile of offcuts in an exaggerated manner.

Susan was still whimpering and the two boys were glaring at each other and pulling faces as the officer walked into the front room.

'Is that gas I can smell?' she asked.

'Yeah, the taters just boiled over,' Don said quickly.

'Look, I won't stop,' the welfare woman said, already feeling uncomfortable in the heat of the flat. 'I've just come to say that I think we've found a nice couple for Susan. I'd like you to take your sister to see them as soon as possible. Can we make some arrangements now?'

Rose hesitated but Don was ready with an answer. 'No, we can't,' he said sharply. 'Yer can see it's the wrong time ter call. Rose 'is trying ter get the tea an' the kids are playin' up. Yer'll 'ave ter come round some ovver time.'

The welfare office made to reply but saw the hard look on Don's face. 'I'll call back tomorrow evening,' she said, glancing at Rose briefly as she left the room.

Freda Arrowsmith had been about to call over to see if everything was all right when the noise and crying started but as she opened her front door she had spotted the officer standing on the landing with her ear pressed against the Farrans' door. Freda recognised the woman and gently closed her own door again. Now, as she heard the officer leaving, she came out on to the landing quickly and confronted her. 'It's not always like that,' she said abruptly.

'Isn't it?' the officer replied coldly.

'No, it's not. There's nuffink wrong wiv that family, luv,' Freda told her.

Peggy Grant walked past the angry woman and hurried down the stairs, feeling that she should put a report in to her district officer as soon as possible. Going by what she had heard at the front door she felt that something might well snap inside the young Farran girl, resulting in her doing the children some harm. The young woman's brother looked a mean, moody person too, she thought. It wouldn't be surprising if he was chastising the children. The youngest child had a frightened look on her face. Anyway, the report would go in and her superior officer would advise on the best course of emergency action to get the children safely into foster homes as quickly as possible.

On Tuesday evening Albert Morgan locked up his ladders and bicycle and walked round the corner to the fish shop. On Tuesday evenings the Gormans had mutton stew for tea and Albert detested mutton stew. As he sat eating cod and chips he thought about his family. He hadn't seen anything of them since the raid but he knew very well that his father would be in the Anchor every night buying drinks for his cronies and bragging about having had another fair-sized win on the greyhounds. It was his way of saying that he had been active, and his friends knew only too well that Frankie's money did not come from betting.

Albert pushed away the empty plate and sipped his mug of tea thoughtfully. His mother had said she intended to go and stay with Joe and Carol and he wanted to see her before she went. His father had forbidden him to go back to the family home and Albert knew that he would make it hard for his mother if he found out that he had visited her. He lit a cigarette and inhaled deeply. His brothers were always out in the evenings and his father usually went out around eight thirty. If he left it until after nine he should be able to have a quiet chat with his mother safely.

Albert left the fish shop and walked slowly home to his lodgings. He could smell the stew as he let himself into the house and put his head round the parlour door. 'I'm just goin' up fer a wash an' brush-up, Mrs Gorman,' he told her. 'I'm gonna try an' see me muvver ternight.'

Sarah Gorman pulled a face. 'You be careful. Yer don't want that farvver o' yours givin' yer anuvver beltin'.'

Albert smiled. 'Don't worry, I'll be careful.'

A few minutes after nine o'clock Albert tapped gently on his mother's front door and when she saw him standing on the doorstep she burst into tears. 'Come in, son,' she said, dabbing at her eyes. 'It's all right, they've all gorn out.'

Albert walked into the tidy parlour and noticed that everything was just as it had always been. The heavy, dark-blue tablecloth covered the wooden table and there was a low fire burning in the grate. A teapot stood in the hearth under a teacosy and the evening paper was lying at the foot of the armchair. 'Yer didn't mind me comin', did yer, Mum?' he said quickly. 'I wanted ter see 'ow you were.'

'I'm all right, boy,' Annie answered. ''Ow are you? Yer look like yer lost weight. Is that Gorman woman feedin' yer prop'ly?'

Albert smiled and nodded as he sat down facing her. 'She does me proud, Mum, there's no need fer you ter worry,' he told her.

Annie shook her head slowly as she studied him and then burst into tears again. ''E shouldn't 'ave turned you out, Albert. I'm never gonna fergive 'im fer that,' she sobbed.

Albert tried not to look uncomfortable. 'C'mon, Mum, stop yer cryin'. I'm fine, really I am,' he said encouragingly.

Annie dabbed at her eyes. 'They'll be the finish o' me, I'm sure they will,' she groaned. 'Yer farvver an' yer bruvvers 'ave bin up ter somefing. I always know. I can sense it.'

Albert suddenly felt very sad for his mother. She looked frail and her face was pale. Her hair was pulled up untidily into a hairnet and the cardigan which she wore over her apron looked shapeless and grubby. He could see the pain and worry in her faded blue eyes.

'I can't stand it 'ere any longer, Albert,' she said tearfully. 'I'm gonna go an' stay wiv yer bruvver. I'm not appreciated 'ere. I never was, but it's got worse lately.'

'It's a good idea, Mum. Joe an' Carol'll be pleased ter see yer,' Albert said comfortingly.

Annie looked down at the wet handkerchief she was absent-mindedly twisting round her fingers. 'I'm glad yer found yerself a young lady. I just 'ope yer can sort fings out about gettin' a place,' she remarked. 'Yer need ter get yerselves settled in somewhere before that baby comes.'

'I'll get somewhere, Ma,' Albert told her with a hopeful smile. 'I'm finkin' o' buyin' ole Frank out. It's a good business an' I can build it up.'

'I'm sure yer will,' Annie said, trying to raise a smile. 'Joe an' Michael 'ave both done well fer themselves. People forget that when they talk about us Morgans. I've 'eard 'em talk an' I've seen their faces when I go out ter get a bit o' shoppin'. If I walk in a shop an' there's a conversation goin' on it all goes quiet. I know they're talkin' about me.'

'Yer shouldn't worry about it, Ma,' Albert said quietly. 'Anyway yer'll be better off at Joe's. Are yer stoppin' fer good?'

Annie shook her head. 'I dunno. Joe's bin on ter me fer weeks now ter go an' stay. 'E knows what sort of a life I've got 'ere wiv yer farvver an' yer bruvvers. They're bad'uns those boys, Gawd fergive me fer sayin' so, but it's the trufe. They ain't never 'ad a steady job an' they 'ang around wiv the bookies an' down the market stalls. I know they're up ter no good.'

''Ave yer told Farvver yer goin' ter stay wiv Joe?' Albert asked.

'No, not yet,' she replied. 'I'll tell 'im ternight when 'e comes in from the pub, that's if 'e does come in at all. 'E's got anuvver woman, yer know.'

Albert looked down at his hands, aware that his father had been seeing one of the stallholders for some time now. 'Yer better shot of 'im, Mum,' he said quietly.

Annie nodded. 'It's bin goin' on a while too, an' it ain't the first one. Soon as 'e got out o' prison 'e was at it wiv a barmaid. It got back ter me, yer see.'

'If 'e 'as a go at yer, let me know an' I'll come round after 'im,' Albert said firmly. 'I don't care if 'e is me farvver. I ain't standin' by ter see 'im start knockin' you about.'

Annie smiled wistfully. 'I don't fink yer need worry about that,' she replied. 'Whatever 'e is or whatever 'e ain't, 'e's never laid a finger on me. I've never bin kept short o' money neivver. It might 'ave bin better if 'e did wallop me or keep me short, then I'd know where I stood. This way I'm just like a bloody 'ousekeeper fer 'im and yer bruvvers. I do the cookin' an' the ironin' an' keep the place nice an' clean, an' never a word of appreciation. Once in a blue moon 'e'll take me out fer a drink, but then 'e leaves me sittin' there while 'e goes over ter chat wiv 'is mates. Last time I went out wiv 'im was goin' on a year back. I wouldn't go any more.'

Albert sat quietly listening, and when his mother lapsed into silence he looked up at her. 'They done a big job this time, Ma,' he told her. 'It was in all the papers.'

'It was that West End jewellery shop, wasn't it?' Annie said, and Albert nodded with downcast eyes. 'I thought as much, but I kept tellin' meself it wouldn't be them. They've never carried guns wiv 'em, not ter my knowledge anyway.'

'They was in it wiv anuvver geezer. 'E was the one wiv the gun,' Albert explained. 'Fankfully that bloke in the shop's out o' danger now, but it could 'ave gone the ovver way.'

'The papers said they pinched some special jewels belongin' to a titled lady,' Annie remarked. 'The papers said they was werf 'undreds o' fousands.'

'Yeah, but all Farvver an' the bruvvers got out of it was two fousand,' Albert said scornfully. 'They was used ter back the ovver bloke up.'

'So that's what 'e was on about then,' Annie replied. 'I over'eard yer farvver talkin'. 'E was sayin' somefing about goin' over an' sortin' it all out.'

'They'd be better off fergettin' all about it,' Albert told her. 'They're dealin' wiv big, powerful people. They'll come unstuck if they mess wiv those sort.'

Annie Morgan got up out of her chair and walked over to the sideboard. 'Albert, I want you ter listen ter what I've got ter say,' she told him firmly, taking a key from the drawer. 'This key fits the trunk in my bedroom. If anyfing 'appens ter me I want yer to open the trunk an' take the box out. It's a big tin moneybox an' there's all the insurance policies in there. I keep the key under the cutlery tray. Yer will remember, son?'

Albert nodded. 'Leave it ter me, Ma.'

''Ave yer seen anyfing of yer Aunt Dolly since she's bin back?' Annie asked him.

'No, but Rose told me she dropped in on 'er,' he replied.

'She's a good woman, is Dolly,' Annie said, leaning back against the sideboard. 'You would 'ave only bin about seven years old when she left ter take a pub in Kent. Dolly's bark's worse than 'er bite, but yer'll no doubt be seein' 'er before long an' yer'll form yer own opinion. Take it from me, she's straight as a die, an' she's bin good ter you kids in the past. Anyway, I'd better not keep yer chattin' in case one of 'em comes in.'

Albert stood up. 'Well, Mum, I'll come an' see you an' our Joe soon as I can. Take care, an' fanks fer everyfing,' he said quietly.

Annie went to him and put her arms around him. He held

her tightly for a few moments, then he stepped back. 'Write to us, Ma,' he said.

Annie nodded and ushered him out of the room. 'Look after yerself, an' look after that young woman. Treat 'er well, son,' she told him.

Albert smiled back at her as he stepped out of the door. 'Don't worry. We'll bring the baby along ter see yer!'

As he walked back through the cold dark streets to his lodgings in Abbey Street, Albert was more determined than ever to go to see Frank Spires first thing next morning about buying the business.

Chapter Twenty-Nine

Dolly Morgan was keen to know what Tommy Caulfield wanted to see her about, and when she walked into his transport yard on Wednesday morning he greeted her with a wide grin.

'C'mon in the office, gel, it's bloody cold this morning,' he said, rubbing his hands together.

He showed her into a chair by his desk and sat himself down facing her. 'I understand yer bin goin' round ter see Gerry's kids,' he began.

Dolly frowned. 'As a matter o' fact, I 'ave. I bin worryin' about 'em,' she replied quickly.

'Jimmy told me the welfare are gonna take the kids away,' Tommy said, leaning back in his desk chair and clasping his hands together in his lap.

'Over my dead body, they will,' Dolly said with venom.

'Yer can't do nuffink about it if the magistrate gives the welfare permission,' Tommy reminded her.

'Well, we'll see about that,' she replied, her eyes widening.

'Jimmy reckons yer gonna try an' get a bigger place an' take care o' the family,' the contractor went on.

'Jimmy's told you a lot,' Dolly said, beginning to feel a little angry. 'More than I realised, in fact. When I asked 'im what it was yer wanted ter see me about 'e went all cagey. What is it, Tommy?'

The contractor got up out of his chair with a smile playing on his wide ruddy face. 'Let me show yer somefing,' he said, taking her by the arm as she stood up.

Together they walked across the yard and entered what had, until the previous day, been Tommy's store room. 'I used ter keep all the 'arness in 'ere,' he told her.

Dolly looked around at the bare room and through into the stone-floored back room. 'Out there as well?'

Tommy nodded. 'When I first took this yard over me an' my missus lived 'ere, but she didn't like it an' I couldn't blame 'er. It was too big for just me an' 'er, so we moved out ter New Kent Road. Since then I put all me stores in 'ere. I kept all me personal fings upstairs, along wiv the 'orses' fodder an' stuff. It was more like a bloody 'ay loft up there. 'Ere, come upstairs an' I'll show yer.'

'Tommy.'

'Yeah?'

'What yer brought me in 'ere for?'

'Can't yer guess?'

'Yer don't mean yer gonna . . .'

'That's right, gel.'

'Rent it out?'

'Yep.'

'Ter me?' Dolly asked excitedly, her eyes growing wide.

'Who else?'

Dolly drew breath. 'Now, let me get this straight,' she said slowly. 'Yer willin' ter let me rent this, fer me an' the Farrans?'

'That's what I 'ad in mind. If yer want it, that is?' Tommy told her with a big smile.

'If I want it! Gawd, Tommy, of course I want it,' she said, feeling as if she could throw her arms around him.

'There'll be a lot o' fixin' up ter do,' he reminded her. 'Upstairs is like a stable an' there's no water or gas, but the electric's on. C'mon upstairs an' see fer yerself.'

Dolly followed the contractor up the creaking stairs and noticed the room leading off on the bend.

'That could do fer a scullery if yer wanted ter turn this inter two separate flats,' he told her. 'Yer see, the bloke who I bought this business off of 'ad a large family, so 'e 'ad an extension built on the back. 'Ere, there's the front room.'

Dolly followed him into the large bare room and noticed the wide brown tell-tale stain in the ceiling, the paper hanging off the walls and the hole in one of the floorboards. A bare light flex hung down from the ceiling and the room door was wedged open on its one hinge. She followed him out on to the dark landing and into the other two rooms which both looked very much the same.

Tommy caught the look in her eye. 'Don't worry too much about the state o' the place, gel,' he said encouragingly. 'The only real problem is the leak in the roof but I'll get that fixed. I'm afraid yer'll 'ave ter do the rest up yerself though. So what d'yer reckon?'

'Tommy, I'm desperate fer somewhere. 'Ow much rent yer gonna charge?' she asked, holding her breath.

'Let's 'ave a proper look downstairs an' then we'll go back over the office ter sort fings out,' he told her.

After they had inspected the three rooms and scullery, Dolly asked him, 'What about the boarded-up winders, Tommy?'

'I'll get them put in, an' a new street door out front so you're independent o' the yard,' he said smiling. 'It's no problem, so don't worry. Let's get over the office an' finalise fings over a drink.'

All day Rose worried and fretted over the coming welfare visit, and when the factory hooter finally sounded after what had seemed the longest day she could remember, she hurried out into the cold evening air feeling sick with apprehension. Peggy Grant had called at the worst moment possible the previous evening. Normally everything would have been quiet and orderly but last night it must have seemed like a mad house to the woman.

As she rounded the corner into Fellmonger Street Rose suddenly remembered that it was Don's birthday the next day and she went into Joe Diamond's shop for a card.

''Ello, luv, 'ow yer feelin'?' Lizzie Carroll asked, her eyes immediately going down to Rose's middle.

'I'm fine, fank you,' Rose answered. 'I want a birfday card fer Don, a quarter o' bullseyes an' two ounces o' dolly mixtures, please.'

'That's the way ter keep the kids quiet,' Lizzie said as she reached up for the large jar of bullseyes.

Rose ignored the remark, guessing that one of the neighbours had mentioned something to Lizzie about the noisy set-to the previous night.

'I was talkin' ter Mrs Stratton this mornin' an' she was sayin' she saw the welfare woman goin' in the block last night,' Lizzie went on. 'I do 'ope everyfing's all right, luv.'

'Yeah, it's fine,' Rose replied, hiding her irritation. 'It was just the usual visit.'

They were alone in the shop and Lizzie looked behind her quickly to make sure Joe Diamond wasn't listening from the store room before she leaned forward over the counter. 'I 'ope yer won't take this the wrong way,' she whispered, 'but people do talk an' it's all round the street about you bein', you know . . .'

'Me bein' pregnant, yer mean?' Rose said in her normal voice.

Lizzie looked a little flustered as she handed her a box of birthday cards and carried on weighing up the sweets. 'Don't get me wrong, luv. It don't do fer any of us ter start castin' stones,' she said after a short pause. 'I just 'ope yer can manage all right, what wiv everyfing.'

Rose sighed with exasperation. People generally meant well, she realised, but they all wanted to know the latest up-to-the-minute information about everyone around them. 'The welfare people are tryin' ter put Susan an' the boys in foster 'omes,' she said flatly.

'Good Gawd, you fight 'em, gel,' Lizzie said firmly. 'They should sort out the ones who neglect their kids. I fink you're ter be praised fer the way yer look after your family. By the way, is the farvver gonna marry yer?'

Rose had to smile at Lizzie's gall. 'Yeah, soon as 'e can,' she replied, passing over the box and the card she had picked out.

As she left the shop and hurried into the Buildings that evening Rose was blithely unaware of what lay ahead. It was going to be an evening she would never forget.

Jimmy Rideout quickly removed the bits and pieces from the table and cursed to himself as he unsuccessfully searched through the drawers for a clean white tablecloth. Dolly had told him how homely it was to see a freshly laundered white tablecloth spread over a table with care with a vase of flowers standing in the centre. Jimmy had managed to get the flowers and he had sorted out a vase, but there was no sign of the tablecloth. Dolly had said she was coming round this afternoon after seeing Tommy Caulfield and he wanted everything to be just right. It was important to show her that he was serious about them getting together permanently, and the little things he did that he knew she liked would surely help to sway her. At the moment she would not take him seriously enough to make any firm commitment and she seemed content to take one day at a time, as she put it.

Jimmy cursed as he shut the last drawer with a bang. He must have given the tablecloth to Fred's wife Muriel to launder for him without realising it. Suddenly he remembered that he had only just that morning changed his bed linen. The sheet would do, he thought, smiling to himself as he quickly pulled it off the bed and spread it over the bare table. With the vase of flowers in place and the room hastily tidied Jimmy felt that he had done a good job of work, and when he heard Dolly's knock on his front door he was ready.

'Jimmy, you're a no-good, schemin', secretive bleeder,' Dolly said loudly as she walked into the flat looking murderous.

Jimmy looked downcast. ''Cos I didn't tell yer what Tommy Caulfield wanted yer for?' he muttered.

'Yer let me stew all last night,' she went on, her face beginning to relax into a smile.

'Tommy made me promise not ter tell yer anyfing till 'e spoke ter yer 'imself,' Jimmy said meekly. 'I couldn't break a promise, now could I?'

Suddenly Dolly threw her arms around him. 'Remember what we said about needin' a miracle?' she said excitedly. 'Well, a miracle 'appened this mornin'. I got the 'ouse! Yeah, that's right. What's more, I've got six weeks rent free while I do it up.'

Jimmy smiled. 'I'm pleased fer yer, Dolly. Yeah, I'm really pleased. I know just what it meant to yer.'

Dolly rested her head against his chest. 'Yer know somefing, Jimmy,' she said quietly. 'When I came back ter Bermon'sey I was full of anger. I couldn't fink of anyfing except 'ow ter get even wiv Frankie Morgan, but now it's not important. Those Farrans are me prime concern, an' I'll die sooner than let 'em be split up.'

Jimmy rubbed his hand gently up and down her spine and she closed her eyes, feeling the comforting warmth of his body pressed against hers. She had gone to him the very first time out of pure physical desire, and out of pity for him. It had seemed right in her moment of need, but she knew that for Jimmy it had not been something he could take lightly. He was in love with her, she knew; she had known before he found the courage to tell her so. She had seen it in his eyes, and she had witnessed the way he had changed so in the very short time since they met that night in the street. Jimmy's physical appearance had shaken her to the core. Her recollection of him was as a proud, upright man, full of himself and with a wicked smile that seemed to hover forever in the corner of his mouth. The man she had met that night just a few short weeks ago had been a shuffling, physical and mental wreck, unable to place one foot before the other with any confidence as he sought relief from his agony and torment in the false succour of the bottle and a dingy public bar.

Jimmy Rideout's transformation had been little short of miraculous. He must have gone through the gates of hell in ridding himself of his dependence on drink, she realised. His eyes were bright and clear now, and his stance upright and proud once more. He had finally asked her to marry him and her laughing refusal had spurred him on. As he held her tight in his arms in the quietness of his flat Dolly could feel his love as if it were electric.

'They're your bruvver's kids, an' Gerry was my best pal, so I've got a stake in this as well. We'll do what we 'ave ter do tergevver, gel,' he told her softly.

'They couldn't take those kids away, not now, could they, Jimmy?' she asked fearfully.

'Not bloody likely,' he replied confidently. 'Jus' let 'em try it.'

Her face was upturned, almost pitiful in its expression of concern, and Jimmy bent his head slightly, gently brushing his lips against hers. His kiss was tender and she locked her arms around his neck, pulling his head down as she opened her mouth and kissed him with all the fire she could muster. She could feel his body pressing hard against hers, his manhood vibrant and ready. Her need now was even greater than before and she allowed him to explore her aching body with his shaking hands. She felt a young woman again, in love and desirous of him to ravish her. The magic of that kiss had set her trembling, and when they moved apart her skin was tingling as he led her to the bedroom. She closed her eyes as he slowly unbuttoned and removed her coat then eased her back on to the bed. She felt his hands on her and groaned with pleasure as his spread fingers travelled slowly up the thickness of her thights. She raised her hips from the bed, allowing him to strip her bare. He was above her now and ready, his hands supporting his trembling body, a ghost of that once-familiar wicked smile haunting his features as he looked down on her hot, flushed face. She closed her eyes once more and felt him as he sought her, delicious feelings coursing as he entered her. She ran her tongue over her hot dry lips, rising in unison with him, and with a quickening, frantic burst of love they reached the pinnacle together.

The pale winter sunshine broke from scattered cloud and pierced the clean net curtain hanging in the small bedroom. Dolly stirred and groaned in her sleep as she nestled closer to him underneath the bedclothes. Jimmy lay on his back, his arm crooked round her in a sleepy embrace. Later they were going to see the Farrans, but for now he closed his eyes and let the sleep of lovers claim them both.

Peggy Grant had submitted her report and was pleasantly surprised when Miss Seaton suggested that it might be prudent if she accompanied her to the Farrans' flat that evening.

'I'm not for one moment implying that you're incapable of dealing with the situation, Peggy, but it is better if a senior officer goes along in cases where there is outright hostility,' Winifred Seaton explained. 'I am quite used to dealing with difficult clients and I have practical experience in making it perfectly clear to such people that our decisions are based on circumstances and need, rather than on pure dogmatism. I know it's sometimes painful to split up a family, but I'm sure we would agree that it is for the best in the long run. To be honest, I'd much rather spend half an hour or so convincing the client of our good intentions than read the riot act and then be compelled to go for a court order.'

Peggy Grant smiled sweetly with a dutiful nod, feeling privileged to be taken into her superior officer's confidence. One day she hoped to be occupying her chair but first she had much to learn, and who better to learn it from than Winifred Seaton. 'I am grateful for your taking the time and trouble with the Farrans, Miss Seaton,' she said meekly. 'I'm sure your experience will be invaluable in dealing with this particular family.'

'It's no trouble, no trouble at all. In fact it's quite nice to get out into the battlefield as it were, on occasions,' her senior replied with a smile.

'As I mentioned in the report, I feel the stumbling block lies with the brother, Donald,' Peggy explained. 'He was positively hostile on my visit yesterday, Miss Seaton.'

'You leave that young man to me, Peggy. And by the way, you can call me Winifred when we're alone together,' the senior officer replied.

Peggy Grant felt a warm glow inside. She had long admired her superior, and to be allowed to use her christian name was indeed a step in the right direction. 'Thank you, Winifred,' she said hesitantly.

Miss Seaton picked up the phone. 'Helen, I'm going to be working late this evening. Would you arrange tea for two, oh, and some of those chocolate biscuits if you will. Thank you.'

Peggy Grant became even more excited and she felt her face colour slightly as she wondered how it would feel to have Winifred take her into her arms and kiss her on the mouth. It was silly to harbour such thoughts, she told herself. Miss Seaton was not a lesbian, at least Peggy didn't think she was. Most senior welfare officers like Winifred Seaton tended to dress in a manly fashion. The mode of dress seemed to go with the position.

'Right, now let's go over the Farran case history once more while we're waiting for our tea,' Miss Seaton said, bringing the younger woman down to earth suddenly.

Rose became more nervous as the evening visit drew near. Susan had been washed ready for bed and she sat in front of the gas fire sipping a cup of cocoa, her eyelids starting to droop. The two boys were being allowed to stay up for the visit but they had been warned that they must be seen and not heard. Don had cancelled a trip to the Troxy cinema with Alice that evening, wanting to be present when the welfare woman called. She had a habit of upsetting Rose and he was going to put his foot down. They had no right to barge in and split up families who were coping very well as they were. He could think of one or two families who might well benefit from a welfare visit, but not his.

On the stroke of seven there was a familiar rat-tat on the front door and Don admitted the Misses Seaton and Grant.

'This is my district officer, Miss Seaton,' Peggy announced proudly as they walked into the front room and sat themselves down at the table. 'She would like to have a talk with you about the fostering of young Susan initially.'

'There's nuffink ter talk about,' Don cut in sharply. 'Susan's not bein' fostered.'

'What do you say, Rose?' Miss Seaton asked. 'It is Rose, isn't it?'

'We both feel the same,' Rose answered positively. 'I'm not lettin' Susan go into a foster 'ome. We can manage quite well, thank you very much.'

'With a baby on the way?' the senior replied curtly, raising her eyebrows.

'We can still manage,' Rose retorted. 'Our neighbours 'ave offered to 'elp an' Don's good wiv the children.'

'Have you considered the amount of space a new baby takes up?' Miss Grant said quickly.

'I'm afraid there's no use you trying to side-step the problem, Rose,' Miss Seaton went on. 'We already have an ideal couple to look after Susan and it will be less painful for you if the children are not all taken from the family home at a stroke. The boys can be fostered at a later date well before your confinement, but it is essential we get Susan settled in as soon as possible.'

'We're not goin' in no bloody foster 'omes,' Billy said suddenly, his face flushed bright red.

'We'll run away,' Joey said in support of his older brother.

'I've already warned you two about bein' quiet,' Rose reminded them sharply.

'Little boys should be seen and not heard,' Miss Seaton said quickly, glaring at them, then she turned to face Rose. 'We have already applied for a court order, due to your reluctance to co-operate. So I should get used to the idea,' she told her.

Don looked hard at the tall, lean figure of Miss Seaton, having felt an immediate dislike for her. He had noticed with distaste how her dark hair was cropped short at the back and how the front was set into a wave and secured by a clip. She was pale-faced and mean-looking, he thought. Her narrow-spaced brown eyes seemed to be constantly darting from one person to another, which made him think of a cat in a roomful of sparrows deciding which one it would pounce on next.

'An' you better get used ter the idea that I'm not lettin' the kids go anywhere, an' we'll fight yer all the way,' Rose said spiritedly.

A knock at the door interrupted Miss Seaton as she was about to reply and after a moment or two she found herself staring up at a tall blonde woman with deep blue eyes and short hair loosely curled round her ears, carrying a dark-brown leather handbag slung over the shoulder of her fawn calf-length coat. Just behind her stood Jimmy Rideout, hands in pockets and looking a little embarrassed. 'It seems I've come at an opportune moment,' Dolly said, smiling at Rose.

'I'm afraid we're in the middle of a private discussion,' Miss Seaton said tartly.

'Don't be afraid, luv,' Dolly replied. 'You carry on, I'm family too.'

Don exchanged a discreet smile with Jimmy while Rose looked up at her aunt with tears in her eyes. 'I've bin tryin' ter tell these welfare women that I ain't allowin' Susan ter be fostered out,' she said, trying hard to control her emotions, 'but they said the court order's already gone frew.'

Dolly pulled up a chair and sat down facing the officers. 'Give me two reasons why the kids 'ave gotta be fostered,' she demanded.

Miss Seaton clasped her hands on the table and glared at her. 'If it's any of your business . . .'

'I'm makin' it my business,' Dolly stopped her sharply, matching her stare.

'Firstly there's a problem of overcrowding which will be compounded with a new baby,' the officer said, flushing angrily, 'and secondly, Rose is responsible for the younger children's welfare. How can she manage to provide for the children's needs with a baby to care for?'

Dolly smiled calmly. 'Granted.'

'You agree?' Miss Seaton said, taken aback.

'Yeah, but the family are gonna move into a bigger place soon, an' I'm movin' in ter take care of 'em all,' Dolly informed her.

Everyone in the room looked at Dolly in amazement, except for Jimmy.

'We're gonna move?' Don queried.

'I've just rented the big 'ouse next ter the transport yard,' Dolly told them all. 'It'll be ready in four weeks, an' unless there's any objections from you Farrans I'll be movin' in wiv yer.'

'I think there will have to be further discussion on what you've just proposed,' Miss Seaton replied.

'I've not proposed anyfing. I've just made a factual statement,' Dolly told her acidly. 'You can talk all yer like. As fer this family, they stay tergevver. So yer can take yer court order an' shove it.'

The two welfare officers left the flat looking angry, embarrassed at the turn of events, and as the front door closed behind them Dolly turned and smiled at the bewildered Farran family. 'We'd better all sit down, there's lots ter talk about,' she said, winking at Jimmy.

There was more to come. Rose answered yet another knock at the door. It was Albert, and as he stepped into the flat he slipped his hands round her waist and kissed her. 'I've just bought the winder-cleanin' business, Rose,' he told her excitedly.

Chapter Thirty

Chief Inspector Bill Grogan walked into the Anchor on Friday evening with a lot on his mind. He was well aware that the pub was frequented by some of the local villains, not least the Morgans, and it made good sense to put in an occasional appearance. It would be noticed, and the landlord Sammy McGarry and his wife Beryl would appreciate it too. Grogan knew that the McGarrys were trying to maintain a respectable watering hole and encourage the local community to consider it as a family pub. Unfortunately, the villains tended to use the Anchor, and they knew that if they avoided causing trouble in the place they had nothing to fear.

Frankie Morgan had leaned on his sons heavily over the affair with Jimmy Rideout, trying to impress on them that it was imperative for them to have a local pub where they were welcome and where they could entertain their friends and plan their clandestine activities. He had told them how important it was to have the respect of the local community. The neighbourhood pub was a place where most of the local news was exchanged and discussed, and nonsense cases and other undesirables could be made to leave the area or suffer the consequences. That way the locals would feel safe, and able to come to the likes of the Morgans with their troubles, Frankie maintained. It would have the effect of keeping the tight-knit community loyal to their protectors, and less inclined to pass on information to outsiders.

Bill Grogan was a long-serving officer and he was well aware of the aims and aspirations of gangs like the Morgans. He had seen it in the East End and other hard areas where he had served. People there lived in fear of being labelled as informants, and they clammed up tight whenever the police made enquiries. As far as the Morgans went, they were a long way from earning the respect they sought. They had made the mistake of upsetting too many of the law-abiding locals by their behaviour, and for the present at least there were occasionally a few snippets of information to be gleaned.

Sammy came over and leaned on the saloon bar counter. ''Ow's tricks, Bill?' he asked.

Grogan shrugged his shoulders and stared down at his half-empty glass of Scotch. 'It's quiet, Sam, too quiet if you ask me,' he said. 'There's normally something going on, but lately, I don't know.'

Sammy looked round the saloon to reassure himself that they were not being overheard. 'Frankie Morgan's bin splashin' money about as usual, but it all comes from the dog tracks, if 'e's ter be believed,' he said quietly.

Grogan smiled cynically. 'They never seem to lose, do they,' he replied.

'We 'ad a turn-out 'ere since yer last visit,' Sammy went on. 'The Morgan boys cut up rough wiv one of our local piss artists but we got it all sorted out. As a matter o' fact one o' the women stopped it. She gave John Morgan a smart back'ander inter the bargain. It's bin very quiet since then.'

'Is Frankie Morgan likely to show his face?' the inspector asked.

''E's due in any time now,' Sammy told him. 'The Morgan boys tend ter stay in the public though.'

Grogan nodded and picked up his drink as Sammy went to serve a customer. Something big was in the wind and he was at a loss to understand why he should suddenly be told that he was required to attend a top-level meeting at Scotland Yard on Monday morning. One thing was certain though: whatever had happened, it involved his manor.

'See yer outside,' the elderly man mumbled as he walked past.

The inspector groaned as he put down his drink and waited a few moments before following him out to the toilet. Dan Beaumont had been giving him bits of information for as long as he could remember and it was all a load of rubbish. At various times Beaumont had had inside information on the whereabouts of Peter the Painter, Jack the Ripper and Charlie Peace, and on one occasion he had found out that the public urinal in Tower Bridge Road was being used as a brothel and was due to be blown up by the Irish Republicans.

Grogan was often of a mind to ignore the crazy old man, but he realised it would only encourage his pestering.

'What you got?' the inspector mumbled as he stood next to Beaumont at the urinal.

'They was in 'ere last night,' the old man hissed, staring straight at the wall in front of him.

'Who was?'

'The Noskies.'

'Russians?'

'Four of 'em.'

'What they up to?'

The old man turned his head slightly. 'They're after the Duchess o' Kent.'

'Assassination attempt?'

'Most likely.'

'I'll see to it,' Grogan replied as he left the toilet, shaking his head sadly.

Sammy came over and watched the old man go back to his seat. ''As 'e bin at it again?' he asked.

Bill Grogan nodded with a smile. 'It's the Duchess of Kent this time,' he said. 'Top it up, Sam.'

A few minutes later Frankie Morgan walked into the bar with two of his associates and there was a flicker of recognition from him as he went to the end of the bar to order.

Grogan drained his drink. His presence had been noticed and that was enough, he thought as he pulled up his collar to leave.

Ethel Price put the letter down and turned to her husband George. 'Well, we know Joe's demob date now so I'd better go round Basin Street an' see the vicar,' she said smiling.

'I'll 'ave a chat wiv Sammy over the Anchor,' George replied. ''E'll give us all the beer we want. I might be able ter get the glasses as well.'

Ethel felt excited as she made her plans. Joe was her eldest son and she doted on him. He was due home from Germany the following week and there was much to do if she was going to give him the welcome home party he deserved. 'I've already seen Joe Diamond,' she went on. ''E's savin' me anuvver tin of 'am an' I've got quite a few tins o' fruit stashed away in the cupboard.'

'Yer better sort out who yer gonna invite,' George told her. 'Yer'll 'ave to ask all those in the block, then there's Joe from the shop an' Lizzie Carroll. Who else yer finkin' of?'

'Well, there's me two mates at the cleanin' job an' ole Mrs Gold from Abbey Street,' she said, pinching her chin thoughtfully.

'What about Fred Albury an' 'is missus?' George reminded her.

'Yeah, I'll 'ave to ask them,' Ethel replied. 'I was wonderin' about Jimmy Rideout as well.'

George pulled a face. 'What d'yer wanna ask 'im for?' he said quickly. ''E's an out-an'-out piss artist. 'E'll be fallin' about all over the place.'

'When did yer last see 'im?' Ethel asked.

'I ain't seem 'im fer ages.'

'Well, yer wouldn't recognise 'im.'

'Oh?'

''E's orf the turps since 'e's bin wiv that Dolly Morgan.'

'Oh.'

'Dolly's bin comin' up ter see the Farrans,' Ethel went on. 'She's their aunt. I was gonna ask young Rose an' Don Farran if they'd like ter come, so I'll 'ave to ask Dolly, an' she wouldn't come if we didn't ask Jimmy Rideout.'

'Yer might as well ask all the bloody street,' George said grinning.

'I've already asked Sadie across the landin' an' she said she'd like ter come, but she said she doubts if 'er daughters will. They're always out an' about wiv their fellers anyway,' Ethel told him.

'As long as it don't upset 'er,' George said. 'Every time she 'as a drink she gets weepy. Remember last Christmas?'

'It's understandable,' Ethel replied. 'She idolised that feller of 'ers an' it was terrible the way 'e went.'

George nodded, feeling suddenly sick inside. Sadie's husband Terry had been in the fire service during the war and at the height of the blitz he had been crushed beneath a falling wall as he helped fight a raging fire at a tanning factory off Abbey Street. George had been in the heavy rescue service and he had been the one who recovered his body. 'Don't worry, we'll look after Sadie,' he said quietly. 'It's the least we can do.'

Ethel got up to put the kettle on, bending down to plant a kiss on her husband's bald crown. 'You're a nice man, George, under that front yer put on,' she said fondly.

Rose sat with Albert Morgan late on Friday evening, her legs curled up under her and her face glowing with excitement. 'I still can't believe it,' she told him. 'It was right out o' the blue. One minute I was ready ter cry an' the next minute I could 'ave jumped fer joy.'

'Yeah, she seems a nice lady,' Albert replied. 'She certainly put those welfare women in their place.'

Rose sighed contentedly. 'I feel so 'appy, I just 'ope I don't wake up an' find it's all bin a dream.'

'It's no dream,' Albert reassured her. 'What wiv me gettin' that business as well, fings seem ter be takin' a turn fer the better. Ole Frank's bin on about sellin' it fer a long time but I never thought I was really gonna get it. Mind yer, 'e's getting' past it now an' 'e told me 'e was gonna move down ter Brighton ter be wiv 'is daughter.'

'I 'ope the welfare don't make trouble though,' Rose added cautiously. 'They was really angry when they left.'

'If we can get that place ready by the time we said there's nuffink they can do,' Albert replied. 'Ter be fair they don't take children away from their families unless they fink it's really necessary. By the time we're finished, that 'ouse is gonna look real smart.'

'There's a terrible lot ter do though,' Rose reminded him. 'Dolly seems ter fink it's no problem, but when she took me over there yesterday evenin' ter show me I could see it's gonna involve a lot o' work. Anyway, I 'ad the chance ter fank Tommy Caulfield. 'E seems a nice man. 'E stayed late just so Dolly could take me ter see the place. 'E's promised ter get the roof fixed next week an' the front door put on as well as the winders fixed up.'

Albert nodded, gazing distractedly into the flames of the gas fire. Rose felt suddenly frightened. He looked so worried and far away. 'Albert, yer not 'avin' second thoughts about us, are yer?' she said quietly.

He suddenly brightened. 'Of course not,' he replied casually.

She was not to be put off. 'What is it that's troublin' yer, Albert? Yer looked so sad all of a sudden,' she told him.

The young man attempted a smile. He had been thinking about his family and had told Don not to let on to Rose about the jewel robbery. He had wanted to spare her any worry while she was carrying the baby but now he realised that it was probably a mistake. She was very perceptive and it was bad if she started taking things personally. 'As a matter o' fact I was finkin' about me family,' he said quietly. 'I didn't want yer ter worry, but yer gotta know some time.'

'Gotta know what, Albert?' she asked, looking puzzled.

He gazed down at his hands for a moment. 'Yer remember that West End jewel raid? Well, it was me farvver an' bruvvers who were involved,' he told her. 'I bin worried sick about it in case that old jeweller took a turn fer the worse.'

Rose shook her head slowly as it sank in. 'You could 'ave bin in on that,' she said to him.

'I could 'ave bin lookin' at a long spell in prison, if it wasn't fer you, Rose,' he told her. 'You an' our baby. I'm really 'appy fer us an' I know we're gonna be very 'appy tergevver, but I still worry over the family, even though they've kicked me out.'

'What about yer mum?' Rose asked him. 'Does she know?'

'Yeah, she knows. She also knows that me farvver's bin

seein' anuvver woman,' Albert replied. 'She's gonna leave 'im an' go ter live wiv our Joe. She liked it at Joe's.'

'Poor woman. It must be terrible fer 'er,' Rose said sadly. 'You'd never cheat on me, would yer, Albert?' she asked him suddenly.

The young man got out of his chair and reached down for her, helping her on to her feet, then he slipped his arms around her and pulled her to him tightly. 'I've always loved yer, Rose,' he said softly. 'I used ter call fer Don, but really I wanted ter see you. I thought we could 'ave got tergevver, until yer muvver chased me away. That night at the dance, I saw yer as soon as yer walked in, an' yer looked really pretty. I couldn't take me eyes off yer. I'm not sorry I loved yer, darlin'. I reckon it was meant ter be. We're tergevver now an' that's the way I want it, fer ever.'

She reached up to him seeking his mouth and he lowered his head. Their lips met in a tender, lingering kiss and Rose slipped her hands up around his neck, running her fingers through his thick dark hair. 'Tell me again,' she whispered as their lips parted. 'Tell me yer love me.'

'I love yer, Rose. I love yer so much,' he sighed, gently stroking his hand down her spine.

'I wish we could go ter bed right now and make love,' she whispered.

'I need you too, darlin',' he said, brushing his lips against her ear and kissing the side of her neck.

Rose suddenly stiffened and moved away as the front-room door creaked open. They both turned to see Susan standing there, rubbing her fingers in her eyes.

'I've 'ad a bad dream, Rose,' she said in a croaking voice.

Albert bent down and swept the child up in his arms. Susan let her head rest on his shoulder as she felt his comforting arms around her, holding her tightly.

'I won't 'ave ter go away, will I, Uncle Albert?' she said in a tiny voice.

'No, darlin'. Nobody's gonna take you away,' he told her firmly. 'We're all gonna live in a nice big 'ouse soon an' every night I'll come in an' tell yer a nice fairy story. I'll tuck you up an' then yer can go ter sleep in yer nice warm bed wiv yer dolly an' yer teddy.'

Rose watched as Albert comforted her young sister, his voice soft and lilting as he walked slowly around the room. She saw the child's eyes droop and she was suddenly filled with a burning love for the young man. How unlike his hard, brutal brothers he was. He was kind and tender, and she could see that Susan felt it too. Her eyes were closed and she rested comfortably against him. Rose went over to them and brushed a strand of hair from Susan's eyes. 'I love you, Albert Morgan,' she whispered.

Don Farran had felt at a loose end that evening. He knew that Albert was coming round to see Rose and he wanted to get out of the flat to give them some time alone. Alice was stopping in that evening to wash her hair and so he decided to go down to the Crown public house at Dockland. He knew a few of the young men there and sometimes there was a chance of a game of darts.

Don strolled along Abbey Street whistling cheerily. Things were looking up and Rose seemed very happy with Albert. He was a good bloke and would take care of her, Don knew. Pity about him being disowned by his family though. He didn't deserve that. Anyway, he was trying hard to better himself and he would no doubt make his new business work. The new year was beginning very well, apart from the one cloud on the horizon. How would the welfare people react to developments, he wondered.

He reached the Crown and walked into the public bar. The piano was being played and a layer of blue tobacco smoke hung in the air. Dockers and factory workers leaned against the counter and sat around iron-legged tables chatting together. The dartboard was being used and Don eased into a space at the bar and waited patiently to be served. He looked down at the red and blue striped tie, the one Rose had bought him for his birthday, and tucked the end into the band of his trousers to keep it away from the beer-soaked counter.

'One pint o' bitter fer the young man in the striped tie.'

Don looked up to see the barmaid smiling at him as she placed the glass of beer down in front of him.

'Who bought it?' he asked her.

She nodded along the counter. Don followed her gaze and saw John and Ernie Morgan standing together a little way off. He raised his hand in acknowledgement and made to join them but they were already coming over to him.

'Well, well, if it ain't our ole pal, Don,' the elder Morgan said. 'Out alone? Where's that no-good bruvver of ours?'

'I dunno,' Don replied, sipping his beer.

'I 'eard that 'im an' your sister was goin' out tegevver. That right, Don?' Ernie cut in.

'Yeah, as a matter o' fact you 'eard right,' Don replied.

John Morgan rolled his shoulders and pulled on his shirt cuffs. 'We'd like yer ter do us a little favour,' he said with a quick glance at Ernie. 'When yer see Albert next, tell 'im our ole man didn't take kindly to 'im goin' round ter see the ole lady while we was out. Tell 'im ter stay away or the ole man'll sort 'im out.'

Don felt the anger rising inside him. 'I'm not yer messenger boy. Tell 'im yerself,' he said quickly.

John Morgan's face hardened, and for a moment it looked

as if he was going to get violent. Then he smiled. 'Yer better warn 'im, fer yer sister's sake. Our ole man can get very mean when 'e's put out,' he said quietly.

Don watched as the two brothers turned away and walked out of the pub. He finished his drink quickly and left, feeling that the night had been soured as he walked home through the gathering fog.

Chapter Thirty-One

Winifred Seaton had spent a number of years in the welfare service and considered herself to be highly professional. She had experience of court procedures regarding care orders, fostering and adoption, she had read books on paediatrics, family planning and office procedures and the currently-favoured textbook, *The Child and Society: A Will to Destroy* by S. J. Prevert, held pride of place on her tidy little bookshelf. Winifred had devoted herself to her chosen vocation and had never wavered in favour of social activities. Men had never interested nor excited her, and the more experienced she became in her profession, the more convinced she was that men were all the same. They were selfish, ignorant pigs and women on the whole would be a lot better off without them.

The district officer had realised early on in her adult life that she was different from her young friends, who all constantly prattled on about the young men in their lives. Winifred only felt at ease in the company of her own sex, and there were occasions when she had had to control her emotions lest she made a fool of herself. Success in her profession became her paramount concern and she buried herself in her work, determined to go to the very top. Now, as a senior officer in

316

her early forties, Winifred Seaton realized that she had fallen in love with Peggy Grant. It had become increasingly difficult to hide her feelings of late, especially when Peggy turned to her for guidance and support over the Farran case. The junior officer was experiencing certain feelings too which were beginning to manifest themselves, Winifred felt sure. Nothing had actually been said, but she sensed it in the young woman's eyes and in the way that she hung on and responded to her every word and action.

Allowing herself to become personally involved with the Farran case and actively to support Peggy was an opportunity for Winifred to impress and excite her junior officer still further. She had wanted to be absolutely sure in her mind that the feelings were mutual before she made any positive move. Unfortunately things had not worked out as she had planned. That atrocious woman Dolly Morgan had really seen to that. How dare she suddenly come on to the scene and threaten and browbeat everyone. Well, if she thought that she was going to pull the wool over this senior officer's eyes with her promises then she had thought wrong, Winifred raved.

Peggy Grant had also been shocked by the turn of events. She had initially felt upset and a little disappointed at her senior's lack of fire in confronting the big blonde woman who had been so bullying and bombastic, but on reflection she realised that Winifred had handled it very pragmatically in the circumstances. Now, as she made her way to the senior's office, Peggy felt little flutters of excitement thrilling inside her. It was silly, she told herself, but she had been able to think of nothing else since last Wednesday evening.

Winifred smiled and motioned Peggy to take a seat. 'I told you I wanted the weekend to think about things, Peggy,' she began. 'Well, this morning I put a letter together. I believe it's the best way forward.'

Peggy Grant took the proffered sheet of paper and read the typescript; then she looked up, her eyes betraying the emotion she felt. 'I think it's perfect,' she purred.

Winifred took the sheet back, carefully folded it and slipped it into an envelope. 'This will catch the last post tonight and should arrive by tomorrow morning,' she said. 'Now Wednesday is the first of February, so the Farrans will have a full month to comply. If by then we see that the situation has not improved, we'll issue the court order and take the three children into care immediately.'

Peggy nodded dutifully. 'I'd like to thank you for your support and guidance,' she began. 'I feel sure we'll be forced to act eventually. I can't see what that horrible woman hopes to gain by making those rash promises. There's no chance of the family being rehoused in such a short time. We know only too well that all the housing lists are closed in this area.'

Winifred nodded, her eyes fixed on her junior; then she suddenly stood up and walked round her desk, laying her hand on Peggy's shoulder. 'I want you to know that I'm always here for you, if you need me,' she said in a measured tone. 'I hope you realise what I mean.'

Peggy felt her face flush and she reached her hand up to touch Winifred's but the older woman grasped it and stood back a pace, gently pulling her out of her chair. Peggy suddenly found herself enveloped in the woman's arms and she caught her breath. It was unreal, almost too wicked, but so delicious and sensuous. Nothing mattered, as long as the loving intent was there, and she could feel it as gentle fingers moved along the length of her spine to her waist, then up slowly until they found the band of her brassiere. Peggy closed her eyes as Winifred's hands explored slowly round her body, her palms pressing against the sides of her hard breasts. The older woman held her firmly, moving her away just enough so that, as Peggy sighed with pleasure, she felt Winifred's lips on hers.

'I love you, Peggy,' Winifred whispered.

'I love you too, Winifred,' Peggy gasped.

'You must come to my home very soon. Say you'll come tomorrow evening,' Winifred said, her eyes pleading.

The young woman nodded, feeling overcome and hardly able to speak.

'We must be very careful, very discreet,' Winifred said, taking Peggy's hands in hers. 'You know my address. Make it after eight. Go now.'

Chief Inspector Bill Grogan had spent many years in the force. He had walked the beats in south London and the East End, receiving three commendations, and the police medal for bravery in disarming a madman who was brandishing a chopper and threatening to kill a policeman lying injured at his feet. Grogan had subsequently risen to the rank of sergeant, and then as an inspector during the war he had been active in helping clean up the Rotherhithe area. For his pains he was promoted to chief inspector and posted to Dockhead in Bermondsey on the retirement of his predecessor, Chief Inspector Ben Walsh.

On the Monday morning, when Grogan attended the meeting at Scotland Yard, he was feeling more than a little puzzled, but when it was over he found it hard to analyse his feelings. More than twenty years of dedicated service had instilled in him a fierce pride in his profession, secure in the knowledge that everyone was equal under the law and no one was above it. Now, as he made his way back to his own patch, Grogan felt that he might have been better advised to go into engineering or banking as a vocation.

As he crossed over Blackfriars Bridge and turned into Southwark Street Grogan felt the need for a stiff drink and he walked into the first pub he saw. The usual customers were standing around chatting together. Market porters, factory and brewery workers stood sipping their pints, all looking to be in rude health and reasonably contented, and that Monday lunch hour Grogan envied them. No one took any notice of him as he sat down in a corner with his large Scotch and soda, going over word for word in his mind the proceedings of that morning.

The Commissioner of Police had opened the meeting, and he had been anxious to impress his feelings on those present.

'Gentlemen, you have all been summoned here this morning on a matter of extreme importance,' he began. 'Every one of you here will understand clearly why your particular presence was required when I have finished. Firstly, I must reiterate and endorse the tenet we all subscribe to, namely that no one is above the law. It is also of paramount importance that, when the whole fabric of our ancient and revered national institutions is threatened, discretion and pragmatic good sense must prevail to maintain order in our free and sovereign nation.'

The Commissioner studied his audience momentarily before going on. 'Gentlemen, you are all aware of the recent Berkeley Street jewel robbery involving Jameson's the court jewellers. You will also be aware that the armed gang made off with the Cape Diamonds, a priceless collection belonging to the Marchioness of Roxburgh. The fact that the Marchioness had deposited the diamonds with Jameson's to be set into a tiara was thought to be a closely guarded secret, but the information was obviously leaked, and consequently the diamonds were removed from the jeweller's safe by the gunman during the very well-organised robbery. No fingerprints were left, nor any clues which could have helped us. The only lead we have is from an eyewitness who saw a suspicious pair lurking outside a wine merchant's opposite the shop at about the time of the raid. The witness is a homosexual who was plying for trade and he was quickly told to move off by the pair, whom he described as looking very villainous. He has been here to the Yard and studied mug shots but he couldn't identify either of the men in question. He was adamant that he would recognise the pair if he saw them again so we have to assume that neither of the men has a criminal record.'

The Commissioner paused and looked around the table before he continued. 'Gentlemen, I can tell you now that we have recovered the Cape Diamonds and on our advice the Marchioness has placed them in a safety deposit box at her bank for the time being. I'm aware that you will all have questions to ask, but I crave your indulgence until I finish. It was sheer chance that the person abducting the diamonds was travelling on the Inverness night express when it was derailed at Glenboig. The Scottish police were called in by an astute medical officer who recognised the jewels which had been removed from the unconscious man.'

The Commissioner saw the look of surprise on the faces of those round the table and he peered over his glasses as he went on. 'I will end by reminding you of my opening remarks, gentlemen. Discretion and good sense must prevail. We have recovered the diamonds and returned them to their rightful owner. The organisation which master-minded the robbery has responded and come forward with names. The armed leader of the raid has, regretfully, already been dealt with by them. He was found at New Fresh Wharf with a bullet in his head, having been assassinated whilst attempting to leave the country. The rest of the gang have been named and they will be brought into custody very soon. Now I'll take your questions.'

'Inspector Bradley, West End Division, sir. Are we to assume that the man carrying the diamonds was a public figure?'

The Commissioner looked at the grey-haired officer, seated to his right. 'We can assume that, inspector,' he replied.

The officer sitting next to Inspector Bradley raised his hand. 'Chief Inspector Lane, City of London Division, sir. The press are getting very suspicious. Can we release the identity of the murder victim?'

'A press release has been prepared,' the Commissioner replied.

Bill Grogan had the next question. 'Chief Inspector Grogan, South London Docks Division, sir. I'd like to know the reason for my attendance here.'

'It will be your division's task to apprehend the rest of the gang members,' came the short reply.

A thin-faced man directly facing the Commissioner raised his hand. 'John Hennessey, Department of Public Prosecutions. With regard to the eventual prosecution of the gang members: names dropped into a hat and fingers pointed at an identity parade do not guarantee conviction, as you must be aware.'

'I am aware, Mr Hennessey,' the Commissioner answered with a brief smile. 'I'm fully confident that your department will be given the necessary information for you to proceed.'

A uniformed officer sitting on the Commissioner's left was next. 'Inspector Johnson, Public Relations Executive Officer, Metropolitan Police, sir. Taking into consideration the delicate situation and press coverage, what of the medical officer's involvement? We might not be able to stop details leaking out.'

'Good point, Johnson,' the Commissioner answered. 'As a matter of fact, the medical officer has already been briefed by our colleagues in Scotland. As far as he's concerned the jewels carried by the Right Honourable Hamish MacKenzie MP were paste replicas and were being taken to the Marchioness on the request of her family after they had been told of the robbery. The old lady is very ill and the family hoped that she would be comforted by believing the paste replicas to be the real diamonds. The medical officer fully understands the need for circumspection and the Scottish press are co-operating.'

It went quiet around the table and as the full implications sank in the Commissioner looked from one to another of them. 'Gentlemen, I need not remind you all that this meeting is strictly confidential,' he told them. 'Last night I was summoned to the Home Office. I was briefed by the Prime Minister as well as the Home Secretary. They both stressed the point that Hamish MacKenzie is of Royal blood and if his involvement in the robbery was made public it would be catastrophic for this country, especially while we are engaged in a cold war with the Soviet Union. We are all enlightened public servants and must be aware that there are forces actively seeking the overthrow of this country's democratic constitution and Royal vestiture. I need hardly add that both the Prime Minister and the Home Secretary will be taking a personal interest in the arrest and subsequent trial of the surviving gang members. I thank you for your indulgence and if there are no more questions, I'll close the meeting. I would like you to stay behind for a few moments if you will, Inspector Grogan.'

Bill Grogan sat staring down into the glass of scotch, his mind racing. The Commissioner had made capital from the danger to the country's security in arguing against implicating Hamish MacKenzie. It was not the first time that a scandal had rocked the throne, and it would not be the last, but for the Commissioner to assert that the whole democratic constitution might well be put in jeopardy was just political claptrap. Powerful, unnameable people were behind it all, using their influence to distort the probity of the British nation. If there were 'active' forces at work, it was they as much as anybody.

Grogan finished his drink and ordered another. He had been privately briefed by the Commissioner after the meeting and made aware of the responsibility resting on his shoulders. Not only was he to organise the arrest of the Morgans; he would have to build up a cast-iron case against them. True, he had been promised the assistance of one of the Yard's top detectives, but the onus was on him.

The inspector swallowed his drink and stepped out into the fresh air. His predecessor, Ben Walsh, whom he had met on a few occasions, was most probably sitting back right now enjoying the quiet life of retirement. In the summer he would be out in his garden, and the only aggravation to worry about on his patch would be the greenfly.

Bernard Collis sat back in his office chair on Monday morning and stared up at the bulging strip of wallpaper over the glass-panelled door. That bitch Copeland started all this, he thought as he gritted his teeth. She was the one who had stirred up the women and got them up in arms. She was the one who went along to the union and persuaded them to cause trouble at the factory. The firm had managed quite well for fifty years without being unionised and he had been on the payroll for the past twenty years. Now, after managing the factory workers and organising the setting-up of the machines for over ten years, he had been relegated to assisting that idiot Penrose. It was all Copeland's fault and he would make her pay, if it was the last thing he ever did.

George Penrose walked into the office and put down a large folder on the table. 'I've been going over the maintenance records, Bernard,' he said, taking off his gold-rimmed glasses and squeezing his eyes between thumb and forefinger. 'The large stamper is due for a strip-down and the cutters need new pulley wheels.'

Bernard hid his annoyance and nodded. 'I'll order the pulley wheels right away an' I'll get the maintenance men ter strip the stamper down after work this evenin',' he replied.

Penrose shook his head. 'No, I'd like the stamper sorted out this afternoon,' he told him. 'That way we can have it back in operation by the morning.'

'What about the production loss?' Collis asked.

'We'll utilise our resources by putting the operator on the spare cutter. We're running behind in that department,' Penrose told him.

When he had ordered the new leather pulley wheels over the phone, Collis went along to the maintenance workshop at the rear of the factory to speak to the engineer in charge. 'Joe, we need the stamper stripped down this afternoon,' he said.

'Bit short notice, ain't it?' the engineer replied irritably.

'Don't nag me, it's that dozy bastard Penrose. I just take orders now,' Collis growled.

'What about that spare cutter? The big-end con-rod's on the blink, an' if that goes it could be dangerous fer the operator,' the engineer told him.

'Let Penrose worry about that,' Collis said sharply. ''E knows it all, or so 'e finks.'

When the factory women came back from their lunch break Collis was standing in the main aisle. 'Prentice, you go on Copeland's machine this afternoon. Copeland, you start up the spare cutter,' he said casually.

Chapter Thirty-Two

True to his word, Tommy Caulfield called in a local building firm, and when Dolly passed the yard on Tuesday afternoon she was very pleased to see the builders hard at work tearing down the planks of wood which had been crudely nailed over the doorway and window openings of the derelict house. As Dolly walked on, intending to call on Jimmy to discuss the problem of ladders and scaffold-planks, she was stopped short by Ethel Price.

'Don't fink I'm bein' nosy, luv, but you are Dolly Morgan, ain't yer?' she asked.

'That's me, luv,' Dolly replied cheerfully.

'I'm Ethel Price,' she began. 'I live over the Farrans. I've seen yer come in the block once or twice. It's nice ter know that yer poppin' in on Rose an' the family. They're well thought of round 'ere, yer know, an' we all worry over 'em.'

Dolly smiled. 'They're my bruvver Gerry's kids. It's the least I can do,' she replied.

Ethel brushed an imaginary piece of fluff from her well-worn coat. 'Me an' my ole man George are organisin' a welcomin' 'ome party fer our eldest boy who's gettin' demobbed,' she went on, 'an' we'd like you an' Rose an' Don ter come. It's on Saturday night at the church 'all in Basin Street.'

'Well, fanks very much, Ethel,' Dolly replied. 'I'm sure Rose an' Don would love ter come, though I'll prob'ly look after Susan an' the boys.'

'Bring the kids as well,' Ethel said with a cheerful grin. 'The more the merrier, I say. They'll be no trouble an' yer can take 'em 'ome soon as they're tired.'

'Yer know Rose an' Don are both courtin',' Dolly remarked tentatively.

'Yeah, I know,' Ethel replied. 'Rose told me she's seein' Albert Morgan. I know that family very well an' 'e's about the best o' the lot, if you ask me. Nice polite lad. I don't know Don's young lady though. She's a friend o' Rose, so I've bin told. Anyway, you tell Rose an' Don they can bring their sweet'earts along as well. They'll be made welcome.'

'Fanks very much, Ethel. I appreciate it,' Dolly said smiling.

'Well, I'd better be on me way. There's so much ter do,' Ethel said with a sigh.

Dolly crossed the street and went into the end block of Imperial Buildings. Jimmy was just locking his front door and he slipped his arm around her and gave her a squeeze. ''Ello, darlin', I'm just off ter see 'ow me stalls are doin',' he told her. 'What's brought you round this time o' the mornin'?'

'Ladders, Jimmy. Ladders an' a couple o' scaffold-planks.'

'Plannin' on 'angin' somebody, are we?' he grinned.

'Be sensible fer a minute,' she chided him. 'I gotta 'ave planks an' ladders ter do the flat up. I gotta make a start next week.'

'Yer don't fink I'm gonna let you do all that yerself, do yer?' Jimmy said quickly. 'I'll sort the decoratin' out.'

'Oh my Gawd,' Dolly mumbled as she raised her eyes to the heavens.

Jimmy gave her a superior look. 'It's men's work, decoratin',' he said, rolling his shoulders.

'What d'yer mean, men's work? Women can do decoratin' just as good as men. Better than most,' she told him firmly.

Jimmy realised he was wasting his time trying to argue with her and he raised his hands in a token of surrender. 'All right, gel, I'll 'ave a word wiv a friend o' mine. I'll see what I can come up wiv,' he said hopefully.

They walked out into the street together and Dolly suddenly laid her hand on his arm. 'By the way, yer don't know of anybody who does a bit o' spare-time carpentry, do yer, luv?' she asked him.

Jimmy pulled a face. 'Not since Jesus,' he replied quickly.

'I gotta get those room doors sorted out an' the cupboards need fixin' up,' Dolly said sighing.

'All right, leave it ter me,' Jimmy told her as he started off.

'I'll call round ternight, luv,' she said. 'Mind 'ow yer go.'

Don Farran had settled in at the sawmills and he had caught the eye of the foreman, who saw him as a sensible lad, strong and willing. He had put the young man in charge of cutting required lengths of wood for trade customers, and for the added responsibility he was paid an extra five shillings per week. Don was happy working there and he decided that the job would suffice until he was called up for National Service the following year. He also decided that he would ask Alice to get engaged before he was called up, and as he took his morning tea break he thought about what she had told him of her strict upbringing and how she had run away from home.

Alice had told him all about herself as they walked home through Rotherhithe Tunnel on Saturday night after visiting the Troxy cinema in Stepney. They had stopped to say goodnight in the shadow of the tunnel steps, and as she snuggled up in his arms she admitted that she was inexperienced in the ways of love but wanted him to make love to her. Her candour had shocked him at first, but it gave him the opportunity to talk to her openly about his feelings and aspirations. They both agreed that it would be a mistake to take any chances, knowing only too well what kind of trouble they might have to face.

Don knew in his heart, though, that Alice was the only girl for him and they would become lovers very soon. Their good-night sessions had become very passionate and he had found it difficult to restrain himself. He would have to be prepared. Alice had told him how her need for him had become almost desperate and that she trusted him more than she trusted herself. He could not let her down, and he promised himself that tonight he would call in at the chemist on his way home from work.

Orders flowed in during the day and Don was kept very busy. It was exacting work that needed his full concentration, and by the time he had placed the last of the required lengths of cut timber on to the appropriate stack it was almost five o'clock. He shut down his machine, put on his reefer jacket and hurried out of the yard towards a parade of shops at Dockhead. The chemist shop was busy, with customers standing around waiting for their prescriptions to be processed, and as he walked through the door Don noticed that there was an attractive young lady serving. There was no way that he could ask her for a packet of Durex, he told himself. He turned on his heel and walked out quickly, wondering why there was not an easier way of buying protectives than having to ask a pretty shop assistant. There should be a man's counter with a man serving there, he thought glumly.

Don crossed the main thoroughfare and walked into Abbey Street. He could see that Tony's barber shop was still open and that seemed a better proposition. Each time he had his hair trimmed and then went over to the till to pay the bill, Tony asked him with a sly wink if there was anything else he wanted.

As Don walked into the shop Tony greeted him cheerfully. ''Ello, me son. Didn't I do yer 'air last week?'

Don was about to ask for a packet of Durex when he noticed that the middle-aged man who was waiting to have his hair cut was looking at him. 'Er, yeah, but I need it short,' he said hesitantly.

Tony held up a mirror behind the customer in the chair and on receiving a satisfied nod he whipped the sheet away and motioned the middle-aged man to take his place. 'Anyfing else?' he asked the shorn young man as he rang the till.

He shook his head quickly and hurried from the shop.

Don sat down with a sigh and picked up a day-old newspaper while Tony turned his attention to the man in the chair.

''Ow's the missus, Ralph?' He asked pleasantly as he tucked the white sheet around him.

'Not too good, Tony,' the man replied.

'Sick is she?'

'She 'as bin.'

'What's bin the matter wiv 'er?' the curious barber asked.

'Gawd knows,' Ralph replied. ''Er face started swellin' all of a sudden. Frightened the bleedin' life out o' me it did.'

'Good Gawd,' Tony said, pushing on the back of the customer's head and running the clippers up the nape of his neck.

'I've never seen anyfing like it,' Ralph went on. 'It looked like 'er 'ole face was goin' out o' shape. 'Er chin seemed ter get bigger an' 'er ears started ter swell up. They looked like bloody pixies' ears.'

'Good Gawd.'

'Yeah, but that wasn't all.'

'No?'

'Nah, 'er face went all funny like.'

'Funny?'

'Yeah. She looked like a bleedin' 'orse, what wiv 'er teef gettin' bigger an' 'er ears sproutin' up,' Ralph told him.

'What did they say it was?' Tony asked, snipping away at the man's hair.

'They couldn't say. The doctor gave 'er some bloody great tablets ter take. One night an' one mornin'.'

'Did they do 'er any good?'

'Well, yes an' no.'

'What d'yer mean, yes an' no?'

'Well, 'er face ain't altered much, but she's stopped drinkin' out of 'orse-troughs.'

Tony looked disgusted as he glanced up at his customer in the large wall mirror and saw that he was grinning widely. 'Yer got me goin' then, didn't yer, Ralph?' he growled as he stretched out a leather strop and proceeded to sharpen a cutthroat razor. 'You ought ter be ashamed o' yerself, puttin' the mockers on yer missus.'

The customer's smile died suddenly as he caught a glimpse of Tony's wild eyes. ''Ere, go easy wiv that razor,' he said quickly.

Ralph left the barber shop intact and then Don was beckoned into the chair. He allowed Tony to snip away at his already tidy and short dark hair, and after the barber had cleaned up his neck with the razor and showed him the results in the hand mirror Don got up and fished into his trouser pocket.

'Anyfing else?' Tony asked as he rang the till.

'Er, er . . .'

'Shavin' soap, razor blades,' Tony suggested. 'I got a nice after-shave fer special occasions.'

'No, I . . . er, a packet o' three please,' Don finally blurted out.

'Sorry, mate, right out o' rubbers. Call in termorrer evenin', they should be in by then,' Tony said, holding out the sixpence change.

Don nodded and ignored the change as he hurried out of the shop, vowing that tomorrow he would call in at the chemist shop regardless.

He walked quickly along Abbey Street, feeling the cold air on his shaved neck, and suddenly he saw the Morgan boys standing outside Joe Diamond's corner shop.

'Bin fer a trim-up then?' John said, leering at him.

'You ain't bin ter that butcher Tony's, 'ave yer?' Ernie added grinning.

Don stopped and stared at them. 'What is it wiv you two? Are yer just out ter wind me up?' he said sharply.

John shook his head solemnly. 'Jus' bein' neighbourly,' he replied. 'By the way, did yer pass on that message to our Albert?'

Don stuck his chin out. 'I told yer before I ain't carryin' your messages,' he growled. 'If it's troublin' yer that much, why don't yer go an' see Albert yerself. Yer both know where 'e's stayin'.'

'I thought our bruv would 'ave moved inter your gaff by now,' Ernie said, still leering.

Don suddenly reached out and grabbed him by his lapels. 'What d'yer mean by that, Dumbo?' he snarled.

Ernie's face drained of colour. 'What's up wiv you? Can't yer take a joke?' he faltered.

'Not that sort,' Don replied quickly, letting go and glaring at him.

John Morgan pushed Ernie aside and stood facing Don, getting ready to hit him, but he noticed the portly figure of PC Kennedy ambling along on the other side of the road. He dug his hands into his trouser pockets and turned away with a sneer. 'If yer wanna do Albert a favour yer better warn 'im ter keep out of our ole man's way,' he said over his shoulder. 'Next time, Farran . . .'

Don turned into Fellmonger Street, furious at being confronted by the Morgans. He found it hard to understand why there should be such bad feeling between the brothers when Albert was only seeking to make a new life for himself and provide for Rose and the coming baby. One thing was for sure, he realised. He would have to put Albert on his guard.

Alice Copeland set to work on the belt-driven cutter on Monday afternoon as ordered, and she soon realised that the lumbering machine was inferior to the one she had operated in the past. It seemed very noisy, and when she pressed the foot pedal there appeared to be a very slight delay before the steel cutter dropped on to the large tin sheet. For the rest of the afternoon she persevered with the ancient contraption and she was glad when the factory whistle sounded and she could finally bring the rattling thing to a standstill.

On Tuesday morning when she arrived at the factory Alice expected to be put back on her usual machine, but Collis had other ideas.

'The main cutter's not fixed yet, so you stay on the spare cutter, Copeland,' he told her.

Alice gave him a cold look as she hurried past to take her place at the machine. It started up sluggishly as usual, but after an hour or so she realised that the noisy rattling was becoming more pronounced. Knowing that any malfunction should be reported immediately, Alice asked the supervisor to fetch Bernard Collis so that he could take a look.

'Up ter yer tricks again, Copeland?' the manager barked as he walked along the aisle.

'Just listen to it,' Alice said angrily. 'We're s'posed ter report any defect in our machines straight away, or 'ave you changed the rules again?'

'Don't get cheeky,' Collis said quickly, glancing up at the vibrating connecting-rod. 'All right, I'll go an' see Mr Penrose, 'e's givin' the orders now.'

'What do I do, shut it down?' Alice asked him.

'Penrose gives the orders, it's up to 'im,' Collis grumbled as he walked away smartly.

Alice slid another sheet of tin into place and pressed her foot down on the pedal. This time the steel knife remained hovering above the metal and the noise became deafening as the machinery shuddered violently. Alice stepped back in fright and before she had time to reach for the control lever the machine ground to a halt. Joe Baines, the foreman engineer, had been working on the adjacent cutter and he came over as it seized up.

'Where's Collis?' he growled as his assistant followed him over.

'I'll fetch 'im, Joe,' the young man said, hurrying off.

When the manager came along the aisle Joe Baines rounded on him. 'What did I tell yer?' he sneered.

Collis took the engineer by the arm and led him out of Alice's earshot. 'It's no good puttin' the onus on me, Joe,' he told him. 'I told Penrose that spare cutter was duff.'

'I 'ave ter take the can back fer breakdowns,' Joe said angrily. 'That main cutter would be workin' by now if I 'adn't 'ad ter strip the main bearin'. Now we've got anuvver big job ter take care of. I ain't a bloody miracle worker.'

'I know you're angry, Joe, an' rightly so,' Collis replied. 'All this trouble's come about since that silly ole fool Penrose started interferin'. I warned 'im we'd 'ave trouble but 'e took no notice. You leave it ter me. I'm gonna go upstairs right away. It's time I sorted Penrose out once an' fer all.'

Before he carried out his threat Bernard Collis hurried into his office and penned two memos which he took into the adjoining office and placed in the desk tray beneath a pile of papers. It was fortunate Penrose was not in that day, he thought smugly, as he slipped out of the office unnoticed and made his way to the main offices above the shopfloor.

Alice had recovered from her ordeal and was given the job of clearing up the metal shavings by a supervisor. She was thankful to get away from the ill-fated machine and she pushed the trolley along to where Rose was working on the large stamper. 'Did you 'ear the racket?' she asked grinning.

'Yeah, one o' the gels told me yer machine broke down,' Rose replied above the general din. 'That's a cushy job yer landed.'

'Wait till Collis finds out,' Alice said, pulling a face. ''E keeps this job fer 'is fancy ladies. I 'ope the gels don't get the wrong idea.'

'I don't fink they will,' Rose shouted. 'Are yer seein' Don ternight?'

Alice nodded. 'We're goin' fer a stroll up the West End ternight. Don said fer me ter call round.'

At four o'clock Collis came down into the factory with a satisfied smirk on his fat face. Ten years without one machine breaking down, and in the short time since Penrose had taken over there had been two machine failures. The directors could hardly ignore the facts, Collis told himself. Penrose would try to wriggle out of taking responsibility and say that he was not kept properly informed of the condition of the machinery, but who would be believed, when there were memos lying in Penrose's tray and carbon copies in his own file?

The smug grin was still there on the manager's face when he stepped out of his office to survey his domain, but it disappeared when he saw Alice Copeland pushing the shavings trolley along the aisle.

'Copeland! Leave that trolley, I've got anuvver job fer you,' he yelled.

When Don arrived home later than usual on Tuesday night the boys both gave him curious looks.

'You 'ad yer 'air cut?' Billy asked.

'Yer look like Checker Bald'ead,' Joey laughed.

Rose came in from the scullery and stared at him strangely. 'What yer done ter yer 'air, Don?' she asked, trying to hide a grin.

'I 'ad it cut,' Don said as casually as he could, taking off his jacket and flopping down into a chair.

'You only 'ad it cut last week,' Rose replied.

'Yeah, but I get a load o' sawdust in me 'air an' I've decided ter keep it a bit shorter,' Don told her.

'I like it better when it's nice an' wavy,' Rose remarked.

Don wanted to tell her he preferred it that way too, but he kept quiet as he picked up the evening paper and quickly scanned through it, noticing the report which said that the man found shot dead at New Fresh Wharf had been identified as Gus Lazaar, a South African who was known to the police.

Later that evening Alice came into the flat and looked at Don with a comical expression on her face. The young man held up his hands. 'I know what yer gonna say, Alice,' he told her, a ghost of a smile playing in the corner of his mouth. 'It was fer a good cause.'

'I fink it makes yer look older, Don,' she remarked, smiling back. 'Who cut it, the butcher?'

Don's eyes twinkled. 'I 'ad it cut at Tony's in Abbey Street.'

''E must 'ave 'ad 'is mind on somefing else at the time,' Alice joked.

'Yeah, so did I, ter tell yer the trufe,' Don replied.

Chapter Thirty-Three

On Wednesday morning as Rose Farran worked at her machine she had another worry to contend with. The previous morning she had left for work before the post arrived and as soon as she arrived home from work in the evening Billy had handed her the letter. The welfare people had been unfair in allowing the family just four weeks to complete the move, she thought angrily. The place needed so much doing to it and it looked an impossible task. Dolly would be incensed when she found out. It seemed that every time the sun came out another rain cloud quickly covered it.

Rose glanced up at the factory clock and sighed. The morning seemed to be dragging on endlessly and as she fed the thin tin sheets into the machine other worrying thoughts drifted into her mind. She would have to report to the antenatal clinic very soon, and it would soon be obvious to everyone at the factory that she was pregnant. Already her belly was beginning to swell and it would be difficult to conceal it, especially under her tight-fitting factory apron. There was also the problem of the rent. Dolly had told her that the new house would not be more than the present flat, but the mysterious benefactor could not be expected to go on paying for them indefinitely.

When the lunchtime hooter sounded Rose hurried along to the canteen and found Alice sitting alone at a table with a miserable look on her face.

'I'm leavin' on Friday, Rose,' she said sadly.

'Leavin'? Why?'

'It's me gran'ma. She's got really frail lately an' she's losin' 'er sight. I gotta get a part-time job so I can look after 'er,' Alice explained.

'I'm really sorry ter see yer go, Alice. This place won't seem the same wivout your cheerful face,' Rose told her, reaching out and squeezing her friend's arm.

Alice shrugged her shoulders. 'Never mind, you'll soon be leavin' 'ere yerself, an' at least we'll still be seein' each ovver,' she pointed out. 'I can't leave me gran'ma by 'erself all day long an' I'm not lettin' 'er go inter one o' those old people's 'omes. As a matter o' fact I got a job as a barmaid in a pub round the corner from where I live. I'll 'ave ter work in the evenin's an' it's gonna be awkward wiv me an' Don, but what else can I do?'

Rose shook her head sadly. It seemed so unfair, she thought. Alice was a good friend with a heart of gold. It was typical of her to put her grandmother before herself. However long the old lady still had, Alice would be sure to make every one of her years on earth as comfortable and as happy as possible, regardless of her own requirements.

'I shouldn't worry too much about Don,' Rose said. ''E's a very understandin' feller an' 'e knows all about family problems. Gawd knows we've got our share, Alice.'

The young woman forced a smile as she looked at Rose. 'At least I won't 'ave ter see that four-eyed ole git Collis every mornin',' she said brightly. 'I 'eard 'e's back in charge now. One o' the loaders told me George Penrose 'as gone back upstairs. Somefing ter do wiv the machinery breakin' down.'

Rose pulled a face. 'I'll be glad when I see the back o' this place,' she replied. 'I don't wanna wait till the last few weeks.'

'I should fink not,' Alice said quickly. 'This sort o' work ain't no good fer anyone in your condition, an' now that Collis is the big-I-am again you could be pushed all over the place. Just look what that ole goat's done ter me. I get all the worst o' the jobs. Mind yer, though, I'm gonna leave 'ere wiv a sting in me tail, all bein' well.'

'What d'yer mean?' Rose asked.

'Didn't yer see the notice board this mornin'?' Alice queried. 'No.'

'There's a union meetin' on Friday lunchtime in the canteen.'

Rose grinned. 'An' our Alice will no doubt be 'avin' a few words ter say.'

'Too true,' Alice grated. 'C'mon, let's take a stroll before we go back ter work an' I'll tell yer what I got planned. C'mon, yer baby needs the exercise.'

On Wednesday evening Don Farran walked into the chemist shop in Dockhead with a determined look on his slightly flushed face. The shop assistant smiled at him pleasantly as he reached the counter. 'Yes, sir?' she asked.

'Packet o' three, er, I mean a packet o' Durex,' he faltered, reddening a little more.

The assistant reached under the counter, her face coming nearer to his. 'Standard or Fetherlite?' she asked.

'Standard, please,' he mumbled, averting his eyes.

With his purchase safely stowed in his hip pocket Don walked home along Abbey Street feeling suddenly at ease. It was stupid to get so nervous about buying a packet of three, he told himself. After all, the woman in the shop must be selling dozens of packets every day and she would be used to it. Why should he get so screwed up about a woman serving him?

'Oi, Don.'

The young man turned quickly to see Tony beckoning from his shop doorway.

'They come in this mornin',' he called out.

Don groaned to himself as he walked over to the barber. 'It's all right, Tony, I've already got some,' he replied.

'Suit yerself,' Tony said, shrugging his shoulders. 'Anyway I'm doin' a promotion. Buy two packets an' yer get one free. Just remember, nine jumps fer the price o' six. Can't be bad, can it?'

Dolly Morgan had told Rose that she could get in touch at any time through Jimmy Rideout, and when Dolly called in on him early on Wednesday evening he showed her the letter.

'It's nuffink more than I expected from the likes o' them,' Dolly said in an angry voice. 'They looked a right pair if you ask me. Well, I'm not gonna be beat, Jimmy. I'm gonna get that place done up in time if it kills me.'

'I told yer, Dolly, I'm in this wiv yer,' Jimmy said quietly. 'We'll get the place sorted out between us. Stop finkin' it's all on your shoulders. I got a stake in this too.'

'Why should you get involved in all this, Jimmy? You've got enough problems of yer own ter sort out,' Dolly replied as she slipped off her coat and sank down into an easychair beside the fire.

'Look, Doll, I don't want yer ter get this wrong,' he said in a steady voice as he sat down in the chair facing her. 'I'm not in this ter make me look good in your eyes. I wanna do this fer Gerry. Yer know me an' your Gerry were good pals an' we often 'ad a few pints tergevver.' Jimmy paused and took a deep breath. 'Well, one night me an' 'im went out fer a couple o' pints. It was just before the invasion. I 'appened ter be between ships an' Gerry was on embarkation leave. 'E knew that 'is mob were goin' in on the initial landin's an' we 'ad a serious chat about it. Gerry was convinced that 'e wasn't gonna make it back 'ome. I tried ter reassure 'im by sayin' that it was the way we all felt in the navy every time we sailed out on convoy duty, but Gerry shook 'is 'ead an' gave me a sad smile. I'll never ferget that smile as long as I live. It's me last real recollection of 'im an' rememberin' that smile keeps 'is face alive in me memory.'

Dolly sighed sadly. 'I remember Gerry's smile,' she said. 'It was a sort o' lopsided smile, like a youngster's when 'e's bin up ter mischief.'

'Yeah, that's it,' Jimmy chimed in. 'Anyway, like I say, I tried ter cheer 'im up an' 'e got a bit narked actually. 'E told me 'e wasn't worried fer 'imself but fer the kids. 'E was aware that Ida 'ad bin seein' ovver men while 'e was away in the army but they'd patched it up fer the kids' sake. Fings were all right fer a time after Susan was born but then Ida started ter get restless. Gerry knew 'er well enough an' 'e told me point-blank that as soon as young Susan was toddlin' around Ida would be up to 'er tricks again. 'E asked me ter promise 'im that if 'e got killed in action I'd keep me eye on the kids. I fink 'e was worried about Ida bringin' the sort o' blokes 'ome ter the 'ouse who'd ill treat 'em, although 'e never said as much. Anyway, I promised 'im I'd watch out fer 'em. I 'ave ter say that as far as I knew Ida never brought a bloke 'ome. I didn't expect 'er ter be in widow's weeds fer long, but I never ever thought she'd run off an' leave those kids. Someone 'ad ter do somefink to 'elp the poor little bleeders.'

'So you decided ter pay the rent for 'em,' Dolly cut in.

'No, yer got it wrong. I . . .'

'Yer don't 'ave ter lie, Jimmy,' Dolly said quietly. 'I've known fer a couple o' weeks now.'

''Ow did yer find out?' he asked.

'On the way back from seein' my solicitor I stopped off at London Bridge ter buy some fruit,' Dolly began, grinning at him. 'The feller on the stall started chattin' me up, until I told 'im I was a good friend o' yours. We 'ad a long chat about yer, Jimmy. 'E finks a lot o' you. In fact 'e told me 'ow you were payin' the rent fer a family who'd bin left ter fend fer themselves after their farvver was killed in the war an' their muvver run off. 'E told me that 'e deducted the rent money from the rent o' the stalls an' gave it to 'is wife ter pay in ter the estate office. 'E asked me not ter say anyfing to yer in case yer gave 'im an ear'ole bashin'. Anyway I would 'ave found out sooner or later. I've gotta see the estate people ter give 'em notice.'

'I'd sooner yer didn't tell the Farrans,' Jimmy said quickly.

'But why, Jimmy?' Dolly asked.

'I don't want 'em ter feel they're indebted ter me, that's all,' he replied, getting up from his chair.

'Well, they are indebted to yer, an' so am I,' Dolly said as she stood up facing him. 'You're a good man, Jim Rideout. I don't know 'ow they would 'ave managed wivout your 'elp.'

Jimmy smiled as she leaned forward and kissed him on his cheek. 'I'd better go an' put the kettle on,' he said, rolling his eyes suggestively.

Dolly followed him out into the scullery. 'I really am grateful. You're a good friend, Jim, an' Gawd only knows I need somebody I can lean on,' she told him.

'I can be more than a good friend, Dolly,' he said quietly, his eyes searching hers.

'Give me some time, luv. I've got so much ter fink about now,' she replied softly.

Jimmy nodded. 'I understand. But when all this trouble is sorted out I'll be askin' fer a straight answer about you an' me. Yer know what I mean.'

'I know, Jim.'

He struck a match, lit the gas jet and lifted the heavy iron kettle over the flame. 'I've made a few enquiries an' I fink I've got a ladder an' a couple o' planks,' he told her. 'This mate o' mine's gonna lend us some brushes an' buckets as well. We'll manage, don't worry.'

Dolly sighed deeply. 'I need ter see young Rose ternight. Come wiv me, Jim.'

He nodded as he picked up the tea-caddy and began spooning the black leaf into a chipped enamel teapot. 'Yeah, all right, but don't go mentionin' anyfing about me payin' the rent, will yer, luv?' he warned her.

'All right, I won't, if that's the way yer want it,' Dolly replied.

'Yeah, it is.'

'Jimmy, 'ave you got somefing worryin' yer?'

'No. Why?'

'You've shovelled 'alf the bloody contents o' that tea-caddy inter the pot,' she told him, shaking her head sadly.

Frankie Morgan summoned his two boys to the saloon bar of the Anchor on Wednesday night for a council of war. The three of them sat in the far corner where they could observe what was going on around them while they talked.

'I dunno what's 'appenin' ter this family,' Frankie said angrily, as he put the drinks down on the table. 'First yer bruvver gives us the elbow, then we do a good professional job an' get took on, then ter crown it all yer muvver pisses off. I reckon somebody's put a poxy curse on us.'

'I thought it was you who give Albert the elbow,' John said, glancing at his father.

'Yeah, after 'e backed out on us,' Frankie replied sharply. 'I've always drummed it inter you boys that we stick tergevver as a family. Albert let us down an' I 'ad ter take 'is place. I'm gettin' too old fer those sort o' capers. S'posin' we'd 'ave got collared. You two are clean but wiv my form I'd be lookin' at a fifteen stretch. What was I s'posed ter do? Go on, tell me. Was I s'posed ter face those two double-dealin' bastards an' say, "sorry, chaps, one o' me boys don't fancy the caper so we'll 'ave ter pass on this one"? No, I 'ad ter convince 'em that I was still capable. As it 'appened, I managed ter persuade 'em in the end but it wasn't easy.'

'It would 'ave bin a good fing if you 'adn't, now,' Ernie piped in.

'That's anuvver fing we gotta get sorted out pretty soon,' Frankie growled. 'I don't like me an' my family bein' took on. Two grand was peanuts, considerin' the value o' those diamonds. Priceless, the bloke on the wireless said. All the papers said the same. We was used, an' if that jeweller 'ad snuffed it we'd be dodgin' the rope right now.'

'What can we do?' John asked. 'We've bin over ter the delicatessen an' got no joy there.'

'I reckon the geezer was lyin',' Ernie said.

'Nah, 'e was bein' straight enough,' Frankie replied. ''E said the room was booked by phone an' I fer one believed 'im when 'e said 'e didn't know the geezers. 'E wasn't gonna ask too many questions as long as 'e got the rent, that's a dead cert.'

'So what do we do about it?' Ernie asked.

''Ow the bloody 'ell do I know,' Frankie hissed. 'Can't you two fink of anyfing, or 'as it always gotta be left up ter me?'

'I reckon we should go over an' 'ave words wiv that Malt, Andretti,' John Morgan said quietly. 'Those geezers who came ter see us said it was Andretti who recommended us in the first place.'

'Yeah, 'e would know 'ow ter contact 'em, surely,' Ernie added.

'I'm glad yer finally pullin' yerselves tergevver,' Frankie said sarcastically. 'That's what I wanna talk ter yer about. I'm plannin' ter go over an' see 'im, but it wouldn't do fer us all ter go. It'd look too much like a show of force an' we'd get nowhere. I plan to 'ave a quiet word in the Malt's ear an' let 'im know we're not too pleased at the outcome.'

'What then?' John asked.

'I wanna meet wiv those two monkeys again,' Frankie snarled. 'Nobody takes us on wiv impunity.'

'If you ask me I'd say we'd do better lettin' it drop,' Ernie cut in. 'We're likely ter bite off more than we can chew.'

'We'll see about that,' Frankie told him sharply.

The three sipped their drinks in silence for a few minutes, then Ernie looked up at his father. 'D'yer want me ter go an' see Albert?' he asked.

'What for?' Frankie asked in return.

'Muvver might 'ave told 'im 'ow long she was gonna stay at Joe's,' Ernie replied.

'She can stay as long as she likes as far as I'm concerned,' Frankie told his son. 'I'm not goin' cap-in-'and to 'er. She'll come 'ome when she's ready.'

Ernie stared down at his drink with a moody expression on his swarthy face. He did not like having to fend for himself and he had already scorched his best shirt while attempting to iron it. It was all right for the old man, he thought grumpily. That floozy barmaid was looking after him. He wouldn't be so flash if he had to cook and wash and iron for himself.

John got up to order fresh drinks and Frankie turned to his younger son. 'Make sure yer stay away from Albert. I don't want yer talkin' to 'im,' he said quickly. 'In fact I don't want any more ter do wiv 'im. 'E's no son o' mine after what 'e did.'

'I'm not gonna argue wiv yer, Farvver, but I can see the sort o' position 'e's in,' Ernie replied. 'After all, 'e's got a kid on the way an' if 'e wants ter go straight it's up to 'im, surely.'

'That's right, but not after sayin' 'e was in on the job,' Frankie retorted. 'I wouldn't 'ave give 'im no grief if 'e'd told me after the job that 'e wanted out. As it was, I got put in a very dicey situation. We could 'ave all lost out over 'im changin' 'is mind at the last minute. Just give 'im a wide berf, an' if yer do bump into 'im warn 'im off callin' round our 'ouse any more, 'cos if 'e does, an' I'm there at the time, I might lose me temper wiv 'im.'

John returned with the drinks and the three sat talking together for a while until Frankie left to visit his barmaid friend at the George, unaware that not very far away last-minute plans were being finalised to take the Morgan family into custody.

Bill Grogan was a patient man, but his patience was wearing thin. He had the Morgan family located and knew that he could seize them all without too much trouble as long as word came through from the Yard within the next few days.

Grogan knew full well that Frankie Morgan tended to move around quite a lot and any undue delay could prove disastrous. At the moment he was staying with Elsie Richards, but her husband was due home from sea at any time now and Frankie would have to move house.

Why did the top brass have to move so slowly, he wondered, already guessing the answer. It all centred on the Right Honourable Hamish MacKenzie MP. According to reports he was making good progress and had spoken to the press about his ordeal. He would have been primed by the powers that be, and after a top-level meeting to co-ordinate matters, permission would finally be given for the arrests to commence.

Bill Grogan was having a quiet chat with Chief Inspector Ray Halleron, his colleague from the Yard, when the phone rang. He picked up the receiver for the umpteenth time that day but this time he stiffened as he heard the brief message.

'It's a green, Ray,' he said sighing with relief. 'I'll tell the sergeant to assemble the team in fifteen minutes and we can do the final briefing. OK?'

Inspector Halleron nodded. He was only too aware that the snatch was just the first part of the operation. A lot of effort was required to put together a watertight case against the villains. There was no margin for error on this one, and, with the most senior echelons taking a personal interest, heads would roll and careers would be ruined if a conviction was not forthcoming due to stupid mistakes on the ground.

'Ready, Ray?'

Halleron got up and crossed his fingers as he followed Grogan along the corridor to the briefing room.

Chapter Thirty-Four

Elsie Richards had a chequered past, but now that she had moved away from Limehouse and found a couple of rooms in Bermondsey she prided herself on the fact that at long last she had become quite respectable. At forty-five, Elsie had felt that she was not able to pick and choose her clients so easily, and after one or two nasty experiences she had seen the light. Her pimp had been disappointed with the money she was making and told her in no uncertain terms that he wasn't going to put up with it for much longer. Elsie had known full well what that meant. Charlie Bass had left his mark on one or two of his unproductive prostitutes and he conducted a reign of terror amongst his girls with impunity, being under the protective umbrella of Andretti, the Maltese gang leader.

One Saturday Elsie Richards had felt unwell and decided to take the night off. It was nothing serious and she felt that Charlie Bass would understand. After all it wasn't often that she felt off colour. Charlie wasn't at all happy with her excuse, however, and after he left the pub that Saturday night he called round to see her. Elsie was in her dressing robe when he barged in, and the smell of whisky on his breath made it plain that he was going to make things difficult for her. It was always the same when Charlie Bass got drunk on whisky.

Elsie did not try to struggle when the pimp dragged her into the bedroom and threw her down roughly on to the bed. To resist him would only make him vicious, and she knew that when Charlie Bass got vicious he not only used his fists, he cut his victims with a taped-up cut-throat razor which he always carried for protection. Elsie closed her eyes and bit on her lip in anguish as he ravished her, praying for him to finish quickly and leave her in peace. Charlie had other ideas that night, and when he demanded of her something that even she as an experienced prostitute found disgusting and depraved she decided that enough was enough and to hell with the consequences. Hiding her disgust she told him that she had to get a drink of water first, and while she was out of the bedroom she concealed a carving knife under her robe.

Elsie still shuddered whenever she recalled that moment when the pimp reached out for her and she plunged the knife deep into his chest. The look of shock on his face and the sight of his wide-open eyes and the spurting blood covering her hand would live in her memory until the day she died. He coughed blood and spume out of his mouth and chest and shuddered violently, finally falling dead at her feet in his own mess.

Elsie was panic-stricken and beside herself with fear, but she knew she had to pull herself together if she were to survive. What could she do? Once Andretti found out that she had killed her pimp he would dispatch his henchmen and they would make sure that she paid the penalty. It was then that she thought of Big Lou. His ship was in dock and she knew that he always spent his evenings at the Elephant's Head, a public house in Limehouse Reach, and on Saturday nights would often go on to the Blue Heaven, a Chinese restaurant in Pennyfields, before returning to his ship.

Big Lou Merrifield was a docile man of enormous strength with the mind of a child. He adored Elsie and had been very helpful to her on a couple of occasions when drunken seamen pestered her. He had never paid for her services but they had often spent time together in the pub, Lou chatting to her in his slow, hesitant way and Elsie listening indulgently. Now she needed his help desperately and there was no time to lose. Fortunately Lou was at his usual Saturday night haunt enjoying a bowl of chicken chow mein, and in no time at all Charlie Bass had been rolled up in Elsie's bloodstained bedroom carpet and bedclothes and dumped in the high-flowing, murky Thames at Limehouse Steps.

Elsie felt as though a huge weight was lifted from her slim shoulders. Charlie Bass had been an evil, vicious man. He had controlled quite a few prostitutes and had many enemies, and no one would have reason to link her with his disappearance. Even if the body was recovered from the river, Andretti would not suspect her of the pimp's murder. After all, it would need a great deal of strength to carry a rolled and roped-up man the size of Bass and chuck him into the Thames. Big Lou could be trusted to keep his mouth shut. Lou was childish, yes, but not stupid, Elsie reasoned. She would have to move away though, as soon as possible. Better if she crossed the river and went where no one knew her.

It was big Lou Merrifield who helped her move her things to Salmon Lane in riverside Bermondsey on a cold January morning in '48. She knew that Lou had saved her life and she felt a great debt of gratitude. Knowing that he was sailing off to Hong Kong the following day, Elsie took him to her bed. Big Lou needed very little in life apart from a full belly, a few pints of ale and a warm bed on a cold night, and he left for sea a contented man. When he returned from the Orient Elsie was waiting, and before he sailed off again she and Big Lou Merrifield were married.

Life had changed so much for Elsie Richards and she now had respectability and a husband who adored her. She did not love Lou in the way he loved her, but she felt comfortable and secure with the docile giant of a man who asked very little of her. Between trips things were good, but the long periods of loneliness when Lou was away at sea began to weigh down on her and she decided to find herself a job behind a bar during the evenings.

It was soon after she started work at the George public house in Dockhead that she met Frankie Morgan. He had started to call in there with a few cronies and they usually discussed their business in the quiet saloon bar. Elsie felt that he was very charming and good-mannered, and handsome into the bargain. Rumours of his lifestyle only served to raise her sense of excitement and before long she found herself openly flirting with him. Frankie Morgan had played his cards well and one Saturday night after the pub closed he took her for a meal and then went back to her house for a goodnight drink. The next morning after he had left, Elsie was filled with a mixture of remorse and cold fear. She felt ashamed of letting Big Lou down and terrified that he might learn of her indiscretion from some trouble-making neighbour when he returned.

As time went on Elsie became more brazen. The neighbours had seemed to turn a blind eye to what was going on, and like the East End folk they knew how to keep their own counsel in such matters. One or two casually mentioned Frankie and Elsie told them that he was a relative who came to stay when he was in the area. No one ever remarked on it being a coincidence that Frankie seemed to turn up in the area every time Big Lou left on a trip, and Elsie accepted that people knew of her dalliance and said nothing, presumably out of regard for Big Lou who would only be hurt by wagging tongues.

On Wednesday night, while the last-minute preparations were taking place at Dockhead police station, Elsie Richards was busy serving behind the bar and she looked visibly shocked when the door opened and Big Lou walked in grinning broadly.

'What you doin' 'ere, Lou? I wasn't expectin' yer 'ome till next week,' she blurted out.

'Yeah, I know, luv, but our ship burst a boiler. We made it ter Naples an' they flew us 'ome ter pick up anuvver ship,' he explained. 'I'm only 'ome fer two nights.'

Elsie filled a pint glass with bitter and handed it to him, her eyes briefly catching Frankie's. 'Well, at least yer 'ome safe an' sound, luv,' she told the gentle giant.

John Morgan left the Anchor and walked home feeling bad-tempered. He had had words with Ernie over something trivial and his brother had stormed out to visit another pub. Things had been strained between them since their mother had packed her bags and left. There were no clean and pressed shirts waiting for them both, and no meals prepared when they came home in the evenings. John Morgan was fed up to the teeth with fish and chips and pie and mash. He longed for a good meal of meat and two veg and yearned to come home to a warm fire instead of having to rake out the ashes and make it up himself in the evenings. Ernie had been getting on his nerves with his constant griping, moaning on about going to find lodgings with someone who could serve him up a decent meal. Maybe he should do the same, he thought.

Ernie was already sitting beside a low fire when he arrived home, and after a few muttered words over a stale cheese sandwich and a mug of tea they both went up to bed. John undressed and slipped between the cold sheets, shivering as he pulled the bedclothes over his head. Ernie sat on the edge of his bed and rolled a cigarette before he undressed, as was his custom. 'I'm bloody well pissed orf wiv this,' he grumbled.

'It's no good to keep moanin' about it,' John growled from under the blankets.

'Our Albert's got it made,' Ernie went on. ''E's got decent lodgin's an' the woman does all 'is food as well.'

'Why don't yer piss off an' find lodgin's too then?' John told him in a sleepy voice.

'Don't worry, I'm goin' to, soon as I can,' Ernie grumbled.

'Yeah, all right.'

'Don't fink I won't.'

'Get in bed an' go ter sleep, fer Gawd sake.'

A loud crash on the front door and the sound of splintering wood startled the two young men and as Ernie jumped to his feet, burly detectives barged into the bedroom and grabbed them both.

'John Morgan, Ernest Morgan, you're both under arrest on suspicion of armed robbery,' Bill Grogan said in a quiet but authoritative voice. 'Read 'em their rights, sergeant.'

Lou Merrifield climbed into bed beside Elsie. She turned over and snuggled up to him, feeling a little disappointed that the night was not going to be as exciting as she had expected. Lou was tired from his long journey, and after a quick goodnight kiss he closed his eyes. For a while Elsie lay awake, listening to Lou's shallow breathing and feeling the slight rise and fall of his chest; then, with her eyelids getting heavy, she yawned and finally started drifting off to sleep. Suddenly she was woken by the sound of wood splintering and heavy footfalls storming up the stairs. The bedroom door burst open and she found herself staring up at two large men. Lou had woken with a start and he sat up quickly. For a few moments he looked up at the two detectives and then he sprang into action.

Bill Grogan and Ray Halleron were well aware of their responsibilities and they had planned the timing of the arrests with precision. They wanted to make a thorough search of the house after the Morgan boys had been taken into custody and then be on hand for the apprehension of Frankie Morgan. With that in mind the first raid took place at exactly one a.m. By one forty the first stage of the operation had been completed and Grogan and Halleron then drove on to Dockhead. The Salmon Lane raid was planned for one thirty and the arresting officers had been ordered to detain Frankie Morgan and hold him at the house until Grogan and Halleron arrived. It took five minutes for the short journey from Basin Street to Salmon Lane and when the police car pulled up outside Elsie Richard's house Grogan felt a pang of anxiety. Glass from an upstairs window littered the street below and lights were on in the adjacent houses. Enquiring faces were peering through curtains and one elderly woman was standing at her front door wrapped in a dressing gown. As the two senior officers hurried into Elsie's house they saw one of the arresting detectives sitting in a chair holding a wet flannel over his eye. The man's colleague came out of the scullery looking even worse, with one eye beginning to close and blood around his nose and mouth. He too was dabbing at his face with a wet cloth and he looked sheepishly at the two inspectors. 'Frankie Morgan wasn't here,' he groaned.

'Who's this?' Grogan asked, pointing to Big Lou.

'His name's Lou Merrifield and he's a bloody maniac, if you ask me.'

The detective sitting in the chair removed the wet flannel and looked up, wincing sharply. 'He didn't give us a chance to explain who we were and what we were doing here,' he grumbled.

'What d'yer expect, breakin' into a bloke's 'ouse,' Lou said in his slow baritone. 'Fink yerself lucky I didn't chuck yer frew the winder.'

'He would have done if Joe here hadn't jumped on his back,' the detective muttered, frowning.

Grogan and Halleron exchanged glances as Elsie Richards walked into the room after hurriedly dressing.

'D'yer mind tellin' me what right yer 'ave burstin' inter my 'ouse in the middle of the night an' scarin' the bleedin' life out o' me?' she asked angrily. 'Ter say nuffink o' the neighbours.'

Grogan raised his hands in a pacifying gesture. 'We're looking for Frankie Morgan and we had reason to believe that he was staying here with you,' he replied quickly. 'I'm sorry if we frightened you, but I think you'll agree that you and your man friend are not the only injured parties here.'

Big Lou looked at the inspector with a puzzled frown and then turned to Elsie. 'You ain't 'ad any men 'ere while I was away at sea, 'ave yer?' he asked her.

'Certainly not,' Elsie replied indignantly. 'You know me better than that, Lou.'

Inspector Halleron hid a smile as he turned to Grogan. 'I think we'd better sort out that broken window,' he said pointedly. 'Can you help us with a few details for our report, Miss – er, Mrs Merrifield?'

Elsie followed the two senior officers into the passage and when they were out of sight of Big Lou, Grogan grabbed her firmly by the arm and glared at her. 'Now listen to me,' he said darkly. 'We know Frankie Morgan's been staying here, and if you don't want to be arrested for complicity in armed robbery I suggest you come clean. Where is he staying?'

'Frankie was gonna stay 'ere ternight but my man came

'ome unexpected,' Elsie said quickly. 'It's the God's trufe. I would 'ave thought 'e went 'ome to 'is own place.'

'Well, he didn't,' Grogan replied sharply. 'Can you give us any idea where he might be?'

Elsie shook her head. 'Look, I'm not gonna get mixed up in anyfing illegal. If I 'ad any idea where 'e might be I'd tell yer, honest I would.'

Grogan nodded. 'All right, I believe you. But if I find out you're holding back on Morgan's whereabouts I'll be back here to let your sailor friend know just what a devious bitch you are. I expect he'll be a bit put out to say the least, and by the look of my two men I'd say he's got quite a violent temper.'

When the police finally left, Elsie turned to Big Lou. 'I bet the man they was after was the one who was stayin' wiv Mrs Gregory at number seven,' she remarked with her fingers crossed behind her back. ''E looked a funny sort o' bloke ter me.'

Lou stood up and flexed his muscles. 'I showed 'em, didn't I, Elsie?' he said grinning.

'You certainly did, luv,' she replied with a sigh of relief.

Frankie Morgan had felt cheated out of a good night with Elsie Richards and he decided reluctantly to go home. He left the pub and walked out into the cold night air, his hands thrust into his overcoat pockets. The main road was quiet, apart from a late-night tram that rumbled past and a taxicab cruising slowly towards him from the opposite direction. Suddenly he had an idea and he hailed the cab. Joe Andretti had told him he was always welcome at his gambling club in Stepney and Frankie wanted to have a chat with the East End villain anyway.

Frankie sat back and lit a cigarette as the taxi drove along Jamaica Road and turned into the Rotherhithe Tunnel. Andretti should be able to locate the two men who hired him for the robbery, he thought. They were going to be told in no uncertain terms that Frankie Morgan did not take kindly to being stitched up, and there was more money due to him and his boys from the proceeds.

The cab emerged from the tunnel and turned right at the traffic lights, moving off in the direction of the West India Dock Road. At the sailors' hostel it swung left and pulled up outside a dimly lit restaurant.

Frankie paid off the driver and entered Joe Andretti's headquarters, to be confronted by a large man who looked as though his face had been worked over at some length with a cricket bat.

'I've come ter see Mr Andretti. The name's Morgan, Frankie Morgan.'

'Wait 'ere, pal.'

Frankie watched the bruiser duck behind a curtain and he cast his eye about the restaurant. All the tables in the large room were occupied and the place was tastefully furnished. Large draperies covered the windows and red candles were burning on every table. Waiters hovered attentively and hurried through the layer of blue tobacco smoke that hung in the air and Frankie noticed that the head waiter was eyeing him curiously.

'This way, pal.'

Frankie followed the doorman up a flight of carpeted stairs and found himself on a wide landing. His escort tapped on a door and then opened it and stood back. The Bermondsey villain felt a little self-conscious as he walked into the lavishly furnished room. Joe Andretti was sitting in a high-backed leather chair behind a large walnut desk and he stood up with a practised smile and held out his podgy hand. 'Nice to see you, Frankie. What can I do for you?' he said, displaying a row of gold-capped teeth.

Frankie shook the big man's hand and sat down beside the desk. 'I need yer 'elp, Mr Andretti,' he told him.

'Call me Joe, all my friends do,' the gang boss said amiably. 'Can I get you a drink?'

Frankie nodded. 'A gin an' tonic, please.'

Andretti walked over to a large cabinet. 'I hope you're not unhappy with the outcome of the venture, my friend,' he remarked, taking up a bottle of Gordon's and pouring out a stiff measure. 'I understand it went off very successfully.'

'That's exactly why I'm 'ere, Joe,' Frankie replied, taking the proffered drink. 'I feel that me an' my boys 'ave bin took on an' I want a meet wiv those contacts o' yours.'

'You were paid?' Andretti queried.

'Oh yes, we were paid,' Frankie told him, anger edging his voice, 'but I reckon the payment ter be way out, considerin' the risks we took an' the value o' the diamonds. They were priceless.'

Andretti seated himself and sipped his drink reflectively. Then he put the glass down and looked at his visitor with steely eyes. 'You understand that I recommended you for the job, but you have to know that I don't make the deals,' he explained. 'That's something you will have to discuss with the two who first spoke to you.'

'I understand,' Frankie said. 'Can you arrange a meet?'

Andretti took another sip of his drink and stroked his chin thoughtfully for a few moments. 'Can you be at the Cutty Sark pub in Greenwich tomorrow at noon?'

Frankie nodded and took up his drink. 'I'll be there.'

'Right then. I'll inform my contacts first thing,' the gang boss told him. 'But tonight you should relax. Why don't you enjoy a spell at the tables. Who knows, you might be lucky. My man will show you the way.'

Frankie gulped down his drink and stood up. 'I'm very

much obliged, Mr Andretti, I mean Joe,' he said, holding out his hand. 'I fink I'll take up your offer.'

As soon as the Bermondsey villain had left the room Andretti picked up the phone.

'My name is Joe Andretti. I'd like to speak to Chief Inspector Halleron.'

Chapter Thirty-Five

Thursday morning began just like every other workday morning for Rose Farran. She roused Don and then woke the children up with cups of tea, made sure that they washed and dressed for school before she and Don left for work, and then finally she knocked at Freda's flat to let her know that she was on her way out. The friendly neighbour would then make sure that the children left for school on time and the flat was securely shut. It was a daily ritual that had gone on ever since the Farrans' mother had left them to fend for themselves, but this particular morning Rose was met on the stairs by a very worried-looking Albert Morgan holding a copy of the *Daily Mirror* in his hand.

'John an' Ernie 'ave bin arrested an' they're lookin' fer me farvver, Rose,' he said breathlessly.

'Oh no!' Rose gasped, her hand coming up to her mouth. 'When?'

'Early this mornin',' Albert told her, showing her the newspaper. 'Look, it's on the second page.'

Rose took the paper and leaned against the iron stair-rail as she read the report.

BERMONDSEY POLICE RAID

Early this morning police investigating the Berkeley Street jewel robbery raided a house in Basin Street, Bermondsey and arrested two men. Another man is being sought in connection with the robbery after a second raid on a house in Dockhead where the man was reported to have been staying. A police spokesman said that an early arrest is anticipated. The police would not confirm or deny that the arrests are linked with the murder of the South African, Gus Lazaar, whose body was recently discovered at New Fresh Wharf in Billingsgate. When pressed about the recovery of the Cape Diamonds, stolen during the robbery, the police would only say that an official statement would be made as soon as possible.

Rose looked up at Albert's ashen face. ''Ow would they 'ave found out?' she asked him.

Albert shook his head. 'Somebody must 'ave shopped 'em,' he replied. 'My bruvvers wouldn't 'ave gone around braggin' about the raid, Rose, nor would the ole man. There was too much ter lose on this one.'

'They wouldn't fink it was you, would they?' Rose asked him anxiously.

'Surely they wouldn't fink I'd shop 'em,' Albert said, his large dark eyes growing hurt. 'After all they're still my flesh an' blood.'

The two young people walked out of the block together and stood on the wet pavement, and Albert looked at Rose appealingly. 'What can I do?' he asked her.

'There's nuffink yer can do fer the time bein,' she said gently, 'unless yer try Dock'ead police station. Yer might be able ter see yer bruvvers.'

'The police wouldn't let nobody near 'em 'cept fer a solicitor,' Albert told her. 'If they get charged an' remanded in custody I can see 'em then, I expect; that's if they'll see me.'

Rose realised that she was going to be late for work and she took Albert's arm. 'Walk wiv me, Alb, it's almost eight o'clock. We can talk on the way,' she said.

They walked quickly out of the turning into Abbey Street through the morning drizzle, Albert holding on to Rose's arm with his free hand thrust into his overcoat pocket. 'I wanted ter make an early start this mornin' so I could canvass fer some extra business when I finished the round,' he explained. 'Anyway, I went into a caff in Bermon'sey Street fer a quick cuppa before I started an' the paper was lyin' on the seat. When I saw that report, Rose, I felt sick ter me stomach. They'll do ten years apiece. As fer me farvver, Gawd knows what 'e'll get wiv 'is record.'

Rose could think of little she might say to make Albert feel any easier, but she was deeply relieved that he was in the clear. Things could have been so different. If he had not found out about her having his baby, he would have been in on the raid. Subconsciously she laid her hand on her stomach and Albert looked at her with concern.

'Is it kickin'?' he asked anxiously.

Rose smiled. 'It's too early yet. I'm only just over three months,' she told him.

'I'm so glad I found out about the baby, Rose,' he said quietly.

'I was just finkin' the same,' she replied. 'P'raps it was all meant ter be. Maybe someone's watchin' out fer us.'

They crossed the main thoroughfare at Dockhead and walked quickly towards the factory entrance. 'I'm sorry if I've made yer late, Rose,' he said, spotting the church clock.

'They don't worry over a few minutes,' Rose lied. 'I'll see yer ternight, Albert.'

The young man kissed her on the cheek and watched her hurry into the factory. Maybe she was right, he thought. Perhaps there was someone watching over them. He turned on his heel and hurried back towards Bermondsey Street. The rain was getting heavier and he felt that he would be better occupied canvassing for the rest of the morning and then see what could be done on the house. The walls had to be stripped and replastered in places, then there were the ceilings to be lined and distempered. So much to do in so little time, he sighed. Just four weeks to turn a ramshackle hovel into a house fit for a young family to live in. As he crossed the Tower Bridge Road at Long Lane and then turned into Bermondsey Street past the old parish church, Albert looked up at the leaden sky and said a silent prayer.

Rose hurried into Bromilow's and immediately saw Bernard Collis standing beside the time-clock, his arms folded and a look of satisfaction on his fat round face. 'You're ten minutes late, Farran. Lose a quarter,' he told her.

Rose handed him her clock card without saying anything and he pencilled in the penalty.

''Ere, yer can do mine as well while yer at it.'

Rose recognised the voice and turned to see Alice grinning mischievously at her.

Collis snatched the card and scribbled on it. 'Appallin' record,' he said in disgust.

'Get stuffed,' Alice mumbled.

'What was that?' Collis barked.

'I was talkin' ter Rose,' Alice replied, keeping a straight face.

'I won't be sorry ter see the back o' you, Copeland,' he grated. 'We don't like troublemakers in this firm.'

'One more day,' Alice told him with a sweet smile.

'Seven more hours an' forty-five minutes an' I'll be out o' the calaboose.'

'All right, that's enough. Get on the cutter, Copeland,' he said sharply. 'Farran, you're on the stamper.'

Alice winked at Rose as she hurried off. 'If I don't see yer at lunchtime I'll see yer at the union meetin' termorrer,' she called out for the manager's benefit.

Collis stormed off to his office in a black mood. The union had only been involved with Bromilow's for a few days and already they were trying to cause trouble, he scowled. They wanted anti-slip mats in the aisles and after the mishap with the cutter they were seeking safety certificates for all machines. Well, if they thought they were going to frighten him into bowing and scraping to a bunch of Bolsheviks then they were barking up the wrong tree. There was only one manager on the shopfloor now, and they would soon see that he was a force to be reckoned with.

As he walked towards his office Collis saw the union convenor standing outside.

'Ah, Mr Brady. What can I do fer yer?' he asked smiling.

'I'm still waitin' fer the management's answer on those proposals we put to 'em yesterday,' the convenor said a little irritably.

'Come along in, Mr Brady,' Collis replied. 'I'll see if I can get an answer this morning.'

Frankie Morgan had spent a pleasant evening at Joe Andretti's gambling house, where he had been introduced to a tall, attractive brunette who paid him a lot of attention. She explained that she was employed to keep the customers company and advise the uninitiated on the rules of roulette, blackjack and other gambling games. She also told him that she could provide other services for a price, which brought a smile to his swarthy face. He was familiar with the various gambling tables and was having a successful spell at roulette, already twenty pounds to the good and feeling mellow on the watered-down whisky.

Frankie left the club in the early hours with the hostess on his arm and left her bed at nine o'clock the next morning. He realised that he needed a shave and clean shirt before he presented himself at the Cutty Sark public house in Greenwich, and he needed time as well to get his brain working properly if he was to present a good argument.

The number 82 bus took him through Rotherhithe Tunnel and when he got off he bought the morning paper before he boarded a tram to Dockhead. As the conveyance rattled along Jamaica Road, the Bermondsey villain opened the paper and immediately caught sight of the news item on page two. His heart missed a beat, and as he quickly devoured the report his hands became hard fists. How could it be? He had been careful not to brag about the robbery and he knew that his two boys had kept silent. They had left no clues, he felt sure. Someone in the know must have turned nark. But who? Why?

Questions mushroomed feverishly in Frankie's mind as the tram neared Dockhead. Suddenly he realised that he was riding straight into the arms of the law. The police would be out in force on his manor and he could not expect to elude them for long. As the tram rumbled to a halt at St James's Church, Frankie got off and quickly slipped into the church gardens. He needed time to think, somewhere quiet and secure.

'Watch'er, Frankie,' a voice called out.

The villain suddenly stiffened as he walked along the quiet path and he turned to see Dan Beaumont grinning at him. 'You ain't seen me, understand,' he growled.

Dan nodded knowingly. 'Got yer, Frankie. Who's after yer, the Elephant mob?'

'Yeah. Now remember what I said if anyone asks yer,' Frankie told him.

The villain hurried up the flight of stone steps and entered the church. Inside the air was musty and redolent of incense. He sat down in a rear pew and bowed his head. What was he to do? Panic gripped at his stomach and he fought to keep control of himself. With shaking hands he opened the morning paper and read the item once more. For a while he stared up at the wide shaft of winter sunshine streaming in through the stained-glass window above the altar and then suddenly something seemed to click at the back of his mind and he shut his eyes as he tried to concentrate. For a time he remained as if in a trance, not moving a muscle, then he expelled his breath with a loud hiss. That was it, the accent. He had been convinced that the man who led the robbery was not English. He had thought at the time that his accent was unusual. The news item had mentioned the possible link between Gus Lazaar, the man found murdered at New Fresh Wharf, and the robbery. There certainly was a link. Lazaar was South African, and that was the accent he had tried to place. He remembered clearly now that during the war a group of South African soldiers had visited the Anchor and he had been intrigued by their guttural accent.

What did it all mean? Was Lazaar murdered to keep him from talking when he realised what he had taken from the jeweller's safe? If that was the case then a lot of double-dealing was going on and he and his two boys were in danger too. Maybe the men who had hired them were doing a deal with the police. That was it, and he had almost walked into a trap. He had been set up by Andretti. The Malt had been very accommodating, even to the extent of providing him with a woman and rigging his winnings, which had amounted to fifty pounds. It had all been arranged to make him feel at ease and less likely to suspect a double-cross. He had really fallen for it too, but thankfully he had seen the newspaper in time.

Frankie slipped out of the church and pulled his coat collar up against the weather as he caught a tram back to Rotherhithe. He would be less conspicuous over the water, he felt. He still had a few friends in the East End who were not in the pay of Joe Andretti, and he was going to need them now.

Dan Beaumont leaned on his stick and watched as the villain boarded the tram to Rotherhithe. ''E'll be makin' fer the East End, a pound to a pinch o' shit,' he mumbled aloud.

Bill Grogan was in a foul mood as he sat with Ray Halleron in his office at Dockhead police station on Thursday afternoon. 'Why, Ray?' he asked in exasperation. 'Couldn't they hold the press off until we had the three of them under lock and key?'

Halleron smiled cynically. 'It's all political, Bill, you know that,' he replied. 'Rumour has it that the top ranks are worried about Duncan Scott of the *Sunday Citizen*. He's been sniffing around and after that article he wrote a few weeks ago on corruption in high places they've a right to be worried. Word is that Scott knows about Gus Lazaar's involvement in the robbery. The man's got a big readership and he won't be bamboozled for long. The press release was a sop to keep the newshounds in general and Scott in particular from blowing the lid right off this case.'

'But it worked against us, Ray,' Grogan said with a sigh of frustration. 'Frankie Morgan obviously read the article and went to ground. There was no way he was going to show up the Cutty Sark today. We're going to have the devil's own job finding him now.'

'Any leads?' Halleron asked.

'Not a one,' Grogan told him. 'We might get something when we interview the Morgan boys, but I doubt it.'

Halleron stood up and puffed. 'I think we've let them sweat long enough, Bill,' he said.

Chief Inspector Grogan nodded. 'I think we should concentrate on Ernie Morgan first,' he replied. 'He's the one most likely to crack.'

Chapter Thirty-Six

It had not taken Dolly Morgan very long to impress her sense of purpose on Jimmy, and he had already managed to get two stepladders and planks from his friend. The reformed character brought them along on a barrow and had them set up in the front room upstairs by lunchtime on Thursday.

'Well, it's no good just standin' there, luv,' Dolly told him, hiding a smile. 'That ceilin' paper's gotta come off. It shouldn't be too difficult. The bloody stuff's 'angin' off as it is.'

Jimmy put on his cap and red cotton choker as a safeguard against the dust and plaster and then he set to work. Dolly left him hard at it and hurried to the market where she managed to buy some cheap lace curtaining for the newly installed front windows, and also found a tin of dark varnish amongst the thousands of bits and pieces on Cheap Jack's stall. As she hurried back to Fellmonger Street Dolly felt happy. It was a start, and with luck the house would be ready in time.

Albert Morgan had soon found to his dismay that everyone in Bermondsey seemed to know of the police raid and he had had to ward off quite a few questions from the neighbours. He felt relieved when he finally arrived at the house in the early afternoon to help with the decorating. There was so much to do if the place was to be renovated inside a month and keeping busy would help stop him dwelling on his brothers' plight.

Dolly was standing in the front room with her hands on her hips, a worried expression on her flushed face. ''Ello, Albert, 'ave yer come ter give us an 'and?' she asked, smiling quickly.

The young man nodded and smiled back. He had been surprised to see Dolly the evening he called to give Rose the good news about taking over the window-cleaning business. She looked very different to the picture of her he had stored away in his mind from when he was a child. She seemed much bigger than he remembered and her hair was shorter. There had been no time to chat with her properly that evening but Rose must have put her in the picture about him, since she did not seem to hold anything against him for what his brother John had done to Jimmy Rideout in the Anchor. It must have taken a lot of courage for her to get involved the way she did and Albert felt a little in awe of her.

'Tell me what yer want me ter do,' he said enthusiastically. 'I'm at yer disposal.'

Dolly grinned and took him by the arm. 'Righto. You've asked for it!' she told him. 'The front room upstairs needs strippin' first of all. There's a scraper on the windersill an' yer'll see a bucket o' water up there ter damp it down. I'll be down 'ere fer a while. I've gotta sort out these winders.'

It did not take Dolly long to hang the lace curtains and when she had finished she went upstairs to survey the progress. 'Jimmy, yer a little luv,' she said encouragingly.

Her suitor looked down from where he was struggling with the last of the ceiling paper and grinned. 'Every man to 'is job,' he joked.

Dolly turned her attention to Albert and saw that he was gritting his teeth as he worked away with the scraper. He had already cleaned off one wall and was making good progress with the area around the fireplace. Unlike the ceiling, however, the wall plaster was crumbling, and Dolly frowned as she looked around the room. 'We'll 'ave ter get this room replastered,' she sighed.

Albert stopped to wipe his hand down his trousers and Dolly suddenly noticed the smear of blood. 'Let's 'ave a look at yer 'and, Albert,' she told him.

The young man tried to pass it of casually but Dolly took his wrist and held his hand up. 'Yer've rubbed a blister raw,' she said. 'Yer've done enough fer one day.'

Albert started to protest but Dolly's eyes widened. 'Now listen, luv. If that 'and goes poisoned yer won't be any use, so get yer landlady ter put somefing on it. Now get off 'ome, go on.'

Jimmy was balancing on the edge of the plank that was stretched between the two ladders when suddenly the large strip of paper he was working on complete with the ceiling plaster underneath came loose. He struggled to regain his footing and fell on to the floor in a heap. Dolly looked down at him with concern and then laughed aloud as he struggled to his feet, cursing loudly.

'Yer should 'ave bin payin' attention ter what yer was doin' instead o' nosin' at us,' she rebuked him.

Jimmy looked up at the large gap in the ceiling. 'That bloody bit's rotten,' he replied quickly.

When Albert had left, Dolly picked up the scraper he had been using. 'Look at this,' she said. 'The 'andle's split. No wonder 'e rubbed 'is 'and raw.'

Jimmy nodded. 'I was lookin' at that distemper brush,' he replied. 'The bloody fing's moultin'.'

'We gotta get some decent tools ter work wiv,' Dolly said anxiously.

Jimmy looked irritated as he took off his cap and banged

it against his leg to remove the dust and plaster. 'Don't worry, I'll sort it out,' he told her quickly.

Dolly felt a little concerned as she saw the look on Jimmy's face. This was just the sort of time when he would have enjoyed a good stiff drink, she realised. He was doing so well fighting it. 'All right, let's call it a day,' she said. 'At least we've made a start.'

Rose had been worried into registering at the antenatal clinic by Dolly, and as she walked back to the Buildings on Thursday evening she glanced over at the house next to the yard and saw that there were curtains up. She found herself thinking about the Saturday morning ritual of step-whitening. Everyone seemed to whiten their front door-steps on Saturday and she vowed that once the family were installed in the house she would make sure she had the whitest front doorstep in Fellmonger Street. Moreover, her windows would be sparkling and the lace curtains always clean, crisp and starched. The children would be able to play outside the front door instead of on a grimy landing and she would be able to peg out her washing in the backyard instead of having to dry it round the gas fire or on that unsafe clothesline Don had put up in the scullery.

Things would be good, Rose dreamed as she climbed the creaking wooden stairs to her flat. It would be summertime when the baby arrived and she would be able to put it out in its pram. She smiled to herself as her imagination took wing. People always called a baby 'it'. She hoped 'it' would be a boy. It was what Albert wanted, and he would take him out for walks while she cooked meals and did the washing and ironing. Albert's business would prosper, of course, and the baby would be dressed very well. There might even be enough money to manage a holiday to Margate, or Ramsgate. The weather would be glorious, and they could all go for a paddle in the sea and walk along the sea front. Their son would be able to watch the Punch and Judy show and Albert would put his arm around her and whisper sweet words of love in her ear. At night, with their son sleeping soundly, Albert would hold her in his arms and love her tenderly.

Maybe it would be a daughter, Rose thought as she reached into her handbag for the key. Things would be the same, except that she would dress the child in lovely dresses and plait her long fair hair. Albert would be protective, and when the girl grew into a beautiful young woman he would vet all the young men who came knocking.

Rose was suddenly jerked back to the present as she saw the look on Don's face when she entered the flat.

'They're in there,' he hissed between clenched teeth.

'Who?'

'The welfare people.'

Rose hung up her coat and took a deep breath before she went into the front room.

'Ah, Rose. I'm sorry to disturb you this evening but we need to have a few particulars,' Winifred Seaton said rather curtly.

'About what?' Rose countered, feeling irritated by their intrusion.

'We need to know where you intend to move and the expected date, you see,' Peggy Grant cut in. 'It's information the court needs.'

'Now, just a minute,' Don said sharply. 'What's it got ter do wiv the court?'

'There's an order pending, you see,' the district officer replied, glancing at Miss Grant quickly.

'No, I don't see,' Don told her.

Miss Seaton took a deep breath in an effort to stay calm as she began to explain. 'Court orders have to be applied for, and in this case we were in the process of serving your family with an order of fostering. The pending move into a larger home, and the fact that you now have a relative to take responsibility for the family, changes things somewhat. A report has to be filed along with reasons for rescission, or in this instance an extension of validity.'

Both Don and Rose stared at the two welfare officers, trying to unravel the official jargon. Their worried and puzzled expressions touched Peggy Grant and she held up her hands in front of her in a calming gesture. 'All it means is that should things not work out and your relative fail to become involved, then we have the power to remove the children into care without further delay,' she said quietly.

Winifred Seaton had been angered by Don's aggressiveness however, and she retained her haughty manner. 'To be frank, Rose,' she began, ignoring the young man, 'we often hear promises that we know cannot be kept. We have a finger on the pulse of the community and we are aware of the current housing crisis. People are desperate for better and more modern accommodation, and larger houses and flats are at a premium. As I said before, we have to monitor the situation for the sake of our legal charges, you understand. Now, to keep up with events I would like the address of the accommodation you intend to rent and the date of entry.'

Rose looked quickly at Don and then fixed Miss Seaton with a confident stare. 'Number twelve, Fellmonger Street, an' we'll be movin' in on the last day o' the month,' she answered.

The two welfare officers exchanged puzzled glances and the senior frowned as she opened her notepad. 'I didn't know there were any vacant houses in this street,' she remarked.

'It's the big 'ouse next ter the transport yard,' Rose replied.

'But that's a derelict house,' Miss Seaton said. 'It's all boarded up.'

'Was boarded up,' Don cut in. 'It's got a new front door an'

374

winders in now, an' the decoration is already started. Like Rose said, we'll be in by the end o' the month.'

As Rose showed the two officers to the door, Miss Seaton turned and smiled coldly at her. 'We are only doing our job, you know.'

'Yeah, but sometimes compassion gets locked away in a drawer, doesn't it?' Rose retorted. 'One month is 'ardly time enough. We need two months really.'

'I'm sorry but it has to be one month,' Miss Seaton replied. 'Goodnight, Rose.'

When the front door closed behind them Rose turned to her brother and puffed loudly. 'We can't let 'em win, Don,' she said angrily.

The young man curled his mouth and waved his hand dismissively at the front door. 'It's not a case o' them winnin', sis. It's all about us losin',' he told her. 'We won't though. I'm gonna go over the 'ouse termorrer night wiv Albert. We're gonna really get ter work. By the way, I've managed ter talk the foreman inter lettin' me 'ave some offcuts. They'll come in 'andy fer the cupboards an' fings.'

Rose gave a heavy sigh and smiled. 'I dunno what I'd 'ave done wivout you,' she said.

'Now, don't go an' get all soppy,' Don replied, grinning. 'What was I s'posed ter do, run off like Muvver an' leave yer ter get on wiv it?'

'No, I mean the way you accepted it when yer found out I was pregnant,' Rose said quietly. 'If you'd 'ave gone on about it I might 'ave decided ter get an abortion.'

'You're my sister, Rose,' he replied. 'I gotta take care o' yer, until Albert puts the ring on yer finger. Mind yer, I'll still look out for yer, an' if Albert don't treat yer right 'e'll 'ave me ter contend wiv. I'll break 'is bloody neck.'

Rose grinned. 'Albert's a good feller, Don. I just know it.

Trouble is, 'e's a Morgan, an' there's a lot o' people who ain't gonna let 'im ferget it. It's up to us ter make sure we stand by 'im, no matter what.'

'Yeah, yer right, sis,' Don said smiling. 'Anyway I can't stand 'ere chattin' all night. I've got a date.'

'Don?'

'Yeah?'

'Promise me somefing.'

'Yeah, what?'

'Promise me you'll let yer 'air grow longer.'

Don gave her a contemptuous look as he hurried into the scullery.

Bill Grogan stood outside the Anchor and took a deep breath before pushing open the saloon bar door. He was feeling very angry and frustrated with the way things had gone that day. The Bermondsey villain had eluded capture yet again, and Ernie Morgan had remained sullen and unco-operative during the interview. Perhaps it might be useful making another appearance in the area that had spawned the Morgans, he thought. He had nothing to lose. Experience had taught him, however, that when the police became active in areas like this the local folk tended to clam up. Information was hard to come by at such times, partly due to a fear of reprisals, but also because of a more deeply ingrained suspicion amongst the locals that maybe an injustice had been done. People who knew the Morgan family would probably realise that they were small-time villains whose devious activities were confined to their own manor, and it was telling, if ironic, that their first criminal venture outside had landed them in so much trouble.

The bar was empty except for one or two customers who sat alone and a group of elderly men who Grogan knew well by sight. Dan Beaumont was amongst them and the detective winced as he walked to the bar. The old man would most probably sidle over soon with another piece of rubbish for him to act on. It was a regular charade and Grogan knew that he had no choice but to play along with the elderly man's ramblings. At least it might encourage any hesitant informant to take a leaf out of Beaumont's book and support the local police, he thought hopefully.

Sammy McGarry smiled a greeting. 'I see you've been 'ard at it,' he remarked.

Grogan wiped a hand over his tired face. 'Yeah. Give us a large Scotch, Sammy,' he replied.

'Word 'as it Frankie Morgan's left the country,' the publican said as he put the glass down in front of the inspector.

Grogan smiled at the joke. 'We'll 'ave 'im soon, don't worry,' he replied.

''Old tight, 'ere comes ole Beaumont,' Sammy warned him.

'Outside,' Dan said out of the corner of his mouth as he walked slowly past the policeman.

Sammy grinned as Grogan swallowed the contents of his glass and pushed it forward on the counter with a silent look that said fill it up.

Beaumont was waiting in the toilet. 'Frankie Morgan's on the run,' he hissed.

'Yeah?'

'I saw 'im this mornin'.'

'Yeah?'

'The Elephant mob's after 'im.'

'They're not the only ones.'

'I saw 'im gettin' on a tram.'

'Is that so?'

Dan Beaumont nodded and glanced quickly at the door. 'Gotta go, in case they twig I'm spoutin',' he whispered. 'They don't like people spoutin' round 'ere, yer know.'

'So I gathered,' Grogan replied with a sigh of exasperation.

'Frankie's gone over ter Shoreditch, a pound to a pinch o' shit,' Dan muttered in his low staccato. 'Prob'ly sleepin' rough in Spitalfields. Never find 'im there.'

'Oh and why's that?' Grogan asked to his peril.

'Gawd blimey, am I wastin' me time wiv you lot,' the old man said in disgust. 'Fink on it. Jack the Ripper led the peelers a merry dance over Spitalfields. Cut 'em up like nobody's business, 'e did. They couldn't find 'im though. Sleepin' rough 'e was. Yeah, amongst all the riffraff, the footpads an' all the rest o' life's downers. Searched everywhere fer ole Jack the Slicer. Everywhere except the churchyard. That's where 'e was.'

'If you say so,' Grogan replied, feeling that it was about time he went back to the bar.

'Before yer go, a word of advice. The man yer lookin' for drinks rum, so be careful 'ow yer approach 'im. Rum makes a man violent.'

'I didn't know Frankie drank rum,' Grogan said as he made to leave.

'Not Frankie, yer silly git. Jack the Slicer.'

Grogan returned to the saloon and raised his eyes to the ceiling in response to Sammy's quizzical look.

'Ole Dan's gettin' worse,' the landlord remarked with a sad shake of his head.

Grogan swallowed his drink and buttoned up his coat. 'Well, I'm off, Sammy,' he said. 'By the way, if he asks you to sell him rum, turn him down.'

'Who, ole Dan?'

'No, Jack the Slicer.'

Chapter Thirty-Seven

From the moment when Bromilow's machinery started up on Friday morning there had been an air of expectancy amongst the workforce, and now as the lunchtime hooter sounded the women hurried into the large canteen, eager to hear what progress the union had made with their various demands and suggestions. A long queue formed at the tea counter with most of the women opting to forgo a meal today in favour of sandwiches.

Alice was standing together with Rose in the line and she had a look of excitement on her face. 'I'm gonna give ole four-eyes somefink ter be goin' on wiv if I get the chance,' she told her.

Rose smiled at her friend's look of distaste as she mentioned the manager. 'It's a shame yer not stayin' on ter do the shop steward's job, Alice. That would really please 'im,' she remarked.

The two took their mugs of tea and found a seat at the far end of the canteen. Alice looked up at the large clock on the wall above them. 'I 'ope they're gonna turn up,' she said anxiously.

On the half hour the union convenor and his assistant entered the canteen and made their way to the far end where they could be seen by everyone. A buzz of excitement grew as the convenor climbed up on to a chair and looked around at the assembly.

'My name's Wally Scott, folks, an' this is the branch secretary, Jack Fletcher,' he began. 'Now, I know that you're due back ter work at one o'clock, so I'll not waste time. We've bin given permission by the management to 'old this meetin' wiv the proviso that we don't overrun, so let's start by sayin' 'ow pleased we are that this firm 'as finally stepped inter line wiv the ovver sheet-metal firms in the area an' agreed ter become unionised. Secondly, I want ter tell yer that we've 'ad a good response to your demands fer safer workin' practices. The company 'ave categorically stated that they'll co-operate in improvin' safety standards where possible. Non-slip mats are bein' installed in the workin' areas an' as from today all machinery will be periodically inspected ter prevent a repeat o' the recent occurrence when a machine broke down through lack o' maintenance.'

Instant applause greeted the announcement and the convenor raised his hands for silence. 'Now we need volunteers ter put their names forward fer the two posts o' shop steward. Jack'll take the names an' 'e'll organise a ballot. The successful candidates will be briefed on their duties an' terms of reference at the union offices one evenin' ter be arranged. Is that understood?'

The buzz of approval rose again to a loud crescendo and once again the convenor raised his hands for order. 'Now, don't let's waste time, folks,' he requested forcibly. 'Are there any points any of you would like to raise?'

Rose Farran was sitting next to Alice and she immediately looked at her for a response. Alice gave her a wink as she put her hand up. A few other hands were up but the convenor pointed over to Alice.

'I'll take your question first,' he said.

'I've got a point ter raise,' Alice replied, her face flushing slightly. 'Some o' the gels feel that they're not treated fairly by the shopfloor manager. They get all the bad jobs an' never get on the best machines. I'd like ter suggest that in future we work a rota system which would distribute the work more fairly.'

Bernard Collis was hovering outside the door of the canteen and from his vantage point he could see quite clearly who was making the point. His face grew angry and he cursed under his breath. Alice Copeland had been a thorn in his side from the very first and now she had the gall to cause more trouble on the day she was leaving, he fumed. The very idea of a rota system filled him with dread. It would mean his leverage over the women would be all but eradicated, and it would take a great deal of extra effort to organise an efficient system.

The union official nodded in agreement to Alice's request. 'It seems a good idea,' he replied. 'We'll be goin' back ter the management this afternoon an' I'll make the point. One fing ter remember though. Once we 'ave union stewards operatin' in this factory you'll all 'ave the opportunity ter put yer grievances ter them. Anuvver important fing ter keep in mind is that solidarity is the keyword. Stick tergevver an' support the union an' yer'll get results. Our aim is ter promote a good workin' relationship wiv the management, an' in doin' so we expect ter make progress in improvin' conditions fer all of yer. Right then, the next question.'

Bernard Collis had heard enough. He stormed back to his office and sat down heavily, his frustration and anger growing by the minute. The union was going to undermine his power and authority and it was all Copeland's doing, he raged. She had stirred up the workforce into getting the union in and she had never shown him any respect whatsoever. She had ruined his chances with Mary Burton too and had turned other women against him with her Bolshy attitude. She needed a good lesson. She needed to be taught that he was not going to take that sort of behaviour from a slut like her. She was just like all the rest. They all thought men were there to be despised and ridiculed. It was bad enough having to take that sort of treatment from his wife and her friends without getting it from the likes of Copeland.

Collis tried to make progress with his production figures but he found his thoughts constantly dwelling on the tall dark young woman. He felt a shiver of excitement run down his spine and a strange stirring in his loins as he pictured Alice Copeland standing before him, pleading for his forgiveness. He could see himself standing above her as she sank down on the floor at his feet. Her dark eyes opened wide with pleasurable expectation as he slowly and deliberately undid his leather belt and wrapped the end of it around his hand. He knew how to handle women and Copeland would be no exception. He could see by her face that she wanted him to chastise her, to arouse her most repressed sensations of pleasure with his punishment, and he would not disappoint her. First the beating to stimulate her and then, with her pleading for him to satisfy her sexual craving, he would take her. She was young and vigorous, eager for a strong, dominant man, not like that dried-up prune of a wife who had never shown him any loving, who refused to allow him near her. It was his wife who had driven him into the arms of other women and she who had to bear the blame.

The afternoon dragged on, and at four o'clock a messenger brought the weekly correspondence down to the manager's office. Amongst the papers and forms were Alice Copeland's insurance cards, and as Collis glanced at them he smiled evilly to himself.

*

Albert felt pleased that the day had broken fine and cold. At least he would be able to catch up with his window-cleaning round. He had managed to get two new customers in Tooley Street, but as he pedalled along Abbey Street to begin work he felt the soreness in his hand. His landlady had bathed and bandaged his raw palm the previous night and she had warned him to make sure the wound stayed clean. Albert ignored the soreness as he started work but by lunchtime his hand was giving him considerable discomfort. During the afternoon he felt sharp pains shooting through his damaged palm, and by the time he had finished cleaning the last of the office windows at the foot of London Bridge Station he felt decidedly off colour. He could see a red line running along the length of his forearm and he found himself sweating.

Albert reluctantly decided to go to Guy's Hospital, and as he sat waiting in the casualty department he thought about his brothers and his father. He had expected to read of charges being brought but there was nothing in the morning newspapers. His mind turned to Rose and the baby she was carrying inside her and he gritted his teeth in exasperation. He had wanted to go back to the house during the evening to carry on with the scraping but it was now out of the question. There was so much to be done and the days were slipping by. Dolly would do all she could and so would Jimmy Rideout, but it was too much to ask of them to complete all the tasks in time. Rose would be devastated if the boys and young Susan were put into foster homes. They would fret and be terribly unhappy and it would be difficult to get them back without a lot of red tape. Rose was tormented by the thought of failure and she was counting on everyone to rally round her. He was responsible for her and the baby, and it was he who had brought her all the worry by making her pregnant. Now he was helpless unless the hospital could fix him up quickly.

'I got a splinter in me finger. Went right down the nail it did,' a voice said.

Albert turned to see the old man next to him holding up his index finger. 'They'll sort it out,' he replied, not wanting to get into a conversation.

'Cut yer 'and, did yer?' the old man asked.

'Nah. It's poisoned,' Albert told him.

'Yer'll 'ave ter watch that. I knew somebody who got a poisoned 'and,' the man said. 'It travelled right up to 'is 'eart. 'E was dead inside a week.'

With a sinking feeling Albert turned away, hoping no other cheerful disclosures were on the way.

Finally he was ushered into the surgery and the doctor pressed and prodded at the festering spot. 'I'll need to lance that and then we'll give you a shot of penicillin,' he said perfunctorily.

Ten minutes later Albert left the hospital with his hand bandaged and his arm in a sling. He could still feel a soreness in his rump where the stern nursing sister had prodded him unceremoniously with a syringe. He walked back to his lodgings feeling depressed. He had just started out in his own business and was now incapacitated for at least a week, according to the doctor's reckoning.

Things had been moving at Dockhead police station. John and Ernest Morgan had been formally charged with armed robbery and their application for bail had been refused. As the Morgan brothers left for Brixton Prison under escort to await the trial, Bill Grogan breathed a sigh of relief. It had been touch and go for a few hours but a stroke of luck had changed the outcome and he felt confident that before the trial date more evidence would be forthcoming. The turning point had hinged on two cinema ticket stubs, which John Morgan had tried to use as evidence of them being elsewhere at the time of the robbery. Grogan had visited the Trocadera cinema and discovered through the serial numbers on the stubs that the tickets were indeed issued on the day in question. The cinema manager was not able to give an exact time of purchase and for a few moments Grogan had felt that the case against the brothers was precarious. His spirits soared, however, when the young woman who had been on duty at the kiosk on that particular day suddenly remembered that she had had to change the ticket roll a few minutes after she had gone on duty at five thirty. She had noticed when she opened the new pack of ticket rolls that the paper was purple as opposed to the normal yellow, for the simple reason that it was almost the same colour as her new amethyst engagement ring. Her evidence proved that the purple stubs offered in evidence by the Morgans had been issued after five thirty, and not at four o'clock as the brothers had stated in their statements.

Inspector Halleron had followed up with another damning piece of evidence. The young homosexual who had propositioned the brothers opposite the jeweller's had been arrested since the raid in a public lavatory and charged with gross indecency. He had demanded to see Inspector Halleron and had given him further details, in return for an assurance that the charge against him would be dropped. It was now recorded in a sworn statement made by the young man that he and a colleague had been talking together further along Berkeley Street just after he had been sent packing by the Morgans and the two actually saw the brothers don their masks as they entered the jeweller's shop along with another man.

Halleron had been reluctant to drop the charges at first, but after interviewing the second man he had been swayed.

'If it got in the papers about Francis misbehaving in the lavatory I'd die, I know I would,' his friend said in a camp voice. 'Our neighbours know us to be a respectable couple and if they found out about Francis I'd simply die of shame.'

Halleron added the second man's sworn statement to his armoury and was assured by the two homosexuals that they were both willing to appear in court to substantiate their statements. Like Grogan, the inspector was feeling pleased that it was all coming together and he was going back to Scotland Yard that very day to liaise with the Chief Commissioner. He felt that a further deal might be possible if influence was brought to bear on the presiding judge to knock a few years off the sentences of all three if the Morgan boys co-operated in the swift arrest of their father. Frankie Morgan was facing a very long term of imprisonment with his previous record, and his sons knew it. They had to realise that their father could not evade capture for ever, and their failure to co-operate in his arrest would mean maximum sentences for them all.

At five o'clock on Friday evening the Bromilow factory hooter sounded and a tired workforce hurried out into the cold evening air, looking forward to another brief weekend away from the constant clatter and din of machinery. Alice Copeland had mixed feelings as she slipped her time card into the clock for the last time. She had made good friends at the factory and through her friendship with Rose she had met Don. Things would be better at the factory now that they had unionised, she felt sure, and Bernard Collis would have to watch himself in future.

Alice waited for Rose to reach the time-clock, waving to friends and smiling as they wished her good luck. The supervisor had told her that afternoon that she could collect her cards from the manager's office when she clocked off and Alice was not looking forward to her final confrontation with the obnoxious Bernard Collis. He would no doubt have some nasty comments to make and she had prepared herself with a few sharp words in reply.

Rose came along the passageway and took Alice by the arm. 'Try an' get someone ter keep an eye on yer gran, termorrer, Alice,' she said. 'It should be a good night, an' Don's gonna be really pleased if yer can make it.'

'I'll try, Rose,' the young woman replied. 'I'll see yer then, all bein' well. I've gotta go an' see four-eyes ter collect me cards.'

The factory had suddenly become very quiet as Alice walked quickly along the stone corridor and tapped on the manager's office. She heard his peremptory voice bid her enter and as she walked into the room she noticed that he looked flushed. She could see beads of sweat on his forehead and a strange look in his eyes. At first she thought that he might be ill, but he smiled uncharacteristically and pointed to a chair beside his desk. 'I'll be wiv yer in a minute,' he said, getting up and going over to the door.

Alice watched as Collis quickly opened the door and looked both ways along the corridor, and when he shut the door again and walked back to his desk she felt suddenly afraid. It was a vague intimation of vulnerability at being alone with the detestable little man now that all the women had left.

'There's bin a delay in gettin' yer cards stamped up,' he said, mopping his brow with a grubby handkerchief. 'They should be 'ere any minute now.'

Alice cursed under her breath. It was deliberate, she thought. His last attempt to make things difficult for her.

'It's warm in 'ere, why don't yer take yer coat off while yer waitin',' he suggested.

Alice shook her head. 'I'm all right,' she replied coldly.

Footsteps sounded outside and Collis looked quickly at the door. A shadow passed the frosted glass panelling and the sound faded.

The manager screwed up his mouth and his eyes widened as he slowly rose from his seat and walked round the desk to face the young woman. 'That was the supervisor. There's no one left in the factory now, Copeland, except you an' me,' he said in a gravelly voice. 'I fink it's time you faced the music.'

'What yer talkin' about?' Alice asked, her stomach knotting as she saw the maniacal look in the manager's eyes.

'You know very well,' he replied. 'Ever since the first day you've bin out ter make me look stupid in front o' the women. On top o' that yer've bin out ter discredit me with yer Bolshy carryin's on. Well, now it's time ter take yer medicine. Don't try an' fight me, Copeland. Just take yer punishment an' it'll purify yer.'

Alice gasped in horror. It was her father all over again. It was the same evil look, the same wild manner of a man who had lost all sense of decency becoming God's avenging messenger. She jumped up and made for the door, terrified by his evil eyes, but Collis was too quick for her. He dashed in front of her and stood leering as he slowly unbuckled his leather belt.

'First the punishment, an' then the pleasure. You 'ave 'ad the pleasure before, I take it?' he said in little more than a whisper.

'Let me go!' Alice shouted. 'Yer mad, stark ravin' mad!'

Collis wrapped the buckle end of his belt around his hand and quickly brushed the back of his other hand across his wet forehead. 'Take yer coat off,' he ordered.

'I'll do no such fing,' Alice said with spirit.

Suddenly he moved forward and grabbed her by her coat collar. 'Do as you're told, slut,' he hissed.

Alice tried to fight back but he threw her roughly against the wall.

'I'll go ter the police. They'll lock you up!' she gasped.

Collis smiled crookedly. 'The police? Who would they believe, you or me? I'm a respected works manager an' you're nuffink but a trouble-makin' slut. Just take yer coat off and bend over the desk. You'll enjoy it, yer know yer will.'

Alice gulped, playing for time as she slowly unbuttoned her winter coat. She cast her eyes around the office, searching for something to defend herself with. Suddenly she spotted the heavy glass ashtray lying on the desk.

'Do yer like beatin' women?' she asked him slowly.

Collis took a step forward and tore her coat open. 'I won't tell yer again. Take it off!' he ordered.

Alice dashed towards the desk but he was too quick for her. He pressed her face down over the desktop and the first blow from the strap landed across her kidneys. Her clothes cushioned it a little but the next blow was delivered with more power and a sharp pain burned across her shoulder blades. She squirmed round, trying to ward him off, but Collis pulled roughly at her coat, attempting to peel it from the shoulders. Alice felt tears of temper and she gritted her teeth as she tried to fight him off.

'Sluts! Yer all sluts!' he shouted as he wrestled with her.

Alice fell to the floor with one arm out of her coat and she raised her hands over her face in an effort to ward off the vicious strap. Collis raised the thong high over his head.

'Beg, Copeland!' he screamed out. 'Beg for mercy!'

Alice gritted her teeth and closed her eyes tightly, waiting for the next searing blow, but it never landed. She felt the pressure suddenly leave her and she looked up quickly to see Collis stagger backwards and fall into a heap.

'Get up, Collis!' a deep voice called out.

Alice saw George Penrose standing in the doorway holding on to the leather belt he had snatched away as Collis raised it above his head.

'She went for me,' the works manager stuttered. 'She tried ter tear me eyes out.'

'Pity she didn't succeed,' Penrose said, winding the belt round his fist. 'I've a good mind to flay you alive.'

He reached down to help the terrified young woman to her feet. 'Did he hurt you, my dear?' he asked kindly.

Alice shook her head. 'I came in ter get me cards an' 'e said they wasn't down yet. Then 'e attacked me,' she blurted out.

Collis cowered as George Penrose went over to the metal tray on the filing cabinet and seached through the papers before pulling out the cards. 'Buried,' he said pointedly. 'Just like the memos you buried under a pile of papers in my office. Remember, Collis?' He turned to Alice. 'Do you want to press charges, young lady?'

Alice had struggled back into her coat and she shook her head. 'No, it's OK. You came in just in time,' she replied in a voice that shook with emotion.

'If you'll wait outside my office, my dear, I'll take you home in my car,' Penrose told her quietly.

Alice walked off quickly down the corridor and Penrose listened to her retreating footsteps, his eyes averted from the shopfloor manager. When she was out of earshot he pulled the leather belt tightly round his fist and, leaning back, with all his strength smashed Collis in the face.

The manager crashed back against the desk and fell to the floor, blood smothering his face. Penrose stepped forward and booted him in the groin and Collis screamed a high-pitched screech of agony.

'I'll expect you in my office at nine sharp on Monday morning,' Penrose told him, gritting his teeth. 'I don't think I'll have any trouble with the board this time, do you?'

Chapter Thirty-Eight

The St Mark's Church hall in Basin Street was not part of the original eighteenth-century church, having been constructed with money donated by the fellmongers who once frequented the area. Its founding purpose was to bring together the local working community in their leisure pursuits, but unfortunately the poor people of the Bermondsey area had had neither the time nor the money to indulge in such pursuits. During the depression years leading up to the Second World War it served as a soup kitchen and a secondhand-clothes distribution centre for the poor and needy, but once upon a time it had been the venue for the Abbey Ladies' Choir.

Every Wednesday evening the respectable ladies had met to rehearse Gilbert and Sullivan operas, oratorios and other choral arrangements; lanterns burning brightly to dispel the gathering gloom. The upstanding nightingales were for the most part wives and daughters of the middle-class managers and supervisors who lived in the fine Victorian houses of Bermondsey, which were tucked away in tidy streets on the edge of the melting pot of tanneries, factories and warehouses. The ladies sang with gusto every Wednesday evening and their dulcet tones would carry out into the mean streets. The riffraff and the guttersnipes, as the ladies tended to label them, would be out in force, their sallow, lean faces screwed up with mirth at the ladies' efforts to sing in perfect unison. The children of the workers gathered outside the church hall and gleefully mimicked the fine, upright ladies who stood shoulder to shoulder, their bonnets and straw hats swaying in time with the thumping of the piano and the cymbals.

The music was like nothing the workers' children had heard at piano parties, and they had never heard such singing at the music halls. The kids would begin to bray, and the braying would be joined by other farmyard sounds until the noise could clearly be heard inside the hall. The upright ladies responded with more gusto and the children replied by hammering sticks and stones against old dustbin lids and hollering even louder. One or the other of the musical groups had to give way and it was not the children. The Abbey Ladies' Choir retreated to a more appreciative location, while the children looked for some new mischief to fill the emptiness.

The church hall survived the London blitz, becoming a gas-mask fitting centre, rest centre for the homeless, temporary mortuary and first-aid training centre. Only after the war did the hall revert to what it had originally been built for, a meeting place for leisure activities of the working class, and on a cold Saturday in February 1950 a large sign was erected over the front door of the hall which said, WELCOME HOME JOE.

Ethel Price and her husband George wore their Sunday best as they welcomed their neighbours to the hall. Trestle-tables lined one wall and crates of light ale, brown ale and stout along with a few bottles of Guinness were stacked high against the opposite wall. The tables were covered with paper tablecloths upon which a variety of food was laid out. Jellies, fairy cakes and jam tarts, sandwiches of ham, cheese and brawn were piled high on variously coloured plates. On the stage facing the entrance there was a battered piano and stool with a chair placed alongside for the accordionist. Ethel had hoped that her son Joe would be there to welcome the neighbours but he had told her he could not face it and would slip into the hall once the festivities were underway. Joe felt that eighteen months' national service in Germany as a corporal in charge of a clothing store was hardly reason for his parents to parade their son to all the neighbours as though he were a conquering hero returned.

Ben Fagan sat himself down at the piano and looked quickly at the accordionist, Vic Thomas, before his practised fingers picked out a few opening bars. Ethel and George Price started the dancing by gliding out across the parquet flooring in a slow foxtrot and then they went round the edge of the hall encouraging other couples to take the floor. Jack Smithers got up and did a very well-received rendering of 'The Gang's All Here' and then Ivy Campbell and Rene Stratton got up and sang 'Needle and Thread'.

The cordial enthusiasm of Ethel's neighbours helped to relax the atmosphere, and when Rose and Albert walked in arm-in-arm, followed by Don and Alice and the three younger Farrans, the welcome-home party was in full swing. Rose wore a loose-fitting, calf-length dress in a sea-green shot silk with a square neckline and puffed three-quarter sleeves. Her legs were clad in nylon stockings which Albert had bought for her and she had on a pair of high-heeled black patent shoes. Albert looked smart in his single-breasted grey suit with a light-blue shirt and blue and black diagonal-striped tie. His black shoes were highly polished and his thick dark hair was neatly groomed around his ears and neck. His poisoned hand was on the mend after the trip to casualty and he had forsaken his sling, though his hand was still heavily bandaged. Alice looked rather pale and serious after her ordeal at the hands of Bernard Collis, and as she stood beside Don she forced a smile for him. She wore a calf-length navy-blue dress which flared from the waist and had a plunging neckline. The children wore their Sunday clothes and looked a little overawed, but their faces lit up when they saw the display of food and cakes. Ethel shepherded them over to the tables along with other children and filled paper plates with goodies, and the youngsters then hurried over to a vacant corner to eat their fill away from the interfering grown-ups.

At eight o'clock a sheepish-looking Joe Price walked in with a young lady on his arm and the music struck up with 'Backstreets'. He moved quickly through the gathering, taking slaps on the back and good wishes from his neighbours with some embarrassment, to the obvious amusement of his young lady. Ethel smiled proudly and George Price winced in sympathy with his son's discomfort.

'Good luck, son,' someone called out.

'Give 'er a kiss,' another voice called out.

'When's the weddin'?'

'Give 'em a chance!'

So it went on until Joe grabbed his lady friend and tried to disappear amongst the dancers.

Albert had steered Rose towards the table near the beer crates and after getting served he found them a seat. Rose hesitantly sipped her stout, which Albert had insisted was the ideal drink for a pregnant woman. The music changed to a waltz and Albert took Rose gently by the arm and led her on to the floor. They moved close together and set off with Albert leading confidently.

'Yer dance very well,' Rose told him softly.

'You're a good mover too. I fink we make an attractive couple,' Albert joked, his bandaged hand limp at her shoulder.

Rose let her head rest against the side of his face and she closed her eyes, savouring the moment. It seemed a very long time ago that the two of them had danced together, she thought, realising that it was in fact only a short few months since that eventful night at the club dance. The baby she was carrying inside her had been conceived on that night, but Rose felt neither regretful nor anxious as she let Albert glide her round the dance floor. She knew that he loved her and the baby she was carrying. He had proved it by standing up to his father for her sake. He was trying very hard to make a go of his newly acquired business, and as they moved smoothly together Rose felt very happy and content.

Don Farran had never considered himself to be a dancer, and when Alice encouraged him to take the floor he did so with much trepidation. Alice snuggled close to him, her head resting against his chest as she tried desperately to shut out the memory of lying helpless over the office desk as Collis assaulted her. She had not been able to get his contorted face out of her mind and when she arrived home the previous evening she had been physically sick. She had kept her ordeal to herself, fearing Don's wrath and knowing that he would most definitely seek out her assailant for revenge, which would only serve to bring more trouble on to the family.

The evening was well under way, with little groups of neighbours and friends chatting and laughing happily together as they got merry. The beer was flowing and most of the food had been eaten. Ethel breathed a sigh of relief as she stood talking to her friends in the block, Ivy and Rene. 'It's such a worry,' she said. 'Yer never know if yer done it right. Our Joe didn't want this turnout yer know, but still it's a chance fer us all ter get tergevver.'

'Yeah, it's really nice,' Ivy replied as she handed her husband Bill her empty glass with an instructive nod towards the beer table. 'It must 'ave cost a few bob, this do.'

'We've bin savin' up,' Ethel told her. 'Ole Joe Diamond got

us a few extra bits an' pieces. Nice bloke, ole Joe. I wonder why 'e never married?'

Ivy nodded as she folded her arms over her short ample figure. 'I used ter fink 'im an' Lizzie Carroll would get tergevver, 'er workin' in that shop wiv 'im,' she remarked.

'She drives 'im ter drink more like it,' Ethel said chuckling. 'The pair of 'em are always arguin'.'

Rene Stratton came up looking flushed. 'Luvverly turnout, ain't it,' she said grinning widely. 'My ole man just whisked me round the floor. 'E ain't done that since my youngest boy's weddin'. Gave me a peck too. Fings are certainly lookin' up.'

Her friends laughed at Rene's expression. ''Ere, you be careful, gel, or yer might find yerself bein' whisked 'ome fer an early night,' Ethel told her with a suggestive wink.

'Gawd 'elp us, luv. Chance would be a fine fing,' Rene laughed.

Ivy's husband came back with a full glass of stout. ''Ere, get that down yer,' he said, turning away to seek out his pals.

'Don't it make yer sick wiv 'em at times,' Ivy remarked. 'Anybody'd fink 'e's givin' me a dose o' jollop.'

'Yeah, 'e's certainly got a way wiv 'im, Ivy,' her friend Rene joked. 'Like my ole man. We went ter Margate once fer a day out an' 'e took me in this posh restaurant. White tablecloths an' flowers on the table, you know what I mean. Well, we 'ad our tea. Fillet o' plaice an' chips, an' those little peas. Very nice it was. Luvverly bit o' fish. Anyway, I looked at my Ken an' 'e was shovellin' those peas on 'is knife an' they was fallin' all over the floor. I didn't know where ter put me face. Then the waiter came up an' said to 'im, "Would yer like a strawberry tart an' custard, sir?"

'"Nah fanks, mate," my Ken ses. "The pips get under me plate." I wanted the floor to open up, Ivy. I thought everyone was lookin' at me. They do show yer up at times.'

Ethel glanced towards the door. 'I thought Dolly Morgan

would be 'ere by now,' she remarked. 'She said she'd come ternight.'

'P'raps she's 'avin' a bit o' trouble gettin' ole Jimmy Rideout ready,' Rene remarked caustically.

'Aw, don't be cruel,' Ivy cut in. 'That man's really pulled 'imself tergevver lately. It's nice ter see it.'

'Yeah, yer right,' Ethel said. 'Look 'ow 'e let 'imself go. Like a bleedin' tramp 'e was before Dolly come back on the scene. The change in that man is somefing ter see. I saw 'im the ovver day. Nice suit an' tie, an' 'is shoes were polished. Even 'is 'air was parted an' brilliantined.'

'I'm only jokin',' Rene replied. ''E looks a treat now, fanks ter Dolly. She's a good gel, that one.'

'Yeah, an' she's always in an' out the Farrans' place,' Ethel said. 'Those kids need 'er. She won't let nuffink 'appen to 'em.'

'I 'eard the welfare was gonna take those kids away,' Rene remarked.

'Dolly won't stand fer that,' Ethel said quickly. 'They're 'er bruvver's kids, after all.'

Freda Arrowsmith and her husband Ted came up to say hello and Ivy immediately took the opportunity to glean some information. 'We've bin talkin' about Dolly an' those Farrans,' she told her. 'I 'eard Dolly's doin' that place up next ter Tommy Caulfield's yard.'

'Yeah, Tommy's rented it out to 'er by all accounts,' Freda replied. 'Mind yer though, there's so much ter be done there. I don't fink they'll be able ter get it up ter scratch in time, if you ask me.'

'What d'yer mean?' Ethel asked.

'Well, young Rose was really upset the ovver night when I popped in fer a chat,' Freda went on. 'It seems the welfare 'ave give 'em a month ter get it liveable, an' if it ain't ready by then they're gonna take the kids away.'

'That's bloody terrible,' the women chorused.

'Well, you know what they're like. 'Alf of 'em 'ave never 'ad kids 'o their own. They ain't got a bloody clue,' Freda said with disgust. 'It's all over young Rose bein' pregnant. They reckon she can't manage the kids what wiv the baby comin'.'

'What's got ter be done ter the new place then?' Ivy asked her.

'It's like a pigsty in there,' Freda replied. 'Caulfield's 'ad a new front door put on an' new winders, as yer know, but inside it's fallin' ter pieces. 'E 'ad it fer a store'ouse fer donkey's years.'

'If it's a question o' time, I s'pose I could do a bit o' cleanin' over there, an' my ole man could put a bit o' paper up. 'E's a dab 'and at paper 'angin' is my man,' Ivy said with enthusiasm.

'I s'pose I could 'elp out as well,' Rene added. 'I can do a bit o' paintin'. I don't mind paintin'. I'm the one who does it all in our place. My Ken's bloody useless at paintin', though 'e's good wiv tools, 'im bein' a gas fitter.'

'P'raps 'e could 'elp out wiv the gas,' Ethel said quickly.

Freda suddenly nodded towards the door. 'There's Dolly an' Jim,' she said.

They looked over to see the big blonde woman come in holding on to Jimmy Rideout's arm. She was wearing a long white dress, pleated and flared, which reached down to her ankles, with a thin gold edging around the square neckline and hem. She had on a pair of high-heeled bronze-coloured shoes and she carried a small bronze clutch bag to match. A hip-length, white blazer-style coat was slung over her shoulders and her waved hair was neatly set away from her forehead. She seemed to stand out in the crowd and her happy smile exposed a row of large white teeth.

Jimmy looked proud and happy too as he stood beside her. He wore a blue serge suit, the single-breasted jacket unbuttoned to expose a waistcoat and a grey tie with red polka-dots; his white shirt looked immaculate and his black patent shoes glistened. His hair was sleeked down and parted in the middle, which prompted an appreciative smile from Ivy.

'Jimmy looks like George Raft, what wiv those shoes an all,' she said.

Dolly and her escort went over to talk to Rose and Albert, and as Ethel watched her a ghost of an idea was forming in her mind. She was feeling good that evening. The party was proving to be a success and all her friends were there. Her son Joe had relaxed and was chatting comfortably with her neighbours, George was passing to and fro, encouraging the guests to take to the floor, and the music made everything seem special. It was time to take stock, she thought. A time to be grateful for good neighbours and friends. A time to close ranks and spread a little happiness and help where possible. Ethel felt herself getting quite emotional as she sipped her stout and looked around the hall. Yes, she would talk to George immediately, before he got up to make his little speech of thanks.

The pianist and his partner had just finished playing 'Home in Pasadena' and Jimmy Rideout smiled winsomely as he led Dolly from the dance floor. 'Yer look like a film star, Doll,' he told her.

'Yer look a bit tasty yerself,' Dolly replied as she squeezed his arm. 'Yer can still do a nifty few steps too.'

'Yeah, I was pretty good when I was a lad,' he said with a debonair narrowing of his eyes. 'See these shoes? They must be twenty years old at least. I used ter wear these when I went up West dancin' ter the big bands. I coulda gone professional at one time.'

'Yeah, well don't go over the top,' Dolly reminded him with an affectionate grin.

Suddenly George Price climbed up on to the stage and raised

his hands for attention. 'Right, everyone,' he began. 'Settle down now, please. Fank you, it won't take long. My ole dutch felt I should get up 'ere an' fank you all fer comin' ternight. It's good ter see yer all enjoyin' yerselves an' I've gotta say that it warms the cockles o' me 'eart, an' Efel's too. We wanted to 'ave a bit of a do ter celebrate our Joe's 'omecomin'. 'E wants me ter say fanks ter you all an' fer yer to 'ave a very nice evenin'.'

The guests applauded and Ethel walked over to tug on her husband's coat sleeve. 'Don't ferget the ovver bit,' she hissed.

George raised his hands again for silence. 'While we're all tergever there's somefing else I'd like ter say,' he went on in a serious voice. 'We all know that the war years took their toll on all of us. We've all lost someone, be it friends or loved ones. But as bad as it was, the war taught us one important lesson. It taught us ter stick tergevver. It taught us that we all depend on somebody.'

Ethel turned to Ivy and Rene and puffed loudly. 'I 'ope 'e don't go on too much. Once 'e gets started there's no stoppin' 'im,' she told them.

'Leave 'im,' Rene said quickly. ''E's all right.'

'It's all right ter feel fer people, but a little 'elp is werf a great deal o' pity,' George continued. 'A lot of us knew Gerry Farran. 'E was a good bloke was Gerry, an' we miss 'im. 'Is kids still live round 'ere an' they're a credit to 'im. Since their muvver left 'em they've 'ad ter fend fer themselves, an' now it seems that the welfare are tryin' ter break the family up. Luckily, Gerry's sister Dolly is back wiv us an' she's fightin' like a tiger ter keep that family tergevver. Now Dolly's 'ere ternight, but I know she won't mind me sayin' this. She's managed ter get that 'ouse next ter Tommy Caulfield's yard an' she's doin' it up fer 'em. The trouble is, she's only got one month. Yes, folks, one month. If the place ain't finished by then the welfare are gonna take those kids away. Do we stand by an' let that 'appen?'

Angry voices were raised and George smiled as he looked around at the gathering. 'As I just said, a little 'elp is werf a great deal o' pity, so what about it? Let's all muck in, just like we did durin' the war. We can all do our little bit. I'm gonna sort out a few o' me tools, an' if there's anyone 'ere who can do a bit o' plasterin' or paper 'angin' I'm sure Dolly an' Jimmy will be very grateful.'

Dolly dabbed at her eye with a handkerchief and Rose lowered her head with emotion as Don put his arm round her. People were beginning to mill round them.

'I'll do yer plasterin',' one man said.

'I'll sort the woodwork out,' another said.

Rene and Ivy came over. 'We got time on our 'ands, ain't we?' Rene said. 'We'll do some clearin' up an' scrubbin'.'

'I don't use me barrer on Thursdays,' an elderly man said. 'I'll dump yer rubbish round the Council yard an' bring anyfing 'eavy.'

An old man hobbled up, leaning heavily on walking sticks. 'I can't do much now, luv,' he told Rose, 'but I used to 'ave me own decoratin' business. I've got a lot o' brushes an' fings, an' yer welcome to 'em.'

Dolly came up and put her arms round Rose and Don. 'I would say the people round 'ere 'ave come up trumps, if you ask me,' she said quietly. 'They won't let us fail, kids.'

The music struck up again as George climbed off the stage to receive a kiss on the cheek from Ethel. People went out on to the dance floor, stirred by George Price's remarks, and the musicians played with zest. Old party favourites rang out and the guests linked arms as they danced a knees-up and then formed into a chain to perform the conga. Rose and Albert joined the chain for a snaking lap of the hall and then they broke away to find the children. The two young brothers were discovered sitting under one of the tables sampling beer, and Rose found Susan sitting in a corner with some other youngsters. Don picked the child up in his arms and together with Alice and Albert they all left the hall with good wishes ringing in their ears.

Outside, the moon had risen high in the sky and fleeting clouds drifted across a star-filled heaven. Don hummed a tune to Susan as he held her in his arms and Alice walked at his side, still unable to forget the horror of her ordeal. Rose was holding Joey's hand as he trudged along yawning but Billy lagged a few paces behind, protesting furiously at having been made to leave the hall at such an early hour.

'It's not over yet, why did we 'ave ter leave?' he grumbled.

''Cos it's past yer bedtime,' Rose told him sharply.

'But I ain't tired,' Billy replied.

'Yeah, but Joey an' Susan are,' she told him.

'It's not fair.'

'Stop moanin', Billy.'

'All the ovver kids are still there.'

'Never mind about the ovver kids.'

Billy lapsed into a moody silence, then as they entered the block he turned to his older sister. 'Rose, when we move in that new 'ouse can I 'ave a rabbit?' he asked.

'We'll see,' Rose said smiling.

'It's gotta be a boy rabbit.'

'Why a boy rabbit?'

''Cos my mate Jackie's got a gel rabbit, an' 'e said that if I get a boy rabbit we can breed 'undreds o' rabbits an' share 'em out.'

Susan heard Billy's remarks and she looked up. 'I'd love to 'ave a little bunny ter play wiv,' she said sleepily.

'They won't be fer playin' wiv,' Billy said quickly.

'What yer wanna breed 'em for, then?' Don asked him.

'Ter sell ter the butcher shop,' Billy replied, as he plodded up the stairs in the rear.

'That boy worries me at times,' Rose said to Alice.

'I wouldn't worry about Billy,' Don told her. ''E'll be a millionaire one day.'

Chapter Thirty-Nine

On the Sunday following the Price family's party, Dolly sat down with the Farrans to discuss their future plans. The first consideration was the response from the neighbours. Promises of help had been freely given and Dolly was keen to keep the momentum going. Jimmy was going along to see the old man who had promised them decorating materials and George had been asked if he could fix the cupboards and re-hang the room doors. Help was also urgently needed with scraping the old wallpaper from the walls and making the plaster good. A gas stove would have to be bought and Dolly made a mental note to ask Rene Stratton's husband Ken if he could lay the gas piping. Jimmy had mentioned too that all the chimneys would need sweeping before the new wallpaper was put up and the electric lights and power points should be installed as well before the decoration was started.

Dolly sighed as she looked at the notes she had made, and while she sipped her tea thoughtfully Rose told her of the plans she and Albert were making for the wedding.

'We wanna get wed as soon as possible, Dolly,' she said. 'If I leave it too long I'm gonna be too big.'

'You can get a nice loose-fittin' weddin' gown,' Dolly told

her. 'I've seen a lovely one in that shop next ter the pie shop in Tower Bridge Road.'

'I dunno about white,' Rose said, pinching her lip.

'Why ever not?' Dolly asked her. 'It's yer big day an' yer wanna look yer best. All right, I know what yer finkin', but let me tell you, my gel, there's plenty o' young gels gone up the aisle in the family way. The Good Lord knows it an' I'm sure 'e ain't worried. Don't ferget 'e made it all possible, so don't get all moody about it. You wear white. Anyway me an' Jimmy are buyin' yer weddin' outfit so yer got no say in it.'

'I can't let yer lay all that money out,' Rose said, looking uncomfortable.

'Now, you listen ter me,' Dolly replied firmly. 'You're all my kids now, an' I ain't gonna let any o' mine go up the aisle lookin' like a dog's dinner. I'm all right fer a few bob. I stuck the money I got from the pub in a bank account an' there was my ole feller's insurance too. What do I need the money for?'

Rose reached out and squeezed Dolly's arm. 'We all love yer, Dolly, an' if it wasn't fer you I dunno where we'd be.'

'We'll be up shit creek if we don't get our fingers out an' get movin',' Dolly said forcefully. 'Termorrer I'm gonna go an' see Tommy Caulfield first fing. I want that roof fixed an' the back door replaced. That's 'is job. Next fing we've gotta sort out is that poxy job o' yours. It's about time yer put yer notice in. The work's too 'eavy fer someone in your condition, an' besides, there's a lot fer you ter do round 'ere while yer still can.'

Rose nodded. 'I was finkin' o' puttin' me notice in at the end o' the month. That way I can save a few more shillin's,' she explained. 'Albert wants me ter pack in work right away though. 'E said 'e could make up the difference.'

'Well, you should take notice o' what 'e's sayin',' Dolly told her. 'Albert seems a sensible sort o' bloke, if you ask me. 'E knows what that job's doin' to yer.'

Rose sighed in resignation. 'P'raps yer right. I'll fink about it.'

'There's nuffink ter fink about. Go in termorrer an' put yer notice in right away,' Dolly insisted.

Rose pondered what her aunt had said and realised she was right. The hustle and bustle of the factory and having to stand in one spot for eight hours were not conducive to health for someone who was pregnant. Collis would be surprised, she thought. He would probably growl at her and remark how ungrateful she was. Well, he could say what he liked. Her baby was the most important thing now.

On Sunday morning Jimmy Rideout strolled along Basin Street whistling tunelessly and knocked at number 26. It was some time before he heard a scraping in the passageway, then the door opened and he saw the old man standing there with a vacant look on his face.

'Mr Williams?'

'Yeah, what yer want?' he asked irritably.

'I've come round about those decoratin' tools yer promised us.'

'Tools? I didn't promise yer any tools,' the old man said, making to close the door.

'You was at the party at the church 'all on Saturday night, wasn't yer?' Jimmy asked him quickly.

'Party, what party?'

'I just told yer. At the church 'all.'

'I don't remember any party.'

Jimmy was puzzled. 'Let me ask yer one fing,' he said quickly. 'Was you a decorator once?'

'Yeah, years ago. Why?'

''Cos I remember you clearly tellin' us that you 'ad some decoratin' tools we could borrer.'

'I don't remember.'

Jimmy puffed loudly. 'Blimey, mate, I was standin' there

alongside yer when George Price got up to ask fer volunteers to 'elp the Farrans, an' you came up an' said about givin' 'em yer tools that yer don't use any more. I ain't after keepin' 'em. I only wanna borrer 'em.'

'George Price? Why didn't yer say yer come from George Price?' the old man growled. 'You coulda bin anybody. I was just puttin' me feet up ter listen ter the organ music when you come knockin'. That bloody rat-tat frightened the bleedin' life out o' me.'

'What d'yer fink it was, the police?' Jimmy said grinning.

'Police me arse. They don't frighten me. I don't get frightened very easy,' the old man went on angrily.

'Unless someone knocked on yer poxy door,' Jimmy mumbled under his breath. 'Anyway I'll be very grateful if there's anyfing in the way o' decoratin' tools yer can spare. It's fer a good cause after all.'

'I s'pose yer better come in then,' the old man told him. 'Mind the mat, it's a bit frayed.'

Jimmy stepped into the dark passage and immediately caught his toe in the holed mat. He staggered forward and steadied himself against the wall.

'I told yer ter be careful,' the old man shouted as he hobbled back into his parlour and sat down.

Jimmy followed him in and stood looking down at him, but the old man seemed to be ignoring him.

'Well?'

'Well what?'

'Ain't yer gonna show me the tools?'

'Tools, what tools?'

'The tools George Price asked yer for,' Jimmy said in a measured voice.

The old man pinched his chin between thumb and forefinger. 'I got some brushes, an' a few scrapers an' fings,' he replied almost to himself. 'They're all in me toolshed. I cleaned 'em all only the ovver day. Gotta keep yer brushes clean is what I always say.'

Jimmy looked down sadly at the hunched-up figure. 'Yeah, they taught me that in the services durin' the war. Keep yer equipment clean at all times,' he said. 'I s'pose you was in the first one wasn't yer, mate?'

'Royal West Kents,' the old man said without taking his eyes from the fire.

'I was in the navy,' Jimmy told him.

The old man continued to stare into the low flames. 'I used ter love the ole Armistice parades. I missed the last one though.'

'Yer old pins playin' yer up, were they?' Jimmy asked.

'Nah, me legs ain't too bad, considerin',' the old man replied. 'I lost me poxy medals. An Ole Contemptible can't go on a parade wivout 'is medals.'

'Lost 'em?'

'Lost 'em, or mislaid 'em. I dunno.'

'Well, I'm sure they'll turn up,' Jimmy told him.

'Mrs Jacobs next door reckons I must 'a' pawned 'em,' the old man went on. 'I don't fink I would 'ave pawned 'em though. Anyway we looked everywhere fer the pawn ticket, me an' 'er. She reckons I must 'ave put it in the fire by mistake when I was 'avin' a clear-out.'

'All right if I borrer a few o' yer tools then?' Jimmy asked.

The old man got up with a grunt and reached for his walking sticks. 'I'll ave ter find me torch, it's bloody dark out there,' he moaned. 'Now where did I put that bloody torch?'

Jimmy waited until his host had discovered his torch, which was hidden under a pile of newspapers, then he followed him out into the scullery and waited as patiently as he could while he fiddled with the door bolts.

'I don't go out there in this weavver. Got no need to,' the old man said.

''Ere, let me do the bolts,' Jimmy offered.

'All right, all right, I can do 'em. I ain't exactly useless, yer know,' the old man grumbled.

'I didn't mean any disrespect.'

'Well, that's all right then.'

The door creaked open and the old man shone his torch into the darkness. Jimmy could see the pile of rubbish stacked high against the back wall and the rusting old wringer with its split wooden rollers. A tin bath was set up in a corner and it was full of earth and sprouting weeds.

'I ain't bin out 'ere since the war, ter tell yer the trufe,' the old man said matter-of-factly.

'Since the war!' Jimmy repeated incredulously.

'Bin no need. Anyway, all the tools are in that there shed. 'Elp yerself, I'm goin' in. It's too bloody cold out here fer me,' the ancient told him.

Jimmy followed the beam of light and saw the tiny shed. He took the torch and nodded. 'Fanks mate, I won't take long,' he said smiling.

Once the old man had left him Jimmy warily opened the shed door and held his hand up to his mouth as the stench reached his nostrils. Everything looked full of rust. There were tobacco tins, biscuit tins and various other containers all in the same state of corrosion. At his feet he saw what he took to be a pile of rotting vegetables in a small wicker basket, and beside them was a large jar which contained brushes and scrapers. He picked up a large pasting-brush and felt the bristles. They were rock hard, and every other brush he felt was the same. They had all been put into the jar with paraffin or some other cleaner to soak and the fluid had long since dried out.

Jimmy shook his head sadly. The old man had no doubt been sincere in offering his equipment but his mind was addled. As far as he was concerned it must seem like only yesterday that he put the brushes in the jar until he had time to wash them out. The torch beam started to dim and Jimmy quickly took down a couple of tins from the narrow shelf. Inside the first one he found nails and screws of all sizes, all rusted. The other tin contained an assortment of rusted nuts and bolts. Before he left Jimmy took down one more larger tin. He could still make out the faded legend which once proudly advertised a brand of chocolate biscuits. The lid came off with some difficulty, and in the failing beam of the torch Jimmy found himself staring down at a clip of rusty war medals.

The old man was sitting beside the low fire, his head drooping on his chest as he contemplated the coals, and he did not look up as Jimmy came back in.

'Fanks fer yer trouble, old son,' the younger man said cheerfully. 'They'll come in very 'andy.'

'I knew they would,' the old man replied, still looking into the fire.

'Well, I'd better be off,' Jimmy told him. 'Take care o' yerself. I'll see meself out.'

The old man did not look up, and when Jimmy stepped out into the quiet street he smiled to himself as he felt the clip of medals resting in his coat pocket.

Bill Grogan and Ray Halleron had been summoned to Scotland Yard for a top-level meeting and they left one hour later harbouring no illusions. All stops were being pulled to make sure that nothing hindered the vigorous execution of the law. Pressure was being brought to bear on various villains in the know to help bring about the swift arrest of Frankie Morgan, who seemed to have vanished into thin air. The Commissioner related that he had been called to the Cabinet Room at Number 10 and told that a certain Right Honourable Gentleman was making good progress after being transferred to a private clinic, where he was out of reach of newshounds, and the Honourable Gentleman's resignation was imminent.

Inspector Halleron had been pleased with the Commissioner's reaction when he mooted the idea of sentence reduction if the two Morgan boys co-operated in the apprehension of their father. It seemed to Halleron that anything was possible now that top-level careers were on the line and Grogan shared his view. The two men immediately decided to go across the river and shake up Joe Andretti, the Maltese gang boss. He had to be made to see that he too was living on borrowed time, powerful as he was, if this case was not quickly brought to a successful conclusion.

Andretti was only too well aware of what was at stake, and when the two senior police officers called in at his gambling club in Limehouse he was very accommodating, though eager to make a very important point.

'I will always be ready to help you in any way I can,' he began as the three men sat down together for lunch. 'But you have to understand I can't be expected to take the blame for Frankie Morgan not showing up at Greenwich. I laid everything on here. He was ready and primed, and then you let the newspapers in on the act. What went wrong? Surely you don't issue a press release before the arrests are complete? You should have waited until you had all of them safely locked away.'

Halleron shrugged his shoulders. 'I take your point, Mr Andretti, but you have to understand our dilemma. The papers were threatening a scandal exposure. We had to give them the story when we did.'

'The point is, we need you to flush him out for us,' Grogan said in his usual forthright manner.

'What makes you think Morgan's on my manor?' Andretti asked quickly.

Grogan waited until the waiter had finished placing the fresh fillets of sole on the plates before answering. 'Frankie Morgan's done business in this area before.'

He saw the lock of feigned horror on Andretti's face. 'We're not following that line of investigation,' he told him. 'Not yet anyway. We just feel that it might occur to Morgan to lie low in the East End. We know he's still got a few old pals on this manor and he might imagine it to be the last place we'd think of looking for him, considering that you set him up.'

'Does he suspect?' Andretti asked.

'Why else didn't he make the meet at the Cutty Sark?' Halleron cut in.

'Anything could have happened,' the gang boss said with a shrug of his shoulders. 'He could have been ill, or got knocked down.'

Both officers smiled and Halleron leaned forward in the manner of a familiar. 'Frankie Morgan's no fool,' he said tartly. 'He knows full well that the Cape Diamonds were targeted at the robbery, and he probably worked out from the newspapers that the man found murdered at Billingsgate was the man who led the raid. The swift arrest of his sons must have made him realise what was going on. He knows it's a question of survival – the mugs get offered up and the big boys walk away.'

Andretti smiled slyly as he picked up his knife and fork. 'We all do what we can, but sometimes harsh measures are the only answer,' he replied.

Grogan took a sip from his Chianti. 'So you'll put word out,' he said bluntly.

Andretti nodded slowly as he broke a bread roll in two. 'I'll have word out as far as Whitechapel and east to Barking. If Frankie Morgan is holed up in the East End, you can rest assured he'll be flushed out,' he said confidently. 'One thing you might be able to do for me in return.'

Halleron raised his eyebrows.

'It would be very nice if I could go to Weissman today and tell him that the investigation into that consignment of cloth he obtained was now completed and no further action was anticipated,' Andretti said with an amicable expression. 'After all, what are we talking about here? Two, maybe three hundred quid?'

'I'll see what I can do, but of course I can't promise anything,' Halleron replied.

'Of course, gentlemen. Now I suggest we enjoy our fish,' Andretti said smiling broadly. 'I would recommend the syrup pudding too.'

One hour later Halleron and Grogan climbed into a taxicab and sat back in the seat as the driver fought his way through the evening dock traffic.

'Oh, what a tangled web we weave,' Grogan said sighing.

'I would imagine Frankie Morgan feels the same as we do,' Halleron replied, smiling cynically.

The two police officers lapsed into silence, then suddenly Grogan chuckled to himself.

'What's the joke?' Halleron asked.

'Oh, I was just thinking,' Grogan replied. 'We go as civil as you please to a criminal like Andretti and sit down eating with him like we're all respectable businessmen.'

'A trade for a trade,' Halleron said smiling. 'It's the way the world's going.'

'It leaves a bad taste in the mouth though,' Grogan replied.

Halleron reached into his coat pocket and took out an envelope. 'Andretti handed this to me while you were in the gents,' he said, passing it over.

'A cheque for £500 made out to the Police Widows and

Orphans Fund,' Grogan said shaking his head slowly. 'Bribery and corruption.'

'It depends which way you care to look at it,' Halleron replied. 'I prefer to call this a bonus.'

Chapter Forty

Jimmy Rideout walked back to his flat deep in thought. The experience of meeting the forgetful old man had brought a lot of memories back. His own father would have been about his age now, had he lived. He too had had a clip of medals but unlike the old boy he had been in no doubt about where they went. He had taken them over to the pawnshop during the depression years and with the pittance he received he bought a loaf of bread and a few other items of food which had become luxuries during those years. Jimmy remembered the day well. His mother had shed a few tears, knowing how proud of those medals his father was, and out of the few pennies left she encouraged him to go and buy himself a pint of ale.

Jimmy entered his flat and carefully laid the medals down on the table, then he put the kettle over the gas ring, spooned some tea leaves into the enamel teapot and finally took off his coat. While he waited for the kettle to boil he put on his glasses and studied the rusting campaign honours. The first one had a ribbon coloured in a rainbow of red, yellow, green and blue, which identified it as the 1914–19 Victory Medal. The second Jimmy knew to be the British War Medal 1914–18. The third one he recognised too. His father had had that medal. It was the Mons Star, which was issued to troops who had served in France at the beginning of the war. The old boy had certainly seen his share of the mud and blood, Jimmy thought.

The fourth medal puzzled him. Its ribbon was of green, white and yellow stripes and the clasp of the medal had two bars which the ribbon was looped around. Like the other medals it was covered in rust and grime which hid the details. Jimmy studied the last of the five. It was different from all the rest, being an intricate design of a compass star laid over a diagonal cross with a small disc centred uppermost. The ribbon was of yellow and black stripes, and like the others the wording on the medal was hidden beneath the rust.

Jimmy made the tea and after his second cup he was ready to commence work. He found some sharp scissors and set to work removing the first ribbon by picking the stitches on the back of the fold. Next he gently washed it in soapy water and carefully scrubbed away the grime. While the ribbon was drying he set to work with a cloth and metal polish. The job proved to be tedious but he persevered. Time passed without him realising and suddenly he heard Dolly's knock.

'I thought yer was gonna be ready ter go up the Anchor,' she said, giving him a puzzled look as she walked in.

When Jimmy told her of his encounter with the old man, Dolly's face took on a sad look and she sat down to examine the medals. The visit to the pub was forgotten as she took the scissors and picked at the second ribbon while Jimmy went on with his polishing.

As the clock moved towards midnight Dolly sat back sipping her tea, staring at Jimmy as he studied the gleaming medals lying in front of him on the table. The ribbons were all clean and pressed flat and the wording on each medal was clearly discernible.

'Just look at that one,' Jimmy said enthusiastically. '"Ashanti

1896". I remember readin' about the Ashanti War on the Gold Coast. And this one. South Africa 1901 an' 1902. That was the Boer War. Gawd Almighty, that old sod must 'ave seen some action.'

'Fancy 'im losin' 'em,' Dolly replied. 'I bet 'e'll be over the moon when yer take 'em back to 'im all shiny an' new.'

'I wouldn't bet on it,' Jimmy told her, smiling as he remembered the old man's manner. "E'll most prob'ly tell me ter piss orf.'

"Ow old would yer say 'e was?' Dolly asked as she dipped a digestive biscuit into her tea.

'Well, yer can get some idea by those medals,' Jimmy replied. 'Take that Ashanti Medal. If 'e went in the army at eighteen and that one was fer service in 1896 'e woulda bin born in '78, which makes 'im seventy-two at least. I'd say 'e was nearer eighty.'

'Well, we got the medals cleaned up but we didn't get the brushes,' Dolly remarked with a smile.

'Don't you worry, gel,' Jimmy told her. 'I'll go an' see my ole pal first fing. 'E won't let me down.'

"E better not,' Dolly replied quickly. 'We've only got three weeks left now.'

On Monday morning Winifred Seaton, district officer of Bermondsey welfare services, paid a flying visit to Tommy Caulfield's transport yard.

The large, jovial contractor led her into the office and found her a seat. 'Now what can I do for yer, Mrs?' he asked.

'Miss,' Winifred corrected him.

'Sorry, Miss.'

Winifred smiled coldly. 'I understand you have rented a property to one Dolly Morgan,' she began.

'I might 'ave done,' Tommy replied, already feeling irritated by the woman's officious manner.

'The welfare services are involved with the Farran family and I was told by Rose Farran that the family intend to move in as soon as the house is ready,' she went on. 'Is that correct?'

'You are correct,' Tommy said smiling.

'Would you mind if I take a look round?' Winifred asked.

'Certainly not. Come this way,' Tommy told her.

The two crossed the greasy yard and Winifred sniffed. 'What's that awful smell?' she asked.

'I transport skins an' 'ides,' he explained. 'A couple o' the lads 'ave just scrubbed out an 'orse cart. That's what yer can smell.'

Winifred scribbled a few words in her notepad and then followed the contractor into the house through the side door. She went up the stairs and passed from room to room making notes, then she came down and walked out into the scullery, looking around with a smug expression on her pale, angular face. She tried the water tap and pulled a face as she peered into the stone sink. 'Um. Have you any gas laid on?'

'Not yet.'

'What about the electric?'

'That's workin'.'

'I see that there is direct access from the house into the yard,' the officer remarked.

'Yeah, that's right,' Tommy answered. 'I used ter use that entrance when I kept me stores in the 'ouse. I 'ad the front all boarded up, yer see.'

'Yes, I saw the new front door and windows,' Winifred replied. 'Tell me, Mr Caulfield. Would you say that those skins and hides which you transport posed a risk of disease and sickness?'

'Oh yes,' he told her with a vigorous nod. 'You can get anthrax from skins. Those 'ides can be dangerous too. I've known men ter get nasty illnesses from 'ides. Some o' the car men get skin complaints, an' one bloke's started 'avin' fits.'

'Thank you very much, Mr Caulfield,' Winifred said smugly. 'I have to make a report, you see. We are responsible for the Farran children while their mother is absent from the family home. The three youngest are under age.'

'Before yer leave I'd like to 'ave a word, if I may,' Tommy said, looking the officer in the eye.

'Of course,' she replied smiling, wondering what other revelations the man was going to come out with.

'Shall we go in my office?'

Winifred sat down and crossed her legs, pulling her skirt down over her knees. Her notepad rested on her lap and she toyed with her pencil as the contractor made himself comfortable at his desk.

'I expect you'll be a mite anxious about those children comin' 'ere ter live, what wiv me 'andlin' skins an' 'ides,' he began.

Winifred raised her eyebrows and blinked once or twice. 'To be quite frank, yes,' she answered.

'Well, yer needn't worry yerself on that score,' Tommy told her. 'All my carts get steam-washed an' disinfected at the tanneries every evenin' before they come back 'ere. They 'ave ter be, 'cos o' my yard bein' in a residential street. It's a sanitary law.'

Winifred looked suspicious. 'What about that awful smell in the yard?' she asked.

'Oh that's nuffink ter worry about,' the contractor replied smiling amiably. 'That was one o' Mark Vice's carts. 'E's a local contractor who does skins as well, yer see. The cart split an axle on the corner o' Basin Street an' we pulled it in ter do a repair job on it. Luckily it was empty at the time but we 'ad ter wash it out before we could work on it. Mark Vice asked me if I could do the repair for 'im. 'E was worried about the smell if the van 'ad ter wait fer the wagon firm ter come down. It could 'ave bin stuck outside the 'ouses fer hours.'

Winifred struck out a few lines in her notepad and looked up. 'I see there's a door from the house leading directly into the yard. Will that door remain?'

'Oh yes,' Tommy replied.

'Now, can I ask you how much rent you'll be charging the family?'

'You can ask, but I ain't gonna tell yer,' Tommy replied sharply. 'Ter be honest I don't see that it's any o' your business.'

Winifred coloured slightly and shifted uncomfortably on her chair. 'I'm concerned that the family will be able to afford the rent,' she said quickly.

'So am I,' the contractor replied, feeling that the interview had gone on long enough.

Winifred put her notepad into her handbag and stood up. 'Well, thank you for your time,' she said.

'It's quite all right,' Tommy told her. 'I'm only glad yer called while the dogs were bein' exercised. I got two Alsatians an' they need a run every day. They get ferocious if I don't exercise 'em regularly.'

'Where do they sleep?' the officer asked, looking quite shocked.

'In the stable along wiv the 'orses. I let 'em run loose in the yard normally. It deters rustlers, yer see,' Tommy explained, desperate to keep a straight face. 'There was a spate o' rustlin' round 'ere not so long ago. Like the ole Wild West it was. I put it down ter the Gyppos. They know a good 'orse when they see one. 'Ave you ever seen a Gypsy doin' a deal wiv the 'orses? Yer should go down Kent. That's the place ter see the Gypsies. When they do a deal they spit on their 'ands an' shake on it. Never see 'em sign anyfing. They can teach us a fing or two. They got their pride, yer see. A deal's a deal an' the 'andshake seals it.'

Winifred felt her head beginning to buzz as she edged for

the door. 'Well, I must leave. I've another call to make,' she said with a note of desperation in her voice.

'Any time yer got a few minutes ter spare drop in,' Tommy told her, hiding a grin. 'Just be careful o' the dogs though.'

'The man's a raving lunatic, I'm certain,' Winifred said aloud as she hurried back to her office. There was a full report due and she would have a few pertinent comments to make about the Farrans' prospective landlord.

When the Morgan boys were first arrested they felt confident that their solicitor would soon have them released, but as the interviews continued they realised that their brief was becoming less optimistic. The case against them had grown stronger and the alibi they offered had been turned against them. What was more, there were now two witnesses who had placed them in Berkeley Street at the time the raid took place and had seen them don masks as they entered the shop, and at an identification parade the witnesses had had no trouble in pointing them out.

Now, having been formally charged with the robbery, both John and Ernest Morgan had been brought from their cells at Brixton Prison to face Inspectors Grogan and Halleron. The Morgans' solicitor had also been present and the interview was soon over. The brothers were allowed to converse with their solicitor in the interview room for a few minutes, then when he left they were allowed thirty minutes to think things over.

'Our brief's bin got at. It stands out like a sore thumb,' John sneered.

'I dunno what 'e's finkin' about, askin' us ter plead guilty,' Ernie replied.

'Yer gotta admit it looks bad though,' John said miserably. 'All right, so we plead guilty an' bank on a lighter sentence, an' we go along wiv the Law an' turn the ole man in. But 'ow do we know the beak's gonna deliver the goods. 'E might give us the maximum anyway.'

'That bastard Grogan said we're likely ter go down fer ten ter fifteen if we plead not guilty an' then lose the case, an' the brief didn't bovver ter challenge it,' Ernie reminded him.

'It's not pleadin' guilty or not guilty that bowers me. It's 'avin' ter turn the ole man in. 'E'd never fergive us,' John said, puffing loudly.

'They said 'e could be starin' at a twenty stretch wiv 'is form though,' Ernie replied, shaking his head.

'We've bin took fer mugs, Em,' John said bitterly. 'We were just 'ired muscle an' we're bein' done fer armed robbery. We should 'ave seen it coming.'

'But 'ow did they get on to us, that's what I'd like ter know?' Ernie grouched.

'Well, yer don't need ter be a poxy Einstein ter work it out,' John replied bitterly. 'The Law told us they got the diamonds back an' yer can bet yer life there's big names involved. We've bin put in the frame ter keep it all nice an' sweet.'

'What we gonna do, John?' his younger brother asked anxiously.

'I reckon we should ask ter see our brief again an' we'll tell 'im ter contact Albert,' John told him. ''E'll be able ter locate the ole man an' tell 'im what's bein' said. If Farvver's got any sense, 'e'll give 'imself up. Albert's gotta make 'im see that it's the best fer all of us.'

'Yeah, that's if 'e'll even let Albert talk to 'im,' Ernie remarked. 'Yer know what the ole man's like. 'Specially after kickin' Albert out too.'

'It's our only 'ope,' John said firmly. 'Albert won't let us down. 'E'll make the ole man see sense.'

Ernie nodded. 'Yer right, John. Let's do it.'

*

Tommy Caulfield soon realised that he might have gone just a little bit too far in his baiting of the welfare officer and he was keen to put things right when Dolly called on him. 'P'raps I shouldn't 'ave wound 'er up like that, but she got my back up wiv 'er bloody attitude, Dolly,' he told her. 'Yer can bet yer life she's got it all down in that notepad.'

Dolly could not help smiling at the thought of the welfare officer's prim face when she was told of the two wild Alsatians running loose in the yard, and she was quick to put the contractor at ease. 'Look, they can't stop us doin' the place up,' she pointed out, 'an' they can't stop me takin' the family on, providin' there's no risk ter the children, an' there won't be.'

'Yeah, but there's somefing else we gotta get sorted out,' Tommy told her. 'I need ter get a tall fence put up about six feet from the side o' the 'ouse so it isolates it from the yard. That way there's no risk o' the kids runnin' out an' 'avin' an accident wiv the 'orse-an'-carts. It'll also give yer a bigger yard space fer the washin' an' fings.'

'It's a good idea,' Dolly replied. 'We don't want the dogs to eat the kids, do we?'

Tommy laughed aloud as he reached into the desk drawer for his bottle of Scotch and glasses. 'Let's you an' me drink to a successful outcome,' he suggested.

'What about that roof?' Dolly asked as he poured two large measures of spirit.

'It's bein' sorted out this week, so don't concern yerself,' he replied.

Dolly took the proffered glass and sipped, her face screwing up as the fiery spirit burned her throat. 'I s'pose yer bin followin' the news o' Frankie Morgan,' she said finally.

'Last I 'eard was that the police were 'untin' for 'im,' Tommy said, staring at his drink.

'I bet those two boys of 'is are wishin' they'd done the same as Albert an' turned the job down,' Dolly remarked.

''Ow's 'e an' young Rose gettin' on?' the contractor asked.

'They're busy sortin' out their weddin' plans, but Albert's upset about 'is family, which is only natural,' Dolly told him.

'What about your plans?' Tommy asked suddenly.

'I've got it all worked out an' organised,' Dolly replied. 'I just need a few more hours in the day.'

'I didn't mean about the 'ouse. I meant about yer own personal plans.'

'Me an' Jimmy, yer mean?'

'Yeah.'

'We get on like two peas in a pod, but tyin' the knot's somefing else,' she told him. 'I still miss my feller. I miss 'im like mad, an' I can't bring 'im back. I know that right enough, but I need time on me own sometimes, time ter dwell, an' time ter bring up all the nice memories. I can't put Jimmy's emotions frew the mangle by me actin' up. Mind you, Jimmy wants me ter marry 'im. 'E's asked me a couple o' times, ter be honest.'

A faraway look came into the contractor's eyes as he stared down at the drink he was holding. 'Do you ever wish yer could turn the clock back, Dolly?' he asked.

'I s'pose we all do sometimes,' she sighed.

'I know I do,' he said. 'All we can do though is learn from our mistakes an' try ter put fings right where we can.'

'We also 'ave ter know that some fings can't be put right an' we 'ave to accept it. I fink it's knowin' the difference that's important,' Dolly replied.

Tommy downed his drink and quickly refilled his glass. 'Another?'

Dolly shook her head. 'I'd like to, Tommy, but I need ter keep sensible. There's so much ter do.'

The big friendly character sat slumped in his office chair,

a serious expression sitting like a mask on his ruddy face as he contemplated his drink. Dolly glanced at him, aware that there was something troubling the man. She moved to make herself more comfortable and caught his eye. 'Yer look like yer got the troubles o' the world on yer shoulders, Tommy,' she remarked.

'My ole dutch ain't too well, an' I bin givin' this business a lot o' thought,' he replied. 'A local carter made me an offer a few weeks ago although nuffink come of it, but it got me finkin'. Me an' Doris would be far better off livin' away from the Smoke. Maybe we could sell up an' buy a little place somewhere in Kent or Sussex. Doris likes Eastbourne. Anyway, whatever I decide, I want yer ter know that the 'ouse won't be in the deal. That place is gonna be yours as long as yer want it, I'll make sure o' that, gel.'

Dolly watched while he finished his drink, then she held out her empty glass. 'I fink I will 'ave that drink,' she told him.

Chapter Forty-One

The women of Fellmonger Street had decided to hold their own council of war and they gathered together in Rene Stratton's front room on Monday morning to make their plans.

'It's no good just sayin' we'll 'elp, we've gotta get out there an' do it,' Rene declared.

'Yer dead right, luv,' Ivy replied. 'It stands ter reason. Dolly Morgan ain't gonna come round an' lead us over there by the 'and, now is she?'

Ethel Price nodded. 'I reckon we should all go over the 'ouse an' get stuck in,' she said with passion. 'There's scrapin' an' paintin' an' Gawd knows what ter be done over there.'

Freda Arrowsmith sipped her tea. 'Yer right, luv. There's no time like the present.'

Sadie Jones looked around at the women. 'It's all gotta be done by the end o' the month. It only gives us three weeks,' she added.

'We can do it, can't we, gels?' Rene said in a loud voice.

The enthusiastic response impelled Rene out of her chair. 'Right then. We're gonna need scrapers an' fings so look around an' see what yer got,' she told them. 'I'll just make us all a fresh cuppa first an' then we'll sort it out wiv Dolly.'

Across the street Dolly and Jimmy were busy scraping the last of the wallpaper in the upstairs front room. 'We better make a start on the back room this afternoon,' Jimmy said as he took a breather.

Dolly sat down on the scaffold-board and sighed dejectedly. 'I thought we'd be more in front than this,' she replied.

Jimmy nodded. 'No worry, luv, it'll get done,' he said encouragingly.

Dolly was about to make a sharp reply when there was a loud knock on the front door. She got up reluctantly and went down the bare wooden stairs, her footsteps sounding loudly in the empty house.

'Right then, what yer want us ter do?' Rene asked, grinning widely.

Dolly looked around at the group of smiling women for a moment, then she almost pulled Rene in through the door. 'C'mon in, you lovely lot,' she told them with a beaming smile. 'Yer'll be sorry.'

The house was suddenly filled with laughter and joking as the women got to work. Jimmy had been made foreman in charge and he allocated the tasks, giving the women a quick demonstration of how to get the best results with a scraper.

'Right now, you piss orf an' get on wiv yer own work,' Rene told him. 'We ain't exactly stupid, yer know.'

Dolly's spirits lifted as she watched the women set to work in pairs. Sounds of singing came from the other rooms and she turned to Jimmy who was sweeping up the scrapings. 'It makes yer feel good, don't it?' she said.

'Ten minutes ago I was feelin' a bit anxious about doin' this place up in time, but now I ain't worried in the slightest. Not now that lot's on the scene,' he said smiling.

*

427

Rose had been dreading having to go and see Bernard Collis to put her notice in and it was a big surprise to find George Penrose now in charge of the factory floor.

'Four-eyes must be out sick or somefing,' one of the girls said. 'There ain't bin nobody standin' round the clock.'

Rose clocked in and walked along the long corridor to the manager's office. When she tapped on the door a more pleasant voice bade her enter and she walked in to see the grey-haired director sitting at Collis's desk.

'I wanna put me notice in, Mr Penrose,' she told him.

'I'm sorry,' he said. 'Is there any special reason?'

'I can't stay 'ere now, the way fings are,' she replied, looking embarrassed.

'Look, I know you and Alice Copeland are friends, but I can assure you that we are treating this matter very seriously, and we are taking action,' Penrose said quietly. 'Alice herself still has the right to make an official complaint to the management, and I've already advised her to report the matter to the police. We'll give her our backing.'

Rose's face looked shocked as she shook her head slowly. 'I'm afraid I don't know what yer talkin' about,' she replied. 'What matter are yer treatin' seriously?'

George Penrose put his elbow on the desktop and rested his head in the palm of his hand. 'Oh dear! Oh dear, oh dear,' he muttered. 'You don't know, do you? I misunderstood when you said you couldn't stay here now, the way things were.'

'I meant I couldn't stay 'ere now 'cos I was pregnant,' Rose explained. 'What's 'appened to Alice?'

'I'm afraid Collis attacked Alice in this office last Friday evening,' Penrose told her. 'As a matter of fact, I came in to the office in time to prevent your friend getting injured, but I have to say she was badly shaken up. Collis is appearing in front of the board this morning and he will be dismissed instantly, I can assure you. As for Alice, she may decide to go to the police, and I will support her if she does. In any case the board will be sending her a personal letter.'

Rose stood looking down at the white-haired director, trying to take it all in. Alice had not said a word on Saturday evening about being attacked, though Rose recalled her looking pale and drawn.

'Why did Collis attack 'er?' she asked.

'I don't know, my dear. I can only assume the man's mind snapped,' Penrose replied.

''Ow did yer know I was Alice's friend?' Rose asked him.

'Well, you see I needed to know how Alice was feeling and I made some enquiries as the women arrived for work,' he told her. 'As a matter of fact, I was going to send for you this morning for a quiet chat. Did you happen to see her over the weekend?'

'Yeah, I did an' she seemed all right, but I knew there was somefing troublin' 'er,' Rose replied. 'She's obviously feelin' the shock.'

'And she didn't tell you anything about what happened on Friday?'

'No, she didn't.'

'That's strange.'

'No, it isn't, Mr Penrose.'

'I'm sorry?'

Rose took a deep breath. 'Alice is a special person,' she said slowly. 'She 'ad a very bad time at 'ome an' she ran away ter live wiv 'er gran'muvver about a year ago. She doesn't pour out 'er troubles very easily. She bottles 'em up like a lot of us do. Alice worries over people. She worries over me, an' she knows I worry over 'er. That's why we tend ter keep troubles from each ovver.'

'I would have thought sharing troubles was what friends were for,' Penrose said kindly.

'Yeah, that's true, but we get ter recognise when people are laden down wiv their own burdens an' we don't go givin' 'em our bundles ter carry,' Rose explained, colouring slightly to hear her own pronunciation.

Penrose nodded his head slowly. 'Of course Alice would know that you have your own burden, being, er, pregnant,' he said hesitantly.

'Partly that, yes. I'm also lookin' after a family,' Rose told him.

Penrose got up and slid a chair towards the desk. 'Sit down a moment, Miss Farran,' he said quietly. 'I'd like you to tell me about your family.'

Jimmy Rideout knocked loudly on the door of number 26 Basin Street on Monday afternoon and stood waiting patiently for Mr Williams. He heard a crash, then a curse, and finally the sound of a bolt being drawn.

'What d'yer want?' the old man asked as he peered round the door.

'Remember me? George Price sent me,' Jimmy told him.

'Why's 'e keep sendin' people round ter me for?' the old man grouched. 'There was a dopey git come round 'ere last night. Gawd knows what for.'

'That was me,' Jimmy replied, trying to keep a straight face.

'Well, yer better come in then,' the ancient said grudgingly.

Jimmy followed him into the parlour and reached into his coat pocket as the old man eased himself down into an armchair.

'I found yer medals an' I took the trouble o' givin' 'em a bit of a clean-up,' he said cheerfully. 'There we are.'

The old man's eyes widened as Jimmy laid the clip of medals down on the bare wooden table. 'Good Gawd! Where d'yer find it?' he asked.

'Them,' Jimmy corrected.

'The ticket. Where d'yer find it?'

'Out in the yard.'

'I knew it. I told that scatty mare who does my cleanin' the ticket might be in the yard. Look in the yard, I told 'er, but no. She wouldn't 'ave it. She's a right know-all ole cow. Wait till I see 'er. I'll give 'er what for.'

'Well, yer got yer medals back, that's the main fing,' Jimmy said, smiling brightly.

'I owe yer a few bob,' the old man said, getting out of his chair.

'Nah, it's OK.'

'I ain't bein' be'olden'. 'Ow much did it cost ter get 'em back?'

''Alf a dollar,' Jimmy told him.

The ancient fished into his waistcoat pocket and pulled out a ten-shilling note. 'Got change?' he grunted.

Jimmy took the note and carefully counted out ten shillings in change which he put down on the table. 'There we are,' he said. 'All squared up.'

Without looking the old man put the coins in his trouser pocket and sat down again. 'I'll be able ter go on the next parade now, Gawd willin',' he said with a ghost of a smile.

'Don't go mislayin' 'em again,' Jimmy warned him.

'What d'yer take me for?' the old man said sharply. 'I ain't that stupid. It's 'er. She does it out o' spite. I could tell yer fings about that cleaner o' mine. D'yer know, one day she 'id me teef. I couldn't chew me meat an' I couldn't eat me crust o' bread. I love a crust o' bread wiv me dinner. That's not all neivver. She took me trousers away one day so I couldn't get out o' bed. I did though. Soon as she left I got up an' stuck a blanket round me. Mind yer, I nearly got meself inter trouble.'

''Ow was that, then?' Jimmy asked, stifling a yawn.

'Well, there was a knock on the door an' when I opened it there was this smart-lookin' woman standin' there. She'd come from the church. She wanted ter know if I'd like ter join the Jover's Witnesses,' the old man went on. 'Anyway, she was sellin' this magazine called the *Watch Tower* so I said I'd buy one. As I reached out ter take it me blanket fell down. She took one look at me an' screamed. Then she ran orf like the devil 'imself was after 'er. She must 'ave thought I'd done it on purpose.'

'Course yer didn't, did yer?' Jimmy asked, grinning.

'Nah. Ten years ago I might 'a' bin able ter raise a gallop but not these days,' the old man replied with a toothless smile.

'Well, anyway yer'll be all right fer the parade,' Jimmy told him as he made for the door.

The old man picked up the medals and followed Jimmy into the passage.

'I'm gonna 'ide these where that 'orrible old cow can't get 'er 'ands on 'em,' he said, grinning evilly.

'Just remember where yer put 'em,' Jimmy told him.

'Don't worry, I'll stick 'em in a tin in me toolshed,' the old man replied. 'She'll never fink o' lookin' there for 'em.'

Word had got around about the house Tommy Caulfield was going to rent to the Farrans, and Joe Diamond had been given an update by Lizzie Carroll. She had made it her business to find out all there was to know about the details and progress of the deal, and she was keen to keep abreast of developments. It was with this purpose in mind that Lizzie positioned herself near the door when she heard two of the neighbours discussing the subject on the corner.

'Dolly was tellin' me about what Tommy told the welfare woman,' Rene was saying. 'Apparently 'e said 'e 'ad these wild dogs an' they was bein' exercised somewhere else when the woman called ter see 'im about the 'ouse.'

'I bet she was shocked,' Ivy replied.

'I expect the woman was worried in case Tommy's dogs got loose an' went fer the kids,' Rene went on. 'After all she's gotta be careful. Tommy might be a ravin' lunatic fer all she knows an' 'e could put the dogs on the poor little bleeders.'

The distance between the two chatting women and Lizzie Carroll, and the wood and glass door separating them, made it difficult for the shop assistant to hear every word. She had pieced enough together, though, to be thoroughly shocked. Joe Diamond was used to his assistant's ramblings and he turned a deaf ear, but there were others who hung on Lizzie's every word.

'What's the latest on the Farrans?' Martha Cork asked her as she stood watching her weigh up a quarter of cheese.

'I dunno, I'm sure,' Lizzie replied with a worried look on her flat round face.

'What d'yer mean?'

'Well, far be it from me ter cast aspersions, but that Tommy Caulfield makes me fink.'

'Fink what, Lizzie?'

'Well, keep it ter yerself, but I 'eard that 'e's got two wild dogs in the yard an' 'e's threatened ter put 'em on the Farran kids.'

'Good Gawd.'

'Frightened the welfare woman away when she called ter look at the 'ouse, 'e did.'

'Who, Tommy Caulfield?'

'Yeah. 'E threatened ter put the dogs on 'er, 'e did.'

''E could get locked up fer that.'

Lizzie was getting into her stride. 'D'yer know, Marfa, I always reckoned there was somefing wrong wiv that Caulfield feller.'

'What d'yer mean?'

'I dunno exactly. Ain't you ever 'ad a feelin' about somebody? A fing yer can't put yer finger on?'

'Yeah, as a matter o' fact I 'ad that feelin' about my first ole man,' Martha replied, slipping her hands into the fur cuffs of her tatty coat. ''E used ter go out every Friday night an' never come back till Saturday mornin'. 'E used ter say 'e was playin' cards all night but I 'ad this feelin'. Call it intuition but I just knew 'e was up ter no good. Anyway one Friday night 'e never went out, so I ses to 'im, ain't yer goin' out ternight fer yer cards, an' 'e just shook 'is 'ead. 'E looked worried out of 'is life. Now I'm sittin' round the fire wiv me sewin' an' all of a sudden there was a loud bangin' on the door. "Come out, yer bastard, I know yer in there," this voice calls out. My ole man went white as a sheet an' 'e runs up the stairs an' shouts down fer me ter say 'e's gorn out. Yer can guess, can't yer, Liz. 'E'd bin playin' about wiv this bloke's missus an' 'e got found out. Anyway I opened the door an' spoke ter the feller. 'E 'ad a carvin' knife in 'is 'and. I managed ter calm 'im down an' 'e told me 'ow 'e'd caught the pair of 'em in bed an' 'ow my ole man got away out the winder. Apparently 'e finally forced it out of 'is wife where we lived an' 'e come lookin'.'

'Good Gawd,' Lizzie exclaimed. 'What did yer do then?'

'Well I said 'e's upstairs. 'Elp yerself.'

'Good Gawd. What 'appened then?'

'This woman's 'usband goes flyin' up the stairs an' my ole man takes a penn'orth frew the winder. Lucky git lands on 'is feet, would yer believe, an' legs it down the turnin'. That was the last time I ever saw 'im. No, tell a lie. I did see 'im once after that.'

'Oh, where?'

'I was wiv my second ole man at the time. We was goin' over north London ter see 'is bruvver an' as we passed

Pentonville Prison there 'e was, the cheatin' bleeder, on an outside workin' party mendin' the walls.'

'Well, I never,' Lizzie exclaimed.

'Nor did I,' Martha replied, grinning slyly. 'Not since my second ole man pissed orf.'

Chapter Forty-Two

Don Farran had had a miserable weekend, but now as he sat on the tram on Monday evening on his way to Rotherhithe he understood everything, the reason why Alice had been so secretive and why she had not wanted him to kiss her and hold her. She had been very quiet and preoccupied when he escorted her home on Saturday night and she had shrugged off his concern by saying that she felt a bit off colour. He had accepted her excuse and made arrangements to take her to the pictures on Sunday evening, but during the whole time they sat in the back row of the Troxy cinema Alice had been quiet and unresponsive to his shows of affection. It had seemed to him that she was trying to make him aware her feelings towards him were cooling. All day Monday he had worried over her attitude towards him that weekend, and her coldness when he kissed her goodnight in the shadows near her grandmother's house. She had seemed impatient to go inside and he had said goodnight abruptly, saying that he would meet her from work on Tuesday evening.

Rose had told him everything when he got home from work that evening, and his hands balled into tight fists as the tram trundled along the Jamaica Road towards Rotherhithe Tunnel. He understood now why Alice had kept her ordeal from him.

She knew that he was headstrong and would have wanted to seek revenge on Bernard Collis when he reported to the factory on Monday morning. Don was impatient to see Alice, to hear her account of the assault on her on Friday evening, and he wanted to tell her how relieved he was that her strange behaviour did not mean she wanted to end their friendship. He wanted to tell her that she was the only girl for him and he needed her so much.

The tram swung round at the tunnel entrance and continued along Lower Road towards Surrey Docks Station. Don let his hands relax on his knees and he drew deep breaths to calm himself. He would take his sister's advice and be calm and supportive to Alice, but if he ever saw that maniac of a manager he would jump on him and give him the hiding of his life, he swore he would.

As the conveyance shuddered to a halt at the Surrey Dock gates Don realised that his hands were screwed up again into angry fists and he fought to control his feelings as he stepped down into the cold night air. Redriff Road was quiet now that the docks were closed, and Don walked quickly along the wide thoroughfare which led Downtown thinking about what Alice had told him when they first walked out together. Her early years had been miserable and loveless. Her father had ruled the family with a rod of iron, and now, after she had torn herself free and begun to carve out a new life, she had had the misfortune to fall foul of a maniac who could have ruined her, were it not for the timely intervention of George Penrose.

Don walked into Schooner Street, a narrow turning leading down to the river wall, and knocked on the door of number 17. The cold river fog was swirling in and he shivered as he waited.

Alice looked surprised as she opened the door and saw him standing there. 'I didn't expect yer, Don,' she said. 'C'mon in.'

Don followed her into the warm parlour and stood beside

the table feeling a little uncomfortable as she looked at him enquiringly.

'Rose found out what 'appened to yer on Friday evenin',' he begun. 'I 'ad ter come round ter see yer, Alice. I couldn't wait until termorrer.'

'I wanted ter tell yer, Don, but I knew what yer reaction would be,' she explained, her eyes dropping.

'I understand but I was worried all weekend,' he replied. 'I thought you was gettin' fed up an' wanted to end it.'

'I don't know what I'd do wivout yer, Don,' Alice said quietly. 'I was feelin' terrible on Saturday night an' I never slept a wink. On Sunday it was like I was relivin' a nightmare. I wanted you to 'old me in yer arms, but I knew that if yer did I'd break down, an' it'd all come out. I knew that if I told yer it'd only cause trouble. You would 'ave sorted 'im out an' got yerself locked up.'

Suddenly he reached out and pulled her into his arms. 'Yer should 'ave told me anyway,' he said quietly, holding her close and gently caressing her.

Alice let her head rest on his chest and closed her eyes. 'I love you, Don,' she whispered, relishing the comforting warmth of his strong arms around her.

Don bent his head and softly nuzzled her ears and neck with his lips and she shivered with pleasure. For a few moments they stayed locked in each other's arms, then Alice pushed him gently away.

'Let me take yer coat,' she said. 'I'll put the kettle on.'

Don slipped out of his reefer jacket and pulled the wine-coloured woollen scarf from around his neck, slipping it into the jacket pocket. Alice hung it behind the room door and hurried into the scullery.

'Sit yerself down by the fire an' get warm. I won't be long,' she called out.

Don looked around the cosy room. Heat came from a kitchen range which he could see had been recently black-leaded. The hearth had been whitened and the ornate brass fender shone brightly in the firelight. A pair of ornamental brass tongs and a shovel hung from a stand at one side of the hearth, and above on a high stone mantelshelf a pair of iron statuettes of Greek maidens held flaming torches aloft. Between them was a large clock encased in carved oak, its figured hands set in a Roman numeral clockface of intricate design. Above the clock a sepia picture of a young maiden with flowing golden hair looked down into the room from an oval frame of polished ebony. The table in the centre of the small parlour was covered with a tasselled tablecloth of a green and red floral design on a brown background, and the oaken sideboard facing the fire was laid with an embroidered cloth and crowded with photographs of children in stand-up metal frames. Dark brown tongue-and-groove panelling lined the lower halves of the walls, and the pink and silver striped wallpaper that covered the upper halves was hung with paintings of rural scenes from a wooden picture-rail. Heavy drapes of brocade shut out the cold, foggy night, and a single lightbulb hanging in a yellow shade shone brightly from the centre of the grimy ceiling.

Don felt at ease in the homely room and he spread out his feet on the hearthrug as he waited for Alice to make the tea. He could feel the heat of the fire on his legs and he sighed contentedly.

'I'll let the tea brew fer a minute while I pop upstairs an' see if Gran'ma's all right,' Alice said as she put her head round the door.

Don heard her light footsteps on the stairs and then a creaking sound above his head.

He raised his eyes and stared at the sepia photograph above the mantelshelf. Probably the old lady when she was young, he thought. She would have been about Alice's age then. Maybe she lived in this very house with her parents. They would have been strict and God-fearing and anxious to keep her from the dangers of Downtown Rotherhithe in an age of squalor and deprivation. Outside, in the mean dockland streets, drunken seamen from the Russian and Scandinavian timber ships would stagger back to their berthed vessels and tarry in search of women to spend the night with. The river fog would drift in and the cobbled byways would be wet and greasy underfoot. Sounds of piano music and loud voices would come from the rough riverside taverns and local young villains would no doubt prowl the alleyways and backwaters looking for unsuspecting tars who would eventually stagger back to the docks with no money in their pockets. The area would have its own distinctive sounds. Foghorns, ships' bells, clattering gears and clanking chains as the pontoon bridges over the basin were raised and lowered.

'She's sleepin' soundly,' Alice said softly as she came back into the room. 'I'll pour the tea.'

Don sat up straight in his comfortable armchair and moved his legs away from the fire, his eyes straying back to the sepia photograph. She would have been around twenty then, he guessed. The pretty face was sad, and there was a yearning look in the eyes.

'There we are.'

Don took the large mug of tea and smiled. 'I was just lookin' at that picture,' he said. 'Is it yer gran?'

Alice shook her head. 'It was 'er older sister,' she told him. 'She died in childbirth.'

Don sipped his tea. 'She looks so sad,' he remarked. ''Er eyes seem ter pull yer, if yer know what I mean.'

'Yeah, I do,' Alice replied. 'It's always bin there, as long as I can remember. I used ter love comin' ter see me gran. She's bin on 'er own since I was very young. 'Er 'usband died when she was a young woman. 'E was a merchant seaman, lost at sea.' She paused and looked around. 'I love this room. I feel safe an' 'appy 'ere. That's why I came 'ere when I run away from 'ome. Gran made me welcome an' said I could stay 'ere as long as I liked. She told me a few weeks ago that all this is mine when she dies, but I just want 'er ter get better. She's very weak though.'

Don gazed at the young woman as she talked, cupping her mug of tea in both hands. Her thick raven-coloured hair, pulled back from her forehead with clips, sat on her shoulders in light curls, and the lips of her small mouth were full and sensuous. She had large, dark eyes, wide apart below fine eyebrows in an oval face, and patches of colour were growing on her prominent, high cheekbones as she sat in the heat of the fire. She was slim like his sister, with long shapely legs and pretty ankles. Her skirt had ridden up slightly and he discreetly glanced at her knees, his eyes quickly travelling along the outline of her thighs to her wide hips. She leaned forward, pulling her sweater taut to display the bulge of her full round breasts. She was a beautiful, desirable young woman, a virgin who wanted him to initiate her with love, and he was suddenly filled with trepidation.

'Penny fer yer thoughts,' she said, making him smile.

'I was just finkin' about us,' he said.

'Was it nice?' she asked, smiling wickedly.

'I was lovin' yer, an' it was very nice,' he replied, returning her smile.

'I love the way yer smile,' she told him, taunting him as she saw the colour rise in his cheeks.

Don's face broke into a wide grin and he looked round the room quickly, trying to recover his composure under the frank intensity of her gaze. 'Yer look much better, d'yer wanna tell me about what 'appened?' he asked.

Alice shook her head slowly. 'No. I want yer ter kiss me,' she said, fixing him with her dark eyes.

Don put his empty mug down and stood up, his arms going out to her as she came to him. Their lips met as their bodies touched and he felt her open mouth crushing his in a passionate kiss. Her body was pressing against him, moving very slightly as she felt his passion growing. The kiss was long and sensuous and he felt the tip of her tongue snaking along his bottom lip.

'I want yer ter make love ter me, Don,' she breathed as their lips parted.

'It's all I've bin finkin' about,' he said in a husky voice.

Alice moved away, her eyes never leaving him as she took his hand and led him towards the door. 'Gran's fast asleep. We can go ter my room,' she whispered.

Don followed her into the dark passageway and up the steep flight of stairs, wincing as the floorboards creaked. When they reached the landing Alice led him through the first door and turned on the light. The bed was made and covered with a candlewick bedspread. On each side there was a small cabinet with a tiny table lamp, and Alice turned one on before she turned off the ceiling light. A warm pink glow suffused the room and Don's breath came fast with expectation. This was the first time for both of them and he must not fail her, he told himself.

Alice came up close to him as they stood beside the bed. Slowly and deliberately she adjusted her sweater and pulled it over her head. Don could see her white brassiere showing beneath her slip and he quickly took off his heavy jumper. Alice was pressing against him, slowly unfastening the buttons on his shirt. Their lips met and he struggled to keep his passion under control. She was undoing his belt now and his hands caressed her soft, satiny shoulders and bare arms. Alice deftly loosened her skirt and let it fall to her feet, urging him to remove her slip. Don felt clumsy as he helped it over her head and she pulled his hand on to her flat belly above her flimsy knickers. He could smell her perfume and felt her hot breath on his cheek.

'I've got the fings wiv me,' he whispered, feeling silly.

Alice took a step backwards and pulled him down on to the bed, remembering what she had heard the girls at work say. 'Don't worry, it never 'appens the first time,' she told him in a low urgent voice as she reached out and turned off the lamp. In the blackness Don moved his hands over her hips, gently slipping her knickers down her thighs. She moaned as his fingers felt her silky mound of hair and strayed lower, sliding in between the very tops of her thighs. He could feel her wetness and he struggled out of his clothes, desperate to love her fully before he exploded with passion.

They came together, Alice enticing him with sensual caresses. Suddenly he thrust his hips forward, entering her, and she groaned, her fingernails digging into his back as she felt him suddenly inside her. Don gasped, biting on his lip and trying to contain his hot desire as they began to move in rhythm. Alice moved her fingers through his thick dark hair and pulled his head down until their lips met. His whole body shuddered, and it was all over.

They lay in each other's arms for some time, kissing gently, and tears brimmed in Alice's wide eyes as she realised that she had taken her first bite from the forbidden fruit.

Don sighed as he turned and laid his hand across her firm breasts. 'I really love you, Alice,' he whispered. 'Are you glad it 'appened?'

'Yes, Don,' she said. 'I didn't think it could be so good.'

'I wasn't careful, Alice,' he said.

'Don't worry, it wasn't the right time o' the month anyway.

I've not fallen, believe me,' Alice told him as she kissed him on the side of his mouth.

Don raised himself on to his elbow and looked down at her in the darkness. 'I want yer ter know that I'd never leave yer, Alice,' he said quietly. 'You're my gel ferever.'

'Ferever's a long time, Don,' she replied. 'You've gotta go in the army soon as yer eighteen an' yer might feel different about fings by then.'

'No, I won't,' he said in a resolute voice. 'I want us ter get engaged before I go in. I want ter know that yer waitin' for me. Yer will wait fer me, won't yer?'

Alice rolled on top of him, pressing him down with her weight. 'There could never be anyone else,' she told him. 'Now kiss me. Kiss me like a lover.'

Outside the fog swirled through the little backwater by the river, and the wail of a tug whistle filtered into the room as the two young lovers lay wrapped in each other's arms.

Chapter Forty-Three

Frankie Morgan had managed to hide out in a grotty flat belonging to an East End pimp named Johnnie Gordon, who was known to everyone as Flash. Gordon had come to know Frankie in prison, and after his release he had gone to the Bermondsey villain for help. He was homeless and his women had found themselves a more reliable protector, an ex-heavyweight wrestler who had made it quite plain to Flash Gordon that if he ever showed his face in Stepney again with the intention of picking up where he left off he would find himself bound and gagged with his feet set in concrete, staring up from the bottom of the canal.

Johnnie Gordon had taken Frankie's handout with profuse thanks, promising that if ever he could repay the kindness he would be only too delighted. Frankie had been embarrassed by the pimp's reaction to the few pounds he had given him. He was not in the habit of being cuddled and kissed on the cheek by another bloke, and certainly not in the saloon bar of the Anchor. He felt that the man invited ridicule by his way of dressing too. He wore expensive suits with outrageous ties, black and white shoes more suited to the music hall, and a fedora that seemed totally out of place on his pin-sized head.

When Frankie Morgan crossed the river and found himself in Whitechapel he had had two addresses to look up. One was an old friend who he had known for a number of years and had done quite a bit of business with in the past. Enquiries led Frankie to a pub in Brick Lane where he discovered that his friend was doing ten years on the Moor for manslaughter. The second address was located nearby and the Bermondsey villain was pleased to discover that Flash Gordon was home, though he was getting ready to take an enforced holiday at his sister's in Clacton where he would be safe from the wrath of a team of a card players to whom he owed a large sum of money. Frankie gave Flash Gordon a month's rent for his grotty flat which was wedged between a bespoke tailor's shop and a Jewish baker's in Cubitt Street, a little backstreet off Brick Lane. The location suited Frankie. The back of the flat looked out on to a morass of brick walls, corrugated sheeting and ruined houses. It would be very easy for him to disappear through the back of the flat into the maze beyond, should the police find out where he was.

When Frankie Morgan left Joe Andretti's Stepney gambling club he had had most of his winnings with him, as well as his original stake, but now the cash was running short. He knew that he would have to go back to his house in Basin Street, Bermondsey, where he had a large amount of money stashed. The problem was that the house and the surrounding area were obviously still being watched and there was no one outside the family he could trust to fetch the money. John and Ernie were in prison awaiting trial and he was determined not to bow and scrape to Albert. He would starve first, he vowed.

Frankie sat in the dingy bedroom overlooking the street and pondered his predicament for a long time. Maybe he was being too rash in discounting his wayward son, he thought. The boy owed him anyway. It would only mean him dropping the money through the letterbox. It was the least he could do to make up for what had happened. He could get a message to Albert through Tommy Caulfield. He was the only contact he could safely trust to pass on the message, and Caulfield owed him too.

Frankie spent most of the day trying to think up different plans but he finally came to the conclusion that there was no other way of getting his money. As the light failed he drew the curtains, switched on the light and hastily scribbled a list of instructions to his son, sealing the sheet of paper in an envelope. He wrote a short note to the contractor, placed it in a bigger envelope together with Albert's letter and then got up and put on his coat. The post office was just round the corner and it was dark and foggy enough for him to feel reasonably confident of getting there and back without being recognised.

Frankie had just turned into Cubitt Street on his way back from posting the letter when a scruffy-looking individual accosted him.

'Gawd 'elp us if it ain't Frankie Morgan,' the man said. 'Remember me?'

The villain cursed his luck as he stared at the grinning figure. 'Yeah, I remember yer. Ike Wigley,' he replied without enthusiasm.

The man had on a greasy overcoat held together with string and his worn-out boots stuck out below old trousers that barely reached his ankles. He wore a tattered trilby with a poppy sticking out of the hatband and a meatcloth tied round his neck.

'Bin a bit down on me luck lately,' Ike said. 'Fings are gonna be movin' soon though. Ain't got the price of a cuppa, 'ave yer, mate?'

Frankie had shared a cell with Ike Wigley in Wandsworth Prison for a few months until the man's release and he had been constantly going on about things looking up once he got out. Ike was a loser, Frankie thought, and the last person he wanted to meet. He fished into his pocket and took out a pound note. 'Don't let on to anyone yer've seen me,' he warned the tramp.

'I was just gonna ask what you're doin' over this side o' the water,' Ike remarked, slipping the note into his pocket without thanks.

'Just payin' a visit,' Frankie replied quickly.

Ike nodded and turned on his heel. 'See yer about, cocker,' he said cheerfully as he walked off.

Frankie waited while the tramp strolled out of the turning then he entered his flat, unaware that Ike Wigley had turned back to watch him.

Ike smiled to himself as he went on his way. Some days are good days on the road and others are bad days. This could prove to be one of the better ones, he thought to himself as he walked into Tubby Goldberg's cafe and ordered a large bowl of pea soup.

'Yer got money, Ike?' Tubby asked him.

'Course I got money. I'm not lookin' fer charity,' Ike replied indignantly.

'One bowl o' pea soup comin' up.'

'Two fick slices o' bread as well.'

'Lashin' out, ain't yer?'

'Yeah, I just 'ad a stroke o' luck.'

'Backed a winner, then?'

'Yer could say that.'

Tubby ladled steaming soup into a deep bowl and cut two thick slices of crusty bread. ''Ere we are. Don't burn yerself, it's very 'ot,' he said, scratching his forearm.

Ike picked up the bowl and the bread and Tubby shook his head disapprovingly as he caught sight of the tramp's filthy hands. He had known Ike for a number of years and did not have the heart to bar him from his cafe. The man was no trouble, he told himself. He always sat in the far seat away from other customers and he never loitered either.

'Seen anyfing o' Moishie?' Ike asked.

''E's bin in earlier,' Tubby replied.

Ike ate his soup ravenously, wiping the last smears from the bowl with a hunk of bread. When a man takes to the open road, he reflected, there are always priorities to consider. The most important thing a bloke needs is a full belly to sustain him through the cold night in the churchyard at Spitalfields, and everything else comes after. The next important matter would soon be taken care of, once he located Moishie Fishman. The information was worth a fiver at least, he estimated. After all, he had been hunting through the streets of Whitechapel for two days in his quest for the Bermondsey villain since the word had gone out, and he had been confident that if Frankie Morgan was in the area then he would find him somehow.

The house next to the transport yard in Fellmonger Street was a hive of industry. In every room women were hard at it, while outside, a builder's barrow was parked in the kerbside. Workmen scrambled over the roof, replacing missing slates, and down below Tommy liaised with the building foreman who had just measured up for a heavy wooden fence along the side of the house. Dolly had just taken two jugs of tea into the women and Jimmy discussed the next move with her.

'When's the gas stove comin' in then?' he asked.

'As soon as Ken gets the pipes laid an' connected,' she told him. 'I've picked out a nice grey one wiv one o' those new automatic gas lighters. It's much better than 'avin' ter rely on matches.'

'When's Ken gonna lay the pipes?' Jimmy enquired.

'All bein' well, termorrer night, so Rene told me,' Dolly replied.

'I'll give 'im an 'and,' Jimmy announced.

'I fink you'll be better off keepin' out of 'is way,' Dolly said quickly. 'Ken knows what 'e's doin', an' after all it is 'is job.'

'All right, don't go on about it,' Jimmy replied irritably.

Dolly looked at him with concern. ''Ere, you all right?'

'Course I'm all right. Why d'yer ask?'

'Well, yer seem sort of edgy.'

'I ain't edgy. What makes yer fink I'm edgy?' Jimmy asked.

Dolly shrugged her shoulders dismissively. She had noticed the change in Jimmy over the past few days and felt worried. It was the drink, or lack of it, she felt sure. He had done wonders in kicking the habit but there must be times when he still had to do battle with John Barleycorn. He was obviously aware that it was a fight he dared not lose, and he was most probably going through a bad period.

'What about that rubbish in the backyard?' she asked him after a while.

'Oh yeah. I'll go an' see if I can borrer the barrer,' Jimmy offered, appearing to brighten.

'Off yer go then.'

Dolly turned her attention to the women. 'Right then, 'ow we doin'?' she asked.

'We're on the downstairs next,' Rene told her. 'Termorrer I should fink.'

Ivy came up to Dolly. ''Ere, Doll, I was talkin' ter Mrs Palmer last night,' she said. ''Er ole man told 'er that 'e'll do yer plasterin' soon's yer ready.'

'That's a load off me mind, Ivy.'

'Bill said 'e can lay a few slabs in the backyard too.'

'Smashin'. 'Ave a word wiv 'im, will yer?'

'Leave it ter me.'

Dolly sat down on an upturned beer crate and sighed. Things were moving swiftly and all being well the whole house could be papered during the last week of February, providing the painting was completed in time.

Winifred Seaton had been hard at work on her report, and when Peggy Grant answered a summons to the office the district officer looked up with a smile. 'Hello, Peggy. Take a seat,' she said, getting up to give her subordinate a hug.

Peggy sat down and crossed her legs. 'The meal was lovely,' she said coyly.

'I really enjoyed last night. I hope you did too?'

'You know I did,' Peggy replied in a quiet voice.

Winifred placed her hand on Peggy's shoulder. 'I meant everything I said last night. You're part of my life now, a very important part,' she said with conviction.

'I want you to know that I feel the same way too,' Peggy replied. 'I never knew it could be so good. You see, I've never . . .'

'I know, my dear, but you must trust me. I wouldn't do anything to hurt or upset you. I do love you.'

'I love you too, Win.'

Footsteps outside the office sent Winifred hurrying back round the desk and as the sounds faded she looked up from a folder hastily thrown open in front of her. 'We must try not to get sidetracked,' she sighed. 'I've just finished the report on the Farrans. I'm afraid I've had to be very forthright. It's the children we're worried about, after all. I'd like you to read my comments. They'll go on file in case there are any comebacks. We must cover ourselves.'

'Good Lord!' Peggy exclaimed as she studied the report. 'Dogs? Wild dogs? Children running loose in a transport yard? What can we do about it?'

'Quite a lot,' Winifred replied firmly. 'As you know, the Farrans are a registered case which we have investigated and taken certain action on. That makes us responsible until we can be sure that the family are no longer in need of support and guidance. There is a court order in abeyance and we can invoke the order to come into operation immediately, if need be. So what I propose is this. You and I will ask for the police to escort us on to the Caulfield's premises while we carry out an inspection. If the dogs are at the yard I will make it quite plain to Caulfield that under no circumstances must he let the adjoining house until he gets rid of them. We can carry out a full inspection of the house to establish suitability for the Farrans' occupation, and we can ascertain the rent required.'

'The landlord will be aware of the Rent Restriction Acts, I take it?' Peggy queried.

'Frankly, I doubt it. The man's an idiot, if you want my opinion,' Winifred replied passionately. 'You see, the Rent Acts are very complicated. Rents depend on a number of factors. Was the house previously decontrolled? Has the house been recontrolled under the 1939 Act or was it ever controlled? You see it all depends on the age and rateable value. What we do know is that if the house is furnished then the rent can be as high as is agreed by tenant and landlord.'

'I'm still a little confused,' Peggy said.

Winifred smiled indulgently. 'Fortunately we have something to go on,' she continued. 'In this case the house was never let for rent. It was part of the business ownership. Now, if we discover that the Farrans are paying more for the house than other tenants in the street are for their houses then we can apply on behalf of the family to the rent tribunal for a rent reduction. I believe we might well be forced into that course of action.'

Peggy sighed. 'I really admire you, Winifred,' she said sweetly.

'You're so in control of everything. I must admit I wouldn't know where to begin.'

'It's training. Training and a lot of experience out there in the battlefield, so to speak,' the district officer replied with a demure smile. 'We do what we can, and hope we make the right decisions. That's all anyone can ask of us, my dear.'

Peggy nodded dutifully. 'I'm really looking forward to watching you confront our Mr Caulfield,' she enthused.

The phone rang and Winifred's face suddenly became angry as she listened to the message. 'I'll be right down,' she said quickly. 'Ask the young lady to wait, will you? Yes, that's right. No, I won't delay. Yes, I understand.'

Peggy looked enquiringly at her superior officer and was rewarded with a grunt of satisfaction.

'What was I saying to you just a few moments ago? The man's mad. He needs putting away,' Winifred raged.

Marion Knowles considered herself to be a good mother and a good neighbour. She had never to her knowledge stood gossiping while there was work to be done and she had never, as far as she could remember, had a bad word to say about anyone, unless they deserved it. Marion had two young children whom she adored, and she made sure that her children got their regular supply of orange juice and cod liver oil and malt. Every second week Marion went to the welfare centre to get the children weighed and checked over, and on the way there she invariably stopped off at Joe Diamond's to get them a Golly bar to suck on while they waited their turn to see the nurse.

It came as a great shock to Marion when she was told in confidence that Tommy Caulfield, the skins and hides contractor in Fellmonger Street, was intending to set his wild Alsatian dogs on the Farran children. She had to agree with Lizzie Carroll that the man must have gone stark raving mad even to contemplate such a thing. Marion had had to pass the yard on many occasions and whenever the contractor was standing by the gate he had always had a cheery word for her and a pat on the head for her two children. Now she would be compelled to take a roundabout route to the clinic in case those dogs were on the loose.

Marion could not help thinking about what Lizzie Carroll had told her, and after waiting for over an hour in the centre with the children covered in sticky toffee she was feeling on edge. Norman would be home for his tea at seven minutes past five and she always insisted on having the tea on the table when Norman walked in after a hard day at the Council rent office. When the nurse told Marion that Golly bars were bad for children's teeth and she would be better off buying them an apple each, her anger towards the monster of Fellmonger Street spilled over.

The duty nurse calmed Marion and promised to pass on her information, assuring the agitated young woman that Golly bars were not even half as bad for children as ravening wild dogs. Marion felt better after being categorically told that action would be taken, and she felt better still when the nurse praised her for her good sense in reporting the lunatic.

As Marion took a diversion to her house she knew that for the first time since she had married Norman there would be no tea on the table when he walked in. He would no doubt have something to say about it but she would have quite a lot to tell him too.

Back at the centre, Winifred Seaton took out her folder and added another damning report concerning the transport contractor, who seemed to be growing in notoriety with every day.

'Tomorrow, Peggy. We will confront the man tomorrow without fail,' the district officer promised.

'I'm beginning to feel terrified of him,' her subordinate confessed.

'Never you worry. We'll have protection. I'm getting on to the police right away,' Winifred said quickly. 'I'll have a word with Chief Inspector Grogan. He's a friend of mine.'

At six o'clock that evening Inspector Halleron walked into Dockhead police station feeling worried. He had had to face the wrath of the Commissioner that afternoon over the lack of progress in discovering the whereabouts of Frankie Morgan. He wanted a word of encouragement or hope from his colleague and a dram of Grogan's pure Scotch malt to calm his jagged nerves. Instead he had to listen to a monologue of despair.

'I've been out since seven this morning,' Grogan growled. 'I've leaned on all the informants I could worm out and I've phoned a dozen different police stations on both sides of the river for information and assistance, and I've got sweet Fanny Adams. Then just when I could do with a little bit of peace and quiet, the welfare start playing merry hell. They want police protection to visit Caulfield's transport yard in Fellmonger Street. Apparently the bloke's gone off his head and started feeding kids to his pack of wild dogs.'

Chapter Forty-Four

Tommy Caulfield was happy with the progress made and he leaned back in his office chair on Thursday morning and stared out of the window at the workmen erecting the fence. The mail lay unopened on his desk and there were the accounts and invoices to be dealt with. Tommy felt confident that he would bring everything up to date by evening and he hummed contentedly to himself as he picked up the first of the letters.

The second letter he opened made him sit up straight in his chair. Inside, along with a smaller envelope addressed to 'Albert', there was a note which said briefly,

> 'Tommy, I want you to pass this letter to my son Albert soon as possible. This is urgent.
>   Regards, Frankie'

Tommy got up and walked quickly over to the house. 'Anyone seen Dolly?' he called out.

'She's gone ter sort some paint out,' Ivy shouted from upstairs.

''Ow long's she likely ter be?' he asked.

'I dunno. She's gone over Shoreditch ter Nicholls an' Clarke's. She reckons it's the best place fer paint.'

Tommy cursed under his breath. The letter in his pocket needed to be dealt with urgently. Any delay in Albert getting it might cause Frankie serious problems, considering the police were looking for him; and Frankie would blame him if things went wrong.

'Tell Dolly I wanna see 'er urgent soon as she gets back,' Tommy called out.

He walked back across the yard and his heart missed a beat as he saw a police car draw up outside. He took a deep breath and walked casually to the gate as the policemen got out of the car.

One of the officers knew him quite well and had often popped into the yard for a cup of tea on cold mornings. ''Ow yer doin', Tommy?' he said amiably.

'Not so bad, John. What's occurrin'?' he asked.

'Well, it appears that yer feedin' yer dogs on children,' the officer said with a broad grin. 'I'd stick ter the normal diet if I were you. Kids can be 'ard ter chew.'

Tommy groaned aloud. 'I know 'ow that little story got out,' he said. 'I was 'avin' a joke wiv the welfare officer who called on me about that 'ouse I'm doin' up.'

'They're the wrong people ter joke wiv, Tommy, you should know that,' the policeman told him.

'Don't tell me yer come along just ter check it out,' Tommy said disbelievingly.

'Nah, the welfare wanted us to escort 'em,' the policeman replied. 'Just in case you 'ave got wild animals on the place. They should be 'ere soon.'

''Ow the bloody 'ell could I keep dogs on the premises wiv the 'orses I got 'ere?' the contractor said with disgust.

'Ours is not ter reason why. We've just bin told ter do escort, that's all,' the officer said.

'Fancy a cuppa,' Tommy asked, 'or somefing stronger?'

'No fanks, I'll sit in the car till little Dolly Daydreams arrives.'

At eleven o'clock Winifred Seaton marched resolutely into the yard accompanied by her subordinate, who looked a little frightened, and behind them two police constables who were grinning widely.

'I'd like to see where you keep your dogs,' the district officer said firmly.

'Dogs? What dogs?' Tommy replied.

'You told me on my last visit that you had dogs and that they were being exercised,' Winifred said.

'I've never owned a dog an' I don't intend ter start now,' the contractor replied. 'They'd scare the 'orses.'

'Why tell me different then?'

'It was just a bit o' fun.'

'A bit of fun? I don't call that funny.'

'Nah, I don't s'pose you would.'

Winifred looked across the yard and saw the workmen busy erecting the fence. 'I suppose it didn't occur to you to let me know that you intended putting that fence up,' she said acidly.

'Why should it?' Tommy replied. 'I unblocked the shit'ole this mornin'. Should I 'ave phoned yer?'

'There's no need to adopt that attitude,' Winifred said quickly.

'Look, I'm a busy man an' I ain't got time ter piss around wiv you people,' he countered angrily. 'Now, if yer wanna inspect the 'ouse again feel free, but leave me alone, will yer?'

The two welfare officers exchanged shocked glances and then Winifred turned to the policemen who were trying desperately to keep straight faces.

'We'll sit outside. Call us if yer need to,' one of the policemen told her, going red with the effort not to laugh.

Winifred stormed over to the house, followed by her devoted subordinate.

'Mind yerself, luv, I'm strippin' 'ere,' Ivy told her.

''Ave yer come ter lend an 'and?' Rene asked the two officers.

'Give 'em a couple o' scrapers,' Ivy joked.

Freda Arrowsmith and Ethel Price came hurrying down the stairs. 'The poxy wall's gonna need a ton o' plaster,' Freda remarked, and seeing the two officers standing by the side door she said, 'You two any good at plasterin'?'

'No, they're a couple o' busybodies, if you ask me,' a voice said from the door.

Winifred and Peggy turned to see Dolly standing with her arms akimbo.

'We have our jobs to do,' Winifred said quickly.

'Well, I suggest yer go back ter yer office an' get on wiv 'em then,' Dolly replied coldly.

The two officers left abruptly and Dolly had a quick chat with her helpers for a few minutes before she strolled over to talk to Tommy.

'Just the person,' he said quickly, as she walked into the office. 'Look what I got in the mornin' post.'

Dolly read the brief few words and shook her head. 'I don't want Albert gettin' 'imself in trouble over that no-good bastard,' she grated.

'I gotta see the lad gets the letter, Doll,' Tommy replied anxiously.

'All right I'll give it to 'im, but if it's what I fink it is I'll be 'avin' a few words wiv Albert,' Dolly said firmly.

'Did yer see the police outside when yer come in the yard?' Tommy asked her.

'Yeah, what was that all about?'

'Dogs.'

'Dogs?'

'Yeah, remember I told yer I was jokin' wiv those silly mares from the welfare about keepin' wild dogs in the yard?' Tommy said grinning. 'Word's got out I'm feedin' the dogs on kids.'

'I don't believe it,' Dolly said laughing aloud.

'It's bloody true!'

'Tommy, yer a bloody disgrace,' she told him, her eyes twinkling wickedly. 'Can't yer get 'orsemeat for 'em?'

Albert had been working hard all week to catch up with his window-cleaning round and Dolly had told him to rest up in the evening.

'If that 'and turns septic again an' yer get blood poisonin', it'll be a long stay in 'ospital an' goodbye weddin',' she warned him.

Albert was relieved to know that the neighbours had rallied round and were doing a marvellous job. Things were beginning to come together, he thought, and if he was successful in getting window-cleaning contracts with a couple of the firms in Dockhead he would be well on his way. He would be able to take on two hands and really go out to establish his company. He was toying with the idea of going into the lucrative industrial cleaning, though it would mean applying for a bank loan to buy the heavy cleaners and polishers. He might even be able to buy a small van to transport the equipment and spread his net down to the factories in Rotherhithe and Deptford.

Albert arrived home to his lodgings on Thursday evening to be given the envelope by his landlady Mrs Gorman.

'Dolly Morgan brought it round this afternoon, Albert,' she told him. 'She seemed very concerned that yer got it soon as yer come in.'

'Fanks, Sarah. I wonder who this can be from,' he said, looking at his scrawled name. The writing looked vaguely familiar.

'Yer better open it then,' Sarah told him, smiling as she walked out into the scullery to boil the kettle.

Albert tore the envelope open and unfolded the thin sheet of paper.

I would sooner not ask you to do this for me but I'm desperate for money. Take all that's in the tin box and bring it over to me on Friday evening at 75, Cubitt Street. (It's off Brick Lane). There's no need for us to meet. Just put it through the letter box. Make sure the law don't follow you or I'm done for. I couldn't stand another spell in the nick.

Your Father.

Sarah Gorman looked into the room. 'Trouble?' she asked.

Albert shook his head. 'Nah, it's business,' he replied, trying not to give himself away.

'Yer better wash up, luv, tea'll be dished up in ten minutes,' she told him.

Albert ate his tea in silence, his mind on his family's problems, and Sarah and Bert Gorman occasionally exchanged knowing glances. At seven o'clock he walked the short distance to Fellmonger Street and as he entered the Buildings he passed a smartly dressed young man on the stairs.

Rose greeted him with a kiss and took his arm as she led him into the front room. 'There was a young feller just called, Alb. Yer must 'ave passed him on the stairs,' she said.

'Yeah, I did. What did 'e want, Rose?' he asked anxiously.

''E left this.'

Albert tore open the envelope and read the typed message.

Dear Mr Morgan,

I am empowered as the solicitor acting on your brothers' behalf to request that we meet at my offices at the above address tomorrow morning at ten a.m.

It is imperative that we converse, following important developments. I do apologise for the short notice given but I trust that you will understand.

Yours sincerely,

Robert S. Murray

Albert handed Rose the letter and as soon as she had read it he showed her the letter from his father before she had time to comment.

Billy and Joey were aware that something was wrong and they sat quietly in a corner of the room playing draughts. Susan came up and put her arms round Albert's leg, however, eager for her usual hug and kiss, and she was not disappointed. Albert swept her up in his arms and made the usual fuss of her.

'What yer gonna do, Albert?' Rose asked him. 'S'posin' you do get followed. They'll take you in as an accomplice.'

'If I don't 'and this letter in ter the police I'm an accomplice anyway,' he replied. 'What do they expect? I couldn't turn me own farvver in. You can see what 'e said. 'E'd die in prison if they banged 'im away again.'

'I know, an' I understand, Albert. Just be careful,' she warned him.

'I wonder what the solicitor wants me for?' he remarked.

Rose shook her head. 'P'raps yer bruvvers wanna see yer,' she suggested. 'It might be somefing they wanna tell yer. They'd 'ave ter do it frew their solicitor, I would 'ave thought.'

Susan was tickling his chin and Albert pretended to bite her ear, which sent the child into a fit of giggling.

'Don't get 'er too excited or she'll be up 'alf the night,' Rose said as she went out into the scullery to pour out the tea.

Albert sat down and was immediately accosted by the boys who were having an argument over the rules of draughts.

'If yer take yer 'and off yer can't carry on wiv the move, can yer, Albert?' Billy said.

'I didn't take me 'and off. It slipped,' Joey replied with spirit.

'Well, it's still the end o' the move,' Albert told him.

'See, I told yer.'

'You don't know everyfing.'

'I know more than you.'

'All right, then. What goes ninety-nine bomp?'

'I dunno?'

'A centipede wiv a wooden leg.'

Billy tipped up the draughtboard and Joey flew at him, his fists flailing. Rose screamed at them from the scullery to stop and Albert leapt out of his chair to separate them. 'If you two carry on like this I might stop away. I will, won't I, Rose?' Albert said with mock severity.

Rose smiled wryly at him, giving him a sly wink as he kept the lads apart at arm's length. 'I could understand it,' she said. 'Who wants ter listen to arguin' an' fightin' every night.'

Joey realised that he had gone too far and he ambled round to Albert's side. 'I'm sorry, but 'e does torment me sometimes, Albert,' he said quietly. 'You wouldn't stop away, would yer? Rose'd miss yer.'

'I expect she would, sometimes,' he answered, returning Rose's wink.

'I'm sorry too, Albert, but I couldn't let Joey clout me wivout givin' 'im one back,' Billy said. 'Yer told me yerself I gotta 'it back if someone clouts me.'

'Yeah, but you started it by tippin' up the board,' Albert told him.

'Well, 'e told me that stupid joke.'

'Yer should 'ave just shrugged yer shoulders.'

'I will next time.'

'Good lad.'

'But if 'e 'its me first I'll smack 'im right on the nose.'

'But Joey's yer bruv.'

'Well, 'e should know better, shouldn't 'e?'

Rose listened at the scullery doorway and a warm glow grew inside her. Albert was wonderful with the boys, she thought, and Susan adored him. He was so patient and understanding. How nice it would be to spend some time alone with him and let him love her fully again, instead of having to make do with sneaked kisses and hugs, and the lingering goodnight kiss in the darkened passage. How nice it would be to show him her feelings and lie all night in his strong arms, and how lovely to let him hold her round her growing belly, let him feel the first movements and marvel with her at the tiny child growing inside her, the baby that they made together.

'Rose is crying,' Susan said suddenly, noticing the solitary tear that ran down on to her cheek.

'No, I'm not, I got a bit o' dirt in me eye,' she replied quickly as she turned and hurried back out into the scullery.

The moon was high in the clear night sky as Albert walked cautiously along Basin Street to his family home. He had kissed Rose goodnight and held her tightly, promising her that he would take care. It would be better to get the money that night, he had decided. He had a very busy Friday, and besides, there was less chance of being spotted at night, and less chance of a neighbour seeing him going into the house.

When he reached the front door Albert looked around carefully and made sure that the street was deserted, then he reached down into the recessed footscraper beside the doorstep and retrieved the spare key which was wedged into a crack in the concrete. It was then that he noticed the damaged door-frame and suddenly realised that the landlord might have changed the lock when he secured the house after the forced entry by the police. Albert held his breath as he inserted the key. It turned easily, and with a sigh of relief he let himself in quietly and gently closed the door behind him.

The familiar smell of his home made him sigh sadly and he pulled the curtains before switching on the light. When he saw the state of the room he swore aloud. The police search had obviously been thorough and there had been no one to tidy up after they left. The distinctive armchair cushions that his mother had made were tossed on to the floor and just about everything seemed to have been moved, including the ornaments and pictures on the walls. The footstool that his mother always used was lying on its side, and her sewing box had been emptied on to the table. Ashes lay in the grate, and the coal scuttle stood empty. An old newspaper lay opened on the table, and Albert recognised John's favourite donkey jacket hanging behind the door.

There was no time to dwell, Albert told himself, and he hurried out into the scullery. Had the police search uncovered his father's cache? he wondered fearfully. He quickly moved the small table to one side and rolled up the cord mat to expose the small grey stone slabs. It was immediately obvious to him that the police had not found the hiding place. He took a spoon and used the handle to scrape the dirt from around one of the stones, then he prised it up with little difficulty and reached down into the darkness below, his fingers touching the oblong tin box.

Albert was surprised at the amount of money: two bundles wrapped in brown paper and secured with adhesive tape. He put them in his jacket pocket and laid the stone slab back, brushing the dirt back along the joins before replacing the mat and moving the table across. Then he turned off the light in the parlour and opened the curtains.

As he made his way back to his lodgings Albert was well aware of the task in hand. He might have been observed going into the house by the police, who would be expecting him to fetch and carry for his father. Perhaps he had been watched and followed ever since his brothers had been arrested. He might be followed over to Whitechapel and then his father would obviously blame him for bringing the Law down on his head. He might even think that his own son had deliberately led the police to him, out of revenge for being disowned.

Albert reached his lodgings safely and Sarah Gorman made him a cup of cocoa and cut him a thick cheese sandwich which he took to his room. Later, as the moon started to dip down in the heavens, Albert twisted on to his back in bed and stared up at the dark ceiling. No matter how careful and vigilant his father was, one day he would be captured. He could expect to spend many years behind bars and perhaps die while locked away. His brothers too were facing long years in jail. What had happened to his family? How had they come to this? He thought of his mother. Would she ever come back to Bermondsey, to face the cruel taunts and dark looks of her neighbours?

Albert's head was throbbing when sleep finally took him, plaguing him with nightmares.

Chapter Forty-Five

The sun was clearing the rooftops on a bright clear Friday morning when Albert Morgan finished the last of the windows in Tooley Street. He had been out since seven o'clock in an effort to catch up on his work before going to see the solicitor in Dockhead. There were two more large offices to be taken care of in Bermondsey Street and then maybe time for a quick cup of tea in Mario's cafe, he calculated.

The usual wharf traffic was passing to and fro and horse carts and lorries were parked on both sides of Tooley Street, the horses munching into their nosebags and the lorry drivers standing around in little groups as they waited their turn to be called on to the quays and wharvesides. Trams clattered by and a constant stream of pedestrians hurried back and forth, going about their business with serious faces on a normal Friday morning. For Albert, however, today was not a normal day. He was feeling apprehensive about meeting the solicitor, and about the task facing him that evening. He was also worried about his mother. She would have read about her two sons being arrested and the police hunt for her husband. What would her reaction be? Would she return to Bermondsey, or stay with Joe for good? She would want to visit John and Ernie while they were in custody and might decide to return home to be nearer the prison, though Albert hoped she would remain where she was, away from the hostile neighbours.

At five minutes to ten that morning the young man parked his bicycle and ladders in a side street off Jamaica Road and entered the offices of Friedman and Murray. The middle-aged receptionist gave him an enquiring look over her rimless glasses and then lowered her head again to continue writing in a large appointments book, a telephone balanced on her shoulder as she crooked her head to one side.

'I've got an appointment at ten,' Albert said, after standing at the desk for a few moments.

'Name, please?' she asked him.

'Albert Morgan,' he said quickly.

'Take a seat, will you,' she said without looking up.

Albert tried to relax as he sat down on an upholstered bench seat and picked up a tattered copy of *John Bull*. He flipped through the pages and then discarded it for another magazine which was over a year old and had been mutilated by someone with a sharp pencil. Occasionally he glanced up at the receptionist, who totally ignored him. When he looked up at the wall clock he found that barely two minutes had passed.

At ten fifteen a heavily built man emerged from a door beside the reception desk, hobbling along with the aid of two walking sticks, and the receptionist looked over towards Albert. 'You can go in now,' she told him.

Albert found himself in the presence of a nervous-looking character whom he estimated to be in his late thirties. The man was thin and balding, with a shirt collar that seemed to be two sizes too large. He wore a pair of tortoiseshell glasses which made his eyes look enormous and he coughed nervously as he held out his hand. 'I'm Robert Murray, a partner in the firm,' he said. 'Take a seat. You're Albert Morgan, I take it, brother of John and Ernest Morgan.'

Albert nodded. 'Yeah, that's right,' he replied.

The solicitor blinked nervously and moved a pencil in his fingers as he studied his visitor. 'I'm sorry that I had to ask you to come at such short notice, but it is very important that I pass on some information to you,' he began. 'I have to tell you that with regard to your brothers' position the news is not very good, I'm afraid. The evidence against them is very damning and we feel that the best recourse for them both is to plead guilty. A plea of not guilty would not stand up, I'm sorry to say, and under the circumstances our advice to your brothers is for them to throw themselves on the mercy of the court. The advice was not given without first looking at all the aspects of the case and then seeking certain assurances.'

'Assurances?' Albert cut in.

'The barrister whom we have engaged to represent your brothers at the trial is first class,' Murray continued. 'He will be seeking to make representations to the judge for a compassionate overview. The case will be put that your father and brothers were dupes in the criminal conspiracy to steal the Cape Diamonds and that they themselves were in ignorance of the nature of the intent. Also, counsel will press home the point that they were unarmed and had no knowledge beforehand that the gang leader was carrying arms. Furthermore, the case will also be put that only the gang leader used violence which put the jeweller's life in danger, and that your family have expressed their shock and remorse at the injuries inflicted. We hope that the judge will be swayed by the argument and that he bestows a much lighter sentence than would otherwise be the norm. Now you have to understand that unless we can get your father to give himself up to the police, and very soon, our hands will be tied. Frankly, that's why I asked you to come in this morning. Without your help, I'm afraid there's little we can do.'

Albert was silent for a few moments while the words sank in, then he matched the solicitor's earnest stare. 'You want me ter find my farvver an' persuade 'im ter give 'imself up?' he said slowly.

'Yes,' the solicitor replied. 'I've spoken to your brothers and they feel that you might know where to locate your father.'

''Ow should I know where 'e's 'idin'?' Albert said quickly.

'Does the name Gordon mean anything to you?' Murray asked. 'Flash Gordon?'

'Yeah, me farvver knows 'im. I've seen 'em tergevver in the past,' Albert replied frowning.

'Mr Gordon is from the East End. Whitechapel to be exact. Your brothers feel that you will be able to ask about and locate your father through Gordon. Can you try?' the solicitor asked.

'Yeah, I'll try, but I honestly don't 'old out much 'ope of 'im givin' 'imself up,' Albert said with a deep sigh.

'You're our only hope, Mr Morgan. Please try.'

'I'll do me best,' Albert said, unwilling to take the solicitor into his confidence.

'Good man. I can be contacted at the office or you can leave a message. There's my card if you need to contact me out of working hours. Feel free anytime, should you get news,' Murray said, standing up and extending his hand.

Ike Wigley picked up his bundle of personal belongings wrapped in a filthy cloth and looped it over his shoulder. He had searched everywhere for Moishie Fishman and felt as if he had been given the run-around. It wasn't as though Moishie was out of the area. Moishie never went anywhere, to his knowledge. He earned his money working a stall in Wentworth Street and when he wasn't there he could usually be found either at the fish shop or in one of the cafes in the neighbourhood. In fact Ike had always been able to contact Moishie within minutes in the past when he had had snippets of information to give him. Why should he be so difficult to locate on this particular occasion, Ike fumed.

Tubby Goldberg sighed with relief when Ike Wigley prepared to leave his cafe. Being friendly and neighbourly was fine, he felt, up to a point, but Ike looked as if he was starting to overdo it a bit. He paid for his bowl of soup and his mug of tea, it was true, but it wouldn't be good for the business to have the tramp sitting around when custom was brisk. He might start getting the cafe a bad name.

'If yer see Moishie tell 'im I've bin lookin' all over for 'im,' Ike told the cafe owner. 'Tell 'im I got the needle wiv all this pissin' about.'

'Right you are. Mind 'ow yer tread,' Tubby replied, grinning with relief as his grubby customer left the premises.

Ike strolled along Brick Lane deep in thought. He had tried everywhere to find his contact and he began to imagine that Moishie was hiding from him, peeping round doorways and alleys in an attempt to avoid him. Well, if that was the case he would go straight to the big man himself. Joe Andretti would be more than pleased with the information, and it would put him in good stead with the big boss who would know for sure then that Ike Wigley was a man of his word.

The tramp hoisted his bundle higher on to his shoulder as he ambled along, and he smiled to himself as he recalled the first time he had chanced to meet the big man himself. It was the night the Hoxton mob came down to Whitechapel and busted up the Green Man public house. Andretti was fuming that outsiders had muscled in on his manor and word got out that all hell was going to break loose in the East End. As it was, the trouble was sorted out quite quickly and with little bloodshed, apart from one of the Hoxton boys being thrown under a tube train and two others being taken to the London Hospital to have ears sewn back on again. Andretti had looked pleased with himself when he drove up to Brick Lane and got out of his posh car to survey the scene, Ike remembered. The tramp had gone up to the gang boss with a bit of information about a remaining Hoxton villain who was hiding out in a tailor's shop. He had offered the information to Andretti for a couple of quid, whereupon Andretti had merely laughed at him and asked him why he should pay for the information when he could get a couple of his boys to take him into an alley and beat it out of him for nothing. Ike had been very diplomatic in his reply, saying that if that was the case then he would surrender the information before the beating but it would be the last time he would have anything to trade in the way of news, and by using strong-arm tactics Andretti would lose the best pair of ears in the East End.

Ike recalled the gang boss laughing aloud and handing him two pounds for the information. In return Ike had promised his loyalty and assured him that he would keep his ears and eyes open for anything that might be of use to him. Since that particular night Ike had often passed on bits and pieces of news, only asking for payment when it was important information. The knowledge of Frankie Morgan's whereabouts was about as important as it got, Ike knew for a fact. Word had circulated that the Bermondsey villain might be hiding in the area and he was to be considered a nuisance, as his presence would compel the police to swamp the area and in consequence disrupt the usual run-of-the-mill business.

Ike Wigley strolled along until he reached Bishopsgate, intending to look in one or two pubs for Moishie, and as he turned the corner he saw Andretti's man getting off a bus.

'I bin lookin' all over fer you,' Ike said with irritation. 'Yer gettin' 'arder ter find than a vacant bench in Spitalfield's.'

'What yer want?' Moishie asked impatiently. 'I can't stand 'ere chewin' the fat all day, I got fings ter do.'

'I got somefing werf a fiver,' Ike said, tapping the side of his nose with his index finger.

'Piss orf,' Moishie said sharply.

'S'posin' I was ter tell yer I knew where Frankie Morgan was 'oled up,' Ike replied, grinning craftily.

'I'd 'ave ter tell Joe Andretti that you was comin' the old soldier,' Moishie said calmly.

'All right then, two quid. Gis two quid an' I'll give yer the address,' Ike told him.

'This better be kosher or I'll get yer dial changed so yer own muvver wouldn't recognise yer,' Moishie growled.

'Did I ever let yer down?' Ike asked humbly.

Moishie Fishman handed the tramp two new one-pound notes and took up a fistful of coat collar. 'Just remember what I said about yer boat race,' he warned.

Ike passed on the information and sauntered away, feeling pleased with his day's work. He knew that five pounds was asking too much, but he also knew full well that if he had originally asked for two pounds he would only have got one. It was a case of survival in a cruel, hard world, Ike reasoned to himself. Frankie Morgan would have to take his chances just like everybody else.

Moishie hurried to Jack Levy's tailor's shop to use his phone. Ike Wigley had come up trumps this time, he thought. Andretti was going to be very pleased with the news.

Bill Grogan leaned back in his office chair and blew a cloud of cigarette smoke towards the ceiling. It was nearing six o'clock and he had been at the station since seven a.m. Everything had been left to fall apart while all available men were put to work scouring the areas for clues to Frankie Morgan's whereabouts, and he was feeling increasingly frustrated. He could not remember a time in the twenty-odd years he had been in the force when so much importance had been placed on one case and so much flak had come his way. It was obvious to him that big wheels were in motion, and everyone involved with the Berkeley Street jewel robbery was travelling down a very precarious path. Even the Commissioner was not above scrutiny and questions had been asked by campaigning members of parliament, themselves lobbied by people who had become suspicious about the lack of news coverage. A week had passed since the press release stating that the Cape Diamonds had been recovered and two men had been charged with the theft while another was being sought in connection. What preoccupied the campaigners most was the involvement of the South African found murdered in Billingsgate, and one of the Sunday newspapers was building up a case which was worrying the top ranks. Ray Halleron had looked positively white with worry when he came back from his briefing yesterday at Scotland Yard, and he had told Grogan that the Commissioner and the Home Secretary were going to be challenged by an eminent journalist to answer one or two very important questions in the next Sunday edition. Time was running short and still there was not a glimmer of light.

Grogan stubbed out his cigarette butt and lit another. The station sergeant tapped on the office door and came in carrying a bundle of papers and a mug of coffee.

'Thought yer might like a fresh one, sir,' he said, putting the papers down with a look of sympathy.

The inspector nodded his thanks. It seemed more and more probable to him that there was a weak link in the whole affair and the top brass were anxious in case the newspapers got a sniff. It would not take them long to piece everything together if they found it, and once that happened all hell would break loose.

Suddenly the door was thrust open and Ray Halleron came in looking flushed. 'We're in business, Bill,' he said breathlessly. 'I've just had a phone call from Andretti. Morgan's been located. He's holed up in Whitechapel.'

Grogan leapt out of his chair. 'Who's handling the operation, Leman Street?' he asked quickly.

Halleron nodded. 'I've been on to Dan McSweeney and he's setting up a briefing.'

'Have you told the Commissioner?' Grogan asked.

'Yeah. He's told them to hang fire until we get there.'

'What are we waiting for?'

'We're to draw firearms,' Halleron replied.

Albert Morgan kissed Rose goodbye and left the flat with her warning ringing in his ears. 'Be careful, Albert. I don't want anyfing 'appenin' ter you.'

The young man walked quickly along to Tower Bridge Road and waited at a bus stop for a number 42 which would take him to Aldgate bus garage. Brick Lane was just a few minutes walk from the garage, and as he waited Albert felt the bundles resting inside his shirt. He had his reefer jacket on over it with the collar pulled up against the cold night air, and while he stood waiting his mind was racing. His father had instructed him to put the money through the letter box but now things had changed. It was imperative he relay the information the solicitor had given him but how was his father going to react?

The bus came into view and Albert took a few deep breaths to calm himself. His father might well get angry and blame him for his predicament. It was true that he had taken his place on the raid and because of that he was now facing a long prison sentence. Surely he could see though that his son had needed to keep out of trouble now that he was going to become a father. The problem was he did not see things in a reasonable way. His solution would have been either to deny that he was the father, or else pay off the woman and absolve himself from all responsibilities. Well, his father would have to change his thinking, Albert told himself. He had responsibilities too, to his own sons, and if he decided not to give himself up then John and Ernest would quite likely get maximum sentences.

The bus drew up at the stop and Albert jumped on, deciding to go up on the top deck where he would have a better view in case he was being followed by another vehicle. He glanced at his wristwatch and saw that it was nearing seven o'clock. The bus was almost empty and the conductor seemed irritated as he came up the stairs to collect his fare, grunting his thanks as Albert handed him tuppence. The Tower Bridge Road was quiet now that the rush hour traffic had passed through. Albert could smell the familiar tang of vinegar from the Sarson's factory and then the smell of hops as the bus trundled up the incline towards the majestic Tower Bridge. To his left he saw the Tower of London illuminated, its battlements sharp-edged against the clear night sky and spot-lamps casting a yellow glow across the surrounding moat. The bus reached the far bank of the river and turned left, pulling up sharply outside the Crooked Billet public house. Normally Albert would have enjoyed the ride, a journey he had taken so often, but tonight his heart was beating fast and he felt an anxious knot in his stomach.

The bus continued through the Minories and finally turned into the terminal. It was there someone might be lurking, Albert thought. The terminal was deserted, however, and the young man looked carefully around him as he walked out into the wide thoroughfare. It took him only a few minutes to reach

Brick Lane and as he walked briskly along past the shuttered shops he felt as though he was experiencing a dream, a bad dream in which he could not extricate himself from some unseen danger that was lurking.

As he crossed Brick Lane and turned into Cubbit Street Albert glanced around and saw that the area was deserted apart from two women who were walking along arm in arm chatting quietly. He reached the front door between two shuttered shops and took a deep breath before bringing the iron doorknocker down sharply on its strike plate.

A hundred yards or so away a plain box van turned into Brick Lane and pulled up silently just short of Cubitt Street. Another van made a detour and parked in a backstreet, its human cargo spilling silently from the back and fanning out as they clambered over the debris of ruined houses.

Halleron turned to Grogan in the darkness of the first vehicle and patted his revolver. 'I really believe the top brass would prefer us to bring a body in,' he whispered.

Chapter Forty-Six

Frankie Morgan glanced at the battered alarm clock ticking noisily on the mantelshelf and saw that it was ten minutes after seven. Albert should be here any time now, he thought, standing up and going over to the back room window. He eased the filthy curtain back carefully and looked down into the gloomy expanse of wasteland and ruined houses which spread out beyond the rubbish filled backyard. It all seemed quiet, apart from a mangy-looking dog sniffing round a rotten tree stump in what was left of a garden behind some derelict houses. Frankie watched as the dog cocked its leg against the stump and trotted off across the rubble.

He walked up and down the room, gnawing at his lip, his hands thrust deep in his trouser pockets while he waited. His son would be careful, he had no doubt, but the police had ways of following people without being spotted and they may have had a tail on Albert for some time. If they did follow him to this house then they would burst in as soon as he dropped the money through the letter box, or else they might grab him before he had time to get rid of the money. In either case Frankie had to be ready to make his getaway, and he smiled to himself at Flash Gordon's ingenuity. The man had been hunted himself and went in fear of his life, and he had been very careful in preparing his hideaway. He had reinforced the front door by fitting brackets against the framework in which thick blocks of wood were dropped to prevent anyone shouldering their way in. The back door from the scullery had been secured with large nails hammered into the jambs and lintel and it would take some time to break it down; enough time to use the special escape route, another of Gordon's innovations.

At twenty minutes past seven Frankie heard the loud knock at the street door and hurried into the empty first-floor front room. He peered down into the quiet street and saw his son standing there. 'Put it in the letter box,' he mumbled aloud, his eyes searching the street for any sign of movement.

Albert knocked again and Frankie gritted his teeth in irritation as he rushed down to let him in. 'I told yer ter put the money frew the letter box,' he said quickly, as he threw open the door. 'Yer did get it, didn't yer?'

Albert stepped into the passageway and watched as Frankie quickly replaced the blocks of wood. 'I 'ad ter see yer, Dad,' he replied, feeling uncomfortable under his father's hard stare.

'Are yer sure yer wasn't tailed?' Frankie asked.

'It's all quiet out there,' Albert told him as he passed over the two packets and followed his father up the steep flight of stairs. 'I made sure I wasn't followed.'

'It's a fine bloody mess I'm in,' the older man grumbled as he walked into the back room and sat down on a rickety chair.

Albert looked around the untidy room and noticed how dirty and unlived-in it seemed. Old newspapers lay about and the table was badly stained. The two armchairs were tattered and torn, and the fireplace was full of ash and cinder. A low fire burned in the grate and beside the chair which his father was using a cardboard box full of coal had spilled on to the floor. The wallpaper was hanging down in places and the distempered ceiling was flaking and covered with water stains. The bare floorboards were grimy and the curtains looked to Albert as though they had been up for years. How different this was from their family home, where everything had always been spotless.

'What yer wanna see me for?' Frankie asked quickly. 'We've got nuffink ter talk about. You let me down an' I ain't fergettin' it. If it wasn't fer you gettin' that bint up the duff I wouldn't 'ave done the job, an' I wouldn't be in the shit I'm in right now.'

'Look, I don't wanna argue wiv yer, Farvver,' Albert replied quietly. 'I made a decision an' that's that. I wanna go straight an' build a future fer me an' Rose.'

'Oh I see. Rose, is it? An' I s'pose yer gonna marry 'er an' settle down wiv a tribe o' kids ter keep yer poor,' Frankie said in a bitter voice. 'I know, I've 'ad a basin of it.'

'As a matter o' fact, I bought the winder-cleanin' round an' I'm building it up,' Albert told him. 'I won't starve.'

'I wouldn't bank on it,' Frankie retorted. 'Anyway I ain't got time to argue the toss. Now say what yer wanna say an' leave me in peace, will yer.'

'I've bin ter see John an' Ernie's solicitor,' Albert said quietly. ''E wants yer ter give yerself up an' . . .'

'Yer gotta be more stupid than I took yer for if yer fink I'm gonna go out there an' 'old me 'ands up,' Frankie cut in. 'I done enough time wivout goin' back fer anuvver ten ter fifteen. You dunno what it's like bein' banged away in the nick.'

'I know 'ow yer feel, Dad,' Albert replied, 'but John an' Ernie 'ave bin offered a lighter sentence if they plead guilty, an' you too, if yer turn yerself in. The solicitor said the barrister'll plead that you was all set up an' yer didn't know that the bloke who was wiv yer 'ad a gun.'

'We was set up right enough,' Frankie growled. 'I've seen

The Farrans of Fellmonger Street

the papers. They got the diamonds back an' that geezer who was wiv us is dead. The Law must 'ave bin leanin' on the people who planned the caper an' me an' yer bruvvers 'ave bin put in the frame. What's more, yer can bet yer life that the geezer was murdered ter keep 'im quiet. 'E knew too much about who was be'ind it all.'

'All fer a lousy couple o' grand,' Albert said, shaking his head slowly.

'I'll find those two geezers who roped us in fer the job, an' when I do . . .'

A sound of falling rubble stopped Frankie in mid-sentence and he got up quickly and hurried over to the window, crouching down and peering through the curtains at the ruins below. It all looked deserted, but when he came away carefully and stood up his shoulders were still hunched.

''Must 'ave bin kids playin' around,' he said, glaring at Albert. ''Ave yer seen yer muvver?'

'No, not since she left,' the young man replied.

'I read in the papers the boys are in Brixton on remand. 'Ave yer bin ter see 'em?' Frankie asked.

'No, but I'm gonna see if the solicitor can get me a visitor's pass,' Albert replied.

'Are the boys gonna plead guilty?'

'I dunno. It depends on you, I reckon.'

'Oh yer do, do yer?'

'Yeah I do, Dad,' Albert said firmly. 'They'll get yer sooner or later. Why don't yer turn yerself in an' nick a few years back?'

'Don't yer start preachin' ter me about what I should do,' Frankie said sharply. 'Yer let me an' yer bruvvers down when yer got in tow wiv that Farran gel. My bruvver married inter the Farran family, an' that no-good wife of 'is kept naggin' at 'im ter move away. Now 'e's dead she's back causin' trouble.

She always blamed me fer the business goin' down the drain. Anyway, I ain't got time ter sit 'ere arguin'. Yer can go an' tell the boys that I ain't givin' meself up. They can plead whatever they like an' take their chances same as I gotta do.'

Suddenly there was a loud clatter down in the backyard and at the same moment a heavy hammering on the front door. 'They followed yer! Yer stupid little bastard!' Frankie shouted, his face draining of colour as he ran to the window and heaved it open wide. He hurried back and motioned Albert to follow him. 'Quick! 'Elp me wiv this,' he barked as he dashed into the bedroom and struggled to move the heavy wardrobe away from the wall.

Albert could see the wide hole in the plaster and the exposed laths of the adjoining property which had been concealed by the wardrobe. Frankie quickly kicked away enough of the plastered lattice for him to pass through, then he turned to face his son.

'Push this back after me an' tell 'em I went over the roof,' he hissed.

As Albert struggled to push the heavy piece of furniture back into place he heard the front door splinter and he barely had time to get into the back room before heavy footsteps bounded up the stairs and uniformed police officers crowded through the door. He was grabbed and pushed against the wall. 'Where is 'e?' the hefty policeman spat out.

''E went out the winder!' Albert gasped, fighting to get his breath as the officer's huge hand pressed against his windpipe.

The next few minutes were a blur as uniforms dashed in and out of the rooms. Albert remembered being pushed into a chair and ordered to stay where he was. Other officers climbed out on to the rusting iron fire escape and lights seemed to be flashing constantly from outside.

'Do you know who I am, Albert?' a voice said in his ear.

The young man looked up to see Inspector Bill Grogan standing over him. 'Yeah, I've seen yer in the Anchor,' he replied quickly.

'We know you weren't in on the raid, son, so what the bloody hell are you doing over here?' Grogan said in a gruff voice. 'Come to warn the old man, did yer?'

Albert shook his head. 'I come over 'ere ter try an' persuade me farvver ter give 'imself up,' he replied, looking up at the heavily built man. 'I was told by me bruvvers' solicitor that if I could persuade the ole man ter give 'imself up the judge might go easy on 'em all. That's the trufe.'

'All right, son. I'm not disputing what you said,' Grogan told him quietly. 'How did you know where to find your father?'

'I got a letter from 'im.'

'Did you bring him money? A gun?'

'No. Definitely not. My old man's never carried one.'

'Money then?'

''E wanted me ter try an' raise some money, but I couldn't,' Albert said. 'I really wanted 'im ter turn 'imself in.'

'That's commendable,' Grogan replied, nodding sagely. 'Anyway we'll get him soon. He can't get far.'

Albert was left alone with his thoughts for a while as the police came in and out and he wondered where his father was now. Had he succeeded in getting out of the immediate neighbourhood, or was he trapped?

'We've been up on the roof. It's clear,' a uniformed policeman said to the inspector.

'Are the streets properly sealed?' Grogan asked.

'No one can get in or out, sir,' the policeman answered.

Albert sat quietly thinking. The concealed bolt hole must lead into the baker's shop next door, he reasoned. Would the police suspect that his father was inside the shop? If so would they wait until morning before going in, or would they break in now? Albert tried to calm his misgivings as he sat quietly waiting, worrying about the outcome. The detective was carrying a revolver. He had caught a glimpse of the shoulder holster as the officer bent over him.

Ray Halleron came into the room and shook his head as he caught Grogan's eye. 'Nothing. We've searched the ruins and all the backyards,' he said with a sigh. 'We could have done with a moon tonight. It's as black as the ace of spades out there.'

Albert looked over, wondering what rank the officer was. He seemed to be the one in charge.

Halleron suddenly glared at him. 'Is this the son?' he asked Grogan.

'Yeah, he's clean,' Grogan replied. 'He came over to persuade his father to turn himself in, didn't you, son?'

Halleron stood over the young man. 'Does your father know anyone else in this area?' he asked suddenly.

'Nah, not as far as I know,' Albert answered.

'How come you knew where your old man was hiding?' Halleron said.

'I've already asked him,' Grogan cut in. 'He got a letter from his father. Morgan asked the boy to bring him some money. He told me he couldn't get any.'

'I hope you're not lying to us,' Halleron said, glaring at Albert.

Grogan looked at the young man and frowned. 'What about the shops next door. Could he have gone in there?' he asked his colleague.

Halleron shook his head. 'They're secured with padlocks and the windows are barred up. There's no sign of entry.'

'We'd better get the lad out of here, then we can secure the flat,' Grogan said, winking at Halleron.

The sign was picked up immediately. 'Yeah, let him go,' he said casually.

Grogan looked down at Albert. 'Right, lad, you can go now.'

As soon as the young man had left the room Halleron called a detective in. 'Follow the boy and don't lose him,' he ordered. 'He should be making for Bermondsey. Make sure he doesn't do any detours.'

Frankie Morgan found himself on the plaster-strewn landing above the baker's shop and he trod carefully, waiting for his eyes to become accustomed to the darkness. With luck the police would not try to break in, he reasoned. They would see that there had been no forced entry. Tomorrow would be a different story though. They would make a search after the baker arrived for work to make sure he hadn't slipped in. There was nothing to do but rest until the early hours. He would try to slip away after the shop was opened up.

Frankie pushed open a door that led off from the landing and found that it was the store room. The light of a street lamp shone in through the barred windows and he could make out a square-shaped trough in the middle of the room. There was flour in it and sacks of flour stacked round about. Frankie knew enough about bakers' shops to realise that the flour was fed down on to the bench in the room below by the pull of a chain or a rope, which would open the vent at the bottom of the trough and allow a quantity of flour to pour through, much like an hourglass.

The Bermondsey villain found some empty sacks in a corner of the room and tried to make himself comfortable. It would be a long wait until the baker arrived. In the meantime it would be a good idea to recoup his energy, he told himself, in case he had to fight his way out.

*

Samuel Cohen was nearing fifty, shortsighted and bald-headed, with a wife and two grown-up children and a distinct sense of pride in his profession. All his family had been bakers. His grandfather had been a baker in Cracow, Poland, until political upheaval forced him to leave the country. The old man's eldest son, Samuel's father, had founded Cohen's of Whitechapel in 1880, and ever since the shop had produced the finest bread and bagels in east London. Gold medals and diplomas adorned Samuel Cohen's shop and customers came from far and wide to buy his fresh hot wares. Samuel was reasonably happy with his lot, although he sometimes wished that he did not have to get up at such an early hour on cold mornings and walk from Stepney Green to his shop off Brick Lane to get the ovens started.

Samuel was surprised to see a large police presence as he turned into Brick Lane at four a.m. He walked along with his coat collar turned up against the wind, his shoulders hunched and his head held low, and he had almost reached Cubitt Street when he found his way barred by a huge policeman.

'I'm sorry, sir, but I must ask yer what yer doin' out at this time o' the mornin'.'

Samuel blinked once or twice. As far as he could remember it was the first time he had ever been stopped by the police on his way to work.

'I'm going to open my shop, constable. I'm Mr Cohen the baker, of Cubitt Street. You might have heard of Cohen's. Most people have,' he replied rather haughtily.

'Well, Mr Cohen, I'm afraid we've got a criminal on the loose in the area an' under the circumstances I'd better accompany yer ter the shop, just in case 'e tries ter sneak in,' the policeman told him.

'That's very considerate of you,' Samuel said in a more hospitable tone of voice.

Frankie had dozed fitfully and he was rudely awakened by the heavy scraping of metal as the padlock came off the front door and the hasp was swivelled and pulled back. He crept to the trough and heard voices directly below him.

'I'll keep the bolt on so no one can get in, officer.'

'Right you are, sir.'

'By the way, I'm expecting a delivery of sundries around six o'clock.'

'That's quite all right, we'll be outside just in case.'

'Pop in before you go off duty, officer and I'll give you a nice loaf and some bagels to take home.'

'Fank yer, sir, that's very nice of yer.'

Frankie crept back on to the flour sacks and sat pondering. It seemed that the police were still out in force on the street, and if the baker came upstairs for any reason it would probably be all over.

Police Constable Harper walked along Cubitt Street to the junction of Brick Lane and turned to retrace his steps. Night duty was something he did not care for and it would be nice to get home round the fire and warm up before Glenda cooked him his breakfast. The constable held his hands behind his back and plodded along slowly, placing his feet between the paving stones to regulate his step. It was an old trick of his and it helped to pass the time. There were two hundred and twenty-four paving stones in Brick Lane on the left-hand side walking from Whitechapel to Bishopsgate, he recalled, and thirty-two on each side of Cubitt Street. There were two lampposts in the little turning and one cracked sewer cover, which he had reported on two occasions to the Council works manager. It was good training too. The job required an alert mind and an eye for detail.

At ten minutes to six a Bedford three-ton box van drove

into Cubitt Street and pulled up outside the baker's shop. The driver stepped out of the cab and went round to the back of his vehicle where he hoisted up the shutter and dropped the tailboard. PC Harper did not take his eyes off the entrance to the shop as he counted his steps. He saw the driver carry in a sack of flour and then return to the lorry for smaller packets. The policeman glanced in the shop as he strolled by and he could see the reflection of the oven fire in the back of the shop.

PC Harper made sure that there was no one around and then he strolled along to the end of the street where he turned and started counting again as he walked back towards the shop. He saw the driver come out and secure the back of the van before driving off. Ten minutes later PC Harper's replacement entered the street. The two officers exchanged a few pleasantries and then the night duty constable walked into Samuel Cohen's baker shop for his promised bread and rolls.

When he walked into the back of the shop PC Harper let out a loud curse. The baker was trussed up with rope and gagged with a towel. The driver of the van was sitting next to him, gagged and bound too. His overalls and cap were missing.

Chapter Forty-Seven

It was inevitable that the comings and goings at the house next to the transport yard would be a constant topic of conversation and gossip for the people who lived in the street, whether or not they were directly involved in lending their labour. Folk spoke about it in the Anchor and in the local corner shops; women in the know were stopped in the market and approached as they stood chatting at their front doors, and word spread.

Surprising things began to happen. An aspidistra in a china pot was left on the doorstep, and the very next morning Dolly discovered a brown paper shopping bag which contained a set of plain white dinner plates. Someone else left a rolled-up coconut mat which was almost new, and another morning Dolly found a tiny spray of heather on the doorstep to which a note was pinned that simply said, 'Good luck'.

It was as though the front doorstep was becoming a shrine, where people came in secrecy to give their votive offerings to Providence and maybe take away a little good luck for themselves. For most, though, it was simply an expression of neighbourliness and support, a chance for local folk to play their part in what had come to be in their eyes a struggle against the powers that be. Elderly women with tired feet and laden shopping baskets made the extra effort to walk through Fellmonger Street on their way home from the market to see the progress being made, and maybe hear a little gossip. Everyone seemed to know about the struggle to get the house ready by the end of February, and those who were not aware of the reasons for the haste were soon enlightened when an article appeared in the local press. Dolly Morgan had been approached by reporters and was only too happy to respond.

During the middle of the last week of February Albert and Rose walked over to the house hand in hand and saw the latest developments. The front door had been varnished and a black number 12 had been fitted, as well as a lion's head doorknocker and a letter-box frame. Inside, the house smelt of paint and varnish where the stair rails had been treated to match the front door. The walls of the rooms on the ground floor had all been papered and there were new light fittings hanging from the ceilings. Out in the scullery there was a brand new gas stove, and sea-green linoleum covered the cold flagstones. On the upper floor the tawny evening light shone through the clean windows and lit up the rooms where freshly applied plaster was drying out.

Albert slipped his arm round Rose as they stood together in the front room overlooking the street. 'This room's gonna be ready fer paintin' termorrer,' he said. 'I'll come in straight from work.'

The young woman brushed a loose strand of fair hair from her face and smiled. 'It will be ready in time, won't it, Albert?'

'Course it will,' he replied, gently kissing her cheek. 'In any case they couldn't do anyfing about the kids now, not after the work that's bin done.'

Rose let her head rest on his shoulder. 'Well, they'll be callin' the banns out fer the last time this Sunday, an' the followin'

Saturday I'll be walkin' down the aisle on Don's arm,' she said with a sigh.

'You've got no regrets, 'ave yer, Rose?' he asked.

'I love you, Albert,' she whispered.

'I love you too, Rose, but I meant about the baby,' he said.

'I've no regrets,' she told him. 'It's our baby an' I'm anxious ter feel it movin' inside me.'

'Should it 'ave moved by now?' Albert asked quickly.

Rose laughed at the note of anxiety in his voice. 'The doctor told me I should feel the first movements between four an' four an' 'alf months, so it won't be long now.'

Albert lapsed into silence as he stood with his arm round her and Rose knew that he was thinking about his family. There had been no news of his father's whereabouts since he had escaped from the house in Cubitt Street, and she knew that Albert was worried about not hearing from the solicitor, who had promised to get him a visiting order.

'Would yer like me ter come wiv yer when yer visit yer bruvvers?' she asked him, hoping to draw him into unburdening himself.

'I expect they've told the solicitor they don't wanna see me,' he replied quietly.

'I don't fink so,' she said reassuringly. 'I reckon it's just all the red tape. The order's gonna come very soon now.'

'I'd sooner go on me own, Rose,' he told her. 'Prisons are not very nice places ter visit, an' I don't want yer ter take our baby in a prison.'

'I don't s'pose it'll make any difference ter the baby,' Rose replied smiling.

'No, but it might get you depressed,' Albert pointed out.

'Will they try yer bruvvers if yer farvver's still missin'?' Rose asked him.

'They've not set the trial date yet,' he replied. 'It might be that they're 'opin' me dad's gonna give 'imself up soon. If 'e doesn't, an' 'e won't, I expect they'll fix a date.'

Rose walked over to the window and looked down into the quiet street. 'Yer don't reckon yer dad finks you led the police to 'im on purpose, do yer?' she asked.

'I would 'ope not,' Albert said. 'Surely 'e wouldn't fink I'd turn against me own flesh an' blood.'

''E did, when 'e turned you out,' Rose said quickly.

'Well, wherever me farvver's 'idin' 'e'll 'ave plenty o' time ter mull fings over,' Albert replied. 'If I was after gettin' 'im put away I only 'ad ter show the police where 'e got frew the wall. No, 'e'll just fink I was careless an' they follered me.'

'I 'ope so,' Rose sighed. 'I don't want anyfing ter spoil fings fer me an' you.'

'Nuffink will,' Albert said, crossing the room and taking her into his arms. 'I've come to accept that me bruvvers are gonna go away fer a long time an' there's nuffink I can do about it. As fer me dad, I don't fink 'e'll be on the run fer much longer. 'E's runnin' out o' people who'll take 'im in. Anyone who 'elps 'im is puttin' themselves on the line.'

Rose stretched up and kissed him on the mouth. 'We will be 'appy, Albert,' she said softly. 'I know fings 'ave bin difficult lately an' we've 'ad no time to ourselves, but we'll soon be married.'

Albert hugged her close, feeling the bulge of her stomach, savouring the clean sweet smell of her hair, and he kissed her ear and neck. Rose shivered and raised her head as his lips moved round to her throat.

'I love yer, Rose,' he gasped. 'I need yer bad.'

'I need yer too, more than I can tell yer,' she whispered.

Albert closed his eyes as she laid her head on his chest, trying to still his rising emotions at the feel of her soft body pressed next to his, and for a while they stood in the middle of the bare room as the light failed. Eventually they moved apart, both realising that it was not the time or the place to let their passions flow unbridled.

'Let's take a look outside,' Albert suggested.

They walked down to the scullery and opened the side door. They could see the newly laid flagstones and the high fence which reeked of creosote.

'We can fix a line across 'ere, an' maybe get a wringer,' Rose said enthusiastically.

'I reckon I could put a small shed up out 'ere, an' I could put me ladders along the fence,' Albert added.

Rose looked up at the late evening sky, at the lone star uncovered by a fleeting cloud, and she took his hand.

> 'Starlight, star bright,
> The first star I see tonight.
> I wish I may, I wish I might,
> I wish my wish came true tonight.'

'What's the wish, Rose?' he asked her quietly.

'I can't tell yer, you'll only laugh,' she replied, turning her head away from his amused gaze.

'I won't. I promise,' he said, his face becoming serious.

Rose looked up at the sky. 'I wished that whoever's bin lookin' out fer us all will bless this 'ouse ternight,' she replied.

Jimmy Rideout had spent much of the last two weeks working at the house. He had cleared up after the women, helped Ken Stratton lay the gas pipework for the cooker and travelled back and forth scrounging tools and bits and pieces. He had helped George Price distemper the ceilings and Albert and Don with the painting. Now, as he sat alone in his groundfloor flat in Imperial Buildings, Jimmy was feeling exhausted. He realised too that he had become edgy and twitchy. He had been sharp with Dolly over the past few days, though she had made little of it. Dolly would be aware that he had not yet won his battle with the spirit bottle and he could understand why she put him off each time he proposed to her. She had to be sure he was truly master of himself again, and it was still early days. Tonight she had gone back to her lodgings to soak in a hot bath and then get to bed early, and she had urged him to do the same. He had intended to take her advice, but after preparing a meal of egg and chips and washing it down with two cups of sweet tea Jimmy had fallen asleep in his armchair. He had roused himself at nine o'clock and could not face the task of heating up the copper for a bath. His eyes went over to the sideboard where he kept the spirits and he licked his tongue across his dry lips, fighting off the strong urge to reach for a bottle. It would be madness to go back on to the spirits now, he knew. He would lose everything.

He got up and splashed cold water over his face, then he brushed his hair and slipped into his overcoat. A quiet couple of pints at the Anchor would take away the craving and help him get a good night's sleep, he reasoned.

Jimmy let himself out of his flat and walked the short distance to the pub. As he reached the public bar door Dan Beaumont came past, making for the saloon bar.

''Ello, Jimmy boy. 'Ow yer doin'?' he asked.

'Not so bad, Dan. What about you?' Jimmy replied.

The old man leaned towards him. 'Frankie Morgan's back,' he whispered. 'In Abbey Street last night. Mum's the word.'

Jimmy shook his head slowly as he watched Dan Beaumont enter the saloon, then he pushed open the door of the public bar. It was quiet tonight and Sammy McGarry nodded a welcome. 'What'll it be, mate?'

'Give us a pint o' bitter, an' one fer yerself,' Jimmy replied.

Sammy held a glass under the tap and pulled down on the pump. 'I 'eard the 'ouse is comin' on well,' he said.

'Yeah, it's nearly ready,' Jimmy replied. 'I'll be glad ter see the back o' that paintbrush. I bin at it nonstop, an' Dolly as well. We've 'ad a lot of 'elp though. The women in the Buildin's 'ave come up trumps. I dunno what we would 'ave done wivout them.'

Sammy handed over the brimming glass and watched as Jimmy picked it up gratefully and sipped at the froth, wiping his mouth with the back of his hand.

'There was a couple of ole dears talkin' to our Beryl in 'ere last night,' Sammy told him. 'They was sayin' 'ow everybody's bin muckin' in. It's an eye-opener 'ow the people round 'ere pull tergevver when there's trouble.'

'Yeah, like when the war was on,' Jimmy replied.

'That Bill Grogan was in 'ere last night,' Sammy went on. ''E looked like 'e 'ad the world on 'is shoulders.'

'I s'pose 'e 'as, as long as Frankie Morgan's still on the loose,' Jimmy remarked.

Sammy leaned forward over the counter. 'They nearly caught 'im the ovver night in the East End,' he said in a low voice. 'Frankie got away in a baker's van, accordin' ter Grogan. Keep it ter yerself though. Grogan wouldn't 'ave told me, except that 'e was pissed at the time. 'E was goin' on about the pressures 'e's under wiv the top brass. I fink it's really gettin' to 'im. 'E must 'ave sunk six double whiskies, an' that was on top of a couple o' pints. I've never seen 'im so pissed, nor so talkative. Gawd knows 'ow 'e got 'ome. I offered ter call 'im a cab but 'e said 'e wanted ter walk it off.'

Jimmy took a large gulp of his drink. 'I wonder if 'e's slipped back over this side o' the water,' he thought aloud.

'Who, Frankie?'

'Who else.'

''E might 'a' done,' Sammy said, stroking his chin.

'Ole Dan Beaumont seems ter fink 'e 'as,' Jimmy told him. ''E reckons 'e spotted Frankie in Abbey Street the ovver night.'

'That silly ole sod reckoned Peter the Painter's crowd was in 'ere last weekend an' 'e over'eard 'em plannin' ter blow the Trocette up,' Sammy replied, grinning from ear to ear. 'I ses to 'im, who in their right minds would wanna blow that fleapit up, Dan, an' 'e give me an ole-fashion look. "It's 'cos o' those bloody ole pictures they're showin'," 'e told me. Can yer believe it? Dan's gettin' worse an' worse. If 'e keeps this up they'll end up certifyin' 'im.'

Jimmy sat at the bar sipping his drink, beginning to feel irritated by the sound of Sammy's voice. Tiredness was washing over him and his stomach was starting to knot up. The pangs felt stronger than they had for a long time and he could feel his hands shaking. Another pint would do the trick, he thought. He would sleep like a top then.

As he drained his glass Beryl came into the bar. 'Yer wanted in the saloon, Sammy,' she told him.

Jimmy nodded to Beryl as she went round to take Sammy's place. ''Ow's tricks?' he asked, pushing his empty glass across the counter.

'Not so bad, Jimmy,' she replied. 'I 'ear the 'ouse is comin' on well.'

'Yeah, but it's bin a slog,' Jimmy told her. 'Sammy was just tellin' me about the plot ter blow up the Trocette.'

Beryl raised her eyes to the ceiling in exasperation. 'Ole Dan's in there arguin' the toss,' she said, jerking her thumb over her shoulder. ''E's goin' on about the Blackshirts now. 'E's sayin' that Oswald Mosley's got Jewish blood in 'im. It's a good job ole Benny Israel ain't in there ternight.'

Jimmy shivered suddenly and Beryl looked at him for a minute or two. ''Ere, you all right?' she asked him quickly.

'Yeah, it's just a bit of a cold comin' on, I expect,' Jimmy replied.

When Beryl put a fresh pint down in front of him she leaned her elbows on the counter. 'I know Dan Beaumont talks a lot o' nonsense at times, but Sammy was tellin' me somefing the ovver night an' it got me finkin',' she said.

'Oh an' what was that then?' Jimmy prompted.

'Well, apparently Dan button'oled Bill Grogan the ovver night. Yer know who Bill Grogan is, don't yer?'

'Yeah, I know 'im,' Jimmy replied.

'Well, Dan's always passin' on these bits an' pieces in confidence an' Grogan tends ter humour 'im,' Beryl went on. 'Anyway, the ovver night 'e told Grogan that Frankie Morgan was 'idin' out in the East End. Mind yer it was funny really, 'cos Dan slipped out ter the toilet ter pass on the info in secret, like 'e always does, then as soon as Grogan left Dan comes over an' tells my Sammy exactly what 'e's told Grogan. The fing is, they nearly caught Frankie when they raided this flat in the East End last week, but 'e got away. Grogan told my Sammy about it. Like I say, it makes yer fink.'

'Just a coincidence, Beryl, nuffink more,' Jimmy said, suddenly wincing at the gripping pain that seemed to be twisting his stomach.

''Ere, you could be goin' down wiv the flu,' the observant landlady told him, turning to the optics.

Jimmy looked at her as she handed him a large Scotch. Part of him was screaming out at her to take it away, but all he could do was stare down at the fiery spirit, imagining what it would be like.

'It's on the 'ouse,' she said smiling. 'Drink it down an' then go ter bed wiv an extra blanket an' sweat it out.'

Beryl was right, he thought. It would settle his stomach and help him sleep. As he nodded his thanks and took up the glass Jimmy knew in his heart that it was a mistake. It was too late. The burning feeling rolled over his tongue and scorched his throat, and he felt it numbing the pain in his stomach. It was all so easy. Another Scotch would settle him down nicely, and besides, a man could not let a woman buy him a drink without reciprocating.

It was nearing half past ten when Jimmy finally left the Anchor after Beryl had stoutly refused to serve him any more drink. He made a little detour, and after downing two more whiskies in the Horeshoe in Tower Bridge Road he bought a small bottle of Johnny Walker and set off for home in a very unsteady manner, pulling the collar of his overcoat up around his ears as he made his way along a cold and windy Abbey Street. He could feel the warm glow in his insides though, and he smiled inanely as he turned into Fellmonger Street and walked into the block. He fumbled in his pocket for his key, and after swaying back and forth and thrusting unsuccessfully a few times Jimmy finally found the lock. He cursed loudly as he put pressure on the key. It would only turn a little bit. The lock must be busted, he told himself. Try as he would he could not get the lock to move and finally he pulled the key out and tried to look at it. When he finally managed to focus his eyes, Jimmy chuckled at his silly mistake. In his hurry to get to the Anchor he had picked up the wrong key. The key in his hand was the one for the new house.

There were two things he could do, he thought hazily. He could knock Fred Albury up for a spare key and feel the wrath of his nagging wife, who would also make it her business to tell Dolly that he was pissed, or he could let himself into the house, where he could at least enjoy the bottle of Scotch in peace and then wrap himself up in the dustsheets for a good night's sleep.

With exaggerated secrecy, his finger held up over his lips, Jimmy Rideout slipped out of the block and crossed the deserted street, weaving a tortuous path to the house next to the transport yard.

Chapter Forty-Eight

Tommy Caulfield leaned back in his office chair and rubbed his hand over his tired and aching eyes. Outside the wind was getting up and he could hear the constant flapping of the tarpaulin sheet which he had recently fitted over the leaking roof of the cart shed. On the desk in front of him a large ledger lay opened, and for the past two hours or so Tommy had been bringing it up to date. His head felt heavy and his eyes had become bleary from poring over the columns of figures but he was determined to finish the task he had set himself. On Saturday morning the directors of Bailey's Transport were meeting him and he wanted to be in a position to present them with accurate and comprehensive figures.

As he reached into his desk drawer for the bottle of whisky Tommy felt the pain again. It seemed to drag at his chest and he found his throat beginning to tighten, as though someone was squeezing his windpipe. He poured out a large measure of spirit and gulped it down quickly, then he slumped back in his seat, brushing an unsteady hand across his forehead to wipe away the cold beads of sweat. No, he wasn't having a heart attack, he tried to convince himself. It was just stress and overwork. It had been relentless for months now and the books had got into a mess. He had worked himself up into a state over the previous bid to buy him out and now out of the blue he had had another, a more promising offer from Bailey's. This time it looked as though he would finally achieve what he had set his heart on for so long, a nice house in the country and a few pounds in the bank, enough to see him and Doris out.

Tommy pushed his head back against the upholstery and waited until the pain began to subside before going back to the figures. When the previous offer was made for his business Doris had been very much against it, he remembered, but now she had come round to his way of thinking. It was most probably her sister Gladys who had been influential in her change of heart. Her husband had laboured in the Bermondsey tanneries all of his working life and he died just before last Christmas, only six months after retiring on a small pension. Gladys had been a regular visitor lately and she was currently staying with him and Doris, which had afforded him the opportunity to work late at the yard all this week without worrying over his wife being alone, and he was confident that by Friday night he would have the books ready for the Bailey directors.

Tommy puffed loudly as he bent over the figures once more. They had not been making much sense but he had finally spotted the error, a wrong entry which had shown up in the balances. The contractor glanced at his silver pocketwatch which was lying beside his arm and saw it was fifteen minutes after eleven. He had decided to leave the yard by eleven o'clock at the latest, but now that he had spotted the error he wanted to total up the columns. The constant noise of the tarpaulin sheet was beginning to irritate him and when he had finished the first column he got up and looked out the window at the moonlit yard. Across the way he could see the shadowy cart shed and it appeared that one of the sheet-ropes had come undone. It would have to be secured, he realised. A loose rope cracking in the wind would sound like a whip to a horse and one of the animals might get nervous and kick its way out of the stall, upsetting the rest.

The contractor took down a hurricane lamp from a corner shelf and shook it to make sure it contained enough paraffin, before putting a lighted match to the wick, then he slipped on his heavy overcoat and went out into the cold night with the lamp down by his side. At the back of the shed was the hay store, hidden behind the carts, and Tommy went inside and glanced up at the roof. It looked secure, and he felt the hay bales to make sure they had not become sodden after the recent rain. As he came out of the store he put the hurricane lamp down in the doorway out of the wind while he set about securing the loose rope. He was knotting it round a cleat on one of the upright roof supports when he felt the pain again. This time it was severe, so much so that he gasped for breath and clutched at his throat in panic. His chest laboured in a hoarse whistle and he staggered towards the lighted lamp, realising even in his agony that he could not leave it where it was. His legs gave way under him and he went down on his knees; starved of air, he suddenly blacked out and fell forward on his face as he reached out clutching blindly. A few inches from his outstretched hand a trail of burning paraffin ran from the toppled lamp towards the hay bale and within seconds the whole store was burning. Flames reached up to the tarpaulin sheet and as it started to burn black smoke poured into the yard.

Jimmy Rideout felt the warm glow in his insides as he sat down against the wall in the bare front room of the house. He could see that the curtains were drawn and he chuckled to himself as he unscrewed the bottle of whisky. It would not be very clever of him to sit there in full view of an inquisitive neighbour while he indulged himself. It would be all round the street by morning. He could imagine them all shaking their heads and tutting to each other. Someone would tell Dolly and she would raise the roof, at the very least. As it was he could have a couple of tots and then sleep it off. Next morning he would get Fred Albury to let him in the flat and then he could wash and shave before Dolly called round. With a bit of luck she would be none the wiser, unless Beryl spilled the beans. No, she was a shrewd one, was Beryl. She knew when to hold her tongue.

For some time Jimmy sat resting against the wall with his legs spread out as he sipped the whisky, and the call of nature slowly got more urgent. He staggered to his feet and leaned against the wall until the room stopped spinning, then he made for the yard. As he stepped out into the night air he shivered and tottered sideways, reaching out to steady himself. The cold air seemed to revive him a little bit and after he had used the yard toilet he went back into the house, pulling the latched yard door to behind him.

Jimmy sat back against the wall of the front room, his eyelids dropping as he thought about Dolly and the impact she had made on his useless life. He was unworthy of her, he told himself. He had let her down by taking that dreaded first sip of whisky, but this was just a one-off little lapse. He would not let it get a hold of him this time. There was too much at stake and Dolly was too important for him to lose her again.

Suddenly he blinked and sniffed loudly as he hauled himself up straight. Through the fumes of drink that befuddled his brain the acrid smell of smoke brought it all back. He could hear the call to abandon ship and he was staggering up a Jacob's ladder on to the deck. The mine-sweeper was burning from stem to stern and dead and wounded were everywhere. The ruptured diesel tanks were fuelling the inferno and the ship was listing to the starboard at a crazy angle. Men were trapped and screaming for help and he could do nothing for them. He heard a comrade cry out and as he staggered over towards him he felt himself lifted into the air as a second torpedo struck the doomed ship. He screamed in terror as he hit the freezing water and fought to free himself from his heavy sea boots as he sank down beneath the waves.

Jimmy found himself on his feet, jerked back to the present by sheer instinct and he staggered into the passageway as the terror of imminent peril hit him with the same force as the cold sea. The yard was ablaze and he could see the flames and sparks rising up. He was alert now and thinking clearly and he knew that unless he acted immediately the fire would spread and the whole house would go up in flames.

Jimmy's drunkenness was gone as he climbed up on to the dustbin and clambered over the fence into the yard, feeling the heat from the fire and hearing the stamping and whinnying of the terrified animals in the stable to his left. Once he had not been able to help anyone, but this time it was different. This time he could do something.

A hosepipe was hanging just outside the lighted office, already connected to a tap. As he grabbed it down from the hook and turned on the water Jimmy glanced into the office but there was no time to wonder about the light being left on all night. The fire was taking hold.

Jimmy directed the fierce jet of water at the roof and then into the shed itself as he inched forward against the intense heat. He could see that the heart of the fire was at the back and he pulled on the hosepipe, gasping as smoke billowed out towards him.

He spotted the boots first through the thickening smoke, and then as he edged still further towards the flames he saw the prone figure of Tommy Caulfield. Most of the oxygen had burned off inside the large shed and Jimmy held his breath and crouched low as he reached the unconscious contractor. He remembered throwing the hosepipe down and grabbing at Tommy's ankles, pulling with all his might and almost crying with frustration as he inched backwards from the flames.

The rest was vague. He heard shouting and bells. The ship was turning turtle and going down fast. ''Ere, mate, take a few deep breaths o' this,' someone said and Jimmy was struggling, fighting to clamber aboard the life raft, but the more he tried the more difficult it became. Hands were bearing down on him and he stopped struggling. It was the end, he knew, but the sea was not cold and he was not sinking. He was being borne away with the sea birds whose cries encircled him, lifting up from the troughs and skimming the crests of huge waves as they glided past, floating effortlessly away, way above the bridge and radio mast. Blackness was swallowing him as he descended and he heard the bells again. Eight bells tolling from the doomed ship as it rested on the ocean floor.

Rose and Albert sat together in the flat discussing their coming wedding. The children were sleeping soundly and Don had gone over to Rotherhithe to be with Alice. Outside, the wind gusted along the narrow backstreet and rattled the windows, and a loose chimneypot blew down from one of the houses opposite. The two young people heard the clatter in the street below and they got up from the armchair they were sharing to gaze out through the curtains.

'Somebody could 'ave bin killed wiv that,' Albert remarked as he saw the large pieces of fired clay lying in the road.

'Yeah, it's a nasty night,' Rose replied, slipping her arm round Albert's waist. 'Shall I make us some cocoa?'

'Not just yet,' Albert told her. 'Let's just sit fer a while. It's nice ter be on our own fer a change.'

Rose pushed a strand of her long hair away from her forehead as she went back to the armchair. 'Yer won't change when the baby comes, will yer, Albert?' she asked him quietly.

The young man smiled as he squatted at her feet. 'Yeah, I'll always be out, an' when I come 'ome I'll expect the little brat ter be tucked up fer the night, and I'll expect you ter get up if it cries,' he told her with wild eyes, and, seeing her face drop, he chuckled. 'Course I won't change, darlin'. All the neighbours are gonna say, "Look at those two walkin' down the street arm in arm. They're a proper Darby an' Joan."'

'Would yer push the pram?' Rose asked him, running her fingers through his thick dark hair.

'Course I will,' Albert said positively. 'I ain't too proud ter be seen pushin' me own kid in a pram, an' if any o' the lads ses anyfing I'll sort 'im out good an' proper.'

Down in the street below an urgent voice shouted out and the sound of running feet carried up to the flat. Albert got up quickly and went to the window followed by Rose, and they gasped as they saw the flames rising from the rear of the transport yard.

'Oh my Gawd!' Rose cried out.

Albert gripped her hand tightly. 'It'll catch the 'ouse!' he gasped.

They could see Fred Albury running along the street and they heard Rene Stratton shout up to Freda Arrowsmith. 'Fred's gorn ter phone the fire brigade.'

'Please Gawd, don't let it reach the 'ouse,' Rose cried.

Albert was putting on his reefer jacket. 'I'll go over there,' he said quickly. 'I can douse the flames, stop 'em takin' 'old.'

'Be careful, Albert!' Rose called after him as he hurried out and ran down the stairs.

Ken Stratton and Bill Campbell had managed to kick the bolt off the inside of the wicket-gate as George Price ran up. They tore into the yard and saw the bent figure of Jimmy

Rideout dragging the unconscious contractor from the blazing shed, and as they reached him he dropped down in a faint, gasping for breath. The three men pulled Jimmy and the contractor a safe distance from the flames before lying them on their sides in the cobbled yard. Other men were beginning to arrive and they started tackling the blaze. Horses were stamping madly in the stable opposite the shed as Horace Carter the stableman arrived, alerted by Rene Stratton who had run the length of Abbey Street to fetch him.

The sound of fire bells grew louder and the fire tender roared down the narrow turning. Albert had already let himself into the house and was dowsing down the backyard fencing adjoining the rear of the cart shed, which had begun to smoulder. In the yard firemen struggled to bring the blaze under control and one of their crew fitted breathing masks over the two unconscious figures. A shriller sound of bells rang out as an ambulance drove into the turning and people stood with shock on their faces as Tommy and Jimmy were eventually stretchered from the yard into the waiting vehicle.

It was some time before the fire was finally put out, the task being made more difficult by the strong gusting wind, and when it all finally seemed to be over Albert Morgan stood back, panting, in the backyard. It had been a near thing, he thought. Another few minutes and the house would have been destroyed.

Out in the street the rumours were beginning to circulate. Lizzie Carroll stood outside the Imperial Buildings talking to Ivy Campbell. 'I 'eard someone say they reckon Tommy Caulfield put a match ter the place 'imself,' she was telling her. 'Done it fer the insurance, I s'pose. Mind yer, it don't do ter believe all you 'ear. Could 'ave bin one o' those wild dogs 'e keeps over there. They could 'ave knocked a lamp over or somefing.'

'Jimmy Rideout saved 'im,' Ivy told her. 'Pulled 'im out o' the fire by 'is feet, so my Bill reckons. 'E was first in there after

Jimmy, was Bill, along wi' Rene's Ken. They've both gone in the 'ouse ter see if Albert Morgan's all right.'

'Was Caulfield badly burned?' Lizzie asked.

'Nah. Bill said 'e was out cold though,' Ivy told her.

'What about Jimmy Rideout?'

''E got a lungful o' smoke, by all accounts.'

'Gawd knows what Caulfield was doin' in the yard so late,' Lizzie went on. 'Mind you it ain't easy when yer got yer own business ter run. I expect 'e was doin' 'is books. I've noticed a light on in that yard at all hours every night this week. Joe Diamond's the same. 'E works hours an' hours on 'is books. I should 'ave thought it'd be more sensible ter get an accountant ter do the books, but there yer go. It takes all sorts.'

Bill Campbell came out of the house next to the yard and walked over to the women. 'Albert's all right,' he said. 'The fire chief just looked in ter make sure nuffink was gonna take. 'E said Tommy Caulfield could 'ave 'ad an 'eart attack while 'e was in the yard. That's 'ow the fire could 'ave started. Mind yer, it's all conjecture at the moment. They'll know more when Tommy comes round, if 'e does.'

Rose had been watching the unfolding drama from her window. She had seen Albert dash into the house and the frenzied activity in the yard, then the ambulance arrive and two bodies carried from the yard. She quickly checked that the children were still sleeping and then hurried down into the street.

'Who's gone in the ambulance?' she asked as she saw Rene.

'Jimmy Rideout an' Tommy Caulfield,' Lizzie butted in.

Rene saw the look of horror on the young woman's face and she laid a hand on her arm. 'Jimmy's gonna be all right but they don't know about Caulfield yet,' she told her.

Albert emerged from the house and walked over to Bill and the woman. 'We was very lucky there,' he said. 'The fence is scorched but ovver than that everyfing's OK.'

'We'd better let Dolly know,' Rose said, as Albert slipped his arm around her shoulders.

The young man nodded. He had spoken briefly to the fire chief when he was checking over the house and the officer had told him that Jimmy Rideout had managed to contain the fire before dragging the contractor from the shed. Bill Campbell had remarked that Jimmy must have spotted the fire and got in via the backyard of the house because he and Ken Stratton had had to break in through the bolted wicket-gate. Albert wondered what Jimmy would have to say about it all and as he escorted Rose back into the Buildings he looked thoughtful. 'I'll go ter the 'ospital right away ter see 'ow Jimmy is, then I'll go an' see Dolly,' he told her.

'Wouldn't it be better ter tell Dolly first?' she queried.

'They may not let anybody visit till mornin',' Albert replied, trying to sound convincing. 'It's no good knockin' Dolly up ternight unless she can see 'im.'

'Yeah, you're right,' Rose agreed.

Albert felt relieved. He had to speak with Jimmy before Dolly, to let him know that the half-empty bottle of Johnny Walker had been removed from the front room and was now in a secure hiding place.

Chapter Forty-Nine

On a bright Friday morning Dolly Morgan walked quickly into Guy's Hospital and climbed the white-tiled stairs to Lister Ward. Her face was full of concern as she approached the ward sister. 'I've called ter see James Rideout,' she said breathlessly.

The sister gave her a cold look. 'James Rideout discharged himself early this morning,' she replied.

Dolly sighed and shook her head slowly. 'It's no more than I should 'ave expected.'

'I wanted him to wait until the doctor did his rounds but Mr Rideout thought otherwise,' the sister told her.

'Was 'e all right?' Dolly asked.

'Well, before he left he gave the night nurse a kiss and he offered to take the morning tea round,' the sister told her, hiding a smile. 'So I suppose we could presume that Mr Rideout has recovered somewhat.'

'Well, you're well rid of 'im,' Dolly flared. 'The man's a bloody idiot.'

The sister seemed taken aback by Dolly's outburst. 'Are you related?' she asked.

'No fear. I'm just a reluctant friend,' Dolly replied.

The sister dropped her formality a little. 'To be honest, your reluctant friend appears to be something of a hero, according to the information we've gathered,' she said, smiling. 'Apparently he tackled a fire and brought a man out alive.'

'So I've 'eard,' Dolly said, returning the smile.

'As a matter of fact the man Mr Rideout rescued is in the ward below,' the sister added.

'Fank you, sister,' Dolly replied. 'I fink I'll go an' ask if I can see 'im. Mr Rideout can wait.'

The sister glanced quickly at the watch pinned to her starched apron front. 'As a matter of fact Mr Rideout came back here less than an hour ago,' she said, and seeing Dolly's puzzled frown she added, 'He brought us a large bunch of flowers and said that he was going to sit down in the tea room for a while. If you're snappy you might just catch him.'

Dolly hurried down the stairs and into the large hall. The tea room was situated near the reception desk and concealed by screens, and when she put her head round the corner she saw Jimmy sitting in a corner with a large grin on his face.

'You took yer time,' he joked. 'I could 'ave bin drawin' me last.'

'You wicked git,' Dolly almost spat out, feeling relieved to see him so chirpy. 'Do you realise I've 'ad a bad fright? Albert knocked me up early this mornin' an' told me you was in 'ere.'

'Yeah, but 'e told yer there was nuffink ter worry about, didn't 'e?' Jimmy asked, still smiling.

'Yes 'e did, but 'ow was I ter know 'e wasn't keepin' somefing from me?' Dolly countered.

'Would yer like a cuppa?' Jimmy asked.

'No, I don't want a cuppa. I wanna get back ter the 'ouse,' Dolly replied sharply. 'Yer do know we gotta get that place liveable by the end o' the month, don't yer?'

'Yeah, I know,' Jimmy said in a subdued voice. 'Sorry if I upset yer, gel.'

Dolly's eyes suddenly filled with tears. 'You could 'ave bin killed,' she said softly. 'What would I 'ave done then?'

'I know,' Jimmy replied. 'I couldn't stand back though, luv. That 'ouse would 'ave gone up in smoke, an' poor ole Tommy would 'ave bin burned to a cinder.'

'Yer do know Tommy's in the ward under where you was?' Dolly queried.

'Yeah, I tried ter see 'im before I came down 'ere but they wouldn't let me,' Jimmy told her. 'They might let you in, though.'

'Come on then, let's try,' Dolly said quickly.

Frankie Morgan seemed to have disappeared from the face of the earth as far as the police were concerned, but in fact the fugitive was now taking the sea air in Clacton, as a guest of Flash Gordon. It had been touch and go from the moment Frankie drove out of Brick Lane in the baker's van early on that Saturday morning. He had been aware that the police would have put a call out and all the local police cars would be scouring the area and with that in mind he had abandoned the vehicle in a backstreet, discarded his borrowed overalls and caught a bus to Bethnal Green.

Frankie was making for the Bell public house, hoping that the landlady, Maisie Thompson, would put him up for a few nights until the heat died down. Maisie was an old friend and Frankie had learned from Flash Gordon that she had had one or two arguments with Andretti and detested the man. He could feel safe staying with Maisie, providing her husband had not decided to return to the nest. As it happened, Frankie was not disappointed and after spending a very pleasant week with the buxom publican he had moved on to Clacton.

Now, as he sat in his bedroom at the Sea View guest house on Friday morning, Frankie penned a letter to Tommy Caulfield, unaware of what had happened the previous night. The villain was feeling incensed that a son of his would stoop so low as to rob his own father and he blamed Dolly Morgan. She had been a bad influence on the boy, that was obvious, he fumed. She must have encouraged and nagged him into accepting responsibility for the baby, and in doing so she had split his family and turned him against his own father. It was hard to believe that Albert would have dipped into the money he had been asked to bring to Cubitt Street but there was no getting away from the fact. There had been seven hundred pounds stashed away under the floor and when Frankie counted the money there was two hundred pounds missing. Neither John nor Ernie would have touched it, nor would Annie. No, it could only have been Albert. Well, he was going to answer for it, and Dolly too.

Dolly had been unable to see Tommy Caulfield that morning as the doctor was with him, and after insisting that Jimmy rested up she went over to the house to finish hanging the curtains. On Friday evening she and Jimmy visited the hospital once more, and this time they were successful. The contractor was propped up against the pillows looking pale but cheerful after the doctor's report.

'Apparently it was just overwork,' he told them. 'The doctor said me 'eart's strong an' everyfing else seems all right. I've just gotta take it easy fer a while. I s'pose I'm a lucky bloke. I gotta be fankful it ain't me 'eart, an' am I bloody fankful ter you too, Jimmy mate. If it wasn't fer you I'd be charcoal by now.'

'Don't give it anuvver thought,' Jimmy said with a comical air of modesty. 'Anyway, what about yer missus, Tommy? 'As she bin in ter see yer?'

'Yeah, she come in this mornin', just after the doctor left,' the contractor replied. 'I tole 'er not ter come runnin' back 'ere this evenin'. All bein' well I'll be out of 'ere on Monday.'

'An what about yer business, Tommy?' Dolly cut in. 'What's gonna 'appen?'

The big man sighed in resignation. 'The ward sister let me use the phone, wiv a bit o' persuasion,' he told her. 'I've got me foreman car man ter sub the work out terday an' next week. 'Im an' the stableman are gonna sort out the damage ter the carts and they'll get the insurance company in ter do an estimate. It'll all work out. One fing's fer sure, I'm not gonna lose no sleep over it. That's what the trouble's bin all along. I bin strongin' it too much.'

'P'raps yer should fink about sellin' the business,' Dolly suggested. 'Yer not gettin' no younger.'

Tommy laughed ironically. 'I was in the process,' he replied. 'That's why I was workin' late. I was bringin' the books up ter date, but it's all gone by the board now.'

'I am sorry,' Dolly said sympathetically. 'Still, never mind, they'll be back.'

'What about yer mail? D'yer want me ter pick it up an' bring it in for yer?' Jimmy asked.

'No fanks, pal,' Tommy told him. 'I'll call in the office on Monday, all bein' well. There's nuffink that can't wait.'

Dolly and Jimmy sat chatting with the big man until the visitor's bell sounded and then they walked home through the backstreets to the Anchor. Jimmy was hoping that Beryl would not mention his last visit, and as he walked into the saloon bar with Dolly he gave the landlady a warning look. He need not have worried, for Beryl was indeed the soul of discretion and she gave him a secret smile.

Word had spread around the neighbourhood of Jimmy's heroic rescue and he was finding it increasingly embarrassing as folk came up to shake his hand and offer him drinks. Dolly refused the drinks on his behalf and jokingly whispered into his ear that she wanted him awake, alert and sensible as she intended staying the night. Jimmy's feigned yawn was returned with a look of mock contempt, but secretly Dolly was feeling very happy. What could have been a disaster had been prevented and she had Jimmy to thank. Things were coming on well at the house, she felt, and with a last concerted effort that weekend the family would be able to move in on time.

On Friday evening in the public bar of the Anchor, Bill Campbell eased his heavy bulk against the corner seat and picked up his pint of ale. He was feeling a little anxious as he waited for Percy Purvis to arrive and he was beginning to think that his conversation with his workmate that morning in the coffee shop had been a mistake. Along with Bill, the devious Percy worked in the building department of the Bermondsey Borough Council, and if anything was required in the way of plumbing materials then Percy seemed able to supply it, providing there were no questions asked.

It had all begun the previous evening after the fire. Ivy and Rene were chatting late into the night at Rene's flat while he and Rene's husband Ken had been enjoying a drink together in the front room. The women were saying how fortunate it was that the house had not been damaged, especially after the work they were all putting in, and Rene mentioned the state of the stone sink in the scullery. It was badly chipped and Ivy had said it was a pity they couldn't get one of those nice white porcelain sinks they were fitting into the new flats that were being built. Bill recalled how he had mentioned casually that his pal Percy Purvis could probably get one and Ivy had jumped at the suggestion.

Before he left for work that morning Ivy had reminded him to have a chat with his friend about the sink, and although in the cold light of day Bill wished he had kept his mouth shut he knew that he was duty-bound to see the resourceful Percy.

'No sweat,' Percy had told him over a mug of tea and two pieces of dripping toast. 'I fink I can get just the fing. Firty bob should do it.'

Bill had agreed to the price and thought that he had done his bit, but Percy had other ideas. As they clocked off at the Council offices that afternoon the plumber had sidled up to him and whispered in his ear that they had to collect it that evening and Bill was to meet him in the Anchor at eight o'clock.

As he finished his pint Bill Campbell saw that it was already eight thirty and there was still no sign of Percy. He walked up to the bar to get a refill and saw the plumber put his head round the door.

'Sorry I'm late. C'mon, we gotta go right now,' he said urgently.

When Bill stepped out into the street, Percy was already climbing into a Council van. 'It's all right, I booked this motor out on an emergency job,' he said grinning.

Bill sat back in the passenger seat feeling nervous as his friend pulled out of the turning and drove along Abbey Street.

'Where we goin'?' he asked.

Percy steered the van into Spa Road. 'Just sit back an' look like a foreman. Ole Stan the night man won't know the difference,' he said out of the corner of his mouth.

Bill Campbell gasped as Percy swung the van up to the barrier and waited while the depot attendant shuffled out of the weighbridge office and lifted the bar. 'You ain't finkin' o' nickin' the sink out o' the depot, are yer?' he said under his breath.

Percy ignored the question. 'Watch'er, Stan ole mate. Just gotta pick up a monkey wrench. The poxy boiler's packed up,' he said to the attendant. 'Yer can leave the bar up, we sharn't be a few minutes.'

Bill slumped down in his seat in case the attendant recognised him but he need not have worried. The man was quite used to the comings and goings of emergency repair teams during the late evening and it was just another entry to go down in the book.

Percy drove down the length of the yard and pulled up outside a back door. 'It's OK, I've left it undone,' he said, climbing quickly from the van and opening the back to take out a heavy tool bag. 'C'mon, Bill, let's go.'

Fifteen minutes later the van pulled out of the Council yard with a brand new porcelain sink resting in the back. If Bill was nervous at first, he had become even more worried when Percy hurried into the toilets at the end of a long corridor and promptly began to dismantle the sink pipes. ''Ow the bloody 'ell are yer gonna get away wiv this caper?' he asked incredulously.

'Piece o' cake,' Percy told him. 'I'm booked in on overtime termorrer ter get that new toilet ready fer the staff on Monday. I'll just indent fer a fresh sink from the stores first fing in the mornin'. A pal o' mine works in there. By the way, where we takin' the sink, round your gaff?'

Bill nodded. 'Yeah, but it's all right. There's no stairs ter climb.'

Percy turned into Fellmonger Street. ''Ere, Bill, d'yer know why they asked fer a large sink ter be put in that carsey?'

'No.'

'So they can wash their cups up,' Percy said with disgust. 'Why they can't use the poxy 'and basins I'll never know. Anyway yer got a bargain there.'

Bill Campbell sat back in the seat and shook his head slowly as the van pulled up outside Imperial Buildings. 'Percy, you're incorrigible,' he said with feeling.

'Nah, I'm not,' the plumber replied, looking hurt. 'I would 'ave thought firty bob was a fair price.'

Chapter Fifty

During the last weekend in February the street volunteers were out in force. On Saturday morning the gas was laid on and Freda, Ethel, Ivy and Rene went into the house with buckets, scrubbing-brushes, bars of Sunlight soap and house flannels and set to work on the stained and grimy floorboards. The task proved to be a difficult one and the four willing scrubbers worked up a sweat but by lunchtime they had finished. Dolly went through the house cleaning all the windows while Don and Albert were hard at it painting the woodwork in the last of the rooms. Jimmy had gone to the market pushing a barrow he had borrowed to collect rolls of oilcloth picked out by Dolly and put aside for collection. George Price was busy in the backyard white-washing the lower part of the brickwork, and during the morning Bill Campbell and Ken Stratton staggered into the house carrying the gleaming white porcelain sink between them.

'That's a nice sink. Where d'yer get it?' Ivy asked.

'Don't ask. Just don't ask,' Bill said firmly.

At four o'clock on that Saturday afternoon the decoration and renovation were finally completed, and while the rolls of oilcloth were being carried into the house Dolly slipped across the street to collect Rose and the three children. The young woman's eyes widened with delight as she saw the results of her neighbours' efforts and Billy and Joey scampered up the stairs to look around, while Susan clung to Rose looking rather overawed by it all. Dolly had boiled a kettle on the new gas stove to the delight of everyone and she and Rene handed out mugs of tea to everybody.

'I just wanna say 'ow grateful us Farrans are fer all the 'ard work you've put in,' Dolly said, smiling as she looked around the tired and dishevelled group. 'We couldn't 'ave managed wivout your 'elp an' I'd like ter say that every one o' yer will be welcome visitors in this 'ouse at any time.'

Ivy nudged Rene. 'Go on then, gel,' she urged her. 'Say yer bit.'

Rene got up from the plank she was sitting on and brushed her hands down the front of her soiled apron. 'We would all like ter wish you an' your family a very 'appy life in this 'ouse,' she began. 'We all know what a struggle it's bin fer Rose ter keep 'er family tergevver, an' we know the part Dolly's played in makin' this all possible. She's bin a very 'ard taskmaster but she rolled 'er sleeves up as well, which leaves me just ter say, may God bless this 'ouse an' all who live in it.'

Handclaps and good wishes rang out and Ivy went to a cupboard and took out a large flat brown-paper parcel which she laid on the floor in front of Dolly. 'It's just a little movin' in present,' she said.

Dolly tore off the wrapping and saw that it was a thick brown coconut mat emblazoned with the word 'Welcome' in big black letters. 'That's very nice of yer,' she said, smiling happily. 'I just 'ope yer'll all be wipin' yer feet on this mat at some time or anuvver in the near future.'

Finally the volunteers drifted off home and then Rose collected the excited children. 'I'd like to add mine an' Don's fanks, an' the children's too fer everyfing, Dolly,' she said. 'I don't know what we would 'ave done wivout yer.'

'It's all right, luv,' she replied, slipping her arm around the young woman's shoulders. 'We're all family, an' we've bin very lucky to 'ave such nice, carin' neighbours, they've bin wonderful. Now I fink we'd better all get off 'ome. It'll need ter be an early start termorrer. There's all that oilcloth ter lay.'

'Yeah, an' I'm gonna take great pleasure in writin' ter the welfare an' tellin' 'em we're movin' in on Monday,' Rose said, smiling broadly. 'I'll pop round an' slip it frew the door, then they'll be sure ter get it first fing Monday mornin'.'

Once Rose and the children had left, Dolly took a last look round before locking up the house. She did not relish the thought of going back to her lonely lodgings, and she crossed the street and entered the Buildings. Tonight she needed company, and Jimmy's warm bed.

Early on Sunday morning Don and Albert went over to the house armed with a pair of scissors and a carving knife. The prospect of laying the oilcloth was daunting. Neither of them had tackled such a job before and they both stood looking with trepidation at the tubes lined up on their ends along the passageway.

'Well, at least they're marked,' Albert said.

Dolly had had the foresight to scribble on each of the brown paper wrappings which room that particular roll was meant for, and when the two young men dragged the first roll into the front room and tore it open they stood scratching their heads in confusion.

'Which way is it meant ter go?' Don wondered aloud.

'Gawd knows. Any way, I s'pose,' Albert suggested.

'Nah, yer gotta get it right,' Don told him.

'Well, I dunno.'

''Ere, let's turn it round.'

'Nah, I fink it should go longways.'

'Yeah, yer right.'

'Just a minute, let's go crossways, 'cos o' that fireplace.'

'Turn it round this way; no, not that way.'

The two frustrated young volunteers sat down on the bare floorboards with their backs against the wall while they tried to work it out. Albert took out a packet of Player's Weights and offered Don one. They smoked in silence, both feeling that they had taken on a little more than they could handle.

'I've never laid oilcloth before,' Albert admitted.

'Me neivver,' Don replied, flicking his ash into an empty paint tin.

Albert stubbed out his cigarette and stood up. 'Well, we can't sit 'ere lookin' at it or we'll never get it done,' he sighed.

Don stood up and stretched. ''Ere, Albert. I bin finkin' about that fire on Thursday night.'

'Yeah?'

'Yeah. I was wonderin' 'ow Jimmy just 'appened ter be on 'and that time o' night,' Don remarked.

'As a matter o' fact, I asked 'im that when I called inter the 'ospital ter see 'im,' Albert replied, trying to look casual. ''E told me 'e couldn't sleep an' 'e was goin' fer a stroll around the 'ouses. 'E just 'appened ter be passin' at the time the fire broke out.'

'That was lucky fer all of us,' Don said with feeling. 'I was wonderin' whevver 'e might 'ave took it in 'is 'ead ter do a bit o' night work on the 'ouse an' didn't want Dolly ter know in case she rucked 'im fer overdoin' it.'

'Yeah, if Jimmy 'ad come in 'ere that night 'e certainly wouldn't 'ave wanted Dolly ter know, that's fer sure,' Albert replied, hiding a grin.

'Well, I s'pose we'd better get crackin',' Don said without much enthusiasm.

Fortunately help was on its way. Ethel Price had been pleasantly surprised at her husband's hidden talents during the past two weeks, and she confronted him as he sat reading the *News of The World*.

'Couldn't you an' Ken give the boys an 'and wiv that oilcloth, George?' she asked him. 'It's a big job if yer don't know what yer doin'. P'raps you could give 'em a few tips.'

George felt flattered by Ethel's confidence in his abilities and he stroked his chin for a few moments. 'I s'pose I could, but yer know me an' Ken always meet Bill Campbell up the Anchor on Sunday mornin's,' he replied.

'Why don't you an' Ken go an' collect Bill an' all pop over the 'ouse before the pub opens,' Ethel suggested. 'The boys'll be ever so grateful, I'm sure.'

The two amateurs had got themselves into a mess unrolling the heavy tube of oilcloth and they found themselves backed up against the wall.

'Don't stand on that bit, yer'll split it,' Albert warned.

''Ow the bloody 'ell am I gonna get over there then?' Don grumbled.

'It looks like yer got yerselves in a right ole state,' George Price said, grinning, as he and his two drinking partners popped their heads round the door. 'Come 'ere, let's sort you out.'

It did not take very long before the front room downstairs was finished, with the oilcloth trimmed and tacked along the joins. Meanwhile Ken Stratton and Bill Campbell had set to work upstairs, both aware that their precious drinking time was at stake.

'There's that room on the stairs ter do yet,' Bill said with a frown.

George had carried the appropriate roll up to the small room on the bend of the stairs and was tearing the wrapping off when his friends appeared from the front bedroom. 'Right then, this is the last room,' he said. 'What I suggest is, you two 'old it up while I cut the right length off.'

Bill glanced at his wristwatch. 'It's ten minutes ter twelve,' he announced. 'Why don't I go up the Anchor an' get the drinks in before the rush?'

'Bloody good idea,' George replied. 'Tell them two lads to 'urry up, will yer, Bill? They've bin ages on that passage.'

Dolly had slipped out of bed early that Sunday morning and after waking Jimmy with a large mug of tea she started to cook their breakfast. She could hear him singing loudly in the scullery as he ran the razor over his lathered stubble and she smiled to herself. He had proved to be a good lover, and he was very understanding. He knew that she was finding it hard to adjust after her husband's death and he seemed to know instinctively when to bring her out of herself and when to remain quiet and leave her to her own thoughts. She realised that marriage was very much on his mind and he wanted a straight answer soon.

Dolly turned over the bacon and cracked two eggs on the side of the large frying pan, suddenly feeling Jimmy's arms come round her from behind.

'Yer a lovely woman, Doll,' he said, rubbing his smooth chin along her neck.

'Don't just stand there,' she said with mock irritation. 'Go an' do somefing useful, like layin' the table.'

Once breakfast was over Jimmy collected the plates up and began to wash up while Dolly got dressed. She was soon back, her shoulder-length fair hair neatly groomed and her fresh plump face shining with good health. She had put on a black satin dress which accentuated her full figure and black nylon stockings with patent high-heeled open-toed shoes. Jimmy shook his head slowly as he put down the teacloth. 'Yer look nice enough to eat, darlin',' he said, coming towards her.

Dolly allowed him to kiss her and then stepped back a pace. 'Jimmy, when was the last time yer went ter church?' she asked him.

'Gawd knows,' he replied, a puzzled look on his face.

''E will, an' 'E won't be too 'appy I should fink,' Dolly said, smiling as she raised her eyes to the ceiling. 'C'mon, let's go an' 'ear the banns bein' read out.'

The church bells were ringing as Dolly and Jimmy stepped out of the Buildings into the early sunshine and walked arm in arm into Abbey Street, Dolly wearing a heavy grey coat with a fur trim and Jimmy dressed in his best grey pinstripe suit. Ahead they could see the parish church of St Mary Magdalene, its ancient yellow stonework dark and pitted in the sun.

'I could get used ter this,' Jimmy said as they crossed Tower Bridge Road and walked along by the high railings that surrounded the church gardens.

'We should do it more often,' Dolly remarked.

As they entered through the arched stone doorway Jimmy leaned his head towards hers. 'Dolly?'

'Yeah?'

'Do us a favour.'

'What?'

'Marry me.'

'Jimmy, you do pick some funny times ter propose,' she whispered. 'The last time it was four o'clock in the mornin'.'

'Well?'

'I can't give yer an answer now,' she hissed as the verger smiled a welcome.

Throughout Saturday night Chief Inspector Bill Grogan had steadily drunk himself into a stupor and he had finally passed out in the armchair. The near-empty decanter and a brandy bowl rested on a side table by his elbow and at his feet was the letter he had read over and over again. Outside, the cold winter sun was shining and the sound of distant church bells drifted into the room. The fire had burned out during the night and Bill Grogan shivered as he roused himself. For some time he sat with his head in his hands, then he refilled the brandy bowl, reached down for the letter and went over to the large mahogany desk where he slumped down in his leather-bound chair.

He wanted it to be just a bad dream, but he had awoken to see the letter still lying there at his feet. Now, as he stared down at it on the desk in front of him he knew this was stark reality. The letter was from his wife Anna and the neatly penned words swam and wavered before his eyes as he read it once more. Anna had threatened so often to leave him but he had never taken her seriously. This time she had done it; but to leave him for that pathetic excuse of a man, Bruce Tynan, was something he found hard to believe. The Tynans had often been guests in his house and he had always felt that Bruce Tynan and his wife Mandy were a happy couple, though a little scatterbrained. How wrong he had been. The affair must have been going on right under his nose, but then he had been away from the house for long hours, especially since the Cape Diamond case. He had often returned home late at night and sometimes into the early hours and flopped into bed totally exhausted. He would have missed the signs.

Grogan took a large gulp from the glass and raised a hand to his forehead. It all seemed so unreal. Their marriage had been shaky for years though, he had to admit. It would have been different had he been able to give Anna the thing she most craved for, a child. They had tried for so long, and when finally out of frustration she had consulted a private clinic the tests had confirmed that she was quite capable of conceiving. She had then persuaded him to go and see his doctor, and when he found out that he was sterile Anna began to change. It was gradual, but painful for them both nevertheless. His career had been a crutch, something which sustained him through the bad years of their relationship, and now it was certain that he would not get the promotion he had been so desperate to achieve.

Bill Grogan took another gulp from the glass. The Commissioner had been scathing on Friday morning. He had made it quite clear that there could be no excuse for allowing a petty criminal to make utter fools of the police force by escaping for the second time when surrounded by an operation team large enough to form a battalion of troops. The Commissioner had also instructed him to work under Ray Halleron and had threatened to take him off the case altogether if a result was not forthcoming in the next few days. It would mean disgrace, and a transfer to some second-rate post with little chance of stepping up the ladder. He might have been able to cope even with that, if Anna had stayed with him. They could have worked at improving their marriage and regaining the happiness they once knew together. It was all too late now. He could forgive her almost anything, but not infidelity.

A cold bright sun was climbing up into the Sunday sky and the church bells sounded clearly as Chief Inspector Bill Grogan scribbled out a short letter and sealed it in an envelope. He then drained his glass, reached into his desk drawer for his police revolver and pressed the muzzle against his temple.

Chapter Fifty-One

Winifred Seaton sat in her office on Monday morning with the Farran file open in front of her and the various papers spread over the desk. On top of them was the brief letter from Rose Farran. There seemed little more to do now, Winifred had to admit. The house was ready for occupation and there was no reason to proceed with a fostering order. That in itself was satisfying. It was never possible to foster out children without some distress, she reflected.

Winifred's training had taught her to follow up every clue, look at things from every angle and seek indefatigably to alleviate family problems and hardship even if the remedy caused short-term distress. She felt confident that all avenues had been explored in the Farran case and all the decisions she had taken had been made with due consideration and fore-thought. She was satisfied that pressures had been brought to bear for all the right reasons. The crucial points always to remember, she reminded herself, were child welfare, safety and protection, and she felt that she had been thorough and profes-sional in her handling of the case.

Winifred gathered up the papers and tucked them neatly into the file, which she marked 'Closed' before slipping it into her filing cabinet. It was almost lunchtime and there was much to do. This afternoon she would go to see Rose Farran and inform her of her decision, then she would go through her in-tray. There must be no outstanding problems to worry over. Peggy was coming round for a meal this evening and she wanted to feel at her best. If she could confine her professional cares to the office then she would have more energy to concentrate on developing their relationship. She had a nice, comfortable home with lots of room, and it would be wonderful if Peggy could be persuaded to move in, she sighed.

Monday morning was the big day for the Farrans and it began with a heated discussion between Rose and her younger brothers, who were eager to do their share.

'Look, I know you both want to 'elp wiv the movin',' she said as she sat brushing out the protesting Susan's long raven hair, 'but that welfare woman is bound ter be callin' round ter see if everyfing's all right, an' if she finds out that I've kept yer both 'ome from school there's gonna be trouble. She'll get on ter the school board man an' I'll 'ave ter go ter court.'

The boys looked glum as they put on their coats, and Billy screwed up his face as he turned to his brother. 'We know where we're not wanted, Joey,' he grouched.

Don had taken the day off work to help Albert move the family's possessions into the new house and he hustled Billy out of the flat, watching with amusement as the lad went down the stairs mumbling to himself. Joey stood waiting until Susan was ready and when they finally left for school holding hands, Rose breathed a sigh of relief.

'I've gotta get the crockery packed up an' then there's the beddin' ter bundle up,' she said, suddenly holding her side.

'You all right?' Don asked with concern.

'Yeah, it's a movement. I've just felt a movement!' she told him excitedly.

Don took her arm. 'Yer better sit down fer a minute. I'll do the packin' while I'm waitin' fer Albert,' he said solicitously.

Rose gave him a reassuring smile. 'It's nuffink ter worry about. It's quite natural ter feel a baby move at this time in a pregnancy,' she told him. 'Anyway, I got no time ter sit down, there's too much ter do.'

A few minutes later Albert walked in and Don immediately took him aside. 'The baby's moved,' he said matter-of-factly. 'Don't worry though, it's about the time.'

Rose was amused as a worried-looking Albert put his arm around her and gave her a gentle kiss on the cheek. 'We're gonna 'ave a lively baby, I reckon,' she told him, smiling happily.

The removal soon got under way with the two young men dismantling the beds and manhandling them down the stairs and across the street. Rose had been scrounging empty cartons from Joe Diamond's shop for the past week and she set to work packing the crockery and bric-a-brac. Later that morning Dolly and Jimmy came to lend a hand and gradually the rooms were stripped bare. The two women finished packing and then went over to the house to supervise the setting up.

'Tommy Caulfield's mindin' a few bits an' pieces o' mine,' Dolly said. 'I'll see 'im about it if 'e shows up terday. I reckon we can make this place look really nice by the time we're finished.'

Don and Albert had brought over the table and chairs, and at one o'clock Dolly called out into the scullery where Jimmy was assembling the large Welsh dresser which had been dismantled and brought into the house in pieces. 'Do us a favour, luv,' she said in her most persuasive voice. 'Can yer go over ter Manzie's an' get some pies an' mash before we all flake out? An' don't ferget the liquor.'

As soon as the meal was over, the work began again in earnest, and it was while Rose and Dolly were unpacking a box of ornaments that the welfare officer arrived. She looked around and nodded her approval. 'I think it looks very cosy,' she said, smiling to defuse any feelings of resentment. 'I'm sure you'll be comfortable here.'

'Yeah, I'm sure we will,' Dolly replied, casting Rose a long-suffering glance.

Rose offered Winifred a chair but she declined to sit. 'The reason I called is to let you know that we are closing our file on you, Rose,' she said smiling.

'Ter be honest there's no reason ter do ovverwise, is there?' Dolly cut in aggressively.

'I do need one more bit of information, however,' the officer went on, ignoring Dolly as she addressed Rose. 'It's just to clear things up. I need to be sure that you are not paying an excessive rent. There is a rent tribunal with powers to re-adjust excessive rents.'

Rose looked at Dolly and the older woman put down the bronze statuette she had just taken out of the cardboard box.

'Look, we've not got the rent sorted out yet,' Dolly said in a bothered voice. 'If we find it's too much, then I'll do what I 'ave ter do fer the family.'

'Isn't that rather unusual?' Winifred replied.

'What?'

'Well, taking tenancy of a house without first agreeing a rent.'

'Not really,' Dolly retorted. 'We've already bin given four rent-free weeks an' we've also bin promised that it won't be any more than the family paid fer the flat.'

'Perhaps I ought to see Mr Caulfield,' the officer said. 'After all, you've got nothing in writing.'

Dolly became incensed at the officer's attitude. 'Now you

listen ter me,' she started. 'I know that you people 'ave got a job ter do, but what gets right up my nose is the bloody way yer go about it at times. There was no need ter put a month's notice on us gettin' this place sorted out. All you did was put us all under a lot o' pressure. Anyway, despite you we got it finished in time, an' yer've only gotta look around ter see the sort o' job we've done, an' . . .'

'Yes, but . . .'

'Never mind about yes,' Dolly shouted. 'Just leave us ter get on wiv our lives, an' go where yer needed. Now if yer don't mind, we've got work ter do.'

Winifred paused at the front door. 'I hope everything's going to work out for you,' she said curtly.

'Don't you worry about us,' Rose replied in the same vein.

Don and Albert had been upstairs when the welfare officer called and they had listened from the landing. 'Good fer you, Dolly,' Albert said, grinning, as he hurried down the stairs.

'I fink we've seen the last of 'er,' Don remarked.

Dolly smiled back as she sought to calm herself. 'I reckon so, unless Tommy Caulfield starts windin' 'er up again.'

At four o'clock the contractor arrived at the yard, and after inspecting the damage caused by the fire and discussing the pressing problems with his foreman he decided to open his mail. Ten minutes later he knocked on Dolly's front door, looking very serious.

'C'mon in, Tommy, I've bin expectin' yer,' Dolly said amiably. ''Ow yer feelin' now?'

'I'd prefer it if yer came over the office,' Tommy replied quietly. 'It's pretty important an' we can talk in private.'

Dolly followed the contractor across the yard and sat down in his office with a sigh. 'It's bin nonstop all day,' she said, smiling wearily.

Tommy leaned forward on his desk. 'Dolly, I got anuvver letter from Frankie Morgan this mornin',' he began. 'It's post-marked Clacton.'

'What's 'e doin' in Clacton, as if I didn't know?' Dolly cut in.

'I expect 'e's got one of 'is ole pals ter take 'im in,' Tommy replied.

'Or a brassy landlady,' Dolly suggested. 'Anyway, what did 'e 'ave ter say?'

'It was only a few lines. 'E's give me a telephone number ter ring. 'E wants me ter contact 'im soon as possible,' Tommy told her.

Dolly looked closely at the big man, and although he was still clearly suffering the effects of his ordeal the previous Friday she could sense a new uneasiness. 'When yer gonna call 'im, Tommy?' she asked quietly.

The contractor stared down at his clenched hands for a few moments, then he looked up at Dolly with concern in his eyes. 'I'll call 'im this evenin',' he replied, and after a pause he said, 'p'raps Frankie wants me ter set somefing up. 'E wanted ter know if you were still on the manor. Maybe 'e's after gettin' ter you before the police catch him.'

'Ter shut me up, yer mean,' Dolly replied quickly.

'Look, Dolly, Frankie don't know 'ow much yer got on 'im,' Tommy said. 'As far as 'e's concerned yer might 'ave enough evidence ter finish 'im.'

'Finish 'im?' Dolly said disdainfully. 'The man's finished already wivout my 'elp. But ter be honest I've come up against a brick wall, Tommy. I need more evidence o' money transfers, I need bank statements an' accounts records before I can nail 'im, an' what's the use? When they catch Frankie Morgan 'e's gonna be banged up fer years.'

'Well, that's as it may be, but I'd be careful if I were you, Dolly,' the contractor warned her.

'Pity yer couldn't give that phone number ter the police an' let 'em trace it,' she replied quickly.

'Believe me, I thought about it,' Tommy told her. ''Ow long would I last though? Frankie'd put the word out an' I'd get done over. Besides, I got my Doris ter fink of. She's a sick woman. I gotta be there ter take care of 'er.'

Dolly looked at the big man with compassion in her large blue eyes, and she glanced out of the window at the scudding clouds for a few seconds. 'I understand 'ow yer must feel, Tommy,' she said after a while. 'Look, I might be able ter sort somefing out, an' at the same time keep you out of it all. Will yer go along wiv me?'

Tommy looked at her enquiringly for a moment or two. 'Yeah, all right, I'll go along wiv yer, but don't screw it up fer Gawd sake, Dolly,' he said anxiously.

Tommy leaned back in his chair and let his face relax. 'Before yer go yer might be interested ter know that I've decided ter charge the grand sum of ten shillin's an' sixpence per week on the 'ouse,' he told her. 'I've seen my solicitor an' 'e's sortin' out the legal side of it. I'm gettin' the 'ouse removed from the business property as a safeguard ter you, if an' when I sell up.'

'That's a very generous fing ter do,' Dolly said gratefully.

The contractor smiled briefly. 'One day yer might 'ave reason ter re-evaluate the gesture in the light o' knowledge gained, an' if you ever do, I 'ope I come out favourably,' he replied.

Dolly nodded her head, looking a little puzzled as she stood up. 'I'd better be gettin' back, Tommy,' she told him. 'I really am grateful. We all are.'

She walked to the yard gate and turned to the tired-looking contractor as he stood in the office doorway. 'I'll see yer in a while,' she called out.

Tommy waved and then went back into his office, praying

that Dolly knew what she was doing. Frankie Morgan was a hard, callous man with many associates, and if things went wrong they would all suffer badly.

Even before the Monday newspapers hit the streets everyone in Bermondsey knew of Bill Grogan's suicide, and it had come as a deep shock to his many friends in the dockland area. Tommy Caulfield learned of the tragedy through his foreman, who had himself heard the news from one of the car men, and the big man was deeply saddened. He had known Grogan for many years, and after reading the account of the suicide in the *Daily Mirror* he was shocked at what the paper had made of it all. The article said that the inspector had had marriage problems and his wife had left him for another man, all of which Tommy found hard to believe. Bill had never indicated to him that anything was wrong with his marriage and he always seemed to be on top of things.

Sammy McGarry was shocked when Beryl gave him the news, but unlike Tommy Caulfield he had a firm conviction. 'I knew there was somefing wrong wiv 'im the last time 'e came in 'ere, luv,' he remarked.

''Ow d'yer mean?' Beryl asked.

'Well, 'e was knockin' the whisky back like there was no termorrer, an' 'e was unusually talkative,' Sammy told her. 'I'd never known Bill Grogan ter let on about what 'e was doin' but that last time 'e came in 'ere 'e was goin' on about Frankie Morgan givin' 'im the slip. I reckon it was the pressure that got to 'im in the end. That's what I fink.'

'It ses in the papers that Bill's wife left 'im,' Beryl pointed out. 'That would 'ave bin enough, surely.'

'I'm not sayin' it didn't add to it, but I'm convinced it was the pressure o' work more than anyfing else,' Sammy insisted. 'I saw the change in the man over the past few weeks.'

'If that's the case, Frankie bloody Morgan's got a lot to answer for,' Beryl replied.

'I bet 'e's laughin', wherever 'e is,' Sammy told her.

'Yeah, an' I 'ope 'e gets struck by a bolt o' lightnin' at the same time,' Beryl sneered. 'I dunno why you ever suffered the no-good whoreson.'

Sammy ignored the comment. Frankie Morgan was not going to remain at large for ever, and with him and his boys locked away for a long time things were going to be a little quieter around the neighbourhood, until some other chancer moved in to take his place.

Chapter Fifty-Two

As night closed in over the Bermondsey backstreets the family gathered together at number 12 Fellmonger Street to hear what Dolly had to say. The big woman's face was serious as she sat back in her armchair and looked around the parlour. 'Are the kids all settled, Rose?' she asked.

'Susan's sound asleep an' the boys are nearly off,' Rose told her.

Dolly took a deep breath and looked directly at Albert. 'When yer farvver got on the phone 'e asked Tommy a lot o' questions,' she began. ''E wanted ter know what my involvement wiv this famiy was an' 'e also wanted ter know about your plans too.'

''E knows where I stand,' Albert replied sharply. 'I shouldn't 'ave thought 'e'd be interested. What's it got ter do wiv 'im anyway?'

'An' why should 'e wanna know about you, Dolly?' Rose cut in. 'It's none of 'is business.'

'Unfortunately, 'e's makin' it 'is business,' Dolly told her.

'What did Tommy tell 'im?' Jimmy asked.

''E just said that I was movin' in ter take care o' you lot an' Albert an' Rose were gettin' married on Saturday,' Dolly replied.

'Tommy Caulfield should 'ave told 'im ter take a runnin' jump,' Don said angrily.

'It's not as simple as that,' Dolly replied quietly. 'Tommy's not a well man an' 'e's also got a sick wife.'

'I still can't understand why Frankie should be so interested,' Rose remarked.

'Look, luv, Frankie knows very well why I came back ter Bermon'sey in the first place, an' so do you,' Dolly said. She looked at Albert. 'I believe 'e finks that I've turned you against 'im by pressin' yer ter marry Rose, an' it was my way o' gettin' back at 'im. I s'pose 'e feels that if it wasn't fer me interferin' the police wouldn't be lookin' fer 'im right now.'

'No, they'd be lookin' fer Albert instead,' Rose said quickly.

'All right, so Tommy's put 'im in the picture,' Albert cut in. 'What can 'e do about it, though? If 'e shows up round 'ere the police are sure ter nab 'im.'

''E might be desperate enough ter try it, just ter get at me,' Dolly told him. ''E might reckon this is the last place the police'll expect 'im ter be. There's somefing else too.' She looked closely at Albert. 'That night you took the money over to 'im. Did yer count it?' she asked him.

'No, I didn't. It was wrapped up in two separate packets wiv tape round it,' he replied.

'Well, yer farvver told Tommy you short-changed 'im ter the tune of two 'undred quid,' Dolly revealed.

Albert looked shocked. 'All that was stashed away were those two packets an' I never interfered wiv 'em,' he said fervently, appealing to her. ''Ow could 'e believe I'd turn me own farvver over?'

Dolly drew breath as she looked around at all the serious faces. 'Now listen ter me, all of yer,' she said in a firm voice. 'We've gotta get this business sorted out, once an' fer all, an' I fink I know 'ow it can be done.' The silence prompted her to continue. 'I asked Tommy ter see if yer farvver would agree ter meet us somewhere, you an' me, Albert, an' I said it 'ad ter be before you an' Rose get wed. Anyway, 'e's gonna fink about it, so all we can do is wait.'

Jimmy was the first to speak. 'Yer gotta be mad! Stark ravin' mad!' he exclaimed.

Dolly smiled indulgently. 'If an' when I do get ter see 'im, I'm gonna give 'im an invite ter the weddin',' she said lightly.

'You are bloody crazy,' Jimmy said, shaking his head.

''E'll fink it's a trap,' Albert said, frowning at Dolly's audacity.

'Maybe 'e will an' maybe 'e won't, but if 'e wants ter get ter me an' you, Albert, 'e'll take that chance, I'm sure,' she replied.

'You can't set yerself up like that,' Jimmy said angrily. 'I won't stand fer it.'

'Yer can't stop me,' Dolly countered, eyeing Jimmy sharply. 'Anyway, I fink we can sort fings out in a sensible manner. The alternative is that Albert'll always be cut off from 'is family an' I'm gonna be constantly lookin' over me shoulder.'

'I don't like it one little bit. It'll be like walkin' up to a lion's cage an' puttin' yer bloody 'ead frew the bars,' Jimmy said with passion.

'I got one little ace up me sleeve, or I 'ope to 'ave,' Dolly told them all. 'Albert, me an' you 'ave gotta 'ave a private chat.'

'Well, I still fink it's a bad idea, an' I still fink you're bloody mad,' Jimmy growled.

On Tuesday morning Rose opened her eyes to see the sun streaming through the curtains and she turned on to her back and stretched. She could smell the freshness of the bedroom and the delicious aroma of frying bacon wafting up from the scullery, and she sat up in bed and sighed happily. It felt wonderful to have the opportunity of sleeping through without being woken up by the loud alarm bell and having to rush off to work. Dolly had been adamant in insisting that she would get the children off to school and make sure that Don got off to work on time that first morning in the new house.

Rose threw back the covers and slid her legs over the edge of the bed, casting her eyes around the room. It had been agreed that she should have the large front bedroom upstairs, which was most suited to take a cot. The upstairs back bedroom had been given to Billy and Joey, and the small bedroom on the bend of the stairs above the scullery had been decorated and furnished with Susan in mind. Don slept downstairs, in the bedroom which had been built alongside the scullery when the house was extended, and Dolly had the bigger bedroom which was situated behind the parlour.

The sounds of crockery downstairs and the rumble of iron wheels on the cobbles outside made Rose feel guilty for sleeping so long, and she reached for her candlewick dressing gown and slid her feet into her slippers. She hurried down to the scullery to find Dolly standing over the gas stove dressed in her long blue quilted dressing robe.

'Did yer sleep well?' Dolly asked her with a warm smile.

'I went out like a light,' Rose replied, yawning widely.

'The kids were up bright an' early,' Dolly told her. 'Don was out on time too. I thought I'd let yer sleep. Anyway, it's only just turned nine.'

Rose and Dolly sat down to a leisurely breakfast of bacon and eggs, followed by toast and marmalade and hot sweet tea, and they sat chatting about the coming wedding and their plans for the day.

'We'll go down Tower Bridge Road an' look at that weddin' dress in Marley's,' Dolly said. 'We'll find out about the bridesmaids' dresses as well. If we can see what we want we'll take

Susan wiv us after school ter try it on. What about Alice, though?'

'Don's gonna bring Alice round this evenin' ter make arrangements,' Rose told her as she reached for the last slice of toast.

Dolly slipped her hands into the wide sleeves of her robe and leaned back in her chair. 'When I was talkin' to Albert last night I asked 'im if 'e'd bin in contact wiv 'is muvver about the weddin',' she said. ''E just shrugged 'is shoulders an' said she'd prefer not ter come. That's all 'e'd say about it.'

'Albert wrote to 'er last week sayin' 'ow much 'e'd like 'er ter be there,' Rose replied, her eyes very briefly straying up to the mantelshelf clock, 'but she wrote back sayin' that it'd be better if she didn't come.'

'But why?' Dolly asked quickly, following Rose's glance at the clock and seeing the envelope poking out from behind it. 'Didn't she say why?'

'She said that wiv two of 'er boys in prison an' 'er 'usband on the run she couldn't face bein' seen in Bermon'sey,' Rose went on. 'She wished 'im luck though an' said 'e was doin' the right fing. Can you believe that, Dolly?' she said in disgust. 'Can you believe that she'd miss out on 'er own son's weddin' just because o' what people might fink?'

'Ter be honest, I didn't get ter know 'er very well,' Dolly replied. 'She always seemed a strange woman ter me. I could never get ter the bottom of 'er. 'Ow 'er an' Frankie ever got tergevver in the first place I'll never know. 'E was always a smart Jack-the-lad an' she was very quiet an' reserved. There must 'ave bin somefing there though in the beginnin', some attraction.'

'Albert told me 'is dad was always gettin' involved wiv ovver women,' Rose said. 'Why did she put up wiv it? Why didn't she leave 'im?'

'We're a funny breed when yer weigh it all up, Rose,' the older woman remarked. 'Maybe it was pride wiv Annie Morgan. Maybe she put on a brave face fer the neighbours' benefit, or p'raps she was secretly glad that Frankie was playin' the field. At least 'e wouldn't make unwanted demands on 'er. I don't s'pose we'll ever know the trufe of it all.'

'Frankie Morgan must be wicked ter carry on like that,' Rose said with feeling. ''E treated 'is wife like a doormat an' 'e's disowned 'is own son, just 'cos Albert wouldn't go along wiv the rest of 'em. The way I see it, a man who'd carry on like that is capable of anyfing. That's why you should be very careful if yer do get ter meet wiv 'im. I'm really worried about that, Dolly. If anyfing 'appened ter you I dunno what I'd do.'

The big woman smiled warmly and touched Rose's arm reassuringly across the table. 'There's no need ter worry, luv,' she said quickly. 'I know what I'm doin'. I just 'ope Tommy Caulfield gets a phone call soon.'

Rose sat up straight in her chair and rubbed her side as she felt a sudden movement. 'It's not only us who's worried,' she told her. 'Jimmy's worried too. 'E really cares fer you, Dolly.'

'I know. 'E's a little luv, but 'e does go on at times,' Dolly replied with a grin.

'What about you an' Jimmy?' Rose asked her. 'Are you two likely ter get tergevver permanently?'

'Married, yer mean?'

'Yeah.'

'Maybe one day, maybe not,' Dolly said with a shrug. ''E 'as asked me, more than once, but I've bin too wrapped up in all what's bin goin' on. One day 'e might pop the question again an' catch me at a weak moment. Who knows? Anyway, enough o' that. Let's us get dressed an' take a stroll down the market. I want yer ter see that weddin' dress I was tellin' yer about.'

*

Jimmy Rideout was in a thoughtful mood as he strolled along Bermondsey Street in the afternoon sunshine. He had been very lucky, there was no question of that, but all in all things had worked out very well. It was providence that had made him pick up the wrong key on his way out of the flat last Thursday night, and it was providence which had sent him into the house to spend the night. There was no other answer, he told himself. Tommy Caulfield had survived, and the house had been spared because he had been on hand when the fire started. If he had been sober on his return from the pub he would no doubt have knocked Fred Albury up for a replacement key. As it was he chose not to, and the rest was history.

Jimmy walked under the long railway arch and smelt the familiar vinegary tang of stale wine as he passed a team of warehousemen who were busy loading a lorry outside one of the wine vaults. His mind was still going over events as he turned left into Tooley Street and made for London Bridge Station. Thanks to Albert Morgan he had been spared Dolly's wrath, but it had been a near thing. If she, and not Albert, had discovered the half-empty bottle of whisky lying in the house it could well have been the end, as far as his matrimonial aspirations went. His addiction to drink was the reason Dolly had found it so difficult to give him a positive answer on each occasion he proposed to her, and it was understandable. She obviously wanted to be sure he had kicked the habit before she committed herself. As it was he had had plenty of time to think while he was lying in the hospital bed, and he had made a vow then that never again would a drop of spirit pass his lips.

The forecourt of the station was alive with activity as Jimmy walked up to his stallholder friend and stood to one side while a customer was being served.

'Well, if it ain't our little 'ero 'imself,' the stallholder said, grinning widely. 'We all 'eard about it, an' it's in the *South*

London Press this mornin'. Good job you was passin' the yard. It must 'a' bin an act o' providence.'

'I s'pose yer could say that,' Jimmy replied casually. 'It could 'ave bin anyone passin' by at the time.'

'Yeah, but it wasn't, was it?' his friend went on. 'Good job you 'ad yer wits about yer. A few weeks ago an' you'd 'ave bin in no fit state ter do anyfing about it. That bloke yer pulled out would 'ave fried, that's fer sure.'

Jimmy nodded, suddenly realising just how lucky he himself had been. If the fire had started a little later he would have been in a drunken sleep and would certainly have perished along with Tommy Caulfield.

''Ere, you all right? Yer've gorn white,' the stallholder said quickly.

'Yeah, it's just the effect o' the smoke. The 'ospital said it'd take time ter wear off,' Jimmy told him.

'C'mon then, Jimmy, let's go an' get a cuppa an' I can settle yer up,' his friend suggested. 'Bert, keep yer eye on me stall fer a few minutes, will yer?'

One hour later Jimmy walked back into Fellmonger Street and saw Rene Stratton talking to her friend Ivy outside Joe Diamond's corner shop.

''Ere, Jimmy, you're in the paper,' Ivy called out as he passed by on the other side of the street.

'Fred Albury's slid the *South London* under yer door,' Rene called out.

Lizzie Carroll could not bear to be left out of any important disclosures and she stepped out on to the front step and pretended to be busy restacking the bundles of firewood which were piled up against the wall, her ears cocked.

'Fanks, Rene. I'll 'ave a read of it when I get in,' Jimmy replied, waving a hand.

'Are yer feelin' all right?' Ivy asked him.

'Top o' the world,' Jimmy told her grinning.

'Tommy Caulfield looks rough,' Rene shouted over. 'I see 'im come past this mornin'. I told 'im 'e didn't look too good an' 'e said the doctor reckons it was overwork. 'E's bin told ter take it easy.'

Lizzie could restrain herself no longer. 'It was a good job you was passin' at the time,' she called out.

'Providence,' Jimmy shouted in reply.

'I mean ter say, yer could 'ave bin anywhere,' she said with a smile, probing.

'I could 'ave bin pissed at the time,' Jimmy replied with a forced grin.

'Funny you should say that,' Lizzie went on. 'Someone came in the shop only this mornin' an' said they thought they saw yer in the 'Orseshoe last Thursday evenin'. They said you looked a bit unsteady on yer feet. I told 'em they must 'ave bin mistaken.' She turned to Joe Diamond who had stepped out to see what all the shouting was about. 'Didn't I, Joe?'

The shopkeeper gave Lizzie a blinding look. 'I don't fink those bundles o' firewood are gonna run away,' he remarked sarcastically. 'It might be better if yer give the bacon slicer a clean-up.'

Rene and Ivy were already on their way home to the Buildings, and as Jimmy set off he saw Dolly hurry out of the house and go into the adjoining yard. It could only mean one thing, he thought. Frankie Morgan was on the line.

Chapter Fifty-Three

Dolly awoke early on Friday morning to the sound of horse carts clattering out of the transport yard. Tommy had soon managed to get things back to normal, she thought, sleepily glancing up at the window as the grim light filtered through the partly drawn curtains. Outside, rain was beating down and she listened to the metallic drumming as the heavy spots fell on the upturned tin bath in the backyard. She slipped quietly out from the covers and shivered as she laid her feet on the small patchwork mat and reached under the bed for her slippers. The clock showed ten minutes to seven and she yawned widely and scratched her head as she pressed the alarm button down. There was no sense in waking the household just yet, she thought. The day was going to be a long one, and if all went well, please God, she would be able to have a celebratory drink or two with Jimmy that evening.

Dolly wrapped her thick dressing robe around her ample figure and went into the parlour to light the gas fire before going into the scullery to put the kettle on. She sighed nervously as she thought about the evening ahead. Had she done the right thing in forcing the issue with Frankie Morgan on the eve of Rose and Albert's wedding? She could have waited until afterwards, perhaps, but then the wedding would have had a dark shadow over it, and events might have taken their own fateful course anyway. No, it was the right decision, she told herself. Once things had been sorted out, the two young people could start their married life a little more securely in the expectation of a happy future together.

Rose walked into the scullery as the kettle was starting to boil and she leaned against the dresser yawning. ''Ello, Dolly. What a nasty mornin',' she said. 'I 'ope it's gonna brighten up fer termorrer.'

'It'll be fine, you'll see,' Dolly replied, pouring the boiling water into the enamel teapot.

'I 'ope you're right,' Rose sighed, glancing out of the window.

Dolly put the tea cosy over the pot and adjusted the collar of her robe. 'Albert told me 'e'll be round early ternight,' she said. 'I do 'ope this rain stops.'

'Yer won't let Albert do anyfing silly, will yer, Dolly?' Rose said anxiously as she took down the tea mugs from the dresser. ''E's bin like a coiled spring ever since that phone call.'

'Now, I don't want you worryin'. It'll all work out,' Dolly told her firmly. 'Remember yer gotta keep yerself calm an' collected wiv that baby inside yer. They can sense it if yer feelin' screwed up, yer know.'

Rose hid a smile and nodded dutifully. Dolly had never had children and she was going on as though she had a house full of kids. But that was the way she was, and how nice it was to have her around. 'You will be careful though, won't yer?' she said anxiously.

Dolly got up and began to pour the tea into the large mugs. 'You sound like my Jimmy. That's all 'e's bin sayin',' she replied. ''Ere, take Don's tea in or 'e'll be late fer work.'

After the young man had wolfed down his Shredded Wheat,

he grabbed his reefer jacket from behind the door and gulped the last of his tea as he stood beside the table. 'I gotta dash, I'm late,' he spluttered.

While Rose roused the children for school Dolly boiled the porridge and refilled the teapot. Outside the rain lashed down, beating against the windows, and they heard the sound of distant thunder. The children came into the room and sat down at the table, watching with fresh faces and bright eyes as Dolly served up the porridge into blue china bowls. Heat from the gas fire had made the room pleasantly warm and the reflection of the flames played on the blue china crockery and the red and gold tin biscuit barrel.

'Yer know, I get a nice feelin' when I come down an' start a new day in this 'ouse,' Rose said to Dolly as the two sat sipping their tea in front of the fire. 'It's so different from the Buildin's. Every mornin' over there it was just a mad scramble, an' then there was the thought o' goin' in ter the factory an' facin' all the noise o' the machines.'

'Well, that's all be'ind yer now,' Dolly replied. 'Yer've got the weddin' ter look forward to an' you an' Albert settin' up 'ome tergevver in this 'ouse. Fings are gonna be good from now on, believe me. Your Albert's doin' well wiv 'is round an' 'e's gettin' more customers. 'E said 'imself if it keeps up the way it's goin' 'e'll be needin' anuvver pair of 'ands.'

The children were beginning to make themselves heard after their quiet entrance. Billy had finished his breakfast and was grinning at Susan as she tried to wipe a smudge of porridge from the side of her mouth with her spoon, while Joey was noisily scraping out his bowl.

'Rose, Billy's laughin' at me,' Susan said pouting.

'Billy, stop laughin' at yer sister,' Rose scolded him.

'I dunno why yer 'avin' Susan as a bridesmaid,' Billy said. 'She can't even eat prop'ly.'

'As long as she looks pretty an' don't pick 'er nose in church she'll be all right,' Rose told him.

'Why are yer 'avin' cars?' Joey asked suddenly.

''Cos it's the fing ter do at weddin's,' Dolly cut in.

'Yeah, but it's only a little way ter the church,' Joey queried.

'It doesn't matter,' Rose told him. 'Brides an' bridesmaids go in cars an' everybody else walks.'

'Cor! It's a swizz,' Joey moaned. 'I don't fink the bride's own bruvvers should 'ave ter walk. It's not fair jus' me an' Billy not gettin' a ride in the car.'

'Well, Susan's a bridesmaid an' Don's givin' me away so that's why they're both goin' in the cars,' Rose replied quickly. 'Now if you two wanna be bridesmaids you can get a ride too.'

'No fear,' Joey said with disgust. 'I'd sooner walk any time.'

'Boys can't be bridesmaids,' Billy piped in.

'But yer could 'ave bin page boys,' Dolly reminded them.

'All our mates would 'ave took the mickey,' Billy replied. 'Anyway, I don't mind walkin' ter the church.'

'My dolly's gonna be a bridesmaid too,' Susan said, hugging the tattered doll.

'Yer can't take that in church,' Billy told her quickly.

'Yes, she can. I'll look after it for 'er,' Dolly replied.

'Can I take my pop gun?' Joey asked.

'No, you can't,' Rose replied firmly.

'Why not?'

''Cos a church is not the place ter take guns.'

'My mate Charlie took 'is frogs an' snails ter church in a cardboard box,' Joey said.

'What for?' Billy asked.

'So the priest could say a prayer for 'em,' Joey explained.

'Did 'e?'

'Nah. 'E called Charlie a dirty little boy fer bringin' such fings inter the place,' Joey told him.

'Well, I s'pose the priest was worried in case the snails an' frogs got out an' frightened the congregation,' Dolly suggested.

'They couldn't get out, Aunt Dolly,' Joey replied.

'They might 'ave done.'

'Nah, they were dead.'

'Well, I can understand the priest bein' upset, if that was the case.'

'Yeah, but we sing hymns at assembly,' Joey went on, 'an' one o' the hymns ses, "All fings bright an' beautiful, all creatures great an' small, all fings bright an' beautiful, the Lord God loves them all." So why couldn't the priest say a prayer fer the little creatures?'

Dolly exchanged amused glances with Rose and then she stood up. 'P'raps the priest fergot ter be nice that particular day, Joey,' she told him. 'Now you lot 'ad better go an' get yer coats on ready fer school, an' I 'ope you won't ferget ter be nice ter people terday.'

When Albert left his lodgings that morning the rain had already washed out any chance of him getting forward with his round and he decided to utilise his time by canvassing once more. The last time he was forced to go canvassing the response had been good, and it was better than sitting around doing nothing. As he walked quickly through the driving rain he thought about the coming evening. When his father phoned Tommy Caulfield back on Tuesday he had said he was not going to chance coming back to Bermondsey, but he would meet them at the St David Refuge in Spitalfields at nine o'clock on Friday evening.

Albert could see the reasoning behind it. Spitalfields was an East End fruit and vegetable market which would be coming to life at that time of night. The area was full of market porters, transport drivers, and down-and-outs who earned a few coppers helping with the loading and unloading. Many of the hard-up characters slept rough in Spitalfields churchyard and they were usually ignored by the police. His father would obviously feel less exposed in an area like that, and if he dressed accordingly he could expect to be reasonably safe from being recognised.

Albert's mind turned to his mother and he thought how sad it was that she had decided not to come to the wedding. He could understand her feelings though, after reading the letter she had sent to him. It was terrible how his father's and brothers' last escapade had destroyed everything. Albert had a bad sense of foreboding about the coming meeting. His father was desperate and it was going to be hard facing him, but as Dolly had been quick to remark, unless things were sorted out once and for all, there would always be a cloud hanging over his and Rose's future together.

As night settled in over the east coast town Frankie Morgan prepared himself for the journey to London. He stood looking into the mirror at his unshaven face and felt satisfied that he would be in character with the lost souls who frequented the Spitalfields area. Flash Gordon had told him that the St David Refuge For the Poor, where he used to work as a care-taker, was an ideal meeting place and bolt hole. Frankie put on the scruffy overcoat which Flash had found for him and tied the red spotted handkerchief into a knot round his throat, then he slipped into a black plastic mackintosh and grey trilby hat to disguise his unkempt appearance and picked up a small package which he fitted into his overcoat pocket. Before he left he reached into the bedside drawer and took out a flick-knife, and at the thought of Dolly Morgan a filthy dark rage rose up, blinding him.

'I'll slice that interferin' bitch if it's the last fing I do,' he muttered, gritting his teeth.

*

At eight thirty Dolly left the house with Albert and they walked quickly to Tower Bridge Road where they caught a number 78 bus to Shoreditch. Dolly estimated the journey taking about twenty minutes, which would give them ten minutes to find the refuge. Albert was looking very serious and Dolly gave him an encouraging smile as they sat on the lower deck of the bus.

'Don't worry, luv, it'll turn out OK,' she said bravely, but Albert merely nodded.

The river fog was descending as the bus trundled over the white stone bridge and passed the Tower of London. Albert glanced at the big woman sitting next to him and she looked quite composed. He had to admire her courage. When she had first moved back into Bermondsey he remembered how taken aback his father had been. He had told him and his brothers about her and the motive behind her return, and he had sworn to stop her one way or another. Now that he was on the run from the police he might be desperate and wild enough to carry out his threat while he still could, and Dolly would have realised that, though he could not see any outward sign of fear on her face as she stared ahead stonily.

The bus turned into Bishopsgate and passed the railway station before pulling up on the corner of Spitalfields. As they got off, Dolly pulled her coat collar up against the cold and Albert thrust his hands deep into the pockets of his reefer jacket and they walked purposefully into the market. The fog was beginning to close in and up ahead they saw the grimy-looking church looming up, its spire already shrouded in a sulphurous blanket. The area was slowly awakening, with shop shutters going up and laden lorries beginning to arrive from all corners of the country. In front of the churchyard a mobile canteen gushed steam and a few men stood beside it waiting for the urns to heat up. Albert stopped to talk to one of them and he nodded as he caught up with Dolly. 'It's just round the corner,' he said quickly.

'Don't rise ter the bait, Albert,' Dolly warned him as they rounded the corner into a narrow turning that ran along the side of the church. 'Just let me do the talkin'.'

'You just be careful,' Albert replied. 'Me farvver can be vicious an' yer gotta remember yer not 'is favourite person.'

'I know what 'e's like, don't worry,' Dolly told him.

They reached the end of the churchyard and turned into a narrow street that ran from east to west, its run-down houses empty and boarded up ready for demolition. Albert's heart sank as he saw why his father would have chosen such a place to meet. Not even a brave policeman would relish spending much time in such a dark, dismal street which had breathed its last and been left abandoned, facing its extinction.

A lone gas lamp flickering in the fog stood like a silent sentinel outside the looming two-storeyed building which backed on to the churchyard, feverish yellow light falling on a faded sign above the boarded-up windows: 'St David Refuge For the Poor'. Albert and Dolly carefully walked round to the side, and when the young man pushed on the decrepit wooden door it opened with a loud creak. They went inside very tentatively, stung by the strong musty smell and conscious of their own breathing in the eerie quiet. There was a light burning in the room to their right.

Suddenly they heard Frankie's gruff voice. 'In 'ere.'

Albert and Dolly walked slowly into the room and saw Frankie sitting down beside a desk white with dust. Four lighted candles gave off a faltering light which played on his wide flat face, casting shadows that turned his features fiendish.

''Ello, Dad, 'ow are yer?' Albert said as he stood beside Dolly.

'Well, if it ain't my dutiful son, or should I say my prodigal son,' Frankie replied with a look of disgust. 'And concerned fer me welfare as well. It's touchin'. It really is.'

'We've not come over 'ere ter trade insults,' Dolly cut in. 'We've come ter clear a few fings up. Remember Albert's gettin' married termorrer an' 'e'd like your blessin'.'

'Yer better sit down,' Frankie told them, nodding towards some chairs to his right.

'We prefer ter stand,' Dolly said coldly.

'Sit down!' he shouted.

Albert immediately sat on a rickety chair but Dolly stood for a few moments, challenging Frankie, before she followed Albert's lead.

'That's better,' Frankie said, getting up and folding his arms. 'So yer'd like my blessin', would yer?' He glared at Albert. 'Yer rob yer own farvver out o' two 'undred quid, an' then yer've got the cheek ter come crawlin' to 'im fer 'is blessin'.'

'I never robbed yer,' Albert replied quickly. 'Surely yer wouldn't suspect me o' that.'

Frankie walked slowly around the pair, his eyes darting from one to the other. 'Oh, wouldn't I?' he sneered. 'I bundled up seven 'undred quid an' when I opened the packets there was two 'undred short. I s'pose yer gonna tell me John an' Ernie took the money.'

'All I'm sayin' is, I never took it,' Albert replied ardently. 'I just did what yer said. When I brought it to yer it was the way I found it. Both packets were wrapped an' taped up.'

'All right then, so the mice must 'ave got to it. Now what about you?' Frankie said, bending down behind Dolly till his face was level with hers. ''Ave you come 'ere ter tell me yer gonna wipe the slate clean as far as I'm concerned? Let's all be friends. Is that what yer sayin'?'

'Exactly that,' Dolly replied calmly.

Frankie Morgan suddenly stood up straight and started

slowly pacing the room. 'Yer come back ter Bermondsey an' fronted me in the pub, remember?' he said to her gruffly. 'Yer made it plain ter me what yer wanted. You was out ter screw me fer everyfing, wasn't yer?'

'That's right,' she told him, matching his stare. 'Everyfing. Everyfing yer screwed out o' my Bob, yer own bruvver.'

Frankie laughed, a dry, humourless laugh. 'The business was goin' down fast an' Bob couldn't see it,' he replied. ''E was pourin' good money after bad ter prop that business up – our money, the family's money. If it'd bin left ter Bob we'd 'ave all gone down the drain.'

'You was just a leech, a bloodsucker,' Dolly said in a measured voice, 'but it was 'is lifeblood.'

Frankie suddenly bent down and crooked his arm round Dolly's neck, pulling her backwards against the chair, and as Albert got up to stop him he pulled out the flicknife. Dolly blinked as the weapon clicked open and she felt the light pressure of its tip against her neck.

'Try an' take this away from me an' I'll slit 'er froat,' Frankie hissed.

'Put it away, Dad,' Albert pleaded. 'Ain't you in enough trouble already?'

Frankie's face looked evil in the light of the candles as he bent closer to Dolly. 'You came back ter Bermon'sey wiv one fing in mind. Yer wanted ter finish me, an' when yer couldn't dig up enough evidence yer decided ter turn me own boy against me. I'm gonna do yer, you whore,' he growled menacingly.

'She didn't 'ave anyfing ter do wiv it,' Albert cut in quickly. 'I made me own mind up about gettin' married an' settlin' down.'

'An' I'm s'posed ter believe she didn't encourage yer ter nick that money o' mine?' Frankie snarled.

'God Almighty, Dad! 'Ow many more times 'ave I gotta tell yer,' Albert cried. 'I never took the money!'

Dolly felt the villain's arm tightening round her neck and she found it difficult to swallow. She closed her eyes and offered up a silent prayer. Please God, don't let Jimmy fail.

As if in answer there were sounds in the passageway and Jimmy walked in. His eyes nearly popped as he saw Frankie with the knife pressed to Dolly's throat. 'Don't be silly now,' he said pleadingly, with his hands held out. 'Take that knife away, yer'll only make fings worse.'

'Two 'undred quid, she an' that no-good son o' mine done me out of, an' yer tellin' me ter ferget it?' Frankie snarled.

Jimmy turned and motioned anxiously to the shadowy figure standing behind him in the passageway and Annie Morgan walked in.

'Yer can put that knife down, Frankie,' she said calmly. 'Albert never took that money. I did.'

The villain looked shocked as he stared at his wife. 'You? You took it?'

'That's right,' Annie replied. 'I never wanted ter lay eyes on yer again, but Dolly persuaded me ter come 'ere ternight. It's a good job she did. Yer no good, Frankie, yer never was.'

'Why d'yer take the money?' he asked, slowly releasing his arm from Dolly's neck and standing up straight. 'I never kept yer short. Yer know I never.'

Everyone's eyes were on the diminutive woman as she stood in the doorway. Her long coat hung on her like a sack, and above her ashen face her mousy hair was pulled back from her narrow forehead. Her grey eyes looked almost lifeless and her shoulders were hunched as she stood staring at her husband, her arms hanging limp at her sides.

''Ow long 'as it bin now? Thirty years? That's 'ow long I've cleaned an' cooked an' skivvied fer you lot,' she began. 'Oh no, yer never saw me short o' money. There was always enough ter provide a good table, an' in yer favour yer never lifted a finger against me. But I wish you 'ad kept me short. I wish you 'ad raised yer 'and ter me, 'cos then I would 'ave got out years ago. Instead I've bin used like a mop, a dishcloth ter clean up after yer. Thirty years I've suffered yer insults, yer indifference, knowin' all the time about the ovver women who took me place in yer affections. I've suffered the scorn o' me neighbours an' I've 'ad ter put up wiv their snide remarks. That's bin my life, Frankie,' Annie told him, tears beginning to form in her staring eyes. 'Six sons I've given yer. One's doin' five years, an' two more are waiting' ter go down. But yer not satisfied wiv that. Yer wanted this boy ter go the same way, an' yer can't bring yerself ter see that 'e's tryin' ter make a decent life fer 'imself. Yes, I took the money, but it wasn't fer me. It was ter spend on yer gran'children, the ones yer never bovver ter go an' see.'

Frankie stood with his head bowed, unable to find any words.

'I'm leavin' yer fer good, Frankie,' Annie went on, 'an' there's only two fings left fer you ter do, if yer've got one spark o' decency left inside yer. Give yerself up an' make it easier on the two boys, an' ask Dolly ter fergive yer. Show 'im, Dolly.'

Dolly's face was sad as she reached into her handbag and took out a bundle of papers. 'The trouble between us is over as far as I'm concerned,' she said as she stood up.

Everyone in the room watched in silence as she slipped the elastic band from the bundle and let the papers fall into a metal wastepaper bin. Then, taking up a lighted candle and applying it to one of the sheets, she stood back a pace.

'It was all there, Frankie, all the accounts, letters an' bills o' sale, all the stuff yer told me ter get rid of over the years,' Annie told him.

Albert looked at Dolly incredulously. 'Yer went ter see me mum?' he said in a shocked voice.

Dolly nodded slowly. 'I didn't tell yer, Albert; I couldn't, in case yer mum decided against comin' 'ere ternight,' she explained. 'Yer see, yer mum told me about the money, an' if you'd known you'd 'ave took the blame, wouldn't yer?'

Albert lowered his head in the heavy silence of the room, then he went to his mother, his arm going around her shoulders. 'Don't go back ternight, Mum,' he said in a soft voice. 'Stay fer the weddin'.'

Annie shook her head slowly. 'I wish yer luck, boy, an' look after yer wife an' baby. Make 'em proud of yer,' she said as she turned away.

Jimmy took his cue from Dolly and followed Annie into the passage, while Frankie sat down heavily in the chair, dropping his head in his hands. Dolly watched the flames die in the metal bin before she slipped her arm through Albert's and walked out into the dense fog.

'C'mon, luv, Jimmy's lookin' after yer mum. Let's get back 'ome,' she said quietly. 'We've got a weddin' ter go to.'

Chapter Fifty-Four

Saturday dawned bright and clear, and as the first rays of the sun reached into the front bedroom at number 12 Rose opened her eyes and stretched luxuriously. She felt sure that it was going to be a wonderful day, the day that she would remember for the rest of her life. Downstairs on her old chairbed, the man in her life was sleeping soundly. Delicious, wicked thoughts brought a smile to the young woman's face and she turned over to stare down at sunbeams lighting up a patch of carpet, then she closed her eyes once more to recapture that magic moment when Albert had come into her bed.

It was nearing eleven o'clock with the yellow fog hanging like a blanket when Albert and Dolly had finally arrived back home, Rose recalled. She had been half out of her mind with worry, but when she saw Albert's tired face she knew that everything was all right. The three of them had sat up chatting till very late and then Dolly had said she wanted to go over to Jimmy's flat to discuss a few things with him and would stay the night. Don was out visiting Alice, and with the fog thickening quickly it was not likely he would come home. Once they were alone in the quiet parlour Rose reached out and took the emotional young man into her arms. He looked drained of colour and his voice was shaking as he told her how he had felt when his mother opened her heart to them all.

It was the night when everything was right. When the love she felt for him had threatened to overwhelm her. He too had needed her arms around him and the feel of her warm rounded body close to him. They had kissed and caressed with complete abandon and then, when their passion was soaring, they had crept up the stairs quietly, and made love. Rose sighed with pleasure as she recalled the moment he had actually entered her. He was terrified of hurting the baby and she had had to reassure him by pulling him on to her, moving her hips sensuously until she could feel him high inside her. She had felt her feelings rising up until she wanted to scream out with the exquisite pleasure and suddenly, at the very moment he climaxed, she felt a river of passion pour through her. Rose knew then that they had sealed their love for ever and tears of happiness welled up in her eyes.

Footsteps on the stairs and excited voices brought Rose back from her reverie and suddenly Joey and Susan burst into the room.

'It's today, the weddin's terday, an' I'm gonna wear my special dress,' Susan said excitedly.

Joey looked a little put out. 'Aunt Dolly told me an' Billy we can sit in the front row,' he said as he leaned against the bed.

Rose ruffled his fair hair and kissed him on the cheek. 'Of course yer can,' she told him fondly.

Susan jumped into bed beside Rose and began to chatter excitedly, and after a few minutes Joey felt that it was time for him to leave. There were more exciting things to be doing than listening to girl talk, he decided.

The morning seemed to fly. First there was breakfast, and Dolly was on hand to make sure they all ate. 'Yer'll be sick if yer don't eat anyfing,' she warned the children.

Jimmy came over later that morning and was immediately captured by the efficient matriarch. 'Don't stand there like a lemon, 'elp me get that trestle-table up, then I can start preparin' the food,' she ordered.

Freda Arrowsmith came over with jellies she had made and later Rene and Ivy walked in with trays of cakes and sandwiches they had prepared together. Sadie Jones and Ethel Price followed hard on their heels with more sandwiches, and then a few minutes later Lizzie Carroll knocked. 'Joe Diamond thought these little bits an' pieces might come in 'andy,' she said, passing over a laden carrier bag.

It was as though all the street had found some reason to pop round and every caller was shown the wedding dress which was hanging up in Dolly's bedroom. Susan was feeling very grown-up that morning and she too was eager to show off her pretty bridesmaid's dress. Jimmy struggled with the trestle-table and then Don walked in, looking rather guilty as Rose fixed him with a knowing smile.

'It was a pea-souper down Rovver'ithe last night,' he said quickly. 'The buses was stopped runnin' an' Alice said I could sleep on 'er settee.'

'Oh I see,' Rose replied with mock seriousness. 'It was better than tryin' ter walk 'ome frew the fog, I s'pose. I mean ter say, yer might 'ave ended up in the river.'

Don ignored the comment. 'Alice said she'll get 'ere soon as she can,' he told her. 'She's gotta make the ole lady comfortable an' get someone in ter sit wiv 'er.'

Jimmy had finished setting up the table and Dolly threw a tablecloth at him. 'C'mon, Jimmy, there's no time ter stand scratchin' yerself,' she said quickly. 'Let's get this grub laid out and then I can 'elp Rose get ready.'

Billy and Joey left the house with Rose's sharp reminder ringing in their ears. 'Don't you two get into any trouble now, an' don't ferget I want yer back by twelve o'clock ter start gettin' ready, understand?'

Dolly quickly spread the plates of food out on the long table which Jimmy had set up in the parlour, and after making sure that everything was under control she slipped into her coat. A very worried-looking Tommy Caulfield had knocked on the door as soon as he arrived at the yard that morning, but she had been quick to reassure him that everything was fine. She had told him that she would pop in for a chat when things quietened down a bit, and now as she made her way to the yard office Dolly was smiling to herself.

''Ow did it go?' Tommy asked anxiously before she had time to sit down, 'I bin worried sick all night. Gawd, gel, I was 'alf expectin' ter be goin' to a funeral instead of a weddin'.'

'It was better than I expected,' Dolly told him. 'It got a bit nasty at first though.'

The contractor listened in silence while Dolly recounted the events of the previous night, but when she told him about the bundle of papers which Annie Morgan had given her his expression changed visibly. 'So yer got all the evidence yer need then,' he said, his throat becoming suddenly dry.

'Yeah, it was all there, Tommy. Bills, accounts, receipts an' lots of ovver papers. Annie 'ad saved the lot,' Dolly replied. 'Don't ask me why she kept 'em all after Frankie ordered 'er ter burn 'em. She must 'ave 'ad good reason.'

''Ave yer 'ad time ter go frew 'em all?' Tommy asked, trying to hide the fearful note in his voice.

Dolly looked down at her clasped hands for a few moments, then she met his troubled gaze. 'Yer know somefing, Tommy. When I brought those papers back ter the 'ouse on Thursday night I put 'em on me dressin' table an' I sat lookin' at 'em fer quite a while,' she told him. 'I was intendin' ter go all frew 'em so I could confront Frankie, so I could 'ave the pleasure o' tellin' 'im that I 'ad enough on 'im ter squeeze im dry like 'e did wiv my feller, Gawd rest 'is soul. But I couldn't bring meself ter look at 'em. Some'ow I just felt that I'd 'ad enough of it, all of a sudden. Anyway they stayed there bundled up, an' when me an' Albert went over ter meet Frankie I just stuck 'em in me 'andbag.'

'Yer still got 'em then?' Tommy queried.

Dolly smiled with mixed emotions, taking pleasure in the man's discomfort and feeling a little guilty at the same time.

'I burned 'em all,' she said, after a lengthy pause.

'Wivout lookin' frew 'em?' Tommy replied.

'Yeah, I burned 'em in front o' Frankie. Call it a peace offerin' if yer like,' Dolly told him. 'It's all water under the bridge anyway. There's no malice left in me now, Tommy, only concern fer those kids o' Gerry's. What 'appened can't be undone, but people live ter regret their actions an' wish they could turn the clock back. We can't, though. None of us can. Suffice it ter say I'm 'appy to 'ave put a match ter the 'ole bloody lot of it.'

Tommy reached into his desk drawer and took out a bottle of Scotch and two glasses. 'Dolly, I'm gonna insist yer take a drink wiv me,' he said firmly.

Dolly smiled as he handed her a filled glass. 'To us, Tommy,' she said, putting the glass to her lips.

''Ere's ter you, gel. What a diamond,' he said with feeling.

The sun was high in the clear Saturday sky and church bells peeled as the bride's car pulled up outside the parish church of St Mary Magdalene in Bermondsey Street. The driver stepped out and hurried round the car to open the door, and as Rose stepped out and allowed Don to adjust her train she could see the two bridesmaids standing just inside the porch and she heard the organ playing. The white satin, empire line wedding dress that she wore was softly gathered at the bust, hanging loosely at the front and concealing her condition. She had a circlet of pearls and satin leaves set on her softly curled fair hair. The tulle veil was secured from the crown and hung in folds, framing her face with its embroidered scalloped edging.

Don took her hand and looked into her eyes. 'Rose, yer look a picture,' he said softly. 'Just like a fairy princess. Dad would 'ave bin proud of yer. C'mon, let's go.'

The bridesmaids followed on as Rose took Don's arm, walking elegantly through the arched portals and down the aisle towards the altar. Susan looked very serious and Alice smiled shyly as they heard the strains of the wedding march. Their white taffeta dresses reached almost to the floor, displaying tiny pink rosebuds along the hemlines and on the lower part of the bodices. The wired head-dresses of matching pink rosebuds and ribbon streamers sat delicately poised on both girls' dark shining hair, and they each carried a tiny posy of carnations.

As the two young lovers joined hands at the altar, Annie Morgan stepped quietly into the church and took her seat in the back row of the pews. She could see them all there. Dolly Morgan sitting with Jimmy Rideout, Rene Stratton and Ivy Campbell with their husbands, Ethel and George Price, and Lizzie Carroll too. Tommy Caulfield was there, and the Alburys, and there were others amongst the congregation she knew well, people she had once been proud to know as neighbours but could no longer face. This was the church in which she had married and had her children christened, and now she was sitting with a heavy heart and a prayer on her lips for her sons' salvation.

Across the narrow street in a deep doorway the sad, forlorn figure of Frankie Morgan had watched the arrival of the wedding group and then seen his wife Annie go into the church. Two minutes later he left his meagre refuge and hurried across into the ancient place of worship. He stood just inside the doorway, shielded from view by a stone pillar but able to see along the aisle to the altar. He stood impassive as the wedding vows were exchanged, and when the bride took her husband's arm and turned to leave the altar he slipped out into the porch.

Albert walked erect, smiling self-consciously at the well-wishers on each side of him and his bride. They reached the porch and suddenly he stopped dead as he caught sight of his father. They looked into each other's eyes for a moment, then Frankie stepped forward. He held out his hand and clasped Albert's in a firm grip. 'Good luck, son,' he said in a low gruff voice. In a spontaneous gesture Albert held out his arms and his father stepped forward. He could feel the deep sigh, almost like a groan of anguish and he felt his father shudder.

The photographer was fussing at the kerbside, arranging the group and gesticulating excitedly with his hands: first the bride and groom, then the bridesmaids. As the main group moved and shuffled into position Frankie saw his wife. She came over to him with a pained look on her pale, gaunt face. 'I was 'opin' yer'd show up, but I didn't fink yer would,' she said.

The camera clicked again and Frankie turned to Annie. 'I'm goin' down ter Dock'ead nick,' he told her quietly. 'Tell those kids I'm not all bad, an' wish 'em luck from me.'

'I'm goin' back ter the 'ouse,' Annie said in a flat voice.

'You are?'

'Yeah. Yer'll be needin' a few fings.'

'I dunno why yer bovverin',' Frankie said.

'I'm bovverin' 'cos I fink that maybe, just maybe, there is a spark o' decency left in yer, Frankie.'

The house was filled with happy voices as people milled about and chatted together. Toasts were drunk and then Albert banged a knife against a plate. 'I feel I should say a few words,' he began. 'Me an' my wife would like ter say 'ow much we owe to everybody, ter you, our good neighbours an' friends, an' especially ter you, Dolly an' Jimmy, for all yer've done fer us durin' the past few weeks. I'd also like ter say that terday was very special fer me, 'cos not only did I gain a beautiful wife, I gained a family an' regained me own family. There's just one ovver fing Rose wants me ter say,' he went on. 'She an' Don, Billy, Joey an' little Susan all wanna say a very big fank you ter their fairy godfarvver fer all 'e's done fer the family ever since last spring. I'd like to add my fanks. So I ask you all ter raise yer glasses ter Jimmy Rideout, ter yerselves, ter the future, an' ter peace an' 'appiness fer each an' every one of us.'

The hour was late when Dolly kicked off her shoes and stretched out leisurely in front of a brightly burning fire. Albert and Rose had left earlier for a few days' honeymoon at Cliftonville, the last of the revellers had gone and the clearing up was done and finished. The children were sleeping soundly upstairs and Jimmy sighed contentedly as he flipped over the page of his newspaper.

'Anyfing in the news?' Dolly asked him.

'Nah, not a lot,' Jimmy replied. 'The Russians are kickin' up a stink again about the Berlin airlift an' Manny Shinwell reckons 'e may 'ave ter put up conscription from eighteen months ter two years.'

'Blimey! That'll please Don,' Dolly remarked. 'Anyfing else?'

'There's a bit 'ere about some MP committin' suicide,' Jimmy told her.

Hamish MacKenzie, MP, former Secretary to the War Office, was found dead at his London flat early this morning. Foul play is not suspected. The Right

Honourable Member for Worsden Central had recently resigned from his post at the War Office after suffering multiple injuries in last month's train derailment in Scotland. A Government spokesman said this afternoon that Hamish MacKenzie had been a dedicated and hard-working minister and an example to us all. He will be sorely missed.

The fire had started to die and Jimmy yawned as he folded the paper up. 'Well, darlin', it's bin a grand day,' he said quietly, 'but I wish you 'adn't told Rose about me payin' their rent.'

Dolly looked at him with a big smile. 'A family shouldn't 'ave secrets from each ovver, an' after all you're family, Jimmy. Well, almost.'

'Yeah, the almost man,' he replied wistfully. 'Well, I s'pose I'd better get off 'ome,' he said.

Dolly glanced at him. 'Well, luv, it's up ter you, but it's all quiet on the western front an' Don said 'e'll be stayin' at Alice's ternight. Why don't we make the most of it? An' if yer really good I'll let yer propose ter me again.'

Jimmy's eyes lit up and he swallowed hard. 'That's the best proposition I've 'ad all week,' he said grinning.

Epilogue

They walked along together in the warm autumn sunshine, Rose pushing the pram and Albert looking proud as he nodded to a neighbour. They had just left Annie Morgan's house after the weekly visit and were both pleased to find that she was looking perky. Annie had smiled broadly as she held baby Roseanne, and she and Rose had chatted incessantly about babies while Albert sat back in the armchair and nodded off to sleep.

Rose and Albert had both pledged to be there for Annie, knowing the bleak time she was facing. There would be long years of loneliness, having to live with the knowledge that when Frankie finally did come home they would both be entering their sixties. Albert realised that in making the choice she had, his mother had provided his father and two brothers with a family future, something they would all seize upon to sustain them through their years of incarceration.

Things had moved swiftly after his father walked into the police station at Dockhead and surrendered himself to the very surprised desk sergeant. A plea of guilty was subsequently submitted by the family solicitor, and in his address to the three prisoners the presiding judge acknowledged that Frankie

Morgan had given himself up to expedite justice, and accepted that the three had been used as pawns in a serious crime of armed robbery perpetrated by a syndicate whose identity remained unknown. The judge had gone on to say that due consideration had been given to the fact that all three defendants were unarmed and had not been party to any violence against the victim of the crime.

Albert had felt his mother's hand tighten like a vice on his arm as the judge pronounced sentence. John and Ernie had each been given five years and their father seven years. The terms of imprisonment were less than the young man had expected. He had feared that the judge would be harsh, especially when his father's previous convictions were read out in court.

As Albert escorted his mother into High Holborn and down the stairs to Blackfriars to catch the bus home that day, he had been comforted by the memory of his father turning to give her a brief smile of encouragement before he was escorted from the dock. John and Ernie had also sought her with their eyes and waved before disappearing from her sight down the stairs to the holding cells. Although the coming years would be very hard for his mother, Albert knew that somehow she would survive. As she had told him earlier that morning, 'I must keep a fire burnin' an' the place clean, fer me, fer all of 'em, no matter 'ow long they're away.'

Rose could see a new moon rising over the rickety chimney tops of Imperial Buildings as she stood by the window. She had fed and changed baby Roseanne and settled her, then she had looked in on Billy, Joey and Susan and seen that they were all sleeping soundly. Downstairs Dolly and Jimmy were listening to the wireless and Don had taken Alice to the Trocadero cinema to see James Cagney in *White Heat*. Albert came up behind her and slipped his arms around her waist, his lips brushing her neck. 'It's a nice night,' he said softly.

Rose leaned her head back on his shoulder and sighed deeply, savouring the pleasure for a few magic moments. It had been a very eventful and worrying year so far for them all and now, as autumn set in, another worry had begun to encroach on the young woman's mind.

The War Minister had spoken on the wireless that night and he had announced that National Service had been extended from eighteen months to two years. The Security Council had sanctioned sending United Nations troops into South Korea to aid the beleaguered American forces and Britain had pledged help. It was all far removed from the uneventful daily life in dockland Bermondsey, Rose had to admit, but she knew in her heart that life had a way of reaching out, and fate was mysterious and inscrutable. No one was immune.

'Penny fer yer thoughts.'

'Oh, I was just finkin'.'

'Yeah?'

'Don's eighteen next March,' Rose said quietly.

Albert held her tight, sensing her thoughts. 'Always the little mum,' he said tenderly. 'Just remember, it wasn't so long ago when you Farrans were nobody's children, but it's different now. This family's got a special star up there an' it's watchin' out fer us – fer all of us. Look, yer can see it. There, over the Buildin's. The first one on the right.'

Rose looked up into the night sky and smiled, touched by a strange sadness. 'Yeah, but there's so many nobody's children out there,' she said quietly.

Have you read every novel by Harry Bowling, the 'King of Cockney sagas'?

headline